O F
L O V E
A N D
L I F E

OF
LOVE
AND
LIFE

Three novels selected and condensed
by Reader's Digest

CONDENSED BOOKS DIVISION

The Reader's Digest Association Limited, London

With the exception of actual personages identified as such, the
characters and incidents in the fictional selections in this volume
are entirely the product of the authors' imaginations and have no
relation to any person or event in real life.

The Reader's Digest Association Limited
11 Westferry Circus, Canary Wharf, London E14 4HE

www.readersdigest.co.uk

For information as to ownership of copyright in the material of
this book, and acknowledgments, see last page.

CONTENTS

Kristin Hannah
ON MYSTIC LAKE

When Annie Colwater's world falls
apart, she heads for Mystic, the small
town in Washington State where she grew
up, hoping that there she can find the
woman she once was.
In Mystic, she is quickly reunited with her
first love, Nick Delacroix, recently
widowed and unable to cope with his
grieving, silent, six-year-old daughter, Izzy.
Together the three of them begin to
rebuild their lives, but just as Annie
believes she has found herself again, she
is faced with a choice no woman should
ever have to make.

Chapter 1

RAIN FELL LIKE tiny silver teardrops from the tired sky. Somewhere behind a bank of clouds lay the sun, too weak to cast a shadow on the ground below.

It was March, the doldrums of the year, still and quiet and grey, but the wind had already begun to warm, bringing with it the promise of spring. Trees that only last week had been naked and brittle seemed to have grown six inches over the span of a single, moonless night, and sometimes, if the sunlight hit a limb just so, you could see the red bud of new life stirring at the tips of the crackly brown bark. Any day, the hills behind Malibu would blossom, and for a few short weeks this would be the prettiest place on earth.

For nineteen years, Annie Colwater had awaited spring with the breathless anticipation of a young girl at her first dance. But now, all she felt was dread, and a vague, formless panic. After today, nothing in her well-ordered life would remain the same, and she was not a woman who liked the sharp, jagged edges of change. She preferred things to run smoothly, down the middle of the road. That was where she felt safest—in the centre of the ordinary, with her family gathered close around her.

Wife. Mother. These were the roles that defined her, that gave her life meaning. It was what she'd always been, and now, at thirty-nine, it was all she could remember ever wanting to be. She had got married right after college and been pregnant within that same year. Her husband and daughter were her anchors; without Blake and Natalie, she would be a ship without captain or destination.

But what did a mother do when her only child left home?

She shifted uneasily in the front seat of the Cadillac. The clothes she'd chosen with such care this morning, navy wool trousers and a pale rose silk blouse, felt wrong. Usually she could take refuge in fashionable camouflage. Designer clothes and carefully applied make-up could make her *look* like the high-powered corporate wife she was supposed to be. But not today. Today, the waist-length brown hair she'd drawn back from her face in a chignon—the way her husband liked it, the way she always wore it—was giving her a headache.

She drummed her manicured fingernails on the armrest and glanced at Blake, who was settled comfortably in the driver's seat. He looked completely relaxed, as if this were a normal afternoon instead of the day their seventeen-year-old daughter was leaving for London.

It was childish to be so scared, she knew that, but knowing didn't ease the pain. When Natalie had first told them that she wanted to graduate early and spend her last term in London, Annie had been proud of her daughter's independence and courage, but she hadn't realised how hard it would be to watch Natalie leave. They'd been like best friends ever since Natalie had emerged from the angry sullenness of the early teen years. They'd had hard times, sure, and fights and hurt feelings, but all that had only made their bond stronger. They were a unit, the 'girls' in a household where the only man worked eighty hours a week and sometimes went days without remembering to smile.

She stared out of the car window. The concrete-encrusted canyons of downtown Los Angeles were a blur of high-rise buildings, graffiti, and neon lights that left streaking reflections in the misty rain. They were getting closer and closer to the airport.

She reached for her husband, touched the pale blue cashmere of his sleeve. 'Let's fly to London with Nana and get her settled with her host family. I know—'

'*Mom*,' Natalie said sharply from the back seat. 'Get real. It would be, like, so humiliating for you to show up.'

Annie drew her hand back and plucked a tiny lint ball from her expensive wool trousers. 'It was just an idea,' she said softly. 'Your dad has been trying to get me to England for ages. I just thought . . .'

Blake gave her a quick look, one she couldn't quite read. 'I haven't mentioned England in years.' Then he muttered something about the traffic and slammed his hand on the horn.

'I guess you won't miss the California traffic,' Annie said into the awkward silence that followed.

In the back seat, Natalie laughed. 'No way. Sally Pritchart said it was way cool. Not like California, where you need a car to go anywhere. In London, all you do is get on the underground.' She poked her blonde head into the opening between the two front seats. 'Did you take the underground when you were in London last year, Dad?'

Blake slammed on the horn again. With an irritated sigh, he flicked on his indicator and jerked the car into the fast lane. 'Huh? What was that?'

Natalie sighed. 'Nothing.'

Annie squeezed Blake's shoulder in a gentle reminder. These were precious moments—the last they'd see of their daughter for months—and, as usual, he was missing them. She started to say something to fill the silence, but then she saw the sign, LAX, and she couldn't say anything at all.

Blake pulled onto the exit ramp and drove into the dark silence of the underground parking lot, killing the engine. For a long moment, they all sat there. Then he opened his door. As always, Annie followed his lead. She got out of the car and stood twirling her sunglasses in her cold, cold fingers. She looked down at Natalie's luggage—a single grey duffle bag and a green canvas backpack.

She worried that it wasn't enough, that it was too unwieldy . . . she worried about everything. Her daughter looked so young suddenly, her tall, thin body swamped by a baggy denim dress that stopped an inch above her scuffed black combat boots. Two metal clips held her long, silver-blonde hair away from her pale face. Three silver earrings formed a curved ladder up her left ear.

Blake walked on ahead, carrying the two lonely pieces of luggage, as Natalie and Annie followed silently in his wake. She wished he'd slow down and walk with them, but she didn't say anything—just in case Natalie hadn't noticed that her dad seemed to be in a rush. At the ticket counter, he handled everything, and then the three of them headed for the international terminal.

At the gate, Annie clung to her navy handbag as if it were a shield. Alone, she walked to the huge, dirty window. For a split second, she saw herself reflected in the glass, a thin, flawlessly dressed housewife standing by herself.

'Don't be so quiet, Mom. I can't take it.' The words contained a tiny wobble of anxiety that only a mother would hear.

Annie forced a laugh. 'Usually you guys are begging me to keep quiet. And it's not like I can't think of a million things to say right now. Why, just yesterday I was looking at your baby picture, and I thought—'

'I love you, too, Mom,' Natalie whispered.

Annie grabbed her daughter's hand and held on. She didn't dare turn towards Natalie, afraid that her heartache would show. It was definitely not the image she wanted her child to carry onto the plane.

Blake came up beside them. 'I wish you had let us get you first-class tickets. It's such a long flight, and it would have been more comfortable.'

'This isn't about comfort,' Natalie answered. 'It's about *adventure*.'

'Ah, adventure,' Annie said, finding her voice at last. Once again she was envious of her daughter's independence.

A voice boomed over the loudspeaker. 'We will now begin boarding flight three-five-seven to London.'

'I'm going to miss you guys,' Natalie said softly.

Annie placed a hand on Natalie's soft cheek, trying to memorise everything: the tiny mole beside her daughter's left ear lobe, the exact hue of her straight blonde hair and blue eyes, the cinnamon sprinkling of freckles across her nose. 'Remember, we'll call every Monday—seven o'clock your time. You're going to have a great time, Nana.'

Blake opened his arms. 'Give your old dad a hug.'

Natalie hurled herself into her father's arms.

Too soon, the voice came over the loudspeaker, announcing the boarding of Natalie's row.

Annie gave Natalie one last long, desperate hug—not nearly long enough—then, slowly, she drew back. Blinking away tears, she watched Natalie give her ticket to the woman at the doorway, and then, with a last, hurried wave, her daughter disappeared into the jetway.

'She'll be fine, Annie.'

She stared at the empty doorway. 'I know.'

One tear, that's how long it took. One tear, sliding down Annie's face, and her daughter was gone.

Annie stood there long after the plane had left, long after the white trail of exhaust had melted into the sombre sky. She could feel Blake beside her. She wished he'd take her hand or squeeze her shoulder or pull her into his arms—any of the things he would have done five years ago.

She turned. In his eyes, she saw her own reflection, and the misty mirror of their life together. She'd first kissed him when she was eighteen years old—almost Natalie's age—and there'd never been another man for her in all the years since. His handsome face was as serious as she'd ever seen it. 'Ah, Annie . . .' His voice was a cracked whisper of breath. 'What will you do now?'

She was in danger of crumbling, right here in this sterile, crowded airport. 'Take me home, Blake,' she whispered unevenly.

'Of course.' He grabbed her hand and led her through the terminal and into the garage. Wordlessly, they got into the Cadillac and slammed the doors shut. The air conditioning came on instantly.

As the car hurtled down one freeway after another, Annie felt exhausted. She leaned heavily in her seat and stared out of the window at this city that had never become her city, although she and Blake had moved here right after college. It was a sprawling labyrinth of a town, where gorgeous, elaborately appointed dowager buildings were demolished daily. In this city of angels, too few noticed the loss of one more landmark. Within months, a sleek, glass-faced child of a building would rise higher and higher into the smoggy brown sky.

Annie was seized by a fierce, unexpected longing to return home. Not to the crowded, affluent beauty of Malibu, but to the moist green landscape of her youth, that wild part of western Washington State where mushrooms grew to the size of dinner plates and water rushed in silver threads along every roadside, where fat, glossy raccoons came out in the light of a full moon and drank from mud puddles in the middle of the road. To Mystic—where the only skyscrapers were Douglas firs that had been growing since the American Revolution. It had been almost ten years since she'd been back. Perhaps she could finally talk Blake into a trip now that they were no longer tethered to southern California by Natalie's school schedule.

'What do you think about planning a trip to Mystic?' she asked.

He didn't look at her, didn't respond to her question, and it made her feel stupid and small. She pulled at the large diamond stud in her ear and stared outside. 'I was thinking about joining the Club. You're always saying I don't get out of the house enough. Aerobics would be fun, don't you think?'

'I haven't said that in years.'

He turned off the freeway and eased onto the twisting, traffic-clogged Pacific Coast Highway. At the gated entrance to their road, he waved to the guard and passed into the Colony, the beachfront jewel of Malibu. Rain beaded the windshield and blurred the world for a split second, before the wipers swept the water away.

At their house, he slowed, inching down the brick-paved driveway. He stopped in front of the garage. Annie glanced at him. It was odd that he hadn't hit the door's remote control. Odder still that he'd left the car running. He hated to leave the Cadillac out in the rain . . .

He's not himself.

The realisation sanded the hard edges from her anxiety, reminded her that she wasn't as alone as she felt. Her high-powered, ultra-competent husband was as fragile as she was right now.

She twisted round to face him, and brushed a lock of hair from his eyes. 'I love you. We'll get each other through this.'

He didn't answer. The awkward silence stung. She tucked the disappointment away and opened the car door. Tiny shards of rain slipped through the opening, mottling her sleeve. 'It's going to be a lonely spring. Maybe we should—'

'Annie.' He turned to her, and she saw that there were tears in his eyes.

She leaned over and touched his cheek in a fleeting, tender caress. 'I'm going to miss her, too.'

He looked away and sighed heavily. 'You don't understand. I want a divorce. I meant to wait to tell you . . . at least until next week. But the thought of coming home tonight . . .' Blake let the sentence trail off.

Very slowly, Annie closed the car door. She couldn't have heard right. Frowning, she reached for him. 'What are you talking about . . .'

He lurched against the window, as if her touch—the touch he'd known for so long—were now repugnant.

It all became real suddenly, with that gesture he wouldn't allow. Her husband was asking for a divorce.

'I should have done this a long time ago, Annie. I'm not happy. I haven't been happy with you in years.'

The shock of it was unlike anything she'd ever experienced. It was everywhere, spreading through her in wave after numbing wave.

'I can't believe I'm saying this,' he said softly, and she heard the choked-up thickness of his breathing. 'I'm seeing someone else . . .'

She stared at him. He was having an *affair*. The word sank through her, hurting all the way to the bone. A thousand tiny details slipped into place: dinners he'd missed, trips he'd taken to exotic locations, the new silk boxer shorts he'd started wearing, the switch in colognes from Polo to Calvin Klein after all these years, the love they made so rarely . . .

How had she been so blind? She *must* have known. Deep inside, she must have known what was happening and chosen to ignore it.

She turned to him, wanting to touch him so badly it was a physical ache. For half her life, she'd touched him whenever she wanted, and now he had taken that right away. 'We can get over an affair . . .' Her voice was feeble, not her voice at all. 'I mean . . . it'll take me some time to forgive you, time to—'

'I don't want your forgiveness.'

This couldn't be happening. Not to her. Not to *them*. She heard the words and felt the pain, but it all had a dizzying sense of unreality about it. 'But we have so much. We have *history*. We have Natalie. We can work this out, maybe try counselling. We can get through it.'

'I don't want to try, Annie. I want out.'

'But *I* don't.' Her voice spiked into a high, plaintive whine. 'We're a *family*. You can't throw twenty years away . . .' She couldn't find the words she needed. It terrified her; she was afraid there were words that could save her, save them, and she couldn't find them. 'Please, *please* don't do this . . .'

He didn't say anything for a long time—long enough for her to find a strand of hope and weave it into solid fabric. *He'll change his mind. He'll realise we're a family and say it was just a midlife crisis.*

'I'm in love with her.'

Annie's stomach started a slow, agonised crumbling.

Love? How could he be in love with someone else? That declaration— love—and everything it meant diminished her. She felt as if she were a tiny, disappearing person, a million miles away from the man she'd always loved. 'How long?'

'Almost a year.'

She felt the first hot sting of tears. A year in which everything between them had been a lie. Everything. 'Who is she?'

'Suzannah James. The firm's new junior partner.'

Suzannah James—one of the two dozen guests at Blake's birthday party last weekend. The thin young woman in the turquoise dress who'd hung on Blake's every word.

'But after the party, we made love . . .'

Had he been imagining Suzannah's face in the darkness? Was that why he'd clicked off the bedroom lights before he touched her? A tiny, whimpering moan escaped her. 'Blake, please . . .'

He looked helpless, a little lost himself, but he wouldn't meet her gaze. 'I love her, Annie. Please don't make me say it again.'

The sour remains of his confession tainted the air, left her with nothing to breathe. *I love her, Annie.*

She wrenched the car door open and stumbled blindly down the brick walkway to her house. Rain hit her face and mingled with her tears. At the door, she pulled the keys from her handbag, but her hand was shaking so badly she couldn't find the lock on the first try. Then the key slipped into the slot and clicked hard.

She lurched inside and slammed the door shut behind her.

Annie walked dully through her house, sipping her third glass of wine and trying to figure out what she'd done wrong, how she'd failed.

If only she knew that, maybe then she could make it all right again.

She'd spent the past twenty years putting her family's needs first, and yet somehow she had failed, and her failure had left her alone, wandering around this too-big house, missing a daughter who was gone and a husband who was in love with someone else.

Somewhere along the way, she'd forgotten what she should have remembered. It was a lesson she'd learned early in life—one she'd thought she knew well. People left, and if you loved too deeply, too fiercely, their swift and sudden absence could chill you to the soul.

She climbed into her bed and burrowed under the covers, but when she realised that she was on 'her' side of the bed, she felt as if she'd been slapped. The wine backed up into her throat, tasting sour enough that she thought she would vomit.

What was she supposed to do now? It had been so long since she'd been anything but *we*. She didn't even know if there was an *I* inside of her any more. Beside her, the bedside clock ticked . . . and she wept.

The phone rang. Annie woke on the first ring, her heart pounding. It was him, calling to say it was all a mistake, that he was sorry, that he'd always loved her. But when she picked up the phone, it was Natalie, laughing. 'Hey, Mom, I made it.'

Her daughter's voice brought the heartache rushing back.

Annie sat up in bed. 'I can't believe you're there already.' Her voice was thin and unsteady. She took a deep breath, trying to collect herself. 'So, how was your flight?'

Natalie launched into a monologue that lasted for a steady fifteen minutes. Annie heard about the plane trip, the airport, about the strangeness of the London underground, and the way the houses were all connected together—like, San Francisco, you know, Mom—

'Mom . . .?'

Annie realised with a start that she'd lapsed into silence. She'd been listening to Natalie—she truly had—but some silly, pointless turn in the conversation had made her think of Blake, of the car that wasn't in the garage and the body that wasn't beside her in bed.

'Mom?'

Annie squeezed her eyes shut, a feeble attempt to escape. There was a white, static roar of sound in her head. 'I . . . I'm right here, Natalie. I'm sorry. You were telling me about your host family.'

'Are you all right, Mom?'

Tears leaked down Annie's cheeks. 'I'm fine. How about you?'

A pause crackled through the lines. 'I miss you guys.'

Annie heard loneliness in her daughter's voice and it took all of her self-control not to whisper into the phone, *Come home, Nana. We'll be lonely together.*

'Trust me, Nana, you'll make friends. In no time at all, you'll be having so much fun that June 15th will come much too quickly.'

'Hey, Mom, you sound kinda shaky. Will you be OK while I'm gone?'

Annie laughed; it was a nervous, fluttery sound. 'Of course I will. Don't you dare worry about me.'

'OK.' The word was spoken so softly Annie had to strain to hear it. 'Before I start crying, I better talk to Daddy.'

Annie flinched. 'Dad's not here right now.'

'Oh.'

'He loves you, though. He told me to tell you that.'

'Yeah, of course he does. So, you'll call Monday?'

'Like clockwork.'

'I love you, Mom.'

Annie felt tears flood her throat again, squeezing until she could hardly talk. 'Be careful, Natalie. Love you.'

'Love you.'

And the phone went dead.

Annie placed the handset back on the base and crawled out of bed, stumbling blindly into her bathroom. She stared in horror at her reflection. She was still wearing her clothes from the airport, and they were wrinkled into something she didn't recognise. Her hair was stuck so tightly to her head it looked as if she'd used glue as conditioner.

She slammed her fist onto the light switch. In the blessed darkness, she stripped down to her bra and panties and left the wrinkled clothes in a heap on the tile floor. Feeling tired and old and swollen, she walked out of the bathroom and crawled back into bed.

She could smell him in the fabric of the sheets. Only it wasn't him. Blake—her Blake—had always worn Polo. She'd given him the cologne for Christmas every year. He'd worn it every day . . . until Calvin Klein and Suzannah changed everything.

Annie's best friend showed up bright and early the next morning, pounding on the front door, yelling, 'Open up in there, goddamn it, or I'll call the fire department.'

Annie slipped into Blake's black silk bathrobe and stumbled tiredly towards the front door. She felt like hell from the wine she'd drunk last night, and it took considerable effort simply to open the door. The expensive stone tiles felt icy cold beneath her bare feet.

Terri Spencer stood in the doorway, wearing a baggy pair of faded denim overalls. Her thick, curly nimbus of black hair was hidden by a wild scarlet scarf. Bold gold hoops hung from her ears. She looked exactly like the gypsy she played in a daytime soap. Terri crossed her arms, cocked one ample hip, and eyed Annie. 'You look like shit.'

Annie sighed. Of course Terri had heard. No matter how much of a free spirit her friend claimed to be, her current husband was a dyed-in-the-wool lawyer. And lawyers gossiped. 'You've heard.'

'I had to hear it from Frank. You could have called me yourself.'

Annie ran a trembling hand through her tangled hair. They had been friends for ever, she and Terri. Practically sisters. But even with all they'd been through together, all the ups and downs they'd weathered, Annie didn't know how to begin. She was used to taking care of Terri, with her wild, over-the-top actress lifestyle and her steady stream of divorces and marriages. Annie was used to taking care of everyone. Except Annie. 'I meant to call, but it's been . . . difficult.'

Terri curled a plump arm round Annie's shoulder and propelled her to the overstuffed sofa in the living room. Then she went from window to window, whipping open the white silk curtains. The twenty-foot-tall, wall-to-wall windows framed a sea and sky so blue it stung the eyes, and left Annie with nowhere to hide.

When Terri was through, she sat down beside Annie on the sofa. 'Now,' she said softly. 'What the fuck happened?'

Annie wished she could smile—it was what Terri wanted, why she'd used the vulgarity—but Annie couldn't respond. Saying it out loud would make it too real. She sagged forward, burying her puffy face in her hands. 'Oh, God . . .'

Terri took Annie in her arms and held her tightly, rocking back and forth, smoothing the dirty hair from her sticky cheeks. It felt good to be held and comforted, to know that she wasn't as alone as she felt.

'You'll get through it,' Terri said at last. 'Right now, you think you won't, but you will. I promise. Blake's an asshole, anyway. You'll be better off without him.'

Annie drew back and looked at her friend through a blur of stinging tears. 'I don't . . . want to be without him.'

'Of course you don't. I only meant . . . Look, Annie, I know I'm harsh and pessimistic, and that's why my marriages fail, but remember what I used to be like? Remember in college?'

Annie remembered. Terri used to be a sweet little Pollyanna; that's why they'd become best friends. Terri had stayed innocent until the day her first husband, Rom, had come home and told her he was having an affair with their accountant's daughter.

'You stayed with me every day,' Terri said softly, slipping her hand into Annie's and squeezing gently. 'You got me through it, and I'm going to be here for you. Whenever you need me.'

'I didn't know how much it hurt. It feels like . . .' The humiliating tears burned again. She wished she could stop them, but it was impossible.

'Like your insides are bleeding away . . . like nothing will ever make you happy again? I know.'

Annie closed her eyes. Terri's understanding was almost more than she could bear. It was terrifying to think that this was . . . ordinary. As if the loss of twenty years was nothing at all, just another divorce in a country that saw a million breakups a year.

'Look, kiddo, I hate to bring this up, but I have to. Blake's a hotshot attorney. You need to protect yourself.'

It was bruising advice, the kind that made a woman want to curl up into a tiny, broken ball. Annie tried to smile. 'Blake's not like that.'

'Oh, really. You need to ask yourself how well you know him.'

Annie couldn't deal with this now. It was enough to realise that the past year had been a lie; she couldn't fathom the possibility that Blake had become a complete stranger. She stared at Terri, hoping her friend could understand. 'I know it's naive—stupid, even—to trust him, but he's been my best friend for more than half my life.'

'Some friend.'

Annie touched her friend's plump hand. 'I love you for worrying about me, Terri. Really, I do, but I'm not ready for this advice. I hope . . .' Her voice fell to a whisper. 'I still hope I don't need it, I guess.'

Terri forced a bright smile. 'Maybe you're right. Maybe it's just a midlife crisis and he'll get over it.'

They spent the next few hours talking. Time and again, Annie pulled a memory or an anecdote out of the black hat of her marriage and tossed it out, as if talking about her life, remembering it, would bring him home.

Terri listened and smiled and held her, but she didn't offer any more real-world advice—and Annie was thankful. Some time around noon they ordered a large lamb sausage pizza from Granita's, and they sat on the deck and ate the whole thing. As the sun finally set across the blue Pacific, Annie knew that Terri would have to go soon.

Turning to her best friend, she asked the question that had been hovering for the better part of the afternoon. 'What if he doesn't come back, Terri?' She said it so quietly that, for a moment, she thought the words were buried in the distant sound of the surf.

'What if he doesn't?'

'I can't imagine my life without him. What will I do? Where will I go?'

'You'll go home,' Terri said. 'If I'd had a dad as cool as Hank, I would have gone home in an instant.'

Home. It struck her for the first time that the word was as fragile as bone china. 'Home is with Blake.'

'Ah, Annie,' Terri sighed, squeezing her hand. 'Not any more.'

Two days later, he called.

His voice was the sweetest sound she'd ever heard. 'I need to see you.'

She swallowed hard, felt the sudden sting of tears. *Thank you, God. I knew he'd come back.* 'Now?'

'No. My schedule's tight this morning. As soon as I can break free.'

For the first time in days, Annie could breathe.

When Blake stared at the soaring white angles of the house, he felt an unexpected pang of loss. It was so beautiful, this home of theirs, so stunningly contemporary. Annie had conceived, created, and designed this place. She'd taken the view—sea and sand and sky—and translated it into a home that seemed to have grown out of the hillside. She'd chosen every tile, every fixture. There was no place inside that didn't reflect her bubbling, slightly off-centre personality.

He tried to remember what it had felt like to love her, but he couldn't any more. He'd been sleeping with other women for ten years, seducing them and bedding them and forgetting them. He'd thought sooner or later Annie would notice that he'd fallen out of love with her, but she was so damn trusting. She always believed the best of everyone, and when she loved, it was body and soul, for ever.

He sighed, suddenly feeling tired. It was turning forty that had changed his outlook, made him realise that he didn't want to be locked in a loveless marriage any more.

Before the grey had moved its ugly fingers into his hair and lines had settled beneath his blue eyes, he thought he had it all—a glamorous career, a beautiful wife, a loving daughter, and all the freedom he needed. He travelled with his college buddies twice a year, went on fishing trips to remote islands with pretty beaches and prettier women; he played basketball two nights a week and closed the local bar down on Friday nights. Unlike most of his friends, he'd always had a wife who understood, who stayed at home. The perfect wife and mother—everything that he thought he wanted.

Then he met Suzannah. What had begun as just another sexual conquest rolled into the most unexpected thing of all: love.

For the first time in years, he felt young and alive. They made love everywhere, all times of the day and night. Suzannah never cared what the neighbours thought, or worried about a sleeping child in the next room. She was wild and unpredictable, and she was smart—unlike Annie, who thought the PTA was as vital to world order as the EC.

He walked slowly down to the front door. Before he could even reach for the bell, the hand-carved rosewood door opened.

She stood in the doorway, her hands clasped nervously at her waist. A creamy silk dress clung to her body, and he couldn't help noticing that she'd lost weight—and God knew she couldn't afford it.

Her small, heart-shaped face was pale, alarmingly so, and her eyes, usually as bright and green as shamrock, were dull and bloodshot. She'd pulled her long hair into a tight ponytail that accentuated the sharp lines of her cheekbones and made her lips look swollen. Her earrings didn't match; she was wearing one diamond and one pearl, and somehow that little incongruity brought home the stinging pain of his betrayal.

'Blake . . .' He heard the thin lilt of hope in her voice, and realised suddenly what she must have thought when he called this morning.

Shit. How could he have been so stupid?

She backed away from the door, smoothing a non-existent wrinkle from her dress. 'Come in, come in. You . . .' She looked away quickly, but not before he saw her bite down on her lower lip—the nervous habit she'd had since she was young. He thought she was going to say something, but she turned and led the way down the hallway and out onto the huge, multitiered deck that overlooked the Colony's quiet patch of Malibu beach.

Christ, he wished he hadn't come. He didn't need to see her pain in sharp relief.

She crossed to the table, where a pitcher of lemonade—his favourite—and two crystal glasses sat on an elegant silver tray. 'Natalie's settling in well. I've only talked to her once—and I was going to call again, but . . . well . . . she'll ask for you. Maybe later . . . while you're here . . . we could call again.'

'I shouldn't have come.' He said it more sharply than he intended, but he couldn't stand to hear the tremor in her voice any more.

Her hand jerked. Lemonade splashed over the rim of the glass and puddled on the grey stone table. She didn't turn to him, and he was glad. He didn't want to see her face.

'Why did you?'

Something in her voice—resignation, maybe, or pain—caught him off guard. Tears burned behind his eyes; he couldn't believe this was *hurting*.

He reached into his pocket and pulled out the interim settlement papers he'd drafted. Wordlessly, he leaned over her shoulder and dropped them on the table. An edge of the envelope landed in the spilt lemonade. A dark, bubbling splotch began to form.

'Those are the papers, Annie . . .'

She didn't move, didn't answer, just stood there with her back to him.

She looked pathetic, with her shoulders hunched and her fingers curled round the table's edge. He didn't need to see her face to know what she was feeling.

'I can't believe you're doing this.' Annie hadn't meant to say anything, but the words formed themselves. When he didn't answer, she turned towards him. She couldn't bear to meet his eyes. 'Why?'

That's what she really wanted to understand. She'd always put her family's needs above her own, always done everything she could to make her loved ones feel safe and happy. It had started long before she met Blake, in her childhood. Her mother had died when Annie was very young, and she'd learned how to seal her own grief in airtight compartments stored far from her heart. Unable to comprehend her loss, she'd focused on her grieving father. It had become, over the years, her defining characteristic, Annie the caretaker, the giver of love. But now her husband didn't want her love any more, didn't want to be a part of the family she'd created and cared for.

'Let's not rehash it again,' he said with a heavy sigh.

The words were like a slap. She snapped her head up and looked at him. 'Rehash it? Are you *joking*?'

He looked sad and tired. 'When did you ever know me to joke?' He shoved a hand through his perfectly cut hair. 'I didn't think about what you'd . . . infer from my phone call this morning. I'm sorry.'

Infer. A cold, legal word that seemed to separate them even more.

'I'll take care of you. That's what I came to say. You don't have to worry about money. I'll take good care of you and Natalie. I promise.'

She stared at him in disbelief. 'February 19th. You remember that date, Blake? Our wedding day. You said—you *vowed*—to love me till death parted us. You promised to take care of me on that day, too.'

'That was a long time ago.'

'You think a promise like that has an expiry date, like a carton of milk? God . . .'

'I've changed, Annie. Hell, we've both changed. I think you'll be happier without me. I really do. You can focus on all those hobbies you never had time for. You know . . .' He looked acutely out of his depth. 'Like that calligraphy stuff. And writing those little stories. And painting.'

She wanted to tell him to get the hell out, but the words tangled with memories in her head, and it all hurt so badly.

'I've drafted a tentative settlement. It's more than generous.'

'I won't make it that easy for you.'

'What?'

She could tell by his voice that she'd surprised him, and it was no wonder. Their years together had taught him to expect no protest from Annie about anything. She looked up at him. 'I said, I won't make it easy for you, Blake. Not this time.'

'You can't stop a divorce in California,' he said in his lawyer's voice.

'I know the law, Blake.' She moved towards him, careful not to touch him. 'If you were a client, what advice would you give?'

He tugged at his starched collar. 'This isn't relevant.'

'You'd tell yourself to wait, spend some "cooling off" time. You'd recommend a trial separation. I've *heard* you say it.' The words tripped her up in sadness. 'Jesus, Blake, won't you even give us that chance?'

'Annalise—'

She kept tears at bay one trembling breath at a time. Everything hung on the thread of this moment. 'Promise me we'll wait until June—when Natalie gets home. We'll see where we are after a few months apart. I gave you twenty years, Blake. You can give me three months.'

She felt the seconds tick by, slicing tiny nicks across her soul.

'All right.'

The relief was overwhelming. 'What are we going to tell Natalie?'

'Christ, Annie, it's not like she's going to have a heart attack. Most of her friends' parents are divorced. That's half of our goddamn problem, all you ever think about is Natalie. Tell her the truth.'

Annie felt her first spark of true anger. 'Don't you dare make this about motherhood, Blake. You're leaving me because you're a selfish prick.'

'A selfish prick who's in love with someone else.'

The words cut as deeply as he intended them to. Tears burned behind her eyes, blurred her vision, but she'd be damned if she'd let them fall. She should have known better than to fight with him—she had no practice, and hurtful words were his profession. 'So you say.'

'Fine,' he said in a clipped, even voice, and she knew by the tone of it that this conversation was over. 'What do you want to tell Natalie?'

This was the one answer she had. She might be a complete failure as a wife and lover, but she knew how to take care of her daughter. 'Nothing for now. I don't want to ruin this trip for her. We'll tell her . . . whatever we need to . . . when she gets home.'

'Fine. I'll just collect a few of my things.' He picked up the envelope from the table and held it out to her. 'Open it.'

'Why? So I can see how generous you've been with our money?'

'Annie, please . . .'

'Please what—please don't make this hard on you?'

'Look at the papers, Annie. I'll be living at Suzannah's house if there's an emergency.' He pulled out a pen and wrote on a scrap of paper from his wallet. 'Here's the number.'

She wouldn't take the paper. He let go and it fluttered to the floor.

Annie lay perfectly still in her king-size bed, listening to the familiar sound of her own breathing, the steady rhythm of her own heart. She wanted to pick up the phone and call Terri, but she'd already leaned on her best friend too much. They'd talked daily, for hours and hours, as if talking could ease Annie's heartache, and when their conversations ended, Annie felt more alone than ever.

The last week had passed in a blur, seven endless days since her husband had told her he was in love with someone else.

Throwing back the covers, she climbed out of bed and went to her walk-in closet. She yanked open her lingerie drawer and pulled out a big grey box. Clasping the box to her chest, she moved woodenly back to the bed. A lifetime's collection of photographs and mementos lay at her fingertips. At the bottom of the box, she found a small bronze compass, a gift from her father. There was no inscription on it, but she still remembered the day he'd given it to her, and the words he'd said: *I know you feel lost now, but it won't last for ever, and this will make sure that you can always find your way home again . . . where I'll always be waiting.*

She clutched the bit of metal in one hand, wondering when and why she'd ever taken it off. Very slowly, she slipped it round her neck again, then she turned to the photographs, beginning with the black and white ones, the Kodak trail of her own childhood. Small, dogeared photos with the date stamped in black across the top. There were dozens of her alone, a few of her with her daddy. And one of her with her mother.

One.

She could remember the day it was taken; she and her mom had been making Christmas cookies. There was flour everywhere, on the counter, on Annie's face, on the floor. Her dad had come in from work and laughed at them. *Good God, Sarah, you're making enough for an army. There's just the three of us . . .*

Only a few months later, there were only two of them. A quiet, grieving man and his even quieter little girl.

Annie traced the smooth surface of the print with her fingertip. She'd missed her mother so often over the years—at high school graduation, on her wedding day, on the day Natalie was born—but never as much as she missed her now. *I need you, Mom,* she thought for the millionth time. *I need you to tell me that everything will be all right . . .*

She replaced the treasured photograph in the box and picked up a coloured one that showed Annie holding a tiny, blotchy-faced newborn wrapped in a pink blanket. And there was Blake, looking young and handsome and proud, his big hand curled protectively round his baby girl. She went through dozens more pictures. Natalie's whole life lay in this box, but somewhere along the way, Blake had stopped appearing in the family photos. How was it that Annie had never noticed that before?

But Blake wasn't who she was really looking for.

She was looking for Annie. The truth sank through her, twisting and hurting, but she couldn't give up. Somewhere in this box that held the tangible memories of her life, she had to find herself. She went through print after print, tossing aside one after another.

There were almost no pictures of her. Like most mothers, she was always behind the camera. Now, it was as if she'd never been there at all. As if she'd never really existed. The thought scared her so badly, she lurched out of bed, shoving the photographs aside with a sweep of her hand. As she passed the French doors, she caught sight of a dishevelled, desperate-looking middle-aged woman in her husband's bathrobe. It was pathetic what she was becoming. Even more pathetic than what she'd been before.

How dare he do this to her. Take twenty years of her life and then discard her like a sweater that no longer fitted.

She strode to the closet, ripping his clothes from their expensive hangers and shoving them in the garbage. Then she went to his study. Wrenching the desk drawer open, she yanked everything out. At the back of one drawer she found dozens of recent charge slips for flowers and hotel rooms and lingerie.

Her anger turned into an honest-to-God fury. She threw it all— charge slips, bills, appointment reminders, the chequebook register— into a huge cardboard box. On it, in bold letters, she wrote his name and office address. In smaller letters, she wrote: *I did this for twenty years. Now it's your turn.*

She felt better than she had in days. *What would she do now? Where would she go?* She touched the compass at her throat and she knew.

Perhaps she'd known all along. She'd go back to the girl she'd seen in those rare black and white photos . . . back to where she was someone besides Blake's wife and Natalie's mother.

Chapter 2

AFTER HOURS OF FLYING and driving, Annie was finally steering her rental car across the long floating bridge that connected the Olympic Peninsula to the rest of Washington State. She rolled down the window and flicked off the air conditioner. Sweet, misty air swept into the car, swirling tiny tendrils of hair across her face.

Mile by mile, the landscape rolled into the vivid greens and blues of her childhood world. She turned off the modern freeway and onto the two-lane road that led away from the shore. Under a purplish layer of fog, the peninsula lay hidden, a pork chop of land ringed by towering, snowcapped mountains on one side and wild, windswept beaches on the other, untouched by the hustle and bustle of modern life. At the heart of the peninsula was the Olympic National Park, almost a million acres of no-man's-land, ruled by Mother Nature and the myths of the Native Americans who had lived here long before the white pioneers.

When Annie finally reached the town of Mystic, she slowed her speed, soaking in the familiar sights. Main Street ran for only six blocks. She didn't have to reach its end to know that at Elm Street the rutted asphalt gave way to a puddled, pockmarked gravel road.

Downtown wore the shabby, forgotten look of a white-haired old man left out in the rain. Fifteen years ago, Mystic had been a booming town supported by fishing and logging, but the intervening years had obviously been hard ones that had driven merchants to more lucrative communities and left in their wake several vacant storefronts.

It was an exhausted little logging town, but to Annie, whose eyes had grown accustomed to steel and concrete and glass, it was gorgeous. The sky now was grey, but she could remember how it looked without the cover of clouds. Here, in Mystic, the sky started deep in the palm of God's hand and unfurled as far as the eye could see. It was a grand land of sublime landscapes, with air that smelt of pine needles and mist and rain.

Annie had roots in this county that went deep and spread far. Her grandfather had come here almost seventy years ago, a block-jawed German with an appetite for freedom and a willingness to use a saw. He had carved a good living from the land and raised his only son, Hank, to do the same. Annie was the first Bourne to get a college education.

She followed Elm Street out of town. The road began its slow, winding crawl up the hillside, thrusting deeper and deeper into the forests. One by one, the houses receded, giving way to trees. Miles and miles of scrawny, new-growth trees huddled behind signs that read: CLEARCUT 1992. REPLANTED 1993. There was a new sign every quarter-mile or so; only the dates were different.

Finally, she reached the turnoff to the gravel road that meandered through fifteen acres of old-growth timber.

As a child, this woodland had been her playground. She had spent countless hours climbing through the dewy bushes and over crumbling logs, in search of treasures: a white mushroom that grew only by the light of a red moon, a newborn fawn awaiting its mother's return, a gelatinous cache of frog's eggs hidden in the bogs.

At last, she came to the two-storey clapboard farmhouse in which she'd grown up. It looked exactly as she remembered: a gabled, fifty-year-old structure painted a pale pearl grey with white trim. A white-washed porch ringed the whole house, and baskets of winter-spindly geraniums hung from every post. Smoke spiralled up from the brick chimney and merged into the low-slung layer of grey fog overhead.

She manoeuvred the rented Mustang to the parking area behind the woodshed and shut off the engine. Grabbing her bag, she walked up to the front door.

Only a moment after she rang the bell, her father opened the door.

The great Hank Bourne—all six feet three inches and 220 pounds of him—stood there for a second, staring with disbelieving eyes. Then a smile started, buried deep in his silvery-white moustache and beard.

'Annie,' he whispered in that scratchy, barrel-chested voice of his.

His arms opened for a hug, and she launched herself forward, burying her face in the velvety folds of his neck. He smelt of woodsmoke and Irish Spring soap and of the butterscotch hard candies he always kept in the breast pocket of his work shirt. Of her childhood.

Annie let herself be carried away by the comfort of her father's embrace. At last, she drew back, unable to look at him, knowing he'd see the tears in her eyes. 'Hi, Dad.'

'Annie,' he said again.

She forced herself to meet his probing gaze. He looked good for his sixty-seven years. His eyes were still as bright and curious as a young man's, even tucked as they were in folds of ruddy pink skin. He placed a scarred hand—cut long ago by blades at the lumber mill—into the bib of his faded denim overalls. 'You alone, Annie?'

She flinched. The question contained layers and layers. There were so many ways to answer. He looked at her so intensely she felt uncomfortable, as if he were seeing into her soul.

'Natalie left for London,' she said weakly. 'She's staying with a family called Robertson. It's raining every day, cats and dogs from what I und—'

'What's going on, Annie Virginia?'

She swallowed. 'He . . . he left me, Dad.'

He looked hopelessly confused. 'What?'

She shrugged. 'It's an old story. He's forty . . . and she's twenty-eight.'

Hank's lean, wrinkled face fell. 'Oh, honey . . .' She saw him search for words, and saw the sadness fill his eyes when he came up empty. He moved towards her, pressed a dry-skinned palm against her face. For a heartbeat, the past slid into the present; they were both remembering another day, long ago, when Hank had told his seven-year-old daughter that there'd been an accident . . . that Mommy had gone to Heaven . . . *She's gone, honey. She won't be coming back.*

In the silence that followed, Hank hugged his daughter. She laid her cheek against the comforting flannel of his plaid work shirt. 'He'll be back,' he said quietly. 'Men can be pretty damn stupid. But Blake will realise what he's done, and he'll be back, begging for a second chance.'

'I want to believe that, Dad.'

Hank smiled. 'Trust me, Annie. That man loves you. He'll be back. Now, how about if we settle you into your old bedroom?'

'That'd be perfect.'

Hank reached out and grabbed her hand. Together they walked through the sparsely decorated living room and up the rickety stairs that led to the upper floor.

At Annie's old bedroom, Hank turned the knob and pushed the door open. The room was a wash of yellow-gold wallpaper lit by the last rays of the fading sun; it was a young girl's floral print, chosen by a loving mother and never changed. Neither Annie nor Hank had ever considered peeling the paper off, not even when Annie had outgrown it. A spindly white iron double bed dominated the room, its surface piled high with yellow and white quilts. Beside a narrow double-hung window sat a twig rocker, the one her father had made for her on her thirteenth birthday. *You're a woman now*, he'd said, *you'll be wanting a woman's chair.*

He'll be back. She wrapped Hank's words around her, letting them become a shield against the other, darker thoughts. She wanted desperately to believe her dad was right. Because if Blake didn't come back, Annie would have no idea who she was or where she belonged.

The night had passed in fitful waves. She'd spent the past four days wandering around this old farmhouse like a lost spirit, feeling restless and bruised. She knew she should do something, but she had no idea what. All her life she'd taken care of people, she'd used her life to create a perfect setting for Blake's and Natalie's lives, and now, alone, she was lost.

There was a knock at her door. 'I'll be out in a while,' she mumbled.

The door swung open. Hank stood in the opening. He was wearing a red and blue plaid flannel shirt and a pair of bleached, stained denim overalls. He was holding a tray full of food. Disapproval etched his face, narrowed his eyes. He carefully set down the tray and crossed the room. 'You look like hell.'

Stupidly, she burst into tears. She knew it was true. She was thin and ugly—and no one, including Blake, would ever want her again. The thought made her sick to her stomach. She clamped a hand over her mouth and raced to the bathroom. It was humiliating to know that her father could hear her retching, but she couldn't help it. Afterwards, she brushed her teeth and moved shakily back into her room.

The worry in Hank's eyes cut like a knife.

'That's it,' he said, clapping his hands together. 'You're going in to see the doctor. Get your clothes.'

The thought of going out, of *leaving*, filled her with horror. 'I can't. People will . . .' She didn't even know what she was afraid of. She only knew that in this room, here in her little girl's bed, she felt safe.

'I can still throw you over my shoulder, kiddo. Either get dressed or go into town in those pyjamas. It's up to you. But you're going to town.'

She wanted to argue, but she knew her father was right, and frankly, it felt good to be taken care of. 'OK, OK.'

Annie stared out at the hand-painted sign which read MYSTIC MEDICAL CLINIC. DR GERALD BURTON, FAMILY PRACTITIONER.

Annie smiled. She hadn't thought about old Doc Burton in years. He had delivered Annie into the world and seen her through almost two decades of childhood infections and accidents. Hitching her bag over her shoulder, she strode up the concrete steps to the clinic's front door.

Inside, a blue-haired old lady looked up at her. Her name tag read, HI! I'M MADGE. 'Hello. May I help you?'

'I'm Annie Colwater. I think my father made an appointment.'

'He sure did, darlin'. Have a seat. Doc'll see you in a jiff.'

After she filled out the insurance forms, Annie took a seat in the waiting room, flipping idly through the newest issue of *People* magazine. She hadn't waited more than fifteen minutes when Dr Burton rounded the corner and strolled into the waiting room. The twenty years she'd been gone showed in the folds of red skin along his neck and in the amount of hair he'd lost, but he was still old Doc Burton, the only man in all of Mystic who religiously wore a tie to work.

'Well, Annie Bourne, as I live and breathe.'

She grinned up at the old man. 'It's been a long time.'

'So it has. Come, come.' He slipped an arm round her shoulder and led her into his consulting room.

He sat opposite her, eyeing her. 'So, what's going on with you?'

She managed a smile. She found it hard to begin. 'I haven't been sleeping well . . . headaches . . . sick to my stomach . . . that sort of thing.'

'Any chance you could be pregnant?'

She should have been prepared for the question. If she'd been ready, it wouldn't have hurt so much. But it had been years since any doctor had asked the sensitive question. Her own doctors knew the answer too well. 'No chance.'

'Any hot flushes, irregular periods?'

She shrugged. 'My periods have always been irregular. In the last year, I've skipped a couple of months. My own gynaecologist has warned me that menopause could be just around the corner.'

'I don't know . . . you're a little young for that . . .'

She smiled. 'Bless you.'

He sighed. 'Is there something going on in your life that would lead to depression?'

Depression.

One word to describe a mountain of pain. One word to steal the sunlight from a person's soul and leave them stranded in a cold, grey landscape, alone and searching for something they couldn't even name.

'Maybe.'

'Would you like to talk about it?'

Tears slipped unchecked down her cheeks. 'My husband and I recently separated. I haven't been . . . handling it very well.'

Slowly, he pulled his glasses off, laid them on top of his papers, and tiredly rubbed the bridge of his beaked nose. 'I'm sorry, Annie. I see too much of this, I'm afraid. It happens in little ole Mystic as often as it does in the big city. Of course you're blue—and depression could certainly explain sleeplessness, lack of appetite, nausea. Any number of symptoms. I could prescribe some Valium, maybe start you on Prozac. Something to take the edge off until you come out on the other side.'

He slipped his glasses back onto his nose and peered at her. 'This is a time when you want to take dang good care of yourself, Annie. Depression isn't a thing to trifle with. I'll give you a prescription but if you have too many sleepless nights, you come on back. Now, how long are you sticking around?'

'I have to go . . . home in mid-June.' *Unless Blake calls.* She shivered inwardly at the thought. 'I guess I'll be here until then.'

'Mid-June, huh? OK, I want to see you here just before then. No matter what. I'll set you up with an appointment, OK?'

It felt good to have someone care about her progress. 'OK. I'm sure I'll be better by then.'

He walked Annie out of the clinic. Patting her shoulder, he reminded her again to take care of herself, then he turned and disappeared back down the hallway.

Annie felt better as she headed across town to the river park where she had arranged to meet her father. The crisp air rejuvenated her. It was one of those rare early spring days that held all the promise of summer.

She found Hank sitting on the same wooden bench that had always been alongside the river. She sat down beside him.

'What did the doc say?' he asked.

'Big surprise . . . I'm depressed.'

'Are you pissed off yet?'

'Last night I pictured Blake being eaten by piranhas—that seems angry, don't you think?' He didn't answer, just stared at her until, more softly, she said, 'I was for a while, but now, I'm too . . . empty to be angry.' She felt tears rise and she couldn't stop them. 'He thinks I'm nothing, Dad. He expects me to live off alimony and be . . . nothing.'

'What do you think?'

'I think he's right.' She squeezed her eyes shut. 'Give me some advice, Dad. Some words of wisdom.'

'Life sucks.'

She laughed in spite of herself. 'Thanks a lot, Dad. I ask for wisdom and you give me bumper stickers.'

'How do you think people come up with bumper stickers?' He patted her hand. 'Everything is going to work out, Annie. Blake loves you; he'll come around. But you can't keep spending all your time in that bed. You need to get out. Do something.'

She knew he was right. She couldn't go on the way she had been, waiting for a phone call that wasn't going to come, crying constantly.

'You've got to take some risks, honey.'

'I take risks. I don't floss every day, and I mix floral and plaids.'

'I mean—'

Annie laughed—the first real, honest-to-God laugh since the shit hit the fan. 'Haircut.'

'What?'

'Blake always liked my hair long.'

Hank grinned. 'Well, well. I guess you're a little angry after all.'

Lurlene's Fluff 'n'Stuff was not the kind of salon she usually patronised. It was an old-fashioned, small-town beauty parlour. Annie parked beneath a hot pink sign that read: PARKING RESERVED FOR LURLENE'S CUSTOMERS ONLY. VIOLATORS WILL BE SUBJECT TO A CUT AND PERM. She followed a walkway of heart-shaped cement stones up to the front porch, then stopped, suddenly afraid. She'd had long hair for ever. What was she thinking? *Calm down, Annie.* She took a deep breath, draining away everything except what she needed to take a single step forward, to walk up those steps and get a haircut.

She had almost reached the top step when the front door whooshed open and a woman appeared. She had to be at least six feet tall, with a pile of red hair that pooched up to the doorway. Someone had poured her statuesque body into a pair of sparkly red spandex pants (either that, or it was a coat of glitter paint). A tight-fitting angora sweater in a black and white zebra print strained across breasts the size of the Alps. A huge zebra earring dangled from each ear.

'You must be Annie Colwater . . .' She pronounced it *Colwatah* in a Southern drawl as thick and sweet as corn syrup. 'Why, darlin', I been waitin' on you! Your daddy called and said you wanted a new look.' She bounded down the creaking stairs. 'I'm Lurlene, sweetie. Big as a moose, you're thinkin', but with twice the fashion sense. Now, sugar, you come on in.' She patted Annie and took hold of her arm, leading her up the steps and into a bright, white and pink room with a few wicker-framed mirrors. Pink gingham curtains shielded the view and a pink hook rug covered the hardwood floor.

'Pink is my colour,' Lurlene said proudly, her drawl spinning the sentence into *Pink is mah colah.* 'The twin shades of cotton candy and summer glow are designed to make you feel special and safe. I read that in a magazine, and ain't it just the God's truth?' She led Annie past two other customers, both older women with their grey hair twined on tiny multicoloured rods.

Lurlene kept up a steady chatter as she washed Annie's hair. *Oh, Lordie, I ain't seen this much hair since my Disco Barbie doll.* After she'd settled her into a comfortable chair in front of the mirror, Lurlene peered over Annie's shoulder. 'You sure you want this cut? Most women'd give their husband's left nut for hair like this.'

Annie refused to give in to the flutter of nerves that had settled in her stomach. 'Cut it off,' she said evenly. 'All of it.'

Lurlene's painted mouth dropped open. 'Off? As in . . . *off?*'

Annie nodded.

Lurlene recovered quickly. 'Why, darlin', you're gonna be my crownin' achievement.'

Annie took one look at her own chalky, drawn face in the mirror, with her hair slicked back from her thin face, and slammed her eyes shut . . .

She felt a tug on her hair, then a snip of steel blades and a whoosh of hair fell to the floor.

'I sure was surprised when your daddy called. I've heard stories about you for years. Kathy Johnson—you recall her? Well, Kath and I went to beauty school together. 'Course Kath never actually finished— something about the scissors bothered her—but we got to be best friends. She told me tons o' stories about when y'all were kids. I reckon you'n Kathy were wild and crazy.'

Kathy Johnson.

It was a name Annie hadn't heard in years. *Kathy and Annie, friends 4-ever. 2 good 2 be true.* That's what they'd written in each other's yearbook, what they'd promised as the end of high school neared.

Annie had always meant to stay in touch, but somehow she never had. Christmas cards for a few years, and then even that had stopped. Annie hadn't heard from Kathy in years. The separation had started before high school was over, when Nick proposed to Kathy.

Nick.

Annie could still remember the day she'd first seen him. Junior English. He'd walked in arrogantly, his blue eyes challenging everyone in the room. He was wearing ragged Levi's and an overwashed white T-shirt, with a packet of cigarettes rolled up in his sleeve. He wasn't like anyone she'd ever seen before, with his wild, too-long black hair and don't-mess-with-me attitude. Annie had fallen in love on the spot; so had every other girl in the room, including her best friend, Kathy.

But it was Kathy he had chosen, and, with that choice, Annie had tasted the first salty wounds of a broken heart.

She smiled at the memory, faded and distant as it was. Maybe she'd go and see them, try to kick-start the old camaraderie—God knew it would be nice to have a friend right about now. If nothing else, they could laugh about the old days. 'How are Nick and Kathy?'

The scissors abruptly stopped clipping. 'You ain't heard? Kathy died about eight months ago.'

Annie opened her eyes. A pale, chalky woman with hacked-off hair stared back at her from the oval mirror. She slammed her eyes shut again. When she found her voice, it was thin and soft. 'What—'

'I been helpin' out as much as I can—baby-sittin' an' such, but that child of his, Isabella, well . . . she just ain't right in the head any more. Got herself kicked out of school yesterday. Can you imagine that? A six-year-old gettin' kicked outta school? Just what're they thinkin', I ask you? They all know about her mama. You'd think a little pity'd be in order. Nick's been lookin' for a nanny, but he finds fault with everyone I send him.'

'How did it happen?' Annie's voice was a whisper.

'Just called her into the principal's office and said, kiddo you're outta school.' Lurlene made a tsking sound. 'That child don't need to get rejected again. What she *needs* is a daddy. 'Course a rabbit's a better parent than he is right now—and they eat their young. I wish I could do more for 'em but Buddy—that's my husband—he says he's done raisin' kids. I don't mind watchin' her after school—she's actually quite a help around the place—but she scares me, if the truth be told, what with her problems and all.'

It was all coming at Annie too fast. She couldn't make herself really comprehend it. *Kathy*.

How could Kathy be dead? Only yesterday they'd been best friends, playing together in the schoolyard at recess in elementary school, giggling about boys in junior high, and double dating in high school. They had been friends in the way that only girls can be—they wore each other's clothes and slept at each other's houses and told each other every little secret. They promised to always stay friends.

But they hadn't taken the time and energy to stay in touch when their lives went down separate roads . . . and now Kathy was gone. Annie hadn't meant to forget Kathy. But she had, and that's what mattered now. She had gone to Stanford, met Blake, and exchanged the past for a future.

'Nicky's fallin' apart, pure and simple,' Lurlene said, snapping a big bubble of gum. 'Him and Kathy bought the old Beauregard house on Mystic Lake—'

The Beauregard house. An image of it came to Annie, wrapped up in the tissue-thin paper of bittersweet memories. 'I know it. But you still haven't told me how Kath—'

The hair dryer blasted to life, drowning out Annie's question. She thought she heard Lurlene still talking, but she couldn't make out the words. Then, after a few minutes, the dryer clicked off.

'Lordie, you do look fine.' Lurlene squeezed her on the shoulder. 'Open your eyes, honey, and take yourself a peek.'

Annie opened her eyes and saw a stranger in the mirror. Her brown hair was so short there was no curl left. The pixie cut emphasised her drawn, pale skin, and made her green eyes look haunted and too large for the fine-boned features of her face. Without lipstick, her unsmiling mouth was a colourless white line. She looked like Kate Moss at fifty— after a lawn-mower attack. 'Oh, my God . . .'

All Annie wanted was to get out of this room without crying. *It'll be all right. It'll grow back*, she told herself, but all she could think about was Blake, and what he would say about what she'd done when—if—he came back to her. Shakily, she reached for her purse. 'How much do I owe you?'

'Nothin', honey. We've all had bad weeks.'

Annie turned to Lurlene. In the woman's heavily mascaraed eyes, there was real, honest-to-God understanding.

If she hadn't felt so sick, Annie might have managed a smile. 'Thanks, Lurlene. Maybe I can return the favour some time.'

Lurlene grinned. 'Why, honey, this here's Mystic. You hang around long enough and a favour's gonna come beggin'.'

Annie thanked her again and made for the door. She escaped into her rented Mustang and cranked up the engine, barrelling out of the drive-way in a spray of gravel and a cloud of smoke. She made it almost a mile before she felt the sting of tears.

It wasn't until almost fifteen minutes later, as she drove with her hands white-knuckled round the steering wheel and tears leaking down her cheeks, that she remembered the question that had been left unan-swered. What had happened to Kathy?

Annie drove round Mystic, down the rain-rutted back roads, up the bare, harvested hills, until the tears on her cheeks had dried to thin silver streaks. She knew she had to put on a happy face when she saw her dad. Finally, when she'd regained some measure of self-control, she went home.

Hank was seated in one of the old butter-yellow chairs beside the fire-place. A book of crossword puzzles lay open on his lap. At her entrance he looked up. The smile on his face fell faster than a cake when the oven door was slammed. 'Holy hamhock,' he said slowly.

Annie couldn't help laughing. 'I've been cast in *GI Jane*, the sequel.'

Hank gave her a crooked grin. 'Your haircut is stunning. It'll just take a little getting used to.'

'Well, I *feel* like a new woman, and that's what I wanted.'

'Of course it is.' He patted her shoulder. 'Now, how about a rousing game of Scrabble?'

Annie nodded and let him lead the way. He pulled the Scrabble box out from the armoire in the corner of the living room, dusted off the box and set out the board on the coffee table.

Annie stared at her seven smooth wooden squares. 'So, Dad, you didn't tell me about Kathy Johnson.'

He didn't look up. 'Didn't I? I thought I wrote you about it. Or maybe I told you when I was down for Christmas?'

'No.'

He shrugged, and she could tell that he wasn't going to look up. 'Oh, well. I guess you know now. That Lurlene's the mouth that roared in Mystic. Sorry you had to find out about it that way.'

Annie could tell that Hank was uncomfortable. He was staring at his letters as if they were the original Ten Commandments. He was not the kind of man who liked to discuss death. Anyone's. But certainly not the untimely death of a woman he'd watched grow up.

Annie let the subject rest. Forcing a thin smile, she plucked up four letters and started the game. Anything she wanted to know about Kathy's death, or her life, would have to come from somewhere else.

Chapter 3

NICK DELACROIX STOOD in his front yard in the pouring rain, staring down at the limp, sagging, half-dead cherry tree he'd planted last year. Slowly, he fell to his knees in the muddy grass and bowed his head.

He hadn't cried at his wife's funeral, or yesterday when his daughter had been kicked out of school, but he had the strangest goddamn urge to cry now—and over this stupid little tree that wouldn't grow. He pushed to his feet and then turned away from the tree, walking tiredly back up to the house where Izzy waited for him.

Yesterday had been a bad day—and in the past eight months he'd had enough of them to know. His Izzy had been kicked out of school. Yesterday, his Izzy had stood in the principal's office, her brown eyes flooded with tears, her full, little girl's lips quivering. Her pink dress was stained and torn, and he'd known with a sinking feeling that it had been like that when she'd put it on. Her long black hair—once her pride and joy—was tangled because no mother's hand had combed through it.

He'd wondered fleetingly, absurdly, what had happened to all those pretty ribbons she'd once had.

We can't have her in school any more, Nick. Surely you see that?

Izzy had stood there, motionless. She hadn't spoken—but then, she hadn't spoken in months. That was one of the reasons they'd expelled her . . . that and the disappearing. A few months ago, she'd started to believe she was disappearing, one tiny finger at a time. Now she wore a small black glove on her left hand—the hand she could no longer see or use. Recently she'd begun to use her right hand awkwardly, as if she believed some of those fingers were 'gone' now, too.

She hadn't looked up, hadn't met Nick's eyes, but a single tear had streaked down her cheek. He'd wanted to say something, but he had no idea how to comfort a child who'd lost her mother. Then, like always, his inability to help his daughter had made him angry. It had started him thinking that he needed a drink—just one to calm his nerves. And all the while, she had stood there, too quiet and still for a six-year-old, staring at him with a sad, grown-up disappointment.

Now, the thought of facing her, seeing that tiny black glove . . .

Maybe if he had a little drink. Just a short one—

The phone rang as he entered the house. He knew even before he answered that it was Lurlene, wondering where he was. 'Heya, Lurl,' he drawled, leaning tiredly against the wall. 'I know, I know, I'm late. I was just leaving.'

'No hurry, Nicky. Buddy's out with the boys tonight—and before you jump down my throat, Izzy's fine.'

He released a sigh, unaware until this moment that he'd tensed up. 'You don't care that I'm late, and Izzy is fine. So, what's up?'

Her voice fell to a stage whisper. 'Actually, I was callin' with an interestin' bit o' gossip.'

'Good God, Lurl. I don't give a shit—'

'I met an old friend of yours today—Annie Bourne. She's back in town, visitin' her daddy.'

Nick couldn't have heard right. 'Annie Bourne is back in town?'

Lurlene babbled on about haircuts and cashmere sweaters and diamonds the size of grapes. Nick couldn't keep his focus. *Annie Bourne.*

He mumbled something—he had no idea what—and hung up.

Jesus, Annie Bourne. Picking his way through the debris in his living room, he went to the fireplace and grabbed a picture off the mantel. It was one he'd seen daily but hadn't really looked at in years. A bit faded, the colours sucked away by time and sunlight, it was of the three of them, taken in the last rosy days of the summer before their senior year. Annie and Kathy and Nick. The gruesome threesome.

He was in the middle, with an arm round each girl. He looked young and carefree and happy—a different boy from the one who'd lived in a cramped, dirty car only a few months before. In that perfect summer, when he'd first tasted the rain-sweet elixir called normal life, he'd finally understood what it meant to have friends, to *be* a friend.

And he had fallen in love.

The photograph had been taken the day he'd first understood it would have to come to an end, the day he realised that sooner or later, he'd have to choose between the two girls he loved.

But there had never really been any doubt. Annie had already applied to Stanford, and with her grades and test scores, everyone knew she'd be accepted. She was on her way in the world. Not Kathy. Kathy was a quiet, small-town girl given to blue moods . . . a girl who needed desperately to be loved and cared for.

He still remembered what he'd told Annie that day. After the life he'd lived with his mother, he knew what he wanted: respect and stability. He wanted to make a difference in people's lives, to be part of a legal system that cared about the death of a lonely young woman who lived in her car.

He'd told Annie that he dreamed of becoming a policeman in Mystic.

Oh, no, Nicky, she had whispered, staring into his face. *You can do better than that. If you like the law, think big . . . big . . . you could be a Supreme Court justice, maybe a senator.*

It had hurt him, those words, the quiet, unintentional indictment of his dreams. *I don't want to be a Supreme Court justice.*

She'd laughed, that soft, trilling laugh that always made his heart ache with longing. *You've got to think bigger, Nicky boy. You don't know what you want yet. Once you start college—*

No college for me, smart girl. I won't be getting a scholarship like you.

He'd seen it dawn in her eyes, slowly, the realisation that he didn't want what she wanted, and that he wouldn't reach that far. He didn't have the courage to dream big dreams. All he wanted was to help people and to be needed. It was all he'd ever known, all he was good at.

But Annie hadn't understood. *Oh,* was all she'd said, but there'd been a wealth of new-found awareness in the word, a tiny unsteadiness in her voice that he'd never heard before.

It was so simple to him back then. He loved Annie . . . but Kathy needed him, and her need was a powerful draw.

He'd asked Kathy to marry him just a few months before graduation, but it didn't matter by then, because Annie had known he would. They tried, after the engagement, to keep their friendship together, but inevitably they'd begun to drift apart. It had become Nick-and-Kathy, with Annie a bystander. By the time Annie left for college, amid a shower of promises to keep in touch, Nick had known there would be no lifelong friendship, no gruesome threesome any more.

By the time he got back from Lurlene's it was almost nine thirty. Well past a six-year-old's bedtime, but Nick didn't have the heart to put her right to bed.

Izzy sat cross-legged on the floor in front of the cold, black fireplace. She was holding her rag doll, Miss Jemmie, in one arm—the best she could do since she'd begun 'disappearing'. The silence in the room was overwhelming, as pervasive as the dust that clung to the furniture.

It shredded Nick into helpless pieces. 'I'm sorry about what happened at school, Izzy-bear,' he said awkwardly.

She looked up, her brown eyes painfully dry and too big for the milky pallor of her tiny face.

The words were wrong; he knew that instantly. He wasn't just sorry about what had happened at school. He was sorry that he was such a failure, that he had no idea where to go from here.

Izzy was watching him warily, waiting and worrying about what he would do next. Sadly, he knew how that felt, to wait with bated breath to see what a parent would do next. He knew how it twisted your insides into a knot and left you barely able to draw breath.

He closed his eyes. He was fifteen years old, a tall, quiet boy with too many secrets, waiting on the street corner for his mother to pick him up from school. The kids moved past him in a laughing, talking centipede of blue jeans and backpacks and psychedelic T-shirts. He watched enviously as they boarded the yellow buses that waited along the kerb.

At last, the buses drove away, heading for neighbourhoods Nick had never seen, and the schoolyard fell silent. The grey sky wept. Cars rushed down the street. None of the drivers noticed a thin, black-haired boy in ragged, holey jeans and a white T-shirt.

He had been so damned cold; he remembered that most of all. There was no money for a winter coat, and so his flesh was puckered and his hands were shaking.

Come on, Mom. That was the prayer he'd offered again and again.

He hated to wait for his mother. As he stood there, alone, his chin tucked into his chest for warmth, he was consumed by doubt. How drunk would she be? Would it be a kind, gentle day where she remembered that she loved him? Or a dark, nasty day where the booze turned her into a shrieking, stumbling madwoman who hated her only child with a vengeance? She wailed that welfare cheques didn't cover gin and bemoaned the fact that they'd been reduced to living in their car—a swallow away from homelessness. He could always read her mood immediately. A pale, dirty face that never smiled and watery, unfocused eyes meant that she'd found her way to a full bottle.

She never came that day. Or the next. He'd wandered round the dark, dangerous parts of Seattle all night, and finally, he'd fallen asleep in the garbage-strewn doorway of a tumble-down Chinese restaurant. In the morning, he'd rinsed out his mouth and grabbed a discarded bag of fortune cookies from a Dumpster, then made his way to school.

The police had come for him at noon, two unsmiling men in blue uniforms who told him that his mother had been stabbed. The policemen told Nick that there were no suspects, and he hadn't been surprised. No one except Nick had cared about her when she was alive; no one was going to care that another scrawny, homeless drunk, turned old before her time by booze and betrayal, had been murdered.

Nick wished he could forget, but of course, the past was close now. It had been breathing down his neck ever since Kathy's death.

With a tired sigh, he turned and faced his utterly silent child. 'Time for bed,' he said softly, trying to forget, too, that in the old days—not so long ago—she would have mounted a protest.

But now, she got to her feet, held her doll in the two 'visible' fingers on her right hand, and walked away from him. Without a single backward glance, she began the long, slow climb to the upper floor. What was he going to do now that Izzy was out of school? She had nowhere to go and no one to take care of her. He couldn't stay home from work every day with her and Lurlene had her own life. What in the hell was he going to do?

Annie woke early from her solitary bed and paced the room. Kathy's death had reminded her how precious time was, how fleeting. How sometimes life snipped the edges off your good intentions and left you with no second chance to say what really mattered.

She didn't want to think about her husband—*I love her, Annie*—but the thoughts were always there.

She glanced at the clock beside the bed. It was six o'clock in the morning. She sat down on the edge of the bed, grabbed the phone and dialled Terri's number.

She answered on the fifth ring. 'This better be important.'

Annie laughed. 'Sorry, it's just me. Is it too early?'

'No, no. I love getting up before God. Is everything OK?'

Annie didn't know if things would ever be OK again, but that answer was getting stale. 'I'm getting by.'

'Judging by the hour, I'd say you weren't sleeping well.'

'Not much.'

'You need to find something to do. Something that gets you out of your bed—or into someone else's. Go buy some new clothes. Something that changes your look.'

Annie rubbed her shorn hair. 'Oh, I've changed my looks all right.'

They talked for another half-hour, and when she hung up, Annie felt, if not stronger, then at least better. She took a long, hot shower.

Dressing in a white cashmere, boat-necked sweater and winter-white wool slacks, she went downstairs and cooked Hank a big breakfast of scrambled eggs, pancakes and turkey bacon. It wasn't long before the aroma drew her dad downstairs.

He walked into the kitchen, tightening the grey cotton belt round his ankle-length robe. He scratched his scruffy white beard and stared at her. 'You're up. Are you out of bed for long, or just roving until the headache starts again?'

The perceptiveness of the question reminded Annie that her father had known tragedy himself. She pulled some china plates from the old oak dresser in the corner and quickly set two places at the breakfast table. 'I'm moving on with my life, Dad. Starting now. Starting here. Sit down.'

He pulled out a chair. It made a grating sound on the worn yellow linoleum. 'I'm not sure feeding a man is a big leap forward.'

She gave him a crooked grin and took a seat across from him. 'Actually, I thought I'd go shopping.'

'In Mystic? Unless you're looking for the ideal steel-head lure, I don't know how much luck you'll have.'

Annie stared down at her eggs. She wanted to eat—she really did—but the sight of the food made her faintly nauseous. She hoped her dad didn't notice. 'I thought I'd get a few books, catch up on my reading. And the clothes I brought won't work up here.'

'Yeah, white's not a very practical colour up here in mudland.' Reaching for his fork, he glanced across the table at Annie. She could tell that he was doing his best not to grin. 'Good for you, Annie Virginia.' Then, softer, 'Good for you.'

Annie strolled down Main Street, peeking into the various stores. She passed stores that sold trinkets for tourists, hardware, fabric, and fishing tackle. But there wasn't a single bookstore. At the H & P Drugstore, she picked up the latest Pat Conroy best seller but couldn't find anything else that interested her. There wasn't much of a selection. It was too bad, because she needed a manual for the rest of her life.

At last, she found herself standing in front of Eve's Leaves Dress Emporium. A mannequin smiled down at her from the display window, wearing a bright yellow rain slicker and matching hat. Annie pushed through the glass door. A tiny bell tinkled at her entrance.

A woman squealed. 'It *can't* be!' Molly Block, her old high-school English teacher, came forward, her fleshy arms waving.

'Annie?' she said, grinning. 'Annie Bourne, is that you?'

'It's me, Mrs Block. How are you?'

Molly planted her hands on her wide hips. 'Mrs Block. Don't make me feel so old, Annie. Why, I was practically a *child* when I taught your class.' She grinned again, and shoved the wire-rimmed glasses higher on her nose. 'It's grand to see you again. Why, it's been years.'

'It's good to see you, too, Molly.'

'Whatever brings you up to our neck of the woods? I thought you married a hotshot lawyer and were living the good life in California.'

Annie sighed. 'Things change, I guess.'

Molly cocked her head to the left and eyed Annie. 'You look good; I'd kill to be able to wear that haircut, but I'd look like a helium balloon. That white cashmere won't last long in this country, though. One good rainstorm and you'll think you left the house wearin' a dead rabbit.'

Annie laughed. 'That's the truth.'

Molly patted her shoulder. 'Follow me.'

An hour later, Annie stood in front of a full-length mirror. She was wearing a nineteen-dollar pair of jeans (who knew they still made jeans at that price?), cotton socks and tennis shoes, and a baggy sweatshirt in a utilitarian shade of grey.

The clothes made her feel like a new woman. She didn't look like the thirty-nine-year-old soon-to-be-ex-wife of a hotshot California lawyer; she looked like an ordinary small-town woman, maybe someone who had horses to feed and porches to paint. A woman with a life. For the first time, she almost liked the haircut.

'They suit you,' Molly said, crossing her beefy arms and nodding. 'You look like a teenager.'

'In that case, I'll take everything.'

While Molly was ringing up the purchases, Annie glanced out of the window. She listened vaguely to the small-town gossip, but she couldn't really concentrate. She turned back to Molly. 'I heard . . . about Kathy Johnson . . . Delacroix.'

Molly paused, her pudgy fingers plucking at a price tag. 'It was a true shame, that. You all used to be awfully close in high school.' She smiled sadly. 'I remember the time you and Nick and Kathy put on that skit for the talent show—you all sang some silly song from *South Pacific*. Nicky wore that outrageous coconut bra, and halfway through the song you all were laughing so hard you couldn't finish.'

'I remember,' she said softly, wondering how it was she'd forgotten it until this very second. 'How's Nick doing since . . .?' She couldn't bring herself to actually say the words.

Molly made a tsking sound and snipped the price tag from the jeans with a pair of scissors. 'I don't know. He makes his rounds and does his job, I guess—you know he's a cop, right? Don't see him smile much any more, and his daughter is in pretty bad shape, from what I hear. They could use a visit from an old friend, I'll bet.'

After Annie paid for her new clothes, she thanked Molly for the help and carried her purchases out to the car. Then she sat in the driver's seat for a while, thinking, remembering.

She shouldn't go to him, not now, not spur-of-the-moment, she knew that. A thing like this needed to be thought out. You didn't just go barging into a strange man's life, and that's what he was: a stranger. Besides, she was broken and battered herself. What good could she be to a man who'd lost his wife?

But she was going to go to him. He and his wife had once been her best friends. And she had nowhere else to go.

It was approaching nightfall by the time Annie gathered the nerve to go and see Nick. A winding brown ribbon of road led to the Beauregard house. Towering old-growth trees edged the road and every now and then, through the black fringe of forest, she could see a glittering silver reflection of the lake. The road twisted and turned and finally ended in a big circular dirt driveway. Annie parked next to a police squad car, turned off the engine, and stared at the beautiful old house, built back at the turn of the century, when woods were solid and details were hand-carved by craftsmen who took pride in their work.

A pale yellow fog obscured half of the house, drifting on invisible currents of air from the lake. It crept eerily up the whitewashed porch steps and wound around the carved posts.

Annie remembered a night when this house had been spangled in starlight. It had been abandoned then; every broken window had held jagged bits of shadow and moonlight. She and Nick had ridden their bikes here, ditched them alongside the lake, and stared up at the big, broken house.

I'm gonna own this house some day, Nick had said, his hands shoved deeply in his pockets.

He'd turned to her, his handsome face cut into sharp angles by the glittering moonlight. She hadn't seen the kiss coming, hadn't prepared for it, but when his lips had touched hers, as soft and tentative as the brush of a butterfly's wing, she'd started to cry.

He had drawn back, frowning. *Annie?*

She didn't know what was wrong, why she was crying. She'd felt foolish and desperately naive. It was her first kiss—and she'd ruined it. It was the first and last time he'd ever kissed her.

She brushed the memory aside.

Nick and Kathy had fixed up the old house—the windows were all in place and sunshine-yellow paint coated everything. Shutters bracketed each window, but still the whole place looked . . . untended.

Last year's geraniums and lobelia were still in the flower boxes, now a dead, crackly bunch of brown stalks. The grass was much too long and moss had begun to fur the brick walkway.

And still it was one of the most beautiful places she'd ever seen. Annie tucked her bag under her arm and slowly crossed the squishy wet lawn, climbing the white porch steps. At the oak door, she paused, then took a deep breath and knocked.

No answer.

She was just about to turn away when suddenly the door swung open, and Nick was standing in front of her.

She would have recognised him anywhere. He wasn't wearing a shirt, and the dark, corrugated muscles of his stomach tapered down into a pair of bleached Levi's. He looked as tough and sinewy as old leather, with pale, lined skin stretched across hollowed-out cheeks. His hair was unkempt, and either time or grief had sucked its colour away.

But it was his eyes—an eerie, swimming-pool blue—that caught and held her attention. His gaze flicked over her, a cop's look that missed no detail, not the brand-new tomboy haircut or the newly purchased small-town clothes. Certainly not the Buick-size diamond on her left hand. 'Annie Bourne,' he said softly. 'Lurlene told me you were back in town.'

An uncomfortable silence fell as she tried to figure out what to say. She shifted nervously from side to side. 'I'm . . . sorry about Kathy.'

He seemed to fade a little. 'Yeah,' he answered. 'So am I.'

'I know how much you loved her.'

He looked as if he were going to say something, but in the end he said nothing, just cocked his head and swung the door open wider.

She followed him into the house. It was dark—there were no lights on, no fire in the fireplace—and there was a faint musty smell in the air.

Something clicked. Brilliant white light erupted from a shadeless lamp. The living room looked like someone had dropped a bomb on it. There was a Scotch bottle lying beside the sofa; open pizza boxes littered the floor; clothes lay in heaps and on chairbacks. A crumpled blue policeman's shirt hung across the television screen.

'I don't seem to spend much time at home any more,' he said into the awkward silence. Reaching down, he grabbed a faded flannel shirt from the floor and put it on.

She glanced around. The sprawling living room was floored in beautiful oak planks and dominated by a large brick fireplace, blackened by age and smoke. It looked as if there hadn't been a fire in the hearth in a long, long time. The few bits and pieces of furniture—a faded brown leather sofa, a tree-trunk end table, a Morris chair—were scattered haphazardly around the room, all wearing tissue-thin coats of dust. A stone archway led into a formal dining room, where Annie could see an oval maple table and four scattered chairs, their seats cushioned by red and white gingham pads. She supposed that the closed green door led to the kitchen. To the left, an oak staircase hugged the brightly wallpapered wall and led to a darkened upper floor.

Annie felt Nick's gaze on her. Nervously, she searched for something to say. 'I hear you have a daughter.'

Slowly, he nodded. 'Izzy. Isabella. She's six.'

Annie's gaze landed on a photograph on the mantel. She picked her way through the rubble on the floor and touched the photo. 'The gruesome threesome,' she said, smiling. 'I can't remember this one . . .'

Lost in her own memories, Annie vaguely heard him pad out of the room. A moment later, he was back. 'Would you like a drink?'

She turned away from the fireplace and found him directly behind her, holding a bottle of wine and two glasses. 'A drink would be great. Where's your daughter? Can I meet her?'

An unreadable look passed through his eyes. 'She's staying with Lurlene tonight. Let's go sit by the lake.' He grabbed a blanket from the sofa and led her out of the house. Together, not too close, they sat down on the blanket.

Annie sipped at the glass of wine Nick had poured for her. A pale half-moon spread a blue-white veil across the navy-blue surface of the lake. Tiny, silvery peaks rippled against the shore, lapped against the pebbly ground. Memories sifted through the air. She remembered how easy it had once been with them, as they sat together at sporting events, watching Kathy cheerlead at the sidelines. They'd known how to talk to each other then—she'd believed she could tell him anything.

And now, all these years later, with the bumpy road of their separate lives between them, she couldn't think of how to weave a fabric of conversation from a single thread.

She sighed, sipping her wine. She couldn't stand the silence any more. 'It's beautiful—'

'Nice stars—' They both spoke at the same time.

Annie laughed. 'When in doubt, mention the weather or the view.'

'We can do better than that,' he said quietly. 'Life's too damned short to spend it making small talk.'

He turned to her, and she saw the network of lines that tugged at his blue eyes. He looked sad and tired and infinitely lonely. It was that, the loneliness, that made her feel like they were partners somehow, victims of a similar war. So, she put the small talk aside, forgot about plundering the shared mine of their teenage years, and plunged into intimacy. 'How did Kathy die?'

He gulped down his glass of wine and poured another. 'She killed herself.'

Annie stared at Nick, too stunned to respond. 'I . . .' She couldn't say the pat, *I'm sorry*. The words were too hollow, almost obscenely expected. She gulped a huge swallow of wine.

Nick stared out at the lake, sighing heavily. 'Remember how moody she used to be? She was teetering on the edge of despair even then—her whole life—and none of us knew it. At least, *I* didn't know it . . . until it started to get bad. The older she got, the worse it became. Manic-depressive. That's the technical term. She started having episodes right after her twentieth birthday, just six months after her folks were killed in a car accident. Some days she was sweet as pie, then something would happen . . . she'd cry and lock herself in a closet. She wouldn't take her medication most of the time, said it made her feel like she was breathing through Jell-O.' His voice cracked.

'I bought this place to make her happy, hoping maybe it would help her remember what life used to be like. I thought . . . if I could just give her a home, a safe place where we could raise our kids, everything would be OK. Christ, I just wanted to help her . . .'

His voice cracked again, and he took another drink of wine. 'For a while, it worked. We poured our hearts and souls and savings into this old mausoleum. Then Kathy got pregnant. For a while after Izzy was born, things were good. Kathy took her medication and tried . . . She tried so hard, but she started to hate this place—the heating that barely worked, the plumbing that pinged. About a year ago, she gave up the medication again . . . and then everything went to hell.'

He finished his second glass of wine and poured another. Shaking his head, he said softly, 'And still, I didn't see it coming.'

She didn't want to hear any more. 'Nick, you don't—'

'One night I came home from work and found her. She'd shot herself in the head . . . with my gun.'

Annie's fingers spasmed round the stem of her glass. 'You don't have to talk about her.'

'I *want* to. No one else has asked.' He closed his eyes, leaning back on his elbows. 'Kathy was like the fairy tale—when she was good, she was very, very good, and when she was bad, you wanted to be in Nebraska.'

He gave Annie a tired smile. 'One day she loved me with all her heart and soul, and the next day, she wouldn't even speak to me. It was worst at night; sometimes she'd kiss me, and other times she'd roll towards the wall. If I even touched her on those nights, she'd scream for me to get away. The more she pulled away, the more I reached out. I knew I wasn't helping, but I couldn't seem to stop myself. I kept thinking that if I loved her enough, she'd be OK. Now that she's gone, all I can think about is how selfish I was, how stupid and naive. I should have listened to that doctor and hospitalised her. At least she'd be alive . . .'

Without thinking, Annie reached for him, touched his face gently. 'It's not your fault.'

He gave her a bleak look. 'When your wife blows her brains out in your bed, with your baby daughter just down the hall, believe me, she thinks it's your fault.' He made a soft, muffled sound, like the whimpering of a beaten pup. 'God, she must have hated me . . .'

'You don't really believe that.'

'No. Yes. Sometimes.' His mouth trembled as he spoke. 'And the worst part is—sometimes I hated her, too. I hated what she was doing to me and Izzy. She started to be more and more like my mother . . . and I knew, somewhere down inside, I knew I wasn't going to be able to save her. Maybe I stopped trying . . . I don't know.'

His pain called out to her. She took him in her arms, stroking him as she would have soothed a child. 'It's OK, Nick . . .'

When he finally drew back and looked at her, his eyes were flooded with tears. 'And there's Izzy. My . . . baby girl. She hasn't said a word in months . . . and now she thinks she's disappearing. At first it was just a finger on her left hand, then her thumb. When the hand went, she started wearing a black glove and stopped talking. I've noticed lately that she only uses two fingers on her right hand—so I guess she thinks that hand is disappearing, too. God knows what she'll do if . . .' He tried to smile. 'What can I do? My six-year-old daughter hid under her bed one night because she heard a noise. She wanted to go to her mommy and get a hug, but thank God, she didn't. Because if Izzy had walked down the hall that night, she would have seen bits and pieces of her mommy on the mirror, on the headboard, on the pillow . . .' Tears streaked down his unshaven cheeks.

His grief mingled somewhere in the darkness with her own pain. Nick gazed at her, and she knew he was seeing her through the blur of his tears. He touched her cheek, his hand slid down to coil round her neck and pulled her closer.

The kiss she pressed to his lips was meant to comfort; of that she was sure, a gentle commiseration of understood heartache. But when their lips touched, soft and pliant and salty with teardrops, everything changed. The kiss turned hot and hungry and desperate. She was thinking of Blake, and she knew he was thinking of Kathy, but it didn't matter. What mattered was the heat of togetherness.

She fumbled with the buttons on his shirt and pressed her hands beneath the worn flannel as quickly as she could, sliding her open palms against the coarse wiry hairs on his chest. Touching him felt secret and forbidden, dangerous, and it made her *want* . . .

With a groan, he wrenched his shirt off and tossed it aside. Annie's clothes came next. Cool night air breezed across her bare skin. She closed her eyes, embarrassed by the intensity of her desire. His hands were everywhere, touching her, rubbing, stroking, squeezing, sliding down the curve of her back. In some distant part of her mind, she knew that this was a bad idea, but it felt so good. No one had wanted her this badly for a long, long time. Maybe ever . . .

He brought her body to a throbbing edge between pleasure and pain. Her breathing shattered into choppy, ragged waves, until she was gasping for air and aching for release. 'Please, Nick . . .' she pleaded.

She clung to him and when he entered her, she had a dizzying, desperate moment when she thought she would scream . . .

Her release was shattering. He clung to her, moaned, and when she felt his orgasm, she came again, sobbing his name. He gathered her into his arms, stroking her hair, murmuring soft, soothing words against her ear. But her heart was pounding so hard and her pulse was roaring so loudly in her ears she had no idea what he said.

When Annie fell back to earth, she landed with a thud. She lay naked beside Nick, her breathing ragged. Very slowly, Nick pulled his hand away from hers. Without the warmth of his touch, her skin felt clammy and cold.

She grabbed one end of the blanket and pulled it across her naked breasts, sidling away from him. 'Oh, my God,' she whispered. 'What have we done?'

He curled forward, burying his face in his hands.

She grabbed her shirt. She had to get out of here, now, before she fell apart. 'This didn't happen,' she said in a whispery, uncertain voice. 'This did *not* happen.'

He didn't look at her as he scooped up his clothes and hurriedly dressed. She was shaking and doing her best not to cry as she dressed. He was probably comparing her to Kathy, remembering how beautiful his wife had been, and wondering what the hell he'd done—having sex with a too-thin, too-old, too-short-haired woman who had let herself become such a nothing . . .

Finally, she stood. She stared down at her own feet, wishing the ground would open up and swallow her. 'I better get—' She'd been about to say *home*, but she didn't have a home any more than she had a husband there waiting for her. She swallowed thickly and changed her words. 'Back to my dad's house. He'll be worried—'

At last, Nick turned to her. His face was lined and drawn. 'I've never slept with anyone but Kathy,' he said softly, not quite meeting her eyes.

'Oh,' was all she could think of to say, but his quiet admission made her feel a little better. 'This is a first for me, too.'

'I guess the sexual revolution pretty much passed us by.'

Another time it might have been funny. She nodded towards her car. 'I guess I should get going.'

Wordlessly, they headed back to the car. She was careful not to touch him, but all the way there, she kept thinking about his hands on her body, the fire he'd started deep inside her . . .

'So,' he said into the awkward silence, 'I guess Bobby Johnson was lying when he said he nailed you after the Sequim game?'

She stopped dead and turned to him, fighting the completely unexpected urge to laugh. '*Nailed* me?'

He shrugged, grinning. 'He said it, not me.'

'*Nailed* me?' She shook her head. 'Bobby Johnson said that?'

'Don't worry—he said you were good.'

This time she did laugh, and some of her tension eased. They started walking again, across the wet grass, to her car. He opened the door for her, and it surprised her, that unexpected gesture of chivalry. No one had opened a car door for her in years.

'Annie?' He said her name softly.

She glanced up at him. 'Yes?'

'Don't be sorry. Please.'

She swallowed hard. For a few moments, Nick had made her feel beautiful and desirable. How could she feel sorry about that? She wanted to reach out for him again, anything to stave off the cold loneliness that would engulf her again the moment she climbed into her rented car and closed the door. 'Lurlene told me you were looking for a nanny . . . for Isabella. I could watch her . . . during the day . . . if that would help you out . . .'

He frowned. 'Why would you do that for me?'

'It would help me out, Nick. Really. Let me help you.'

He stared at her for a long time, that wary cop's look again. Then slowly, pointedly, he took hold of her hand and lifted it. In the pale moonlight, the three-carat diamond glittered with cold fire. 'Don't you belong somewhere else?'

Now he would know what a failure she was, why she'd come running back to Mystic after all these years. 'My husband and I have recently separated . . .' She wanted to say more but her throat closed up.

He dropped her hand as if it had burned him. 'Jesus, Annie. You shouldn't have let me act like such a whiny asshole, as if no one else in the world had a problem. You should have—'

'I *really* do not want to talk about it.' She saw him flinch, and was immediately sorry for her tone of voice. 'Sorry. But I think we've had enough shoulder-crying for one night.'

He nodded, looking away for a minute. He stared at his house. 'Izzy could use a friend right now. I'm sure as hell not doing her any good.'

'It would help me out, too. I'm a little . . . lost right now. It would be nice to be needed.'

'OK,' he said at last. 'I have to pick Izzy up from Lurlene's tomorrow. I could meet you at her house—she lives down in Raintree Estates—you remember where that is? Pink house with gnomes in the front yard. It's hard to miss.'

'Sure. What time?'

'Say one o'clock? I can meet you there on my lunch break.'

'Perfect.' She stared up at him for a long minute, then turned and climbed into her car, started the engine, and slowly pulled away. The last thing she saw, out of her rearview mirror as she drove away, was Nick looking after her.

Long after she'd driven away, Nick remained on the edge of the lawn, staring down the darkened road. Slowly, he walked back into the house, letting the screen door bang shut behind him. He went to the fireplace and picked up the photograph of the three of them again. He looked at it for a long, long time, and then he poured himself a stiff drink. He knew it was dangerous to use alcohol to ease his pain, and in the past months, he'd been reaching for that false comfort more and more.

What he and Annie had done tonight didn't change a thing. He had to remember that. The life she'd stirred in him was ephemeral and fleeting. Soon, she'd be gone, and he'd be left alone again, a widower with a damaged child who had to find a way to get through the rest of his life.

There was a light on in the living room when Annie pulled up to her dad's house. She winced at the thought of confronting him now, with her clothes all wrinkled and damp. God, she probably smelt like sex.

She climbed out of the car and headed into the house. Hank was in the living room, waiting up for her. He looked up from the book he was reading. 'Well, well,' he said, easing the bifocals from his eyes.

Annie self-consciously smoothed her wrinkled clothes and ran a hand through her too-short hair, hoping there was no grass stuck to her head. 'You didn't need to wait up for me.'

'Really?' He closed the book.

'There's no need to worry. I'm a hell of a long way from sixteen.'

'Oh, I wasn't worried. Not after I called the police and the hospital.'

Annie sat down on the leather chair beside the fireplace. 'I'm sorry, Dad. I guess I'm not used to checking in. Blake never cared . . .' She bit back the sour confession and forced a thin smile. 'I visited an old friend. I should have called.'

'Yes, you should have. Who did you go see?'

'Nick Delacroix. You remember him?'

Hank's blunt fingers tapped a rhythm on the cover of the book, his eyes fixed on her face. 'I should have expected you'd end up there. You three were as tight as shoelaces in high school. He's not doing so good, from what I hear.'

Annie imagined that Nick was a delectable morsel for the town's gossips. 'I'm going to help him out a little. Take care of his daughter while he's at work, that sort of thing. I think he needs a breather.'

'Didn't you two have sort of a "thing" in high school?' His gaze turned, assessing. 'Or are you planning to get back at Blake?'

'Of course not,' she answered too quickly. 'You told me I needed a project. Something to do until Blake wakes up. What am I supposed to do—cure cancer? I'm a wife and mother. It's all I know. All I am.' She leaned forward, ashamed that she couldn't tell him the whole truth—that she didn't know how to be this alone. 'Dad, if I don't do *something* I'm going to explode. This seems as good as anything. Nick and Izzy need my help.'

'The person you need to help right now is you.'

Her answering laugh was a weak, resigned little sound. 'I've never been much good at that, now have I?'

Chapter 4

ANNIE THREW BACK the covers and stumbled out of bed. Her first thought when she woke was always *Blake?* But, of course, he wasn't beside her in bed. It was getting harder and harder for her to believe that he would ever come back to her, and the loss of that transient hope made her feel as hollow as a reed sucked dry by the summer heat.

Tears stung her eyes. Last night she had broken her marriage vows for the first time in her life; she had shattered the faith she'd made with the only man she'd ever loved. And the hell of it was, he wouldn't care.

Nick was just getting ready to sign off for his lunch break when the call came in, a domestic disturbance on Old Mill Road.

The Weaver place.

With a sigh, Nick radioed the dispatcher and asked her to put a call in to Lurlene. He wouldn't make his meeting with Annie and Izzy.

Flicking on his siren and lights, he raced down the rutted strip of asphalt that led out of town. He followed Old Mill Road along the winding curves that sidled along the Simpson tree forest, and came at last to the driveway. A lopsided, dented mailbox, rusted to the colour of Georgia mud, hung precariously from an arched piece of weathered driftwood. He turned cautiously down the road, a narrow, twisting swatch cut by hand from the dense black forest around it, to the clearing where a rickety mobile home squatted in the mud.

Nick radioed the dispatcher again, confirming his arrival, and then he hurried from the squad car and charged up the wooden crates that served as the front steps. He was about to knock when he heard a scream from inside the trailer.

'Police!' he yelled as he pushed through the door. It swung inwards and cracked on the wall. A shudder reverberated through the room. 'Sally? Chuck?' He peered through the gloomy interior. Avocado-coloured shag carpeting muffled the sound of his boots as he moved forward. 'Sally?'

A shriek answered him.

Nick ran through the kitchen and shoved through the closed bedroom door.

Chuck had his wife pinned to the fake wood panelling. She was screaming beneath him, trying to protect her face. Nick grabbed Chuck by the back of the neck and hurled him sideways. The drunken man blinked up at him, obviously trying to focus. 'Goddamn it, Nicky,' he whined in a low, slurred voice. 'What in the fuck are you doing here? We was just havin' a argument . . .'

Nick holstered a fierce, sudden urge to smash his fist into Chuck's fleshy face. 'Stay here, goddamn it,' he said as he cautiously made his way to Sally. She was leaning against the wall now, her torn, stained dress splattered with blood. A jagged cut marred her lower lip, and already a purplish bruise was seeping across her jaw.

He couldn't readily recall how many times he'd been here, how many times he'd stopped Chuck from killing his wife. It was a bad situation, this marriage, and had been long before Chuck got laid off at the mill, but since then, it had become a nightmare. Chuck spent all day at Zoe's Tavern, downing beers he couldn't afford and getting mad. By the time he crawled off his bar stool and pulled his broken-down pick-up into his driveway, he was ready to do some serious damage. The only one around was his wife.

Nick touched Sally's shoulder. 'Sally, it's me. Nick Delacroix.'

She slowly opened her eyes, and when she did, he saw the bottomless well of her despair, and her shame. She brought a shaking, bruised hand to her face and tried to push the blood-matted hair from her face. Tears welled in her blackened eyes and streaked down her battered cheeks. 'Oh, Nick . . . Did the Robertses call you guys again?' She edged away from him and straightened, trying to look normal and in control. 'It's nothing, really. Chuckie just had a bad day, is all . . .'

Nick sighed. 'You can't keep doing this, Sally. One of these days he's going to kill you.'

She tried to smile. It was a wobbly, unbalanced failure, and it tore at Nick's heart. As always, Sally made him think of his mother, and all the excuses she'd made for alcohol over the years. 'Oh, no, not my Chuckie. He gets a little frustrated, is all.' She patted his forearm. 'I don't need no help, Nick. But thanks for comin' by.'

Nick stood there, staring down at her. She seemed to be shrinking before his eyes, losing weight. The ragged cut of her cotton dress was too big for her; it hung off her narrow shoulders and lay limply against her body. He knew as certainly as he knew his own name that one day he would answer one of these calls and Sally would be dead. 'Sally—'

'Please, Nick,' she said, her voice trembling, her eyes filling with tears. 'Please, don't . . .'

Nick turned away from her. There was nothing he could do to help her. The realisation caused an ache deep inside him, and left him wondering why in the hell he did this job. There was no success, or damned little of it. He stepped over an upended laundry basket and took hold of Chuck's collar. 'Come on, Chuck. You can sleep it off downtown.'

He ignored Chuck's whining and refused to look at Sally again. He didn't need to. Sally would be following, whispering words of apology to the husband who'd broken her bones, promising to be 'better' when he came home, vowing to have dinner on the table on time.

It didn't sicken Nick, her behaviour. Unfortunately, he understood Sally. He had been like her in his youth, had followed his mother around like a hungry dog, begging for scraps of affection, taking whatever attention she would occasionally fling his way.

Yes, he understood too well why Sally stayed with Chuck. And he knew, too, that it would end badly for both of them. But there was nothing he could do to help them.

Izzy Delacroix lay curled in a tight little ball on Lurlene's guest bed clutching Miss Jemmie to her chest, stroking the doll's pretty yellow hair with the two fingers she had left on her right hand.

At first it had sorta scared her, when she'd figured out that she was disappearing. She'd started to reach for a crayon, and halfway there, she'd noticed that her pinky finger was sort of blurry and grey. The next day it was invisible. She had told her daddy and she could tell by the way he looked at her that it scared him, too. And that icky doctor—it had made him look at her like she was a bug.

She stared at the two fingers that remained on her right hand. *It's goin' away, Mommy.* She waited for an answer, but none came. Lots of times, she imagined her mommy was right beside her, and she could talk to her just by thinking the words.

She wished she could make it happen right now, but it only seemed to happen at special times—at the purply time between night and day.

She needed to talk to her mommy about what had happened the other day. It had been so bad. One minute, she'd been looking at the pictures in her book, and the next thing she knew, there was a scream inside her. She had felt so scared and so lonely she couldn't breathe right. The scream had started as a little yelp that slipped out. She had clamped a hand over her mouth but it hadn't helped. The scream had come out. Loud, louder, loudest. She'd clamped her hands over her ears so she couldn't hear it. She'd known she was crying, but she hadn't been able to stop that, either.

The teacher had grabbed Izzy's hand, and led her down the hallway into the principal's office. The grown-ups looked at her like she was crazy—but she couldn't help herself.

As quickly as the scream had come, it went away. It left her shaken and weird-feeling, standing in the middle of the principal's office, with everyone staring at her. The grown-ups' voices whispering . . .

Then her daddy had walked into the principal's office. The grown-ups shut up instantly. He wouldn't have come to the school if she hadn't started screaming, and for a second, she was glad she'd screamed. Even if it made her a bad girl, she was glad to have her daddy here.

She wanted to throw herself in his arms, say, *Hi, Daddy*, in that voice she used to have, but he looked so sad she couldn't move.

He was so handsome; even since his hair had changed colour after the bad thing, he was still the most handsome man in the world. She remembered what his laugh used to sound like, how it used to make her giggle right along with him . . .

But he wasn't really her daddy any more. He never read her stories at night any more, and he didn't throw her up in his arms until she laughed. And sometimes at night his breath smelt all mediciney and he walked like one of her wobbly toys.

'Izzy?' He said her name softly, moving towards her.

For one heart-stopping minute, she thought he was going to touch her. She leaned towards him, just a little teeny bit, but enough so maybe he'd see how much she needed him.

He gave a sharp sigh and turned back to face the grown-ups. 'What's going on here, Bob?'

Izzy almost wished for the scream to come back. The grown-ups talked a bunch more, saying things that she wasn't listening to. Then Daddy went away, and Izzy went home with Lurlene. Again.

'Izzy, sweetheart, are you in there?'

She heard Lurlene's voice, coming through the closed bedroom door. 'Come on out, Izzy. There's someone I want you to meet.'

Izzy wanted to pretend she hadn't heard, but she knew there wasn't any point. She sighed. *Miss Jemmie, we gotta go.*

The bedroom door swung open. Lurlene stood in the opening, her big feet smacked together, her body bent at the waist. 'Come on, sweetheart.' She reached out and tucked a tangled chunk of hair behind Izzy's ear.

Wordlessly, Izzy followed her down the hallway.

Annie stood in the entryway of Lurlene and Buddy's home, on a patch of pink carpet. Buddy sat sprawled in a burgundy velours lounger. He was watching Annie carefully.

She shifted from foot to foot, trying not to think about the fact that she wasn't a psychiatrist, or that the child's trauma was a dark and bottomless well, or that Annie herself was lost.

She knew that love was important—maybe the most important thing—but she'd learned in the past weeks that it wasn't a magic elixir. Even Annie wasn't naive enough to believe that every problem could be solved by coating it in love. Some pain couldn't be assuaged, some traumas couldn't be overcome. She'd known that since the day her own mother had died.

'Nick ain't comin'. Did Lurlene tell you that?'

Annie frowned and glanced at Buddy. 'Oh. No. I didn't know.'

'He don't never show up when it matters.' He paused. 'You're taking on a hell of a job, you know. That Izzy's got the kind of pain that sucks innocent bystanders under and drowns 'em.'

In other words: *You're out of your depth here, city girl.*

'Annie?'

It was Lurlene's voice this time. Annie slowly turned.

Lurlene appeared at the end of the hallway, clad in a neon-green sweater and a pair of skin-tight purple imitation snakeskin leggings. She clashed with everything in the house.

A child hung close to her side, a small girl with big brown eyes and hair the colour of night. She was wearing a too-small pink dress that had seen better days. Her thin legs stuck out from the hemline like twin beanpoles. Mismatched socks—one pink, one yellow—hugged her ankles and disappeared into a pair of dirty Beauty and the Beast tennis shoes. An ordinary little girl who missed her mother.

Annie smiled. Maybe she didn't know about traumatic muteness but she knew about being afraid, and she knew about mothers who disappeared one day and never came back.

Slowly, with her hand out, she moved towards the girl. 'Hey, Izzy,' she said softly.

Izzy didn't answer; Annie hadn't expected her to. She figured Izzy would talk in her own sweet time. Until then, Annie was just going to act as if everything were normal. And maybe, after what Izzy had been through, silence was the most normal thing in the world.

'I'm Annalise, but that's a mouthful, isn't it? You can call me Annie.' She knelt down in front of the little girl, staring into the biggest, saddest brown eyes she'd ever seen. 'I was a good friend of your mommy's.'

A response flickered in Izzy's eyes.

Annie took it as encouragement. 'I met your mom on the first day of kindergarten.' She smiled at Izzy, then stood and turned to Lurlene. 'Is she ready to go?'

Lurlene nodded, then whispered, 'God bless you for doing this.'

'Believe me, Lurlene, this is as much for me as anyone. See you later.'

Annie led the way to the car, settled Izzy in the front seat, and clicked the seat belt in place. She started the car and backed out of the driveway, steering carefully past a crowd of ceramic gnomes. She kept talking as she drove. She talked about anything and everything—the best colours, her favourite movies, the Girl Scout camp she and Kathy had gone to—and through it all, Izzy stared and stared.

When they reached the end of the winding lake road, Annie found herself unable to move. She sat behind the wheel of the car and stared at the old Beauregard place. Nick's home, now.

I'm gonna own this house someday.

It had sounded like a silly dream to Annie then, all those years ago. Something to say on a starlit night before he found the courage to lean down and kiss the girl at his side.

Now, of course, she saw the magic in it, and it cut a tiny wound in her heart. She pulled into the gravel driveway and parked next to the wood-pile. The house sat primly in the clearing before her. Sunlight, as pale and watery as old chicken broth, painted the tips of the lush green grass and illuminated the daffodil-yellow paint on the clapboard siding.

Izzy's seat belt unhooked with a harsh click. The metal fastener cracked against the glass. She opened the door and ran towards the lake, skidding to a stop at a picket-fenced area beneath a huge, moss-furred old maple tree.

Annie followed Izzy across the squishy lawn and stood beside the child. Within the white fence lay a beautiful square of ground that wasn't nearly as wild and overgrown as everything else on the property. 'This was your mom's garden,' she said softly.

Izzy remained motionless, her head down.

'Gardens are very special places, aren't they? They aren't like people . . . their roots grow strong and deep into the soil, and if you're patient and you care and you keep working, they come back.'

Izzy turned slowly, tilted her head, and looked up at Annie.

'We can save this garden, Izzy. Would you like that?'

Very slowly, Izzy reached forward. Her thumb and forefinger closed round the dead stem of a Shasta daisy. She pulled so hard it came out by the roots. Then she handed it to Annie.

Izzy clutched Miss Jemmie under her arm; it was the best she could do without all her fingers. She lagged behind the pretty, short-haired lady.

'Come on, Izzy,' the lady called out from the porch.

The front door creaked open, and Izzy trudged reluctantly up the porch steps. The lady—Annie—she had to remember that the lady's name was Annie—clicked on the lamp beside the sofa. Light landed in streaks on Daddy's mess. Bottles, pizza boxes, dirty clothes were lying everywhere.

'As Bette Davis would say, "What a dump."'

Izzy winced. But Annie didn't turn and walk away. Instead, she picked her way through the junk and flung open the curtains in a cloud of dust. Sunlight poured through the two big picture windows. 'That's better,' she said, glancing around. 'I don't suppose you know where the brooms and dustpans are? A bulldozer? How about a blowtorch?'

Annie winked at Izzy. 'I'll be right back.' She hurried out of the living room and disappeared into the kitchen.

Izzy stood very still. Annie came back into the living room carrying a black garbage bag, a broom and a bucket of soapy water.

Slowly, Izzy moved towards Annie, waiting for the lady to throw her hands up and say, *It's too goddamn much work, Nicky*, like her mommy used to. But Annie didn't say that. Instead, she bent over and picked up the garbage, one piece at a time, shoving it into the black bag.

Cautiously, Izzy moved closer.

Annie didn't look at her. 'It's just junk, Izzy. Nothing permanent. There's nothing done here that can't be undone. My daughter's room used to look like this all the time—and she was a perfectly lovely teenager.' She kept talking, and with each unanswered sentence, Izzy felt herself relaxing. 'Why, I remember this place when I was a little girl. Your mom and daddy and I used to peek in the windows at night-time, and we'd make up stories about the people who used to live here.' She paused long enough to smile at Izzy. 'Maybe when the weather warms up, we could have a picnic on the lawn. Would you like that?'

Izzy felt the weirdest urge to cry. She wanted to say, *We could have milk shakes and Jell-O salad*, but she didn't. She couldn't.

'In fact,' Annie said, 'we could have a mini-picnic today. When I get the living room cleaned up, we'll have cookies and juice outside—iced raisin cookies and Maui punch. That sounds good, don't you think? "Yes, Annie, I think that would be terrrrrific." That's my Tony the Tiger impression. Natalie—that's my daughter; she's almost a grown-up now—she used to love Frosted Flakes. I'll bet you do, too.'

Izzy bit back an unexpected smile. She liked the way Annie didn't wait for her to answer. It made Izzy feel like she wasn't so different, like not talking was as OK as talking.

Tiny step by tiny step, she inched sideways. When she reached the sofa, she sat down, ignoring the dust that poofed up around her. Bit by bit, the garbage disappeared, and it began to look like home.

Annie tapped lightly on Izzy's bedroom door. There was no answer. Finally, she pushed open the door and went inside. The room was tucked under an overhang in the roofline. A charming dormer reached outwards, capturing the last pink light of day behind pale, worn lace curtains. The walls were done in a beautiful lavender-striped paper, and a matching floral print covered the bed.

Annie didn't know much about manic-depression, or how it had twisted and changed Kathy, but she knew that Kathy had loved her daughter. Every item in this room had been lovingly chosen, from the Winnie-the-Pooh nightlight to the Peter Rabbit book ends.

She crossed the clothes-strewn wooden floor to where Izzy was playing with Miss Jemmie.

'I thought you'd like to take a bath before your daddy gets home.' Annie smiled and held up the bag of treats she'd bought that morning. 'I got you some new clothes and a few surprises—Lurlene told me what sizes to get. Come on.' She led Izzy to the bathroom, where she quickly ran some water into the tub.

Then she knelt in front of the child.

Izzy eyed her warily.

Annie looked down at Izzy's gloved hand. 'How, exactly, do we undress the invisible parts?' Slowly, she pulled the sleeve along the 'invisible' arm. Then she reached for the glove.

Izzy made a choking sound and wrenched away from her.

'Oh, sorry. The glove can't come off?'

Izzy stared intently at a spot somewhere behind Annie's left ear.

'I understand. There is no glove, is there, Izzy?'

Izzy bit down on her lower lip. She still didn't look at Annie.

Annie stood. Carefully taking Izzy by the shoulders, she steered the child towards the bathtub and helped her in. Izzy hugged the side of the tub, where her left arm hung limply over the edge.

'That's not too hot, is it?' Annie asked. 'No, Annie, that's just right. Just exactly the temperature I like.'

Izzy stared at her.

Annie grinned. 'I can carry on a conversation all by myself. When I was a girl—I was an only child, too—I used to do it all the time.'

Annie poured bubble bath into the falling water, then lit a trio of votive candles she'd found in the kitchen. The sweet aroma of vanilla rose in the air. 'Sometimes a girl needs a romantic bath—just for her. OK.' She reached into her brown bag. 'Look at my goodies. I've got Pocahontas shampoo and soap, a Hunchback of Notre Dame towel, and a Beauty and the Beast comb. And this *darling* playsuit. It's lavender with little yellow flowers—just like your mom's garden will be—and a matching yellow hat.'

She kept up a steady stream of dialogue, asking questions and answering them herself as she washed Izzy's long hair and lathered and rinsed her body, and finally helped her out of the tub. She wrapped the tiny girl in a huge towel and began combing her hair. 'I remember when my daughter, Natalie, was your age. It used to make my heart ache just to look at her.' She wove Izzy's hair into a pair of perfect French braids and finished them off with two yellow satin bows.

'Turn around.'

Dutifully, Izzy turned.

Annie dressed her in new white cotton underwear and helped her into the lavender blouse and overalls. When she was finished, she guided Izzy to the full-length mirror in the corner.

The little girl stared at herself for a long, long time. Then, very slowly, she lifted her right hand and touched the satin ribbons with her forefinger. Her rosebud mouth wobbled uncertainly. She bit down hard on her lower lip. A single tear trickled down Izzy's flushed pink cheek.

Annie understood. It was what she'd been hoping for, at least in part. 'I bet you always used to look like this, didn't you, Izzy?'

She placed a tender kiss on Izzy's forehead. 'Now, I could use some help in the kitchen. I've started dinner, but I can't find the dishes *any-where*. Maybe you could help me?'

Together, they went down to the kitchen. Izzy walked dutifully towards the table and sat down. Her little feet dangled above the floor.

Annie talked the whole time she made dumplings, then dropped them into the simmering chicken stew. 'Do you know how to set the table?' she asked as she put the lid on the big metal pot.

Izzy didn't answer.

'This isn't going to work, you know, Miss Izzy.' Annie picked up a spoon and handed it to the girl. 'Here you go—this is for you.'

Izzy used her thumb and forefinger to take hold of the spoon. She stared at it, then frowned up at Annie.

'One shake of the spoon is yes. Two shakes is no. That way we can talk . . . sort of in code, without ever having to say something out loud. Now, do you think you could show me where the plates are?'

Izzy stared unblinking at the spoon for a long, long time. Then, very slowly, she shook it once.

'**H**ey, Nicky, I hear Hank Bourne's daughter is back in town.'

Nick glanced up from his drink. There was a headache pounding behind his eyes, and he couldn't quite focus. He'd had it ever since the fiasco at the Weaver place and he thought that if he stopped in at Zoe's for a quick drink—just one to steady his nerves—he'd be OK to face Annie and Izzy at home. But, like always, one drink led to another and another and another . . .

What he'd seen in Sally's eyes opened a wound in his soul, a dark, ugly place that was bubbling with painful memories.

He closed his fingers round the glass and took another long, soothing pull of the Scotch. 'Whatever you say, Zoe.'

Joel Dermot scooted closer to him. 'I remember Annie Bourne. Annie and my daughter, Suki, used to be in Girl Scouts together.'

Nick closed his eyes. He didn't want to think about those days, long ago, when the three of them had been best friends. When he thought of those days, he remembered how much he used to care about Annie, and then he wound up thinking about the previous night, when she'd been in his arms, naked and wild, fulfilling all the fantasies he'd ever had about her. The memory invariably pushed him down a long and treacherous road, a road that made him question all the choices he'd made along the way. How he'd chosen Kathy because she needed him . . . and how he'd let her down, and how loving her had ruined him. Then he'd find himself having dark, dangerous thoughts—like what would his life have been like if he'd chosen Annie, or what it *could* be like if she were the kind of woman who would stay in Mystic.

Another man's wife.

Nick shot unsteadily to his feet, in a hurry to outrun that thought.

Tossing a twenty-dollar bill on the bar, he turned and hurried out of the smoky tavern. He jumped into his patrol car and headed for home. By the time he pulled into his driveway, his head hurt, and he longed for one more drink to ease the way.

What in the hell would he say to Annie now, after what had happened between them?

Slowly, he got out of the car, walked across the gravel walkway and up the sagging porch steps, and went inside.

Annie was stretched out on the sofa. When the door clicked shut behind him, she sat up and gave him a bleary-eyed smile. 'Oh,' she said. 'I guess I fell asleep.'

Her beauty left him momentarily speechless. He glanced away. 'Sorry I'm late. I . . . meant to show up at Lurlene's, but we had an emergency call, and, well . . .'

She threw the blanket back and got up. 'It's no problem. Izzy and I had a good time today. I think we're going to get along great.' She plucked her bag from the coffee table. She was careful not to look at him for too long. 'If you want . . . I could make you and Izzy a nice dinner tomorrow night. I think she'd like that.'

'That would be great. I'll be home at six o'clock.'

She edged past him but stopped at the door, turning back. 'From now on . . . if you're going to be late, I'd appreciate a phone call.'

'Yeah. I'm sorry.'

She gave him a last smile and left the house.

He stood at the window, watching her drive away. When the tiny red dots of her taillights disappeared round the bend in the road, he slowly climbed the stairs and went into the guest bedroom, the one he'd moved into eight months ago and still used when he didn't fall asleep on the couch. Stripping out of his blue uniform, he slipped into a pair of ragged old sweats and tiredly walked down the hallway. Outside Izzy's door, he paused for a moment, gathering his strength.

A tiny nightlight glowed from the wall next to her bed. It was Winnie-the-Pooh's face in vibrant yellow. He picked up her favourite book—*Where the Wild Things Are*—and lowered himself slowly to the edge of her bed. As the mattress sagged beneath his weight, he froze. Izzy wiggled in her sleep, but didn't waken.

He opened the book, staring down at the first page. In the old days, when he'd read to her every night before bed, she'd curled her little body so trustingly against his, and cocked her smiling face up. *Daddy, what're yah gonna read me tonight, Daddy?*

He shut his eyes. It had been a long time since he'd remembered her habit of saying *Daddy* at the beginning and end of every sentence. He leaned down slowly and kissed the softness of her forehead. The little-girl scent enveloped him, made him remember giving her bubble baths . . .

He let out a long, slow breath. Now, all he did was read to her when she was asleep, just a few pages from her favourite book. He hoped the words soaked through her sleeping mind. It was a tiny, stupid way of saying he loved her; he knew that. Still, it was all he seemed to have left.

He read the book in a soft, singsong voice, and then gently placed it back on the bedside table. 'Good night, Izzy-bear,' he whispered, placing a last kiss on her forehead.

Back downstairs, he went to the kitchen and poured himself a stiff drink. He kicked open the front door and slumped onto a chair on the porch.

It came to him then, as he'd known it would. He could recall the bruise on Sally's cheek, how it had been spreading already, seeping like a spot of blood through a bit of tissue paper.

Once, long ago, he had believed he could rescue people like Sally. He'd thought that when he put on his uniform, he would be invincible. God, he'd been such an idiot, believing in the words that meant so little today: honour, respect, justice. He'd actually thought that he could save people who had no desire to be saved.

But life had taught him a lot. Between his job and Kathy, his idealism had been hacked away, bit by bit, until now there was nothing left but rusted scraps. Without it, he didn't know who he was.

He took a long drink and leaned back in the chair, looking up at the night sky. Once, he'd thought that his needs were simple and easily met. He'd wanted only his family, his job, his home. He'd imagined that he would grow old in this house, sitting in this chair on his porch, watching his children grow up and move on. He'd thought then that age would pull the black from his hair, and that it would take years. He hadn't known then that grief and guilt could age a man and turn his hair silver in the span of a single season.

He drank until his head began to spin, until his vision blurred. The empty bottle slipped through his numb fingers and rolled away, clattering down the steps one by one to land silently in the grass.

The next morning, Izzy woke to the sound of her mommy's voice. She kicked the covers away and sat up, blinking. *Mommy?*

There was no answer, just the creaking sound of the house. Izzy crept out of her bedroom. She moved silently down the stairs, hoping not to wake her daddy. He was asleep on the couch, with his bare feet sticking out from the end of his blue blanket.

She tiptoed past him, her heart thudding in her chest as she eased the front door open and closed it silently behind her. She stood on the porch, looking out. A pink mist floated across the lake. *Mommy?*

She walked through the grass, to the edge of the lake. She squeezed her eyes shut and pictured her mommy. When she opened her eyes, her mommy was there, standing in the middle of the water, too far away for Izzy's hands to reach.

Mommy didn't seem to move, but all at once, she was beside Izzy, so close that Izzy could smell her perfume.

It's OK now, Izzy. Her mom's voice mingled with the breeze. *It's OK now*, Mommy said again. *I have to go.*

Izzy panicked. It felt as if she were losing her mommy all over again. *Don't go, Mommy. I'm disappearin' as fast as I can.*

But her mommy was already gone and the mist went away.

Izzy waited and waited, but nothing happened. Finally, she went back into the house. Crossing the living room, she wandered into the kitchen and started making herself breakfast.

In the other room, she heard her daddy wake up. She'd seen it a bunch of times, and it was always worse when he fell asleep in the living room. First he'd sit up on the sofa, then he'd grab his head and make a little moaning sound. When he stood up, he always hit his shin on the coffee table and yelled a bad word. Today was no different.

'Shit!'

Izzy hurried to put the pink tablecloth on the table—the one her mommy always used for breakfast. She wanted her daddy to notice how smart she was, how grown up. Maybe then he'd finally look at her, touch her . . . maybe he'd even say, *Heya, Sunshine, how did you sleep?* That's what he used to say in the mornings, and if he talked to her, maybe she could find her own voice, answer, *I'm fine, Daddy-O*, and make him laugh again. She missed hearing him laugh.

He stumbled into the kitchen and came to an unsteady stop. 'Izzy. What are you doing up?'

She blinked at him in surprise. *You c'n do it*, she thought. *Just answer him. I'm makin' you breakfast, Daddy.* But the words tangled in her throat and disappeared.

He went to the refrigerator and poured himself a glass of orange juice. Then he headed towards her. For one heart-stopping moment, she thought he was going to pat her shoulder and tell her she'd set the table real pretty. Or that *she* looked pretty—just like she used to look, with her hair all braided. She even leaned slightly towards him.

But he moved on past, and she had to squeeze back tears.

He looked at the table again. Not at her. 'I don't have time for breakfast, Izzy-bear.' He touched his forehead and closed his eyes.

She knew he had a headache again—the same one he'd had ever since Mommy went to heaven. It scared her, thinking about that.

Her daddy smiled—only it wasn't his real smile. It was the tired, shaky smile that belonged to the silver-haired daddy—the one who never looked at her. 'Did you have a good time with Annie yesterday?'

Izzy tried and tried but she couldn't answer. She saw how her daddy looked at her, like he was gonna cry, and it made her ashamed of herself.

Finally, he sighed. 'I'm gonna go take a shower. Annie should be here any minute.'

He waited a second—as if she was going to answer—but she didn't. She couldn't. Instead, she just stood there, holding two bowls, and watched him walk away.

Annie came bright and early and started cleaning the house again. All the time Annie was working, she talked to Izzy. She talked so much that sometimes Izzy couldn't listen to it all.

Izzy liked the way her house looked now, after Annie had finished cleaning it up.

It made her feel safe.

She closed her eyes, listening to the soothing sound of the broom. It made her think of her mommy, and all the times she'd sat by herself, looking at a book while her mommy cleaned the house.

Before she knew it, a sound had slipped from her mouth. It was a faint *schk-schk* noise, the same sound that the broom was making on the floor.

Her eyes popped open. It shocked her to hear her own voice after all this time. Even if it wasn't words, it was *Izzy*. She thought that part of her—the talking part—had disappeared, just like her hand and arm. She hadn't meant to stop talking, but one day after her doctor's appointment, she had opened her mouth to speak and nothing had come out.

It had terrified her, especially when she realised that she couldn't change it. After that, everyone treated her like a baby and pretended she couldn't hear, either. Annie was different. Annie didn't look at Izzy like she was a broken doll that belonged in the trash.

Annie looked at her the way her mommy and daddy used to.

Izzy smiled, and the sound kept coming, softly, barely louder than the sound of her own breathing. *Schk-schk-schk.*

Chapter 5

B<small>Y THE TIME</small> N<small>ICK</small> finally got home from work—late, as usual—Annie was exhausted. She drove home and stumbled into bed. Almost immediately, she fell into a deep sleep, but some time in the middle of the night she awoke and reached out for Blake.

Once awake, she couldn't fall back asleep again. It was an unfortunate symptom of her depression that she was tired all the time, but rarely slept well. As usual, she spent the hours until dawn trying not to think about the big empty house on the Pacific, and the man who had been a part of her life for so long. The man who'd said, *I love her, Annie.*

She went into the kitchen and ate a bowl of cereal, then she picked up the phone and called Natalie—an unscheduled call. She listened to her daughter's stories about London for several minutes, and then quietly told her about the move to Mystic. *To see Hank and help out an old friend*, she'd said.

Natalie had asked only one question: 'What does Daddy say?'

Annie had forced a fluttery laugh that sounded false to her own ears. 'You know Dad, he just wants me to be happy.'

'Really?'

It made Annie feel inestimably old, that single, simple question that seemed to know too much. After that, they'd talked for almost an hour, until Annie could feel bits and pieces of herself returning. It anchored her to talk to her daughter, reminded her that she hadn't failed at everything in her life.

At the end of the conversation, she made sure Natalie had Hank's phone number in case of an emergency, and then she hung up.

For the next hour, Annie lay in her lonely bed, staring out of the window, watching the darkness until, at last, the sun came to brush away the bruising night.

It was thoughts of Izzy that gave Annie the strength to get up, get dressed and eat something. The child had become her lifeline. Izzy touched something deep and elemental in Annie, and it didn't take a psychiatrist to understand why. When Annie looked down into Izzy's frightened brown eyes, she saw a reflection of herself.

She knew the hand Izzy had been dealt. There was nothing harder than losing a mother, no matter what age you were, but to a child, a girl especially, it changed everything about your world. In the years since her mom's death, Annie had learned to talk about the loss almost conversationally, the way you would remark upon the weather. *My mother died when I was young . . . I really don't remember her . . .* Sometimes, it didn't hurt to say those things—and sometimes the pain stunned her.

No mother.

Two small words, and yet within them lay a bottomless well of pain and loss, a ceaseless mourning for touches that were never received and words of wisdom that were never spoken. No single word was big enough to describe the loss of your mother. Not in Annie's vocabulary, and certainly not in Izzy's. No wonder the girl had chosen silence.

Annie wanted to say all of this to Nick, to make him understand all that Izzy must be feeling, but every time she looked into Nick's pale blue eyes, or at his grief-whitened hair, she knew that he understood all too well.

They were still awkward around each other. Uncertain. For Annie, at least, the memory of their passion underscored every look, every movement, and if she spoke to him too intimately, she found that it was difficult to breathe evenly. He seemed equally unnerved around her.

But slowly, things had begun to improve. Yesterday, they had spent ten minutes together, standing at the kitchen counter, sipping coffee while Izzy ate breakfast. Their conversation crept along the perimeter of their old friendship, dipping now and then into the shared well of their memories. In the end, they had both smiled.

It had given Annie a new strength, that single moment of renewed friendship, and so, today, she pulled into the driveway a half-hour early. Grabbing the bag of croissants she'd picked up from the bakery and the bag of surprises she'd bought for Izzy, she climbed out of her car and went to the front door, knocking loudly.

It took a long time, but finally Nick answered, wearing a pair of ragged grey sweatpants. Swaying slightly, he stared down at her through bloodshot eyes.

She held up the bag. 'I thought you might like some breakfast.'

He stepped back to let her in, and she noticed that he moved unsteadily. 'I don't eat breakfast, but thanks.'

He disappeared into the bathroom and came out a few minutes later, dressed in his policeman's uniform. He looked sick and shaky, with his silvery hair slicked back from his face. The lines under his eyes were deeply etched.

Without thinking, she reached for him, touched his forehead. 'Maybe you should stay home . . .'

He froze, and she could see that he was startled by the intimacy of her touch. She yanked her hand back, feeling the heat of embarrassment on her cheeks. 'I'm sorry. I shouldn't—'

'Don't,' he said softly. 'I have trouble sleeping, is all.'

She almost went to him then, almost started a conversation that wasn't for her to begin. Instead, she changed the subject. 'Will you be home for dinner? It would mean a lot to Izzy.'

'You think I don't know that?' In his eyes was a bleak desperation that wrapped around her heart. 'I'm sorry—'

He shook his head, held a hand up, as if to ward her off. 'I'll be home,' he said, then he pushed past her and left the house.

Their days together followed a comfortable routine. Annie arrived early and spent the day with Izzy, playing, reading, walking round the forest. In the early evening, she made dinner for the two of them, and afterwards, they played games or watched videos until bedtime.

Every night, Annie tucked Izzy into bed and kissed her good night.

Nick consistently missed dinner, forgot to call, and showed up around nine o'clock, smelling of smoke and booze. Even when he promised to be home, as he did almost every night, he didn't make it.

She was tired of making excuses for him. Once again, it was bedtime and this beautiful child was going to have to go to bed without a kiss from her father.

She went to Izzy, who stood now at the big picture window, and knelt beside her on the hardwood floor. She chose her words with care. 'When I was a little girl, my mom died. It made my daddy and me very quiet for a long time. When my dad saw me, all he could think about was my mama, and the hurt made him stop looking at me.'

Izzy's brown eyes filled with tears. Her lower lip trembled and she bit down on it.

Annie reached up and caught a single tear on the tip of her finger. 'My daddy came back to me, though. It took a while, but he came back because he loved me. Just like your daddy loves you.'

Annie waited for Izzy to respond—so long the waiting became noticeable. Then she smiled and pushed to her feet. 'Come on, pumpkin. Let's get you to bed.'

Izzy fell into step beside her. Annie slowed her steps to match the child's as they climbed the stairs. Halfway up, Izzy inched closer and slid her hand into Annie's. It was the first time Izzy had touched her.

Annie clung to the tiny fingers, squeezing gently. *That's it, Izzy . . . keep reaching out. I won't let you fall.*

Upstairs, after Izzy brushed her teeth, they knelt beside the bed together. Annie recited the 'Now-I-lay-me' prayer and then tucked Izzy into bed, kissing her forehead.

As so often happened, the nightly ritual made Annie remember. When her own mother had died, she'd been much too young to handle her grief. All she knew was that one day her world was bright and shining and filled with love, and the next, everything fell into a gloomy, saddened, tear-stained landscape. She could still recall how much it had scared her to see her father cry.

It had taken her years to grieve. Her first year away from home had been incredibly lonely. Stanford was no place for a small-town mill-worker's daughter. It had shown her—for the first time—that she was poor and her family uneducated.

Her love for Hank was the only reason she stayed at that big, unwelcoming school. She knew how much it meant to him that she was the first Bourne to attend college. And so she kept her head down and she did her best to fit in. But the loneliness was often overwhelming.

One day she started her car, and the sound of the engine triggered something. All at once, she felt her mother beside her in the car, and Annie's Volkswagen 'Bug' had become the old station wagon they'd once had, the one with the wood-grain strip along the side. She didn't know where they'd been going, she and her mom, or what they'd talked about, and she realised with a sharp, sudden pain that she couldn't recall the sound of her mother's voice. The more she tried to slip into the moment, to immerse herself in the memory, the more flat and one-dimensional it had become.

Until that moment, she had actually—naively—thought she'd overcome the death of her mother, but on that day, more than ten years after they'd placed her mother's coffin in the cold, dark ground, Annie fell apart. She cried for all the missed moments—the night-time kisses, the spontaneous hugs, the joy that would never be as complete again. She grieved most of all for the loss of her childhood innocence, which had been taken without warning, leaving behind an adult in a child's body.

It was not surprising that she fell in love almost immediately after that. She had been a walking wound of loneliness. When she met Blake, she showered him with all the pent-up love that was inside her.

Annie was halfway down the stairs when the phone rang. She jumped down the last few risers and dived for the phone, answering it on the third ring. '*Nick?*'

There was a moment of silence, then a woman's voice said, '*Nick?*'

Annie winced. 'Hi, Terri.'

'Who in the hell is Nick and where are you? I called Hank and he gave me this number.'

Annie sank onto the sofa. 'It's nothing, really. I'm baby-sitting for an old friend and he's late getting home.'

'I had *hoped* you'd changed. A little bit, at least.'

'What do you mean?'

'You just spent twenty years waiting for a man to come home—now you're waiting for another man? That's insane.'

It *was* insane. Why hadn't Annie seen that on her own? It made her angry suddenly, both that she'd lost the ability to really get mad, and that she'd allowed herself to take from Nick what she'd spent a lifetime accepting from Blake. 'Yeah,' she muttered more to herself than to Terri. 'I only have to take this kind of shit from men I'm in love with.'

'Well, that answers my next question. But what—'

'I've got to run, Terri. I'll call you later.' Annie could still hear Terri's voice as she hung up the phone. Then she punched in another number.

Lurlene answered on the second ring. 'Hello?'

'Lurlene? It's Annie—'

'Is everything all right?'

'Fine, but Nick isn't home yet.'

'He's probably down at Zoe's, havin' a drink—or ten.'

Annie nodded. That's what she'd suspected as well. 'Could you come watch Izzy for a little while? I want to go talk to him.'

'He ain't gonna like that.'

'Be that as it may, I'm going.'

'Give me ten minutes.'

True to her word, Lurlene showed up in ten minutes, wearing a puffy pink chenille bathrobe and green plastic clogs.

'Heya, honey,' she said quietly, stepping into the house.

'Thanks for coming,' Annie said. 'This won't take long.'

Annie stood on the sidewalk below a cock-eyed pink neon sign that read: ZOE'S HOT SPOT TAVERN. It sputtered and gave off a faint buzzing sound.

Clutching her handbag, she went inside. The tavern was bigger than she'd expected, a large rectangular room, with a wooden bar along the right wall. Pale blue light shone from tubes above a long mirror. Dozens of neon beer signs flickered in shades of blue and red and gold. Men and women sat on bar stools, drinking and talking and smoking.

Keeping her back to the side wall, she edged deeper into the place, until she saw Nick in the back corner. She pushed through the crowd.

When he saw her, he lurched to his feet. 'Is Izzy—'

'She's fine.'

'Thank God.'

He was unsteady on his feet as he backed away from her. He plopped into his chair. Reaching out, he grabbed his drink and downed it in a single swallow. Then he said softly, 'Go away, Annie. I don't . . .'

She squatted beside him. 'You don't what?'

He spoke so quietly she had to strain to catch the words. 'I don't want you to see me here . . . like this.'

'Did you know that Izzy listens for you every night, Nick? She sits beside the front door for as long as her little eyes can stay open, waiting to hear your footsteps on the porch.'

'Don't do this to me . . .'

Her heart went out to him, but she didn't dare stop, not now when she'd finally found the courage to begin. 'Go home to her, Nick. Take care of your little girl.'

The look he gave her was sad and hopeless. 'I can't take care of her, Annie. Christ, I can't take care of anyone.' In an awkward, jerking motion, he pushed to his feet. 'But I'll go home and pretend. It's what I've been doing for the past eight months.' He walked out of the bar.

She rushed after him. At the kerb outside, he finally stopped and looked at her. 'Will you do me one more favour?'

'Anything.'

A quick frown darted across his face, made Annie wonder why it was so hard for him to believe that she wanted to help him.

'Drive me home?'

She smiled. 'Of course.'

The next morning, Annie arrived at Nick's house an hour early. She slipped through the unlocked door and crept up the stairs. She checked on Izzy, found her sleeping peacefully, then went to Nick's bedroom. It was empty. She went down the hall to a guest room and pushed the door open.

The curtains were drawn, and no sunlight came through the heavy Navajo-print drapes. Against one wall was an old-fashioned four-poster bed. She could just make out Nick's form beneath a mound of red wool blankets. In sleep, he looked young and innocent; more like the boy she'd known so long ago than the man she'd recently met.

It came to her softly, whispering on the even, quiet sound of his breathing, how much she had once loved him . . .

'What are you doing here so early?'

With a start, Annie realised that he was awake, and that he was looking at her. 'I . . . I thought you might need me.'

Frowning, he sat up. The covers fell away from his body, revealing a chest that was covered with coarse black hair.

She waited for him to say something, but he just sat there, his eyes closed. A fine sheen of sweat had broken out on his forehead and upper lip.

She pulled up a chair and sat beside the bed. 'Nick, we've got to talk.'

'Not now.'

'You've got to make a better effort with Izzy.'

He looked at her finally. 'I don't know how to help her, Annie. She scares me.' The words were spoken softly, and they were steeped in pain. 'I mean to have one drink with the boys after work, but then I start thinking about coming home . . . to my empty bedroom and my disappearing daughter, and one drink turns into two . . .'

'You'd be fine if you'd stop drinking.'

'No. I've always been shitty at taking care of the women I love.' A low, tired sigh slipped from his lips. 'I'd rather not talk about this now. I don't feel good. I need—'

'Izzy loves you, Nick. I understand your broken heart—at least to the extent anyone can understand such a thing—but nursing it is a luxury. You're her father. You simply don't have the right to fall apart. She needs you to be strong. But mostly, she needs you to be *here*.'

'I know that,' he said softly, and she could hear the heartache in his voice, the hushed admission of his own failure. 'I'll be home for a family dinner on Friday night. OK? Is that what you want from me?'

Annie knew that it was another lie, a promise that would be broken. Nick had lost faith in himself. 'It isn't what I want from you that matters, Nick,' she said softly, and in the deep sadness that seeped through his eyes, she knew that he understood.

Nick limped out of his bedroom. With one hand on the wooden wall for support, he made his way down the hallway. Clutching the slick wooden handrail, he went down the stairs, one painful step at a time. It was a miracle that he reached the bottom of the stairs without falling or puking. Still holding the banister in a death grip, he paused, sucking in air, trying to keep the bile from rising in his throat, and looked at the changes Annie had made in his home. A fire leapt and danced in the grey river-rock opening. The two leather chairs had been shined up and now sat opposite the sofa, and between them the rough-hewn wooden coffee table glowed a beautiful reddish brown. On the table was a polished silver water pitcher full of fern fronds and white blossoms.

He had often dreamed of a room just like this one, filled with the sounds of laughter . . . instead of the hushed silences and sudden outbursts that had been Kathy's way.

With a heavy sigh, he moved away from the stairway.

That's when he saw his Izzy. She was standing beside the big windows that overlooked the lake; golden sunlight created a halo round her face. Time drew in a sudden breath and fell away, leaving Izzy as she once was, a porcelain doll dressed in pretty clothes, with satin ribbons in her braided hair. She looked at him from across the room, her eyes wide.

'Hey, Izzy,' he said, trying to smile. 'You look gorgeous.'

She blinked and didn't move.

He wet his dry lips. A bead of sweat slid down his temple.

Just then, Annie came bustling out of the kitchen, carrying a steaming pot of coffee and a covered serving dish. 'Nick! This is wonderful, you can join us for breakfast.'

The thought of breakfast sent his sour stomach into revolt.

'Izzy, go help your daddy into the sunroom. I've got breakfast set up in there. I'd better add another place at the table.'

She apparently had no idea he was about to throw up. She just kept on talking—about what, he had no idea—and fluttering between the kitchen and the sunroom.

'Annie, I don't—'

'Izzy,' she said again. 'Go help your daddy. He doesn't feel well.' And she was off again, scurrying towards the sunroom.

Izzy looked up at him when they were alone in the room. Her brown eyes were wide with uncertainty.

'I don't need help, Izzy,' he said. 'I'm just fine, really.'

She looked at him a moment longer, then slowly she moved towards him. He thought she was going to walk past him, but at the last second, she stopped and looked up at him.

It killed him to see the fear in her eyes, and that damned black glove almost did him in. Annie was right. He *had* to be a better father. He had to take care of his baby. Feeling awkward and unsure, he smiled down at her. 'Come on, Izzy-bear. Let's go.'

Slowly, he covered her one bare hand with his larger, calloused one. Together, they walked towards the sunroom. His steps matched hers perfectly. It was sadly silent between them, the daughter who no longer spoke and the father who had no idea what to say.

Annie was beaming when they walked in. The sunroom looked like a picture from one of those women's magazines. There was a bright blue tablecloth on the table, with a centrepiece of huckleberry and dogwood in a crockery vase. Plates were heaped with scrambled eggs and pancakes. Beside the three empty plates were glasses of orange juice.

'Sit down,' she said to both of them.

Nick slowly sat down, trying to ignore the drums beating inside his head.

'Just coffee for me,' he croaked. 'I feel like shi—' He glanced at Izzy. 'I feel bad. A headache, is all.'

Izzy's eyes told him that she knew all about daddy's headaches. Guilt came at him hard, riding on the crest of shame. He turned to Annie, ready to tell her that he had to get the hell out of here, but her smile stopped him. She looked so damned . . . hopeful. He couldn't bear to disappoint her. He swallowed the thick lump in his throat and wiped the sheen of sweat from his brow with a weak hand.

Annie began dishing out food. She served herself a man-sized portion of eggs and a stack of pancakes a logger couldn't finish.

He tried to concentrate on that, her food—anything but his headache and the tremors that quaked through his limbs. 'Are you going to eat all that?'

She laughed. 'I'm from California. I haven't had an egg in fifteen years, and lately I've been eating like a pig. I'm hungry all the time.' Still smiling, she began eating and talking, eating and talking.

Nick curled both shaking hands round a thick porcelain coffee cup. When he thought he was steady enough, he brought the cup to his lips and took a slow, thankful sip. The hot coffee soothed his jittery nerves and took the shine off his headache. After a while, he managed to eat a bit of breakfast. Through it all, Annie talked and laughed and carried on as if they were a family who ate breakfast together every morning, instead of a silent, disappearing child and her hung-over father.

He couldn't take his eyes off Annie. Every time she laughed, the sound moved through Nick in a shiver of longing, until he began at last to wonder how long it had been since *he* had laughed, since his Izzy had laughed . . . how long since they'd had something to laugh about or a moment together in which to find joy . . .

'I thought we'd go to the Feed Store today and buy some gardening supplies,' Annie said brightly. 'It's a good day to get that flower garden into shape. Why, if the three of us worked, it would take no time at all. What do you think, Izzy?' Annie said. 'Should we let your dad help?'

Izzy picked up her spoon, holding it in two tiny fingers—the only ones his baby thought she had left—and shook it hard.

Annie gazed at him across the flowers. 'That means your daughter would love to garden with you, Nick Delacroix. Can she count on you?'

Even as he nodded, Nick knew that it could end up being a lie. Another promise made by a man who'd kept too few.

Chapter 6

NICK SAT IN HIS SQUAD CAR on the edge of downtown Mystic. He used to love walking these streets. He'd known everything about the people he was sworn to protect: when their daughters were getting married and their sons were preparing for bar mitzvahs, when their grandparents were moved into nursing homes and when their kids started day care. He'd always taken pride in how well he did his job.

He knew he'd been letting everything that mattered slip away from him, but he was terrified to start caring again. He failed those he loved. Even when he tried his best. It was *his* fault Izzy was disappearing, *his* fault she didn't feel safe or loved; he knew that. It would be difficult, finding his way back, but Annie was right. He had to. For the first time in months, he felt a stirring of hope.

He eased out of the car and took a first cautious step into his old life. He merged quietly into the crowd of late-afternoon shoppers. Every person he saw waved at him, said 'Heya, Nick' as he passed, and with each greeting, he felt himself coming back to life. It was almost like the old days, before Kathy's death. Back when his uniform had always been clean and starched, and his hands had never trembled.

He walked past the stores, waving at shopkeepers. At the kids' clothing store, he saw a beautiful little pink dress in the window. It was exactly what Izzy needed. As he opened the door, a bell tinkled overhead.

Susan Frame squealed from her place at the cash register and came at Nick like a charging bull, her pudgy pink hands waving in the air. 'Good Lord, I can't believe it's you.'

He grinned. 'Hi, Susan. Long time no see.'

She swatted him on the shoulder and laughed, her triple chins jiggling. 'How are you doing?'

'Better. I saw that little girl's dress in the window—'

She clapped her hands together. 'Ooh-ee, that's a beautiful thing. Perfect for Miss Isabella. How old is she now?'

'Six.'

'Ooh, I'll bet she's growing like a weed. I haven't seen her since her mama—' She shut up abruptly and took him by the arm, propelling him through the store. He let himself be carried away by her steady, comforting stream of words. He wasn't listening to her; she knew it and didn't care. She seemed to sense that it was a major event for him to be here.

She plucked the dress off the hanger. It was a pink and white gingham with a white lace underskirt and a pale blue yoke embroidered with tiny pink and white flowers. It reminded him of Kathy's garden—

It hit him like a blow, the memory. He winced and squeezed his eyes shut.

'Nick? Are you feeling well?'

A little unsteadily, he pulled a twenty-dollar bill from his trouser pocket and tossed it on the counter. 'The dress is perfect, Susan. Can you wrap it up?'

She answered, but he wasn't listening. All he could think about was Zoe's, and how a single drink would calm the shaking in his hands. He wet his dry lips and tried to smile.

'Here you go, Nick.'

Gripping the package, he pushed through the glass door and went outside. It had started to rain. He glanced longingly towards Zoe's.

No. He wouldn't go that way. He'd finish out his rounds and head home. Izzy and Annie were waiting, and he didn't want to disappoint them. Taking a deep breath, he straightened his shoulders and kept moving down the street. With each step, he felt better, stronger.

He returned to his patrol car and got inside, ducking out of the hammering rain. He reached for the radio, but before he could say anything, a call came out. Domestic disturbance on Old Mill Road.

'Shit.' He answered the call, and headed out of town.

When he reached the Weavers' he knew it was bad. The mobile home was already surrounded by two patrol cars and an ambulance.

Nick slammed the car to a halt and jumped out. The first person he saw was Captain Joe Nation, the man who had given Nick a place to live all those years ago. Joe was walking out of the trailer, shaking his head. Across the clearing, he caught sight of Nick, and he stopped.

'Joe?' Nick said, out of breath already.

Joe laid a thick, veiny hand on Nick's forearm. 'Don't go in there, Nicholas. There's nothing you can do now. Nothing anyone can do.'

Nick shoved past Joe. Inside, several people were milling about, searching for clues in the green shag carpeting. Nick went into the bedroom, where Sally lay on the bed, her thin floral dress shoved high on her rail-thin legs, her face bloodied almost beyond recognition. A red-black blotch of blood seeped across her chest.

Nick felt as if pieces of him were crumbling away. He was thrown back suddenly to another time, another place, when he had had to identify a similarly beaten body . . .

'Goddamn it, Sally,' he whispered in a harsh, fractured voice.

He went to her, knelt beside her bed, and brushed the bloodied, matted hair away from her face. Her skin was still warm to the touch, and he could almost believe that she would wake up suddenly and smile and tell him that it was nothing.

'Don't touch her, sir,' said someone. 'The evidence . . .'

Nick drew his shaking hand back and got awkwardly to his feet. He wanted to pull her dress down—give her that final dignity at least—but he couldn't. No one could do anything that mattered for Sally any more.

He turned blindly away from the bed and stumbled through the cluttered trailer. Joe came up to him, pulled him away from the trailer. It felt strangely as if it were years and years ago, back when Joe had met a skinny, freezing fifteen-year-old boy at the bus station in Port Angeles. 'There was nothing you could do, Nicholas,' he said. 'She didn't want our help.'

Nick felt as if the life were slowly, inexorably draining out of him. Buried images of another night, not long ago, were oozing to the forefront of his mind, images that were also stained in blood and violence and tragedy. He'd spent eight months running from the images of that night, burying them deep in his subconscious, but now they were back, killing him. 'It's too much,' he said, shaking his head. 'Too much.'

Joe patted his back. 'Go home, Nicholas. Go home to the little girl who loves you and your beautiful house and forget about this.'

Unable to move, Nick stood there, in the rain, knowing there was only one thing that could help him now.

Nick hadn't shown up for dinner again.

Annie had tried to pretend it meant nothing. She'd made a great show of cheeriness for Izzy, but she knew that the child wasn't fooled. She held the girl in her lap, gently rocking back and forth in a rocking chair on the porch. 'Your daddy will be back soon, Izzy,' she said softly, praying it was true. 'He loves you very much.'

Izzy didn't move, didn't respond.

'Sometimes grown-ups get confused . . . just like kids do. And your dad's confused right now. He doesn't feel like he belongs anywhere, but if we're patient, and we give him time, I think he'll figure it out. It's hard to be patient, though, isn't it? Especially when the waiting hurts.'

Annie's voice faded. She closed her eyes and leaned back in the rocker, listening to the rhythmic scraping of wood on wood and the echo of rain on the porch roof. It took her a moment to realise there was a sound coming from the child, a tiny, reed-thin whisper that sounded like *png-png-png*.

She was mimicking the sound of the rain hitting the tin roof overhead. Annie smiled. Izzy was trying to find her way back.

Izzy was scared. She couldn't remember her dream but her whole body was shaking.

She threw the covers back and slithered out of bed. She crept down the hallway and peeked over the railing, and saw Annie asleep on the sofa. Very slowly, she went down the stairs and tiptoed to the sofa. Izzy wasn't sure what to do. When she was little, she used to climb into her mommy's and daddy's bed whenever she was scared, and it felt so good, so warm. Mommy would curl Izzy up in her arms and tuck the blanket round them both, and Izzy would go to sleep.

Annie made a quiet snoring sound and stretched out, leaving an empty space along the edge of the sofa. Just enough space for Izzy.

Izzy cautiously peeled back the scratchy blue blanket and gingerly crawled onto the couch. She lay stiffly on her side, hardly breathing. She was afraid Annie would wake up and tell her to go back to her room. But she didn't want to be alone in her room.

Annie made another quiet sound and rolled towards Izzy. She curled her arm protectively around Izzy's body and pulled her close. Izzy felt as if she were melting. For the first time in months, she felt as if she could breathe right. She snuggled backwards, poking her bottom into the V of Annie's bent body, so they were like two spoons pressed together.

With a quiet, happy sigh, she closed her eyes.

In the early hours of the morning, Annie woke to the feel of a small, warm body tucked against hers. It brought back a flood of memories— days long ago and a child that was now far away and hadn't been a baby in years. She gently stroked Izzy's sweaty hair and kissed her small, pink ear. 'Sleep well, princess.'

Izzy snuggled closer. A quiet sound answered Annie, so quiet she might have missed it if they'd been outside or if it had been raining or she had been talking. In her sleep, Izzy laughed.

Annie glanced at the clock on the mantel. It was five thirty in the morning. 'Damn you,' she whispered.

This time, Nick hadn't come home all night.

The phone rang at five forty-five. Annie reached over Izzy and answered softly, 'Hello?'

'Hello. Annie Bourne, please.'

She frowned, trying to place the male voice. 'This is she.'

'This is Captain Joseph Nation, of the Mystic police force.'

Annie's stomach clenched. She eased away from the sleeping child and sat down on the cold floor.

'Nick was in an accident last night.'

'Oh, my God. Is he—'

'Fine. Apart from a few bruises and . . . a hell of a hangover, he's going to be fine. He's at Mystic Memorial.'

'Was he driving?'

'No. He was smart enough to get a ride home with someone—but not smart enough to pick a sober driver.'

'Was anyone else hurt?'

Captain Nation sighed. 'No. They hit a tree out on Old Mill Road. The driver walked away without a scratch, and Nick just bonked his head a good one. He has a slight concussion. He was lucky . . . this time. I'm calling because he's going to need some fresh clothes and a ride home from the hospital.'

Annie glanced over at Izzy, sleeping so peacefully on the sofa. She couldn't help remembering the way Izzy had waited and waited for a daddy who didn't come home—because he was getting drunk again.

Enough was enough. She answered, 'Oh, I'll come get him all right.'

Nick moaned. He was lying in a narrow, metal-rimmed bed. Fluorescent tube worms crisscrossed the ceiling, sending blinding pyramids of light into the white-walled room. A bright yellow privacy curtain hung in folds from ceiling to floor.

He felt like shit. His head hurt, his eyes ached, his mouth was dry, and his stomach felt as if it had been scraped clean by a rusty scalpel. His whole body was shaking and weak.

'So, Nicholas? You back among the living?'

All in all, it was not a good sign to wake up in a hospital bed with your boss standing beside you. Even worse when that boss was as close to a father as you'd ever known.

Joe had offered Nick the first real home of his life. Nick had been young and scared and ready to run; his mother had taught him early that policemen were the enemy. But he'd had nowhere else to go. His mother's death and Social Services had given him no options.

You must be Nicholas, Joe had said that day. *I've got a spare bedroom . . . maybe you wouldn't mind hanging out with me for a while. My daughters have all got married and Louise—my wife—and I are sorta lonely.* And with those few welcoming words, Joe had shown Nick the first frayed edges of a new life.

Nick pushed up to his elbows. It hurt to move; hell, it hurt to breathe. 'Hey, Joe.'

Joe stood quietly beside the bed, staring at Nick through sad, disappointed eyes. Deep wrinkles lined his forehead and bisected his round, dark-skinned cheeks. 'You were in a car accident last night. Do you remember it? Joel was driving.'

Nick went cold. 'Christ. Did we hurt anyone?'

'Only you . . . this time.'

Nick sagged in relief. He rubbed a trembling hand over his face, wishing he could take a shower. He smelt like booze and smoke and vomit. The last thing he remembered was taking a drink at Zoe's—his fourth, maybe. He couldn't remember getting into Joel's car at all.

With a high-pitched scraping sound of metal on linoleum that almost deafened Nick, Joe pulled up a chair and sat down next to the bed. 'You remember the day we met?'

'Come on, Joe. Not now—'

'*Now.* I offered you everything I had to give. My home, my family, my friendship—and this is what you give me in return? I'm supposed to watch you turn into a drunk? If Louise—God rest her soul—were alive, this would kill her. You blacked out, you know.'

Nick winced. That was bad. 'Where?' It was a stupid question.

'At Zoe's.'

Nick sank back onto the bed. In public. He'd blacked out in public. 'Jesus Christ,' he moaned. He could have done it in front of Izzy.

He didn't want to think about that. He threw the covers back and sat up. At the movement, his stomach lurched and his head exploded. He cradled his head in his hands and leaned forward, staring at the floor through burning eyes until he could breathe again.

'Nicholas, are you all right?'

Slowly, he looked up. It came back to him in bits and pieces: Sally Weaver . . . all that blood . . . Chuck's wailing voice, *It's not my fault . . .* 'Remember when you talked me into going into the academy, Joe?

You told me I could help people like my mother . . .'

Joe sighed. 'We can't save 'em all, Nicholas.'

'I can't do it any more, Joe. We don't help people. All we do is clean up bloodstains. I can't . . . not any more . . .'

'You're a damn fine cop, but you have to learn that you can't save everyone—'

'Are you forgetting what I came home to last year? Hell, Joe, I can't save anyone. And I'm sick to death of trying.' He climbed out of bed. He stood there like an idiot, swaying and lurching in a feeble effort to stand still. His stomach coiled in on itself, just waiting for an excuse to purge. He clutched the metal bed frame in boneless, sweaty fingers. 'You'll be getting my resignation tomorrow.'

Joe stood up. Gently, he placed a hand on Nick's shoulder. 'I won't accept it. I'll agree to a vacation—for as long as you need. I know what you're going through, and you don't have to do it alone. But you do have to stop drinking.'

Nick sighed. Everyone said that. *I know what you're going through.* But they didn't know; how could they? None of them had come home to his blood-spattered bedroom. Even Joe, who had been a full-blown alcoholic before his eighteenth birthday, and who had grown up in the blackened, marshy shadow of a drunken father. Even Joe couldn't completely understand. 'You're wrong, Joe. In the end, we're all alone.'

'It's that kind of thinking that got you into this mess. But you've got to trust *someone*, Nicholas. There's a whole town here that cares about you, and you have a little girl who needs you. Stop thinking about what you've lost, and think about what you have left. You want to end up like your mother, half starved on a park bench, waiting to be killed?' He pulled a business card out of his pocket and handed it to Nick. 'When you're ready to sober up, here's the number for you to call. I'll help you—all of us will—but you have to take the first step by yourself.'

You look like warmed-over shit soup.'

Nick didn't even look at Annie. 'Nice language. They teach you that at Stanford?'

'No, but they did teach me not to drink and drive.'

He glanced around, ran a shaking hand through his dirty, tangled hair. 'Where's Izzy?'

'Ah, so you do remember her.' Annie had dropped her at Lurlene's.

'Goddamn it, Annie—'

'We—your *daughter* and I—were worried about you last night. But you don't care about that, do you?'

Suddenly he was tired, so tired he didn't think he could stand up much longer. He pushed past her and stumbled out of the building. Her Mustang was parked in the loading zone in front of the electronic glass doors. Half falling, he grabbed the cold metal door handle and stood there, his eyes closed, concentrating on each breath.

He heard her walk past him. Her tennis shoes made a soft scuffing sound on the cement. She wrenched her car door open, got inside and slammed the door shut. He wondered dully if she had any idea how loud it sounded to a man whose head was ticking like a bomb ready to go off.

She honked the horn, and the sound sliced painfully through his eardrums. He opened the door and collapsed onto the red vinyl seat.

The car lurched onto the rutted road. She sped up at every bump and pothole in the road, Nick was sure of it. He clung to the door handle for dear life, his knuckles white and sweaty.

'I spoke with your police captain while you were getting dressed. He told me you were taking some time off from the force. And he mentioned your blackout.'

'Great.'

She made a low, whistling sound. 'What a high time you must have had yourself. God knows, it's better than being at home with your daughter.'

He winced, feeling shame sink deep into his gut. He slanted a look at Annie. She was sitting perfectly erect, her hands precisely placed on the steering wheel, her gaze focused on the empty road in front of them. 'Would you do me a favour, Annie?'

'Of course.'

'Take me to the Hideaway Motel on Route 7,' he said quietly. 'And watch Izzy for a few days.'

She cast a quick, worried look at him, then turned back to the road. 'But Izzy—'

'Please?' The word came out soft and swollen, unmanly, but he couldn't help it. 'Could you please stay with her while I get my act together? I know it's a lot to ask . . .'

She didn't answer; the silence was uncomfortable. After a mile she flicked on her signal and turned off the highway. Within minutes, she had pulled into the parking lot at the Hideaway Motel. A neon sign flickered in the window. It read: SORRY. VACANCY. That pretty much summed it up.

'Here we are, Nick. I don't know . . .'

'Home sweet home,' he said, smiling weakly.

She turned to him then, and there was a softness in her expression that he hadn't expected. She leaned towards him, gently brushed the hair from his eyes. 'I'll help you. But you'd better not screw up this time, Nicky. That beautiful child of yours doesn't need to lose her daddy, too.'

'Christ, Annie,' he whispered in agony.

'I know you love her, Nick.' She leaned closer. 'Just trust yourself.'

He climbed out of the car and stood there, watching her drive away. When she was gone, he jammed his hands into his pockets and turned towards the motel. Fishing his credit card out of his front pocket, he signed the register and got himself a room. Finally, after eight months of drifting, he'd come to the end of the line. There was only one thing that might make a difference. He reached into his pocket and pulled out the card Joe had given him.

Annie kept Izzy busy all day, but as the night began to fall, she couldn't pretend any more. After dinner she pulled Izzy into her arms. 'I need to tell you something, Izzy,' she started softly, trying to find the right words. 'Your daddy is going . . . to be away for a while. He's sick. But he'll be back. He loves you more than the world and he'll be back.'

Izzy didn't respond. Annie didn't know what to say, what words could soothe this situation. She held Izzy for a long, long time, humming tunes and stroking her hair, and then, finally, she sighed. 'Well, it's bedtime.' She pulled away from Izzy and got to her feet. She started to head for the stairs but Izzy grabbed her hand.

Annie looked into the sad, frightened brown eyes, and it broke her heart all over again. 'I'm not going anywhere, honey. I'm right here.'

Izzy held on to her hand all the way up the stairs and down the hall, and into the bathroom. In the bedroom, she still wouldn't let go.

Annie looked down into the girl's huge brown eyes. 'You want me to sleep with you?'

A quick smile darted across Izzy's face. She nodded.

Annie climbed into Izzy's single bed, without bothering to brush her teeth or change her clothes. She left the Winnie the Pooh nightlight glowing next to the bed as Izzy snuggled close.

Annie stroked Izzy's soft cheek, remembering suddenly how much she'd missed talking about her mom when she was young. After the accident, no one ever mentioned her: it was as if she'd never existed in the first place. And so, Annie had begun, day by day, to forget. She wondered if poor, quiet Izzy was facing the same fears.

She pulled up a memory of Kathy, concentrating until she could *see* Kathy, sitting in that old rocking chair on her porch. 'Your mom had the prettiest blonde hair I ever saw; it was the colour of a ripe ear of corn. And it was so soft. When we were little, we used to braid each other's hair for hours. Her eyes were almost black, and when she smiled, they crinkled up in the corners like a cat's. You remember that?'

Izzy twisted round to see Annie. There were tears in her eyes, but she was smiling.

'You'll never forget her, Izzy. You remember her laugh? The way it used to spike up at the end, just before she started snorting? And the perfume she liked to wear? And the feel of her hand in yours? You remember how it used to feel to snuggle in her lap and hear her read you a bedtime story? All of that is your mom. My mom's been gone a long, long time, and I still think of her every time I smell vanilla. I still talk to her at night, and I believe she hears me.' She brushed a lock of black hair from Izzy's earnest little face. 'She hears you, honey. You snuggle under your blankets with Miss Jemmie and close your eyes and remember one thing about your mom—just one—and the next thing you know, she'll be in bed beside you. You'll feel yourself getting warmer, or you'll see the moonlight get a little brighter, or the wind will moan a little louder, and you'll know. In her own way, she's answering you.' Annie took Izzy's cheeks in her hands and smiled down at her. 'She's always with you.'

She held Izzy close until she slipped into a deep and peaceful sleep.

Against her father's pointed advice, Annie had packed a small suitcase and moved into Nick's house. They spent all their time together, she and Izzy. They went to town, baked cookies, and made jewellery boxes from egg cartons. They worked out of kindergarten and first-grade work-books, to ensure that Izzy was still learning what she needed for school. And every evening Nick called to say good night.

Today, Annie had special plans. It was time to revive Kathy's garden.

She stood at the wobbly white picket fence that framed the garden, and Izzy was beside her. The earth was a rich brown, soggy to the touch from last night's heavy rain.

Annie set down her big cardboard box and began extracting her tools: spades, hand shovels, trowels, scissors.

'I wish I'd paid more attention to the gardeners at home,' she said. 'Come on, Izzy.' She led her across the necklace of stepping stones that formed a meandering trail through the large garden. They stopped at a patch of dead stuff.

Annie knelt. She could feel the moisture seeping from the soil into her trousers, squishing cold and clammy against her skin. Pulling on a pair of gloves, she attacked the dead plant and yanked a handful out by the roots. 'Bulbs,' she said with a triumphant smile. 'I knew it.'

She separated and replanted the bulbs, then attacked the dead stalks of perennials with her clippers, hacking everything down to ground level. 'You know what I love about gardening? Paying someone to do it for me.' She laughed at her own joke and pulled up everything that looked like a weed and divided and replanted all the bulbs. As she worked, she hummed. She tried to think of a song that Izzy would know, but all she could come up with was the alphabet song, and so she sang that. 'A-B-C-D-E-F-G . . . H-I-J-K . . . L-M-N-O-P.'

She frowned suddenly and looked down at Izzy, keeping her gaze averted from the tiny black glove. 'My goodness, I've forgotten the alphabet. I keep getting stuck on P.'

Izzy reached slowly for a trowel. It took her a while to pick it up with only two fingers, and after the first fumbling attempts, Annie couldn't watch. She kept singing. 'H-I-J-K . . . L-M-N-O-P . . . darn it. There's that block again. Oh, well. I think we're—'

'Q.'

The spade fell from Annie's hand and hit the ground with a thunk. She looked at Izzy, who was still kneeling in the dirt, awkwardly pulling up weeds with her two 'visible' fingers as if nothing had happened.

Annie released her breath in a slow sigh. *Stay calm, Annie.* She decided to act as if speaking were as normal as not speaking. 'Why, I do believe you're right. L-M-N-O-P . . . Q-R-S . . .'

'T-U-V.'

'W-X-Y . . . and Z.' Annie felt as if she would burst with pride and love. She forced herself to keep digging weeds for a few more minutes. She wanted to shriek with happiness and pull Izzy into her arms, but she didn't dare. She didn't want to scare Izzy back into silence.

'There,' she said at last. 'That's enough for now. My arms feel like they're going to fall off.' She wiped a dirty hand across her forehead. 'What do you say we have a picnic dinner out here? I could make us milk shakes . . .'

When Izzy looked up at her, there were tears in her eyes.

At last, Annie pulled the little girl into her arms.

Nick stood in the open doorway of a long, narrow room in the windowless basement of the Lutheran church. Two wood-grain Formica tables hugged the back wall, their surfaces covered with coffeemakers and Styrofoam cups and boxes stacked with packaged sugar and instant creamer. There was a crowd of people at the Coke machine, and an even larger crowd at the coffeepot. The smell of burnt coffee mingled with the bitter stench of cigarettes.

People sat in folding metal chairs, some comfortably stretched out, some perched nervously on the edge of their seats.

He didn't know if he could go through with this, if he could stroll into this smoky room and throw his vulnerability on one of those cheap-ass tables and let strangers dissect it . . .

'It's harder than hell the first time. All the tension of first sex, with none of the fun.'

Nick turned and saw Joe standing behind him.

The older man's shoe-leather-brown face was creased into a relieved smile. 'I hoped you'd show up. It was sort of a shock to my system after all those years of hoping you'd *never* show up.'

'I'm sorry to disappoint you, Joe,' Nick said.

Joe laid a hand on Nick's shoulder and squeezed gently. 'I'm *proud* of you, Nicholas. Not disappointed. Life's thrown a lot of curves your way—enough to crush a weaker man. I couldn't be prouder of you if you were my own son. If Louise were here, she'd say, "Give that boy a hug, Joseph," and I think I will.'

It was the first time Joe had ever hugged him. When he drew back, his black eyes were moist. 'It's going to get tougher before it gets better. You've just jumped into the deep end, and you'll think you're drowning. But I'm here to keep your head above water.'

'Thanks, Joe.' He didn't say *for everything*, but he could see that Joe understood.

'Come on,' Joe said. 'Let's sit down.'

They headed into the room. Over the next few minutes, more people wandered in, some talking among themselves, others noticeably silent.

Nick shifted in his seat. His feet tapped nervously on the floor.

A man introduced himself: 'Hi, I'm Jim. I'm an alcoholic.' The crowd of people answered back like good Catholics on Sunday, 'Hi, Jim.'

Jim stood in the front of the room and started talking. First there was the 'God grant me' prayer, then stuff about meetings and twelve steps and more on serenity.

A young woman stood up suddenly. She was tall and rake-thin, with bleached yellow-white hair and skin the colour of candlewax. She looked as if she hadn't eaten in a year. Nick had been a cop long enough to recognise the signs of long-term drug use. 'I'm Rhonda,' she said, nervously eyeing the crowd, 'and I'm an alcoholic and an addict.'

'Hi, Rhonda,' said the crowd on cue.

'Today's my seventh sober day.' There was a round of applause.

Rhonda gave a wan smile. 'I've tried this before—lots of times. But this time'll be differ'nt. The judge said if I can stay clean for one year, I can see my son again.' She paused and wiped her eyes, leaving a black trail of mascara down one white cheek. 'So, here I am, and this time I mean it. I'm gonna do anything to see my son again. This time I'm gonna get clean and stay clean.'

When Rhonda was finished, someone else started talking, then another and another. They all used different words, but the stories were the same, tales of loss and pain and anger.

Nick was one of them, he knew it by the close of the meeting, and there was a strange comfort in admitting that, in knowing he wasn't the only one in the world trying to wrestle with a bottle of booze.

Izzy couldn't sleep. She went to her window and stared outside. Everything was dark and scary-looking. The only light was tiny white flecks on the black lake. Annie said those were stars fallen from the sky.

She turned away from the window. All week long, ever since Annie had told her that her daddy wasn't coming home, she'd been scared. Yesterday, she'd stood at the window for a long time, waiting. So long that Annie had come up to her.

I don't know when he'll be coming home, Izzy. That's what Annie had said to her. *You remember I told you that your daddy was sick? The doctors say he needs a little time—*

But Izzy knew the truth about doctors. Her mommy had seen lots and lots of them, and none of them ever made her mommy feel better.

They wouldn't help her daddy, either.

Izzy hadn't been able to stop crying. *I miss him*, was all she said to Annie, but there was a lot more she didn't say. She didn't say that she'd been missing him for a long, long time, and she didn't say that the man with the silver hair wasn't really her daddy—because her daddy never got sick and he laughed all the time. She didn't say that she thought her real daddy had died when her mommy died, and that he wouldn't ever be coming back.

Izzy crept down the stairs and sneaked outside. It was raining gently, and a mist floated on the top of the grass, so thick that she couldn't see her feet.

'Mommy?' she whispered, hugging herself. She closed her eyes and concentrated really, really hard. When she opened her eyes, she saw her mommy standing in a layer of soft, hazy fog that clung to the sides of the lake. The vision was shimmering and out of focus.

You should be sleeping, little girl.

'I miss you, Mommy.' Izzy reached for her, peering into the mist.

It's getting harder for me, Izzy, coming to see you.

Izzy felt a rush of panic. 'I'm disappearin', Mommy. Just like you. I'm comin' as fast as I can!'

She felt the softness of her mother's hand in the coolness of the breeze. *It won't work, Izzy-bear. You can't follow me.*

Tears stung Izzy's eyes, blurred everything until she couldn't see anything any more. She blinked away the tears.

The fog was moving away from her. Izzy knelt down on the cold, gravelly bank and cried.

Annie made sure that Izzy was busy all the time. She was talking regularly now; it no longer seemed hard for her to remember the words. They were gaining strength from each other.

Annie had finally learned to sleep alone. She knew it didn't sound like much, but to her it was momentous. Sometimes, when she left Izzy and crawled into her empty bed, she didn't even think about the man who used to sleep with her; sometimes she went for whole days without thinking about him. Oh, the ache was still there, and the loneliness, but day by day, she was learning that she could survive without him. She still didn't want to, but she knew now that she could.

Every Monday, like clockwork, she called London and heard about Natalie's week. In her daughter's voice, she heard a burgeoning maturity that filled Annie with pride. Natalie wasn't a child any more, and when she learned of the divorce, she would be able to handle it.

And Annie finally understood that she could handle it, too. Last night, when Terri had called (after ten minutes of grilling Annie about who this Nick character was and why Annie was staying at his house), she had finally settled down and listened to Annie, and when the conversation was over, Terri had said quietly, *Of course you can handle it, Annie. You're the only one who thought you couldn't.*

Easter Sunday arrived wrapped in clouds and drenched in rain, but Annie refused to let the uncooperative weather ruin her plans. She dressed Izzy warmly and drove her to Hank's, where the three of them had a huge brunch and a world-class egg hunt. Then they went to church in town. Afterwards, Annie and Izzy drove back to the house, and Annie gave her a small, wrapped gift. 'Happy Easter, Izzy.'

Izzy tried to open the package with her two good fingers, and the failing effort pinched at Annie's heart. 'Here, I'll do it, sweetheart. It's hard when your fingers are gone.'

Annie unwrapped the shiny paper, then placed the box on the table.

Biting back a grin, Izzy flipped open the box top. Inside, on a bed of white tissue paper, was a bronze medallion the size of a quarter, resting on a coil of thin silver chain. At Izzy's frown, Annie took the compass from the box and placed it in Izzy's hand.

'When I was a girl, I thought I was lost all the time. Then my dad gave me this compass, and he told me that if I wore it, I'd always know where I belonged.' Annie sighed softly. She hadn't kept wearing the compass. Instead, she'd gone all the way to California and lost her sense of direction again. 'So,' she said at last, 'do you want to learn how it works?'

Izzy nodded.

'I knew you'd say that. OK, grab rain gear, and I'll show you.'

With a quick smile, Izzy ran to the coat closet and grabbed her still-wet coat and hat. Annie quickly explained to Izzy how the compass worked, and when she was convinced that Izzy understood, she slipped the compass round the girl's neck. 'Let's go exploring.'

Outside, the weather was horrible. Stuttering gusts of wind blew across the lake, sending silvery ripples onto the gravel shore. They veered away from the lake, and started down the wide, needle-carpeted trail that led into the rain forest. At every bend in the trail, Izzy stopped and checked her compass.

By midafternoon, Izzy had a sense for true north, and the quiet confidence that came with knowledge.

They walked down one trail and then another and another. Suddenly, the trees opened up, and they found themselves in an overgrown clearing deep in the oldest part of the rain forest. Tucked in one corner was an old ranger station, obviously abandoned for years. Its shingled roof was furred with moss, and grey fungus peeked out from cracks in the log siding.

Izzy blinked up at her. 'Can we go in?'

Annie looked questioningly at the cabin. 'OK, but go slow . . . and don't touch anything icky.'

With a shriek, Izzy raced for the cabin. Annie hurried along behind her. Together, they eased through a broken door.

Inside, buried under a gauzy net of spider's webs and dust, were two twin beds, complete with musty blankets; a flimsy, handmade wooden table and two chairs; and a long-forgotten black iron woodstove.

Izzy let out a squeal and pulled something out from under the bed. 'Look!' She thrust her hand at Annie.

It was a silver coin, dated 1899.

'Oh, my,' Annie said. 'What treasure. You'd best put that in a safe place.'

Izzy frowned, then very solemnly looked up at Annie. Wordlessly, she shoved the coin towards her.

'It's yours, Izzy. Don't give it to me.'

'You'll always be here, won'tcha, Annie? That makes you a safe place.'

Annie knew she should give the child the gift of honesty. But then she looked into Izzy's liquid brown eyes and she was lost. 'Always is a lot longer than you'll need me, Izzy, but I'll keep the coin until you're ready to give it to your daddy, OK?'

''K. Don't lose it.' Izzy grinned and nodded and started to run for the door. Halfway there, she skidded to a stop and turned round. She was staring at her right hand.

'Izzy, what is it?'

Slowly, Izzy turned. Frowning, she stuck her right hand up in the air. 'I can see all my fingers on this hand again.'

'Oh, Izzy . . .' Annie went to Izzy and knelt beside her, pulling the child into her arms. But Izzy was stiff and awkward, and she couldn't seem to take her eyes away from her hand.

Izzy started to cry. 'She said I couldn't follow her.'

Annie stroked the child's soft, soft cheek and smiled. 'Who said that?'

'Mommy. I . . .' She bit her quavering lower lip and looked away.

'Tell me, Izzy,' Annie said softly. 'I can keep a secret.'

Izzy stared at Annie for a long, silent moment, then said quietly, 'I . . . I see her sometimes . . . in the fog. I was disappearin' to be with her . . . but last time I saw her . . .' Huge tears welled in Izzy's eyes and spilled over, streaking down her pink cheeks. 'Last time she said I couldn't follow her.'

Annie took Izzy's hand and led her outdoors. Side by side they sat on the rickety, moss-haired porch of the cabin.

'You can't follow your mom, Izzy, and you know why?'

Izzy turned to her. 'Why?'

'Because she's up in Heaven now, and she wants to watch you grow up. She wants you to have fun and make friends and go to school—to do all the things she did when she was a little girl.'

'How do you know she's watchin' me?'

Annie smiled at her. '*You* know. In your heart. That's why you see her in the fog. You know she's watching over you, and when it rains . . . that's when she's missing you. The rain is her tears, and the sunshine is her smile.'

Izzy stared out at the trees a long, long time. 'I miss her, too.'

Annie curled an arm round Izzy's narrow shoulders and drew her close. 'I know, baby, I know.'

Chapter 7

IT WAS RAINING on the day Nick came home. He paid the cabdriver and got out of the car, watching the town's only taxi drive away. He could have had the cab drive him to the front door, but he needed the time to approach slowly. Blinking against the rain, he began the long walk home. At last, he turned the corner. Soft, golden light poured through the windows of his home. The chimney puffed smoke into the purple sky. It was how he'd always imagined it . . .

This house had seized his imagination from the start. He could still recall the night Annie had brought him here. And he knew he had to own it. It had taken him years, but he'd finally saved enough money to buy the place. It had been summer then, August, when he'd signed the papers and written the down-payment cheque. Yet even on that hottest day of the year, this road had been cool and shaded, and a breeze had swept along the banks of the lake.

The memory was as sharp as broken glass. He'd raced to bring Kathy here, but it was night by then and shadows lay thick and dark along the porch rails. He'd grabbed her hand and dragged her through the murky, musty interior.

Can't you just see it, Kath? This'll be the sunroom—where we'll have breakfast . . . and that's the kitchen, they don't make stoves like that any more . . . and check out that fireplace—I bet it's one hundred years old . . .

He smelt hope and home and possibilities.

She smelt must and dirt and work.

How had he failed to notice? And why hadn't he stopped talking long enough to ask her opinion? Why had he just thought, *She's having one of her bad days*, and let it go at that?

With a tired sigh, he straightened his shoulders, crossed the grass, climbed the porch steps, and knocked on the front door.

There was a flurry of footsteps behind the door, and a muffled 'Just a minute', then the door opened and Annie stood before him.

He wished he could smile, but he was afraid. He looked away, before she could see the sudden longing in his eyes.

'Nick.' It was just a whisper of sound; he imagined he could feel the moist heat of her breath on his neck. Slowly, slowly, he looked at her.

She was standing so close he could see the smattering of freckles that lay along her hairline, and a tiny white scar that bisected one eyebrow. 'I've been going to AA twice a day,' he said quickly, without even adding a mumbled hello. 'I haven't had a drink since you dropped me off at the motel.'

'Oh, Nick, that's wonderful. I—'

It was as if she suddenly realised how close they were standing. In the pale glow of the porch light, he saw a sweet blush colour her cheeks.

She broke eye contact and cleared her throat, moving back a respectable few feet. 'Izzy is in the family room. We were painting. Come on in.'

'Painting. Sounds fun. I wouldn't want to—'

'You can do this, Nick.' She took hold of his hand—her grasp was solid and comforting—and pulled him into the house. The door banged shut behind him.

Her 'family room' was what Nick used to think of as the shit room. Years ago, probably in the fifties, somebody had tried to remodel this room on a skimpy budget. Pressboard wood panelling hid the log walls underneath. The only nice thing in the room was a big old brick fireplace, in which Annie had a fire going.

Multicoloured jars and paintbrushes cluttered a portable card table. Spilt paint lay in bright blemishes on the newspaper that protected the floor. Izzy stood with her back to them, one gloved hand hung limply at her left side. There was a huge easel in front of her, with a piece of white paper pinned in place. He could see splashes of colour on the paper, but her body blocked the picture.

He realised suddenly that Annie was gone. His hand felt cold and empty. Turning slightly, he saw her in the hallway. She gave him a quick thumbs up and disappeared. He sighed. Turning back towards the room, he took a cautious step inside. 'Izzy.' He said her name softly.

She dropped a jar full of blue paint. The colourful liquid splashed across the newspaper. Slowly, clutching her paintbrush, she turned round.

She looked like an angel. She was wearing a paint-stained pair of yellow overalls, but there were no streaks of colour on her hair or face. Her jet-black hair lay in two evenly plaited braids, tied at the ends with bits of yellow ribbon.

She looked like she used to.

It was that thought, more than anything, that brought him fully into the room. His knees felt weak, and fear was a cold knot in his stomach, but he kept moving, going towards his little girl, who stood so silently beside the easel, her big brown eyes fixed on his.

Beside her, he knelt. His knees squished in the puddle of blue paint.

She looked down at him, her eyes unblinking, her pink lips drawn in a serious line, with a wary, worried expression.

Only a year ago, she would have leapt into his arms and smothered him with kisses. Even when he'd had a hangover, or after a fight with Kathy, Izzy had always adored him.

He realised with a sudden tightening in his chest how much he'd missed her kisses . . . the sweet smell of her hair . . . the gentle softness of her hand as she slipped it into his.

'Hey, Sunshine,' he said, his eyes avoiding the tiny black glove that evidenced his failure and her heartbreak.

It was his pet name for her. He hadn't called her Sunshine in a long time. Since Kathy's death, and probably even before that. She remembered. A little jumping smile tugged one side of her mouth.

There were so many things he could say to her right now, promises he could make, but in the end, he knew it would only be words. Promises made by a man who'd broken too many to be trusted.

One day at a time; that was one thing AA definitely had right.

So he made no promises, saying only, 'What are you painting?'

She cocked her head towards the paper and stepped back. It was Izzy's self-portrait: another figure, Annie, stood beside her, wearing a broad brushstroke of a smile.

Nick grabbed a clean paintbrush from the card table and dipped it into a jar of brown paint. 'Can I add something?'

She stared up at him. Then slowly she nodded.

He drew a quick, misshapen circle alongside Annie. Another four strokes and he had a body of sorts. 'This is Daddy,' he said, without looking at her. Then he added eyes, a nose and a flat line of a mouth. 'I don't need to paint the hair—it's almost the same colour as the paper. We'll just imagine it.' Lowering the brush, he looked at her.

Her gaze was level and steady.

'Can I come home, Izzy?' He waited a lifetime for her answer, a nod, a blink, anything, but she just stood there, staring at him through those sad, grown-up eyes in her little-girl's face.

He touched her velvet-soft cheek. 'I understand, Sunshine.'

He started to get to his feet. She grabbed his hand.

Slowly, he lowered himself back to his knees. He stared at her, losing himself in the chocolate-brown eyes. 'I love you, Izzy,' he said, remembering then how simple loving her used to be.

Nick stood on the porch, his legs braced apart, his arms crossed. He was hanging on to his world by a fraying thread. He'd noticed that Izzy was using her right hand again—and not in that pathetic two-fingered way. Every time he looked at his daughter, he felt a hot rush of shame, and it took all his self-control not to turn away. But he hadn't taken the coward's road tonight, and that was something of a triumph. He'd looked Izzy square in the eye, and if he flinched at the wariness in her gaze, he did it inwardly, so she couldn't see.

Behind him, the screen door screeched open and banged shut.

It took him a second to find the courage to turn round. When he did, Annie was standing there, alongside the old rocking chair. Her fingers trailed lightly across the top rail, and her wedding ring glittered in the orange glow of the outdoor bulb. The size of the diamond reminded Nick once again of how different her world was from his. As if he needed reminding.

She was holding a small designer suitcase.

'Izzy has brushed her teeth. She's waiting for you to tuck her in.' Her voice was as soft and cool as spring rain, and it soothed the ragged edges of his anxiety. Even with that Marine-issue haircut, she was beautiful. A tired grey sweatshirt bagged over a pair of oversized jeans, but it didn't camouflage her body. Suddenly he could remember her naked, recall vividly how she'd lifted her arms and pulled off her shirt . . . the moonlight kissing her breasts . . .

'Nick?' She took a step towards him. 'Are you all right?'

He forced a weak laugh. 'As well as a drunk who has stopped drinking can be, I suppose.'

'You're going to make it.' She started to reach for him, and he leaned slightly towards her, needing that touch more than air, but at the last minute, she drew back. 'It's not easy to start over. I know . . .'

He saw the haunted look in her eyes and wondered what he'd done to her, the man who'd put that egg-sized diamond on her left hand. He wanted to ask, but it felt wrong, presumptuous, to probe her wounds. 'You saved my life, Annie. I don't know how to thank you.'

She smiled. 'I always knew you'd be back for her, you know. It wasn't much of a risk. I could see how much you loved Izzy.'

'Such optimism.' He glanced out at the darkened lake. 'I loved Kathy, too, and look what happened.' He sighed and leaned back against the porch rail, staring out at the yard. 'You know what haunts me? I never really understood my wife. The sad thing is—I do now. I know what hopelessness feels like; before, I thought I did, but I was skimming the surface. She used to tell me that she couldn't feel the sunlight any more, not even when she was standing in it, not even when it was hot on her cheeks.' It surprised Nick that he could talk about his wife so easily. For the first time, he remembered *her*, not the illness or the crumbling of their marriage over the last few years, but Kathy, his Kathy, the bright-eyed, big-hearted girl he'd fallen in love with. 'She didn't want to live in the darkness any more . . .'

When he turned back to Annie, she was crying. He felt awkward and selfish. 'I'm sorry . . . I didn't mean to upset you.'

She gazed up at him. 'You're so lucky.'

'What?'

'It doesn't matter how you felt about Kathy by the end, or since the end. You obviously loved her. No matter what she did, or why she did it, she must have known.' Her voice fell to a throaty whisper. 'Most people are never loved like that in their whole lives.'

He stepped towards her. 'Have you known that kind of love?'

She gave him a fleeting, sad little smile and looked away. 'No. I have loved that way . . . but been loved . . . I don't think so.'

'You deserve better than that.'

She nodded and nonchalantly wiped her eyes. 'Don't we all.'

Silence fell between them, awkward and uncomfortable. 'Annie—'

She turned to him. 'Yes?'

'Maybe you'd like to come over tomorrow—spend the day with us.'

'I'd like that,' she answered quickly, then she looked away.

'Thank you.'

'You're welcome, Nicky.' There was another moment of awkwardness as she stared up at him. 'You should know that Izzy started talking while you were gone.'

Nick frowned. 'She didn't talk to me.'

Annie touched his arm in a brief, fleeting caress. 'She will. Give her time.'

He couldn't meet Annie's gaze. Instead, he stared out at the lake.

She moved nervously from foot to foot, then said, 'Well, I should be getting home . . .'

'See you tomorrow.'

She nodded and hurried past him. With a quick wave, she climbed into her Mustang and drove away.

Reluctantly, Nick went back into the house and climbed the stairs. Outside Izzy's room, he paused, then knocked.

Answer, baby . . . you can do it.

But there was no response. Slowly, he turned the knob and opened the door. She was sitting up in bed, her right arm curled round Miss

Jemmie. The black glove on her left hand was a tiny blotch against the white and lavender lace comforter.

He went to the bed and sat down beside her.

Silence spilled between them, and every heartbeat plucked at the fragile strands of Nick's self-confidence. 'I thought I'd read you a story.'

She let go of Miss Jemmie and pulled a book out from under the covers, handing it to him.

'Ah, *Where the Wild Things Are*. I wonder how Max has been doing lately. He probably turned into a wart hog.'

Izzy made a small, hiccuping sound, like a hacked-off laugh.

Curling an arm round her tiny shoulders, he drew her close. With the book open on his lap, he began to read. And as he slipped into the familiar story, he felt for the first time as if he might have a chance.

For the first week, Nick was shaky and short-tempered and afraid that if he made one wrong move, he'd end up back on a bar stool at Zoe's. Every moment of every day was an agonising test of his will.

Annie arrived every day with a smile on her face and an activity planned. By sheer force of will, she was turning the three of them into a patchwork family, and it was that connection that kept Nick going to his AA meetings. He'd be damned if he'd let Annie and Izzy down. But wherever he went, whatever he said, he felt Izzy's eyes on him. She was waiting for the inevitable screw-up.

She hadn't spoken a word to him yet, and this time, the silences were worse than before, because she was talking to Annie—though he'd never heard the sweetness of his little girl's voice.

Their days followed a familiar pattern. Monday through Friday, Annie showed up at Nick's house bright and early. He made pancakes and eggs for breakfast, and then the three of them spent the day together. Today they had hiked deep into Enchanted Valley, and now, several hours and even more miles later, each of them was exhausted. Izzy had fallen asleep almost before her head hit the pillow.

Annie kissed Izzy's forehead, murmuring a quiet good night.

''Night, Annie,' Izzy mumbled back, her eyes closed.

Annie drew back. This was the time of the week she hated most. Friday night. She wouldn't see Nick and Izzy again until Monday, and though she enjoyed the time she spent with Hank, she couldn't wait to get back here on Monday morning. She didn't often let herself think about how much she liked Nick and Izzy, or how *right* it felt to be with them. She had come to the sad realisation that Blake wasn't going to change his mind, that she wasn't going to receive the apologetic phone call she'd fantasised about for weeks. Without even that slim fantasy to cling to, she was left feeling adrift.

She started to turn away, when she noticed something through the window, a movement. She pushed the patterned lace curtains aside.

Nick was standing down alongside the lake, his shadow a long streak across the rippling silver waves. He was as lonely as she was. She saw it in his eyes all the time, a sadness that clung even when he smiled. He was trying so hard. Yesterday, he'd spent two hours playing Candy Land with Izzy. Every time Izzy smiled, Nick looked like he was going to cry.

So often, during the day, she was reminded of Blake, and the kind of father he'd been. Never there, physically or emotionally, for his daughter, taking so much of his life for granted. It was partially Annie's fault; she saw that now. She had blindly done everything he'd asked of her. Everything. She'd given up so much—everything of herself and her dreams; she'd given it up without a whimper of protest . . . and all because she loved him so much.

Her life, her soul, had faded into his, one day, one decision at a time. She'd done what they 'agreed' she should do. She'd stayed at home and become the perfect suburban wife and mother, and in her quest for quiet perfection, she'd let Blake become a bad husband and bad father. Only now she saw how wrong she'd been: she'd made all those sacrifices not out of strength and love, but out of weakness. Because it was safer and easier to follow. She had become what she'd set out to be, and now she was ashamed of her choices. But still she had no true understanding of where she would go from here. She wished she had Nick's strength, his willingness to shove past his fear and *try*.

She closed the bedroom door behind her and went downstairs. Plucking her bag from the sofa, she headed for the door. Outside, the cool night air breezed across her cheeks.

She stared across the blackened lawn at Nick. It was at times like these, at the quiet end of the day, that memories of their lovemaking floated to the surface of her mind. She remembered the feel of his hands on her naked skin . . . the softness of his lips . . .

'Annie?'

Her eyes popped open. He was in front of her, and when she looked at him, she was certain that it was all in her eyes: the naked, desperate need for companionship and caring. She was vulnerable now, longing to be held and touched by a man . . . even if it was the wrong man . . . even if she wasn't truly the woman he wanted.

She forced a smile. 'Hi, Nick . . . 'bye, Nick. I've got to run.'

Before he could answer, she ran to her car.

Sunday was the kind of day that tricked people into moving into this damp, soggy corner of the world. When Nick flung back the living-room curtains and looked outside, a bright yellow sun had just crested the trees; lemony streamers of light backlit the forest and gave it a translucent, otherworldly glow. Lake Mystic swallowed the surrounding images and held them against its blue mirrored surface.

It was a perfect day for a father–daughter outing. He hurried up the stairs and woke his sleeping child. Within the hour, they were driving down the winding coastal road and Nick parked in one of the lay-bys that were designed to showcase the view to tourists. Taking Izzy's hand, he led her down the trail towards the beach. Below them, huge, white-tipped waves crashed against the rocks. When they finally dropped onto the hard-packed sand, Izzy grinned up at him.

Nick set their picnic basket down on a grey boulder near the land's end. 'Come on, Izzy.'

They ran across the sand, laughing, creating the only footprints for miles, searching for hidden treasures: sand dollars, translucent quartz stones and tiny black crabs. When the sun reached its peak in the sky and sent its warmth through their layers of wool and Gore-Tex, Nick led Izzy back to where they'd begun. He threw a huge red and white blanket over the hard sand and unpacked the basket. They sat crosslegged on the blanket and ate their lunch.

All the while, Nick told stories—about the Native Americans who had first combed this beach, hundreds of years before the first white settlers appeared; about the time he'd brought Kathy here when she was pregnant.

Once, he'd thought that Izzy was going to say something. She'd leaned forward, her brown eyes sparkling, her lips trembling.

He'd put down his glass of lemonade. *Come on, Izzy-bear*. But in the end, she'd held back.

That silence was worse than the others, somehow. It lodged in his heart like a steel splinter; he felt it with every indrawn breath afterwards. But he forced a smile and went on with another story.

They drove home in the last fading rays of the setting sun. Nick found it difficult to keep talking, to keep spilling his soul into the stony silence that surrounded them, but he forced himself to do it. When they passed Zoe's, the need for a drink rose in him, relentless as the surf. He hit the gas harder and they sped beyond the tavern.

When they pulled into the driveway, day had given way to a pink and gold evening. He held Izzy's hand as they quietly made their way back into the house.

'What do you say we play a game?' he said.

Izzy didn't answer, but scampered away. In a few moments, she appeared again, with the big, multicoloured Candy Land box.

He groaned dramatically. 'Not that—anything but that. How about Pick-up Sticks?'

A tiny smile tilted her mouth. She shook her head.

'OK. One game of Candy Land, then Pick-up Sticks.'

She released a giggle, and the simple sound of that soothed the ragged edges of his nerves. He quickly made a fire, then they set up the board in the middle of the living-room floor.

One game turned into another and another. When Nick had finally lost his fine motor skills, he tossed the tiny blue and yellow board pieces into the oblong box. 'I give up. You're the queen of Candy Land. No one can beat you. Come on, Izzy-bear, it's dinnertime. Even cooking is better than this game.'

In the kitchen, they sat and ate store-bought macaroni cheese. Izzy helped Nick wash and dry the dishes and put them away, and then they went upstairs. He helped her into her nightgown, brushed those white teeth of hers, and together they climbed into her narrow bed.

He pulled the tattered copy of *Alice in Wonderland* off the bedside table, drew his daughter close and began to read.

When he closed the book, her eyes were heavy and she was more than half asleep. 'Good night, Sunshine,' he said softly, kissing her forehead. Slowly, he drew back and stood up.

She reached out suddenly and grabbed his hand. He turned back, stared down at her. 'Izzy?'

'Daddy?'

For a second, he couldn't breathe. It was the first time he'd heard her sweet child's voice in almost a year. Slowly, slowly, he sat down beside her. Tears stung his eyes, turned his precious baby into a blur. 'Oh, Izzy,' he whispered, unable to find any other words.

'I love you, Daddy,' she said, and now she was crying, too.

He pulled her into a bear hug. 'Oh, Izzy-bear, I love you, too,' he whispered over and over again, stroking her hair, feeling her tears mingle with his on the softness of her cheek. He held her tightly, wondering if he'd ever have the strength to let her go.

Monday was a magical day, filled with laughter. Once again the sun banished the clouds from the sky. Nick and Annie and Izzy rode bicycles and collected wild flowers and made crowns from the dainty purple and white flowers that had opened during the night.

Annie couldn't remember when she'd had so much fun. Blake had never spent a day like this with his girls, just the three of them; even when he'd had a rare day at home, he'd spent it in his study. Annie was only now beginning to realise how lonely her life had been.

As she pedalled her bike down the National Park trail, she found herself recalling the old Nick—the young Nick—and how she'd loved him. And when she closed her eyes while he was talking, she saw the boy who'd first kissed her beneath a starry night sky. The boy whose gentle, tentative kiss had made her cry.

She could feel herself drifting into dangerous waters. So many things about Nick touched her, but it was the depth of his love for Izzy that tangled her up inside and left her aching. No matter how hard she tried to forget the life she'd lived in California and the choices she'd made, Nick brought it all up again. Annie had raised a daughter who would never truly know the comforting embrace of a father's adoration.

And she had been a wife in love alone for too many years.

She had felt pathetic and small as she crossed the rickety bridge to that realisation. For years, she'd assumed that the love she gave her husband was a reflection of his love for her, and now, because of her blindness, she was alone, a thirty-nine-year-old woman who faced her 'golden' years without a child at home or a husband in her bed.

Now, as they drove home after their bike ride, Annie prayed that Nick hadn't heard all that loneliness and pain in her voice. Every time he looked at her today, she'd looked away, fast.

By the time they returned to the house, she was a wreck. As soon as dinner was over, she bolted from the table and hustled Izzy up to bed, leaving Nick to wash and dry the dishes.

'Good night, Izzy,' she said, tucking the child into bed. 'Your daddy will be up in a minute.'

''Night, Annie,' Izzy muttered, rolling onto her side.

Annie closed the bedroom door and headed downstairs. She found Nick in the living room, staring out at the lake. Even from this distance, she could see that his hands were shaking.

The last step creaked beneath her foot and she froze.

He spun towards her. His skin was pale in the lamplight, and sweat sheened his forehead.

'You want a drink,' she said.

'Want?' His laugh was low and rough. 'That doesn't even begin to cover it.'

Annie didn't know what to do. It was dangerous to touch him, but she couldn't turn away. Cautiously, she moved towards him. He reached for her hand, his sweaty fingers coiling round hers with a desperate squeeze. After a long minute, she said, 'How 'bout a bowl of Chocolate Chip Mint instead?'

'Great. I'll just go say good night to Izzy, then . . . I'll meet you by the fire.' He gave her a relieved smile before bolting up the stairs.

Annie went to the kitchen and scooped out two bowls of ice cream. The whole time she told herself that it was nothing, just a bowl of ice cream between friends. By the time she was finished, Nick was back downstairs. Together, they sat on the sofa.

In silence, they ate. All at once, he turned to her. 'How long will you be here?'

She sighed. 'About another month and a half. Natalie gets home on the 15th of June.' His gaze caught hers, and she felt as if she were falling into his blue eyes.

'What do you think of Mystic?' he asked slowly, watching her. 'You sure couldn't wait to leave after high school.'

'It wasn't Mystic that sent me running.'

It was a minute before he answered softly, 'I never meant to hurt you.'

'I know.'

'You scared me.'

'You're kidding, right?'

He leaned forward and set the bowl down on the coffee table. Then, slowly, he turned towards her. One arm snaked down the back of the sofa towards her, and she had to fight the urge to lean back into it. 'I think our lives are mapped out long before we know enough to ask the right questions. Mine was cast in stone the day my dad abandoned my mom. She had . . . trouble handling life. Before I even knew what was happening, I was her caretaker. I learned what every child of a drunk learns: don't talk, don't trust, don't care. Hell, I was an adult before I was ten years old. I shopped, I cooked, I cleaned . . . wherever we lived. I loved her, so I took care of her, and when she turned on me or became violent, I believed what she said—that I was worthless and stupid and lucky she stayed with me.' He leaned back into the sofa.

Annie felt his fingertips brush her shoulders.

'Living here with Joe was like a dream for me. Clean sheets, clean clothes, lots to eat. I got to go to school every day and no one ever hit me.' He smiled at her, and the heat of it sent shivers through her blood. 'Then I met you and Kath. Remember?'

'At the A and W, after a football game. We invited you to sit with us.'

'You invited me. I couldn't believe it when you did that . . . and then, when we all became friends, it stunned me. Everything about that year was a first.' He smiled, but his smile was sad and tired round the edges. 'You were the first girl I ever kissed. Did you know that?'

Annie's throat felt dangerously tight. 'I cried.'

He nodded. 'I thought it was because you *knew*. Like you could taste it in me somehow, that I wasn't good enough.'

She wanted to touch him so badly her fingers tingled. She forced her hand into a fist. 'I never knew why I cried. Still don't.'

He smiled at her. 'See? The paths are set before we're aware. Kathy was so much simpler. I *understood* her. She needed me, even then she needed me, and to me that was the same as love. I just plopped into the role I knew. I mean, what was I supposed to do? Ask you to give up Stanford? Or wait for you, even though you hadn't asked me to?'

Annie had never once considered being bold enough to talk to Nick about how she felt. Like him, she'd fallen easily into the role she knew. She did what was expected of her; she went away to college and married a nice boy with a bright future—and lost herself along the way.

'I always figured you'd be famous,' he said at last, 'you were so damned smart. The only kid from Mystic ever to get an academic schol-arship to Stanford.'

She snorted. 'Me, famous? Doing what?'

'Don't do that, Annie.' His voice was as soft as a touch, and she couldn't help looking at him. The sadness in his eyes coiled round her throat and squeezed. 'That's a bad road to go down. Believe me, I know. You could succeed at anything you tried.'

His encouragement was a draught of water to her parched, thirsty soul. 'I *did* think of something the other day . . .'

'What?'

'I'd like to run a small bookstore. You know the kind, with over-stuffed chairs and latte machines and employees who actually *read*.'

He touched her cheekbone, a fleeting caress that made her shiver. It was the first time he'd deliberately touched her since that night by the lake. 'You should see yourself right now, Annie. Your eyes lit up when you said "bookstore". I think it's a great idea. In fact, there's an old Victorian house on Main Street. It used to be a gift shop until a few months ago. When the owner died, they closed it up. They've been trying to find a renter. It could make a great location.' He paused and looked at her. 'If you wanted to open that bookstore in Mystic.'

The fantasy broke apart. They both knew that her life wasn't in Mystic. She stared down at her diamond ring, trying to think of some-thing to say.

He said suddenly, 'Have you seen *Same Time, Next Year*?'

She frowned. 'The Alan Alda movie—the one about the couple who have an affair for one weekend every year?'

'Yeah.'

She found it difficult to breathe evenly. The air seemed electrified by the simple word: affair. 'I—I always loved it.'

'It's starting in ten minutes. You want to watch?'

Her breath expelled in a rush. She felt like a fool for reading something into a simple little question about a movie.

'Sure.'

They watched the movie, but all the while, Annie had the strangest sensation that she was falling. She kept glancing at Nick, whom she often caught staring at her in return. She didn't want to consider how much he had begun to matter. She didn't want to care too deeply about him, and yet she could feel each day bringing them closer and closer.

When the movie ended, she couldn't look at him, afraid of what she'd see in his eyes . . . afraid of what he'd see in hers. So, she grabbed her bag and ran for the door. She hardly even mumbled a goodbye.

Izzy woke up scared. She'd been dreaming about her mommy . . . that was all she could remember. Her mommy had been down by the lake, calling out to her . . . crying.

She threw back the covers and climbed out of bed. She crept out of her bedroom and hurried down the hall. She paused at her daddy's bedroom, then moved past, down the stairs and out of the front door.

She stared at the lake. The mist had thickened into a grey fog spiked with black toothpick trees.

Izzy-bear, is that you?

'Mommy?'

Something white flashed beside the shore. Then she heard the sound of a woman crying. She hurried across the wet grass, her toes squishing in muddy ground, not stopping until she reached the lake.

'Mommy?' she whispered.

A fine mist rose from the water. It was in the mist that she saw her mommy, clear as day, her hands clasped at her waist, her golden-blonde hair a halo around her face. There was a brightness to her mommy that hurt Izzy's eyes, like looking right at the sun.

Izzy-bear, why did you call me?

Izzy blinked. 'I didn't call you this time.'

I heard you calling in your sleep.

Izzy couldn't remember her dream. 'I don't know what I wanted.'

She felt her mother's touch, a breeze on her forehead, brushing the hair away, a kiss that smelt of mist and rain and her mommy's favourite perfume. 'I miss you, Mommy.'

Your daddy's back now.

'What if he goes away again?'

Another touch, softer. *He won't, Izzy-bear.*

This time, when Izzy looked up, her mother was closer. 'I can't follow you, can I?'

For a split second, the mist was gone, and Izzy saw her mom, a sad-eyed, blonde-haired woman, looking down at her little girl. *I'll always be inside you, Izzy. You don't have to disappear or follow me or reach for me. All you have to do is close your eyes and think of me and I'll be there.*

Tears streaked down Izzy's face, plopped on her hands. She stared, blinking, into her mommy's blue, blue eyes. 'I love you, Mommy . . .'

And then suddenly her mommy was gone.

'Izzy!'

Her father's panicked voice sliced through Izzy's thoughts. She twisted round and saw him running towards her. 'Daddy?'

He pulled her into his arms and held her tightly. 'Izzy,' he said her name in a weird way, as if he'd been running for miles. 'Oh, Izzy . . . you scared me. I didn't know where you were . . .'

'I di'n't go anywhere bad, Daddy.'

He gave her a wobbly smile. 'I know, honey.'

He carried her back into the house and put her gently in bed. She scooted under the covers, but she wasn't ready to be by herself yet. She grabbed her father's hand and he climbed into bed beside her.

Izzy looked up into his face. 'Annie says that when it rains, it's Mommy and the angels crying.'

He brushed the hair from her face. 'Annie knows an awful lot.'

She turned away from him, trying to hide the tears that burned her eyes. 'I'm startin' to forget her, Daddy.'

He slipped an arm round her and drew her close, gently stroking her moist cheek. 'Mommy had the prettiest eyes in the world, and when she looked at you, it felt as if the rain had stopped and the sunlight was on your face. And she had a crooked front tooth—it sort of slanted sideways, and a tiny mole right next to her ear. She loved you, Izzy . . .'

'She loved both of us, Daddy.'

He didn't say anything but kissed her, right on the tip of her nose just like he used to. For the first time since her mommy died, Izzy wasn't scared. The scream that had been inside her for months shrivelled up like an old raisin and rolled away. Her daddy loved her again.

She squeezed her eyes shut, really hard so she wouldn't cry like a baby. When she could breathe again, she slowly opened her eyes.

She couldn't believe what she saw. 'Daddy?' she said softly.

'Yeah, Sunshine?'

She slowly lifted her left hand. Clear as day, she could see the little black glove that grew out of her sleeve. She bit down on her trembling lower lip, afraid it was a mistake. Slowly, she took off the glove, and there was her hand. 'Do you see it, Daddy?'

He looked right at her hand—she was sure he saw it—but he didn't smile. Instead, he looked at her. 'What *should* I see?'

She swallowed. 'I see my hand . . . and my arm. Do you see 'em?'

Her daddy made a raggedy sound. 'Yeah. I see your hand.' Very slowly he took the glove from her.

She wriggled her fingers. 'I guess I'm stayin' here with you, Daddy.'

'Yeah, Izzy-bear. I guess you are.'

The Mystic Rain Festival started on schedule, on the first Saturday in May, just as it had for each of the last hundred years. A low-slung grey sky hung over downtown. Rain fell in a stuttering curtain on the storefront awnings. Annie wore a slick yellow raincoat, with her Levi's tucked into high-topped black rubber boots. Hank stood beside her, munching on a homemade scone he'd purchased at the Rotary Club booth.

The parade moved slowly down Main Street, splashing on the wet pavement. There were fire trucks, police cars, Boy Scout troops, and six little girls in pink tutus from Esmeralda's Dance Barn.

Annie was enchanted by the schmaltzy, small-town production. She had missed this. She'd gone to California and raised her daughter behind iron gates and in air-conditioned rooms, in a city where hometown parades had celebrity marshals and corporate sponsors.

She didn't want to go back there.

It surprised her, the sudden certainty of her decision. It was the first time in her life she'd come to a conclusion without thinking of other people's feelings, and it felt good. She didn't want to live in California any more, and she didn't have to. After the divorce, when Natalie went away to college, Annie could return to Mystic, maybe even open that bookstore . . .

Dreams. They were such precious commodities, and she'd given so many of hers away without a fight. Never again. She turned to her dad. 'Let me ask you something, Dad. Do you think this town could use a bookstore?'

He smiled. 'Hell, yes. We've needed one for years. Your mom used to dream of opening one.'

Annie shivered. For a strange, disorientating second, she felt as if her mom were beside her. 'Really? I was thinking the same thing.'

He turned to her, looked at her long and hard. 'You're hurting right now, Annie, and you're running, but don't forget where your real life is.'

She slipped her hand into her dad's and gave him a gentle squeeze. They strolled down the sidewalk, past the artisans' booths and hot-dog stands. Hank stopped at the Lutheran church stand and bought two mocha lattes, handing one to Annie. The pungent aroma of the coffee swirled between them, and the heat of it soothed her scratchy throat. Neither of them noticed the gentle patter of the rain.

'So, Natalie gets home in six weeks.'

Annie took a sip of coffee, then nodded. 'June 15th. I can't wait.'

'What will you say to Blake when you see him?'

The question surprised Annie. It was unlike her father to ask. She shrugged. 'I don't know. For weeks, all I wanted was to see him again, to make him remember what we had together, but now I can't seem to grab hold of what we had.'

'Is it because of him?'

She started to ask what he meant, but when she looked up, she saw Nick. He was standing across the street, with Izzy on his shoulders. They were both eating ice-cream cones. He turned, and across the crowded street, he flashed her a smile, waved, then moved on. She tried to frame an answer for her dad, but she honestly didn't know how Nick fitted into the picture. 'Who knows what causes anything? All I know is that I'm not the same woman I was before.'

'You be careful, Annie.'

She glanced across the street again, but Nick was gone. She felt a pang of disappointment. 'You know, Dad, I'm tired of being careful.'

Chapter 8

On Monday, Annie, Nick and Izzy drove to Sol Duc Hot Springs and hiked deep into the Olympic National Forest. Afterwards, they swam in the lodge's huge swimming pool and relaxed in the steaming, sulphuric hot springs. When dusk started to fall, they piled back into the car and headed home.

By the time they unpacked the car and got everything put away, it was almost midnight. Nick offered Annie his room, and she took him up on the offer. She called her dad, who was waiting up for her again, and told him that she'd be home first thing in the morning.

'Is that wise, Annie Virginia?' he asked in a quiet voice.

She told him not to worry, and hung up the phone. Afterwards, she wasn't so sure she'd made a smart decision, but the truth was that she didn't feel well. She wanted to collapse in a convenient bed and sleep for ten hours. Her back hurt, her head hurt, and she'd felt nauseous for most of the drive home. She was definitely not cut out for hiking.

She was careful to avoid Nick as she hurried upstairs, brushed her teeth, and soon fell into a deep sleep.

The next morning, she woke up feeling even worse. A headache pounded behind her eyes, and she had to lie very still in bed, concentrating on each breath, or she was certain she was going to throw up.

A chill racked her body, and she closed her eyes.

Some time later—an hour? a minute?—a knock sounded at her door. Annie forced herself to sit up. 'Come in.'

Izzy poked her head through the open door. 'Annie?'

Annie manufactured a wan smile. 'Hi, honey. Come on in.'

Izzy slipped into the room, closing the door behind her. 'I was waitin' for you to show up. I thought maybe you'd left us . . . but then Daddy tole me you'd spent the night.'

Annie's heart went out to the girl. 'I wouldn't do that, Izzy. I wouldn't disappear without saying goodbye.'

'Grown-ups do that sometimes.'

'Oh, Izzy . . .' Annie shifted her position, trying to ignore a sudden wave of dizziness. 'I know they do.' She started to say something else, when she sneezed hard. She sagged in bed, trying to remember when she'd felt this rotten.

Izzy's eyes widened. 'Are you sick?'

Annie gave her a weak smile of understanding. 'Not *really* sick,' she answered quietly. 'It's just a cold. I think I'm going to go to sleep for a while, but we'll talk later. OK?'

Izzy nodded slowly. 'OK. See yah.'

Annie smiled weakly. 'See you, pumpkin.' Her eyes closed.

Annie dreamed she was in a cool, dark place. She could hear the cascading fall of water and the buzzing drone of a dragonfly. There was someone waiting for her in the forest's darkness. She could hear the even cant of his breathing in the shadows. She wanted to reach for him, but she was afraid. Where she was felt familiar, safe, and he was waiting for her in a strange world where she didn't know the rules. She was afraid that if she followed, she'd lose the way.

'Annie?'

She woke up suddenly and found Nick sitting on the end of her bed. Trying to smile, she struggled to sit up halfway. 'Hi.'

'Izzy tells me you're sick.' He leaned towards her. 'I've brought you some orange juice and a couple of scrambled eggs. Oh, and Tylenol and a pitcher of ice water.' He handed her two Tylenols. 'Here.'

She stared down at the two little pills in his hand.

He frowned. 'Annie? You're crying.'

She blinked hard.

'What is it, Annie?'

The gentleness in his voice only made her cry harder, and though it was humiliating to sit here crying for no reason, she couldn't seem to stop herself. She couldn't meet his eyes. 'You'll think I'm an idiot.'

He laughed, a quiet, tender sound. 'You're worried about what the town drunk thinks?'

She sniffed hard. 'Don't talk about yourself that way.'

'Is that how the rich people in California do it—am I just supposed to pretend you're not crying? Now, tell me what's the matter.'

Annie closed her eyes. 'No one has ever given me an aspirin before— I mean, without me asking for it.' God, it sounded as pathetic as she'd thought it would. 'I've been a wife and mother for so long. I've always been the one who took care of people when they were sick.'

'But no one took care of you.' He said it as a simple statement, and though she wanted to reject it as being silly, she couldn't.

It was all there, in that simple sentence, everything that had been wrong with her marriage. She'd done everything to make Blake's life safe and perfect; she'd loved him and cared for him and protected him. All those years she'd made excuses for his selfishness: he was tired, or busy, or distracted by business. The marriage she'd had wasn't good enough. She'd never really, truly been loved . . . not the way she deserved to be loved.

With a deep, ragged sigh, she wiped her eyes and smiled up at Nick. 'I'm sorry for being such a baby.' She didn't know what else to say to him, this man who'd accidentally opened a door on her old life and shown her the truth.

'You should drink something.'

She wiped her runny nose and gave him a crooked grin. 'Well, you should know.'

He looked stunned for a second, then he burst out laughing.

The cold hung on for a few days, and when it was over, Annie was left feeling tired and weak. Her stomach stayed queasy afterwards, but she refused to pay any attention to it. Her admiration for Nick increased. His vulnerability and his strength moved her, and the tenderness of his care had almost undone her. She found herself watching him, mesmerised, one evening. He was standing down at the lake again, his body a shadow within shadows. Suddenly she wanted to be with him, and though the realisation frightened her, it also set her heart racing with anticipation. When she was with Nick, she was a different woman. He made her feel beautiful and sparkly and more alive.

The grass was cold and wet on her bare feet. Nick stood motionless, his shoulders rounded, his head dropped forward.

'Hi, Nick,' she said softly.

He spun round, and she saw the pain in his eyes.

'Hi, Annie.' His voice was low, and as rough as old bricks. She had come to know him so well in the past weeks that his longings were obvious to her. 'You want a drink.'

He laughed, but it was a sharp, bitter sound, not his laugh at all. He reached out and held her hand, squeezing hard.

She knew from experience that he needed an anchor to hold him steady. 'Remember the senior party, when Kath disappeared for a half-hour or so?' she said quietly. 'We were at Lake Crescent. You and I sat by the lake, right in front of the lodge, and talked and talked. You said you wanted to be a cop.'

'You said you wanted to be a writer.'

She was surprised that he remembered, and though she didn't want to, she found herself remembering the girl who'd wanted to be a writer. 'That was before I'd learned . . .' Her voice faded into the breeze.

He turned, gazed down at her. 'Learned what?'

She shrugged, unable suddenly to meet his gaze. 'I don't know. How time passes and takes everything in its path—youth, hopes, dreams. Dreams—it takes those most of all.'

She felt his gaze on her again, and she was afraid to meet it, afraid of what she'd see in his eyes.

'Sometimes I don't even recognise you,' he said, gently tilting her chin up. 'You say things like that and I don't know the woman who is speaking at all. What happened to you, Annie?'

The question was startling in its intimacy. The night fell silent, awaiting her answer. She pushed the poisonous words out in a rush. 'My husband is in love with another woman. He wants a divorce.'

'Annie—'

'I'm fine, really.' But when she looked in his eyes, she saw a terrible, harrowing compassion, and it was her undoing. The strength she'd been gathering and hoarding for the past weeks fell away from her. A single tear streaked down her cheek, and in that glittering bead of moisture, he saw reflections of all the distance that separated them. She still looked amazingly like the sixteen-year-old girl he'd first fallen in love with, but like him, the life she'd led and the choices she'd made lay collected in the tiny network of lines around her beautiful face. 'How does it happen? I loved Blake with all my heart and soul and it wasn't enough . . .'

He sighed, and the sadness of the sound bound them together.

She gazed up at him. In the weeks since Blake's confession, she'd trapped the pain inside her heart and kept it there. But now, all at once, the fire of it was gone. In its place was a dull, thudding ache.

Nick didn't know how it happened exactly. All he knew was that he needed Annie. He reached for her. Slowly, watching her, he bent down and kissed her. It was gentle at first, a soft mingling of lips and breath. But then she moved towards him, settled into his embrace.

He deepened the kiss until he was light-headed with longing, and then slowly he drew back.

She stared up at him. He saw sadness in her eyes, but something else, perhaps the same quiet wonder he had felt. 'I'm sorry,' he said softly, even though it wasn't true. 'I had no right—'

'Don't be,' she whispered. 'Please . . . don't be sorry. I wanted you to kiss me. I . . . I've wanted it for a long time, I think.'

She opened the door to intimacy and he couldn't walk away. He didn't care if he was being stupid or asking for trouble. He only knew that he wanted her, heart, body and soul. 'I want you, Annie Bourne. It feels like I've wanted you all my life.'

A tear slipped down her cheek. 'I know,' was all she said in answer, but in the two simple, sadly softened words, he heard the truth: that sometimes, the wanting wasn't enough.

He reached for her hand, lifting it. In the glittering silver moonlight, the diamond ring seemed to be made of cold fire. He stared at the ring saying nothing. Then he turned from her. 'Good night, Annie,' he said softly, walking away from her before he made a fool of himself.

It occurred to Annie that if she were smart, she would leave right then. But all she could think about was Nick, and the way he'd kissed her. The way he'd touched and held her had swept her away. And when he'd said, *I want you, Annie Bourne*, she'd known that she was lost.

She glanced up at his bedroom. A shadow passed in front of the glass, then disappeared. She glanced down at the wedding ring on her left hand. The diamond glittered with colour in the lamp's glow. The ring she'd worn since Blake had placed it on her hand beneath a shower of romantic words on their tenth anniversary.

Gently, she pulled the ring from her finger. 'Goodbye, Blake.' It hurt to say the words, even to think them, but there was a surprising freedom in it, too. She felt unfettered, on her own for perhaps the first time in her life. There was no one to determine her path. No one but her.

Before she could talk herself out of it, she hurried back into the house and up the stairs. Outside Nick's door, she lost her nerve. All the reasons for being here scurried away, cowards leaving a sinking ship. Suddenly she didn't feel sexy; she felt vulnerable and alone.

She was just about to turn away when she heard the music. A radio was playing, a scratchy old rendition of Nat King Cole's 'Unforgettable'.

It soothed her ragged nerves. Nick wasn't some inexperienced teenager; he was a man, her age, and as ravaged by life and love as she was. He would understand why she was here. He would ask nothing of her except the simple, uncomplicated act of sharing.

She rapped sharply on the door.

There was a pause. The music snapped off. 'Come on in, Izzy.'

She pushed on the door; it opened slowly. 'It's me . . . Annie.'

Nick was in bed.

She swallowed hard and moved towards him. She felt as gawky and awkward as a teenager. She thought about the weight she'd gained in the past weeks, and wondered if he'd find her attractive. Blake had always made such cutting remarks when Annie gained a pound . . .

'Are you sure?' He asked it simply, the only question that mattered.

And she was. Utterly, absolutely, positively sure. She felt herself moving towards him, reaching out. Later, she would never be able to remember who had touched first, or how they had come to be naked together on that massive, four-poster bed . . . but she would never forget the soft, singsongy way he whispered her name while he kissed her . . . or the way his arms wrapped round her body, holding her so close that sometimes she couldn't breathe . . . or the shattering intensity of their lovemaking. All she could remember was that at the jagged peak of her pleasure, it was *his* name she cried out. Not Blake's.

Annie lay cuddled alongside Nick, her naked leg thrown across his thigh. They had been together for hours now, talking softly and laughing, and making love. At about midnight, she'd reluctantly called her father and told him that she wouldn't be home tonight—that Izzy was fighting a cold and needed Annie; but her father hadn't been fooled. 'Are you sure that's wise, Annie Virginia?'

She'd brushed him off with a schoolgirl's giggle and told him not to worry. She didn't want to think about whether this was wise. For the first time in her life, she felt wicked and wild, and wonderfully alive.

So much had changed for her tonight. The simple act of removing her wedding ring had transformed her. She'd become younger, braver, more adventurous. Tonight, in the hours she'd spent in Nick's arms, she'd discovered a whole new woman.

Nick slid an arm round Annie and drew her close. For the first time, there was sadness in his blue eyes. 'June 15th, huh?'

Annie caught her breath. Their gazes locked, and she felt her smile weaken. In less than a month, Annie would be going home—such as it was. She would be leaving Nick and Izzy and Mystic, and returning to her real life . . . or whatever was left of it.

He touched her face with a tenderness that made her heart ache. 'I shouldn't have said that.'

'We have what we have, Nicky. Let's not ruin it by looking ahead. The future isn't something I like to think about.'

His hand slid down her bare arm and settled possessively on her left hand. She knew that he was thinking about the ring she no longer wore—and about the tiny white tan line that remained to mark its place. When he finally looked at her, he was smiling again. 'I'll take whatever you have to give, and . . .'

'And what?'

It took him a long time to answer. 'And hope it's enough.'

Every day brought them closer together. In the last week of May, summer threw its multicoloured net across the rain forest. It was an unseasonal heatwave, and everyone in Mystic treasured the new-found warmth.

Annie spent less and less time at her father's house, and more and more in Nick's bed. She knew she was playing with fire, but she couldn't help herself. She was like a teenager again, consumed by her first lover. Every time she looked at Nick she remembered their lovemaking. She couldn't believe how uninhibited she'd become.

During the day, they were careful not to touch each other, but the forced abstinence only increased their desire. All day, Annie waited for the night to begin, so that she could creep into his bed again.

Today they'd had a wonderful time at Lake Crescent. They'd played volleyball on the beach, and rented paddle boats. At home, Annie made a big pot of spaghetti, and after dinner, they sat round the big kitchen table and worked on Izzy's reading skills. Later, when they went upstairs, they all climbed into Izzy's bed for story time.

Annie refused to think about how *right* all of this felt, how much she was beginning to belong here. Nick had read only the first page when the sound of a ringing telephone interrupted them. 'I'd better go answer that,' he said.

'We'll wait for you, Daddy,' Izzy said, snuggling up to Annie.

Nick pressed the book into Izzy's hands and hurried out of the room. He came back a few minutes later, looking solemn. He eased back into the bed, on the other side of Izzy. 'That was your teacher, Izzy-bear. She said there's a class party on Friday—and all the kids want you to come.'

Izzy looked scared. 'Oh.'

Nick smiled at her, a soft, gentle smile that seemed to reach right into Annie's heart. 'She said something about cupcakes.'

Izzy frowned. 'I *do* like cupcakes.'

'I know you do, Sunshine.' He pulled her against him with one strong arm. 'There's nothing wrong with being scared, Izzy. It happens to all of us. What's wrong is if we don't try things because we're afraid. We can't hide away from the things that scare us.'

Annie heard so much in his voice, all the remnants of the lessons he'd learned the hard way. She felt a warm rush of pride for him, and she wondered again how she was going to leave this man, how she was going to return to her cold, sterile life.

Izzy sighed. 'I guess a party would be OK. Will you'n Annie take me?'

'Of course we will.'

'OK.' She looked up, gave Nick a tentative smile. 'Daddy, will you read me another story, Daddy?'

He grinned. Reaching down to the floor beside the bed, he produced another book. 'I thought you might ask that.' After story time was over, Nick went back to his room and waited.

He heard a knock.

He surged to the door and yanked it open. Annie stood in the doorway, wearing an oversized T-shirt and a pair of navy-blue kneesocks.

They barely made it to the bed. Kissing, groping, laughing, they fell onto the pile of wrinkled sheets. The tired old mattress creaked and groaned beneath them.

Nick had never wanted a woman so badly in his life, and Annie seemed to share his urgency. He held her, stroked and fondled and caressed her. She rolled with him, kissing him with a greediness that left him breathless, pulling his tongue deep into her mouth.

When it was over, Nick lay exhausted on his bed, one arm flung out against the wall, the other curled protectively round Annie's naked hip. She lay tucked against him, her bare leg thrown casually over his, her nipple pressed against his rib cage. Her head was resting on the ball of his shoulder, her breath caressed his skin.

He was afraid suddenly that she would pull away now, draw out of his arms and scurry back to her father's house, and that he'd be left with nothing but her lingering scent and the cold chill of her absence along his side. 'Talk to me, Annie,' he said softly, stroking the velvety skin in the small of her back.

She laughed. 'Most people who know me want me to shut up.'

'I'm not Blake.'

'Sorry.' She snuggled closer to him. One pale finger coiled in his chest hair, then absently caressed his skin. 'You . . . bring out something in me. Something I wouldn't have believed was there.'

'Oh yeah? What is it?'

She rolled half on top of him. 'I used to be . . . organised. Efficient. I fed everyone and dressed everyone and went shopping and made lists and kept appointments. Blake and I had sex . . . nice sex, comfortable. It felt good and I had orgasms. But it wasn't like it is with you. I never felt as if I were going to leap out of my skin.' She laughed, that broad, infectious laugh that seemed to come from someplace deep inside her. Kathy had never made him feel this way, as if the whole world was open to him and all he had to do was reach for his dreams.

Dreams. He closed his eyes. They came to him so often now, the dreams he'd long ago put aside. He remembered again how important a family had always been to him, how he'd imagined his life would chug along on a bright and easy road, crowded with laughing children all around him. If he'd chosen Annie, all those years ago, maybe everything would have been different . . .

'How come you and Kathy never had more children?' Annie asked, suddenly.

Her question disconcerted Nick for a second. 'I always wanted to. Hell, I wanted six kids, but we waited so long for Izzy and afterwards, it was obvious that Kathy couldn't handle any more. When Izzy was about two, I had a vasectomy.' He glanced down at her, cuddled so close to him. 'How about you? You're such a wonderful mother.'

It was a long time before she answered. 'Adrian would have been fourteen this year. He was my son.'

'Annie . . .'

She didn't look at him. 'He came prematurely and only lived for four days. After that, we tried everything, but I couldn't get pregnant again. I always wanted more children.'

He didn't say he was sorry; he knew first-hand how plastic the words could sound. Instead, he pulled her into his arms and held her as close as he could, so close he could feel her heartbeat against his skin.

Jefferson R. Smithwood Elementary School sat on a grassy hill surrounded by hundred-year-old fir trees. A long cement walkway started at the double black doors and slid down to the parking lot.

Nick stood close to the kerb, with Izzy beside him. Annie stood on Izzy's other side. His little girl was scared, and it was up to him to make her feel confident. Swallowing hard, he bent to his knees and looked at Izzy. She tried to smile, but it was a quick, jerking little tilt of the mouth. He reached out and plucked up the satiny yellow ribbon that hung at the bottom of her braid.

Her lower lip quivered. 'They'll make fun o' me.'

'They won't make fun of you,' he said.

'I'm . . . different.'

He shook his head. 'No. You've had some . . . sadness. And sometimes that makes a person go a little . . . crazy. But you're going to be OK this time. I promise.'

'OK,' she said at last.

He smiled. 'That's my girl.'

Together, the three of them started up the cement sidewalk towards the school, pushed through the double doors, and entered the hallway.

Izzy stopped. 'I wanna go in by myself,' she said quietly. 'That way they won't think I'm a baby.' She gave Nick and Annie one last, frightened look, then started down the hallway.

Nick fought the urge to run after her.

Annie slipped her hand in his. Nick sighed, watching his little girl. He saw the hesitation in each of her footsteps and knew how hard she was trying to be brave. He knew how that felt, going forward when all you wanted to do was crawl into a warm darkness and hide. Finally, he had to look away. He'd never known it would be so damned hard to watch your child face fear.

'She'll be fine,' Annie said. 'Trust me.'

He looked at her, and at the soft certainty in her gaze, something in his chest felt swollen and tender. 'I do, Annie,' he said softly. 'I do.'

A door opened. A feminine voice said, 'Izzy! We've missed you.' A bubble of applause floated through the open door. Izzy glanced back, gave Nick and Annie a huge grin, then raced into the classroom.

'Well, that certainly took my mind off Izzy,' Nick said when finally he could speak. He rolled off of Annie but kept an arm round her. Gathering her against him, he settled comfortably with his back against the wall and propped his sweaty cheek in his hand, gazing down at her.

She looked incredibly beautiful, with the sunlight from the half-open window on her face and her hair all spiky in a dozen different directions. He wanted to lie with her for hours, talking about nothing and everything, sharing more than just their bodies. It was a dangerous desire, he knew, wanting more from Annie than the body she shared so willingly. No matter how hard he tried to forget it, he remembered that she was leaving on June 15th—now less than three weeks away. She was going back to her real life.

He held her tightly, knowing he should just keep his mouth shut. But he couldn't. 'Are you still in love with Blake?'

She sighed, and he felt the gentle swell and fall of her chest. 'In love? No. But he is . . . was my best friend, my lover, my *family* for almost twenty years. How do you stop loving your family?'

'What . . . what if he wanted you back?'

'Blake's not that kind of man. It would mean admitting that he'd been wrong in the first place. In all our years together, I've never once heard him say he was sorry. To anyone.'

He heard sorrow in the quietly spoken words.

He gathered her into his arms, turning her so that he could lose himself in the green of her eyes. 'I remember a story you wrote in Senior English. It was about a dog who helped a lost boy find his home. I always thought you'd be a famous writer.'

She was silent for a long time, and when finally she spoke, her voice was thick. 'I should have trusted myself, but Blake . . . he thought writing was a silly little hobby, and so I put it away. It's not his fault, it's mine. I gave in too easily. I wrapped up my two unfinished novels and tucked them under my lingerie chest. After a few years, I forgot I'd even had a dream in the first place. I became Mrs Blake Colwater, and without him, I felt like nobody. Until now. You and Izzy gave me my self back.'

He touched her face. 'No, Annie. You took it back yourself. Hell, you *fought* for it.'

She stared at him. 'I lost myself once, Nick. I'm terrified of doing it again.'

There was no point in asking what she meant. He knew. Somehow, she'd seen the secret he was trying so hard to keep from her. He'd fallen in love with her, and they didn't have much time together; that was the truth he'd understood at the outset, the truth that came from sleeping with a married woman, even if she were headed for divorce. She still had Natalie, and a whole life that didn't include Nick. 'OK, Annie,' he said quietly. 'OK for now.'

Annie stood on the porch of her father's house, staring out at the sinuous silver ribbon of the salmon stream. Bright blue harebells danced nimbly through the high grass at the river's edge. She heard the door squeak open behind her, then the banging of the screen door.

'OK, what's going on, Annie Virginia?'

She knew by the quiet tone of his voice that it was the question he'd followed her out here to ask. 'What do you mean?' She played dumb.

'You know what I mean. You blush like a teenager every time you say Nick's name, and I've hardly seen you in the past two weeks. You're doing a hell of a lot more than baby-sitting up there. Are you trying to get back at Blake?'

'No. For once, I'm not thinking about Blake or Natalie. I'm doing this for me.'

'Is that fair?'

She turned to him. 'Why is it that only women have to be fair?'

'It's Nick I'm thinking of. I've known that boy for a long time. Even as a kid, he had eyes that had seen a dozen miles of bad road. When he started dating Kathy, I thanked God it wasn't you. But then he settled down and became the best cop this town has ever had. We all saw how he loved Kathy; and that little daughter of his was the apple of his eye. Then, that . . . thing happened with Kathy, and he . . . disintegrated. His hair turned that weird colour, and every time I saw him, I remembered what had happened. It was like a physical badge of sorrow.'

'Why are you telling me this?'

'You're a fighter, Annie, and—'

'Ha! Come on, Dad, I'm a doormat of the first order.'

'No. You never have seen yourself clearly. You've got a steel core inside you, Annie—you always did.'

'When Blake left me, I fell apart,' she reminded him.

'For what—a month?' He made a tsking sound. 'That's nothing. When your mom died, I didn't hide out for a couple of weeks and then emerge stronger than I'd started.' He paused, shaking his head. 'I'm not good at saying what I mean. What I'm trying to say, honey, is that you don't understand despair or weakness, not really. You can't get your mind wrapped around hopelessness.'

She stared out at the river. 'I guess that's true.'

'You're still a married woman, and if you think Blake is really going to leave you for a bimbo, you're crazy. He'll be back. When he comes to his senses, Blake will come home to you.'

'I don't feel married.'

'Yes, you do.'

She had no answer to that; it was true and it wasn't. As much as she'd grown and changed in the last months, Hank was right: Annie did still feel married to Blake. She'd been his wife for almost twenty years . . . that kind of emotional commitment didn't evaporate on account of a few hastily thrown words, even if those words were *I want a divorce*.

Hank came up beside her, touched her cheek. 'You're going to hurt Nick. And he's not a man who rolls easily with life's punches. I don't mean to tell you what to do. I never have and I'm sure as hell not going to start now. But . . . this thing . . . it's going to end badly, Annie.'

The next night, long after the dinner dishes were washed and put away and Izzy had gone to bed, Annie sat in the rocker on the front porch. The scratchy creak-creak-creak of the rocker kept her company in the quiet. She knew she should go inside; Nick would be waiting for her upstairs. But it was so quiet and peaceful out here, and the lingering echo of her father's words seemed softer and more distant when she was alone.

Nick and Izzy had already been hurt so badly. She didn't want to do anything that would cause them more pain, and yet she knew, as certainly as she was sitting here, that she was going to do just that. She had another life in another town. Her real life was out there, waiting for Annie, circling in the hot, smoggy air of southern California, readying itself for the confrontation that was only a few short weeks away.

Behind her, the screen door creaked open. 'Annie?'

She closed her eyes for a second, gathering strength. 'Hey, Nick,' she said softly, staring down at the hands clasped in her lap.

The door banged shut and he came up beside her. Placing a hand gently on her shoulder, he crouched down. 'What are you doing out here all by yourself?'

She looked at him and, for a second, felt a flash of panic. The thought of giving him up was terrifying.

But it was Nick she had to think of, not herself. She gazed at him. 'I don't want to hurt you, Nick.'

He took hold of her left hand, tracing the white tan line with the tip of his finger. 'Give me some credit, Annie. I know it's not as simple as taking off a ring.'

She stared at him for a long time. The urge rose in her to make impossible promises, to tell him she loved him, but she couldn't be that cruel. She would be leaving in two weeks. It would be infinitely better to take the words with her.

'We don't have for ever, Annie. I know that.'

She heard something in his voice, a little crack in the words *for ever*, but he was smiling at her, and she didn't want to think about what he was feeling. 'Yes,' she whispered.

He swept her into his arms and carried her up to his bed. And as always, once she was in his arms, she stopped thinking about the future and let the present consume her.

On Tuesday morning, they planned a trip to the beach. Annie glanced down at the picnic basket beside her, then she checked her watch. It was already ten thirty. She went to the bottom of the stairs and yelled up at Nick and Izzy to get a move on.

The phone rang. She picked it up on the second ring. 'Hello?'

'Hold for Blake Colwater, please.'

For a moment, Annie couldn't connect the name to her own life. Nick came down the stairs. She threw him a confused look. 'It's Blake.'

Nick froze in mid-step. 'I'll . . . leave you your privacy.'

'No. Come here. Please.'

Nick crossed the room and came up beside her. Turning slightly, she took hold of his hand.

Blake's authoritative voice came on at last. 'Annie—is that you?'

At the sound of his voice, it all came rushing back. She stood perfectly still. 'Hello, Blake.'

'How are you, Annalise?'

'I'm fine.' She paused, trolling for what came next. 'And you?'

'I'm . . . OK. I got your number from Hank. You know Natalie will be getting home soon.'

'The 15th of June. She wants us to meet her at the airport.' She put the slightest emphasis on *us*.

'Of course. We need to talk, obviously, before we meet Natalie. I want you to come down to Los Angeles this weekend.'

'Do you?' It was so like Blake. They hadn't spoken in three months but now he wanted to talk, so she had to get on a plane. 'I'm not ready to see you yet.'

'*What?* I thought—'

'I doubt it. We don't have anything to talk about now.'

'Annalise.' He sighed. 'I want you to come home this weekend. We need to talk.'

'I'm sorry, Blake. I have no intention of coming home this weekend.

We agreed to discuss our separation in June. Let's leave it at that, OK? I'll come home on the 13th.'

'Goddamn it, Annalise. I want—'

'Goodbye, Blake. See you in two weeks.' She hung up the phone.

'Are you OK, Annie?'

Nick's voice pulled her back from the dark edge gathering on her horizon. Forcing a smile, she turned into his arms. 'I'm fine.'

He stared down at her a long, long time. For a second, she thought he was going to kiss her, and she pushed onto her toes to meet his lips. But he just stood there, gazing down at her face as if he were memorising everything about this moment. 'It's not going to be long enough.'

Chapter 9

As Blake drove down Mystic's main street, he remembered how much he'd always disliked this shabby little logging town. It reminded him of the town he'd grown up in, a dingy, forgotten farming community in Iowa—a place he'd worked hard to forget.

He pulled the rented Cadillac into a gas station and parked. Flipping up the collar of his overcoat—who in the hell wanted to live in a place where you needed an overcoat in late May?—he strode through the pouring rain towards the phone booth.

Dropping a quarter in the slot, he punched out Hank's number.

On the third ring, Hank answered. 'Hello?'

'Hi, Hank. It's Blake . . . I wanted to speak to my wi—to Annie.'

'She isn't here. She's *never* here during the day. I gave you a number the other day. You can reach her there.'

'Where is she, Hank?'

'She's out visiting . . . at the old Beauregard place. An old friend of hers lives out there now.'

Blake got a strange feeling in the pit of his stomach. 'What's going on, Hank?'

There was a pause, then Hank said, 'You'll have to figure things out for yourself, Blake. Good luck.'

Good luck. What the hell did that mean?

By the time Blake had asked directions and got back in his car, he was irritated as hell. Something was not right here.

But then, things hadn't been right in a long time.

He'd first realised that something was wrong about a month ago; he'd stopped being able to concentrate. His work had begun to suffer.

And it was little things, nothing really. Like the tie he was wearing today. It was wrong.

It was a stupid, nonsensical thing, and certainly no one would notice, but *he* knew. When Annie had bought him the black Armani suit, she'd chosen a monogrammed white shirt and a silk tie of tiny grey and white and red stripes to go with it. It was a set, and he always wore them together. He'd realised a few weeks ago that he couldn't find the tie. He'd torn the bedroom apart looking for it.

'I hope you're going to pick all that shit up,' was what Suzannah had said when she'd seen the mess.

'I can't find the tie that goes with this suit.'

She'd laughed. 'I'll alert the press corps.'

She thought it was funny that the tie was missing, and that he needed it so much. *Annie would know where it is.*

That had been the beginning.

The road unfurled in front of him. A road that turned and twisted and finally led him to a huge clearing. A bright yellow house sat primly amid a front yard awash in brightly coloured flowers. A red Mustang and a police car were parked beneath an old maple tree.

He parked the car and got out. Flipping his collar up again, he strode across the yard and bounded up the stairs, knocking hard on the front door. It opened almost instantly, and a little girl stood in the opening.

Blake smiled down at her. 'Hello. I'm—'

A man appeared behind the child. His hands rested protectively on the girl's shoulders and drew her back slightly into the house. 'Hello?'

Blake stared at the tall, silver-haired man, then craned his neck to look inside the house. 'Hi. I'm sorry to bother you, but I'm looking for Annalise Colwater. Her father, Hank, told me she'd be here.'

The man tensed visibly. His eerie blue eyes narrowed and swept Blake from head to toe in a single glance. 'You're Blake.'

Blake frowned. 'Yes, and you are . . .'

From somewhere inside the house, Blake heard the clattering of someone running downstairs. 'I'm ready, you guys.'

Blake recognised Annie's voice. He sidled past the silent man and child and slipped into the house.

Annie saw him and skidded to a stop.

He almost didn't recognise her. She was wearing yellow rain gear and a big floppy hat that covered most of her face. He forced a big smile and opened his arms. 'Surprise.'

She threw an odd glance at the silver-haired man, then slowly her gaze returned to Blake. 'What are you doing here?'

He looked at the two strangers; both were watching him. Slowly, he let his arms fall to his sides. 'I'd rather not discuss it in public.'

Annie bit on her lower lip, then sighed heavily. 'OK, Blake. We can talk. But not here.'

The girl whined and stomped her foot. 'But, Annie—we were gonna get ice cream.'

Annie smiled at the child. 'I'm sorry, Izzy. I need to talk to this man for a while. I'll make it up to you, OK?'

This man. Blake's stomach tightened. What in the hell was going on here?

'Don't make this hard on Annie, OK, Sunshine? She has to go for a minute.' It was the man's voice.

'But she'll be comin' back . . . won't she, Daddy?'

The question fell into an awkward silence. No one answered.

Annie moved past the little girl and came up beside Blake. 'I'll meet you at Ted's Diner and Barber shop in about ten minutes. It's right downtown. You can't miss it.'

Blake felt as if the world had tilted. He looked down at her, this woman he barely recognised. 'OK. See you in ten minutes.'

He stood there for an interminable moment, feeling awkward and ill-at-ease. Then he forced a smile. All they needed was a few minutes alone, and everything would be fine. That's what he told himself as he turned and left the house. He was still telling himself that ten minutes later as he parked in front of the sleaziest diner he'd ever seen. Inside, he slipped into a yellow booth and ordered a cup of coffee. When it came, he checked his Rolex: 11.15.

He was actually nervous. Beneath the Formica wood-grain table, he surreptitiously wiped his damp palms on his trousers.

He glanced at his watch again—11.25—and wondered if Annie was going to show. It was a crazy thought and he dismissed it almost instantly. Annie was the most dependable person he'd ever known. If Annie said she'd be someplace, she'd be there.

'Hello, Blake.'

He snapped his head away from the window at the sound of her voice. She was standing beside the table with one hip cocked out and her arms crossed. She was wearing a pair of faded blue jeans and a sleeveless white turtleneck, and her hair . . . it looked as if someone had hacked it off with a weed-eater.

'What did you do to your hair?'

'I think the answer is obvious.'

'Oh.' He frowned, disconcerted by the sight of her and by her answer. It was flip and unlike her. He'd imagined this moment—dreaded and looked forward to it in equal measure—for weeks. But whenever he'd imagined their meeting, it was with the old Annie, impeccably dressed, smiling wanly, a little nervous. This woman standing in front of him was someone he didn't recognise. 'Well, it'll grow back.' Belatedly, he got to his feet. 'It's good to see you, Annie.'

The smile she gave him was reserved and didn't reach her eyes. She sidled into the booth and sat across from him.

With a quick wave of his hand, he signalled a waitress, who hurried to the table. Blake looked at Annie. 'Coffee?'

'No.' She drummed her fingernails on the table, and he noticed that she was wearing no polish and that her nails were blunt, almost bitten-off short. And on her left hand, in the place where his ring belonged, there was only a thin band of pale, untanned skin. She smiled up at the waitress. 'I'll have a Budweiser.'

Annie turned her attention back to Blake. Her gaze swept him in a second, and he wondered what this new woman saw when she looked at the old Blake. He waited for her to say something, but she just sat there with her new haircut and her no make-up and her terrifyingly ringless finger and stared at him.

Into the quiet, the waitress came to the table. She placed a frosted mug of beer on a small, square napkin, and Annie gave her a bright smile. 'Thanks, Sophie.'

'You bet, Miss Bourne.'

Miss Bourne? The address left him winded.

'So,' she said at last, sipping her beer. 'How's Suzannah?'

Blake winced at the coldness in her voice. He knew he had it coming, but still he hadn't expected anger. Annie never got angry. 'I'm not living with her any more. That's what I wanted to talk to you about.'

She stared at him across the rim of her glass. 'Really?'

He wished he'd rehearsed this more, but he hadn't expected her to make it so difficult. In his mind, it always went the same way: he swept into a room and she hesitated, then smiled and cried and told him how much she'd missed him. He opened his arms and she hurled herself at him . . . and that was that. They were back together.

He tried to gauge her emotions, but the eyes he knew so well were shuttered. He tripped through the words uncharacteristically. 'I made a mistake.' He slid his hand across the table.

'A mistake.' She drew her hand back.

He heard the censure in her voice and knew what she meant. It was a mistake to be late on your Visa payment; what he'd done was something else entirely. The way she looked at him, the soft, reserved sound of her voice—not Annie at all—punched a hole in his confidence. 'I want to come home, Annie,' he said softly, pleading with her in a way he'd never pleaded in his life. 'I love you, Annalise. I know that now. I was a stupid, stupid fool. Can you forgive me?'

She sat there, staring at him, her mouth drawn in a tight, hard line.

In the silence, he felt a spark of hope ignite. Memories of their life together refuelled his confidence. He remembered a dozen times he'd hurt her, birthdays he'd missed, nights he hadn't come home, dinners that had been ruined by his absence. She had always forgiven him; it was who she was. She couldn't have changed that much.

She stared straight ahead, her eyes wary and filled with a pain he knew he'd put there. 'Annie?' He took her hand in his, and it was cold. 'I love you, Annie,' he said again.

He saw then that her eyes were flooded with tears. 'You think you can say you're sorry and it's all over, Blake? Like it never happened?'

He clutched her hand, feeling the delicacy of her bones and the softness of her skin. 'I'll spend the rest of my life making it up to you.'

She closed her eyes for a second, and a tear streaked down her cheek. Then she opened her eyes and looked at him. 'You did me a favour, Blake. The woman I was . . .' She drew her hand away from his and wiped the moisture from her cheek. 'I let myself become a nothing. I'm not that woman any more.'

'You're still my Annie.'

'No. I'm *my* Annie.'

'Come back to me, Annie. Please. Give us another chance. You can't throw it all—'

'Don't you *dare* finish that sentence. *I* didn't throw anything away. You did, with your selfishness and your lies and your wandering dick. And now you've figured out that little Suzannah wants to be your lover, not your wife and your doormat and you come running back to me. The woman who'll take your shit with a smile and give you a safe place where nothing is expected of you and everything goes your way.'

He was stunned by her language and her vehemence. 'Annie—'

'I've met someone.'

His mouth dropped open. 'A man?'

'Yes, Blake. A man.'

He took a long gulp of his lukewarm coffee, trying to get over the shock of her statement. A *man*? *Annie with another man?*

The silver-haired man with the sad blue eyes.

Why was it that in the months they'd been apart, he had never considered such a thing? He'd always pictured her pining away for him, inconsolable. He looked up at her. 'Did you . . . sleep with him?'

'Oh, for God's sake, Blake.'

She had. Annie—his Annie, his *wife*—had slept with another man. Blake felt a surge of raw, animal anger, a fury he'd never known before in his life. He wanted to throw his head back and scream out his rage, but instead, he sat very still, his hands fisted in tight, painful blocks beneath the table.

'An affair,' he said quietly, wincing at the sound of the word and the images it brought to mind. Annie, writhing in pleasure, kissing another pair of lips, touching another man's body. He pushed the horrible thoughts away. 'I guess you did it to get back at me.'

She laughed. 'Not everything revolves around you.'

'So . . .' What in the hell did you say at a time like this? 'I guess . . .' He shrugged. 'I guess we can forgive each other.'

'I don't want your forgiveness.'

He flinched. They were the same words he'd thrown at her a few months ago, and they hurt. 'I'm sorry, Annie,' he said quietly, looking up at her. For the first time, he truly understood what he'd done to her. In his arrogant selfishness, he hadn't really thought about what he'd put her through. He'd acted as if their marriage were an inconvenient encumbrance, an irritating lien on property you wanted to develop. The words that truly mattered—*love, honour, and cherish, till death us do part*—he'd slapped aside as if they meant nothing.

He felt the first wave of honest-to-God shame he'd ever experienced. 'I never knew how it could hurt. But, Annie, I love you—you can believe that. And I'm going to go on loving you for the rest of my life. No matter what you do or where you go or what you say, I'll always be here, waiting for your forgiveness. Loving you.'

He saw a flash of pain in her eyes, and saw the way her mouth relaxed. For a second, she weakened, and like any great lawyer, he knew how to pounce on opportunity. He touched her cheek gently. 'You think I don't really love you, that I'm just the same selfish prick I always was, and that I want you because you make my life easier . . . but that's not it, Annie. You make my life complete.'

'Blake—'

'Remember the old days? When we lived in that beach house in Laguna Niguel? I couldn't wait to get home from work to see you. And you always met me at the door—remember that?—you'd yank the door open and throw yourself into my arms. And how about that time on the beach, when you and I made sandcastles at midnight and drank champagne and dreamed of the house we would someday own. You said you wanted a blue and white bedroom, and I said you could paint it purple if you wanted, as long as you promised to be in my bed for ever . . .'

She was crying now. 'Don't, Blake, please . . .'

'Don't what? Don't remind you of who we are and how long we've been together?' He pulled a handkerchief from his breast pocket and wiped the tears from her face. 'We're a *family*. I should have seen that before, but I was blind and stupid and selfish, and I took so much for granted.' His voice fell to a throaty whisper and he stared at her through a blur of his own tears. 'I love you, Annie. You have to believe me.'

She rubbed her eyes and looked away from him, sniffling quietly. 'I believed you for twenty years, Blake. It's not so easy any more.'

'I never thought it would be.'

'Yes, you did.'

He smiled ruefully. 'You're right. I thought you'd hear my apology and launch yourself into my arms and we'd ride off into the sunset together.' He sighed. 'So, where do we go from here?'

'I don't know.'

It was an opening, something at least. 'You have to give me—give us another chance. When you asked for one, I agreed, and I thought about where we'd gone wrong and here I am. You owe me the same consideration, Annie. You owe it to our family.'

'Oh, good. A lecture on family values from *you*.' Her gaze was uncomfortably direct, and he was reminded that in some ways, after almost twenty years of marriage, he didn't know the woman sitting across from him at all. 'On June 14th, I'll meet you at the house. We can discuss . . . this . . . then.' She got to her feet, and he saw that she was a little unsteady, holding herself together with incredible effort.

He took hope from that. 'I won't give up, Annie. I'll do whatever it takes to get you back.'

She sighed. 'Winning was always very important to you, Blake.' On that final, cutting remark, she turned and walked out of the diner.

Nick waited for Annie to return. For the first hour, he told himself he was being an idiot. He knew she couldn't possibly meet with her husband and be back here in less than two hours.

But then two hours had stretched into three, and then four, and then five. Forcing a smile, he'd made a big production out of dinner, for Izzy's sake. But they were both keenly aware of the empty chair at the table.

By the time they'd done the dishes and he'd given Izzy her bath and put her to bed, he was as jittery as a bird. He couldn't even concentrate enough to read her a bedtime story. Instead, he'd kissed her forehead and run from the room.

Blake had been exactly what Nick had expected—and precisely what he'd feared. When he'd seen the handsome, confident, obviously successful man in his expensive black suit, Nick had felt as if he were nothing. Blake was everything that Nick could never be.

He wished he could push his worry aside, think about something else—anything else. But the more he tried to clear his thoughts, the more she was there, inside him. Annie held his heart and soul in the palm of her hand, and she didn't even know it.

Annie saw him standing out at the lake. She got out of her Mustang and eased the door shut quietly, walking slowly across the grass.

Wordlessly, she came up beside him. She waited for him to touch her, move close enough that she could feel the comforting heat of his presence, but he didn't. Instead, he stood stiffly in place. 'How did it go?'

There was no point in lying to him. 'He made a terrible mistake and he loves me.'

'What are you going to do?' he asked softly.

'I don't know. I spent two and a half months trying to fall out of love with him, and now when I've almost succeeded, he wants to take it all back. I can't adapt this quickly.'

He fell silent, and she realised what she'd said. *Almost succeeded.* Almost fallen out of love with her husband.

On the shore, the water lapped quietly against the gravel. Breezes whispered through the leaves of a huge old maple tree.

The thought of leaving here terrified her. She thought of her big, empty house and all the time she'd have alone. 'What if—'

He turned to her. 'What if what?'

She took a deep breath. 'What if I . . . came back here? After . . . everything is settled? I've been thinking more and more about a bookstore. You were right, that house on Main Street would be perfect. And God knows, this town needs one . . .'

He went very still. 'What are you saying?'

'After the divorce . . . and after Natalie leaves for college, I'll be down in southern California all by myself—'

'Don't do that to me, Annie. Don't throw me hope like it was a bone to bury in my backyard. I can't spend the rest of my life waiting for you, watching the driveway, thinking *today, maybe today*. It'd break what's left of my heart. Don't make me any promises if you can't keep them. It's . . . easier for me that way.'

She knew he was right. Her future was uncertain. She had no idea what would happen when she returned home. She wasn't even sure what she wanted to happen. 'I'm sorry,' she whispered.

He didn't say anything. He just stood there, swaying slightly, gazing down at her as if he had already lost her.

The next morning, Annie was so depressed she didn't even go to Nick's. Instead, she lay in bed and alternately cried and stared. Her mind was too full; it was making her crazy, all the things she had to think about. Her husband—the man she'd loved since she was nineteen years old—wanted another chance to make their marriage work. He was sorry. He'd made a mistake.

Hadn't she *begged* him to give their marriage a chance just a few months ago?

Beside her bed, the phone rang. She picked it up. 'Hello?'

'Annie Colwater? This is Madge at Dr Burton's office. I'm calling to remind you of your ten-thirty appointment this morning.'

She'd forgotten all about it. 'Oh, I don't know—'

'Doc Burton told me not to take no for an answer.'

Annie sighed. Last week she'd thought she'd beaten the depression, but now she was there again, slogging through the bleak confusion, unable to break through to the surface. Maybe it would be good to talk to the doctor. If nothing else, it gave her somewhere to go and something to do. She would probably feel better just getting out of bed. 'Thanks, Madge,' she said softly. 'I'll be there.'

With a tired sigh, she rolled out of bed and headed for the shower. By ten fifteen, she was dressed in a pair of jeans and a worn sweatshirt. She grabbed her bag and car keys and left her room.

Hank was on the porch, sitting in his rocker, reading a book. At her hurried exit, he looked up. 'You're running late this morning.'

'I have a doctor's appointment.'

His smile faded. 'Are you OK?'

'Other than the fact that I'm depressed and retaining more water than a Sea World seal tank, I'm fine. Doc Burton made the appointment when I saw him. He wanted to make sure I wasn't still feeling blue before I . . . went home.'

Forcing a smile, she leaned down and kissed his forehead. ''Bye, Dad.'
''Bye.'

She hurried down the steps and jumped into her Mustang.

Downtown, she parked in the shade of an elm tree and left her car without bothering to lock the door. She hurried up the concrete steps and into the brick building she'd visited so often in her youth.

Madge grinned up at her. 'Hello, sweetie. The doctor's waiting for you. Go on back to exam room two.'

Annie nodded and headed down the white-walled hallway. She found a door with a huge black 2 stencilled on it, and she went inside.

A minute later, Dr Burton knocked on the door and pushed it open. 'Hi, Annie. Are you still feeling blue?'

How in the hell could she answer that? One minute she was pink, and the next—especially since Blake's call—the blue was so bad it was a dark, violent purple. 'Sometimes,' she answered. 'I had a bout with the flu. I won, but . . . in the last day or two, the nausea has come back.'

'I told you that this was a time to take extra good care of yourself. When the depression bites, your system has a hard time with bugs. How about if we draw a little blood and see what's what. Then, if everything's OK, we can talk about how you really feel.'

Three hours later, Annie stood in front of her father's house. Shivering, she moved forward. Her legs didn't seem to work; it felt as if she were walking through a dense grey fog that resisted her movements.

Slowly, she climbed the steps and went inside.

Hank was sitting by the fireplace, doing a crossword puzzle. At her entrance, he looked up. 'I didn't expect you until—'

She burst into tears. He was beside her in an instant, scooping her into his big arms and stroking her hair. Holding her close, he guided her onto the sofa, sitting beside her.

'What is it, Annie?'

She sniffed hard and wiped her runny nose on her sleeve.

'I'm pregnant,' she whispered, and at the words, she started to cry again. She wanted to be filled with joy over the news; she was three months pregnant. After years of taking her temperature, religiously charting her ovulation cycles, she had effortlessly conceived a child.

Blake's child.

She'd never been so confused and shaken in her whole life, not even when Blake had asked for a divorce. At first when Dr Burton had given her the results of the blood test, she'd assumed it was a mistake. When she realised it was no mistake, she'd had a moment of gut-wrenching, paralysing fear. She wondered whose baby it was.

Then she remembered what Nick had told her. He'd had a vasectomy when Izzy was two. And then there'd been the pelvic examination, which showed that Annie was three months along.

It was definitely Blake's child.

Hank touched her cheek, gently turned her to face him. 'It's a miracle,' he said, and she knew it was true. She *felt* it, the small seed of a baby growing inside her. She placed her hand on her stomach. It thrilled her and terrified her.

'It changes everything,' she said softly.

That's what scared her most. She didn't want to step back into the cold, sterile life she'd had in California. She wanted to stay here to let the cool green darkness become her world. She wanted to open her own bookstore and be accountable to no one but herself.

But mostly, she wanted to be in love for the rest of her life, to wake up every morning with Nick beside her and go to sleep each night in his arms. But she couldn't do that. She'd called her obstetrician in Beverly Hills and been told to get home. Bed rest was the order of the day. Just like it had been with Adrian. Only this time Annie was almost forty years old; they weren't going to take any chances.

'Have you told Blake?'

This time, she wanted to cry, but she couldn't. She stared at her dad, feeling already as if everything she wanted was moving away, receding just beyond her touch. 'Oh, Dad, Blake will want—'

'What do *you* want?'

'Nick,' she whispered.

Hank gave her a sad smile. 'So, you think you're in love with him now. Just a couple of months ago, you were so devastated by the breakup of your marriage that you couldn't get out of bed. Now you're willing to toss it out like yesterday's garbage?'

She knew her father was right. What she had with Nick was special and magical, but it didn't have the foundation that was her marriage. 'Blake and I tried for so long to have more children. When he finds out about the baby . . .'

'You'll go back to him,' Hank said, and the quiet certainty in his voice tore her apart.

It was the right thing to do, the only thing to do, and Annie knew it. She couldn't take Blake's child from him and move up here on her own. A baby deserved its father. There it was, the truth that stripped her soul and left her with nothing but a handful of broken dreams and soon-to-be-broken promises.

She was crying again; she couldn't help herself. She kept picturing what was to come—the moment when she would tell Nick about the baby—and it hurt so badly she couldn't breathe.

She thought about all their time together, all the moments he'd held her and touched her and kissed her lips with a gentleness she'd never imagined. She thought about Izzy, and how much she'd lost, and then she thought about going back to California, to Blake's bed, to a place where the air was brown and the earth was dry. But most of all she thought about how desperately lonely her world would be without Nick.

Annie finally made her way to Nick's house. When she got there, he was in the garden with Izzy. It would all go on without her, this place, this family. Izzy would grow up and learn to dance and go on her first date, but Annie wouldn't be there to see it. She looked at Nick and was horrified to realise that tears were blurring her vision.

'Annie?'

She took a deep, shaking breath. More than anything, she wanted to throw herself into his arms. She ached suddenly to say the precious words, *I love you*, but she didn't dare. She knew that if Nick could, he'd promise that the sun would shine on them for ever. But neither of them was so naive any more; both had learned that everything could change in an instant.

He stood up, moved towards her. 'Honey, what is it?'

She forced a bright smile, too bright, she knew, but there was no helping that. 'I've got something in my eye. It's nothing. Let me change my clothes, then I'll come out and help you guys.'

Before he could answer—or ask another painful, loving question—she ran into the house.

Nick and Annie lay in bed, barely touching.

After Izzy had been put to bed, they'd circled each other, he and Annie, saying none of the things that seemed to be collecting in the air between them. She'd been quiet all evening, and every so often he'd looked at her and seen a faraway sadness in her eyes. It scared him, her sudden and unexpected quiet. He kept starting to ask her what was wrong, but every time the words floated up to his tongue, he bit them back. He was afraid of whatever it was that lay curled in all that silence.

'We need to talk,' she said softly, rolling towards him.

'God, if those aren't the worst four words a woman can say.' He waited for her to laugh with him.

'It's serious.'

He sighed. 'I know it is.'

Her eyes looked huge in the pale oval of her face, huge and filled with sadness. 'I went to see a doctor today.'

His heart stopped. 'Are you OK?'

The smile she gave him was worn and ragged at the edges. 'I'm healthy . . . I'm also three months pregnant.'

'Oh, Christ . . .' He couldn't seem to breathe right.

'We tried for years and years to get pregnant.'

Blake's baby. Her husband's baby, the man who'd said he'd made a terrible mistake and wanted her back. *I always wanted more children.* Those had been her exact words. He'd known then it was the one thing he couldn't give her. Now it didn't matter.

He knew Annie too well; she was a loving, honourable person. It was one of the things he loved about her, her unwavering sense of honour. She would know that Blake deserved a chance to know his child.

There would be no future for them now, no years that slid one into the next as they sat on those big rockers on the porch.

He wanted to say something that would magically transform this moment into something it wasn't, to forge a memory that wouldn't hurt for the rest of his life. But he couldn't.

Before their love song had really begun, it was coming to an end.

Nick knew that Annie was making her arrangements to return home, but she was careful around him. He tried to erect a shield between them, something that would soften his fall when she left, but it was impossible. She had changed him so much, his Annie. She'd given him a family and made him believe that love was a heavy winter coat that kept you warm all year. She'd shown him that he could pull himself out of the destructive patterns of his life; he could quit drinking and take care of his daughter. She'd given him everything he'd dreamed of.

Except a future.

Now she was standing in the living room, staring at the pictures on the fireplace mantel. Absently, she stroked her abdomen.

As he walked down the stairs, he wondered what she was thinking. The steps creaked beneath his weight, and at the sound, she looked up, giving him a tired smile. 'Hey ya, Nicky,' she said.

He went to her, slipped his arms round her, and pulled her against him. She leaned her head back against his shoulder. Tentatively, he reached a hand out, let it settle on her stomach. For a single heartbeat, he allowed himself to dream that the child was his, that *she* was his, and this moment was the beginning instead of the end.

'What are you thinking?' he asked quietly, hating the fear that came with the simple question of lovers everywhere.

'I was thinking about your job.' She twisted in his arms and looked up at him. 'I . . . want to know that you'll be going back to it.'

It hurt, that quiet statement of caring. He knew what she needed from him right now: a smile, a joke, a gesture that reassured her that he would be all right without her. But he didn't have that kind of strength; he wished he did. 'I don't know, Annie . . .'

'I know you were a good cop, Nick. I've never known anyone with such a capacity for caring.'

'It almost broke me . . . the caring.' The words held two meanings, and he knew that she understood.

'But would you give it all up . . . the caring and the love and trying . . . would you give it up because in the end there is pain?'

He touched her face gently. 'You're not asking about my job . . .'

'It's all the same, Nick. All we have is the time, the effort. The end . . . the pain . . . that's out of our control.'

'Is it?'

A single tear streaked down her face, and though he longed to wipe it away, he was afraid that the tiny bead of moisture would scald his flesh. He knew that this moment would stay with him for ever, even after he wanted to forget. 'I'll never forget us, Annie.'

Annie showed up at her dad's house bright and early. For a moment after she got out of the car, she simply stood there, staring at her childhood home as if she'd never seen it before. The windows glowed with golden light, and a riot of colourful flowers hugged the latticework below the wraparound porch. She wouldn't be here to see the chrysanthemums bloom this year, and though she hadn't seen them flower for many, many years, now it saddened her.

She would miss seeing her dad. It was funny; in California she had gone for long stretches of time without seeing him—sometimes as much as a whole year would slip by without a visit—and she hadn't had the ache of longing that now sat on her chest like a stone. She felt almost like a girl again, afraid to leave home for the first time.

With a sigh, she walked up to the house.

She hadn't even reached the porch when Hank flung the door open. 'Well, it's about time. I was—'

'It's time, Dad.'

'Already.'

She nodded. 'I'm leaving tomorrow morning.'

133

'Oh.' He slipped through the door, closing it behind him. He stepped round her and sat down on the wicker love seat. Then he motioned for her to sit beside him.

Hank stared out at the green darkness of the forest. 'I'm sorry, Annie. About all of it.'

Annie felt her throat tighten. 'I know, Dad.'

Hank turned to her at last. 'I made you something.' He went into the house and came out a moment later, carrying a present.

She took the thin box, wrapped in beautiful blue foil, and opened it. Inside was a thick, leatherbound photograph album. She flipped the cover open. The first page held a small black and white print that had seen better days; a rare photo of Annie and her mom, one she'd never seen before. Her mother was wearing a pair of white pedal pushers and a sleeveless shirt, with her hair pulled back into a ponytail. She was smiling. Beside her, Annie was standing next to a brand-new bike.

Slowly, she turned the pages, savouring each and every photograph. Here she was at last, Annie . . . from the early, toothless days of kindergarten through the midriff-baring teenage years.

The memories crowded in on her, clamouring to be held and savoured, and she wondered how it was that she'd forgotten so much. In every photograph, she saw herself, saw the woman emerging through the freckled, gap-toothed features of the girl in these pictures. The final page of the book was reserved for the family photograph she and Blake and Natalie had posed for only two years ago.

There I am, she thought, gazing at the smiling, bright-eyed woman in the black sweater . . . *and there I'm not.*

'I couldn't find very many pictures of your mom,' Hank said softly.

Annie was surprised to hear his voice. She'd fallen so deeply into her own thoughts, she'd forgotten that her dad was beside her. She flipped back to the beginning of the album, to a five-by-seven black and white copy of her mom's graduation picture. She looked so heartbreakingly young. She wondered now, for the first time in years, what her mom would be like today. Would she be dyeing her hair, or would she have allowed her beautiful blonde to fade into grey?

'She was beautiful,' Hank said quietly, 'and she loved you very much.' He touched Annie's cheek with his papery, old man's hand. 'I should have told you that—and given you these pictures—a long time ago. But I was young and stupid and I didn't know . . .'

There was an emotional thickness in Hank's voice. It surprised Annie, his unexpected journey into intimacy. 'What didn't you know?'

He shrugged. 'I thought you grieved for a few respectable months and then got on with your life. I didn't know how . . . *deep* love ran, how it was in your blood, not your heart, and how that same blood pumped through your veins your whole life. I thought you'd be better off if you could forget her. I should have known that wasn't possible.'

Annie's heart constricted painfully. Never had her father shown his grief and his love in such sharp relief. It moved her to touch his velvety cheek. 'She was lucky to be so loved, Dad. By both of us.'

'She's still loved—and still missed. No one can ever take her place for me, except you, Annie. You're the best of Sarah and me, and sometimes, when you smile, I see your mama sitting right beside me.'

She knew then that she would remember this day for ever. She would buy a wicker love seat for her deck, and she would sit there with her new baby and remember what she had once allowed herself to forget.

'I'll visit more often this time,' she said. 'I promise. And I want you to come down for Thanksgiving or Christmas this year. No excuses.'

'Are you going to be OK, Annie Virginia?'

'Don't worry about me, Dad. That's the one thing I learned up here in Mystic. I'm stronger than I thought. I'm always going to be OK.'

It rained on the day Annie left. All the night before, she and Nick had lain awake in bed, talking, touching, trying in every way they could to mark the memory on their souls. They had watched in silence as the sun crept over the dome of Mount Olympus, turning the glaciers into spun pink glass on the jagged granite peaks; they'd watched as the clouds rolled in and wiped the sunlight away, and as the rain tiptoed along the surface of the lake, turning from a gentle patter to a roaring onslaught, and then back to a patter again. They'd stared at each other, their gazes full of longing and fear, and still they'd said nothing.

When finally Annie rose from the passion-scented warmth of his bed, he reached out and clasped her hand. She waited for him to speak, but he didn't. Slowly, hating every motion, she dressed in a pair of leggings and a long sweatshirt.

'My bags are in the car,' she said at last. 'I'll . . . say goodbye to Izzy and then . . . go.'

'I guess we've said our goodbyes,' he said softly. Then he smiled, a tender, poignant smile that crinkled his eyes and made her want to cry. 'Hell, I guess we've been saying them from the moment we met.'

'I know . . .'

They stood for a long time, gazing at each other. If it were possible, she fell in love with him even more. Finally, she couldn't stand how much it hurt to look at him.

She pulled away from his hand and went to the window. He came up behind her. She wanted him to take her in his arms, but he just stood there, distant and apart. 'I love you, Annie.' He said it like he said everything, with a quiet seriousness. 'It feels like I've loved you for ever.'

The words made her feel fragile. 'Oh, Nick . . .'

He moved closer, close enough to kiss, but he didn't touch her. He just stared down at her through those sad blue eyes and gave her a smile that contained all his joy and sadness, his hope and fear.

'I need to know, Annie . . . am I in love alone?'

Annie closed her eyes. 'I don't want to say it, Nick. Please . . .'

'I'm going to be alone, Annie, we both know that.' He touched her face with a tenderness that broke her heart. 'I don't want to make you cry. I just want to know that I'm not crazy. I love you. And if I have to let you go to make you happy, I'll do it, and you'll never hear from me again. But, God, Annie, I have to know how you feel—'

'I love you, Nick.' She smiled sadly. 'I'm crazy in love with you. Over the moon in love with you. But it doesn't matter. We both know that.'

'You're wrong, Annie. Love matters. It's the only thing that does.'

Without waiting for her to answer, he gave her one last tender kiss— a kiss that tasted of tears and regret, a last kiss that said goodbye.

Biting down on her lower lip, she went to Izzy's room and found the little girl sitting on the end of her bed, her feet swinging just above the floor. She was wearing Annie's white cashmere cardigan with the pearl buttons. A pretty lacquered box lay open on her lap.

'Hey, Izzy-bear,' Annie said softly, 'can I come in?'

Izzy looked up. She tried to smile, but already her brown eyes held a sheen of tears. 'You wanna look through my collection again?'

Annie went to the bed and sat down beside Izzy.

'These buttons were my mommy's.' Izzy picked out a big cream-coloured one. She handed it to Annie. 'Smell it.'

Annie took the button and lifted it to her nose.

'That one smells like my mommy's bedroom.'

Slowly, Annie put the button down. Then she reached into her pocket and pulled out a folded-up handkerchief with a big red *AVC* sewn across the bottom. 'Why don't you put this in your collection?'

Izzy pressed it to her nose. 'It smells like you.'

Annie was afraid she was going to cry. 'Does it?'

Izzy pulled a faded pink ribbon from her box. 'Here. This is one o' my hair ribbons. You can have it.'

Annie took the satin ribbon. 'Thanks, pumpkin.'

Izzy closed her box and clambered into Annie's lap. Annie held her tightly, savouring the feel of her, the smell of her hair.

Finally, Izzy drew back, and her brown eyes were huge in her pale face. Annie could tell that she was doing her best not to cry. 'Today's the day, isn't it? You're leavin' us.'

'Yes, Izzy, today's the day.'

Annie couldn't meet Izzy's earnest, overbright eyes. Forcing a wan smile, she tried to shore up her courage for what was to come. With a sigh, she reached into her pocket and pulled out the antique coin. 'I'm going to miss you something fierce, Izzy.'

'I know, but you gotta go be with your daughter now.'

It was a heartbeat before Annie could find her voice. 'Yes.'

'I wish . . . I wish I was your daughter.'

'Oh, Izzy . . . your mommy loved you very, very much. And your daddy loves you with all his heart and soul.' She twisted Izzy round to face her. 'I need you to do something for me while I'm gone.'

'What's that?'

'You have to take care of your daddy for me. He's big and strong, but he's going to need you sometimes.'

'He's gonna be sad.'

The words stung. 'Yes.' She handed Izzy the coin they'd found at the abandoned ranger's station, the one Izzy had asked Annie to protect. 'You'd better give this to your daddy. He's a safe place now, Izzy. You can trust him with everything.'

Izzy stared at the coin in Annie's hand; then, slowly, she looked up. Tears magnified her brown eyes. 'You keep it.'

'I can't.'

Izzy's tears started to fall. 'You keep it. Then I know you'll be back.'

The next thing she knew, Annie was crying. 'I love you, Izzy,' she whispered, stroking the child's hair. Then, very softly, she said, 'Goodbye.'

Nick left Izzy with Lurlene and followed Annie out of town, keeping the squad car a safe distance behind. He felt like one of those crazy stalkers, but he couldn't help himself. He followed her all the way to the Hood Canal Bridge.

There, he pulled over and got out, watching her red Mustang speed across the bridge, becoming smaller and smaller.

And finally, just as suddenly as she'd come into his life, she was gone.

The urge for a drink came on him, hard and fast.

He closed his eyes. *Please God, help me hold on.*

But the prayer was useless. He felt himself starting to fall, and there was no one to catch him. He lurched for his car and jumped in. The car spun away from the bridge turnout, fishtailing back onto the highway, speeding back towards Mystic.

At Zoe's, he found his favourite chair empty, waiting for him in the darkened corner.

'Jesus, Nick, where yah been?'

Nick looked up and saw Zoe standing by him. She plunked a drink down in front of him. He swirled it round, watching the booze shimmer in the dull light. He brought the drink to his lips, inhaling the sweet, familiar fragrance of the Scotch.

He wanted to guzzle this drink and then order another and another and another, until he could barely remember that he'd loved Annie at all.

But then he thought of Izzy.

Can I come home, Izzy? When he'd said those words to her, he'd wanted her trust more than anything in the world. And he wanted it still.

The booze wouldn't help, the rational part of his brain knew that. He'd get drunk and then what? Annie wouldn't be any closer to coming back to him, and he would have failed his little girl again.

He slammed the drink down, threw a ten-dollar bill onto the table and raced out of the bar. His hands were shaking and his throat felt uncomfortably dry but he was glad to be out of there.

The pain was still there, throbbing on his heart like an open wound, and he recognised that it would be there for a long time, but Annie had helped him to see himself in a different and kinder light. That's what he had to focus on now. He had a life that mattered, a daughter who loved and needed him. Falling apart was a luxury he couldn't afford.

By the time the AA meeting started, Nick had pushed the need for a drink to a small, dark corner of his soul. He filed into the smoke-filled room behind a string of friends.

Joe was right behind him. He felt Joe's hand on his shoulder, heard his rough, sandpaper voice, 'How are you doing, Nicholas?'

Nick was able to smile. 'I'm OK, Joe,' he said, settling onto the hard, plastic seat. 'Can you put me back on the schedule Monday morning?'

'Ah, Nicholas. I never took you off.'

The meeting got under way. Nick listened to the stories, and with each one felt himself grow stronger. When at last the meeting was coming to a close, he motioned to the chairman. 'I'd like to speak,' he said quietly.

There was a flutter of surprise as people turned to look at him.

'My name is Nick,' he said into the quiet. 'And I'm an alcoholic.'

'Hi, Nick,' they answered in unison, smiling proudly at him.

Chapter 10

Heat rose in shimmering waves from the black ribbon of asphalt and melted into the brown, smog-filled air. Annie leaned deeper into the smelly velour upholstery of the taxicab and sighed, resting her hand on her stomach. Already, she couldn't stand being away from Nick and Izzy; it felt as if a vital part of her had been hacked off and left to wither in some other place.

The cab veered off the Pacific Coast Highway and turned onto her road—funny, she still thought of it as her road. Beyond the Colony's guarded gate, they drove past the carefully hidden beach houses, each one a tiny kingdom that wanted to keep the rest of the world at bay.

They turned into her driveway, and the white angles of the house soared towards the blue sky. The yard was in full bloom, a riot of pink and red hibiscus and glossy green leaves. Its beauty was so . . . false. If they stopped watering, this contrived garden would shrivel and die.

The cab pulled up to the garage and stopped. The driver got out of the car and went to the trunk, popping it open.

Slowly, Annie got out. She stared down at the driveway, remembering how she had watched over the placement of each and every brick.

'Ma'am? Is that everything?' The cabdriver was standing beside her Louis Vuitton luggage.

'Yes, thank you.' She flipped her handbag open and retrieved the fare from her wallet, plus a healthy tip. 'Here you go.'

When he was gone, she turned back to the house. For a second, she thought she couldn't do it, couldn't walk down to the hand-carved mahogany door, push it open and go inside. But then, she was moving, walking beneath the arched entrance that smelt of jasmine, pulling the jangle of keys from her bag.

The key slid in; what had she expected? That it would no longer fit here because she didn't? The door whooshed open, and the smell of stale air greeted her.

She walked through the house, room by room, waiting to feel something . . . sad, happy, depressed . . . something. The floor-to-ceiling windows framed the brilliant blues of the sea and sky.

She felt as if she were walking through a stranger's house. Thoughts of Nick and Izzy crowded in on her, begging to be replayed and picked over, but she didn't dare. Instead she focused on the little things: the grand piano she'd purchased at a Sotheby's auction, the chandelier she'd rescued from an old San Francisco hotel, the Lladró statue collection she'd begun when Natalie started junior high.

Things.

She went up to her bedroom. Their bedroom.

There, certainly she would feel *something*. But again, there was only that odd sensation that she was viewing the remains of a long-dead civilisation. This was Annie *Colwater*'s room, and it was all that remained of her. Her closet was full of expensive silks and woollens and cashmeres, skirts in every colour and length, shoes in boxes still marked with exorbitant price tags.

At the bedside table, she picked up the phone. She wanted to call Nick and Izzy, but she dialled Blake's office number. Without waiting to speak to him, she left a message that she was home.

Then she replaced the receiver and sat heavily on the end of her bed.

Soon, she'd see Blake again. In the old days, she would have obsessed over what to wear, but now, she couldn't have cared less. There was nothing in that vast, expensive closet that felt like hers. It was nothing but acres and acres of another woman's clothes.

The office was like the man, understated, expensive, and seething with power. Years before Blake could afford this corner office in Century City, with its expansive views of glass and concrete skyscrapers, he'd imagined it. He always knew it would be stark and unrelieved. It was the kind of office that made a client squirm and reminded him with every silent tick of the desk clock how much it was costing to sit here.

He sighed and leaned back in his chair. He felt odd and out of sorts, and he'd felt this way since his impromptu trip to Mystic.

He'd thought he could apologise to Annie and step back into the comfortable shoes of his old life. Except that Annie wasn't Annie any more, and he didn't know what to say or do to get her back.

On his desk, the intercom buzzed. 'Yes, Mildred?'

'Your wife called—'

'Put her through.'

'She left a message, sir. She wanted you to know that she was home.'

Blake couldn't believe it. 'Right, Mildred. I'm finished for the day.'

He sprinted out of the building and jumped into his Ferrari, speeding out of the parking lot and onto the freeway.

At home, he raced to the front door and jammed the key in the lock, swinging the door open. There was a pile of luggage at the foot of the stairs. 'Annie?'

She was standing at the edge of the archway that separated the living room from the formal dining room.

She was home again. *Now*, at last, everything would be all right.

He moved cautiously towards her. 'Annie?'

She turned away from him and walked into the living room, standing alone at the windows. 'I have something to tell you, Blake.'

It unnerved him, the way she wouldn't look at him. The sight of her, so stiff and unyielding, was a sharp reminder that she was not the same woman he'd left a few months before. His throat was dry. 'What is it?'

'I'm pregnant.'

His first thought was *no*, not again. He couldn't go through that again. Then he remembered the other man, the man Annie had slept with, and he could hardly breathe. 'Is it mine?'

She sighed, and it was a sad little sound that didn't reassure him. 'Yes. I'm three months along.'

He couldn't seem to think straight. He shook his head, sighing. 'A baby . . . Christ, after all these years.'

She turned and gave him a quirky smile, and there she was at last. His Annie. He realised then that it was the baby that had brought her back to him. 'A baby.' This time he could smile. '*Our* baby . . .'

'All those years I thought God wasn't listening. It turns out He's got a mean sense of humour. He obviously wanted me to go through menopause and potty training at the same time.'

'We'll make it work this time,' he said softly.

She flinched at the words. 'Blake—'

He didn't want to hear what she was going to say. 'Whatever happened in Mystic is over, Annie. This is our child you're carrying. *Our* child. We have to become a family again. Please give me another chance.'

Annie closed her eyes. God, how many nights had she lain in her lonely bed, aching to hear those words from him? Yet now they fell against her heart like stones down an empty well. Clattering, bouncing, signifying nothing.

And what had she said to him, all those months ago? *I can't believe you'd throw it all away. We're a family, Blake, a family.*

'Annie—'

'Not now, Blake,' she said in a fragile voice. 'Not now.'

She heard him sigh, a tired, disappointed sound that she knew well. He was confused and more than a little angry; he didn't know how to lose or how to be patient or how to hold his tongue.

'I'll have to have bed rest, just like with . . . Adrian.' She gazed up at him. 'It's going to take some work on your part. I won't be able to be good old Annie, taking care of everyone else. For once, you'll have to put me first.'

'I can do that.'

She wished she could believe it.

'I know it won't be easy for you to trust me again. I screwed up . . .'

'A mammoth understatement.'

His voice dropped to a plaintive whisper. 'I can't believe you don't love me any more . . .'

'Neither can I,' she said softly, and it was true. Somewhere, deep inside of her, a shadow of their love had to remain. She'd loved him for twenty years. Certainly that kind of emotion didn't simply disappear. 'I'm trying to believe in what we had, and I pray we can find our way back to love, but I'm not in love with you now. Hell, I don't even *like* you much.'

'You will,' he answered with a confidence that set her teeth on edge. He leaned towards her. 'Let's go to bed.'

'Hel-*lo,* Blake. Have you been listening to me? I'm not ready to sleep with you yet . . . besides, Dr North said it was risky. Remember? Early contractions.'

He looked ridiculously deflated. 'Oh, yeah. I just thought, if this is a reconciliation, you should—'

'No more telling me what I should and shouldn't do, Blake. I'm not the same woman I was before. And I'm scared to death you're the same damn man.'

'I'm not. Really, I'm not. I've grown, too. I know how precious our life was. I won't make the same mistakes again.'

'I hope not.'

He moved towards her. 'You always used to say that the longest journey begins with a single step.'

He was right; it used to be one of her favourite sayings. Now, that kind of optimism felt far, far away.

He was obviously waiting for her to respond, and when she didn't, he glanced around. 'Well, do you want to watch television for a while? I could make some popcorn and hot chocolate—like the old days.'

The old days.

With those simple words, she saw her whole life flash before her eyes. This spring she'd worked to unearth the real Annie, and now Blake wanted to bury her once again beneath the sand of their old patterns.

Tomorrow, she knew she would have to make an effort, an honest effort to find her way back to Blake, but tonight, she was too damned tired to start. 'No, thanks,' she said quietly. 'I think I'll just go to bed. It's been a long day. You can sleep in the green guest room.'

'Oh. I thought—'

She might have laughed at his expression—so confused and crest-fallen—but it wasn't funny. He was her husband, the father of her children, the man she'd vowed to love, honour and cherish until death parted them, and right now, standing in the house they'd shared for so many years, she couldn't think of a single thing to say to him.

Blake met Natalie at customs.

She gave him a big hug, then drew back, looking around. 'Where's Mom?'

'She couldn't make it. I'll tell you all about it on the way home.'

'Do you have the Ferrari?'

'What else?'

'Can I drive?'

Blake frowned. 'Did someone tell you I'd suffered recent brain damage? I never let—'

'Come on, Dad. *Pleeeeease.*'

He imagined the look on Annie's face if she heard he'd let Natalie drive. Slowly, he pulled the keys out of his pocket and tossed them in the air. Natalie caught them in one hand. 'Come on, Dad!' She grabbed his hand and dragged him through the terminal. Within moments, they were strapped into the sports car and heading for home.

As always, Blake was uneasy around his daughter. He tried to think of something to say to her now, something to break the awkward silence that always stood between them.

'So, Dad, how's Grandpa Hank?'

'How should I know?'

She glanced at him. 'You *did* go up to Mystic?'

He shifted uncomfortably, thankful when her gaze turned back to the road. He wasn't good at handling this stuff. It was Annie's job to put the right spin on their separation. 'I . . . was really busy. There was this big case between a rock star and—'

'So, you were really busy,' she said quietly, her eyes staring straight ahead. 'That must be why you never called me.'

He heard the hurt in her voice and he didn't know what to say. He'd never heard that tone before, but he wondered suddenly if it had been there all along. 'I sent flowers to you every Friday.'

'Yeah. You thought of me long enough to ask your secretary to send flowers every week.'

Blake sighed. He was way out in left field with this one. What was he supposed to tell her? The truth, a lie, or something in between? Annie would know what to do and say. But Natalie was obviously waiting to hear his explanation. 'Your mother's . . . angry with me. I made a few mistakes, and . . . well . . .'

'You two were separated this summer.' She said it in a dull, monotonous voice, without looking at him.

He winced. 'Just a little break, is all. Everything will be fine now.'

'Really? Did you have surgery while I was gone—a personality transplant maybe? Or did you retire? Come on, Dad, how is everything going to get better? You hate being at home.'

He frowned, staring at her stern profile. It was an odd thing for her to say. 'That's not true.'

'Yeah, right. That's why I have no memories of you until high school.'

He sank deeper into his seat. Maybe this was *why* he stayed away so much. Annie and Natalie were masters at piling on the guilt. 'Everything will be fine, Natalie. You'll see. Your mom's . . . going to have a baby.'

'A *baby*? Oh, my God, how could she not tell me that?' She laughed. 'I can't believe it . . .'

'It's true. She's back in bed with this one—just like with Adrian. And she's going to need our help.'

'*Our* help?' It was all she said, and he was glad she'd dropped the subject of the separation, but after a while, the silence began to gnaw at him. He kept thinking about that ridiculous little sentence, *I have no memories of you.* It kept coming back even as he tried to push it away.

He stared out of the window at his whole life. Years ago, when Natalie was a pudgy-faced child who talked incessantly, it hadn't been like this between them. She'd looked at him through adoring eyes.

But somewhere along the way, and for no reason that he could remember now, he'd let it go. He'd never had much time for her, that was certainly true. He was always so damned busy. Blake had told himself his job was to bring home money. And by the time he realised that his daughter had stopped coming to him with her problems—a wiggly tooth, a lost teddy bear—it was too late. By then he barely knew her. One day she was a toothless toddler, and the next, she was off to the mall with a group of girls he didn't recognise.

Sadly, when he thought about it, he had damn few memories of her, either. Moments, yes; pictures in his mind, certainly. But memories, recollections of time spent together, were almost totally absent.

Annie heard the scream first. *Mommmm!*

She sat up in bed, fluffing the pillows behind her. 'I'm in here, Nana!'

Natalie burst into Annie's bedroom. Grinning, laughing, she dived onto the king-size bed and threw her arms round Annie. Blake came in a few moments later and stood beside the bed.

Finally, Natalie drew back. Her beautiful blue eyes were filled with tears, but she was smiling from ear to ear.

Annie drank in the sight of her daughter. 'I missed you, Nana,' she whispered.

Natalie cocked her head, eyeing Annie critically. 'What happened to your hair?'

'I got it cut.'

'It looks *great*. We could be sisters. Talking of which, Dad tells me you're pregnant.' A tiny bit of hurt flashed through Natalie's eyes and then was gone. 'I can't believe you didn't tell me.'

Annie gently touched her daughter's cheek. 'I just found out, honey.'

Natalie grinned. 'I ask for a sister for sixteen years, and you get pregnant just before I leave for college. Thanks a lot.'

'This definitely falls into the "accident" category.'

Natalie laughed. 'Hey, guess what, Mom. Dad let me drive the Ferrari home.'

'You're kidding.'

'It's a good thing you weren't there. You'd have made me wear a crash helmet and drive on the side of the road—preferably with my emergency blinkers flashing.'

Annie laughed, and she couldn't escape how *right* this all felt—the teasing, the joking, the familiarity. How natural.

They were a family. A *family*.

Blake bent closer to Annie. He whispered in a voice so soft that only she could hear, 'People change, Annalise.'

It scared her, that deceptively simple sentence that seemed to promise so much. That's when she knew she was at risk. This man she'd loved for so long knew what to say, always, what to do. If she wasn't careful, she'd slide without a ripple into the gently flowing stream of her old life, pulled back under the current without a whimper of protest.

The shattered pieces of their family fell back together with a surprising ease. Like a glass vase that had been broken and carefully mended, the tiny fissures could be seen only on close examination, when Blake and Annie were alone. In truth, she was glad to spend her days in bed, hidden away from the reality of the marriage. Most days, while Blake was at work, she and Natalie spent long hours talking and laughing and sharing memories.

Annie learned that Blake hadn't called Natalie in London. She heard the hurt and disappointment in her daughter's voice when she spoke, but there wasn't a damn thing Annie could do to fix it. 'I'm sorry' was all she could say. Again and again.

Increasingly, Annie noticed changes in Natalie, a new maturity that hadn't been there before. Every now and then, she zinged Annie with an unexpected observation. Like yesterday.

All you think about is making us happy. What makes you happy, Mom?

Or: *This spring . . . you sounded so different. So happy.*

And the most surprising of all: *Do you love Dad?*

Annie had meant to say, *Yes, of course I love your dad.* But then she'd looked in Natalie's eyes and seen a grown-up understanding. And so, Annie had spoken to the woman her daughter had become.

I've loved your dad since I was a teenager. We're just going through a hard time, that's all.

He loves you, Natalie had said. *Just like he loves me, but . . . his love . . . it isn't very warm . . . I mean . . . it's not like being loved by you, Mom.*

It had brought tears to Annie's eyes, that quiet observation. She was saddened to realise that Natalie would never really understand what a father's love could be. It would be a loss in Natalie's life for ever . . .

Unlike Izzy.

She closed her eyes and leaned back in bed, remembering Nick and Izzy when they'd played Candy Land, Nick hunched over the board . . . or when the two of them had played Barbies on the living-room floor, Nick saying in a falsetto voice, *Have you seen my blue dancing shoes?*

How long would it be this way? How long would she spend feeling that she'd left an essential part of herself in another place and time? No matter how hard she tried to be her old self, Annie couldn't quite manage it. With each day, she saw the future approaching in a low-rolling fog of lost chances and missed opportunities.

Summer blasted through southern California. The Malibu hills dried up and turned brown. Leaves began, one by one, to curl up and die, dropping like bits of charred paper on artificially green lawns.

Blake stood on the deck outside his room, sipping a Scotch and soda. The wood was warm beneath his bare feet.

He hadn't slept well last night. Hadn't, in fact, slept well in weeks. Not since he'd apologised to Annie and discovered that she didn't care.

She was trying to make their marriage work. He could see the effort.

She even touched him occasionally—brief, flitting gestures that were designed to make him feel better, but that had the opposite effect. Every time she touched him, he felt a tiny, niggling ache in his chest, and he remembered the way it used to be, the way she used to touch him all the time and smile at his jokes and brush the hair away from his face, and when he remembered he hurt.

He couldn't stand this much longer. He wasn't the kind of man who liked to work this hard for what he wanted. Enough was enough.

He set down his drink on the table and strode back into the house. He knocked on Annie's door—quickly, before he lost his nerve.

'Come in,' she called out.

He opened the door and went inside. Annie was in bed, reading a book called *How to Run Your Own Small Business*. Beside her, there was a pile of similarly titled self-help books.

Jesus, was she thinking of getting a *job*? He had no idea who this woman was, who sat in bed and read how-to books. He felt unconnected to Annie; he had to do something to get them back together.

She looked up, and he noticed the dark circles under her eyes and grey cast to her skin. In the past month, she'd gained a lot of weight, but somehow her face looked thinner. Her hair had grown out some, and the tips were beginning to curl wildly. Again, she looked like a woman he didn't know. 'Hi, Blake,' she said softly, closing the book. 'Is it time for the movie to start? I thought—'

He went to the bed and sat beside her, gazing down into her beautiful green eyes. 'I love you, Annie. I know we can work all this out if we're . . . together.'

'We are together.'

'Where's your wedding ring?'

She cocked her head towards the chest of drawers. 'In my jewellery box.'

He got up and went to the chest, carefully opening the hand-painted box. There, among the black velvet rolls, was the three-carat diamond he'd given her on their tenth wedding anniversary. Beside it was the plain gold band they'd originally bought. He picked up the two rings and returned to the bed, sitting down beside his wife.

He stared down at the fiery diamond. 'Remember that vacation we took, years ago, at the Del Coronado Hotel? Natalie wasn't more than a year old—'

'Six months,' she said softly.

He looked at her. 'We brought that big old blue and red blanket—the one I had on my bed in college—and laid it out on the beach. We were the only people out there, just the three of us.'

Annie smiled. 'We went swimming, even though it was freezing cold.'

'You were holding Natalie, with the waves splashing across your thighs. Your lips were practically blue and your skin was nothing but goose bumps, but you were laughing, and I remember how much I loved you. My heart hurt every time I looked at you.'

She looked down at her hands. 'That was a long time ago.'

Annie closed her eyes, and he wondered what she was thinking. Could she remember the rest of that day? How often he'd touched her . . . or when he'd leaned over and grazed her neck with a kiss.

'When did we stop having fun together, Annie? When?' He was seducing her with their memories, and he could see that it was working; he could see it in the way she stared at her hands intently, in the sheen of moisture that filled her eyes.

Slowly, he reached down and placed the two rings back on her finger. 'Forgive me, Annie,' he said quietly.

She looked up. A tear streaked down her cheek and dropped onto her nightgown. 'I want to.'

'Let me sleep with you tonight . . .'

She sighed. It was a long time before she answered, time enough for him to feel hope sliding away. 'Yes,' she said at last.

He told himself that nothing mattered but the answer. He ignored the uncertainty in her voice and the tears in her eyes and the way she wouldn't quite look at him. It would all be OK again after they slept together. Finally, the bits of their broken lives would fuse together again.

He wanted to crush her against him, but he forced himself to move slowly. He got up, went into the closet, and changed into his pyjamas. Then, very slowly, he went to the bed and peeled back the coverlet, slipping beneath the cool, white cotton sheets.

It was soothing to hold her again, like easing into a favourite pair of slippers after a long day at the office. He kissed her lightly, and, as always, she was quiet and undemanding in her response. Finally, he turned over—the regular beginning of their nightly ritual. After a long moment, she snuggled up behind him.

Her body spooned against his, her belly pressed into his back. It was the way they'd always slept, only this time she didn't curl her arms round him.

They lay there, touching but not touching in the bed that had held their passion for so many years. She didn't speak, other than to say good night, and he couldn't think of anything else.

It was a long time before he fell asleep.

Natalie set a big metal bowl full of popcorn at the foot of Annie's bed, then she climbed up and snuggled close to her mom. It was Friday afternoon: girls' day. Annie and Natalie and Terri had spent every Friday together since Annie returned home.

'I left the front door open for Terri,' Natalie said, pulling the bowl of popcorn onto her lap.

Annie grinned. 'You know what your dad would say. He thinks criminals spend all day in the rosebushes, just *waiting* for us to leave the door open.'

'How come Dad never talks about the baby?'

The question came out of the blue, smacking Annie hard. She tried not to compare Nick and Blake, but it was impossible at a moment like this. Nick would have been with Annie every step of the way, sharing in the miracle. She would have clung to his hand during the amniocentesis, letting his jokes distract her from the needle . . . and she would have laughed with him later, when they found out it was a girl, skipping through name books and spinning dreams . . .

She sighed. 'Your dad is uncomfortable with pregnancy; he always has been. Lots of men are like that. He'll be better after the baby is born.'

'Get real, Mom. Dad's good at doing his own thing. I mean, you guys are supposedly getting over your "bad patch", but he's never here. He still works seventy hours a week, he still plays basketball on Tuesday nights, and he still goes out for drinks with *the boys* every Friday night.'

Annie gave her a sad smile. 'When you get older, you'll understand. There's a certain . . . comfort in the familiar.'

Natalie stared at her. 'I have almost no memories of Dad—did you know that? All I remember about him are a few hurried goodbye kisses and the sound of a slamming door.' She turned to Annie. 'What about after this summer . . . when I'm gone?'

Annie shivered, though the room was warm. She looked away from Natalie, unable to bear the sad certainty in her daughter's eyes.

'You'll be lonely.'

Annie wanted to deny it. She wanted to be grown up and a good parent and say just the right thing that would alleviate Natalie's worry. But for once, no parental lies came to her. 'Maybe a little. Life can be like that, Nana. We don't always get what we want.'

Natalie glanced down at her own hands. 'When I was little, you told me that life *did* give you what you wanted, if you were willing to fight for it and believe in it. You told me that every cloud had a silver lining.'

'Those were a mother's words to a little girl. These are a mother's words to a nearly grown woman.'

Natalie looked at her. 'You don't have to be this way, you know.'

'What do you mean?'

Natalie shook her head and looked away. 'Never mind.'

Understanding dawned slowly, and with it, pain. It all fell into place: Natalie's desire to study biochemistry at Stanford, her sudden trip to London, her unwillingness to date the same boy for more than a few months. Behind it all was a sad message: I don't want to be like you, Mom. I don't want to be dependent on a man for everything.

'I see,' Annie said.

Natalie turned to her at last, and this time there were tears in her eyes. 'What do you see? What are you thinking?'

'I'm thinking you don't want to grow up to be like your old mom, and . . . as much as that hurts, it makes me proud. I want you to count on yourself in life. I guess, in the end, it's all we have. I'm glad you don't want to be like me, Nana.'

Sadness suffused Natalie's face. 'I don't want to have a marriage like yours, and I don't understand why you stay with him—I never have. That doesn't mean I don't want to be like you. There are only two people in the world who don't respect you . . . as far as I know, anyway.'

She looked at Natalie, shaking her head slightly, as if she could stop her daughter's words.

'Just two,' Natalie said. 'Dad . . . and you.'

You. Annie felt a sudden urge to disappear, to simply melt into the expensive bed linen and vanish. She knew that Natalie was waiting for her to say something, but she didn't know what was the right answer. She felt as if she were the child, and Natalie the mother, and as the child, she'd let her parent down.

She opened her mouth to say something—she had no idea what—when suddenly Terri charged into the bedroom like a multicoloured bull, her body draped in layers of red and gold lamé.

She came to a breathless stop beside the bed. Planting her fists on her meaty hips, she surveyed the bowl of popcorn. 'So, where's *my* popcorn? I mean, that's enough for two skinny chicks like you, but we real women like our popcorn to come in bowls that could double as lifeboats. And I certainly want it coated in butter.'

Natalie grinned. 'Hey, Terri.'

Terri smiled back. 'Hiya, princess.'

'I'll go make another batch of popcorn.'

'You do that, sweetie,' Terri said, uncoiling the gold turban from her head.

When Natalie scurried from the room, Terri sank down on the bed and twisted round to sit beside Annie. 'So, kiddo, how's the ever-growing Goodyear blimp?'

Annie glanced down at her stomach. 'We're doing OK.'

'Well, I've been coming every Friday for weeks now, and we talk on the phone constantly. I think I've been patient as hell.'

'About what?'

Terri looked at her, hard. 'About *what*? Come on.'

Annie sighed. 'Nick.'

'What else? I've been waiting patiently—and we both know that patience is not one of my virtues—for you to bring his name up, but obviously, you're not going to. I'm sick of respecting your privacy. Now, spill the beans. Have you called him?'

'Of course not.'

'Why not?'

Annie turned to her best friend. 'Come on, Terri.'

'Ah . . . that honour thing. I've read about it. We don't see much of it in southern California. But you *are* in love with him?'

'I don't think I want to talk about this.'

'There's no point lying to an old slut like me. Hell, Annie, I've been in love more times than Liz Taylor and I've slept with enough men to protect this country in time of war. Now, do you love him?'

'Yes,' she whispered, crossing her arms. It hurt to say the word aloud, and instantly she regretted it. 'But I'll get over it. I *have* to. Blake is doing his best to put our family back together. Things are . . . rough right now, but they'll get better.'

Terri gave her a sad smile. 'I hope it works that way for you, Annie. But for most of us, when love is gone, it's gone, and all the pretending and wishing in the world can't bring it back.'

'Can't bring what back?' It was Natalie, standing in the doorway with another bowl of popcorn and a bottle of spring water.

'Nothing, honey,' Annie said softly.

Natalie produced a videotape from behind her back. 'I rented us a video.' She put it in the VCR, then climbed up onto the bed beside Terri.

Terri grabbed a handful of popcorn. 'What's the movie?'

'*Same Time, Next Year.*'

'That Alan Alda movie?' Terri gave Annie a sharp, knowing look. 'I always thought that was a hell of an idea. An affair once a year. Yep, sounds like heaven to me.'

Annie tried not to feel anything at all, but when the music came on and the credits began to roll, she sank deeper and deeper into the pillows, as if distance could soften the sharp edges of her memories.

Chapter 11

NICK MADE IT through the summer one day at a time. The last thing he did every night was stand by the lake, where Annie's memory was strongest. Sometimes, the missing of her was so acute, he felt it as a pain in his chest. Those were the nights when he heard the call of the booze, the soothing purr of his own weakness.

But he was making it. For the first time in years, he was actually living life on his own terms. Annie had been right in so many of the things she said to him. He'd gone back to work, and the job had given him a purpose. He was the best policeman he'd ever been. He gave everything to the people under his protection, but when his shift was over, he left the worries behind. He had learned, finally, to accept that there would be failures, and that it was OK. All he could do was try.

And there was always Izzy, waiting for Nick at the end of the day with a smile and a picture she'd drawn or a song she had learned. They'd become inseparable. Best buddies. He never took a moment or a word for granted.

During the week, the second his shift was over, he picked up Izzy from the Raintree Day Care, and they spent all their free time together.

Today, he'd got off work three hours ago and their nightly ritual had begun. First, dinner on the porch (lasagne and green salads from Vittorio's, an Italian restaurant), then they washed the dishes together.

Now, Nick sat crosslegged on the cold plank floor, staring down at the multicoloured Candy Land game board. There were three little pieces at the starting box, a red, a green and a blue.

But there are only two of us, Izzy, he'd said when Izzy put the third man down.

That's Annie, Daddy.

Nick watched with a growing sadness as Izzy stoically rolled for Annie and moved her tiny blue piece from square to square.

'Come here, Izzy,' he said at last, pushing the game away. She crawled across the floor and settled into his lap, hooking her spindly legs round him. He stared down at her. The words congealed in his throat; how could you tell a little girl to stop believing?

'She's comin' back, Daddy,' Izzy said in the high-pitched, certain voice of an innocent.

He stroked her hair. 'It's OK to miss her, Sunshine, but you can't keep thinking that she's going to come back. She has another life . . . she always did. We were lucky to have her for as long as we did.'

Izzy leaned back into his laced fingers. 'You're wrong, Daddy. She's comin' back. So, don't be so sad.'

Sad. Such a little word, no more than a breath; it didn't begin to describe the ocean of loss he felt at Annie's absence.

'I love you, Izzy-bear,' he whispered.

She planted a kiss on his cheek. 'I love you, too, Daddy.'

He stared down at her, lying in his arms in her pink flannel jammies, with her black hair still damp and squiggly round her face, and her big brown eyes blinking up at him with expectation.

He knew then, as he'd known so many times before, that no matter what, he'd always love Annie for what she'd given him.

The air was crisp the next morning, chilly with the promise of fall. A cloudy sky cast shadows across the cemetery, where acres of grass rolled gently towards a curtain of evergreen trees. It was well cared for, this final resting place for most of Mystic's citizens.

Nick walked slowly towards the easternmost corner of the cemetery. Izzy was beside him, holding his hand. With each step, he felt his insides tighten, and by the time he reached his destination, his throat was dry and he needed a drink desperately.

He gazed down at the headstone. *Kathleen Marie Delacroix. Beloved Wife and Mother.*

He sighed. Four words to sum up her life. How could you possibly express the sum of a person's life in a few words cut into smooth grey stone?

He glanced down at Izzy. 'I should have brought you here a long time ago.'

Izzy let go of his hand. She reached into her pocket and pulled out a wrinkled sheet of paper. Last night, when he'd told her they were going to come here, Izzy had picked up a piece of paper and her crayons, then she'd gone into her room alone. When she emerged, she held a picture of her mom's favourite flower. *Daddy, I'll give her this. That way she'll know I was visitin' her.*

He had nodded solemnly.

She walked over to the wrought-iron bench and sat down. Smoothing the paper on her lap, she stared at the headstone. 'Daddy said I could talk to you, Mommy. Can you hear me?' She drew in a ragged breath. 'I miss you, Mommy.'

Nick bowed his head. This place had so little to do with his Kathy. It was why he hadn't come here before, not since the day they placed her gleaming mahogany casket in a gaping hole in the earth. He couldn't stand to look at the evenly clipped carpet of grass and know that she was below it, his wife who'd always been afraid of the dark and afraid of being alone . . .

He reached out, touched the cold headstone with the tip of a finger, tracing the etched canal of her name.

'I came to say goodbye, Kath,' he said softly, closing his eyes against the sudden sting of tears. His voice broke, and he couldn't speak out loud. *I loved you for most of my life, and I know you loved me, too. What . . . what you did was about something else, something I never could understand. I wanted you to know that I forgive us. We did the best we could . . .*

He touched the stone again, felt it warm beneath his fingertips, and for a moment he imagined her beside him, her golden hair streaming in the sunlight, her eyes crinkled in a smile. It was the day Izzy was born, that was the memory that came to him. Kathy sitting up in the hospital bed, her hair all askew, her skin left pale by exhaustion, her pink flannel nightgown buttoned improperly. She had never looked so lovely, and when she looked down at the sleeping infant in her arms, she'd begun softly to cry. 'Isabella,' she'd said, trying the name on her tongue before she looked up at Nick. 'Can we call her Isabella?'

As if Nick could deny her anything. 'It's perfect.'

Kathy had continued to look at him, while tears streamed down her cheeks. 'You'll always take care of her, won't you, Nicky?'

She had known even then the darkness that was coming for her.

But did she know that he loved her, that he had always loved her, and that he always would?

Izzy slipped her hand in his. 'It's OK, Daddy. She knows.'

He pulled her into his arms and held her, looking up at the sky through hot, stinging tears. *I have her, Kath—the best part of us—and I'll always be here for her.*

They placed a wicker basket full of blooming chrysanthemums on the grass, then drove home.

It was time now to let go. But how did you do that, really? Annie had spent seventeen years trying to protect her daughter from the world, and now all of that protection lay in the love she'd given Natalie, in the words she'd used in their talks, and in the examples she'd provided.

The examples.

Annie sighed, remembering the talk she'd had with Natalie and the disappointment she'd felt in realising that she hadn't been a good role model. Now it was too late to change all that she'd been and done as a mother. Annie's time was over.

'Mom?' Natalie poked her head into Annie's bedroom.

'Hey, Nana,' she answered, trying to inject cheerfulness into her voice. 'Come on in.'

Natalie climbed onto the bed and stretched out alongside Annie. 'I can't believe I'm really going.'

Annie put an arm round her daughter. Seventeen years had passed in the blink of an eye. It was too fast. Not long enough . . . She'd been preparing for this day for ages and still she wasn't ready. 'Have I told you today how proud I am of you?'

'Only a billion times.'

'Make it a billion and one.'

Natalie snuggled closer and pressed a hand to Annie's stomach. 'How were the latest stress tests and ultrasounds?'

'Everything shows a healthy baby girl. There's nothing for you to worry about.'

'She's lucky to have you for a mom.'

Annie laid her hand on Natalie's. She wished she could think of one single, flawless bit of advice to hand down like an heirloom to her child.

Natalie leaned against her. 'What are you going to do while I'm gone?'

Gone. Such a hard, cold, uncompromising word. It was like *death*, or *divorce*. Annie swallowed. 'Miss you?' She sighed. 'When I was in Mystic, I started thinking about opening my own bookstore. There was a wonderful old Victorian house at the end of Main Street, and the downstairs was vacant.'

'That's why you've been reading all those business books.'

Annie bit down on her smile and nodded. She felt like a child again, who'd just shown a friend her most precious possession and found that it was as beautiful as she'd imagined. 'Yes.'

Natalie gave her a slow-building grin. 'Way to go, Mom. You'd be *excellent* at that. You could give the Malibu bookstore a run for its money. Maybe I could even work for you in the summers.'

Annie looked away. That wasn't part of her dream at all, doing it here, under the watchful, critical eye of her husband. She could just *hear* his comments . . .

Not like Nick's response.

There was a knock at the door.

Annie tensed. *It's time*. 'Come in,' she called out.

Blake strode into the room, wearing a black silk suit and a bright smile. 'Hey, guys. Is Natalie ready? Mrs Peterson and Sally are here.'

Annie manufactured a brittle laugh. 'I always pictured myself lugging your suitcases up the dorm stairs and unpacking your clothes for you. I wanted you to at least *start* school with your things organised.'

'I would have had to call security to get rid of you.' Natalie started out laughing and ended up crying.

Annie pulled Natalie into her arms. 'I'll miss you, baby.'

Natalie clung to her, whispering, 'Don't you forget that bookstore while I'm gone.'

Annie was the first to draw back, knowing she had to be the one to do it. She touched Natalie's soft cheek, gazed into her precious blue eyes. 'Goodbye, Nana-banana,' she whispered.

'I love you, Mom.' Sniffling, her smile trembling, Natalie pulled away. She gave her dad a weak grin. 'OK, Dad. Walk me out.'

After they'd turned and walked away, Annie kept watching, as the door slowly clicked shut. She surprised herself by not crying. She knew, too, that she would survive. She was stronger than she'd been in March. She was ready to let her daughter go into the world.

'Goodbye, Nana,' she whispered.

Annie went into labour in the first week of November. She woke in the middle of the night, with her stomach on fire. The second cramp hit so hard, she couldn't breathe.

She doubled forward. 'Oh . . . God . . .' She focused on her own hands, until the pain released her. Clutching her belly, she flung the covers back and clambered out of bed. She started to scream, but another cramp sliced her voice into a pathetic hiss. 'Blake—'

He sat upright in bed. 'Annie?'

'It's too . . . early,' she wheezed, clutching his pyjama sleeve. She thought of Adrian and panicked. 'Oh, God, it's too early . . .'

'Jesus.' He lurched out of bed and raced for the clothes that lay heaped over a chair. In a matter of minutes, he had Annie in the car and they were speeding towards the hospital.

'Hang on, Annie. I'll get you to the hospital.' He shot her a nervous look. 'Just hang on.'

She squeezed her eyes shut. *Imagine you're on a white sand beach.*

Another cramp. It was impossible. All she could think about was the red-hot pain that was chewing across her belly, and the life inside her. *Her baby*. She clutched her stomach. 'Hold on, baby girl . . . hold on.'

But all she saw was tiny Adrian, hooked up to a dozen machines . . . being lowered into the ground in a minuscule casket . . .

Not again, she prayed silently over and over. *Please, God . . . not again.*

The sterile white walls of the hospital's waiting room pressed in on Blake. He paced back and forth watching the clock. He kept reliving it in his mind. Annie being rushed into the delivery room, her eyes wide with fear, and her voice, broken and braying, saying over and over again, *It's too early.*

'Mr Colwater?'

He spun round and saw Annie's obstetrician, Dr North, standing in the doorway, wearing a crisp white coat and a tired smile. 'The baby—'

'How's Annie?'

Dr North frowned for a second, then said, 'Your wife is sleeping peacefully. You may see her now.'

He sagged in relief. 'Thank God. Let's go.' He followed Dr North down the quiet white hallway to a private room.

Inside, the curtains were drawn and the room lay steeped in bluish shadows. Annie looked young and frail in the strange bed. It brought back a dozen painful memories of his son.

'When will she wake up?' he asked the doctor.

'It shouldn't be long.'

Blake couldn't seem to move. He stood in the centre of the room, staring at his wife. He'd almost lost her. It was the thought that kept spinning through his head. He'd almost lost her.

He went to the bed and pulled up a chair. Dr North said something—he didn't know what—and then left the room.

After for ever—he'd lost track of time—she opened her eyes. 'Blake?'

His head snapped up. He saw her sitting up, looking at him. She looked scared and broken. 'Annie,' he whispered, reaching for her hand.

'My baby,' she said. 'How's our little girl?'

Shit. He hadn't even asked. 'I'll go find out.' He rushed away from her and hurried down the hall. He found Dr North at the nurses' station, and he dragged her back to Annie's room.

At the doctor's entrance, Annie straightened. She was trying desperately not to cry; Blake could see the effort she was making. 'Hi, doctor,' she said, swallowing hard.

Dr North went to Annie, touched her hand. 'Your daughter is alive, Annie. She's in neonatal intensive care. There were some complications; she was barely five pounds and developmentally that's a problem. We're worried about—'

'She's alive?'

Dr North nodded. 'She still has a lot of hurdles to overcome, Annie, but she's alive. Would you like to see her?'

Annie clamped a hand over her mouth and nodded. She was crying too hard to answer any other way.

Blake stood aside as the doctor helped Annie into the wheelchair stationed in the corner. Then, feeling left out, he followed them down the hallway and into the neonatal ICU.

Annie sat huddled beside the incubator. Inside the clear plastic sides, the baby lay as still as death, a dozen tubes and needles connected to her thin red arms.

Blake came up beside her and laid a hand on her shoulder.

She looked up at him. 'I'd like to call her Kathleen Sarah. Is that OK?'

'Sure.' He glanced around—up, down, sideways, anywhere except at the incubator. 'I'm going to get us something to eat.'

'Don't you want to sit with us?'

He didn't look at the baby. 'I . . . can't.'

Annie didn't know why she was surprised, or why it hurt so deeply. Blake was no good with tragedy or fear; he never had been. If the emotions couldn't fit in a neat little box, he pretended they didn't exist. She would have to handle this in the way she'd handled every upset in her life: alone. Dully, she nodded. 'Fine. Get yourself something. I'm not hungry. Oh, and call Natalie. She'll want to know what's happening.'

'OK.'

After he left, she reached through the bagged opening in the incubator's side and held her baby's hand. She tried not to think about Adrian, and the four futile days she'd sat beside him in a room exactly like this one, mouthing the same useless prayers, crying the same wasted tears.

Katie's hand was so damned small and fragile. Annie tucked her fingers around the minuscule wrist. For the next hour, she talked, hoping that the familiar sound of her voice would soothe her daughter, make her know that even in this brightly lit new world full of needles and breathing machines and strangers, she wasn't alone.

Finally, the nurses came and took her away. They reminded Annie that she needed to keep her strength up, that she needed to sleep and eat. Annie had tried to argue with them but of course, she went back to her room, climbed back into her narrow, uncomfortable bed, and stared at the blank walls. She called Stanford and talked to Natalie, who had booked a flight for Friday evening. Then she'd called both Hank and Terri.

When the calls were done, Annie lost her strength. She kept thinking about those tiny red fists and legs and she closed her eyes. The pain in her chest was so great, she wondered if she could withstand it.

Somewhere, a phone rang. The sudden, blaring sound jarred her from her thoughts. Blinking, she glanced around, realised it was the phone beside her bed. She picked it up and answered dully. 'Hello?'

'Annie? It's Nick. Your friend Terri called me . . .'

'Nick?' That's all she said—just his name—and the floodgates opened. She couldn't hold it in any more. 'Duh-did Terri tell you about the baby? My beautiful little girl . . . oh, Nick . . .' She sobbed into the telephone. 'She only weighs five pounds. Her lungs aren't fully developed. You should see all the needles and . . .' She cried until there were no more tears inside her, until she felt exhausted and drained and old.

'I'll come right down.'

She closed her eyes. 'You don't have to do that. I'll be fine, really . . . Blake's here.'

There was a long, scratchy silence between them, then, finally, Nick said, 'You're stronger than you think you are. You can get through this, whatever happens, you can get through it. Just don't forget.'

She wiped her eyes. 'Forget what?'

'The rain,' he said softly. 'It's an angel's tears. And every glass you've ever seen is half full. Don't let yourself forget that. I know what it does to a person . . . forgetting that hope is out there.'

She almost said, *I love you, Nick*, but she held the words back just in time. 'Thanks.'

'I love you, Annie Bourne.'

It made her want to cry all over again, that soft, quiet reminder of something that was already leaking away. *Colwater*, she wanted to say. *I'm Annie Colwater.* 'Thank you, Nick,' she whispered.

'We'll be praying for . . . all of you,' he said finally.

She sighed, feeling the tears start all over again. 'Goodbye, Nick.'

It was the middle of the night, but Annie couldn't sleep. Though she was no longer technically a patient, the hospital had given her a room so she could be near Katie. She'd tried reading and eating and writing, anything to take her mind off of Katie, but nothing worked.

She'd spent hours hunched alongside the incubator, reading, singing, praying. She'd expressed milk into a bottle, but when she looked at the creamy-coloured liquid, she wondered if her baby would ever get a chance to drink it. Or a chance to grow strong and move out of this sterile world, a chance to grow and snuggle with her mommy . . .

We'll get through this, she said to herself, straightening her spine, but every time a machine buzzed, Annie thought, *This is it, she's stopped breathing.*

Blake had tried to help, in his own way, but it hadn't worked. He'd said, *She'll be OK*, in a quiet voice, over and over again, but when he spoke, his eyes were blank and afraid.

In truth, Annie had been glad when he left the hospital. *I don't have to sleep in a chair to prove my love—do I?*

Of course not, she'd answered, knowing that it was a lie.

The phone rang. She picked it up. 'Hello?'

'Annie? It's me, Nick.'

'Nick.' His name came out on a whisper of longing.

'I thought you might need me.'

It sounded so simple, those few little words, but they wound round her heart and squeezed. She'd spent a lifetime going through crises alone, always being the strong one, always being in control, and she hadn't realised until just now how much she yearned to be comforted.

'How is she doing?' he asked.

She ran a shaking hand through her short hair. 'She's holding on. The neonatologist says she'll be OK if she can just . . . hold on another few weeks . . .' Quietly, she began to cry again. 'I'm sorry, Nick. I'm tired and scared. All I seem to do is cry.'

'You want to hear a story?'

She wanted desperately to be whisked away from reality on the wings of his voice. 'Yes, please.'

'It's about a man who started life as poor white trash, a kid who ate out of Dumpsters and lived in the back seat of an old Impala. After his mom died, the world gave this young boy a singular chance, and he moved to a soggy little town he'd never heard of, where they didn't know about his ugly past. He went to high school there, and he fell in love with two girls. One was the sun and the other was the moon. He was young, and he reached for the moon, figuring it was a safe, quiet place—and he knew that if you reached for the sun it could burn you away to nothing. When his wife died, he lost his soul. He turned his back on his child and his dreams and he crawled into a bottle of booze. All he wanted was to die, but he didn't have the guts.'

'Nick, don't . . .'

'*Then*, a fairy princess came into his life. She changed his world, this woman who wandered uninvited into his life and demanded the very best of him. Before he knew it, he had stopped drinking and he'd taken the first steps towards becoming a parent again, and he'd fallen in love—for the second and last time in his life.'

'You're drowning me, Nick,' she whispered brokenly.

'I don't mean to. I just wanted to let you know that you aren't alone. Love can rise above tragedy and give us a way home. You taught me that, and now you need me to remind you.'

Annie's days bled one into the next in a monotonous flow of hours spent huddled alongside the incubator in a helpless, hopeless confusion. She counted the passing of time in little things: Natalie was here at the weekends and at school during the week; Hank showed up unannounced and came daily to the hospital. Terri and Blake both visited each day after work. The clock ticked. Thanksgiving came and went; they ate pressed turkey and canned gravy off yellow plastic trays in the frighteningly empty cafeteria.

But Annie barely noticed any of it. Sometimes, when she sat beside the incubator, Katie became Adrian, and in those moments, when Annie closed her eyes, she couldn't see anything except that tiny coffin draped in flowers. But then an alarm would go off, or a nurse would come in, and Annie would remember. With Katie, there was hope.

She talked to her baby constantly. *I am sitting beside you now. Can you feel me? Can you hear my breathing? Can you feel me touching you?*

'Mom?'

Annie wiped her eyes and glanced at the door. Natalie and Hank stood there. Her dad looked ten years older than he was.

'We brought Yahtzee,' he said.

Annie smiled tiredly. It must be another week gone by; Natalie was home again. 'Hey, guys. How did the Psych test go, Nana?'

Natalie pulled up a chair. 'That was two weeks ago, Mom, and I already told you I aced it. Remember?'

Annie sighed. She had no memory of that conversation at all.

Natalie and Hank sat beside the bed and started unpacking the game. They kept up a steady stream of chatter, but Annie couldn't concentrate.

Hank leaned towards her, touched her cheek. 'She's going to be fine, Annie. You've got to believe that.'

'She's gaining weight steadily, Mom. I talked to Mona—you know, the ICU night charge nurse—and she said Katie's a champ.'

Annie didn't look at either of them. 'She hasn't been held yet . . . does anyone realise that but me?' It plagued her, that thought, kept her up at night. Her baby, stuck full of needles and tubes, had never felt the comfort of her mommy's arms, had never been soothed to sleep by a lullaby . . .

'She will, Mom,' Natalie said, squeezing her wrist. 'She's going to be fine. Maybe—'

There was a knock at the door, and Dr North pushed through the opening. Dr Overton, the neonatologist, was standing beside her, wearing green surgical scrubs.

Annie's heart stopped at the sight of them. Blindly, she reached out for Natalie's hand, squeezing the slim fingers until she could feel the bones shift. Hank shot to his feet and squeezed Annie's shoulder.

'Oh, God,' she whispered.

The door opened again and a stout, white-clad nurse named Helena swept into the room on a tide of rustling polyester. In her arms she held a small pink-swaddled bundle.

Dr North came to the end of the bed. 'Would you like to hold your daughter?'

'Would I—' Annie couldn't seem to draw a solid breath. She hadn't believed in this moment; hoped, yes, but she hadn't really believed. She'd been afraid to believe; afraid that if she believed and lost, she would never find the surface again.

Unable to say anything, she reached out. The nurse moved towards her and placed her daughter in Annie's arms.

The newborn smell filled her nostrils, at once familiar and exotic. She peeled back the pink blanket and stroked her daughter's forehead, marvelling at the softness of the skin.

Katie's rosebud mouth puckered and yawned, and a little pink fist shot out from the blanket. Smiling, cooing, Annie peeled back the cotton fabric and stared down at her little girl, dressed in a tiny doll's diaper. A network of blue veins crisscrossed her pale chest and dappled her thin arms and legs.

'Oh, Katie,' Annie whispered, stroking her daughter's soft, soft head, laughing quietly at the miracle of it all. 'Welcome home.'

The first days home were crazy. Hank and Terri hovered beside Annie, demanding to help, refusing to take no for an answer. Natalie called home between every class and asked how Katie was doing. Annie couldn't handle it all, not when all she wanted to do was stare at the miracle of her child. At last, Hank went home—but only after he vowed to return at Christmas.

Alone again, Blake and Annie tried to find their way back to the familiar routine, but it wasn't easy. Annie spent all her time huddled on the sofa with Katie, and Blake spent more and more time at the office.

In the third week of December, Hank met Natalie at the San Francisco airport, and they flew down to LAX together. The family shared a tense, quiet holiday dinner that only reminded Annie of how shredded their relationships had become. Even opening the presents on Christmas morning had been a subdued affair.

Hank watched Blake every minute. Annie had heard the questions he jabbed at her husband: *Where are you going? Why won't you be home tonight? Have you spoken to Annie about that?*

Annie had known that Blake felt like a stranger in his own home. Natalie watched him warily, waiting for him to pick up Katie, but he never did. Annie understood; she'd been through it before. Blake simply wasn't one who fell head over heels in love with newborns. They frightened and confused him, and he was not a man who liked either emotion. But Natalie didn't understand that.

Now, Annie lay huddled along the mattress's edge. Beside her, Blake was stretched out, one arm flung her way, one knee cocked against her hip, hogging the bed in his characteristic fashion.

She woke so often, alone, desperate to reach out for comfort in the darkness, but there was no comfort in her marriage. Oh, they'd tried, each of them in their own way. Him, with gifts and promises and quiet conversations about things that mattered to Annie; her, with brittle smiles and rented movies and elegant dinners for two. But it wasn't working. They were like butterflies caught on separate sides of a window, each trying to break through the glass.

With a tired sigh, Blake pushed the Dictaphone aside and shoved the depositions back into their folder. He was having trouble concentrating lately, and his work was beginning to suffer. Katie only slept a few hours at a time, and whenever she woke up, crying or whimpering, Blake couldn't get back to sleep.

He got to his feet and poured himself a Scotch. Swirling the amber liquid around in the Waterford tumbler, he walked to the window and stared outside. The city was a blurry wash of January grey. A few ragged New Year's decorations swung forgotten from the streetlights.

He didn't want to go home to his strangely unfamiliar wife and his squalling newborn daughter. As he'd expected, Annie's whole existence revolved around the baby's needs and when she did finally get the child to sleep, Annie stumbled blindly to bed, too exhausted for anything beyond a quick peck on the cheek and a mumbled *Good night*.

He was too damned old to be a father again. He'd been no good at it when he was young, and he had even less interest now.

There was a knock at the door.

Blake set the glass down. 'Come in.'

The door swung open and Tom Abramson and Ted Swain, two of

Blake's partners, stood in the opening. 'Hey, bud—it's six thirty,' Ted said with a wicked grin. 'What do you say we head on down to the bar and celebrate the Martinson decision?'

Blake knew he should say no. In the back of his mind was the thought that he had something to do at home, but he couldn't for the life of him remember what it was.

'Sure,' he said, reaching for his coat. 'But just one. I have to get home.'

'No problem,' Tommy said. 'We've all got families.'

Annie had set the table beautifully. Candlelight flickered above the Battenberg lace cloth, casting slippery shadows on the sterling silver plates that held all of Natalie's favourite dishes. There was a small stack of multicoloured, foil-wrapped presents at one end of the table, and bright, helium-filled balloons were tied above each chair.

Tonight was Natalie's eighteenth birthday party, and they were all coming together to celebrate. Annie was determined to fit this family back into its groove, at least for these few hours.

Hank came up beside her, put an arm around her shoulder and drew her close. Through the open archway to the kitchen, they could hear Natalie and Terri laughing. Annie leaned against her dad. 'I'm glad you could come down, Dad. It means a lot to Natalie and me.'

'I wouldn't miss it for the world.' He glanced round. 'So, where's that busy husband of yours? We're ready to party.'

'He's only fifteen minutes late. For Blake, that's nothing. I told him six thirty so he'd be here by seven.'

Slowly, Hank withdrew his arm. Turning slightly, he went to the window that overlooked the driveway.

She followed him. 'Dad?'

It was a full minute before he spoke, and then his voice was softer than she'd ever heard it. 'It . . .' His voice trembled and he wouldn't meet her gaze. 'It hurts me to see how you are now. Last spring you were so happy. I miss hearing you laugh. I think . . . when you were in Mystic, I gave you some bad advice. I should have told you that you'd make a wonderful bookseller. Somewhere along the line, I stopped telling you that kind of thing.' He turned to her at last. 'I should have kept telling you that you were the smartest, most talented, most incredibly gifted person I've ever known . . . and that I was proud of you.'

'Oh, Daddy . . .' Annie knew that if she tried to say anything more, she'd start to cry. She stepped into her father's big, strong arms and clung to him. 'I love you, Dad,' she whispered against his warm neck.

When she finally drew back, her mascara was running down her face.

She grinned. 'I must look like something out of *The Rocky Horror Picture Show*. I'd better run to the bathroom and freshen up.'

She spun away and hurried through the kitchen. She passed Terri and Natalie, who were busy arranging candles on the cake.

Natalie looked up. 'Are you OK?'

Annie nodded. 'Fine. My mascara is bothering me.'

'Is Dad home yet?'

'I'm going to try his carphone right now.'

Above Natalie's head, Terri shot Annie an irritated look. Annie shrugged and went to the phone, punching in Blake's cellular number. It didn't even ring; it just patched her through to his voice mail.

Annie turned, faced their expectant looks. 'He's not in the car.'

They waited another forty minutes for Blake, and then by tacit consent, they started the party without him. They came together at the table, talking furiously to cover the awkwardness and disappointment. Still, the empty chair at the head of the table couldn't be ignored.

Annie forced a bright smile all through the meal. Terri regaled them with funny anecdotes about life on the soaps until everyone was laughing. After dinner, they sat round the fire and Natalie opened her gifts.

At ten o'clock, Terri reluctantly went home. She hugged Natalie tightly, then held Annie's hand as they walked to the front door. 'He's a real shithead,' she whispered furiously.

There was no point in answering. Annie hugged her friend and said goodbye, and then walked slowly back to the living room.

Hank rose immediately. 'I think I'll go to bed. Us old guys need our beauty sleep.' He squeezed Natalie's shoulder and bent to kiss her cheek. 'Happy birthday, honey.' Straightening, he threw Annie a frustrated look and strode from the room.

Silence fell.

Natalie went to the window. Annie came up beside her. 'I'm sorry, Nana. I wish I could change it.'

'I don't know why I keep expecting him to be different . . .'

'He loves you. It's just . . .' Words failed Annie. She'd said the same tired thing too many times and she couldn't even pretend tonight that it made a difference.

Natalie turned to Annie. 'What good does his love do me?'

The softly spoken question raised a red, stinging welt on Annie's heart. 'It's his loss, Natalie.'

Natalie's eyes filled slowly, heartbreakingly, with tears. 'Why do you stay with him?'

Annie sighed. She wasn't up to this conversation. Not tonight. 'You're young and passionate, honey. Some day you'll understand. Obligations and commitments build up around you—sort of like plaque. You have to do the right thing. I have other people to think about.'

Natalie snorted. 'I may be young and passionate, but you're naive, Mom. You always have been. Sometimes I feel like the grown-up around you. You always think everything will work out for the best.'

'I used to think that. Not so much any more.'

Natalie's gaze was solemn. 'You should have heard yourself last spring, Mom. You sounded so . . . happy. Now, I know why. He wasn't around, making you jump every time he came into the room and scurry around to do his bidding.'

It took Annie a second to find her voice, and when she did it was soft and hurting. 'Is that how you see me?'

'I see you for who you are, Mom. Someone who loves with all her heart and will do anything to make us happy. But last spring, something made *you* happy.'

Annie swallowed past the lump in her throat. She turned away, before Natalie could see the moisture gathering in her eyes.

'Tell me about that little girl Izzy.'

'Izzy.' Although Annie knew it was opening the door on her pain, she let herself remember. Her thoughts scrolled back to the garden, to a handful of straggling Shasta daisies, and a small, black-gloved hand. 'She was something, Natalie. You would have loved her.'

'And what about Izzy's dad?'

'He's an old friend of mine from high school. He was the first boy I ever kissed.'

'There it is again, Mom.'

Annie frowned. 'There's what?'

'That voice. It's the way you sounded while I was in London. Is he part of what made you happy, Mom?'

Annie felt vulnerable and exposed. She couldn't tell her daughter the truth. 'A lot of things made me happy in Mystic.'

It was a long minute before Natalie spoke. 'Maybe he and Izzy can come down here some time. Or maybe you and I can visit them.'

'No,' Annie said softly. She wanted to say something more, tack an excuse onto the simple word that seemed to make no sense. But she couldn't manage it. Instead, she pulled Natalie into her arms and squeezed tightly. 'I'm sorry your dad forgot your birthday.'

Natalie sniffled. 'You're the one I feel sorry for.'

'How come?'

'In eighteen years you'll be saying the same thing to Katie.'

Chapter 12

SOME TIME AROUND MIDNIGHT, a woman walked up to Blake. She was wearing a skin-tight black catsuit with a huge silver belt and black stiletto heels. With an easy smile, she sat down next to him. She tapped a long fingernail on the bar. 'Vodka martini—two olives,' she said to the bartender.

In the background, a throaty song came on, and the woman asked Blake to dance. He pushed off the bar stool and stumbled back from her, putting as much distance as he could between them. 'Sorry,' he mumbled. 'I'm married.'

But he didn't turn away, he couldn't. He stood there like a man possessed, staring at the woman. He couldn't help wondering how those breasts would feel in his hands—the young, solid breasts of a woman who'd never had children.

At that, Blake felt something inside him shift and give way. He realised the truth, the one he'd been denying for months. He loved Annie, but it wasn't enough. He'd cheat on her. Maybe not tonight, maybe not even this year; but sooner or later, he'd slide back into his old routine. It was only a matter of time.

And when he did, he would be lost again. There was nothing on earth lonelier than a man who betrayed his wife on a regular basis. Blake knew how seductive it was—the temptation to possess a stranger, make love with a nameless woman. But afterwards, it left him broken somehow, ashamed of himself and unable to meet his wife's gaze.

Shaken, he finally left the bar. He drove home and parked in the garage. Tiredly, he went into the dark, cool house. Without bothering to flick on any lights, he headed through the kitchen.

He found Annie waiting for him in the living room. She was sitting on the sofa, with her feet tucked up underneath her. 'Hello, Blake,' she said in a soft, tired voice that seemed to cut through his heart.

He stopped dead. For no reason at all, he thought she'd seen him tonight, that she knew what he'd almost done.

'Hey, Annie,' he said, forcing a smile.

'You're late.'

'A bunch of us went to the sports bar on 4th. We won a big settle—'

'It was Natalie's birthday party tonight.'

Blake winced. 'Oh. *Shit.* I forgot to mark it on my office calendar.'

'I'm sure she'll love that answer.'

'You should have called to remind me.'

'Don't turn it on me, Blake. You're the one who screwed up. You can remember when a client owes an alimony cheque, but you forget your daughter's eighteenth birthday.' She sighed. 'You should go see her now—I'll bet she's still awake.'

'She's probably tired . . .'

'She deserves an explanation.'

He turned and moved to the elegant stone table that hugged the wall, staring at his own reflection in a gilt-framed mirror. 'Natalie's angry with me,' he said softly. 'When she was in London, I didn't call her. I sent flowers every week. A girl loves to get flowers, that's what Suz . . .' he realised what he was going to say and clamped his mouth shut.

'Suzannah was wrong,' Annie said tiredly, reading his thoughts. 'A seventeen-year-old girl needs a lot more than flowers from her father's secretary every Friday.'

He ran a hand through his hair. 'Without you, I was . . . lost with Natalie. I kept thinking I should call, and then a deposition or a court date would come up, and I'd forget. I'll make it all up to her, though, even tonight. I'll get her a laptop.'

'She'll be leaving for school on Sunday. We won't see her again until spring break, and soon . . . we won't be seeing much of her at all. She'll find her own place and she won't be coming home to us as much.'

Us. He tried to take courage from that single, simple word, but he couldn't quite manage it. 'So, what do I say to her?'

'I don't know.'

'Of course you do. You always—'

'No more. If you're going to forge a relationship with your daughter, it's up to you.'

'Come on—'

Annie's face softened. 'You have to talk to her, Blake. But mostly you have to listen.' She gave him a smile that was as sad as it was familiar. 'And we both know you're listening-impaired.'

'OK. I'll go talk to her.'

He said the words, softly and in exactly the right tone of voice, but they both knew the truth. They'd had this same discussion a hundred times before, with Annie begging him to spend time with Natalie.

They both knew he'd never quite get round to doing it.

On the last day of January, Terri showed up bright and early, holding a bottle of Moët & Chandon and a bag of croissants. 'When a woman turns forty,' she said brightly, 'she should begin drinking early in the day. And before you start whining about nursing and alcohol in the breast milk, let me reassure you that the champagne is for me and the croissants are for you.'

They sat together on the big wooden deck.

'So,' Terri said, sipping her champagne. 'You look like shit.'

'Thanks a lot. I hope you'll come by to celebrate my fiftieth birthday—when I *really* need cheering up.'

'You're not sleeping.'

Annie winced. It was true. She hadn't slept well in weeks. 'Katie's been fighting a cold.'

'Ah,' Terri said knowingly, 'so Katie's the problem.'

'No . . . not really, Dr Freud.' Annie glanced out at the glittering surface of the sea, watching the white-tipped waves lick gently at the sand. She didn't have to close her eyes to see another place, a place where winters were real. There, nature would have reclaimed its rain forest. Annie longed to see it now, to feel the crisp winter air on her cheeks.

'Why do you stay with him?'

Annie sighed. She had known the question was coming; she'd expected it every day since the fiasco of Natalie's birthday party. It was the same thing she asked herself at night, as she lay in bed, beside her husband, unable to sleep.

She missed the woman she'd become on the shores of Mystic Lake, the one who dared to dream of her own bookstore, and learned to wager her heart on a game as risky as love. She missed Nick and Izzy and the family they'd quilted together from the scraps of their separate lives.

It was the kind of family Annie had always dreamed of . . . the kind of family Katie deserved . . .

Did you know I have no memories of Dad?

Terri touched her shoulder. 'Annie? You're crying . . .'

She'd been holding it in for too long, pretending that everything was OK, pretending that everyone mattered but her. She couldn't hold it in any more.

'I matter,' she said quietly.

'Well, praise God,' Terri whispered and pulled Annie into her arms. Annie let herself be held and rocked by her best friend.

'I can't live this way any more.'

'Of course you can't.'

Annie eased back, pushing the grown-out hair away from her eyes. 'I don't want some day to hear Katie tell me that she has no memories of her dad, either.'

'And what about *you*, Annie?'

'I deserve more than this . . . Blake and I don't share anything any more. Not even the miracle of our two children.'

It was the truth she'd been avoiding all these months. Their love was gone, simply gone. She couldn't even remember those days, long ago, when they had been in love. She couldn't help grieving for the loss of that fire, and she was as much to blame as he.

Blake wasn't happy, either. Of that she had no doubt. He wasn't ready to let go of Annie quite yet, but the Annie he wanted was Annalise Bourne Colwater, the woman she'd become after years and years of living in a rut of their combined creation.

He wanted back what couldn't be had.

Faint strains of music came from the bedroom speakers. Blake stood in front of the baby's bassinet, staring down at the tiny infant.

He reached into his pocket and withdrew a slim black velvet box. His finger traced the soft fabric as he remembered a dozen gifts he'd given Annie in the past. Always, he'd given her what he thought she should have. He'd never given her what she needed, what she wanted. He'd never given her himself.

'Blake?'

At the sound of her voice, soft and tentative, he turned round. She stood in the open archway, wearing a beautiful blue silk robe he'd given her years ago, and she looked incredibly lovely.

'We need to talk,' she said.

Steeling himself, he moved towards her. 'I know.'

She stared up at him, and for a second, all he wanted to do was hold her so tightly that she could never leave him again. But he'd learned that holding too tightly was as harmful as never reaching out at all. 'I have something for you. A birthday present.' He held the box out to her. It lay in his palm like a black wound.

Tentatively, still staring up at him, she took the box and opened it. On a bed of ice-blue silk lay a glittering gold bracelet. The name *Annie* was engraved across the top.

'Oh, Blake,' she whispered, biting down on her lower lip.

'Turn it over,' he said.

She eased the bracelet from the box, and he saw that her hands were trembling as she turned it over and read the inscription:

I will always love you.

She looked up at him, her eyes moist. 'It's not going to work, Blake. It's too late.'

'I know,' he whispered, hearing the unmanly catch in his voice and not caring. Maybe if he'd cared less about things like that in the past, he wouldn't be standing here, saying goodbye to the only woman who'd ever truly loved him. 'I wish . . .' He didn't even know what he wished for. That she had been different? That he had? That they'd seen this truth a long time ago?

'Me, too,' she answered.

'Will you . . . remember the words on that bracelet?'

'Oh, Blake, I don't need a bracelet to remember how much I loved you. You were my life for more than twenty years. Whenever I look back, I'll think of you.' Tears streaked in silvery lines down her cheeks. 'What about Katie?'

'I'll support her, of course . . .'

He could tell that she was hurt by his answer. 'I don't mean money.'

He moved towards her, touched her cheek. He knew what she wanted from him right now, but it wasn't really in his power to give. It never had been, that was part of their problem. He wouldn't be there for Katie, any more than he'd been there for Natalie. Sadly, he gazed down at her. 'Do you want me to lie to you?'

She shook her head. 'No.'

Slowly, he pulled her into his arms. He held her close. 'I guess it's really over,' he whispered into her sweet-smelling hair. After a long moment, he heard her answer, a quiet, shuddering little 'Yes.'

Natalie's dorm room was cluttered with memorabilia from London. Pictures of new friends dotted her desk, mingled with family photos and piles of homework. The metal-framed bed was heaped with expensive Laura Ashley bedding, and at the centre was the pink pillow Annie had embroidered a lifetime ago, the one that read: A PRINCESS SLEEPS HERE.

Natalie sat cross-legged on the bed, her long, unbound hair flowing around her shoulders. Already she looked nervous and worried—a normal teenage response to *both* parents flying up to see you at college.

Annie wished there was some way to break the news of their divorce without words, a way to silently communicate the sad truth.

Blake stood in the corner of the room. He looked calm and at ease— his courtroom face—but Annie could see nervousness in the jittery way he kept glancing at his watch.

Annie knew this was up to her; there was no use putting it off any longer. She went to the bed and sat down beside Natalie. Blake took a few hesitant steps towards them and then stopped in the middle of the room.

Natalie looked at Annie. 'What is it, Mom?'

'Your dad and I have something to tell you.' She took Natalie's hand in hers, stared down at the slender fingers, at the tiny red birthstone ring they'd given her on her sixteenth birthday. It took an effort to sit straight-backed and still. She took a deep breath and plunged ahead. 'Your dad and I are getting a divorce.'

Natalie went very still. 'I guess I'm not surprised.' Her voice was tender, and in it, Annie heard the echo of both the child Natalie had once been and the woman she was becoming.

Annie stroked her daughter's hair. 'I'm sorry, honey.'

When Natalie looked up, there were tears in her eyes. 'Are you OK, Mom?'

Annie felt a warm rush of pride for her daughter. 'I'm fine, and I don't want you to worry about anything. We haven't worked out all the details yet. We don't know where we'll each be living. Things like addresses and vacations and holidays are all up in the air. But I know one thing. We'll always be a family—just a different kind. I guess now you'll have two places in the world where you belong, instead of only one.'

Natalie nodded slowly, then turned to her father.

Blake moved closer, kneeling in front of Natalie. For once, he didn't look like a $350-an-hour lawyer. He looked like a scared, vulnerable man. 'I've made some mistakes . . .' He glanced at Annie and gave her a hesitant smile, then turned back to Natalie. 'With your mom and with you. I'm sorry, Sweet Pea.' He touched her cheek.

Tears leaked from Natalie's eyes. 'You haven't called me that since I fell off the jungle gym in third grade.'

'There are a lot of things I haven't said—or done—in years. But I want to make up for lost time. I want to do things together—if that's OK with you.'

'*Phantom of the Opera* is coming to town in May. Maybe we could go?'

He smiled. 'I'd love to.'

'You mean it this time? I should buy two tickets?'

'I mean it,' he said, and the way he said it, Annie believed him. Of course, she always believed him.

Slowly, Blake got to his feet and drew back.

'We're still going to be a family,' Annie said, tucking a flyaway strand of hair behind Natalie's ear. 'We'll always be a family.' She looked at Blake and smiled.

It was true. She reached out. He took her hand in his, and together they drew around Natalie, enfolding her in their arms. When Natalie was little, they'd called this a 'family hug', and Annie couldn't help wondering why they'd ever stopped.

She heard the soft, muffled sound of her daughter's crying and knew it was one of the regrets that would be with her always.

It was like going back in time. Once again, Annie and Blake were walking through the Stanford campus. Of course, this time Annie was forty years old and as much of her life lay behind her as lay ahead . . . and she was pushing a stroller.

'It's weird to be back here,' Blake said.

'Yeah,' she said softly.

They'd spent the whole day with Natalie, being more of a family in one afternoon than they'd been in many of the previous years, but now it was time to go their separate ways. Annie had driven the Cadillac up here, and Blake had flown in, renting a car to get to the campus.

At Annie's car, they stopped. Annie bent down and unstrapped Katie from the stroller.

'What will you do now?' he asked.

Annie paused. It was the same question he'd asked her when Natalie had left home last spring. Then, it had terrified her. Now, these many months later, the same words opened a door, through which Annie glimpsed a world of possibilities. 'I don't know. I still have tons to do at the house. Twenty years has to be sorted and catalogued and packed away. I know I want to sell the house. It's not . . . me any more.' She straightened, looking at him. 'Unless you want it?'

'Without you? No.'

Annie glanced around, a little uncertain as to what to say. She had no idea when she would see him again. Probably at the lawyer's office, where they'd become a cliché—a cordial, once-married couple coming in as separate individuals to sign papers.

Blake stared down at her. There was a faraway sadness in his eyes that made her move closer to him. In a soft voice, he asked, 'What will you tell Katie about me?'

Annie heard the pain in his voice, and it moved her to touch his cheek. 'I don't know. The old me would have fabricated an elaborate fiction to avoid hurting her feelings. But now . . . I don't know. I guess I'll cross that bridge when I come to it. But I won't lie to her.'

He turned his head and looked away. She wondered what he was thinking, whether it was about lying, and how much it had cost him over the years. Or if it was about the daughter he had lived with for eighteen years and didn't know, or the daughter he'd hardly lived with at all, and now would never know. Or if it was the future, all the days that lay ahead for a man alone, the quiet of a life that included no child's laughter.

'Will you miss me?' he asked, finally looking at her again.

Annie gave him a sad smile. 'I'll miss who we used to be—I already do. And I'll miss who we could have been.'

His eyes filled slowly with tears. 'I love you, Annie.'

'I'll always love the boy I fell in love with, Blake. Always . . .'

She moved towards him, pressing up on her toes to kiss him. It was the kind of kiss they hadn't shared in years; slow, and tender, and heart-felt. There was no undercurrent of sexuality in it. It was everything a kiss was supposed to be, an expression of pure emotion—and they had let it go so easily in their life together. She couldn't remember when kisses had become something perfunctory and meaningless. Maybe if they had kissed this way every day, they wouldn't be here now, standing together in the middle of the Stanford campus, saying goodbye to a commitment that had been designed to last for ever.

When Blake drew back, he looked sad and tired. 'I guess I screwed up pretty badly.'

'You'll get another chance, Blake. Men like you always do. You're handsome and rich; women will stand in line to give you another chance. What you do with that chance is up to you.'

He ran a hand through his hair and looked away. 'Hell, Annie. We both know I'll screw that up, too.'

She laughed. 'Probably.'

They stared at each other for a long minute.

Finally, Blake checked his watch. 'I have to go. My plane leaves at six o'clock.' He bent down to the stroller and gave Katie a last, fleeting kiss. When he drew back up, he gave Annie a weak smile. 'This is hard . . .'

She hugged him, then slowly she drew back. 'Have a safe flight.'

He nodded and turned away from her. He got into his rented car and drove away.

She stood there watching him until the car disappeared. She had expected to feel weighed down by sadness at this moment, but instead she felt almost buoyant.

'Come on, Katie Sarah. Let's go.' She picked up her almost-sleeping daughter and strapped her into the car seat in the back of the Cadillac. Then, throwing her clunky diaper bag onto the passenger seat, she climbed into the car and started the engine. Before she even pulled out, she flicked on the radio and found a station she liked. Humming along with Mick Jagger, she manoeuvred onto the highway and nudged the engine to seventy miles per hour.

What will you do now?

She still had months of responsibilities in southern California. Closing and selling the house, packing everything up, deciding where she wanted to live and what she wanted to do. She didn't have to work, of course, but she didn't want to fall into that life-of-leisure trap again. She *needed* to work.

She thought again about the bookstore in Mystic. She certainly had the capital to give it a try—and that Victorian house on Main Street had plenty of room for living upstairs. She and Katie could be very comfortable up there, just the two of them.

Mystic.

Nick. Izzy.

The love she felt for them was as sharp as broken glass. She knew she would go to him again when her life was in order; she had planned it endlessly in the past few weeks.

She would buy herself a convertible and drive up Highway 101 along the wild beaches, with her hair whipping about her face. She would play slow tunes and sing at the top of her lungs, free at last to do as she pleased. She would drive when the sun was high in the sky and keep going as the stars began to shimmer overhead. She would show up without warning and hope it was not too late.

It would be springtime when she went to him, in that magical week when change was in the air, when everything smelt fresh and new.

She would show up on his porch one day, wearing a bright yellow rain slicker that covered most of her face. It would take her a minute to reach for the doorbell; the memories would be so strong, she'd want to wallow in them. In her arms would be Katie, almost crawling by now, wearing a fuzzy blue snowsuit—one they'd bought just for Mystic.

And when he opened the door, she would tell him that in all the long months they'd been apart, she'd found herself falling, and falling, and there'd been no one there to catch her . . .

Ahead, the road merged onto the interstate. Two green highway signs slashed against the steel-grey sky. There were two choices: I-5 South. I-5 North.

No.

It was crazy, what she was thinking. She wasn't ready. She had oceans of commitments in California, and not even a toothbrush in her diaper bag. It was winter in Mystic, cold and grey and wet, and she was wearing silk . . .

175

South was Los Angeles—and a beautiful white house by the sea that held the stale leftovers of her old life.

North was Mystic—and in Mystic was a man and a child who loved her. Once, she had taken love for granted. Never again.

Nick had known that. It was one of the last things he'd said to her: *You're wrong, Annie. Love matters. It's the only thing that does.*

She glanced in the rearview mirror at her daughter, who was almost asleep. 'Listen to me, Kathleen Sarah. I'm going to give you lesson number one in the Annalise Bourne Colwater book of life. I may not know everything, but I'm forty years old and I know plenty, so pay attention. Sometimes you have to do everything right and follow the rules. You have to wait until all your ducks are in a row before you make a move.' She grinned. 'And other times . . . like now . . . you have to say "What the hell" and go for it.'

Laughing out loud, Annie flicked on her indicator, changed lanes—

And headed north.

KRISTIN HANNAH

In 1985, while I was in my final year of law school, my mother received the devastating news that she had breast cancer. For months, I spent every spare hour at her hospital bedside. There were so many things I didn't want to think about. That my mother wouldn't be at my wedding, that my children would never know the woman who had shaped my life. So, we talked about other things. Anything.

It just so happened that what my mother wanted to talk about were love stories. In short, romance novels. I was stunned. My mother was a true intellectual, a woman who went back for her first graduate degree in physical anthropology when the oldest of her three children was eight. And I was a college student, on the tail end of seven years of solid study. Like many idiots, I judged the books by their lurid covers. But my mother forced me to read them. Within the first few pages, I was hooked. It wasn't long before we were collaborating on an eighteenth-century pirate romance with—you guessed it—a heroine disguised as a cabin boy. We had a ton of fun researching and plotting it together. I will always remember that time we shared. She said she'd always believed I'd be a writer. I realised that it was her dream, but she gave it to me.

After her death, I continued to write. When I sold my first novel in 1990, there was no one I wanted to call more than my mom, and in the years that followed, as I wrote book after book, I was searching for the one story that would bring her back to me, that I knew would make her smile.

On Mystic Lake is that novel. While I was writing this book, something truly extraordinary happened. The book grew into more than I had ever imagined it could be: a big, emotional novel about all kinds of love. Between men and women. Mothers and daughters. Fathers and families and friends. It became my mother's favourite kind of book: a three-hanky love story with a happy ending.

The character of Annie Colwater began as a tribute to my mother, an intelligent, beautiful woman who gave up most of herself to raise her children and run her household. It's hard for women sometimes to hang on to themselves in the midst of raising kids and keeping a marriage strong and being a part of your community. In Annie, I wanted to explore a woman like that who had to start over, had to uncover the woman she was meant to be. And of course, her memories of her mother . . . well, many of those are my memories.

I hope when you finish *On Mystic Lake*, that you will have enjoyed this very special love story as much as I enjoyed writing it.

Kristin Hannah

Libby Mason is a chameleon girlfriend. When going out with penniless Nick she dresses in jeans and Adidas trainers. But when she meets rich Ed, she can let her designer tastes run wild and wear Prada and Gucci with abandon. If only she loved Ed as much as she loved Nick, her life would be perfect. But perhaps love will grow if she can just persuade Ed to shave off his hideous moustache and learn what foreplay is all about?

Chapter One

NICK WAS NEVER SUPPOSED to be The One, for God's sake. Even I knew that. And yes, I know those who are happily married often say you can't know, not immediately, but of course I knew. Not that he sounded wrong—Nick spoke the Queen's English slightly better than myself, but nothing else was right, nothing else fitted.

There was the money thing, for a start. My job as a PR might not be the highest-paying job in the universe, but it pays the bills, pays the mortgage, and leaves me just enough for the odd bit of retail therapy. But Nick didn't earn a penny. Well, that's an exaggeration, but he wasn't like all the other boyfriends I'd had, wasn't rolling in it, and, although that's not my main motivation, what I always say is I don't mind if he can't pay for me, but I do bloody well mind if he can't pay for himself.

And then there was politics. Or lack thereof, in my case, might be more appropriate. Nick was never happier than when he was with his left-wing cronies, arguing the toss about the pros and cons of New Labour, while I sat there bored out of my mind, not contributing just in case anyone asked me what I voted and I had to admit I voted Conservative because, well, because my parents had.

Speaking of pros and cons, it might be easier if I showed you the list I drew up soon after I met Nick. It might help you to see why I was so adamant that he wasn't right for me, that he was just a fling.

Pros:
I fancy the pants off him.
He's got the biggest, softest, bluest eyes I've ever seen.

He's very affectionate.
He's fantastically selfless in bed. (Make that just fantastic.)
He makes me laugh.

Cons:
He's got no money.
He lives in a grotty bedsit in Highgate.
He's left-wing/political.
He likes pubs and pints of beer.
I hate his friends.
He's allergic to commitment.
He says he's not ready for a relationship. (Although neither am I.)

So there you have it—more cons than pros, and, if I'm completely honest, the cons are much more important. I mean, how could I have even thought of getting involved with someone whose friends I hated?

But then again, I suppose you can't help who you fancy, can you? And that was the bottom line. I fancied Nick. Fancied him more than I'd fancied anyone in years, and somehow, when someone gives you that tingly feeling in the pit of your stomach, you just go with it.

You're probably wondering how I met Nick, because, let's face it, our paths were hardly destined to cross. I'd known him for a while, actually. I used to see him at the odd party I went to with my friend Sally, and I vaguely remember Sal having a crush on him.

I used to work with Sal, indirectly. Years ago, when I first started as a lowly PR assistant, Sal was a journalist on one of the magazines, and she was about the only person who didn't treat me like shit, so we formed a friendship on the basis of that. Not that I don't like her. She's a great girl. Just different to me, that's all. She used to drag me along to these parties, student parties I'd think snootily, except no one had been a student for years, but they were always in dilapidated houses, held by the four, or six, people who lived there, and they were never my scene.

Not that I could have afforded the lifestyle I wanted. Not then. Champagne tastes and beer pockets, my mother always used to sniff, if I made the fatal mistake of wearing a new outfit when I went round to see my parents.

'What's that?' she'd say, in a disapproving tone of voice.

'What? This old thing?' I'd learn to say, dismissing my fabulous designer outfit that I loved so much. 'I've had this for ages.' Or, 'It was lying around the fashion cupboard at work, so they gave it to me. Do you like it?' It took me a while, but eventually I learned that, as long as I didn't admit to it being new, my mother would like it.

I used to have these dreams about being a career woman. I wanted shoulder pads, briefcases and mobile phones. I wanted designer clothes and a fuck-off flat which had wooden floors and white sofas and enormous bowls of lilies on every polished fruitwood table. I wanted a Mercedes sports car and chunky gold jewellery.

Unfortunately, life in PR is probably not the best way of going about it, because PR is one of the worst-paid professions in the world. But when I graduated at the tail end of the eighties, PR seemed like an easy option. It sounded glamorous, exciting, and I wouldn't have to start as a secretary, which I was loath to do, because I would have hated people asking me what I did for a living. In PR I was able to start as a Public Relations Assistant, which made me feel like I'd won the lottery.

I answered an ad in the *Guardian*, and when I went along for the interview I decided that if I didn't get this job I would die. The offices of Joe Cooper PR were in a backstreet in Kilburn, not the most salubrious of areas, I know, and from the outside it looked just like a big warehouse, but inside it was magnificent. A huge loft, wooden floors, brightly coloured chairs, and a constant buzz of phone conversations from some of the most beautiful people I'd ever seen in my life.

And then Joe Cooper came to shake my hand. 'You must be Libby,' he said, and as soon as I met him I knew I'd like him, and, more importantly, I knew he'd like me. And he did. And I started the following week on a pittance, but I loved it. God, how I loved it.

Within a month all my friends were green with envy, because I was already on first-name terms with some of the hottest celebrities on TV, and I spent my days helping the executives, typing press releases, occasionally baby-sitting those celebrities on their excursions to radio and television shows where they plugged their latest book, or programme, or film. And it was so exciting.

My budding champagne tastes were brought to full fruition at Joe Cooper PR. And now, finally, I can just about afford to fund my lifestyle, with the help of a very understanding bank manager, who agreed to give me an overdraft facility 'just in case'. Because I fill my overdraft facility pretty much all the time, but hell, it's only money, and as far as I'm concerned we're only here for about eighty years if we're lucky, so in the grand scheme of things nothing really matters very much, and certainly not money. Or even men, when it comes to it.

Friends are what matter, that's what I've decided. My social life is swings and roundabouts. Sometimes I'm on a social whirl, out every night, grateful for the odd night in watching television and catching up on my sleep. But then everything will slow down for a while, and I'll be in every night, flicking through my address book, wondering why I can't really be bothered to talk to anyone.

Well, not quite anyone. I talk to Jules every day, about five times, even if we don't really have anything to say to one another. She'll phone me up and say, 'I've just eaten half a packet of biscuits and a cheese and pickle sandwich. I feel sick.'

And I'll say, 'I had a toasted bagel with smoked salmon, no butter, and one stick of Twix,' and that will be it.

We never, ever, say goodbye, or talk to you at the weekend, or even tomorrow, because, unless we're speaking to each other late at night when we're in bed (which we do practically every night), we know we are going to talk to each other later, even when we've got nothing to say.

What's really surprising about this is not how close we are, but the fact that Jules is married. She married James, or Jamie as he's more commonly known (good, isn't it? Jules et Jim), last year, and I was terrified I'd never see her any more, but if anything the reverse has happened. It's almost as if she isn't married. Jamie never seems to be there, or if he is he's shut away in his study, working, and for a while I was worried, concerned that perhaps their marriage wasn't all it should be, but, on the rare occasions I see the two of them together, I can see that it works, that she's happy, that marriage has given her the security she never had, the security I long for.

And meanwhile, I've still got my friend, my touchstone. Jules is the wisest woman I know. I'll sit and bore her with my latest adventure and she'll listen very quietly, wait for a few seconds while she thinks about what I've said, then she'll give me advice which is always spot-on, even if it might not be exactly what I want to hear.

She's what my mother would call a true friend, and I know that no matter what happens we'll always be there for each other, so even on those nights when I'm cocooning, when I decide that I'm not quite ready to face the world, Jules is the one person I always phone. Always.

And at least my flat's comfortable for those solitary periods of take-outs and videos. Not quite the flat I've always dreamed of, but I've made it pretty damn nice considering most of my furniture has either been inherited from my parents or bought from junk shops. And if it hadn't been for my parents, bless them, I'd never have been able to afford to buy somewhere. I'd probably be sharing some dilapidated house with four, or six, other girls and spending every evening arguing about the washing-up or just resenting them even breathing.

My flat is tiny. Tiny. The tiniest flat you could ever imagine that's actually a flat and not a studio. It's in a basement in Ladbroke Grove, and you walk in the front door and straight into the living room. But, surprisingly, for a basement it's quite bright. There's an L-shaped kitchen off the living room, a galley kitchen, open plan, and opposite the large window there are French doors leading into a bedroom, and then off the bedroom is a minute bathroom. That's it. Perfect for me, although I haven't lost sight of my dream of huge spaces and high ceilings—it's just that I'll have to marry a rich man to get the sort of lifestyle to which I want to become accustomed.

So. Men. Probably the one area of my life that's a complete disaster. Not that I don't meet them. God, it seems as if they're crawling out of the woodwork, except the ones that crawl out to meet me are always worms. I can't understand it.

I thought Jon was the one. Yeah, yeah, yeah, I know I say that every time. But I really did. He was everything I'd ever been looking for. He was a property developer, which is a bit boring, I know, but he wasn't boring. He was handsome, well-dressed, had a beautiful flat in Maida Vale, a Mazda MX-5, knew brilliant people, was great in bed . . . Well, the list goes on and on, really. The only problem was he didn't like me very much. I mean, sure, he fancied me, but he didn't *like* me, he didn't want to spend time with me, and I kept thinking that if I acted like the perfect girlfriend, he'd fall in love with me. But he didn't. The more I tried to be the perfect girlfriend, the more awful he was to me.

In the beginning he used to call me, but the phone calls practically dwindled away to nothing, and then eventually people used to call me up and ask why I wasn't at that party last night that Jon went to. And he used to go away for weekends without telling me, he'd simply disappear, and I'd spend all weekend in floods of tears, ringing his answering machine and banging the phone down before the end of his message.

Eventually I couldn't deal with the stress of being treated like shit any more, and, I'm quite proud of myself for this, I ended it. The bastard didn't even seem to care. He just shrugged and said he was happy with the way things were, and, when I said I needed more, he shrugged again and said he was sorry that he couldn't give me more. BASTARD.

But no, that was a long time ago. I was apoplectic with grief. I kept bursting into tears at work, and everyone was massively sympathetic. Then after a week Jules said I had to get my act together and she knew from the beginning that he wasn't for me and that there were plenty more fish in the sea and blah blah blah. But I began to see her point.

I started putting myself 'out there' again. Going to bars, parties, launches. And even though I felt like shit I pretended to have a good time, and after a couple of months I realised that I actually was having a good time, and that was when I decided that I'd had enough of men.

Yup, I thought. No more bastards for me. But then about six months on I started getting withdrawal symptoms. Not from Jon, but from cuddles, affection and, all right, I'll admit it, from sex. So I decided I'd have a fling. Not a relationship, I thought. I just want sex. That's all. Because I was in that rare state of mind that women always tell you to aspire to, but which you usually find impossible to reach. That state of mind that is completely happy without a man, isn't looking for anyone, is completely fulfilled by work and friends.

And I really was. I realised, post-Jon-trauma, that I definitely didn't want to be in a relationship with someone unless they were absolutely right, and, let's face it, how often do you meet someone who you really fancy and really like? Exactly.

So that's where I'm at when Sal phones, and I haven't seen her for ages, and she invites me out, breathless with excitement about her new boyfriend, and when I arrive at the bar Nick is there and he remembers me, and that's that.

Well, not quite, but more of that later. So you would have thought I'd have learned my lesson after Jon, but have I? Have I? Have I hell. Except with Nick I knew from the beginning that he could never be The One. And so that night in the bar, when there suddenly seems to be this amazing chemistry, I decide that Nick will be my fling, that he'll be perfect for a few weeks of brilliant sex, that I won't get involved.

And I feel really strong. I feel, for the first time in my life, that I can actually do this. That I can have sex with someone and not get emotionally involved, not suddenly start dreaming of marriage and babies and a happy ever after. I feel like a woman. I feel like a grown-up.

Chapter Two

'Libby!' cries Sal, flinging her arms round me in a huge bear hug. 'God, it's been ages. Look at you! You look fantastic!' This, incidentally, is the way Sally speaks. In exclamation marks.

'Thanks,' I say, believing her because who, after all, wouldn't look fantastic in their brand-new, super-expensive, pale-grey, cotton-ribbed cardigan, teamed with grey flannel trousers and sexy high- heeled black boots. 'So do you,' I add, although Sal always looks the same to me. With her natural auburn hair in a sort of fluffy medium-length layered bob, she always looks good in a timeless sort of way.

'Jesus, Sal,' I say, stepping back, because there's something different about her tonight. 'You've lost so much weight.'

'Have I!' she says, with a cheesy grin, because of course she knows she has. She'd never dare wear those skintight jodhpurs if she hadn't. 'Must be love!' she whispers loudly, taking my hand and leading me to a table in the corner. 'Come and meet the others.'

What an, er, eclectic, bunch. This is something that I've always admired about Sal: her choice in friends, her willingness to mix and match, just to throw people together and not worry about the consequences. I, on the other hand, spend my life in a constant panic about whether people will get on with one another.

'Hi,' I say with a smile to Kathy, Sal's oldest friend, a tall, stunning blonde who oozes style and sophistication and seems to have a constant stream of equally gorgeous men at her side.

'Libby,' she says, stretching out a smooth tanned cheek to kiss the air next to mine. 'How are you? It's been so long. You must meet Phil,' and she gestures to the drop-dead gorgeous hunk at her side.

'Delighted to meet you,' he says, and holds out his hand to shake mine, which floors me for a few moments because outside the office nobody I know shakes hands. I surreptitiously wipe my damp palms on my cardigan, shake his hand firmly and say a businesslike 'How do you do', because I can't be too friendly to someone this gorgeous in case Kathy thinks I'm flirting with him.

'You remember Paul,' says Sal, putting a stool down next to a baby-faced scruffy young man sipping from a pint who I know is her latest boyfriend, but I'm not sure why I should remember him.

'Umm.' I'm not sure I do, actually.

'Yes you do,' she says. 'Paul worked with me on the *Sunday Mail.*'

'Oh, Paul!' I say, suddenly remembering. 'That Paul. Sorry. God, finally I can put a face to the name.'

He grins at me. 'I know what you mean. You must spend all day talking to journalists and never knowing what they look like.'

'Unless,' I say, grinning cheekily, 'the journalist in question has been out for the day wearing a miniskirt to test the latest men's fashion.'

'Shit,' he groans. 'I thought I'd lived that one down.' We both laugh.

'And Nick,' says Sal, making big eyes at me which I don't quite understand, but then I turn to Nick and realise that he's the one she used to fancy and that she's trying to warn me telepathically not to say anything. 'You must remember Nick.'

Nick turns to look at me, and nods. 'Hi, Libby,' he says, and somehow the way he says my name makes it sound really intimate, and I feel a tiny shiver at the base of my spine.

Hello? What's this all about, then? And I look closely at Nick and it's as if I'm seeing him for the first time. God, I think. I never realised his eyes were that blue. And he's had his hair cut. It's not in a straggly pony-tail any more, it's a short buzz cut that brings out these incredible sculpted cheekbones, and Jesus, he's handsome, and in an instant I remember what that shiver is. Lust. Pure and simple.

This could be my fling, I think, settling back into my chair and switching into flirt mode. Nick. Perfect.

'So what have you been up to?' he says, giving me what is definitely an appreciative glance.

'Working hard as usual,' I say, instantly regretting how dull it sounds.

'I like your hair,' he says, and another shiver goes through me. 'You've changed it.'

And I have. I'd had long straight hair and a fringe the last time I saw Nick. Now it's shoulder-length, no fringe, and flicking up at the bottom.

'You're not supposed to remember hair,' I laugh. 'You're a bloke.'

'You'd be surprised at what I remember,' he says with a smile.

'What do you mean?'

'The last time I saw you was at Sal's party two years ago,' he says. 'You had your hair up and you were wearing black leather trousers, trainers, and a bright orange T-shirt which said "Bizarre" on it.'

'Jesus Christ. How the hell do you remember what I was wearing?'

He shrugs. 'Let's just say I have a very good memory for things I want to remember.'

'Oh,' I say in a small voice, as it dawns on me that maybe he wasn't being stand-offish all those times I had met him. Maybe he fancied me?

'So the exciting world of PR is still as exciting as ever, then?' he says.

'I know you think PR's a complete waste of time,' I start, even though I don't know, I just suspect, 'but it suits me. I like it.'

'I don't think it's a waste of time.' He sounds surprised. 'And when my novel is a best seller you'll probably be the first people I come to.'

'You've got a deal?' My voice is high with excitement. This is getting better and better. If Nick's signed a deal, then he's got money, and if he's got money that instantly makes him eligible.

'Nah,' he sighs. 'Still trying.'

'Oh. What's the book about?' I'm being polite, OK? I think he'll just give me a two-minute synopsis, but ten minutes later he stops, seeing my eyes glaze over.

'Shit, I'm sorry. I've bored you.'

'No, no,' I say quickly. 'I just don't know much about politics, so it doesn't mean a great deal to me. But it sounds excellent,' I add enthusiastically. 'I can't believe it hasn't been published.'

'I know,' he says sadly. 'Neither can I.

'What are you drinking?' He stands up, and I tell him a Sea Breeze if they've got it.

'Well,' says Sal in a knowing voice when he's gone off to get the drinks. 'You and Nick seem to be getting on rather well.'

I shrug. 'He seems nice, that's all. I never realised.'

'You should go for it,' she says. 'I could see you two together.'

I laugh. 'Sal! You're crazy. I can't see us together at all.'

'Why not?' She looks startled, and I remember how she doesn't think about the important things, about our lifestyles, how different we are.

'Just look at us,' I say, feebly gesturing at my designer clothes, and then pointing at Nick, at his dirty jeans, his scruffy loose jumper with holes in the sleeves, his scuffed Doc Martens.

'What?' she says again, brow furrowed because she isn't getting it.

'Oh, never mind,' I laugh. 'He's definitely not the one for me, but he is nice. He's really quite sexy.'

'Maybe you should just get together and see what happens,' she says, smiling, leaning back to make way for Nick, who's returning with a fresh round of drinks.

'Maybe I should,' I say, thinking that the getting together bit would suit me just perfectly right now, but I know what would happen. We wouldn't fit. But that's OK, I remind myself. I don't want a potential husband or even a boyfriend. I just want some fun. No strings attached.

'What are you two gossiping about?' says Nick, and I can tell from his smile his ears were burning.

'Er, just work,' says Sal, who is completely crap at lying.

'I see,' he says, sitting down and sliding my drink over to me. 'Not discussing men, then, were you?'

'No!' says Sal, giving me a hugely indiscreet thumbs up and turning to snuggle into Paul's shoulder.

Nick and I talk all evening, and, once the book is out of the way, it turns out that he really is interesting, and funny, and different.

'If you won the lottery what would you do?' he asks at one point, and I practically squeal with pleasure because I love questions like this.

'How much?' I say. 'You have to name a figure.'

'OK,' he says, grinning. 'Five million pounds.'

I sit back, thinking about all the lovely things I could buy with five million pounds. 'Well,' I start. 'I'd buy a house. One of those huge white ones in Holland Park.'

'You do realise that would set you back about three million quid.'

'Oh. OK. A small white one in Maida Vale.'

'For how much?'

'Five hundred thousand?'

He nods. 'And how would you decorate it?'

I describe my dream house, except I get a bit lost after I've done the living room, the bathroom, the kitchen and the bedroom, because I've never had to think about any other rooms.

'What about the dining room?' Nick asks. 'What about bedroom number four? What about the study?'

'Oh, God,' I finally groan. 'Too many rooms. Maybe I'll just settle for an amazing two-bedroom flat with huge rooms and a split-level galleried bit to work in.'

'So. You've got four and a half million left.'

'I'd buy a holiday home in the Caribbean.'

'You're big on homes, aren't you?'

'What do you expect? I'm a child of Thatcher's generation.'

'Hmm,' he sniffs. 'Don't tell me you voted for her?'

'No,' I lie, saying what I always say. 'I voted for the Green Party.'

'Did you?' He looks, well, if not impressed, at least not completely pissed off, and for a moment I think of telling him the truth, that I don't give a stuff about politics and the only reason I voted Tory was because my parents had. I decide to keep lying.

'Yes,' I say, nodding. 'None of the other parties seemed to offer anything, and you know what politicians are like. They're all untrustworthy bastards.' This last line I'd heard at a party, and I thought it sounded rather good, like I knew what I was talking about, and it works. Nick nods in agreement, as if I've just said something very sensible.

'Anyway,' I continue, bringing the conversation back onto more familiar footing. 'My house in the Caribbean.'

'Ah, yes,' he says, smiling. 'That's far more important than politics.'

'Absolutely.' I describe the house I would build on Anguilla.

'So we're about a million down,' he says. 'What else?'

'I'd probably take about a hundred thousand and go on a mad shopping spree,' I admit. 'Armani, Prada, Gucci . . .'

'Top Shop?' asks Nick. 'Oasis?'

'Are you crazy?' I say. 'I'd never demean myself by stepping foot in anywhere like that.'

'Oh, right.' He grins. 'Of course. How stupid of me.'

'Anyway,' I say, 'how come you know about Oasis?'

'I know a lot of things,' he laughs.

'You're not really a bloke, are you?' I say, narrowing my eyes and squinting at him. 'You're a girl.'

'Damn,' he says, laughing. 'And I hoped you hadn't noticed.'

At about three million pounds I run out of ideas. I have, by this point, two homes, a wardrobe that would make Oprah Winfrey jealous, a convertible Porsche, a live-in cleaning woman, and numerous investments in property. I don't know what to do with the rest. 'I'd, er, give the rest to charity,' I say magnanimously, hoping he won't ask which ones, because I couldn't name a charity if my life depended on it.

'Which charity?' he asks. He would.

'I'd give to a few. That breast cancer one. The . . .'—I think hard— 'NSPCC.' I remember those little blue plastic collection boxes they used to give you at school. 'AIDS Research, lots to them. And animal charities! Yes, I'd give loads to animal charities so no more little ponies and horses in my cat food.'

'What about you?' I look at Nick. 'What would you do?'

Nick sits and thinks about it for a bit. 'I don't think I'd move,' he says. 'There's no real point because I'm quite happy.'

'Where do you live?'

'In Highgate. I've got a bedsit. I suppose I could get a one-bedroom flat, but I'm happy where I am.'

'You'd have to buy somewhere,' I say sternly. 'You've got to get your foot on the ladder.' Another phrase I've picked up somewhere.

'Do I? Why?'

'Because . . .' I suddenly don't know why, other than that I've been brought up to believe that everyone should own their own house.

'Because you're one of Thatcher's children, right?'

'Well, so are you,' I say in my defence. 'You grew up during Thatcher's time, didn't you?'

'Does that mean I was supposed to believe in her?'

'No, it's just sometimes hard to go against what you've been brought up to believe in.'

'It wasn't what I was brought up to believe in. My parents were dyed-in-the-wool Labour supporters.'

I'm getting out of my depth. I stand up. 'Another pint?' and he laughs.

'So, OK, you won't buy a mansion,' I say when I come back.

'No, no,' he says. 'But I've been thinking about it and you're probably right. I should buy somewhere, but it wouldn't be anything amazing. I'll buy a one-bedroom flat.'

'What else, what else?'

He sits deep in thought. 'I know!' he suddenly exclaims, his eyes lighting up. 'I'd buy a proper computer.'

'You mean you're writing a novel and you haven't got a computer?'

'I've got one of these typewriter things that has a tiny screen and you can see about three lines of what you've written on it.'

'You must be spending a fortune on Tipp-Ex,' I say.

'There we go,' he grins. 'I'd buy a lifetime's supply of Tipp-Ex.'

'But you wouldn't need Tipp-Ex if you had a computer.'

'I might get nostalgic.'

'OK,' I sigh. 'We've probably spent less than a hundred thousand so far. You're not doing very well.'

'I could donate a million quid to the Labour Party,' he says sheepishly.

'You can't give a million pounds to politicians!' I say in horror.

'Sorry,' he says, looking it. 'I'm just not very money-orientated.'

'Evidently,' and luckily he laughs, and when he does I can't help but notice how his face softens, how goddamned gorgeous he looks.

'So,' says Sal, leaning over and interrupting us. 'Have you got any good stories for me, then, Libby?'

I sit and think. 'Not really stories, but maybe you'd be interested in an interview with Sean Moore?'

'Sean Moore!' Her eyes light up. 'Are you doing him?'

I nod. 'We're doing the PR for his new TV series, and I'm setting up a round of interviews in a couple of weeks. You should have got the press release, I sent it to you last week.'

'Oh,' says Sal, looking guilty. 'I probably did get it, but I get so many press releases, half the time I don't even look at them.'

'What?' I say in mock dismay. 'You mean I go to all that trouble to think up something witty and clever, and it goes in the bin?'

'No,' she says. 'It joins the towering pile on my desk that's threatening to topple over and knock someone out.'

'You're forgiven . . .' I pause. 'As long as you give Sean a good show.'

'Double-page spread?'

'That would be brilliant. Ring me in the office.'

At eleven o'clock everyone starts getting up to leave. We wander outside, and stand around in a big huddle to say goodbye.

'Where do you live?' asks Nick, just as I'm wondering how to say good night to him, and if, in fact, I want to say good night to him at all.

'Ladbroke Grove.' The regret is obvious in my voice. I mean, there's no way I can offer him a lift back to Highgate, it's just too unsubtle. 'Are you driving?' I say.

He shakes his head. 'No. I got the tube here.'

'Oh.'

And then I have a brainwave. 'Do you want a lift to the tube?'

His face glows. 'I'd love one.'

And as we walk off I can see Sal grinning at me, and I can't help it. I start grinning too.

We walk to my car in silence. I stride along next to him, wondering why my heart is pounding. I mean surely this is the perfect fling?

Not that I want a one-night stand with Nick, just maybe a few weeks of delicious sex before saying goodbye with no broken hearts. One-night stands aren't my style. I don't think they're anyone's style, are they? Sure, we've all done it, but even when you can't stand them, even when it's just a drunken mistake after a party, you still want them to call, don't you, even if it's just so you can turn round and tell them you never want to see them again. It's an ego thing.

In normal circumstances, I would never dream of sleeping with Nick on the first night, as it were. If I had looked at him and thought, yes, you could be The One, I would have given him my number and let him take me out a few times before even considering going to bed with him. But because Nick is never going to be my boyfriend, and because it's just sex, the rules change.

When it's just sex, you're allowed to be predatory, to make the first move, to entice them into bed, because it's not necessary to make them fall in love with you.

When it's just sex you're allowed to lead them into your living room and kiss them passionately before they've even had a chance to take their coat off.

And then you're allowed to . . .

Sorry, I'm jumping ahead of myself here. Where were we? Ah, yes, in the car, listening to music, and neither of us is actually saying anything. Eventually we turn into Ladbroke Grove and I have to say something, so I do. 'The tube's just down the road,' I say. Unimaginatively.

'Oh,' he says. And I smile inside.

'Do you want to come in for a coffee?' I say.

'I'd love one,' he says. And he grins.

So I park the car and I can't look at Nick because I'm very aware of his presence, of the chemistry, of this unspoken agreement we are entering into, and I just unlock my front door and we both walk in.

And you know what I love? Even though Nick just isn't boyfriend material, I love the fact that he seems to feel instantly at home.

'You have incredible taste,' he says, wandering around, picking up things and putting them down. 'Really,' he reiterates. 'Such style.'

'Thank you,' I say, going through the motions of putting the kettle on, and watching curiously to see where he'll sit. If he sits on the chair, I think, I'm in trouble, because how can I manoeuvre myself into a position where he'll kiss me? Maybe I can perch on the arm of the chair, I think, watching as he seems to hover ominously by the armchair.

Phew. He seems to think twice about the chair and settles into the sofa. I kick my shoes off, bring the mugs to the coffee table, then panic about my make-up and quickly disappear into the bathroom.

I blot the shine off my nose and forehead, and think about a fresh coat of lipstick, but no, too obvious, so I just shake my hair around a bit to give it a wild, wanton look, then sashay back into the living room to put on some music.

Seduction music, I think. Something soft, jazzy, sexy. Something that will put us both in the mood. I flick through the CDs until I find my fail-safe Sinatra CD. Perfect. It always worked in the past, and I put it on and turn the volume down so it's barely throbbing in the background, then I walk over to the sofa where Nick is sipping his coffee and watching me.

'I need a woman's touch,' he says, as I curl up at the other end of the sofa, not wanting to sit too close, but knowing that I'm only a hop, skip and a touch away from the passion I'm so desperate for.

I raise an eyebrow and he laughs.

'I meant in the home,' he says, and I laugh too, then we both make big shows of drinking our coffee, although it's far too hot to drink.

'What's your flat like, then?' I ask.

'A hovel,' he says, and he laughs.

'Why?' I ask, although quite frankly I'm not that surprised. Bachelor pads seem to fall into two categories. If the bachelor in question has money, it's all black leather and chrome, with huge, fuck-off TVs and stereos. And if he, like Nick, hasn't got a pot to piss in, it will be overflowing with books and papers, and dirty clothes, and rubbish.

'Well,' I say, raising my mug. 'Here's to winning the lottery.'

After this we seem to relax. We talk about Sal, about her boyfriend, about us. I tell him I'm not into relationships, I've had enough of getting my heart broken and I'm not ready for anything serious.

He nods intently while I say this, and says he knows how I feel. He grins and tells me he hasn't had a serious relationship in two years, but that after his last—a miserable five-year relationship with Mary, who loved him but didn't seem to like him very much—he definitely isn't ready for commitment.

And then he looks up at me with those incredible blue eyes and says, 'But I'm very attracted to you,' and even though I'm the one who's supposed to be in control, the one who's made the decision to have a fling with him, my stomach turns over and does a little somersault.

There's a long silence, and then I say, 'Thank you,' because I don't know what else to say, and I can't say that I'm very attracted to him too because it sounds really naff, and anyway he must know that because why else would I have invited him back.

So we sit there in silence for a bit and then I offer him another coffee. When he shakes his head my heart plummets.

Shit, I think. Shit, shit, shit. He's going to go home. But he doesn't. He grins and says, 'You know what I'd really like?'

'No.' I shake my head.

'I'd really like a bath.'

'A bath? Are you mad?'

'I know it sounds bizarre, but I've only got a shower in my flat and I miss baths. Would you mind?'

I shake my head, wondering what the hell this is about, because this is a completely new one on me. What on earth am I supposed to do while he has a bath?

I don't have to think about it for very long because just then the phone rings. 'Hi, babe,' says Jules. 'It's me.'

'Hi,' I say guardedly, in the tone of voice that tells her this is perhaps not the best time to be calling.

'Uh-oh,' she says. 'Something tells me you're not alone. Who's there? It's a bloke, isn't it?'

'Mmmhmm,' I say, eyes widening slightly as Nick starts grinning manically at me, unbuttoning his shirt.

'What's going on?' she pleads, as I start giggling. Nick has started dancing round the room doing a bloody good imitation of a stripper, except it isn't sexy, it's very, very funny.

'OK,' I say. 'There's an extremely gorgeous man jumping round my living room and taking off his clothes.'

Nick wiggles his hips in appreciation of my description of him.

'Oh ha bloody ha,' says Jules. 'Seriously. What's going on?'

'Seriously,' I say. 'He's about to take his shirt off.'

Nick takes his shirt off.

'I don't believe you,' she says, as I hold the phone out to Nick.

'Hello,' he says, as I practically salivate over the sight of his lean, muscular, naked torso. 'Who's this?'

There is a pause. 'Nick,' I hear him say, as he unbuttons the flies of his jeans, giving me minor heart failure. 'Having a bath,' he says next, and then he starts laughing as I grab the phone off him.

'Bloody hell!' says Jules. 'Now I believe you. But who the hell is Nick?'

'It's a long story,' I say. 'Can I call you tomorrow?'

'Just tell me, is he naked?'

'Not yet,' I say, eyes glued to Nick, who is trying to balance on one leg as he pulls off his socks, 'but I think he will be soon.'

Nick wiggles off into the bathroom.

'As long as you know what you're doing,' she says.

'Having fun,' I say. 'Something I haven't had for a while.'

'OK,' she says. 'I'll let you go. And for God's sake use a condom.'

I can hear the bathwater running, so when I've put the phone down I walk through the bedroom, thanking God I made the bed this morning, and gingerly push the bathroom door open before creasing up with laughter.

Nick is sitting in the bath as the water pours in, and he's put in practically a whole bottle of bubble bath—this doesn't bother me because it means I can't see anything, which I've been dreading because I don't know him well enough to take it in my stride—and he's put a plastic shower cap on his head. If he wasn't so damn gorgeous he'd look ridiculous. As it happens, he looks cute as hell, and I pull the loo seat down and sit on it, shaking my head.

'You really are crazy,' I say, as he rubs his face.

'No I'm not,' he says, lying back. 'This is lovely. Why don't you join me? I need someone to scrub my back.'

Oh fuck it, I think, standing up and untying my cardigan. This isn't exactly the way I'd planned it, but what have I got to lose?

Thankfully Nick doesn't watch me getting undressed. He lies back in the bath and closes his eyes, and I keep a close watch on him to check he isn't peeping. I'm not quite ready to take off all my clothes in front of him, so when I'm down to my underwear I grab a towel and go back into the bedroom.

'Libby?' he shouts as I go. 'Have you got any candles?'

I find three, and, after I've taken my bra and knickers off, I wrap a towel round myself, light the candles, and switch the light off in the bathroom, putting the candles round the room.

MR MAYBE

Nick sits up, facing away from me, and I let the towel drop and climb in behind him in the bath. 'Here,' he says, handing me the soap over his shoulder. 'Back-scrub time.'

'You just did this because you wanted a massage,' I say, soaping his back and wondering how on earth I've managed to get so intimate with someone I hardly know in such a short space of time.

'Mmm,' he murmurs. 'A bit lower. Yup, that's perfect.'

I look at my hands circling his back with soap, at the flickering candle-light picking up the definition of his spine, and when his back is covered I put the soap on the side of the bath and slowly rub his back. I have my legs on either side of him, and, as I rub his back, Nick picks up the soap and starts soaping my calves. I catch my breath as I feel his big, strong hands gently soap my legs, over the knee, down to the ankles, holding my feet as he rubs them in silence.

And as we half sit, half lie in the bath, the music coming from the living room seems to take on a distinctly sexual feel, and before I even know what I'm doing I lean forward and kiss his neck. I hear him groan as my lips touch his skin, and I open my lips and suck softly as they travel up to his earlobe. His hand stops circling on my leg. He's stopped moving, and everything seems to be happening very slowly.

He turns as the water sloshes round him in the bath, then looks at me through eyes glazed with lust, before kissing me softly, open lips teasing mine for what seems like hours, before finally licking my upper lip as I moan and slide my tongue into his mouth.

I'm vaguely aware that as he's kissing me he's half standing up, twisting his body round, and when he sits down again in the warm water he's facing me, his legs over my legs, his lips never leaving mine.

And as we carry on kissing, I pull the bathcap off his head and drop it over the edge of the bath, and slink my hands round his neck, pulling him closer as he drops his head and kisses my collarbone.

I shiver.

He sits back and picks up the soap again, still looking at me as if to check this is OK, which it most definitely is, and very gently starts soaping my arms, up towards my shoulders, then slowly he circles my breasts, moving closer and closer to my nipples, which are rock hard, but not quite touching them, not yet.

Then he slides the bar of soap over my left nipple and I gasp, and look down into the water because by this time the soap has made all the bubbles disappear, and I can see his cock, thick and hard, and I slide the soap out of his hand and down the side of his cock, and it's his turn to gasp as I slide it up and down the shaft, round his balls.

The soap slips out of my hand, and he picks it up and traces a line over my nipples, down my stomach, and across my clitoris and all I can think of is that I want him inside me.

I hear a slurping noise and I jerk my eyes open and Nick laughs as he holds up the plug, and it breaks the spell for a second, but just a second, because as the water slips out of the bath Nick pushes me onto my back, and, as my legs rest on either edge of the bath, he kisses his way down my body until I feel his tongue slip in between my legs. As he licks, sucks, laps at my clitoris, I feel a wave of orgasm building up inside me, and after I've come, I lead him out of the bathroom and into bed.

I slip a condom on his cock that is jerking with anticipation, and I push him onto his back and straddle him, positioning myself so I can ease him inside me, and when he's about an inch in I gasp because I really had forgotten how good this feels.

And it's perfect. The perfect fuck. Nick is perfect. And I love that feeling of power, being on top, being in control, and I love watching his face as he finally gives in to an orgasm.

When it's over he puts his arm round me and cuddles me for ages. 'That,' he says, after squeezing me very tightly, 'was lovely.'

'Good,' I say. 'I thought so too.'

'And you,' he says, kissing my nose, 'are one hell of a sexy lady.'

'I aim to please,' I laugh.

'You certainly did,' he says. 'And now shall I tell you a bedtime story.'

'Yes, please!' I say, in a little-girl voice, feeling strangely like a little girl, all safe and warm and protected, encircled in his arms.

'Once upon a time,' he starts, in a soft, low voice, 'there lived a little girl called Libby. Libby lived all by herself in a huge yellow sunflower at the bottom of a beautiful garden.'

I sigh and snuggle up closer.

'At the back of the garden,' he continues, 'was a great big house, and in the house lived Mr and Mrs Pinchnose. They were called Mr and Mrs Pinchnose because every time they went into the garden they pinched their noses because Mr and Mrs Pinchnose hated the smell of anything fresh and beautiful, but what they never knew was that it wasn't the smell of the flowers, or the trees, or the river, it was the smell of Libby.'

'Are you saying that Libby smelt?' I say indignantly, although I'm smiling.

'I'm saying that Libby smelt fresh and beautiful,' he says.

'Oh,' I say. 'That's OK, then,' and I pick up his hand and kiss it as he carries on talking, and before I know it I'm fast asleep.

 # Chapter Three

I HATE THE MORNING after the night before, because you never know how you stand, and even though we wake up and have sex again, I'm still not sure what will happen once we both break the spell by getting out of bed, and, in my case, going to work, so I try to put the moment off for as long as possible by snuggling up to Nick, because let's face it, it's not as if *he* has anywhere to go.

But after the fifth time the alarm goes off I have to get up or I'll be severely late for work, so I wrap myself up in the silk dressing gown that was a present from Jules last year and go into the kitchen to make coffee.

I carry a mug of coffee back into the bedroom for Nick, and when he sees me he holds his arms out and says, 'Come and give me a cuddle,' and as I'm lying in his arms and he's making me laugh by giving me big, punchy kisses, I'm thinking, God, I could get used to this.

No, Libby. No, you could not. He's not what you want. You really think you could spend your life in a grotty bedsit in Highgate? You think you could spend your social life in pubs drinking warm beer? You think you could forget all about your dreams of being a rich man's wife and a lady who lunches? I don't think so. No. I am not going to fall in love with this man. I'm going to be a woman of the nineties and just enjoy the sex, and so what if he happens to be affectionate and quite funny? That's just a bonus.

Nick sits up in bed and drinks his coffee while I get ready for work. Then, as I'm putting my make-up on in the bathroom mirror, he comes in and sits on the edge of the bath to talk to me and, as he puts it, 'see what I'm doing'.

'What's that for?' he keeps saying, as I root around in my make-up bag and pull out yet another alien thing—at least to his eyes.

'I dunno,' he says eventually, shaking his head as I pout at my perfect reflection. 'If you ask me you look far better without anything.'

'Now I know you're joking,' I say, because I'd never dare leave my house without the full appliance of science.

'No, I'm serious,' he says. 'You don't need all that make-up. I know there are some women who look like complete dogs without it, but you're really pretty naturally, and you honestly do look better without.'

I don't know about you, but flattery, for me, will get anyone just about anywhere they want to go, and I could kiss him for saying that. In fact, I do. I completely forget about the make-up bit and just concentrate on the pretty bit. He says I'm pretty! He thinks I'm pretty!

By the time we leave the house and walk up to the tube station, I'm flying as high as a kite. Not that I've fallen in love, not even close, but it's just so nice to have had a night of snuggling up to someone, to have someone to talk to in the morning, to have compliments again.

But as we separate in the tube station, I do feel a tiny twinge, because even though I know this isn't going to go anywhere, I don't think I can stand it if he just says, 'Bye.' I think Nick must see this in my face, because he puts his arms round me and gives me a huge hug.

'That was the nicest night I've had in ages,' he says, while my heart sinks, because surely this is the lead-in to, 'Take care.'

But no. I'm wrong.

'When can I see you again?' he says next, and, despite myself, I feel like doing a little jig on the spot.

'Umm,' I say, pulling away and digging my diary out from my bag. I flick the pages open and have a quick look. 'I'm a bit busy this week,' I say. 'So either the weekend or next week?'

Please say weekend, I think.

'Saturday?' he says.

'Great,' I say, beaming.

'OK,' he says. 'Why don't you come to me?'

'What, and set foot in your hovel?'

Nick laughs. 'We could go out for something to eat. I'll give you a call at work to arrange a time. How's that?'

It's fine. In fact I'm feeling a lot happier than I've felt in months.

'You look like the cat that got the cream,' says Jo, our super-trendy receptionist at the office.

'Do I?' I say innocently, but I can't help it, a huge Cheshire cat grin plasters itself to my face.

'You're in love, aren't you?' she says.

'Nope.' I shake my head. 'Definitely not. But,' and I skip away at this point, just turning back before I disappear through the doorway, 'I may well be in lust,' and I wink at her before making my way to my desk.

Do I get any work done? Do I hell. I sit and moon at my desk, looking out of the window and shivering with lust at the occasional flashbacks of my passion-filled night.

And the flashbacks seem to come at the most ridiculous times. I'll be talking on the phone to a journalist, and suddenly, mid-sentence, a picture of Nick licking my neck slides into my head and I'll pause, grin and lose the plot completely.

It really isn't that I'm falling for him, it's just so damned nice to have had a gorgeous man in my bed, to have been reminded that I am attractive and sexy. Because, to be perfectly honest, I've been starting to doubt myself these last six months. Not hugely, because there haven't been that many men I've been interested in, but I do have a tendency to fall for the ones who will never be interested in me, and the ones that fall for me are generally pretty revolting.

I can't figure out why I fall for the wrong ones. I meet these men, fall desperately in love, and become friends with them in the mistaken hope that one day they'll see the error of their ways and realise they're madly attracted to me. But of course that doesn't happen, and each time I end up feeling like shit.

It feels like ages since I've been attracted to someone who feels the same way about me, and OK, that doesn't mean anything, it certainly doesn't mean Nick's The One, but it just makes me feel good about myself, which is good. Isn't it?

In fact, I'm feeling so good that I'm not the slightest bit stressed about my job, which is a bloody miracle, because lately I've been given more and more accounts and I have to confess that there are times when I really don't know how I'm going to cope.

My accounts? OK, I'm currently working on Sean Moore, which you already know about. A performance artist called Rita Roberts, which is a bit peculiar because I don't tend to do the theatrical stuff as I know nothing about it; the comedian Tony Baloney; and an aspiring television presenter called Amanda Baker. I say aspiring, which isn't really fair, because she is on television, although not nearly as often as she'd like. She presents a showbiz slot on one of the daytime shows, and the minute she got her face on-screen she decided she was a star. Unfortunately, nobody seems to know who she is, and it's a bit of a Catch-22. The papers won't write about her because she's a no one, but without the coverage she can't raise her profile, and it's the hardest account I've got, not just because of that, but because she's such a complete bitch to me, even though I managed to get her into a celeb round-up in one of the nationals, where they wanted celebs to talk about their date from hell. You'd think she'd be over the moon, but all she did was moan about being the smallest quote in there.

But even the fact that Amanda's coming in today for a meeting doesn't ruin my good mood, and when the receptionist buzzes me to tell me she's here, I float down to meet her, and even manage to compliment her. 'I love your suit,' I lie, taking in her tele-friendly pastel trouser-suit, which looks vaguely Armani-ish except I know it's not because Amanda isn't nearly successful enough to afford Armani.

'This old thing?' she says, but I can tell she's pleased.

'Come through.' I hold the door open for her, and say in my best PR voice, 'So how are you?'

'Oh, you know,' she says, running a hand through her mane of streaky blonde hair. 'Busy as ever.'

We sit down, I shuffle some papers around on my desk and ask what she wants to see me about.

'I really feel,' she starts, 'that now is the time we should be blitzing the papers and getting some more coverage.'

'Umm, yes,' I say, digging out the list to show her exactly who has been approached. 'Was there anything specific you had in mind?'

'Well, yes, actually,' she says. 'I noticed in *Hello!* that they've done a profile of Lorraine Kelly with her new baby, and I've just moved house and done it up, and I thought it would make a very good feature.'

'OK,' I say, groaning inside. 'I'll ring them.' Which I will and they will sit on the other end of the phone, doubtless raising their eyes to the ceiling while I start my PR spiel about how brilliant Amanda is, and then they'll say, sorry, we've never heard of her.

'And,' she says, 'I wondered exactly who you had spoken to recently about me?'

Aha! Here's my perfect chance for revenge. I slide the contact sheet over to her and start speaking in my most sympathetic tone of voice. 'Last week I spoke to Femail in the *Daily Mail*, *Sun* Woman, the lifestyle supplement of the *Express*, *Bella*, *Best*, *Woman's Realm* and *Woman*. This week I spoke to *OK!*, *Here!* magazine and *Cosmopolitan*.'

'Oh.' Amanda's voice is very small, and, for the first time ever, and I swear, this must be down to the good mood I'm in, I feel sorry for her.

'Look,' I say. 'I know it's hard,' and I give her my speech about Catch-22. 'We need to come up with an angle, really. Have there been any life-changing events that we might be able to use, something that would make a good story?'

'Not like moving house, then?' she asks hopefully.

'Er, no. Not like moving house.' Like stealing, pillaging, nervous breakdowns, I'm thinking.

'Umm.' She sits there and I can almost see her brain try to kick into gear. Oops, nearly, nearly. Nope, she can't quite manage it.

'OK,' I say. 'As a child, did you ever steal anything?'

'Are you serious?' she asks.

'Absolutely.' I nod my head very seriously.

'No. Not really. Well . . .'

'Yes?' I encourage eagerly.

'Well, I did once take an eyeliner from Boots by mistake. I meant to pay for it but I completely forgot.'

'Perfect! My thieving hell from top TV presenter! I can see it now.'

'Are you sure that will make a story?' she says doubtfully. 'I mean, it was only an eyeliner and I was about fourteen years old, and I wouldn't say it was hell, exactly, except I did feel terribly guilty.'

'We won't say it was an eyeliner, we'll say it was a complete set of make-up, and you won't have been fourteen, it will have happened last year, and the outcome of it was you felt so terrible, you didn't know what came over you, you went back and owned up.'

'But that's lying!' she says.

'That's PR,' I say. 'Hang on,' and I pull the phone over and dial a number. 'Keith? It's Libby from Joe Cooper PR. Fine, fine, you? Great. Listen, you know Amanda Baker from *Breakfast Break*? No, no, the showbiz slot. No, no, she does the weather. No, no, the blonde. Oh well, anyway, she's doing more and more and she's getting really big and she's just confessed the most amazing story which would be perfect for your magazine. It turns out she had the shoplifting experience from hell last year, and she feels the time is right to confess all. Yup.' I nod, listening to what he's saying. 'Yup. Perfect. Full page? Brilliant. OK.' I scribble down the direct line of the journalist he wants to do it, and put the phone down.

'Well, Amanda,' I say. 'You've just got yourself a full page in *Female Fancies*, with photographs and everything.'

'That's fantastic!' she says, almost breathless with excitement. 'Photos! That's brilliant! Will it be a studio shot?'

'We'll sort out the details later,' I say noncommittally, thinking now would not be the time to tell her they want to take pictures of her in a chemist's, furtively slipping a make-up bag into her raincoat.

Amanda is thrilled. 'Libby,' she says, standing up and dusting imaginary dirt from her jacket. 'You are doing the most incredible job. Thank you.' And with that she gives me two air kisses on either side of my face, which throws me somewhat because she's never before offered me anything other than a limp handshake.

'Ciao,' she says, as I wince. 'I'll speak to you later,' and I know she will, because the smaller the star the bigger the pain in the arse they are.

'Libby?' says Jo, as I show Amanda to the door. 'Jules is on the line. It's about the eighth time she's called. D'you want to take it?'

I'm already running back to my desk as she finishes the sentence. 'I'll take it,' I scream, picking up the phone.

'Libby!' shouts Jules. 'I've been dying to speak to you, I can't believe you had a bloody meeting, I can't get any work done, who's Nick and what happened, you had sex didn't you, I know you bloody had sex, how was it, what's he like, tell me everything . . .'

'Calm down,' I laugh, lighting a cigarette and settling back in my chair for a good long chat. 'First of all you can stop planning the wedding because he's definitely not for me. For a start he's got no money. But yes, we did have sex, and fucking hell, Jules, he is gorgeous.'

There's a silence on the other end of the phone. 'Libby, just because he doesn't have money doesn't mean he's not for you. Maybe you should start lowering your expectations.'

'It's not just the money,' I say, feeling slightly guilty. 'It's everything. We're like chalk and cheese.'

'So what happened last night, then?'

And I tell her.

The high-as-a-kite feeling lasts precisely two days. Two days of floating around beaming with love. Sorry, lust. Two days of getting very little done other than daydreaming about the events of my night with Nick. Two days of leaping every time the phone rings.

And then, when he hasn't called, I start to feel sick. Now I know I'm being ridiculous because yes, yes, I know he's not The bloody One, but that doesn't mean I don't want him to want me. I mean, Jesus, he's supposed to be madly in love with me by now, and he's definitely supposed to be phoning me.

I call Jules.

'Jules,' I moan, 'he hasn't called.'

'Stop being so childish,' says Jules. 'Anyway, you know you're seeing him, so of course he'll call, but it will probably be on Saturday, just to confirm the time, as he said he would.'

'OK,' I grumble.

'And,' she continues, 'you don't want him to fall in love with you because that will only make the whole thing far more complicated.'

'OK,' I grumble again.

'So just relax,' she finishes.

'You're right, you're right. I know you're right.'

'Naturally,' she laughs. 'I always am.'

The phone rings at one o'clock on Saturday.

'Hello?' I'm already breathless.

'Hi, babe.' It's Jules.

'Oh,' I say, the disappointment more than clear in my voice. 'Hi.'

'What are you doing now?' she asks, and I decide not to tell her that I'm sitting next to the phone willing it to ring.

'Nothing much. You?'

'Nothing. Jamie's working. Do you want to go shopping?'

Now that sounds more like it. A bit of retail therapy never did anyone any harm. 'Do you want to come and pick me up?' I say.

'No,' she says. 'You come over here and we'll hit Hampstead. How does that sound?'

'Perfect,' I say. 'See you in an hour.'

Once again I sigh with envy as I walk into Jules's flat, because, thanks to being part of a couple, both with nice fat incomes—Jules is an interior designer and Jamie is a barrister—Jules lives in the flat I wish I had. A maisonette in a side road off Haverstock Hill. You walk into a huge, bright, airy living room with maple floors and floaty muslin curtains drifting on either side of French windows that lead to a large balcony. All the furniture is camel and cream, and the canvases on the walls are huge, colourful, abstract and beautiful.

The kitchen's in the basement, and Jules spends most of her time down there. As large as the living room, the kitchen is dominated by a massive scrubbed old French pine table, with enough room left for checked yellow comfy sofas at one end. It's my favourite room in the house, and the one we always end up in, drinking huge mugs of tea at the kitchen table, or curled up on a sofa with the sun streaming in.

'Hi, Libby,' Jamie calls out from his study next to the kitchen.

'Hi, workie,' I call back, the shortened version of workaholic, which is what I've been calling him for years. He appears in the doorway and comes over to kiss me hello, and, even though I know I couldn't stand to be with someone who works all the time, it has to be said that I can see exactly what Jules sees in him because he is, truly, gorgeous.

And before I met Jamie I thought that all barristers were pompous assholes. They were all, from my limited experience, into ballet, opera and theatre. They all spoke like they had a bagful of plums in their mouth and were as patronising as hell.

But Jamie isn't like that. Jamie, when he isn't working, is actually a laugh. And Jamie doesn't wear pompous classically English clothes. Jamie wears faded jeans and caterpillar boots. Jamie smokes like a chimney and drinks like a fish. Jamie, in fact, is cool.

Jamie and I have an odd relationship, in the way that you always have slightly odd relationships with the men your girlfriends subsequently marry. Jules was my friend for years, and then Jamie came along, and yes, we hit it off immediately, but there's always that tiny bit of resentment because they took your best friend away.

But I forgave him. How could I not? And now, we have this lovely, teasing, almost brother-sister relationship, where he sits me down and asks about my love life and then tries to give me advice, which I almost always ignore because at the end of the day he's a bloke. And despite being gorgeously gorgeous, he wasn't exactly Mr Experience before Jules came along and swept him off his feet. He was far too busy building up his career, and yes, he had hundreds of admirers, but never the time to notice them.

Jules was different to all the women setting themselves up to be the perfect barrister's wife. Jules didn't wear designer clothes. Jules didn't go to the hairdresser's once a week. Jules didn't care about going to the best restaurants or the ballet. And, more to the point, Jules never tried to pretend she was anyone different to try to trap her man.

No, Jules has always been one of those women that men go crazy about because she has enough self-confidence to say this is me, take it or leave it. And, invariably, they take it. Or at least try to. They love the fact that she doesn't wear make-up. That her clothes, on her tiny, petite frame, are a mishmash of whatever she happens to pull out of the wardrobe that morning. That her laugh is huge and infectious, and, most of all, that she listens. She loves life, and people, and even before Jamie came along men were forever falling in love with her.

So anyway, Jamie comes out of his study and gives me a huge kiss as I stand by the kettle and then says, 'Tea? Excellent. I need a break. So,' he says, pulling a chair out from the kitchen table, 'how's the love life?'

He always asks me this because he knows I'll have a story to tell, and, if I do say so myself, I tell my stories brilliantly. So, sitting here in the kitchen with Jules and Jamie, I tell them my funny story about Nick, and about him performing a striptease in the living room, and about him sitting in my bath with a shower cap on, and they laugh, and I laugh with them, and Jamie shakes his head and says, 'God, Libby, what would we do without you?' and I don't take offence, I just shrug.

'So where are you two off to today?' he ventures, standing behind Jules and rubbing her shoulders in a gesture that's so affectionate I practically sigh with craving.

'Just up the high street,' she says, as he rolls his eyes to the ceiling.

'Oh, God. I'd better warn the bank manager.'

'No, darling,' she says, 'we're not going for me, we're going for Libby. Except I might see something I like, in which case—'

'I know, I know,' he laughs. 'So, d'you want a lift up there or are you walking?'

Jules looks at me, the disgust already written on her face because she knows exactly how I feel about walking—if God had meant us to walk he wouldn't have invented cars—and I don't have to say anything. She sighs an exasperated sigh and says, 'You're giving us a lift.'

We jump into Jamie's BMW, and he drops us off by the station.

'Jules,' he calls out of the window, just before driving off, 'can you get me some socks?'

She nods and turns to me with a sigh. 'And who said it was glamorous being married to a barrister?'

We go to Whistles, Kookai and agnès b. We mooch round Waterstone's, Our Price and David Wainwright. We ooh and aah for hours in Nicole Farhi, and finally, in a tiny little sports shop tucked away at the top of the high street, I find exactly what I'm looking for.

'You're not seriously buying those,' says Jules in horror, as I stand in front of the mirror with super-trendy Adidas trainers on my feet.

'Why not?' I look innocent as hell, even though I know exactly what she's going to say.

'But they're not you!' she manages in dismay. 'You're Miss Aspiring Prada, Miss Gucci. You're not Miss Adidas.'

'Look,' I say to her slowly and seriously, trying to make her understand, 'I can hardly go to Nick's local pub in my designer togs, can I? These are much more appropriate, and anyway I've wanted a pair for ages. Honest.' So, armed with my wonderful new trainers (and what a bargain, £54.99!), we go for a cappuccino, and as we sit down I pull my mobile phone out of my bag and ring the answering service just in case it rang and I didn't hear it, but no, the recorded voice on the end says, 'You have (pause) no (pause) new messages,' and now I'm starting to get seriously pissed off, but Jules says, 'No. Stop it. He's going to phone,' so I relax a bit, and it's fine.

Over coffee, Jules says, 'Are you sure you're not going to get too involved?'

And I sweep her comment aside with a toss of my hair and laugh in a very grown-up, in-control sort of way and tell her she's being ridiculous.

'What makes you think I can't have a fling?' I say. 'You know, sex with no strings attached?'

'Because you can't,' she says firmly.

'Now that's where you're wrong,' I say. 'I haven't done it for a while, but I've had loads of flings with men when I haven't been emotionally involved. It's just been sex.'

Jules thinks for a minute. 'And when was the last time you did that?'

'Five years ago, but I could have done it loads of times since then.'

'So why haven't you?'

'I just haven't.'

'You don't think that perhaps we change between the ages of twenty-three and twenty-eight or -nine and that what was so easy for us when we're in our early twenties becomes almost impossible when we're nearing thirty, which is why we don't do it any more?'

'What do you mean?'

'The reason women generally stop having flings, or sleeping around, or whatever you want to call it, is because they realise they can't do it, because the older they get the more they see you can't sleep with someone on a regular basis and not want more, not when you've reached an age where society, unfortunately, still tells you that you should be married and having babies.'

'No.' I shake my head. 'I think you're either the sort of person who can or the sort of person who can't, and I'm the sort of person who can.'

Jules doesn't say anything. She just shrugs and changes the subject.

And eventually at five o'clock we wander back down the high street, which I don't mind in the slightest because it's downhill and even my disgustingly unfit body can cope with practically falling down a hill, and I jump in my gorgeous car, Guzzle the Beetle, and drive home, and when I walk in there have been two messages, and, as I press 'play', I'm praying, I'm seriously praying that Nick has phoned.

The first is from my mother. 'Hello, Libby, it's me. Mum.' As if I didn't bloody know.

'Just calling up for a chat,' she says, 'and wondering whether you're coming for tea tomorrow. Call me later if you can, or otherwise in the morning, and if you're going out tonight have a nice time. If not, there's an interesting documentary about magazines at nine o'clock tonight.'

'Oh, shut up,' I shout at the answering machine as she finishes. Anyway, what kind of sad git does she think I am, staying in on a Saturday night? Even if it's only drinking coffee at Jules's kitchen table and watching *Blind Date* it counts as going out because I've left my house, and all I need to tell people is I went to some friends for dinner.

Message number two is a silence. Then the phone's put down. Shit. I pick up and dial 1471.

'Telephone number 0 1 8 1 3 4 0 2 3—' Yes! I don't bother listening to the end of the number because it's a Highgate number, and I don't know anyone else who lives in Highgate! Yes! He rang! And it gives me the burst of energy I need to run the bath so that I'll be ready whenever he calls again.

And to make sure I don't give in to the urge to call him back I jump in the bath, and then, just as I've submerged my head under water, the phone rings and I jump up as if I've had an electric shock and go running into the living room, leaving a trail of sopping wet footprints. I pick it up and, trying to sound calm and collected and sexy as anything, say huskily, 'Hello?'

'Libby?'

'Yes?'

'It's Nick.'

 ## Chapter Four

OH MY GOD, I'm having a serious clothes crisis. The trainers are great, better than great, perfect, but what the hell can I wear with them? I've tried the jeans and T-shirt, and it doesn't look quite right and no, it's not that I'm that excited, but hell, I still want to look nice.

The bed is strewn with clothes, and eventually I settle on a white T-shirt with a babe-type logo emblazoned across the chest, my oldest, most faded, most favourite 501s, and the beloved trainers. I dig out some chunky silver earrings from the bottom of the papier-mâché box I use as a jewellery box and, what the hell, stick on some chunky silver rings as well. Perfect.

I'm meeting Nick at the Flask in Highgate, a pub I vaguely remember from my teenage years, and I know I'm going to be drinking so I leave the car at home and order a minicab, and, just as I'm about to leave, the phone rings.

'Hello, love, it's Mum.'

As if I didn't know.

'What is it, Mum? I'm late and I'm going out.'

'Oh, that's nice. Anywhere special?'

'I've got a date.' Damn, I didn't mean to tell her. Now I'm going to get an onslaught of questions. What car does he drive, where does he live, and, basically, is he good enough for our daughter?

That is the problem with having The Suburban Parents from Hell. Not that I don't love them, I do, it's just that they've got this thing about me marrying way, way above my station, and I try not to tell them anything about my life, except sometimes things have a habit of slipping out. 'Yes, he's very nice,' I sigh, 'but I really have to go.'

'Well,' she stalls. 'You young things. Always rushing around. Dad and I were wondering if you were coming round for tea tomorrow?'

'Oh.' I'd forgotten. 'OK,' I sigh. 'I'll see you about four.'

'All right, darling. What does your date do?'

'Look, Mum, I've got to go. The cab's here.'

'He's not picking you up?' There's horror in her voice.

'No, Mum. I'll see you tomorrow. Bye,' and I gently put the phone down with an exasperated sigh as the doorbell rings announcing the arrival of the minicab.

OK. Got everything? Clean knickers, toothbrush, make-up, moisturiser? Yup. My Prada bag's so full it's practically bursting, and I grab a jacket and run down the stairs.

And the closer we get to Highgate the more nervous I become. At Queen's Park I check my lipstick. At West End Lane I check I'm not shining. At Hampstead I start tapping my feet and trying to ignore the driver staring at me in his rearview mirror.

'You look nice,' he says in a thick Eastern European accent.

'Thank you,' I say, in a tone of voice aimed to discourage him. It works. And then I feel guilty, so when we pull up I give him a two pound tip and then I stand on the pavement for a bit, wondering what it's going to be like, and wondering where he is.

'Libby!' I look up, and there, sitting at a table outside in the large courtyard, is Nick, and as I walk over to him I feel the tension disappear, because, after all, it's only Nick, and he looks gorgeous, and suddenly I'm beaming because everyone turned round to look at him when he shouted, and most of the women are still looking, and hey! He's with me! And then I'm standing in front of him, not sure what to do. Should I kiss him? Should I just say hello? And then he leans forward and kisses me, aiming for my lips, and fool that I am I turn my head out of nervousness, so he just grazes the corner of my mouth, and he looks slightly surprised but then smiles and asks what I'd like to drink.

I can see that he's already halfway through a pint, and vodka and cranberry juice—my usual—would seem completely out of place, so I ask for half a lager and he seems pleased, and then he disappears inside.

'So how has your week been?' he says, as he puts the lager down in front of me. I wonder whether to tell him about Amanda and the pictures she doesn't know she's going to be doing, and I do tell him because it's a good story, and he laughs, and I'm having a good time because Nick's so nice, so easy to be with, so laid-back.

And then Nick tells me about his week. He tells me that once again he did a mailshot, this time to eight publishers, sending them the first three chapters of his masterpiece, and that already he'd had one rejection letter saying interesting concept but 'not for us'.

'Would you ever consider going into another field?' I venture, wondering why he's bothering if he's no good at it.

'Nah.' He shakes his head. 'Well, maybe. If something interesting came along I suppose so, but this has always been my dream.'

'But how do you live? Where do you get money from?'

'Her Majesty's government,' he says proudly, and I blanch.

'You mean you're on the dole?'

'Yup.'

'Oh.' I'm speechless, and as I sit there wondering what to say next I think of how Jules would laugh. From Jon with his Mazda MX-5 to this. Oh dear. What the hell am I doing here?

'I don't mind,' he says, laughing. 'Even though you, apparently, do.'

'It's not that I mind,' I say. 'It's just that it seems a shame to waste your talents.'

'But I'm not wasting them. I'm waiting for them to be recognised.'

'Oh,' I say. 'Well, that's OK, then.'

'So,' he says, after our fourth drink (I got two rounds, I'm not that stingy, particularly given that he's on the dole), 'are you hungry?'

And I realise that I am. Starving.

'There's a really nice pizza place round the corner. I thought we could walk up there and have some dinner.'

'Mmm.' I nod my head vigorously. A little too vigorously, perhaps, because those lagers have gone straight to my head. 'That sounds perfect,' and we get up and start walking, and it's not round the corner, it's practically the other side of bloody London, and after about twenty minutes I say, 'Nick, where is this place?'

'Nearly there,' he says. 'God, you're hopeless.'

'I'm not,' I say, and playfully slap him, and he turns to me and grabs me, saying, 'Don't you slap me, young lady,' and I giggle as he tells me my punishment is to kiss him, and I reach up and give him a quick peck on the lips, and he stands back and smacks his lips.

'Nope,' he says. 'That wasn't enough.'

I give him another kiss, and before I know it it's turned into a huge, delicious, yummy snog, and my stomach turns upside-down.

And it breaks the ice—the little there was left. I don't notice the last twenty minutes of the walk because we're holding hands and stopping every few minutes to kiss each other passionately, and we're giggling like teenagers and I wish this walk could go on for ever.

And we have a tiny cosy table in one corner with a candle in a wax-covered bottle in the centre, and everyone else in there looks exactly like Nick: young, trendy, struggling, but they're all smiling, and I wonder whether perhaps I could get used to this, this world away from the smart, posey bars and restaurants I'm used to.

The waiter comes over to take our order, and he obviously knows Nick and there's much shaking of hands and 'good to see you's, and then Nick tells him what he wants while I sit there thinking, you should have asked me first, and then I think it really doesn't matter, and I say that I'll have a Pizza Fiorentina and a side salad, and Nick orders a bottle of house red.

As soon as the waiter goes, Nick gets a slightly serious look on his face and sighs.

'What's wrong?' I ask.

There's a silence.

'OK,' he says finally. 'Do you think it's time we should have that talk?'

Oh shit. Shit. Shit. Shit. I knew this was too good to be true. This is the time he tells me he doesn't want to see me again.

'Well,' I say hesitantly. 'If there's something on your mind perhaps you'd better get it off your chest.'

'OK,' he nods. And then he sighs. And then he doesn't say anything and I start feeling sick.

'For Christ's sake,' I say, my nervousness giving my voice a loud, sharp edge, 'will you just say it?'

'OK,' he nods. 'The thing is, I'm not ready for a relationship.'

I don't say anything. I don't need to. I've heard it all before.

'But,' and he looks up, 'I really like being with you.'

'So what are you saying?'

'I don't know.' He shakes his head. 'I think what I'm saying is that I need you to know that I'm not ready for commitment. I've been single for a while, and I'm enjoying it and I'm not ready to give that up.'

'So is this it?'

'Well, no,' he says. 'Because I really like you and I want to keep seeing you, but I just don't want you to get the wrong idea.'

'But, I'm not ready for a relationship either,' I say, which is true, and he looks relieved. 'And I know that you're not The One, and I know I'm not The One for you, but that doesn't mean we shouldn't enjoy each other.'

The relief on his face is spreading. I swear, I can practically see his shoulders relax. 'So you're OK with that?' he says.

'Absolutely.' I nod firmly. 'We like being with each other, we have lovely sex, so let's just relax and enjoy it for as long as it lasts.'

'Libby,' he says, reaching over the table to kiss me, 'you're fantastic!'

And I blush and I think to myself, There, that wasn't so bad. And at least it will stop me from falling for him. Not that I would, you understand. It's just that now I definitely won't. There'd be no point.

And we have a lovely dinner. No, that's not actually quite true, because although I can't speak for Nick I know that I hardly noticed the food, I was far too busy kissing him over the table and holding his hand under the table, but it was lovely. The evening was lovely. He was lovely.

And you know the nicest thing about it? The nicest thing was to be with a man on a Saturday night. To pretend that we were a couple. To pretend that I'm as good as the rest of the women in here, that I've got a man too, that I'm not some sad, single, lonely woman out with the girls again on a Saturday night.

You probably think I'm mad. I know Jules thinks I'm mad, because there are advantages to being single. When you're busy and sociable and meeting men and going on dates, it's the best thing in the world and you wouldn't want it any other way. But, when all your single girlfriends suddenly seem to have boyfriends and you're the only one who's on your own, it's as miserable as sin.

But tonight I'm one of them. I belong! And you know what? I love it.

We finish dinner and walk back to Nick's flat, because it's presumed that I'll be staying. What, after all, does 'enjoy each other' mean, if not sex? And Nick leads me up a path to a tall, red-brick Victorian building, and there are slatted blinds on the window at the front. I can just about see through, and it doesn't look horrible, it looks lovely. OK, it's not quite my taste, but it's not the hellhole I expected at all. And I walk through the front door and, as Nick riffles through the envelopes on a table in the hall, I put my bag down by his front door and wait.

Nick looks up and laughs. 'That's not mine,' he says. 'I'm upstairs.'

'Oh,' I say, flushing. And we go upstairs and he unlocks his front door and I walk into his flat, and it's horrible.

Not that it's dirty, at least not on first sight, it's just that it's so messy, and untidy, and uncoordinated. There's an unmade futon at one end, which I presume doubles as a sofa when Nick can be bothered to make it, which he evidently didn't do this morning because the duvet's still crumpled up at the bottom, and there are piles of papers and magazines everywhere. And I mean everywhere. I pick my way across the room, and sit gingerly on an armchair that's obviously seen better days. Far, far better days.

The furniture all looks as if it's falling apart, and shelves have been put up haphazardly everywhere, and there are so many books that they're stacked up instead of neatly lined up, and it's a dump.

A bloody dump.

'Would you like some tea?' Nick says, disappearing into what must be the kitchen, and I get up to follow him in there but he comes back out and says, 'Stay here. The kitchen's a mess. I'll bring it out to you,' and I wonder what the hell the kitchen can be like.

'Sorry it's a mess,' he says, bringing out the tea in two chipped mugs. 'I meant to tidy it today but didn't have time.'

'It's fine,' I say, racking my brain to try to come up with a compliment. 'It's exactly what a writer's flat should look like.'

'You think?' he says, obviously chuffed.

'Definitely.' I nod, and sip my tea.

He comes and sits next to me and starts stroking my back, and I put my tea down and lean into him and after a few minutes forget about the mess, forget about everything except the feeling of his hand on my back, and I turn round to kiss him, and, I suppose, one advantage of this place is that it only takes a second to move to the futon, and I don't even notice the state of the sheets because Nick's pulled my T-shirt up and he's undoing my bra and mmm. This is lovely.

And I unbutton my own jeans, furiously tugging them off, and then I watch as Nick unbuttons his, and I watch, mesmerised, as his cock stands straight out of his boxer shorts, and Nick watches me watching him stroke his cock, and then I lean forward and kiss the tip, and he groans, and I push him back so he's on his knees, and I open my lips and take the tip in my mouth, then the whole of the shaft, and he exhales very quickly.

After a while he whispers for me to stop or he'll come, and he pulls me up and our tongues mesh together with passion, and he strokes my breasts before moving one hand down, and it's my turn to exhale loudly, because his fingers are stroking my clitoris, reaching inside me, and with the other hand he circles my breasts until he reaches the nipples, and he pinches them and I moan and sink back on the bed.

And then all our clothes come off, and I can't take this any more, I insist he puts a condom on and enters me NOW, and he does and it's better, so much better than I remember, and as he moves in and out I suck his neck, and I wonder why it's never felt so good before, and then I stop wondering because suddenly I'm making these incredibly animal-istic sounds as the most intense orgasm of my life sweeps over me.

And afterwards I'm exhausted, and I do something I've never ever done before. I fall asleep in his arms.

'So, Libby dear,' says my mother, pouring the tea out of her best china teapot. 'How was last night?'

You know, it's an extraordinary thing but here I am, twenty-seven, independent, mature, sophisticated, yet the minute I step through my parents' front door I regress to being a surly teenager, and I feel the same exasperation at my parents' questions now as I did ten years ago.

'It was fine,' I say, determined to be nice, not to let them get to me.

'And is he nice?' she says with a smile.

'He's OK.'

'If he's just OK why are you going out with him?' she trills with laugh-ter, and pushes her hair behind her ears—a nervous habit I've unfortu-nately inherited.

'I'm not going out with him,' I grunt. 'We just went out last night.'

God, I think, mentally raising my eyes to the ceiling. What would she say if I told her the truth? If I told her that yes, I went out with someone, and then we went back to his place and shagged each other senseless until we both fell asleep, and then in the morning had tea in bed, then had sex again, and that I came straight here.

'And what does he do?'

'He's a writer.'

'Ooh, a writer. How exciting. What does he write?'

She may be irritating, but I can't tell her the truth. 'He writes, er, he writes articles.'

'What sort of articles?'

'For men's magazines.'

'That's nice. He must be successful. Does your young man have a name?'

'He's not my young man, and yes. His name's Nick.'

'Nick,' she repeats, thinking about it. 'Nicholas. Oh, I do like the name Nicholas. Where does he live?'

'He's got a flat in Highgate.'

'Very posh,' she says, and I think how she'd have heart failure if she saw it. 'Is it a nice flat?'

'Give her a break,' says my dad, putting down the paper. 'It's early days, isn't it, Libby?' and I nod, smiling at him with relief.

'I just worry about you,' says Mum, smoothing down her apron and sitting down. 'When I was your age I was happily married and you were three years old. I don't understand all you girls. So independent.'

'Yup. We're women of the nineties,' I say. 'And anyway I'm not bothered about getting married, I'm far too interested in my career.'

God, if only that were true.

'So how's Olly?' I ask, to change the subject. The only way I know to put her in a truly good mood is to ask about my beloved brother, the apple of her eye.

'Being a rascal as usual,' she says. 'Loving his job, and breaking all the girls' hearts, I shouldn't wonder.'

Much as I hate to admit it, I adore my brother. Twenty-six years old, drop-dead gorgeous, he has me in fits of laughter whenever I see him, which isn't nearly as often as I'd like because he lives in Manchester. He's the kind of person that everyone instantly adores, and, although I sometimes feel I ought to be jealous of that, of his easy-going nature, I'm not, and the only time I get slightly pissed off with him is when he tells me to lay off Mum.

He works for a large TV company as a producer, and hits all the Manchester clubs at the weekend. He's very happy living up there. He doesn't have a serious girlfriend—relationship trouble must run in the family—but he has more than his fair share of flings. I call him every weekend, usually waking him from the depths of yet another killer hangover, and more often than not he has to call me back when the result of last night's session has put her make-up on and gone.

And he's the best person to sort out my love life, other than Jules. He's not as wise as Jules, but he's bloody good at giving the male perspective on things, and I've spent many hours on the phone to him working out strategies for catching the man of my dreams.

'How's his job?' I ask, because I've been a bit too caught up with my own life to call him recently.

'He's got a new programme about food,' she says proudly, puffing out her chest with pride, because television producing is something she knows about, something she understands. At least she should do, the amount of TV she watches. PR, as far as she's concerned, doesn't count. She can't boast about her daughter working in PR because she's never really understood what it's all about, even though I've tried to explain it a million times.

'Food?' I laugh. 'But Olly doesn't know the first thing about food, unless it's about takeaway curries and hamburgers.'

'It's called *The Gourmet Vegetarian*.' Evidently she's decided to ignore my last comment.

'*The Gourmet* what?' Now this I really can't believe. 'But Olly's your classic meat-and-two-veg man.'

'Yes,' she says. 'But you know Olly, he'll be an expert before you know it. I can't think why neither of you has inherited my cooking skills.'

'I can cook!' I practically shout.

'Libby, dear, spag bol is hardly cooking.'

'Excuse me, Mum, but I'm an excellent cook.'

'Are you?' she says, sounding bored. 'So what's your best dish?'

Shit. I try to think of something and nope, the mind's gone blank.

'I can cook anything,' I bluster.

'Yes, dear,' she says, and that's it. I've had enough.

'I've got to go,' I say, standing up and going over to my dad to kiss him goodbye.

'Off so soon?' he says, lowering the newspaper again.

'Yup. You know how it is. Things to do, people to see.'

'But, Libby,' says Mum, 'you've only been here five minutes.'

More like a bloody hour, but whatever it is it's about an hour too long. 'Sorry, Mum. I'll speak to you in the week,' and I dash out before she can start making me feel guilty.

I get in the minicab I called earlier and switch my mobile on immediately. Damn. No messages. But what was I expecting? That Nick would call and say he was missing me? Hardly. But then it starts to ring and Jules's number appears on the little screen and I pick up the phone.

'Where've you been?' she moans. 'Your mobile's been off.'

'Sorry,' I say, settling back into the car seat and lighting a fag before I look up and see my mum twitching at the curtains. 'Shit. Hold on.' I haven't even told the driver where we're going. 'Ladbroke Grove,' I say to him, and I wave at my mum before putting the phone back to my ear.

'So how was it?' Jules says.

'Amazing,' I say. 'It was so nice, he's so nice.'

'And did you stay at his?'

'Yup. And we had fantastic sex again.' I drop my voice to a whisper so the driver can't hear.

'And is his flat as disgusting as you thought?'

'Oh God, Jules,' I groan. 'Worse. Much worse. It's a good job this is just a fling because I couldn't live like that. I don't know how he does.'

'Was it dirty?'

'No, but it was just grotty.'

'OK. The real test is the bathroom. Doesn't matter what the rest of the flat's like as long as they've got a decent bathroom.'

Hmm. Interesting. 'Actually, the bathroom was fine. Sparkling clean, in fact. And he lied about not having a bath!'

'Thank God. I don't care if a man lives in a pit as long as he's clean.'

'He's clean,' I say, remembering his lovely, clean, masculine smell.

'You're not in love, then?'

'God no! We ended up having a chat about things last night.' I relay the conversation, word for word, touch for touch, to Jules, who listens carefully and then says, 'You're sure you can handle it?'

'Of course! Jules, listen, after that talk we both know exactly where we stand and it's fine.'

'As long as you don't get hurt.'

'Shut up, Jules, you know I hate that expression.'

And it's true. I do. Why lock yourself away in an attic and never go out because you're frightened of getting hurt? Bollocks. As far as I'm concerned you have to give every relationship your all because if you're going to get hurt, you're going to get hurt, but at least at the end of it you'll know you gave it your best shot.

Although I'm not planning to give this relationship, or fling, or whatever this is, my all, at least not when we're out of the bedroom. No, this feels good. Healthy. I'm in control, and that's something I have very little experience of. Hell, I haven't even thought of Nick since I left him. OK, not as much as I've thought about boyfriends in the past, then.

You probably think I'm lying, but it's true, because in the past I've thought about new boyfriends every second of every day. Well, almost. This is what I've never understood about men. No matter how crazy they are about you, they can get on with their lives, their work, their friends, and not give you a second thought. When they do think of you, which is generally when they're not thinking of anything else, they'll pick up the phone and call you, completely oblivious to the fact that you've been sitting there crying for a week because they haven't called.

To be honest I find the whole process completely exhausting, and that's why, sitting in the car on the phone to Jules, I decide that I'm not going to do it this time. In fact, I'm fed up with talking about him, remembering him, analysing him.

'Jules, I've got to go,' I say. 'I'm in a minicab and I really can't talk.'

'OK. I'll call you later.'

And when I get home I jump in the bath and, as I lie there, soaking in lavender bubbles, I remind myself that I'm not going to think about Nick, but then I think, a few thoughts wouldn't hurt, so I decide to allow myself three minutes and that's it, at least for today.

So once his three minutes are up I pick up a book and start reading, and every time Nick threatens to creep back into my head (which is about once every two pages) I push him out again until I'm so immersed in the book I genuinely don't think about him, and when Jules calls me later I'm in the middle of a good Sunday night film which, I think you'll agree, is a perfectly valid reason not to talk to your best friend given that TV's normally shit on a Sunday night, and by the time I climb into bed I'm so tired I haven't got the energy to think about Nick even if I wanted to. Which I don't. Just in case you're wondering.

 ## Chapter Five

SAL CALLS THE NEXT DAY about the Sean Moore interview, and, because I'm still basking in that old postcoital glow and feeling more than a little magnanimous, I try Amanda Baker out on her.

'Amanda who?' she says, and I groan.

'You know, Sal,' I say. 'The showbiz reporter on *Breakfast Break*.'

'As if I'm ever up early enough to watch *Breakfast Break*.'

'Well, I suppose you wouldn't be interested in doing a feature on her, then?'

'Libby, you know I can't write about someone nobody knows.'

'Yeah,' I sigh. 'I know. Anyway, how's the big love of your life?'

And sure enough, her voice goes all dreamy. 'He's wonderful,' she says. 'Really, Libby, this is completely different to all of the others.'

'Which others?' I say, because truth to be told I've never heard Sal really talk about men before.

'Just all of them. What are you doing after work?' she says, and I can tell from her voice that she's desperate to talk about Paul, and, even though I know I'll be bored, you never know, I might find something out about Nick, and I don't really have any plans unless you count watching *Brookside*.

We arrange to meet at the Paradise Bar at 7.00pm.

And I get a hell of a lot of work done that afternoon. I sit there phone-bashing, and I manage to persuade two journalists to write about Rita Roberts, as well as organising the launch for Sean Moore's series. All in all, a good day's work, and the best thing about it is I hardly think about Nick at all, except to congratulate myself that I've hardly thought about him at all, if you know what I mean.

And I'm looking forward to seeing Sal. She may not be someone I see that much, but I always have a good time when I'm with her. And I'm really happy that she's found Paul. I've always thought that she would make a perfect wife and mother, because, even though she's only a year older than me, there's something incredibly warm and maternal about her, and I've never understood why she's been single for so long.

She's there when I arrive at the Paradise, sitting at a corner table at one side of the bar, and she gives me a huge hug and kiss on the cheek when I walk over.

'I'm starving,' she says. 'Shall we reserve a table in the restaurant?'

'Fine,' I say, 'I'll do it,' because I'm already standing up, and as I walk off she calls me back.

'Ask for a table for three,' she says. 'Nick's joining us later, is that OK?'

'Oh,' I say, slightly flummoxed, because I don't know whether Sal knows about us, and why didn't he call me, and how should I act when he arrives, but fuck it, Nick's coming!

I get a drink on the way back to the table and sit down, and Sal starts telling me all about Paul.

'He's just so thoughtful,' she says. 'He keeps buying me these little presents,' and she holds out her arm to show off a beautiful silver charm bracelet. I make the appropriate oohing and aahing noises, and though I'm listening to her, I'm suddenly desperate to talk about Nick, to tell her about him, but somehow I don't quite know how to do it.

'So do you think he's The One?' I say, which is a question I always ask my girlfriends when they start going out with someone, not so much because I want to know the answer, but more because I want to know how they know, and whether I'll know too.

'I really think he might be,' Sal says. 'And I've never felt that about anyone before.'

'Really?' This is so alien to my own experience, I'm fascinated. 'You've never thought that you'd marry someone before?'

'God, no!' she laughs. 'And if you'd met them you'd see why. Nah, even the short relationships I've had were with self-obsessed assholes. That's the difference, I've never been treated well before, and before I met Paul I didn't even know what that could be like. I think the reason this is so different is because we were friends for so long, and I never even thought about Paul as anything other than as a good mate.'

'So how did it happen?'

'I hadn't seen him for a while, and then he phoned me for a contact for a story he was doing, and we arranged to meet up for a drink. I hardly bothered making an effort, I mean it was Paul, for heaven's sake, and then, when we met, we had the most brilliant evening and suddenly at the end there was all this weird chemistry which blew my mind a bit.'

'Did you sleep with him?'

Sal starts laughing. 'You're joking! I didn't even kiss him, even though I wanted to, and I could tell he wanted to as well, but I found the whole thing really confusing.'

'So what happened then?'

'He called me the next day to thank me for a really lovely evening. Then he asked me out again, and that night something did happen, and that was that, really.

'And the weirdest thing of all is that it feels so right. I suppose it's true what they say, you never know it's right until it is, although I'm really scared of saying that out loud just in case he turns out to be a bastard, but somehow I don't think he will.

'And you know what?' she continues, as I shake my head. 'I've never had anyone who looks after me before. I've always been the one cooking and cleaning for them, whereas Paul's the one who wants to do every-thing for me.'

'And do you love it?' I say, and grin wickedly.

Sal grins back. 'I love it. Anyway, enough about me. What about you? Who's the latest in your fantastically tempestuous love life?'

'Well, actually . . .' I'm just about to tell her, when the door opens and Nick walks in. Sal sees me looking over her shoulder and turns round.

'Nick!' She stands up and waves, and he comes over to join us.

'My favourite redhead,' he says, giving her a big hug as I sit there feel-ing incredibly awkward and wondering what the hell I should say. And then he looks at me and grins and says, 'My favourite brunette,' and he puts his arms round me and gives me a hug too, and then he goes off to the bar to get a fresh round.

'You don't mind me asking Nick, do you?' Sal whispers once he's gone. 'It's just that we were on the phone this morning and when I told him I was seeing you he asked if he could join us.'

I feel like jumping in the air with joy.

'That's fine,' I say. 'No problem.'

'It's really weird,' she whispers. 'I used to fancy him so much, but I don't even think he's good-looking any more. I must be in love.'

'Yup,' I say, because I can't think of anything else to say and thank God Nick chooses that moment to pull up a chair and sit down.

'So,' says Sal. 'We were just talking about Libby's love life.'

'Oh, yes?' says Nick, visibly perking up. 'What were you saying?'

'She was just going to fill me in on her latest man, and before you say anything, Libby, I know you've got one, it's written all over your face. Yup, you're in love.'

Oh fuck. I can't help it. I feel a bright red, hot flush spread up from my neck until my cheeks are flaming red.

'Now I know you're in love,' she laughs, as I think, shut the fuck up.

'Now this,' grins Nick, 'I've got to hear.'

'I'm not in love,' I say forcefully. 'Definitely not.'

'Go on,' says Nick, shoving me gently and playing completely dumb. 'Tell us. You know you want to.'

'Nick's brilliant at sorting out people's love lives, aren't you, Nick?' says Sal, who, at this precise moment in time, only seems to be opening her mouth to shove her foot further in.

'Sal, I haven't got anything to talk about.'

'I don't believe you,' says Nick, as I kick him under the table.

'Ouch,' says Sal. 'What was that for?'

'Oh God, sorry,' I say, as Nick rocks back in his chair and starts roaring with laughter.

'What is going on?' Sal's now looking confused.

'Classic,' groans Nick. 'OK. Sorry. It's just that Libby and I . . .' He tilts his head and raises his eyebrows.

'Oh my God,' she says, starting to laugh. 'Why didn't you say something?'

'I didn't know how to,' I say, but in truth I didn't really want to.

'So you really did get on the other night?' she says with a smile.

'Very well,' drawls Nick, putting his arm round me and giving me a smacker on the cheek.

'Oh no. Don't start getting all lovey-dovey on me.'

'Sorry,' says Nick, drawing away. 'I just can't seem to keep my hands off her.'

I sit there and smile. And smile. And smile.

The waitress comes over to tell us there's a table waiting for us in the restaurant, so the three of us get up and walk in.

And we turn out to have a really nice evening. I like being with Nick and Sal. I like this feeling of Nick getting on with my friends, even though Sal is as much his friend as mine, possibly even more so. And more than that I like the fact that he spends most of the evening holding my hand under the table, and that he's making me feel like the most special woman in here.

And at the end of the evening, when we've finished our coffees and Sal starts yawning, we get the bill and leave, and I don't bother saying anything to Nick about him staying the night because both of us know he's going to.

We say goodbye to Sal and go back to my flat, and when I walk in there's a slight moment of awkwardness when Nick notices the flashing red light on my answer phone indicating four messages.

I could listen to them now, but I don't, and before you get the wrong idea it's not because there may be other men who are calling me, it's because of Jules. She's probably left a message saying, 'Where are you? I hope you're not out shagging,' or 'How's the big love of your life going?' and I would die, just die, if Nick heard that.

'You've got messages,' he says, sitting down.

'Yeah,' I say nonchalantly. 'Probably my mum or Jules. Anyway, whoever it is it's too late to call them. I'll listen to them tomorrow.'

He jumps up and starts kissing my neck. 'Not calls from tall, dark, handsome strangers, I hope?'

'As if!' I laugh, and then I get quite serious. 'Nick,' I say, and he can tell from the tone of my voice that I have something to say, so he pulls back and says, 'Uh-oh, have I been a naughty boy? What have I done?'

'No,' I laugh. 'It's just that I want you to know that while I'm sleeping with you I wouldn't sleep with anyone else.'

He nods seriously, taking it in. 'I accept that,' he says, 'and I feel the same way. I know this isn't serious between us, but I agree that as long as we're sleeping together we won't be sleeping with anyone else. And the only thing I'd add to that is that if either of us is tempted, or meets someone else, we'll talk about it, be honest with each other.'

'Perfect,' I say, as I kiss him, but even as I say the word I'm hoping that he doesn't ever tell me that, that if anyone meets someone else, or is, as he put it, 'tempted', it's me. I don't think that's too much to ask.

How can I turn down Jules's invitation to a dinner party, when Nick's sitting next to me in my flat, and can hear every word? It's not that I don't want to go, it's that I'm really not sure how Nick will fit in with my friends, not after meeting his the other night. But he's grinning like an idiot and nodding, so I say we'll come.

It has to be said that my friends would be a damn sight more welcoming than his were. Jesus, I felt like I'd been put through the mill, and I didn't come out well, which was hardly my fault.

It was, to put it nicely, a bloody nightmare. I thought it was going to be just Nick and me, and then, when we met, he said he'd arranged to meet some friends of his and did I mind, and I lied and said that no, it was fine. And anyway part of me was curious about his friends, because apart from Sal, I didn't know who they were, or what they were like.

We joined them in a pub (surprise, surbloodyprise), and from the minute we turned up I knew that this wasn't going to be my sort of evening. You don't know what I'm talking about? OK. I don't like pubs, I think I already told you that, but I especially hate the old-fashioned variety. Dark, dingy, smoky places with bottle-blonde barmaids and dodgy customers doing deals at the bar. And this was that sort of pub, and through the haze of smoke I could see a group of people at one end—all of them stopped talking when we walked in, and they waved to Nick before giving me the once-over.

One look at me, one look at them, and you could see, instantly, we weren't going to get on. All the people crowded round the tiny table in the pub looked like overgrown students. Big time. As far as I was concerned, I'd dressed down for the occasion, in my uniform of trainers, jeans and sloppy jumper. And OK, so the jumper did come from Nicole Farhi, but so what? That's casual for me. Not one of the women was wearing make-up, and even though I wasn't wearing much—well, maybe a bit, but applied so it looked as if I was hardly wearing any—I could see them linger on my lipstick, and I felt like running and hiding.

Oh Christ, I thought, I know I'm going to hate them, but I decided I was going to be charming and polite and make them like me, because, after all, they're Nick's friends, and I had to make an effort.

'This is Joanna,' said Nick, as a dirty blonde scowled at me.

'How do you do,' I said, holding out my arm to shake her hand. She looked at her neighbour in amazement, and hesitated with a smirk on her face before finally putting an incredibly limp hand in mine and sort of moving it vaguely, then pulling away.

'This is Pete,' and I did the same thing, except Pete didn't bother taking my hand, he just looked up from his pint and said, 'Awright?'

'Yes, thank you,' I said. 'How are you?'

He didn't say anything. Just smirked.

'Rog, Sam, Chris, Moose.'

'I'm sorry?'

'That's my name,' said Moose. 'Awright?'

Nick went off to the bar to get a fresh round of drinks, and I noticed, with more than a hint of distaste, that all the women were drinking pints, but that didn't mean I had to. No way.

So I stood there awkwardly, waiting for one of the men to offer me a stool, but no one did, they just carried on talking about Tony Blair and

'New Labour bastards', and I stood like an idiot, wishing I were anywhere else but here.

And eventually I went to the table next to them and took a stool, and perched next to Joanna and tried to be friendly.

'I love your jumper,' I lied. 'Where did you get it?'

'Camden Lock,' she said, before turning away in disgust.

'So you're Libby,' said Rog, as I breathed a sigh of relief that someone was actually going to talk to me. 'We've 'eard a lot about you.'

'Oh,' I said, smiling politely. 'Nice things, I hope?'

He shrugged.

'What do you do, Rog?' I ventured, fitting his name in the sentence because I read somewhere that it always makes people warm to you.

He looked at me for a few seconds, then shrugged. 'Nothing.'

'Oh.' I didn't quite know what to say next. 'Well,' I carried on, 'what would you like to do?'

He shrugged again. 'Nothing.'

'You're a bloody liar,' said Joanna, turning to me. 'He's an artist.'

'Really?' I said. 'What do you paint?'

'Abstract.'

Jesus, this is a losing battle.

'You work in PR, don't you?' said Chris, not the male variety, the female variety.

I nodded gratefully.

'Don't you think it's a complete waste of time?' she asked aggressively. 'I mean, you're just pandering to these stupid fucking celebrities.'

'Actually, I quite enjoy it,' I bristled. 'Why, what do you do?'

'I work for Greenpeace,' she said. 'I couldn't stand a job like yours. At least with mine I know I'm making a difference to the world.'

'Why, have you been out rescuing whales?' I asked innocently.

She huffed. 'Not personally, but I have organised it.'

There was a silence as everyone looked into their drinks, but I'm sure I saw Chris look at Pete and raise her eyebrows, and I sat there miserably knowing that that look was about me.

'Do you live locally?' said Joanna, the only one in the crowd who seemed to be OK.

I shook my head. 'I live in Ladbroke Grove.'

'Really?' she said. 'I've got friends there. They've got this fantastic housing association flat, huge. Do you rent or what?'

'No, I bought it,' I said proudly.

'Oh,' she said. 'You must be loaded.' The others all looked at me, waiting to hear what I was going to say.

'Hardly,' I tried to laugh. 'I saved for ages for the down payment. And I try to be careful with money.'

'I wish I had enough money to be careful with,' she said.

'Do you work?'

'Nah.' She shook her head. 'I'm on the dole.'

And I was stuck, because I wasn't going to make the same mistake of asking what she would be doing if she wasn't on the dole.

'So,' said Moose finally. 'We were talking about New Labour. What do you reckon about them?'

'I think they're all a bunch of untrustworthy bastards,' I said firmly.

'Do you?' said Moose. 'Even Blair?'

Oh shit. What do I say now? I think Tony Blair's pretty damn nice, but somehow I suspected that wasn't the thing to say.

'Especially Blair,' I said, and thank God, they started nodding, and I felt like I'd passed some sort of test.

Nick came back, put his arm round me and whispered, 'Sorry, I had to wait for ages at the bar. Are you OK?'

I nodded because I wasn't going to say that I found his friends disgusting, that they were rude and nasty, was I? So Nick thought I was OK, but I didn't say another word all night, which was really all right, because everyone ignored me anyway. Nick kept trying to bring me into the conversation, but it was too political for me anyway, so I sat there wondering what the fuck I was doing there.

Eventually, at around ten o'clock, I couldn't stand it any more.

'Nick,' I whispered. 'I've got a bit of a headache. Do you mind if we go?' Nick looked at me in surprise, because he'd been taking centre stage and was obviously having a great time.

'Sure,' he said. 'Why didn't you say something before?'

'I thought it might go away,' I lied. I stood up. 'Nice to meet you all,' I lied again. When we were outside I breathed a huge sigh of relief.

'You hated them, didn't you?' said Nick.

'I'm really sorry,' I said. 'I'm sure they're really nice people, but they weren't exactly friendly to me, and I didn't feel comfortable at all.'

'God, I'm sorry, Libby,' he said, and put his arms round me. 'I'm so stupid. I just kind of assume that everyone I like will get on.'

'Don't worry.' I snuggled into his shoulder as we walked off down the road. 'Can we stay at mine tonight?'

Nick nodded, and I didn't feel the need to explain that after feeling so bloody insecure all evening I needed to be at home, surrounded by my things, feeling safe and comfortable and secure.

And that's when Jules phones and asks me over for dinner next week.

'And do you want to bring the infamous Nick?' she adds.

Oh God. Nick with a bunch of barristers would be as awkward as me with a bunch of hard-line socialists. I'm about to say no, but Nick starts nodding vigorously because he can hear every word Jules is saying.

'He's sitting next to me,' I warn. 'And he's nodding, so I guess that's a yes.'

'Wednesday night, eight thirty, casual.'

So here I am, in my bedroom, on the evening of Jules's party, and I've arranged to pick Nick up at the tube station, and there are clothes everywhere, and, bearing in mind I've completely changed my look since meeting Nick, I don't know what goes with what any more.

I want to look smart, cool and trendy, and finally I think I've got it. A camel-coloured print dress, hip-hugging, almost see-through, with very high Prada strappy sandals, and I'm not sure about the shoes, they might be a bit over the top, but they make me feel beautiful and the one thing I need tonight more than anything else is a shot of confidence, because I'm nervous as shit of him meeting my friends.

I put my make-up on carefully, only a tiny bit, just to accentuate my eyes and lips, and when I'm ready I stand back, and I know it sounds big-headed, but God, I look amazing. I'd forgotten I could look like this.

I climb into the car to go and pick up Nick.

And bless him, he's made an effort. He's not wearing his usual jeans and trainers, he's wearing chinos and brown lace-up shoes and a soft blue shirt that completely brings out the colour of his eyes, and he looks gorgeous, and God, what a difference clothes can make, because I suddenly fancy him more than ever before.

'You look amazing,' I say, as soon as he gets in. 'Where are all these clothes from?'

'My mother bought me them last year, but I never wear them.'

'I know,' I laugh. 'But Nick you look gorgeous.'

He also looks very uncomfortable. Jesus, I would marry Nick if he looked like this all the time. Well, no, I probably wouldn't. Don't get too excited, it's just a figure of speech.

And then he looks at me, and does a very slow and very sexy wolf whistle. 'Christ,' he says, taking in the outfit. 'You look unbelievable.'

'Unbelievable good or unbelievable bad?'

'Unbelievable sexy,' he says, shaking his head in disbelief, as my head threatens to swell so much it won't fit in the car. 'Why don't we not go, and I'll take you home and ravish you instead.'

And I laugh, but as I look at him I see he half means it.

'You're nervous!' I'm amazed.

'No, I'm not,' he says, and then he pauses. 'OK. Maybe a bit.'

'Why?'

'It's the first time I'll be meeting your friends, and Jules is your best friend, and I want to make a good impression.'

'You are so sweet.'

'Don't say I'm sweet,' he growls. 'I hate that.'

'Sorry,' I say, and reach over and give him a kiss. 'But you are.'

 ## Chapter Six

'I THOUGHT YOU SAID you were having people over for dinner,' I say, pulling Jules aside and whispering to her furiously. 'You didn't tell me you were having a bloody party.'

'You know how it is,' she laughs. 'It was meant to be six of us, and then we invited a couple more, and then someone else phoned and asked if they could bring someone, so before we knew it there were sixteen people. Anyway, what's the problem?'

'Nothing,' I mutter, and there isn't really a problem, but somehow I thought it would be easier to introduce Nick at a dinner party, more intimate, but I suppose, thinking about it, perhaps this is better.

'So where is he?' she says, looking around the room.

'Nick!' I call out to where Nick's already chatting to Jamie. 'Come and meet Jules.'

Jamie's smiling, so I assume whatever it is they were talking about went well, and he comes over with Nick to kiss me hello.

'Jules, Nick. Nick, Jules.' Nick holds his hand out very formally, and I have to stifle a laugh because this is not Nick's way at all, but Jules being Jules just laughs and gives him a kiss on the cheek. 'Welcome to our party,' she says. 'It's so nice to finally meet you.'

'And you,' says Nick, relaxing. 'I've heard so much about you.'

'Not half as much,' she says, winking at me, 'as I've heard about you.'

'Libby says you're a writer,' says Jamie.

Nick nods. 'But it doesn't seem to be getting me anywhere. Unfortunately.'

'It's got to be a novel, then.'

'Yup.'

'I've always wanted to write a novel,' says Jamie. 'I find it amazing that you have the discipline to sit down and write every day.'

'I know, everyone does, but it's getting to the stage where I might have to start looking for other work. TV work, scriptwriting, something like that. Because I just don't know how much longer I can keep sending out letters only to be rejected.'

'You ought to meet Charles,' says Jules, turning to Jamie. 'Isn't he a drama producer for one of the TV companies?'

Jamie nods. 'He's the boyfriend of a friend of ours, Mara. They should be here soon, so I'll introduce you.'

'So who else is coming?' I ask.

Jules reels off a list of names, then says,'Oh, and there's a surprise for you.'

'For me?' I love surprises, even though I pretend to hate them.

'Yup.' She checks her watch. 'In fact,' she says, going to the door to answer the doorbell that's just rung, 'this could be it. Come with me.' I follow her out of the room, and the minute we're in the hallway she grabs me and whispers, 'He's gorgeous! So handsome! And sweet!'

'I know,' I whisper back, as the doorbell rings again.

'All right,' she grumbles, running down to the front door. 'Coming!'

It's Ginny and Richard, a couple I've met before who seem very nice, but he's a bit intimidating in that barrister, legal-ish sort of way.

I stand back as they kiss Jules hello, then Richard gives me a big smile and reaches down to kiss the air on either side of my cheek. 'Libby!' he exclaims. 'How lovely to see you again!'

Ginny does the same thing, then all four of us move into the living room, as Jamie says hello, then goes off to get drinks.

'Nick!' says Richard. 'I don't believe it!' and I stand open-mouthed as Richard gives Nick a manly hug and clasps his hand in both of his. 'What on earth are you doing here?'

'I'm here with Libby,' says Nick.

'I don't believe it.' Richard turns to me. 'I haven't seen Nick in years. We were at school together.'

At school together? But I thought Richard went to . . .

'Didn't you go to Stowe?' I look at Richard, bemused.

'Most certainly did,' he nods. 'Both of us.'

'What a small world,' says Jules, obviously delighted that her guests are getting on so well, and then the doorbell rings again.

More couples file in, some I know, but all well-spoken, well-dressed, and very much at home standing around making small talk.

And there I was worrying about Nick, I think, watching him and Richard roar with laughter as they reminisce about school.

And I'm so impressed that Nick went to Stowe I completely forget about my surprise, and then the doorbell rings, and a familiar face appears in the doorway, and I'm so excited I practically spill my drink, and Jules grins as I shriek, 'Olly!' and my darling brother rushes in and scoops me up in his arms, giving me a massive hug.

'I wanted to surprise you,' he says, and I'm so happy he's here.

'What are you doing here?' I say, breathless with excitement.

'For God's sake, don't tell Mum,' he says. 'She'd kill me if she knew I was down and wasn't staying there.'

'Where are you staying? Will you stay with me?'

'No,' he shakes his head. 'I'm staying with Carolyn,' and then I notice the tall, tanned girl standing in the doorway.

'Carolyn.' He beckons her over. 'This is my sister, Libby.'

I shake her hand and approve immediately of her warm smile, the fact that she's so naturally pretty without make-up, her adoring look at Olly, which tells me that she is definitely not just a good friend.

'I'm so pleased to meet you,' she says. 'Olly talks about you all the time.'

I look at Olly and, without Carolyn noticing, I give him an almost imperceptible nod that tells him I approve, and he grins at me.

'Oh God,' I say. 'Where's Nick?' I look around, but he's disappeared.

'Nick?' says Olly. 'Who's Nick, then? Your latest squeeze?'

And then I see Nick walk in from the kitchen and I call him over to introduce him and it turns out—another amazing fact I didn't know—that Nick's as big a Man United fan as Olly, and within minutes the pair of them are talking animatedly as if they've known each other for years.

Jules introduces Carolyn to Ginny, and then sweeps me into the kitchen to help her get the food ready.

'Everyone seems to be getting on, don't they?' she says, and I know that she is always nervous before bringing together new people, but that she's such a good hostess her evenings always turn out fine.

'I can't believe how Nick's fitting in.'

'Why ever not?' says Jules, opening the oven and pulling out something that smells delicious.

'God, Jules, if you'd have met his friends the other night, you would have known why not. His crowd is so completely different to ours.'

'But he's fitting in perfectly,' she says. 'I don't know why you keep saying there's no future in it. I think you're perfect together.'

'But that's just your first impression, Jules. You don't know him.'

'So what do I need to know? He's handsome, obviously bright, and you seem to get on really well. What's the problem?'

How can I explain what the problem is? How can I tell her that I couldn't marry Nick because how would we live? I'd never be able to give up work, and our children would have to go to the local comprehensive, where they'd probably get in with the wrong crowd and end up taking drugs. How can I tell her that my idea of hell would be to end up a harassed mother who had to try and be the breadwinner as well as bringing up the kids? That I'd have to say goodbye to the designer restaurants and bars I love so much, and on the rare occasions we went out for dinner it would have to be somewhere cheap and cheerful.

Actually, a lot of it doesn't sound so bad, but I know I'm talking myself into believing it's not so bad because I'm growing to like Nick more and more, and I'm trying to change my lifestyle to fit into his.

In fact, I haven't even been to a designer restaurant or bar since before I met Nick, and OK, I don't miss them that much, but I wouldn't want to spend the rest of my life knowing that I couldn't go to them because I couldn't afford it.

'It's too long to go into,' I say. 'But I'm telling you, it's just a fling.'

'Bullshit.' She turns to look at me. 'You may be able to get away with telling other people that you don't care about him, that it's just sex, but not me. Look at you, for God's sake. You're crazy about him.'

'What makes you say that?'

She sighs. 'It's the way you look at him, the way your face lights up every time he says something, the way you hang on his every word. Don't worry,' she says, seeing the dismay on my face. 'I don't think he knows, but I do.'

'So what do you think he thinks of me?'

She shrugs. 'It's much harder to tell with men, but my guess is he probably feels the same way. The only thing that worries me is that he did say at the beginning that he wasn't looking for a relationship, and I just think you have to remember that, because you've definitely fallen for him. He may well have fallen for you too, but, if the timing's wrong, then you might get hurt.'

Jules can see that what she's said has upset me, and her voice softens as she says, 'Look, Libby, I think he probably does feel the same way about you, but you have to be aware that when men say they're not ready for a relationship, nine times out of ten it means that they're not ready for a relationship.

'But,' she adds, almost to herself, 'there are always women who can change their minds, I suppose.'

That's what I needed to hear, and as soon as she says the words I make a decision. I'm going to be the woman who changes his mind. Except I don't share this with Jules, it's going to be my own little secret.

Jules sighs as the phone starts to ring. 'Who the hell is calling us now?' she says, running to pick up the phone.

'Hello? Hello?' There's a pause. 'Hello? Is anyone there?' She puts the phone down and turns to me, annoyed. 'That's the fourth bloody time that's happened this week.'

Jamie comes rushing into the kitchen, looking startled. 'Who was that?' he asks breathlessly.

'God knows,' she says. 'I told you someone keeps ringing and putting it down when I pick up.'

'Oh,' says Jamie, as Jules picks up some bowls and leaves the room, and if I didn't know better I could swear he turns a whiter shade of pale. But no. I must be imagining it.

I bring the rest of the food into the living room and carefully put it down on a table at one end of the room.

'Mmm, this looks delicious,' says Ginny, as Jules laughs.

'This?' she says. 'It was nothing,' and I know for Jules it probably was nothing, but to anyone who didn't know it looks like a bacchanalian feast: mounds of chicken in a curried cream sauce; a huge, whole salmon, decorated with the thinnest slices of cucumber I've ever seen; piles of couscous surrounded by ratatouille; warm potato salad sprinkled with parsley and chives; and bowls of mixed leaf salads.

We all grab plates and tuck in, and then small groups of people seem to gather together, friends naturally gravitating towards friends.

I sit down with Nick, Olly, Carolyn and Jamie. 'So what's all this about the gourmet vegetarian?' I say to Olly.

Carolyn laughs. 'Ridiculous, isn't it?' she says. 'Olly can't cook to save his life and here he is, producing a show about food.'

'Thanks, girls,' says Olly, in mock disgust. 'But actually I can cook.'

'Bollocks!' I say.

'I can, Libby. Tell them what I made you the other night.' He looks at Carolyn.

'He made me Chinese,' she says, trying to suppress a smile.

'Really?' Now I'm impressed. 'How on earth did you do that?'

Carolyn answers for him, which instantly makes me realise that perhaps she's not as transient as all of the other women I've heard about, that perhaps this is serious.

'I chopped the vegetables,' she says, winking at me, 'and Olly opened the packet of oyster sauce.'

'Ah,' says Nick. 'That's exactly how I like to do my cooking.'

'Yeah,' agrees Olly. 'It's a guy thing.'

'You've never cooked for me,' says Nick. 'Can you cook?'

''Course I can cook,' I exclaim. 'I'll make you dinner next week.'

'Damn,' says Olly. 'I needed a laugh. What a shame I'll be back in Manchester.'

I hit him.

'So how long's this been going on?' Olly gestures at Nick and me.

Three months, three weeks and two days, is what I could say, but I'm not supposed to be counting, so I just wait to hear what Nick says.

'A couple of months now?' He looks at me, and I nod.

'Serious, then?' laughs Olly, and Nick blanches slightly.

'Bit of a record for you,' continues Olly, missing the look on Nick's face.

I stand up. 'Time for seconds. Anyone coming?'

We kiss everyone goodbye, and finally I have Nick to myself.

And as we walk home Nick turns to me and says, 'They were so nice! I had such a nice time!'

'Well, what did you expect from friends of mine?'

'They're just so different from the kind of people I mix with. But even though they're all obviously successful, they're really down-to-earth.'

'Success doesn't mean you have to be pompous,' I say.

Nick walks along in silence for a while, and I can tell he's thinking about something. Eventually he says, 'It's just sort of made me think about my life, about what I'm doing with it, about what I could be doing with it. Particularly bumping into Richard after all these years.'

I walk next to him wondering whether just to listen or to give practical advice. I mean, I've bloody read *Men are from Mars, Women are from Venus*, but this is the bit I always get confused about. I can't remember what I'm supposed to do, so I don't say anything at all, because I don't want to alienate him by doing the wrong thing.

'I don't know,' he sighs. 'I feel a bit confused at the moment.'

'Do you want to talk about it?' I say.

'I don't really know what there is to talk about,' he says, and after that he's very quiet. He's quiet all the way home, he's quiet when I make him a coffee, and we get into bed and cuddle before falling asleep. Or maybe I should say, before he falls asleep. Part of me thinks this is good, this is a progression, that it's not only about sex any more, but the other part thinks, why doesn't he want to have sex with me, and I can't help it, I've got this horrible suspicion that he might be going off me.

 # Chapter Seven

THE NEXT MORNING Nick was lovely. OK, we didn't have sex again, but hey, it was a late night, and I know I'm being ridiculous, and insecure, and probably slightly paranoid. So it doesn't bother me that Nick doesn't call me all morning because why would he? He's busy getting on with his life, and I'm busy getting on with mine.

At lunchtime Jo the receptionist buzzes me and asks what I'm doing.

'Nothing,' I reply, looking with distaste at the smoked salmon bagel on my desk that I don't really have the stomach for.

'I want to go shopping,' she says. 'Fancy coming with me?'

'Where?' I ask, feeling that old familiar buzz at the prospect of spending some money, a feeling I haven't had in a while.

'I thought we could get a cab to St John's Wood.'

'St John's Wood? What the hell's in St John's Wood?'

'Joseph, for starters.'

'I'm coming.'

As a receptionist on a completely crap salary Jo really shouldn't be able to afford the clothes she wears every day, but luckily for her she has extremely wealthy parents who never seem to think twice about giving her money for her wardrobe, and, although we know we should all hate her for it, she's so nice we can't help but adore her.

And what's more she pays for the taxi.

'I'll get the one on the way back,' I say, feeling slightly guilty as she puts her Louis Vuitton purse back in her Gucci bag.

'Whatever,' she says, tripping off down the high street, and it is a bit of a revelation for me, like a mini Bond Street in North London.

'How did you discover this?' I say.

'My parents live round the corner,' she says, 'so I spend most of my life here. So much easier than going into town.'

She obviously does spend most of her life here because as soon as we walk into the first shop, the girl in there says, 'Hi, Jo! How are you?' and you just know that she's probably their best customer.

And then we go into Joseph, which is a bit of a scary experience, because the woman in there looks me up and down and evidently decides I'm not good enough to bother saying hello to, so she sticks her nose up in the air and carries on ordering a sales assistant around.

'Aren't you going to even look?' says Jo, and I half-heartedly look, but I can't really be bothered because there wouldn't be any point in buying that 'fabulous' chiffon shirt or those 'wicked' PVC trousers, because my life with Nick just doesn't need those sorts of things.

'This isn't like you,' says Jo, pulling a gold AmEx out of her purse and paying for a pile of tissue-wrapped clothes. 'What's going on?'

I shrug, and think of explaining it to her, but then decide not to because I know she wouldn't understand. 'I'm just a bit strapped for cash at the moment.' I know she won't be able to say anything after this because she feels ever so slightly guilty at having so much money from her parents, and, sure enough, she nods and drops the subject.

And when we get back to the office there's a note on my desk saying Nick called, and my heart, even after three months, etc, etc, still skips a little beat and I call him back immediately, because I'm a bit crap at playing hard to get.

'Hello, my darling,' he says.

'Hello, my darling,' I echo, all my insecurities forgotten because he called, and he didn't just call, he called the next day.

'I'm bored,' he says.

'Why don't you write?'

'I'm not in the mood.'

'Oh. What are you in the mood for?'

'You. On a silver platter. Preferably with nothing on. No, wait, with a pair of red lace crotchless knickers.'

'God, you're such a bloke!' I laugh.

'I thought I was a girl . . .'

'You are, but when it comes to sex you're very much a bloke.'

'I'm sorry about last night. I'm phoning to apologise for being so tired and for not, you know, not ravishing you like I usually do.'

'That's OK,' I say, happily. 'I didn't feel like it either,' I lie.

'Blimey! Are you sure you're not a bloke?'

I laugh.

'I was just worried you'd get the wrong idea,' he says.

'Don't be silly,' I trill with laughter. 'It was lovely just cuddling.'

'You're so damned nice,' he says, sounding serious. 'You're so understanding all the time, and so nice!'

'Stop saying I'm nice.' I'm grinning. I'm grinning so hard any second now I might tell him I love him. Ha! Got you. That was a joke. Of course I don't love him.

'OK. What are you doing tonight?'

'Nothing planned.' Another lie. I said I'd go to the movies with Jo, but hey, it's only the movies. Jo will understand. 'What about you?'

'I'm meeting Rog for a drink. I miss you, will you come with me?'

Shit. Dilemma. I want to see Nick more than anything, but I honestly don't think I could stand another night with one of his vile friends.

'Umm.' I say, stalling for time. 'I'd better not. I kind of said I might go to the movies with Jo.'

'All right,' he grumbles. 'What about later? Why don't you come over when the movie's finished?' he says.

'Tell you what. Why don't you come over to me?'

'You really hate my flat, don't you?'

'It's not that I hate it exactly, I just prefer mine.'

'I know,' he says. 'That's the problem. So do I.'

I don't go to the movies, Jo blows me out, so I get a Chinese takeaway and eat it watching TV.

Afterwards I look in the mirror at my pot belly. 'Bloody hell!' I'm fat. I'm huge. I'm disgusting.

Hmm. Maybe sit-ups would work. I hook my legs under the bed, wondering why on earth I don't exercise more often, because this is easy. And one. And two. And three. And four. And five. And, Jesus, why am I puffing already? And six. And seven. And eight. And nine. And I don't think I can go on any longer.

I stand up and look in the mirror, and my face is bright red and I look seriously unfit and oh, what the hell, I'll have another cigarette, and just when I've lit it the doorbell rings and oh God! I'm a complete state.

'What have you been up to?' says Nick, kissing me hello.

'Exercise.'

'Urgh. I'm allergic to the bloody stuff.'

'You don't need to do it,' I say, rubbing his deliciously firm washboard stomach. 'But look at this.' I push my stomach out, figuring it's better to be up-front about it.

Nick recoils in horror. 'What. Is. That?' He gets down on his knees and presses one ear against my stomach. 'Yup.' He nods sagely. 'I know exactly what that is. It's a food baby.'

I start laughing.

'In fact,' he says, tapping my stomach in a doctor-ish sort of way, 'I'd say it was a Chinese food baby.'

How the hell did he know? 'How the hell do you know?' I ask.

Nick stands up and shrugs nonchalantly. 'I'm paid to know.'

I turn round and see the evidence in the kitchen. Foil cartons and white cardboard lids, which I meant to clear up, but it's too damn late.

'Seeing as we might just about be in time to catch last orders,' says Nick, 'I thought we could go down to the Westbourne for a drink.'

'Sure!' I say enthusiastically, sitting down and pulling my trainers on.

Funnily enough, the Westbourne is about the first place I've been to with Nick where we both feel at home. Enough of a pub to make him relax, and trendy enough to make me relax. It's a warm night, so we sit outside and, just as I think we're having a really nice time, Nick starts sighing again.

'What is it now?'

He sighs again. And then he looks at me.

'I really like you, Libby,' he says, and my heart sinks, because I know what's coming next. What's coming next is a But.

'No, I mean I really like you. But . . .' And he stops.

'I really like you too,' I offer lamely.

'I know,' he says. 'That's what worries me.'

Oh shit. Why didn't I play harder to get?

'I just don't know what to do. I like you more than I've liked anyone for ages. I mean, over the last year there have been several women I could have got involved with, but I didn't because I wasn't ready for a relationship, and I wasn't ready to get involved with you, but I like you so much I sort of couldn't help it.'

'Nick,' I say slowly. 'We're not having a relationship, we're just having fun, so what's wrong with that?'

'But we are having a relationship, you know that.'

There's no point in denying it because he's right.

'And what scares me is that at some point in the not too distant future you're going to want more commitment from me, and I know, quite categorically, that I won't be able to give it to you, even though I want to, more than anything else in the world, but I'm just not ready.'

What can I say? He's right again.

He sighs. 'I like you far too much to hurt you, and I know that inevitably I will.'

'Maybe not,' I bristle. 'Maybe I'm not as involved as you think I am.'

'Aren't you?'

I shrug. 'I don't know.'

'Look.' He takes my hand. 'You are the best person I've met in years, and if I'd met you in a year's time, or maybe even a few months, I know we could be happy together, but I can't give you what you need.' He sighs again. 'I haven't got my life together, and I can't deal with a relationship until I have. I want to get my novel published, but I also know that I need some money, some stability, and I can't keep doing this for ever. If I had a publishing deal, or a job, then it would all be different.'

I think I'm going to start crying, but somehow I manage not to. I think about telling him that it doesn't bother me that he doesn't have money, that I'm prepared to wait, but I know, deep down, that his mind is made up, and it really wouldn't make any difference.

'Is this it, then?' I say.

'No,' he sighs. 'I don't know. I don't want to stop seeing you.'

'So do we carry on?' Hope. Light at the end of the tunnel.

'I don't know. I don't think we can. But I don't want to lose you.'

'You can't have it both ways,' I say, amazed at where this resolve comes from, but praying that if I tell him I'll never see him again as a friend, he'll somehow find a way to work through this, to stay with me. 'I can't be your friend,' I continue. 'I'm sorry, but I just can't.'

'I don't know what to do. What do you think?'

'I think . . .' I stop, and suddenly I feel very grown-up. 'I think it's late. I think we had a late night last night and that we're both tired, and that everything seems so much worse when you're tired. I think we should go home, sleep on it, and see how things are in the morning.'

I think I said the right thing, because Nick relaxes and says, 'Maybe you're right. OK. Shall we go?' And we do.

So we go home, and we make love, and it really is making love, it's not just sex, because it's impossibly tender and throughout it all we gaze into each other's eyes and if I didn't know better I'd say that a couple of times Nick's were swimming with tears, but it was truly beautiful, and afterwards I thought, how could he give this up? How could he say goodbye to me when we are so damn good together?

And we fall asleep cuddled up, and the next time I open my eyes it's ten to eight in the morning and I kiss him awake, thinking that last night must have been a bad dream.

We go to the tube together, but somehow it is different. As we kiss goodbye Nick says to me, 'Are you OK?' and I nod.

'Are you?' I say.

'I'm still confused,' he says. 'Even more so,' and he gives me a hug, and I'm not sure I like this hug because it's so tight, so clingy, if I didn't know better I'd almost think it was the last one, but we stand there for ages, and eventually I break away and he says, 'I'll call you,' and I'm not sure what the hell is going on, but neither of us has said it's over, so maybe it's not, but if it isn't, then why do I feel like shit?

I feel like shit all day. I don't start crying, but I feel as if I'm on the brink every second.

Of course Jules is the first person I call when I get to the office, and she listens quietly while I relay what happened, and eventually she says, 'It doesn't look good.'

'I know it doesn't bloody look good, Jules. But what's happening?'

'I don't know. I think he really is confused, and that you'll need to give him space, and I could be wrong, but I think he'll come back.'

But I don't want to give him space, I want to see him, be with him, convince him that I'm right for him.

'But you can't forget what you've always said,' she continues softly, trying to ease my pain. 'You never thought he'd be The One, so maybe this is a good thing.'

'I know,' I sigh. 'But you can't sleep with someone on a regular basis that you really like and not get emotionally involved.'

Jules laughs. 'That's what I've been saying since the beginning.'

'But I really thought I could,' I groan. 'I've done it before, why can't I do it now?'

'Because things are different in your early twenties. You can afford it, you've got time, but after about twenty-five, there are other things at stake, and unfortunately every man you meet becomes a potential husband, whether you admit it to yourself or not.'

'You're right, I know you're right. But that doesn't stop it hurting.'

'I know, my darling. And it will hurt for a while, but you have to get on with your life. What are you doing tonight?'

'Nothing.'

'Right. I'm coming to pick you up at eight o'clock, and I want you in your best designer togs. We're going to Mezzo for a drink.'

'I'm really not in the mood, Jules.'

'I don't care. We're going to go out and get drunk and have some fun.'

'Can't we do it another time?'

'No way. You are not moping by yourself.'

I can tell there's no getting out of it, so I say yes and miserably put down the phone, only for it to ring again two seconds later.

'Libby? It's Nick.'

'Hi,' I say in a strained voice.

'Hi. I just wanted to phone to check you were OK.'

'I'm OK. Is this it, then?'

He sighs. 'I don't know. But you know, it's not you. It's me.'

I almost laugh. That's what they always say.

'I think I might have to go into therapy or something,' he sighs.

'Good idea.' And hell, maybe I should too. Maybe if I went to see someone they'd help me understand why I keep attracting the bastards. Not that Nick's a bastard, it's just that none of the men I meet seem to be available. They're either physically unavailable, in other words they're not interested in me, or they're emotionally unavailable, see Nick.

'I'd really like it if we could stay friends,' he says. 'You're incredibly important to me, Libby.'

Well, that's it, then, isn't it? He may as well have said it's over, he just didn't have the balls.

'I've got enough friends,' I say. 'Thanks.'

His voice sounds sad. 'Can I phone you?'

'If you want.' Now it's my turn to be harsh.

'Listen, take care.'

'Yup. Bye.' I put down the phone and give in. I start crying. Fuck it. I don't care that I'm at work or that everyone's looking at me, and as I sit there with my shoulders heaving a sob escapes my throat and that's it, moments later I'm crying like a baby and I get up and run to the loo, where I lock myself in a cubicle and just let go.

I hear the door open, but I don't stop. I can't stop.

'Libby? Are you OK?' It's Jo.

I try to answer her but the words don't come out.

'It's Nick, isn't it? Let me in.' She starts banging on the cubicle door, so I get up and unlock it, then sit back down on the toilet seat (closed).

'They're all bastards,' she says vehemently. 'He's not worth it.' She waits for a bit while I try to regain a bit of composure, which is hard when your eyes look remarkably like those of Dracula's daughter.

'I' hiccup 'know' hiccup 'it's just' hiccup 'I' hiccup, hiccup, sob, sob.

'It's OK.' She puts an arm round me, which is pretty damn difficult in the confines of the cubicle, and I can't help it—someone being this nice, this sympathetic, sets me off all over again.

'It's OK,' she keeps saying softly. 'It's OK.'

But it's not OK, I think. It's not OK because I've got used to having Nick around, because I love having him around. Because for the first time in ages I wasn't some sad person who had to go out on the pull with the girls on Saturday nights because there was nothing better to do.

It's not OK because I love, loved, having sex with Nick. Because there was nothing better than waking up and rolling over only to discover that you're not on your own.

It's not OK because he made me laugh. Because I didn't have to pretend to be anything other than who I am when I was with him. Because I believe that what you look for in a relationship is someone who makes you a better person when you're with them, who changes you for the better, who makes you the best person you can possibly be, and because I thought I had found that in Nick.

Even though I don't think I ever quite realised it until now.

And yes, maybe you're right, maybe I'm being overdramatic, maybe I'm blowing this up into something much bigger than it is because I'm feeling sorry for myself, but why the hell not, huh? And whether it's true or not, it certainly feels true right now. And it feels like shit.

And oh my God, I'm never going to wake up next to him again. And I'm never going to look in his eyes as we're making love, and he's going to be doing that with someone else, and probably very soon, and me? I'm going to be on my own for the rest of my bloody life.

I start sobbing again.

I hate myself for losing it at the office. When you set yourself up, as I've done, as this strong independent career woman, always in control, people get very nervous when you lose it, they don't quite know how to react, and sure enough, when half an hour's passed and I've finally managed to get a grip, I walk back in with head held high and everyone stops talking and starts pretending to be very busy.

Somehow I manage to get through the day, and, perhaps because I've immersed myself in work, by the time I actually leave the building I really am starting to feel a lot better, and when Jules arrives I've been so busy reading I haven't even had time to get dressed, and the first thing we do after pouring ourselves a glass of wine is sit down and make a list. Yup, that list. The list I showed you when we first met.

And you know, looking at the list I start to feel one hell of a lot better, because yes, maybe he was nice, and yes, maybe he was sweet to me, but really, how could I ever have even thought of getting seriously involved? And Jesus, the thought of spending even one more night with his revolting friends in a revolting pub turns my stomach.

I leave Jules sitting in the living room as I go and get dressed, and fuck it, I'm going to make an effort. So I pull out a Joseph dress from last season and team it with my gorgeous Prada shoes, and I put on lots and lots of make-up, and I sweep my hair up into a big beehivey-type thing, and when I walk out Jules does a wolf whistle and claps her hands.

'Hooray!' she shouts, as she leaps up and grabs me, dancing round the living room. 'We've got the old Libby back. You look gorgeous, Libby, just like your old self.' Bless her. She doesn't mention the fact that my eyes, despite a ton of mascara and cleverly applied eyeshadow, look like pissholes in the snow.

And off we go, to Mezzo, and it's packed with City boys and glamorous girls, and we haven't been there five minutes before a group of chinless wonders send over some champagne, and OK, so they're not my type, but it's really quite nice to be in this sort of environment again.

'So how come someone as gorgeous as you hasn't got a boyfriend?' says Ed, who is not my type at all. Tall, stocky and with a moustache, and I hate moustaches. He's also very, very straight.

And yes, he's probably rolling in money, and yes, I know that I'm looking for a rich man, but I don't want him to be straight, I want him to be just as comfortable at the opera as he would be at, say, a Lightning Seeds gig, and there aren't too many men around like that. In fact, it may well be that Jules nabbed the last of a dying breed.

I just know this guy Ed is too damn straight for me, but what the hell, I flick my hair around a bit and smile coyly as I say, 'How do you know I haven't got a boyfriend?'

'Oh, umm. Er. Have you?' Inspired or what?

I shake my head and suddenly feel incredibly sad. Jules sees it and grabs me. 'Excuse us, boys. We'll be back in a sec,' she says.

We leave them moaning about why women always go off to the loo in pairs, and once we're in there she asks if I'm OK.

'I am. Really. I'm having quite a nice time. It's just that I miss Nick.'

'What about Ed? He's definitely interested.'

'Nah,' I say. 'Not my type. Too straight.'

'How d'you know? Sometimes people can surprise you.'

'OK. I'll show you.' And we go back to join them.

'So,' I say to Ed. 'Been to any good gigs lately?'

'Gigs?' He looks bewildered. 'Oh, ah. Gigs. Oh yes,' and he starts laughing. 'Hilarious,' he says. I look at Jules and raise one eyebrow.

'You're very funny, Libby,' he says, although I haven't quite got the joke. 'I'd love to take you out for dinner.'

'OK.' I shrug, not really giving a damn whether he does or not.

'May I have your number?'

Jesus, is this guy formal or what? I tell him my number, which he writes down carefully in a leather wallet thing that holds small sheets of white paper and looks desperately expensive.

'I shall call you,' he says. 'And we shall go somewhere wonderful.'

I literally have to force myself not to shrug and say, 'Whatever.' Instead I smile and say, 'Lovely.'

And when we leave, which is shortly afterwards because all the emotion of this morning is starting to make me extremely tired, Ed shakes my hand and says, 'It's been an absolute pleasure meeting you. I'll ring you about dinner.' And that's it. We jump in a taxi and head home.

'I can't believe you pulled,' says Jules. 'You pulled someone on your first night as a single girl!'

'Oh, come on, Jules, he's not exactly a good pull.'

'You're blind, Libby. He was lovely, and obviously smitten with you. He'll probably take you somewhere fantastic, he's obviously loaded.'

'How can you tell?'

She looks at me in dismay. 'Libby, everything I know I learned from you. Don't tell me you didn't notice the Rolex?'

I shake my head.

'The Porsche keyring?'

I shake my head.

'Maybe I will go out for dinner with him,' I say, suddenly quite liking the idea of being driven around in a Porsche. 'But just dinner. That's all.'

Jules sits there and smiles to herself, and I give her a look.

'I know you so well,' she chuckles, and I start laughing too.

# Chapter Eight

THE GOOD MOOD LASTS precisely as long as it takes me to get back to the flat. I turn on the lights, and as I walk around I start fighting off the memories of Nick that seem to be everywhere I look.

The sofa where we curled, that first night, when he came back after Sal's get-together. The bath where he sat in that ridiculous bathcap. The bed. Oh my God. The bed.

I sink to the floor, tears streaming down my face, and I curl up, hugging my knees to my chest, crying like a baby.

Why did this have to happen to me? I try to remember what Nick said, why it's ended, because it doesn't make sense. How can you like someone, really like them, and still want to end it? He said it might have worked if we'd met in a few months' time, so maybe it could work now, maybe I could change his mind.

I stop thinking properly. I stand up, wipe the tears from my eyes and grab my car keys. The only thing that will make this better is seeing Nick. I have to see him. Talk to him. Make him see that this can work.

I climb in the car, filled with resolve, so intent on making this work that I forget to cry, I concentrate on manoeuvring the car through London's streets, until eventually I pull up outside Nick's flat.

I sit for a while in the car, suddenly unsure about confronting him, but I'm here now, and I know that I don't believe it's over, I won't believe it's over, until I can talk to him face to face, and if he sees me, sees what he's doing to me, he'll change his mind. He has to.

Nick takes for ever to answer the door. At one point I start turning back, feeling sick at what I'm doing, but just as I turn I hear a door upstairs, and then the soft clump of footsteps coming down the stairs.

The door opens and there he is. His hair mussed up, his eyes half closed with sleep, and he is obviously shocked to see me standing there.

We look at each other while I try to find the words, the words that will bring him back, but nothing comes out, and I try to blink back the tear that squeezes itself out of the corner of my right eye.

'Libby,' he whispers, as he puts his arms round me, and I can't help it. I break down, sobbing my heart out because as he stands there with his arms round me, gently rubbing my back, I know that I am making a fool of myself, that nothing will change his mind.

'You'd better come upstairs,' he says eventually, gently disengaging himself and leading me upstairs by the hand.

We sit in silence, me on the armchair, Nick on the futon, and all I want to do is climb into the futon with him and cuddle him, make everything OK. I can't believe that I am no longer allowed to do this because it's over, and as I start to think about it the tears roll down my face again.

'God, Libby,' Nick whispers. 'I am so sorry. I never meant to hurt you.'

'I don't understand,' I blurt out. 'You said if we met in a few months it would be OK, we could be together, so why can't we just carry on.'

Nick doesn't say anything at first. Then he says gently, 'This is why. Because neither of us was supposed to get emotionally involved. I never wanted to cause you any pain, and it's killing me to see you like this.'

'So why are you causing me this much pain?' I look up at him, not caring that the tears are now flowing freely down my face.

'Libby,' he says, coming over and crouching down so that his face is level with mine. 'I told you from the beginning I wasn't ready for a relationship. I knew you were getting more involved, but I tried to deny it because I knew I couldn't give you what you want. I am so sorry.'

'OK,' I snuffle, regaining some small measure of composure. 'So you can't give me what I want. So what? Let's carry on anyway. You can't hurt me more than you already have, and now I know exactly where I stand, so I don't see why we can't keep seeing each other, not when we get on so well, when things are so good between us.'

'No, Libby.' He shakes his head sadly. 'I want to, but I can't put you through this again, and it will happen again, because I can't commit to anyone right now. I'm just not ready.'

The tears dry up as I realise that I cannot persuade him. That his mind is made up. That now there is no doubt that it really is over. I stand up and go to the door, trying to regain some self-respect, although even I know it's a little late for that.

'I'll call you,' Nick says, walking down the stairs behind me as I head for the front door, feeling like nothing is real, like this is all a horrific nightmare. I don't bother saying anything. I just walk out and somehow manage to make it home.

'What did you do this time?' My mother's looking at me, and it's all I can do not to jump up and scream at her because this is absolutely typical, it's always my fault. She'd never stop to think that there was something wrong with these men. Oh no. It's always that I've put them off.

'Did you come on too strong?' she says, and I wish I'd never mentioned anything. I wasn't planning to, really I wasn't, but then my mother seems to have some sort of psychic sixth sense, and she could see something was wrong, and before I knew it it just came out. That I'd split up with Nick. Although I omitted the part about turning up at his flat. That's something I'm trying hard to forget.

And yes, I regret it. I regret it because I allowed him to see me at my most vulnerable. In the few days since it happened, I've tried not to think about it, because the only thing I feel when I remember laying myself open in the way that I did is shame. Pure and absolute shame.

'No,' I say viciously. 'I did not come on too strong. He just doesn't want a relationship, OK?'

'Since when does any man want a relationship?' She snorts with laughter at her little joke, and I look at her, wondering when in hell my mother became such an expert at relationships? She's only ever been with my dad, for God's sake. No one else would have her.

'You know you have to play hard to get, Libby. None of this jumping into bed on the first night and being there whenever they want you.'

How the fuck would she know? 'It's not like that, Mum,' I say through gritted teeth. 'You really don't know what you're talking about.'

'That's what you think,' she says firmly. 'Anyway, I'm not saying I'm an expert, all I'm saying is that I can see what you're doing wrong.'

That's it. I've had enough. Again. 'Why is it always me who's doing something wrong?' I practically shout. 'Have you ever considered the fact that it might be men who have the problem? No, no, how stupid of me, of course it's my fault. It's always my bloody fault.'

'No need for that sort of language,' my mum says. 'But have you ever considered why you're still single at twenty-seven?'

'It's only twenty-seven, for God's sake! I've got years.'

My mum shakes her head sadly. 'No, Libby, you haven't, not if you want to get married and have children, and I think it's high time you stopped and had a good long look at yourself.'

'You're amazing.' I shake my head in disbelief. 'Most girls my age would kill to have my life. I've got a flat, a great job, a car and plenty of disposable income. I've got a busy social life and hundreds of friends. Can you not see that having a man is really not that important these days? That I'm far happier being single.'

'Libby, dear,' she says patronisingly. 'You know that's not true and I know that's not true.'

Why does she always have to have the last bloody word? And what's more, the nasty old cow is right. Well, right about me not liking being single, I really don't know about the rest of that stuff.

'Mum, let's just drop it,' I say, getting up to go.

'Oh, you can't go,' she says. 'You've only just got here. And I'm concerned about you, Libby, you look as if you've put on a bit of weight.'

Jesus Christ. Talk about knowing where to hit the weak spot. Trust my mother to notice that in the few days since that night at Nick's flat I've been eating like a pig, although I decided this morning that that was going to stop. Definitely.

'I haven't put on weight,' I say, although I know from the scales that I'm four pounds heavier.

'OK, OK,' she sighs. 'I'm only saying it for your own good.'

'Look. I'm going.'

'Not just yet.' She stands up. 'Tell you what, I've got some of your favourite caramel cakes here, why don't I just go and get them?'

'You just told me I'd put on weight!'

'One won't hurt you,' and she bustles off.

Please tell me I'm not the only one with a completely mad, insensitive mother. Please say that I'm not the only one who goes through hell every time she goes home to see her parents. I don't even know why I bloody go. Every Sunday I'm expected for tea, and when I turn up, I behave like a pissed-off teenager and run away as fast as I can.

She comes back and puts a plate of caramel cakes on the table.

'I. Don't. Want. One,' I say through gritted teeth. 'OK?'

'Libby, I wish you wouldn't always take offence when I try to help.' She looks at me with mournful eyes. 'I'm only saying these things

246

because I can see things from a different perspective, that's all. There's nothing I'd love more than to see you happy and with a good man.'

'Mum,' I say, standing up and giving her a peck on the cheek. 'I really am going now,' and finally, thankfully, I manage to get away.

'Has that guy called?' Jules asks when she rings me later that evening.

'Which guy?'

'Ed.'

He has called. He called the day after I'd met him and left a rather nervous-sounding message on my machine, which was a bit peculiar because he was so self-assured when we met. 'Hello, Libby,' he said. 'Er, it's, er, Ed here. We met last night at Mezzo. I was just wondering whether perhaps you'd, er, like to come out for dinner with me. It was lovely to meet you, and I wondered whether you might give me a call back.' Then he left his home number, his work number and his mobile number, and he said he'd be in all day and at home that evening.

I didn't call back.

I mean, I know I said I'd have dinner with him, but what would be the point? I don't fancy him, there's no stomach-churning lovely lustful feeling like I had with Nick, and right at this moment if I can't have Nick I don't want anyone.

'No,' I lie. 'He hasn't called.'

'Really?' Jules sounds surprised. 'He seemed so smitten. Well, he will.'

'I really don't care.'

'I know,' she says. 'But it would do you good. The only way you're truly going to get over Nick is by going out with other men. And he'll probably take you somewhere incredibly swanky and treat you like a princess and you'll have a good time. No one says you have to sleep with him, or even see him again for that matter, but you never know what his friends are like. You might meet the man of your dreams by being friends with him.'

'Oh, shut up, Jules, you sound just like my mother,' but I know she's right and I decide to call him back after all.

Today is the day I'm going to phone Ed. Definitely. I know he's not really my type, but what the hell. I am, as my mother reminded me, twenty-seven years old and I suppose what it's all about is a numbers game: go out with enough men and one of them's bound to be Mr Right.

But in the meantime I've got my hands completely full at work. I'm trying to organise the launch for this TV series, and I've just finished the press release, when who should call up but Amanda Baker.

Not what I need right now at all.

'Hi, darling,' she says, which throws me ever so slightly, because she's never darlinged me before.

'I thought we could go out for lunch,' she says. 'You know, a girls' lunch. You and me.'

I'm so flummoxed I don't know what to say.

'Are you free today?' she says. 'It's just that I'm so busy at the moment, but I'd love to see you and I thought we might go to Quo Vadis.'

Now that's done it for me, because I haven't been to Quo Vadis yet, and it's one of those restaurants that you really ought to go to at least once, if only to say that you've been there. 'I'd love to,' I say. 'Shall I meet you there?'

'Perfect,' she says. 'Book the table for one fifteen. All right, darling, see you later.' And she's gone, leaving me sitting there wondering why on earth I'm supposed to book the table when she invited me?

So I'm walking round the office, asking if anyone's got the number for Quo Vadis, when Joe Cooper walks out of his office and says, 'That's very posh. How come you're going to Quo Vadis?'

'This is really odd, Joe,' I say. 'Amanda Baker just phoned and invited me out for lunch, which is completely peculiar in itself because up until now I was her worst enemy, and I suddenly seem to have become her best friend, and then she asked me to book the table.'

Joe throws back his head with laughter. 'Libby,' he says. 'This is Amanda's trick, she's done this with every PR she's ever worked with. She starts off mistrusting you and the minute you actually get her some coverage she decides you're her best friend. Don't worry about it, look at it this way, at least it will make your life easier.'

I shrug. 'S'pose so.' And I scribble down the number on a yellow Post-it note and go to call the restaurant.

It's half past one, and I'm sitting at a window table trying to look cool, as if I'm someone famous, because it seems that almost everybody else in here is. I've already spotted three television presenters, two pop stars, and the people at the table next to me are talking about their latest film, and since I don't recognise them I presume they're behind the camera, as it were.

I'm asking for another kir, and wondering where the hell Amanda is, when I suddenly hear a familiar 'Darling!' and look up and see her kiss her way through the restaurant, greeting all the minor celebrities as if she's known them for ever, and to my immense surprise they do all know her. She sweeps up to the table and gives me two air kisses.

'Darling,' she says, as she sits down. 'You look fab.'

'So do you,' I say. 'It's lovely to see you.'

'I thought that we really ought to get to know each other a bit better,' she says, glancing round the room as she speaks, presumably just in case she's missing anything.

She orders a sparkling mineral water from the waiter, and then, once we've ordered, the conversation turns, as it so often does with single women, to men.

'Well, you know'—she leans forward conspiratorially—'my last affair was with . . .' She whispers the name of a well-known TV anchorman, then sits back to note my admiration, because the anchorman in question is indeed gorgeous, and I would normally tell you, but somehow I don't think Amanda would want you to know, because he's married, and it wouldn't do his image any good at all.

But trust me. It's great gossip.

'So what happened?'

'He came out with all the usual shit about loving his wife but not being in love with her, and how they slept in separate beds, and he was only with her because it was good for his profile, and that he was going to leave her, he'd had enough. But of course he wasn't going to.'

'So what made you realise he wasn't going to leave her?'

'When I opened the pages of *Hello!* and read how excited they both were that she was pregnant again with their sixth child.'

'Jesus.' I exhale loudly and sit back. 'That must have hurt.'

'It was a killer,' she says. 'So now I'm back on the dating scene, which is hell, really. I just don't seem to meet any decent men. To be honest, I think they're all a bit intimidated by me.'

'I can understand that,' I say, suppressing a snort.

'Really?' she says. 'Why do you think it is?'

'Oh, er. Well, because you're famous, and you're very bright, and very attractive.' I see her face fall. 'I mean, you're beautiful, and that scares a lot of men off.'

'I know,' she nods. 'You're absolutely right.'

'It's the same for me,' I say, and wait for her to ask me about my own love life, but she doesn't, and then I think how stupid I am to think a celebrity, even one as minor as Amanda, would be interested in anyone other than themselves. But fuck it. I want to talk about this. I need to talk about this, and somehow, I find myself telling her all about it.

'So,' I end, having spoken nonstop for the last twenty minutes, 'now there's this guy Ed pursuing me and I really don't know whether to call him, because even though he's nice enough I just can't see a future in it.'

'Ed who?' Amanda asks, a flicker of interest in her eyes.

'I don't know,' I say, and I laugh, because I'm so uninterested I haven't even bothered to look at his business card. 'Hang on,' I say, fishing around in my bag. 'His card's here somewhere.'

I find my diary and pull out the card. 'Ed McMahon.'

'You're joking!' Amanda gasps. She grabs the card and starts laughing. 'Oh my God, Libby! Don't you know who he is?'

I shake my head.

'He's only one of the most eligible bachelors in Britain. I can't believe you pulled Ed McMahon and you didn't even realise who he was!'

'Who is he, then?'

'He's a financial whiz kid who seems to have appeared out of nowhere. He's single, rich and unbelievably intelligent. I've never met him, but my friend Robert knows him really well. I've been begging him to fix me up with him, but Robert says we wouldn't get on.'

'How come, if he's so rich and so eligible, he hasn't got a girlfriend?'

'That's the odd thing,' she says. 'He doesn't seem to have much luck with women. Robert says it's because he's eccentric.'

'Well,' I say, 'maybe I will call him, then.'

'Call him?' Amanda snorts. 'Marry him, more like.'

By the end of our lunch, and I swear, no one is more surprised by this than me, I've made two decisions. One is to call Ed McMahon this afternoon, and the other is that I quite like Amanda Baker. OK, she's not someone whom I'd normally consider being friends with, but, after our bit of female bonding over lunch, I think she's quite sweet really.

So I go back to the office and pull out Ed McMahon's business card again, and dial his number.

'Hello, is Ed McMahon there, please?'

'Who may I say is calling?'

'Libby Mason.'

There's a silence, and I sit and listen to piped music for a while, and then Ed comes on the phone.

'Libby! I'm so delighted you phoned. I was worried you didn't get my message.'

'I'm sorry,' I say, 'I've been running around like a madwoman, I've been so busy.'

'Never mind. You've phoned now! When are you free for dinner?'

'I'll just look in my diary,' I say. 'When were you thinking of?'

'Tomorrow night?'

Naturally there's nothing in my diary for tomorrow night, but do I really want to see this man so soon? Nah, I don't think I do.

'I'm sorry,' I say, sounding as if I mean it. 'But this week's horrendous. How about next week? That's looking pretty clear.'

'Oh, umm. OK. Actually, what about the weekend? Saturday night?'

Now Saturday night is not a night to give up for just anyone, particularly a man I don't even fancy, but then again, he's bound to take me somewhere nice, and he is one of the most eligible men in Britain, so OK, I'm game on.

And Ed is so excited I can practically hear him jumping up and down. He takes my address and says he'll pick me up at eight.

I say goodbye and ring Jules without even putting down the phone.

'I have a date with one of the most eligible men in Britain on Saturday night!' I say, feeling pretty damn pleased with myself.

'Who?'

'Ed McMahon.'

'Ed? Ed that we met?'

'Yup.'

'What do you mean, one of the most eligible bachelors in Britain?'

I repeat, word for word, what Amanda told me over lunch.

'Jesus. That's a result. And he sounds much more you than that Nick.'

See? Already Nick's become 'that Nick'—someone in my past.

'In what way?'

'Oh, come on, Libby, he'll probably take you to amazing places and buy you wonderful presents and you'll love every minute of it.'

'Jules, I think you're jumping a bit ahead of yourself here. I mean, I hardly know the guy, and I certainly don't fancy him.'

'Fine,' she laughs. 'Let's just wait and see.'

 **Chapter Nine**

AT EIGHT ON THE DOT, the doorbell rings. I walk to the front door of my tiny flat and open it with a gracious smile.

The flat looks perfect. Well, as perfect as it can look. I even bought armfuls of flowers this morning, and I have to say I'm quite proud of the place. I've done away with the clutter. At least, I've swept it under the sofa and into cupboards, so it looks pristine. OK, it wouldn't pass my mother's inspection, but I'm damn sure it would pass everyone else's.

I don't actually see Ed for a while. All I can see, when I open the door, is the most enormous bouquet of long-stemmed creamy white roses that I've ever seen in my life, and they completely take my breath away.

No one's ever bought me flowers before, you see. I know that sounds daft, but none of my boyfriends has ever been the romantic type. Jon bought me flowers once, but it was only because I'd gone over to his flat and he'd obviously been out buying loads of flowers for himself, and I was so upset that he didn't buy me any that I threw a wobbly, and when we left the flat he stopped outside the flower shop and bought me a bunch of wilting chrysanthemums.

But here, on my doorstep, is a bunch of flowers so big it hides the man standing behind, and, as I take the flowers and see Ed, my first thought is that he isn't nearly as bad as I remember him. In fact, apart from the disgusting moustache, he looks rather nice, really. We stand there sort of grinning at one another until he leans forward and gives me a kiss on the cheek and says that I look lovely.

I twirl around and he hands me the flowers and of course I invite him in. He stands in the living room and looks around and doesn't actually say anything, doesn't say how lovely it is, which is a bit strange because most people, when they come to your house for the first time, compliment it out of politeness, even if they hate it.

I take the flowers and dig out a jug, which is the only thing I've got left since I've used up my one vase for the flowers I bought myself earlier, and as I arrange them Ed stands there rather awkwardly, so I try to make small talk with him.

'Did you find it all right?' I say, for want of something better.

'I got a bit lost,' he says. 'It's not really my neck of the woods.'

'Where do you live?'

'Regent's Park.'

'Oh, really? Whereabouts?'

'Hanover Terrace.'

Jesus Christ! Hanover Terrace! That's one of those huge Nash terraces that sweeps along the side of the park next to the mosque. But maybe Ed has a flat there, maybe it's not as impressive as I think.

'Do you have a flat?'

'Er, no, actually. I have a house,' he says. 'So how come you live here, Libby?'

'What, in Ladbroke Grove?'

'Yes.'

'It's the only place I can afford,' I laugh, and wait for him to smile, but he doesn't. He looks horrified.

'But it's not very safe,' he says finally.

'It's fine,' I say. 'You get used to it, and I quite like the fact that there's such a mixture of people, there's always something going on. And it's a great place to score drugs.' I can't help this last comment, it just sort of comes out and I don't know what it is but something about him being so straight makes me want to shock him. It works.

'You take drugs?' Now he looks completely disgusted.

'I'm joking.'

'Oh.' And then, thankfully, he starts laughing. 'Hilarious,' he says. 'You're ever so funny, Libby.'

I shrug and smile, and then the flowers are in the jug, and we're ready to go.

'Libby, I didn't say this before but you really are looking absolutely beautiful tonight.'

'Thank you.' I'm wearing a smart black suit that always makes me feel fantastic. And thank God I've learned to be gracious about receiving compliments. For years I'd say things like, 'What? In this old thing?' but now I accept compliments like the sophisticated woman I try to be.

'And I particularly like the scarf,' he says, gesturing to the grey silk scarf tied softly at my neck.

'What? This old thing?' I couldn't help it. It just came out.

'Is it silk?'

I nod.

'I thought so. Shall we go?'

So we walk out of the front door and I can't help but grin when I see his Porsche—a midnight-blue Porsche Carrera. And not only that. Ed walks round to my side first, opens the door and waits until I get in before closing it gently, and I almost want to hug myself because I can't believe I'm sitting in a Porsche with one of the most eligible men in Britain.

'I've booked a table at the River Café,' he says. 'Is that all right?'

All right? All right? It's fantastic because I haven't been—it's far too expensive for my meagre pockets.

'It's perfect. I haven't been and I really want to go.'

'Oh, good.' He smiles at me. 'I was so worried you wouldn't like it. Shall I put some music on?'

'Definitely,' I say approvingly.

'He reaches over and puts a CD on. '*L'Elisir d'amore*,' he says, in a perfect Italian accent, the R's rolling off his tongue.

He looks at me for approval, and what can I say? It's all right, really, quite melodic, but it's opera, for God's sake, and I'm just not into classical music and opera. But I can't tell him this, so I just smile and tell him he made a good choice.

And then as we stop at some traffic lights I turn my head and notice that in the old Peugeot next to us are two girls my age, and they're looking enviously at the Porsche and at me, and I smile to myself because I'm quite enjoying this. Despite the music.

So I decide that I'm going to make an effort with Ed, even though I suspect he really isn't my type, but surely he could grow to be my type? Surely I could grow to like him? Fancy him? Couldn't I? I sneak a peek at him driving and feel a wave of disappointment, because he's not half as gorgeous as Nick, but then Nick isn't here, and Ed is.

'Tell me about your job, Libby,' he says, trying to be polite.

'Not much to tell,' I say. 'I work in PR on people like Sean Moore.'

'Who?'

I look at him in amazement. 'Sean Moore. You must know who he is. He's the biggest heart-throb since, well, since Angus Deayton.'

'Oh, ha ha. I know who Angus Deayton is! He's the chap on that news programme, *Have I Got News for You.*' Ed nods vigorously. 'Yes, very funny show. Always try and catch it if I'm in on a Friday night.'

'And are you usually in on a Friday night?'

'Not usually,' he laughs. 'Most Friday nights I'm working late.'

'Don't you ever take time off?'

'To be honest with you I suppose I throw myself into work because I haven't met the right woman yet.'

Now this is a first. I can't believe he's telling me this on our first date. And I'm eager to hear more. 'You mean you want to settle down?'

'Definitely,' he says. 'Absolutely. That's why I bought the house in Hanover Terrace. I thought it would be a perfect home for a family and children, but at the moment I'm still rattling around in it all by myself.'

This is getting better and better. The most eligible bachelor in Britain is desperate to get married and he's taking me out! He's with me! For the first time in my life I'm on a date with a man who doesn't appear to be allergic to commitment.

Although to be honest, I'm not too sure about this whole scared-of-commitment business. OK, I do believe there are some men who are genuinely terrified of commitment, but for the most part I think it's that they haven't met the right woman yet. Because if a man met the woman of his dreams, he wouldn't want to let her go, would he?

That's what I think, anyway.

'So how come you haven't married?' I ask, to see whether he really is for real.

'I don't know. I thought I had met the right woman, but then it turned out I hadn't, she wasn't the right one. You see, I suppose I'm quite old-fashioned. I don't understand these career girls, and yes, I think it's fine for girls to have a bit of independence, but I'm really looking for a wife. Someone who'll look after me and our children.'

'So you wouldn't want her to work once she got married?'

He shakes his head. 'Do you think that's too much to ask?'

'No,' I say firmly. 'I absolutely agree.'

'Do you?'

'Yes. I think a mother ought to be at home with her children. I know too many women whose kids are completely neglected because they seem to be more interested in working late at the office.'

This last bit isn't completely true, but what the hell, I know I'm on the right track and Ed's so excited he can hardly contain himself.

'Libby,' he says, taking his eyes off the road and turning to me. 'I'm jolly glad I met you. Jolly glad.' And his grin's so wide, for a second I think it's going to burst off his face.

When we get to the River Café, Ed walks up to the girl standing behind the desk at the front and says, 'Hello!' in such an effusive tone I figure he must know her, but she stands there smiling awkwardly at him, which makes me think that he's this overexuberant all the time. 'Ed McMahon!' he says. 'Table for two!'

'Oh, yes,' she says, scanning her list. 'Follow me.'

'I hope it's a good table!' he says to her. 'I asked for the best table in the restaurant. Are we by the window?'

'I'm afraid not,' she says. 'But you're as close as we could get you,' and she leads us to a table in the middle of the room.

'Oh, jolly good!' Ed says loudly in his public school accent, and I cringe slightly as I notice how other people in the restaurant are turning to look at where this voice is coming from. '*Très bien!*' he then says, in a very, very bad French accent, and I can't help it, I start giggling, because if nothing else he's certainly a character.

'Umm, you speak French?' I say, as we sit down.

'*Mais, bien sûr!*' he says, and it comes out, 'May bienne soor,' and I sit there and wish he'd shut up, and then I mentally slap myself for being so nasty, because he's just a bit eccentric, that's all.

And you know what? I have a really nice time. Ed's quite funny. He tells me lots of stories about investment banking, and admittedly a large part of each story goes completely over my head, but he giggles as he tells them, and it's quite cute, not to mention infectious, and I find myself giggling with him and I'm quite surprised at how well this evening's going.

But just because he's good company doesn't mean I fancy him, but then maybe fancying someone isn't what it's all about? Let's face it, it didn't exactly work with Nick, did it? But as I sit there I allow myself to imagine what it would be like kissing him. I picture his face moving closer to mine, and then, Oh God! That moustache! Yuck, yuck, yuck!

'Do you cook?' I'm brought back to earth by the sound of Ed's voice, and I try to push the thought of him kissing me out of my head. Unfortunately, I don't manage to, but it lodges somewhere near the back, which is OK for now.

'I love cooking,' I say. 'But only for other people. I can never be bothered to cook for myself.'

'Gosh!' he says. 'You can cook too! Libby, is there anything you're not good at?'

'Sex?'

'Oh ha ha!' He rocks back in his chair, gulping with laughter. 'Hilarious!' And I sit and smile, wondering who on earth this man is, but not in a bad way, in more of an intrigued way, and the bill arrives, which is always a bit of an awkward time because I'm never too sure whether to offer, but this time I decide not to because, after all, Ed did say he was old-fashioned, and anyway with the amount of wine we've had to drink, I couldn't afford it even if I wanted to. So I sit back and watch as Ed pulls out a platinum American Express card, and when the waitress takes it away I lean forward and thank him for a lovely evening.

'Libby,' he says earnestly. 'The pleasure was all mine. I think you're fantastic!' And I smile because it feels like a long time since anyone's thought that about me, and I'm not sure whether anyone's really felt that way about me, ever.

I think I could get used to this, and quite frankly if I can't have Nick, then perhaps I can settle for having someone who completely adores me. Even though he hardly even knows me.

We get back in his car and on the way back we have that whole relationship talk where they ask you why you're single, when your last relationship was and what the longest relationship you've ever had has been. I say we have that talk but actually that's slightly wrong—I'm so busy trying to think of how to avoid saying I'm a complete nightmare in relationships because I'm so needy, paranoid and insecure that I forget to ask him anything at all.

But he doesn't seem to mind. In fact, he doesn't say anything as I tell him that I haven't met the right man yet, that I drifted apart from all my previous boyfriends, and that my longest relationship has been a year. And if I didn't know better I'd say he was definitely sizing me up for wife material, but maybe that's a bit ridiculous of me because this is only our first date.

Do I ask him in for coffee? I'm not sure I want him to come in for coffee. I'm not entirely sure how to deal with this whole scenario, but luckily Ed pulls up outside my flat and doesn't switch the engine off so I assume he'll be whizzing home.

'May I see you again?' he says and, without even thinking about whether I really want to, I find myself saying yes.

'Are you free tomorrow?' he says eagerly.

'I'm afraid not,' I say, because OK, I'm only going to my parents, but tomorrow feels a bit too soon, and I'm still not entirely sure how I feel about this anyway. 'I could do next week, though,' I say. 'Tuesday?'

'Marvellous!' he says, without looking at his diary. 'I'll pick you up at eight, how does that sound?'

'Fine,' I say. 'And thank you, again, for a lovely evening.'

Ed leaps out and walks me to my front door. I turn awkwardly as I put my key in the lock, wondering exactly how to say goodbye, and even as I turn he's leaning down to give me two kisses on each cheek.

'Again, Libby,' he says, turning to walk back towards the car, 'the pleasure was all mine.'

I don't mean to say anything, really I don't, but my mother is banging on about me being single again, and before I know it it just slips out that last night I had a date with Ed McMahon, and she's so shocked all the colour practically drains from her face.

'Not Ed McMahon the finance person?'

'Yes, Mum,' I say, and I can't help the hint of pride in my voice. 'Ed McMahon the finance person.'

For one ghastly minute I think she's about to hug me, but thankfully she doesn't. 'How on earth did you meet him?' she says.

'I met him at Mezzo,' I say.

'Mezzo?' she says in awe, because my mother, despite never actually leaving suburbia, dreams of doing so on a regular basis, and consequently reads every style magazine on the shelves. 'What's it like?'

'It's fine.' I shrug. 'Big.'

'And what's he like?' she asks.

'He's nice.'

'Nice? There must be something else you can say about him.'

'OK.' I watch her face closely. 'He drives a Porsche.'

She practically swoons before regaining her composure. 'So where did he take you?' she asks.

'The River Café.'

'Ooh. That's meant to be very expensive. What did you have?'

I tell her, and quite enjoy that she hangs on to my every word.

'And does he want to see you again?'

I nod. 'We're going out on Tuesday.'

And the funny thing is that all day Sunday, when I think about my evening with Ed, I find myself smiling, and it's not a lustful, falling-head-over-heels type of smile, but an I-had-quite-a-nice-time-and-I'm-surprised kind of smile, and although I wouldn't go as far as saying I can't wait until Tuesday, I would say that I'm quite looking forward to it because the man's definitely got something, I'm simply not entirely sure what it is.

'That's so exciting! Well, Libby, all I can say is this time don't blow it.'

'I beg your pardon?'

'You heard me. Don't mess this one up. Ed McMahon's very rich.'

'God, Mum,' I say in disgust, 'is that all you ever think about?'

On Monday morning Jo buzzes me from reception.

'Jesus Christ!' she says. 'You'd better come out here. Now.'

I walk through the office to the reception desk, and there, on the counter, is a forest. Well, OK, not quite a forest, but an arrangement of flowers that's so big it's threatening to take over the room.

'Jesus Christ!' I echo. 'These are for me?'

'They certainly are,' she says, the grin stretching across her face. 'Come on, come on. Open the card. Who are they from?'

I open the card with fingers that are shaking ever so slightly, and I suppose a part of me hopes they're from Nick, though I know they won't be, because Nick could never afford something like this.

'Dearest Libby,' I read out loud. 'Just wanted to thank you for a wonderful evening. Can't wait until Tuesday. With love, Ed.'

'Who the fuck's Ed?'

'Just an admirer,' I say breezily, skipping back into the office with the flowers and loving, loving the admiring glances I get on the way.

And I know this might sound a bit stupid, but I'd quite like to send him something in return, not because I desperately fancy him, but because he did a nice thing for me and I'd like to repay him somehow.

And I suppose if I did fancy him I wouldn't be able to do this, because I'd be far too busy playing games and playing hard to get. But number one, I don't really care if me sending something to him scares him off, and number two, I'm pretty damn sure it won't anyway. I suppose it's Sod's Law, isn't it? The ones that like you are never the ones you're interested in, and the ones you like are always the bastards. But Ed's different. I'm not really sure how I feel. I know that I'm not in lust with him, but I also know that I'd like to see him again. So this is why I want to do something for him.

But what? I go back out to Jo.

'OK,' I sigh. 'You win. I'll tell you everything if you help me out,' and I do.

'Got it!' she says when I've finally finished, although I didn't give her the long version, I kept it as short as I possibly could. 'Send him a virtual food basket!'

'A what?'

'On the Internet! You can go to these places and send virtual flowers and food baskets, they're amazing. It's a seriously cool thing to do, and you'll probably blow his mind. Come on. I'll show you how to do it.'

Ten minutes later Jo's sitting in front of the computer, tapping away, and there it is! A site that shows you pictures of flowers and presents which you can send to people.

'Is this going to cost anything?'

'Nah. Don't be daft. They're virtual, aren't they? That means they're not real.'

She clicks on a picture of a basket stuffed with crisps, cakes and biscuits, then over her shoulder says to me, 'What do you want to say?'

'How about, Dear Ed, thank you for your beautiful flowers. I thought you might be hungry but save the Oreos for me. They're my favourite . . . Looking forward to seeing you on Tuesday. Libby.'

'Love, Libby?' Jo asks, typing in my message.

'Oh, all right then. Love, Libby. So what happens now?'

'You just send it, and they get a message on their email saying they've had a virtual delivery and it gives instructions on where to go to pick up the present.'

'That's amazing.'

'Jesus, Libby!' she says. 'He's going to fall head over heels in love with you! I bet he's never met anyone like you before!'

I bet he hasn't either.

Just before I leave, I check my email, just in case, and sure enough there's a message from EMcMhn@compuserve.com.

'Dearest Libby,' it says. 'I'm now absolutely stuffed! What a delightful surprise, and I'm so pleased you received the flowers. Can hardly wait to see you again. Much love, Ed.'

'Cor,' says Jo, who's standing behind me, reading this over my shoulder. 'Now. He. Is. Keen.'

And I go home with a smile on my face.

I sneaked off early today, to have enough time to get ready, because I want to look good tonight and not necessarily for Ed, more for me, but I could really get used to these flowers and this general feeling of having met someone who could, possibly, adore me.

So it's face-pack time, and deep-conditioning-hair-stuff time, and anyway, there's nothing wrong in trying to look the best you can possibly look, is there? And I'm pretty damned pleased with how I look tonight. A pale grey trouser-suit with little pearl earrings that are really not my style at all, but they were a present from my mum a couple of birthdays ago, and flat cream suede shoes.

God. If my mother could see me now! I look like the epitome of a sophisticated young woman. And it's quite good fun, dressing up. I sort of feel a bit like a child playing a big game. Let's pretend to be sophisticated, smart and mature. What fun!

The phone rings just as I've finished applying a coat of nail polish.

'What have you eaten today?' Naturally, it's Jules.

'Nothing for breakfast. A milk-chocolate Hobnob at about eleven o'clock. A Caesar salad for lunch, and an apple this afternoon.'

'That's good. You've been really good. The biscuit wasn't bad, not if you compare it to what I've had today.'

'Go on.'

'OK. For breakfast I had a huge bowl of cornflakes. Huge. Really. Disgusting. Then at about ten o'clock I was hungry again, so I had three chocolate Bourbons. At lunch I went out with a client and had grilled vegetables swimming in olive oil to start with, then a huge plate of pasta in a creamy sauce, and then we shared a *crème brûlée* but she hardly ate anything, I had practically the whole thing.'

Jules is such a bloody liar. I know exactly what she's like. She probably had a tiny bowl of cornflakes. No Bourbons. Plain vegetables. A couple of mouthfuls of pasta and a taste of the *crème brûlée*. There's no way Jules would be as slim as she is if she really ate what she says she does. She's more than a little obsessed, which is why we have so many food phone calls a day. I don't mind, really I don't, but I wish she'd stop thinking about it quite as much as she does.

Although I suppose I'm not that much better.

'I'm not going to have any dinner,' she says firmly. 'That's it for today. And tomorrow I'm going on a diet.'

'Oh, for God's sake, Jules!'

'What? What?'

'Never mind.' There's no point in telling her she doesn't need to lose weight, if anything she needs to put it on, because she won't believe me.

'So what are you wearing?'

I tell her.

'Mmm. Very sophis.'

'I know. It's not really me, but I couldn't turn up in something dead trendy or he'd faint.'

'You know what you are? You're a chameleon girlfriend.'

'A what?'

'I was reading an article about it. Women who change their image, their hobbies, pretty much everything, depending on the man they're with.'

I wish I didn't have to say this, but as usual Jules is absolutely right. I know it's wrong, even as I'm doing it, but I can't seem to help it.

'So tell me something else I didn't know,' I say bitterly, because, much as I love Jules, I suppose I'm slightly envious of her confidence, the fact that she's never done it. She's never had to.

'Don't take it like that,' she says, sounding wounded. 'I wish I could be more like you sometimes.'

'Jules! You're nuts! You'd like to be single with no self-esteem and a radar that warns off all decent men and only attracts the bastards?'

'Ed's not a bastard.'

'Not yet. Anyway, he's not good-looking enough to be a bastard.'

'And Jon was good-looking?' she taunts. 'Listen, Jamie's back, I gotta go. Have a fantastic evening, and call me first thing.'

'Thanks, sweetie. Bye.'

Ed has booked a table at the Ivy, and he seems to know an awful lot of people in there, and I'm really beginning to enjoy being with this man who's so sophisticated and yet so naive at the same time. His naiveté is probably his most endearing quality.

He orders champagne and, as we raise our glasses, I hear a familiar swooping voice.

'Libby! Darling!' And I turn round and there, resplendent in a tiny black dress, is Amanda. I give her the obligatory air kisses, and then she just stands there, looking at me, then at Ed, and I introduce them.

And it's quite extraordinary, because Ed stands up to shake her hand, and Amanda starts simpering like an idiot.

'Who was that?' Ed asks when she's gone.

'Amanda Baker. She's a television presenter.'

'I see. Is she famous?'

'Not as famous as she'd like to be.'

'Ha ha! That's very good, Libby. How do you know her?'

'I do her PR.'

'So you could make her famous, then?'

'It's sort of Catch-22. You can't be famous without being written about, and nobody wants to write about someone who isn't famous. But I'm trying.'

'I don't watch much TV, that's probably why I didn't recognise her.'

'What do you do if you're at home at night?'

'Work usually. Listen to music.'

'So if I told you I was in love with Dr Doug Ross it wouldn't mean anything to you?'

His face falls. 'Who's Dr Doug Ross?'

'Never mind,' I laugh. 'You wouldn't understand.'

The food's delicious, the champagne's delicious, and I'm loving sitting here star-spotting, although every time I whisper that another celebrity has just walked in, Ed stares at them in confusion, and it's quite amazing that he really doesn't have a clue who these people are.

'Libby,' he says, when we're waiting for our coffees. 'I think you're extraordinary. You're so bright, and sparky, and full of life. I really enjoy being with you. And . . .' He pauses.

'And?' I prompt, because after Nick I deserve to have my ego inflated.

'Well, I'm not sure whether I should say this yet, and it probably sounds ridiculous, but I really like you.'

'That doesn't sound ridiculous.'

'No. I mean I really like you.'

'I like you too.'

'Good. And I think we might have something special here.'

I smile. I mean, what could I say? The guy hardly knows me.

'I thought you might like to see my house,' he says, on the way back.

'I'd love to!' which is true, I want to know more about him, more about where he lives, how he lives. I want to nose around his home and look for clues about who he is, whether I could be happy with him.

Please don't think it's because I've decided he's The One or anything, but I do have a worrying tendency to, how shall I put it, plan ahead. You wouldn't believe the number of times I've sat in bed dreaming of my

marriage to someone I've had one date with. And, although I don't fancy
Ed, it's quite good fun dreaming about it anyway.

So we pull up outside a sweeping terrace, and I can see that Ed's
incredibly proud of his house as he walks me through the hall, one of
those black-and-white marble numbers, and flings open the doors to
the most spectacular drawing room I've ever seen. Huge, airy, with stunning original mouldings on the walls and ceiling, it's completely empty.

'Umm, have you recently moved in?' I ask.

'No. I've lived here for two years!' he says.

'What about furniture?'

'I've never got round to buying any,' he says, shrugging. 'I suppose
I'm waiting for my wife to come in and redecorate.'

'Oh. Right,' I say.

He leads me upstairs to his bedroom. Immaculate and huge, it leads
into an enormous dressing room, lined wall to wall with cupboards, and
then through to an en suite bathroom.

Next door is his study, and upstairs there's a gym, a sauna and more
empty bedrooms. And more. And more. They seem to stretch on for
ever, and I honestly feel as if I've stumbled into a ghost house, because
it's quite clear that none of these rooms is ever used. I start to feel
increasingly uncomfortable here.

We go downstairs to the basement. A country-style kitchen, and I
breathe a sigh of relief because next to the kitchen there are sofas, and
French doors leading onto a garden. Judging by the amount of books
and papers piled around the room, this is the place he lives in.

And it really is quite cosy. Not perhaps exactly as I'd do it, but it's not
at all bad.

Ed goes into the kitchen to make some coffee, and I sit and look
round the room, deciding what I'd change if I lived here. I'd have the
sofas re-covered in a bright blue-and-yellow chequered fabric, I'd get rid
of that revolting limed kitchen table, I'd . . .

'Do you like it?' Ed interrupts my thoughts.

'I think it's spectacular,' I say, because it undoubtedly is, but I decide
against telling him it's a bit like a morgue. 'But don't you get a bit lonely
rattling around in this huge place by yourself?'

'Yes,' he says, suddenly looking like a little boy lost. 'At times I do.'

And he looks so sweet I want to hug him.

He comes to sit next to me on the sofa, and the air suddenly feels a lot
more oppressive, and I know he's going to kiss me, but I'm not sure I
want him to. I try to avoid looking at him, keeping my eyes fixed firmly
on my coffee. He sneaks an arm round the back of the sofa, not yet

touching me, and I want to run out of there screaming because at this moment I know as an absolute certainty that I don't want to kiss him.

This, it has to be said, is a bit of a new feeling for me. If I bother going out with someone again after a first date, then it's because I fancy them, and I spend the rest of the second date praying they'll kiss me. So why am I so desperate for Ed not to kiss me now?

And more to the point, what the hell am I supposed to do? Suddenly, and I'm not really sure how this happens, suddenly he's kissing me, and I wish to God I could tell you that it was lovely, that my stomach turned over with lust, that I suddenly started to fancy him . . .

It was revolting.

I wish I could pinpoint exactly what it was that was so revolting, but I can't. Too much tongue. Too much saliva. Too much moustache. Yuck. Not nice at all. So I pull away, thinking that nothing, nothing will make me kiss him again.

Not even the Porsche.

But I don't mind cuddling him, and he puts his arms round me and that's quite nice, at least it would be if I wasn't so tense at the prospect of him kissing me again.

'Libby,' he says after nuzzling my neck for a while. 'I think I'd better take you home.'

What? What? He's supposed to ask me to stay the night and I'm supposed to turn him down. What is this? He's supposed to be dying of lust for me; he's not supposed to want to take me home. But at least it means I won't have to kiss him again.

We get in the car, and this time Ed keeps a hand on my thigh all the way back, but the funny thing is it's not sexual somehow, more proprietorial, and, although I wish he'd take it off, I'm not quite sure how to tell him, so I do an awful lot of shuffling around and crossing and uncrossing my legs, but the hand stays.

'When can I see you again?' he says, walking me to my front door.

'Well, I'm a bit busy this week,' I say.

'Oh.' His face falls. 'Actually, I wanted to invite you to a ball. Some friends of mine in the country are having their annual ball the weekend after next, and I'd love you to come.'

Jules's voice echoes in my head: go out with him because you never know what his friends are like, so I tell him that I'd love to come.

'Do you have anything to wear?'

'I'm sure I've got something.'

'Look, I hope you don't think this too forward of me, but I'd really like to buy you something special. Would you allow me to?'

What am I, stupid? As if I'm going to turn this down.

'If you're sure,' I say.

'Absolutely. Why don't we go shopping on Saturday?'

My brain starts ticking quickly. Shopping. Daytime. No public displays of affection, therefore no kissing.

'That sounds lovely.'

'Great! I'll see you on Saturday.' His arms encircle my waist and his head moves in again, so I give him a few pecks on the lips, and then with a mysterious smile I move away and go into my flat.

Quite well handled, if I say so myself.

But once I'm home, back in the safety of my flat, I start thinking about that kiss, and then, I can't help it, I start thinking about Nick kissing me, about how it made me feel, and before I know it I'm sitting on my sofa with tears streaming down my cheeks.

I miss him. I can't help it. I just miss him. And Ed, nice as he is, isn't Nick and never will be.

But it's funny how sometimes a little cry makes you feel a whole hell of a lot better, and when I've finished I feel sort of resigned. I know that it's over with Nick, and I know that I don't feel the same about Ed, but maybe I could learn to love Ed. Maybe.

'Nah. I don't think there's any point.'

'But he's so nice, Jules! Maybe it could grow.'

'Libby, when he kissed you, you felt sick. What could grow, exactly?'

'I don't know,' I huff. 'Maybe I need to get used to his kissing.'

'Then go for it.'

'God, you're no help at all.'

'Well, what am I supposed to say? I tell you not to bother and you say he's really nice, so I tell you to keep seeing him and you tell me I'm not helping. I can't win with you.'

'Sorry,' I grumble, curling my feet up under me on the sofa in Jules's kitchen.

'So what's going on now?' Jamie walks in, bends down and gives me a kiss on the cheek before ruffling Jules's hair as he heads to put the kettle on, and something about this affectionate gesture suddenly makes me feel incredibly lonely.

I want this too. I want someone who will adore me so much that they cannot even walk past me without touching me in some way. I want someone who will worship me, even when—as Jules is now—I'm sitting around with no make-up on and hair scraped back.

'More man problems?' Jamie says from the other end of the kitchen.

'Naturally,' I say. 'Isn't it always?'

Jamie brings three mugs of coffee over and sits down. 'Jules said you'd been out with Ed McMahon. Bit of a catch, I'd say.'

'I know,' I moan. 'But I don't fancy him.'

'Ah,' says Jamie. 'That could be a problem. But he's meant to be a nice guy. Maybe you need to give it time.'

'Tell him about the kissing.' Jules prods me.

I tell him about the kissing.

Jamie makes a face. 'I've got to be honest, Libs, it doesn't sound good.'

'And meanwhile,' Jules interrupts, 'he's taking her shopping for a ball-gown on Saturday.'

'Look on the bright side,' Jamie says. 'At least you'll get a designer outfit out of it.'

On Friday morning another bouquet arrives at the office. This is getting silly. My flat's looking less like a florist's and more like Kew Gardens every day.

God, will you listen to me?

Sorry, sorry, sorry. It's typical, isn't it? For twenty-seven years I've wanted someone who adores me and now I've found that person I just can't seem to get excited. Why can't I fancy him? Why can't I make myself fancy him? Maybe I can. Let's just see what happens on Saturday.

And then a very peculiar thing happens. Just after the flowers arrive the phone rings. 'Libby? It's Nick.'

'Nick who?' I'm so distracted by the flowers I'm not thinking straight.

'Thanks a lot. It wasn't that long ago, surely.'

'Nick!' My heart starts pounding. Perhaps he's ringing because he misses me so much he's realised he's made a terrible mistake.

'Libby!'

'Oh my God! I'm so sorry! I was distracted. Hi!' I'm fighting to sound as normal as possible, and it's a hard struggle, but I think I'm winning.

'Hello, my darling. I was just sitting here doing nothing and I was thinking about you so I thought I'd phone and see how you are.'

He called me darling! He was thinking about me!

'I'm absolutely great,' I say, with conviction, because of course, now that he's phoned, I am. 'How are you?'

'Oh, you know. Usual. Trying to write but can't seem to concentrate. Plus, I'm still trying to get over the most mind-blowing hangover.'

'Where did you go? Anywhere nice?' I feel a huge twinge of jealousy at the thought that Nick might have been with another woman, and I pray that he wasn't. My prayers, for once, are answered.

'Just down the pub with Moose and that lot.'

Thank God. At least I know he couldn't have fancied any of those awful women. God. Moose. Those friends. I suddenly feel like laughing, because for the first time I realise I won't ever have to go to a pub with Moose and that lot again. And not only that, I realise that for the first time in my life I might actually be able to stay friends with an ex-lover. And I really don't want anything more from him. Honestly.

'A heavy session?' I laugh, thrilled at this feeling of being set free.

'A very heavy session,' he groans. 'But I'm paying for it now. So what have you been up to? I've been thinking about you.'

'I've been very busy, actually. Everything's going really well.'

There's a short silence before Nick asks, 'How's your love life?'

'Umm. Well . . .' Oh fuck it. Why not? 'I've sort of met someone.'

There's a long silence.

'That's great, Libby!' he says finally, but if I didn't know better I'd say he didn't think it was great at all. 'Who is he?'

'Just a guy. I don't know whether it's anything serious,' I say. 'Really, nothing to write home about, but he's nice, he treats me well.'

'What does he do?'

'Investment banker.'

Nick groans. 'So he can afford to take you to all the places I never could?'

'Yup!' I say, and laugh.

'I knew you hated me not having money,' Nick says suddenly.

'No, I didn't, Nick. I just hated staying in your disgusting bedsit.'

We both laugh.

'I suppose now you're staying the night in Buckingham Palace?'

'Hanover Terrace, actually.' I don't mention that I don't even like kissing my new man, let alone thinking about going to bed with him.

'Seriously, Libby,' he says. 'I'm really happy you've found someone.'

'Are you?'

'Well, OK then, not really. Well, sort of. I am happy, but I'm also really sorry that things didn't work out with us.'

This conversation seems to be going in a very strange direction, but I think it's OK, I think that I'm over Nick, that we probably both have regrets but that it's time to move on.

'I know,' I say. 'So am I, but, let's face it, we weren't exactly a match made in heaven.'

There's a silence.

'I mean,' I continue, 'I'd love to have you as my friend, but in hindsight we should probably never have been together.'

'You're probably right,' he sighs. 'And anyway, I couldn't handle a relationship right now.'

'I know,' I laugh. 'That's what you said when you dumped me.'

'I didn't dump you! We just . . . parted.'

'A bit like the Red Sea?'

'Exactly.'

'And what about you, Nick?' I don't really want to ask this question, I don't really want to know, but I can't help it. 'How's your love life?'

'Terrible.' Thank you, thank you, thank you, God.

'No women, then?'

'Nah. Not since you. But I'm fine. I'm being very introverted and doing lots of thinking about love and life and all that stuff.'

'Come up with any conclusions yet?'

'Yes. I've concluded that I'm completely screwed up.'

'So tell me something else I didn't know.'

'Thanks!' Indignant tone.

'Pleasure!' Light and breezy tone.

'So are we friends now?' A cautious tone.

'Of course! I'd love to be friends with you.'

'Does that mean we could get together for a drink some time?'

'That would be lovely.'

'OK. Listen, I'll call you next week and we'll sort something out.'

'Fine. I've gotta go, Nick, there's another call for me.'

'OK. God, it's so nice to hear your voice, Libby. I've missed you.'

'I've missed you too.'

I ring Jules immediately to tell her that Nick called, but as soon as she picks up the phone I can hear there's something wrong. Her voice is sounding flat, she doesn't sound as bright as she normally does.

'Jules?' I venture. 'Is everything OK?'

I hear a long sigh.

'What's the matter?'

'God, Libby,' she sighs. 'I'm really worried. About Jamie. I know this sounds crazy, and I know he works all the time, but the last couple of weeks he's been working late in the office, and last night I called him and there was no reply. When he got home I casually asked him if he went out, but he said no, he'd been in his office all night.'

'So? He'd probably gone to the loo or something.'

'For three hours? And that's not everything. He's been a bit distant lately but I tried to ignore it and when I did ask him if there was something the matter he said his mind was on a case and he was really busy.'

'Jules, you're not telling me you think he's having an affair, are you? You're crazy, Jamie would never do that.'

'I thought I was going mad,' Jules says slowly, 'but suddenly I've started remembering that over the last few weeks the phone's rung a few times and it's been put down when I've answered.'

'So? Probably a wrong number.'

'I know something's wrong, Libby. I can't explain it, it's almost like a sixth sense. I'm sure he's met someone else.'

'Jules, you're being ridiculous. I saw you together just the other day and he still obviously adores you. And Jamie's hardly the type to have an affair. Jesus, Jules. Are you sure you're not going through an early menopause or something?'

'I don't know. Look, I've got to go. I haven't decided what to do yet but I'll fill you in.'

I put down the phone, wondering whether Jules is going mad, whether Jamie would be unfaithful. But I'll tell you this. If Jamie is having an affair I'll kill him. Even the thought of him causing Jules pain makes me so angry I want to go storming into his chambers now and kick the living daylights out of him. How could he? How dare he?

It seems as if a weight has suddenly descended onto my shoulders, and, if I feel like this, how in the hell must Jules be feeling?

 **Chapter Ten**

'SO YOU'RE ACTUALLY going out with him?'

Amanda and I are once again having lunch, this time at Daphne's, and she's still treating me like her best friend, and I can't figure out why we're having lunch again so soon after the last one, but she phoned up and suggested it and anything to get me out of the office for a while.

Not that I don't enjoy work. I love my job. But recently I've found myself dreaming more and more about not having to work. Lunching at Daphne's and shopping at Joseph every day. Heaven.

'I'm not sure I'd say that,' I say. 'We're just sort of seeing one another.'

'I think he's really quite sexy,' says Amanda in a dreamy sort of voice.

I look at her in horror. 'What? That moustache? Sexy?'

'I don't mind moustaches,' she says. 'Not if they have that much money. But surely if you're seeing him you must find him sexy?'

I shrug. 'I'm not sure how I feel about him, but he treats me well and he's taking me out tomorrow to buy me an outfit for this ball he's taking me to. To be honest, I'm just enjoying being spoiled, no one's ever done anything like this for me before.'

'He's taking you shopping?' Her eyes are wide. 'Where are you going?'

'I don't know. You're probably the best person to ask. Where will I find a black-tie-type dress?'

'Why don't you go to Harvey Nichs? They've got a decent evening wear department, and if you don't find anything you like there, then they've got all the designer concessions.'

'Excellent idea. Harvey Nichs it is.'

'And I have to tell you, Libby, if you decide you don't want him, I'll have him.'

I laugh, but then I look up and realise that Amanda's not laughing with me. She has this sort of strange smile on her face, and Jesus Christ, she's not bloody joking. Oh well, if I decide I don't want him she can have him. With pleasure. And am I going mad or might the fact that she wants him be making me want him just a teeny bit more?

So when Saturday arrives I'm sort of looking forward to seeing him. What I've done, since my lunch with Amanda, is try to picture Ed as being much worse than he actually is. I know that might sound a bit bizarre, but I've pictured him as really ugly, his moustache as really big, his laugh really braying, and that way I'm hoping that I won't be disappointed when I open the door, that I'll actually be pleasantly surprised.

And you know what? It bloody works! I open the door and Ed is far, far better than I remember him, and I grin as I take the flowers—lilies this time—and reach up and give him a kiss on the lips.

'I've really looked forward to seeing you,' he says, putting his arms round me and giving me a hug.

'Good,' I say, as I hug him back.

We drive up to Knightsbridge, park the car, and when we walk to Harvey Nichs he takes my hand and I follow meekly, loving this submissive role of being a wealthy-woman-who-lunches in waiting.

I think we actually look a pretty good couple. Ed in his casual but still oh-so-smart polo shirt, crisp dark blue jeans and brown suede Gucci loafers (of course I bloody noticed them, what do you think I am, blind or something?), and me in my camel silk trousers, brown mock-croc loafers and white linen shirt.

And it gets better! In the evening-wear department in Harvey

Nichols, Ed walks around silently looking at clothes as the sales assistant bustles around showing me dresses. 'Would your husband like this one?' she says at one point, and Ed overhears while I almost faint in alarm, because you should never, ever, bring up the M word when you're with your new boyfriend. But Ed just smiles at me, a very tender, affectionate smile, and I can't help it. I grin back.

'I can see my *wife* in something like this,' Ed says, and my heart turns over, and then it stops completely when I see what he's picked out. It's a twin-set taffeta suit. The jacket's navy, with a nipped-in waist and a flared peplum skirt, and the skirt's probably mid-calf length. It is absolutely disgusting. It's the sort of thing my mother would wear.

'Umm, I don't think that's quite me, actually,' I say, turning away.

'Would you just try it on?' he says. 'For me?'

'OK.' I shrug, and take the outfit into the changing room. Jesus Christ I wouldn't be caught dead in anything like this. I poke my head round the curtain. 'Ed, I don't think this is quite, er, me.'

'Let me see. Come out here.'

I walk out with shoulders stooped, stomach pressed out, trying to look as disgusting as the suit, hoping to put him off.

'You really hate it, don't you?' he laughs.

'I really hate it.'

'I think it's rather nice, but if you don't like it, then we'll find something else.'

Eight more disgusting taffeta numbers and I'm beginning to seriously rethink this whole thing.

And then finally we leave the evening wear department, and, just as we're walking through the designer section, Ed stops and walks over to Donna Karan. There, on a dummy, is the most beautiful shimmering black dress I've ever seen. Long-sleeved, it swoops at the front and sweeps down to the floor in the most gorgeous, slinky, sexy way.

We both stand there for a while, admiring this dress, and then Ed turns to the assistant, who's hovering behind us and says, 'Do you have this in a twelve?' Bless him, he's remembered my size.

'Certainly, sir,' she says, and smiles at me as she goes to get the dress.

And finally I feel like a princess. Actually, make that a queen. I stand straight and proud, admiring the way the dress cleverly hugs my figure, how it makes me look slim and tall and sophisticated. I walk out of the changing room, and both Ed and the sales assistant gasp.

'You look beautiful!' Ed whispers, as the sales girl just nods in agreement, and I can see from her face that she's as thrilled as I am with how the dress looks, and Jesus Christ, this dress has to be mine.

'That's the dress!' Ed says, and I beam as I admire myself in the full-length mirror.

'I love it!' I say. 'It's the most beautiful thing I've ever worn.'

Ed turns to the sales assistant. 'Do you take American Express?'

I go back into the changing room, and I can't help myself, when I finally tug the dress off I sneak a look at the price. And I almost faint.

£1,500.

Jesus Christ. What the hell should I do? I can't let Ed spend this money on me, that's absurd. That's the most ridiculous amount of money I've ever seen in my whole life.

The sales assistant pops her head round, smiles at me and takes the dress, and I figure that if Ed has a problem with it, he'll tell me, because he's going to find out soon enough how much it is.

I finish getting dressed and walk out of the changing room, and Ed's sitting in a chair with a big grin on his face. By his feet is a bag, floaty wisps of tissue paper peeking out from the top.

'There you are, my darling,' he says, handing me the bag. 'A beautiful dress for my beautiful Libby.'

'But, Ed,' I say, flushing because I can't believe he's done this, and I start to say something about the price, but he stops me.

'I don't want to hear another word about it,' he says, so I reach up and kiss him.

'Thank you. No one's ever bought me anything so wonderful before.'

'It's my pleasure,' he says. 'Now. Do you have plans for the rest of the day?'

I know what he means. He means this evening. And you know what? Fuck it. I don't mind spending the rest of my Saturday with him, evening included. I mean, for £1,500 it's the very least I can do.

We go back to Ed's house, and you know this time, the second time, it doesn't seem quite so cold and forbidding. I'm beginning to feel quite at home: I even offer to make tea while Ed makes some business calls. While I'm pottering in the kitchen, opening cupboards to find out where everything is, I'm starting to think that I could live in a house like this. I could, in fact, live in this house.

Oh, for God's sake, Libby! Stop it!

But anyway, this feels very cosy. Very *coupley*. Unbelievable, bearing in mind I hardly know this guy, but I do feel very comfortable with him, surprisingly so, and whether this is because I'm not in love with him and he, I suspect, is crazy about me, I don't know, but it's a nice feeling, really. Bit of a new one for me.

And we have a nice evening. To be honest I would be happy staying in, but we're still in the getting-to-know-you stages, and we're not quite ready for cosy evenings in, and as far as I'm concerned those only happen once you've slept together, and, lovely as I'm beginning to think Ed is, I'm still not ready to sleep with him. Not yet.

So instead of curling up on the sofa and watching a video, we jump in the car and whiz down to the Screen on Baker Street to watch a film, and Ed insists on buying me a huge bucket of popcorn.

And the strangest thing of all is that he is so intent on making me happy, on making sure that I'm all right during every single second that I'm in his company, that I start thinking that maybe he could be The One after all.

The phone's ringing as I walk in the door, but for a while I have no idea who it is, because all I can hear is sobbing.

'Hello? Hello? Who is this?'

'It's me,' and between the hiccups and the sobs I recognise Jules's voice and my face drains of colour as I slowly sit down.

'Jules? What's the matter?'

'I . . .' She can't speak.

'I'm coming over,' I say, and bang down the phone, grab my keys and head out of the door.

Jules looks terrible. Her eyes are so puffy they've almost disappeared, I walk in and put my arms round her, and she leans her head on my shoulder and collapses into a fresh round of tears.

Eventually the tears dissipate into hiccups, and I lead Jules into the kitchen and sit down on the sofa with my arm round her.

'I don't know what to do,' she says eventually, her pain almost break-ing my heart. 'I don't know what to do.'

'What's happened?' Gentle, soothing tone of voice.

'He's gone,' she says, as the tears start flowing again.

An hour later, after countless tears, I have the full story, and it makes me feel sick. Sick, frightened and angry. I had always thought Jules and Jamie were the perfect couple. They had the marriage I aspired to have, the life I had always wanted. They had fulfilled a dream, and now that dream was lying in shreds around our feet.

Jamie, it seems, had walked in last night and said that they needed to talk. Jules had sat there with pounding heart as he told her that he had a confession. He said that he had been having an affair with Laura, a lawyer he had met, but that it wasn't meant to be an affair—they had only slept together three times and he had felt so guilty that it was now over.

He said he was telling her because it was over, and it was only fair that she should know. He said he loved Jules, and, if anything, it had made him realise how important Jules was. He couldn't live with himself any more, with the guilt, and he hoped she would forgive him, and it would never happen again.

And Jules, apparently, sat there speechless, too shocked to say anything, feeling as if she had been physically kicked in the stomach.

After the shock came anger, at which point Jules ran to their bedroom, threw his clothes into a heap and screamed at him to get out.

Jamie had started crying, trying to put his arms round her and telling her that he loved her, that he couldn't live without her, but Jules kept screaming at him to go. She spent the night pacing round the flat, and now anger has been replaced by desolation, and this is why she does not know what to do.

'I hate him,' she sobs, as she finishes. 'I absolutely bloody hate him.'

'Jules,' I say eventually, as once again the crying subsides. 'Are you sure this is over, between you two, I mean? Shouldn't you try and talk about things, give this time?'

There is a silence, and then: 'I don't know. I don't know what to do.'

'He said it was over with this Laura,' and Jules winces at the mention of her name, but I continue nevertheless, 'and he loves you, and is it really worth throwing away your marriage because of a mistake?'

'I don't know if I can forgive him, if I can ever trust him again,' she says. And I sit there as she lets out the anger, lets out the pain, and I think, if this marriage is over, then perhaps I can no longer believe in the dream at all.

'Oll! What are you doing here?' I fling my arms round Olly, and he scoops me off the ground and swings me round.

My mum stands in the living room watching Olly and me, her face beaming because her beloved son is back home this weekend.

'How long are you down for?' I ask.

'Just this weekend, but then I'm coming down soon for a couple of weeks because we're shooting a load of stuff in London.'

'He's going to stay here, aren't you, Olly?' says my mum proudly. 'It'll be just like old times having you back here again.'

'Only if you promise to make a fuss of me and spoil me,' says Olly, with a cheeky grin.

'Oh, you,' says my mother grinning, flicking a dishcloth at Olly's legs.

I sit there and watch them and wonder how in the hell he does it. How he manages never to put a foot wrong in her eyes. How he teases her and she loves it. He never gets her back up, never upsets her. And part of me, I suppose, is slightly envious of that.

I sigh as she bustles into the kitchen to make some tea, and I settle back into the sofa with Olly.

'So how's Carolyn?'

'She's fine,' he says.

'Still going strong?'

'Yeah, I know. Amazing. It's still going strong.'

'So what's her secret?'

'I don't know really . . .' Like a man would ever take the time to analyse, but then Olly surprises me. 'I think the thing is that she doesn't make any demands on me. She's really laid-back. She's happy to get on with her own life, and it's just really comfortable and relaxed, because I know she doesn't expect to see me all the time.'

'So how often are you seeing her?'

'Well, actually,' he laughs, 'I suppose I am seeing her a lot, but that's because she's so easy to be with. And when I'm not with her she's out with her friends.'

'That's brilliant, Olly,' I say, and I wonder whether I could ever be more like Carolyn, whether I could be laid-back, low-maintenance, but then I suppose I am like that with Ed. I'm really not that bothered about where he is when he's not with me.

'And you really like her?'

'I really like her. So what about you, Libby? What's going on with men in your life? Any action?'

'Yes, there is. I'm seeing someone, and he's really nice.'

'Tell me about him.'

'His name's Ed, he's thirty-nine—'

'Thirty-nine? Isn't that a bit old for you?'

'Nah, I like older men.' As it happens I've never liked older men before, but there's something quite sophisticated about being the sort of woman who likes older men.

'So go on.'

'He's an investment banker . . .'

Olly lets out a high whistle. 'Shit. He must be loaded.'

'He is,' I say, smiling happily. 'But more importantly he's really nice to me, he treats me like a queen.'

'You really like him?'

'Ye-es,' I say. 'I do really like him. The only thing is I'm not sure how much I fancy him, but I think I'm beginning to, so that's OK.'

Shit. My bloody mother overheard that last bit.

'You don't know whether you fancy him? *Fancy* him? I've never heard anything so ridiculous, Libby. It's not about fancying someone, it's about liking them and getting on with them. None of that fancying stuff lasts anyway. D'you think I *fancied* your father?'

Olly and I both grimace. Not a thought I particularly want to dwell on, I have to say.

'It's Ed McMahon, Olly,' my mother says. 'He's very rich and very nice, and Libby's worried about whether she fancies him or not. Honestly!'

'How do you know he's very nice?' I taunt. 'You've never met him, he could be a complete bastard for all you know.'

'I won't have that language in my house, Libby, and I've heard he's very nice.'

'Oh right. Of course. Because you do mix in the same social circles.'

My mother harrumphs and walks back into the kitchen.

'What was all that about?' Olly's looking confused.

'Mum's decided that come hell or high water I'm going to marry Ed, because he's rich and because she can boast to all her friends.'

'Uh-oh,' he says. 'Sounds like you're in trouble. So when am I going to meet this Ed?'

My mother's back in the room, evidently having forgotten my last sarcastic remark. 'Ooh, I'd love to meet him too,' she says.

'I think it's a little bit early on to start introducing him to my parents,' I say, feeling physically sick at the thought.

'I don't agree,' she says. 'If he's as nice as you say he is then he'd be delighted to meet us.'

'I don't think so, Mum,' I say. 'Look, Olly, I've got to go.' Even the added attraction of Olly being there doesn't make me want to stay a second longer than is absolutely necessary. 'Why don't you come with me and we can have a drink?'

'Olly's staying here,' my mum says firmly. 'And where are you going that's so important?'

'To Ed's,' I lie, knowing it's the one thing she won't try to stop.

'How lovely,' she trills. 'Ask him if he'd like to come over for dinner.'

'Yeah, really,' I mutter, kissing her goodbye.

And when I get home there's a long, rambly message on my machine from Ed, and I ring him back, and he's so pleased to hear from me it's really sweet. And he asks me about my day, and I tell him I've just got back from my parents. Ed says he'd love to meet my parents.

'You are joking?'

'Of course not. Why don't we all go out for dinner this week?'

'Ed,' I say slowly, not quite knowing what to say next. 'Let's just wait until after the ball, OK?'

'Fine, fine. But I would like to meet them.'

'Umm, don't you think that, umm, it might be a little soon?'

'Libby,' he says calmly. 'When it's right, it's right,' and in a flood of confusion I say goodbye.

What the fuck does that mean, when it's right, it's right? Was he saying that he loves me? Do I feel the same way about him?

Normally I'd talk this through with Jules, but the only thing we talk about now on the phone is Jamie. But I need to know if she's OK, so I put my life on hold for the time being and call her. Her machine picks up and I start talking, and then she picks up the phone.

'How are you feeling?' I venture, surprised and incredibly relieved that she sounds almost, almost, like her normal self.

'Not great,' she says. 'But better than I was.'

'Have you spoken to him?'

'I've left the machine on and he's been leaving pleading messages. I can't face speaking to him just yet, I've still got a lot to think about.'

'So you think you might give him another chance?'

'I don't know. I can't believe what he's done, or how much this hurts.'

'Jules, do you still love him?'

'Of course I still love him. That's the bloody problem.'

A few minutes later the phone rings and it's Sal. 'Listen,' she says. 'I know this may well not be your thing, and Nick's coming, but a few of us are meeting up tonight at the Clifton in St John's Wood, and I wondered if you'd like to come?'

I suddenly have an inspired thought. 'Sal, my brother Olly's in London this weekend. Can he come too?'

"Course he can.'

'And it's fine with Nick. It will be really lovely to see him.'

But after I put the phone down I'm not so sure. I mean, yes, it was lovely talking to Nick on the phone the other day, but seeing him is another matter entirely.

Oh, what the hell, it's not as if I've got anything better to do. I ring Olly and yes, Mum's beginning to get on his nerves a bit, and yes, yes, yes, he'd love to come out for a drink.

I give Olly the details and arrange to meet him there, and once I've put down the phone I look at myself in my jeans and sloppy jumper, and I decide that, as befits a woman of my recently acquired social standing, I will dress up. Smart casual. I will blow Nick's socks off.

Yeah, yeah, yeah, I know. It's that old story again. Nick said he didn't want me any more, so, even though I'm with Ed now, I want to show him what he's missing out on, what someone else is now getting.

Or not, as the case may be, but Nick doesn't need to know that.

What to wear, what to wear? I riffle through my clothes, and eventually pull out some wide-legged navy trousers, which I team with navy shoes and a thin cream cashmere sweater.

Oops, sorry, I forgot to mention that I went on a bit of a shopping spree recently. It's Ed, you see. I can hardly go out with him to the smartest restaurants in London in all my old clothes, so I've bitten the bullet, pushed my overdraft to the very back of my head, and been hitting Joseph in a major, major fashion.

It's only money, for God's sake.

Yup. This is the outfit. Nick will have heart failure.

I walk in the pub, and it's a bit like *déjà vu*, because sitting at a table on the other side of the bar are Sal and Paul, the gorgeous Kathy with an equally gorgeous and evidently new man by her side, and Nick.

And when I see Nick my heart does begin to beat a little faster because—and I know it hasn't been that long—I really had forgotten quite how blue his eyes are, and just how gorgeous his smile is.

He stands up and gives me a huge bear hug, and there's something incredibly sweet and painful about hugging this body that up until recently I knew so well, and I can't help myself, those old loins start stirring and I don't want to let go. Ever.

No! Stop it, Libby! Nick is not for you. Nick has no money. Remember Moose. Remember the bedsit. I remember, and my heart slows down. It slows down even more when I think of the Porsche and the house in Hanover Terrace.

Nick stands back and looks at me, giving me a wolf whistle and a cheeky grin. 'Cor,' he says. 'You're all sophisticated and sexy. Verrrry nice.'

'You like my new look, then?'

'Mmm,' he says. 'I could definitely get used to it.'

I almost laugh when I think of how I only ever wore jeans and trainers with Nick because I thought that's what he wanted. Almost, but not quite, because Jules's description of me as a chameleon girlfriend is still in my mind, and I don't want to think about the fact that I might be doing it again.

'Hi, sorry I'm late.' Olly walks in, and I give him a kiss, then introduce him round the table. I can see Kathy's eyes light up as she shakes his hand, and bless Olly, he barely even seems to notice her. This is when I realise that it really must be serious with Carolyn, because, up until he met her, Kathy would have been just his type.

'Nick! Good to see you again!' Nick stands up and they give each other a really warm, claspy sort of handshake—the sort of handshake that men give each other when they really like one another.

'I was just saying that Libby looks fantastic,' says Nick.

'Yeah. You do look nice. Very smart.' Olly seems to notice what I'm wearing for the first time. 'That looks expensive. Had a pay rise?'

Nick chuckles as I blush. 'No. It's courtesy of my overdraft facility.'

'Who wants what?' Olly goes off to the bar to get the drinks, and I start chatting to Sal and Paul.

But while I'm chatting to them I keep feeling Nick's eyes on me, and I can feel myself holding in my stomach, straightening my back, tossing my hair around as I laugh in what I hope is a sexy and mysterious way.

And then there's a break in the conversation and Nick leans over to me. 'You must be happy with this bloke,' he says. 'You're glowing. In fact you look like you're going to explode, a sort of thermonuclear reaction.'

'Is that supposed to be a compliment?'

'It is a compliment.'

'OK. Well, thanks.'

'And no food babies tonight, then?' He looks at my stomach and I laugh, and suddenly I'm swept back to that night in my flat when Nick knelt down and rubbed my stomach, and I feel this incredible yearning, and I meet his eyes which are watching me curiously, and I suddenly think that this is exactly what he intended.

I change the subject. 'So how's the book coming along?'

'Finished!' he says, thanking Olly for the pint that's just been placed in front of him. 'I'm about to send the finished manuscript off to a load of literary agents. I've had it with publishers. I don't think they even bother to read the bloody thing, so I'm going the agent route.'

'Good luck,' I say, and I mean it. 'What do you think will happen?'

'I don't know,' he says. 'But unless I win the lottery very soon, I'm going to have to do something about a job.'

There. You see? He did it again. Brought up the lottery. Made me think instantly of the night we got together.

'So go on. Tell me everything you've bought in the last week.'

'What?'

'You've obviously been shopping. I want to know exactly what you bought and where you got it from.'

I start to laugh. 'Jesus, Nick. I'd forgotten what a girl you are.'

'It's not that I'm a girl,' he says. 'I just know the way to a girl's heart.'

Chapter Eleven

'SO DID YOU ASK HIM?' Jules says.

Maybe she's just putting on a very good act, but the more we talk the more Jules sounds like her old self. I want so desperately for her and Jamie to get back together. I know he's betrayed her utterly and completely, but I wonder whether three fucks, to put it crudely, are worth a marriage, are worth throwing away a man who might not be perfect, but who loves her, despite everything, and who is a good husband.

'I couldn't. How could I ask Ed whether or not we would be staying the night?'

Because for the last few days I have been terrified of this. The ball is in a country house in Midhurst, which is about an hour and a half's drive from London, so does that mean we'll be driving back, or does it mean we're staying there? And if we are staying, are we staying in the same room, or will they have organised separate rooms for us?

'You are such a wimp!' says Jules. 'What are you going to do?'

'I don't know. I've packed clean knickers and a toothbrush just in case, but I don't want to be forced into a situation where I have to have sex with him before I'm ready.'

'Don't you mean, make lurrrve,' she shrieks, giggling.

'Oh, Jules! Be serious.'

'OK, OK. Sorry. Look, Libby, I doubt very much whether Ed will force you into anything, he's far too much of a gentleman, so I would assume that if you are staying the night you will have separate rooms.'

'You really think so?'

'I really think so. Look, you're going to have a brilliant time. Think of your gorgeous dress.'

'OK, OK. You're right. I will have a brilliant time. I'll ring you tomorrow, either way. Are you sure you're going to be OK?'

'I'm sure,' she says. 'Slowly getting used to enjoying the single life again. It's reminding me how jealous I am of your life.'

'Oh yeah, really—you'd just love to be living in my tiny flat, fending off the bastards, trying to find Mr Right.'

'First of all, I may well be single again. Secondly, my self-esteem's taken the biggest knocking it's ever had and I'm not sure I'll ever feel the same, and thirdly, I thought I had found a decent man. It looks like we are pretty damn similar after all.'

Shit. Why did I have to say that? I've unwittingly brought the conversation back round to Jamie.

'I'm sorry,' Jules says after a pause. 'I didn't mean that. I still feel so hurt. Look, I'd better go. Have a wonderful time tonight, and let me know how it went tomorrow.'

'Are you sure?'

'Sure that you should have a wonderful time or sure that you should let me know tomorrow? On both counts I'm sure.'

'No, are you sure you don't want to carry on talking?'

'No, Libby. I'm tired of talking about Jamie. I need a break.'

'OK. Just look after yourself.'

'I can't tell you how much easier this is, having you there. I couldn't go through this without you, Libby, I really couldn't.'

'You know I love you.' There are tears filling my eyes.

'I know. And I love you too. Oh, and by the way. Give him one for me,' she says, with a faint hint of laughter that brings a smile to my face.

I put the phone down and it rings again immediately. Who the hell is it now?

I might have guessed.

'Ringing to remind you, darling, that if it's a sit-down dinner you work your way in from the outside of the cutlery. I don't want you showing me up.'

'I can't believe you're ringing me to tell me that. What on earth has it got to do with you anyway? You're not coming.'

'I know, but you're still your mother's daughter.'

'Oh, for God's sake.'

'And have you taken a hot-water bottle? You know how these country mansions can get very draughty at night.'

'No, Mum,' I sigh wearily. 'I'm sure they'll have central heating. Look, I really have to go.'

'All right, darling. Have a wonderful time, and ring me tomorrow and tell me everything.'

'Yeah, Mum. I will.'

As if.

Thank God, no flowers this time. And I know this may sound crazy, but Ed seems ever so slightly nervous when he picks me up, which I find odd in a man who's so wealthy and sophisticated.

'Are you nervous?' I venture, as we set off from Ladbroke Grove.

'A little.' He turns to me and grins. 'Are you?'

'A little. But why are you nervous?'

He shrugs. 'I really want you to like my friends, that's all.'

Thank God for that. For one horrible minute there I thought he was worried about his friends liking me, worried that they might see beyond my designer dress to the not-nearly-good-enough suburban girl lurking just beneath the surface.

After a while Ed puts some music on—classical, naturally, and we sit there in this comfortable silence, and it is comfortable, and this feels so much nicer than the times I've spent with men in the past, desperately trying to think of something to say to fill the silences.

And finally we take an exit off the A3 and wind our way down country roads, as Ed tells me about the ball they had last year, and how wonderful it was, except that he didn't have anyone to share it with then, and how happy he is that I'm with him now.

We pull off the road and eventually come to a halt outside a pair of tall, black iron gates, and Ed speaks into an intercom, the gates open, and we're on a magnificent sweeping driveway, and I'm so impressed, and suddenly so nervous I can hardly speak.

Ed gets out of the car and comes round to open the door for me, and as I step out of the car I feel somewhat princess-like, and we both turn as a couple come walking out of the huge, heavy oak front door.

'Ed!' says the petite, blonde woman, who turns out to be Sarah, one half of Sarah and Charlie.

'Sarah!' he says, giving her a kiss on each cheek as she looks interestedly over his shoulder at me, standing there awkwardly smiling because I'm not sure what else to do.

He shakes hands with Charlie and turns to me.

'This is—'

'Libby,' says Sarah warmly, coming over to shake my hand. 'I am so delighted to meet you. We've heard all about you.'

'We certainly have,' echoes Charlie, coming over to give me a huge kiss on the cheek. 'Let me take your bags.'

Uh-oh. Here it is. That bedroom moment. Charlie and Ed lag behind as Sarah leads me up this, well, the only word for it would be magnificent, staircase, as I wonder what on earth I'm going to do.

'So how long have you known Ed?' She turns with a warm smile.

'Not long,' I venture. 'Only a few weeks.'

'He seems to be completely smitten.' She winks, stops and opens a door. 'We thought you might like this bedroom.'

I walk in, mouth wide open, because I can't believe how beautiful it is. There's a huge oak four-poster bed, and for a moment I'm so taken in with the splendour of it I forget to think, fuck! Double bed.

'We've put Ed next door,' she whispers, as the men approach. 'We weren't sure . . .' She tails off as I breathe a sigh of relief and grin.

'That's perfect,' I say, feeling as though I want to hug her. 'Thank you.'

She puts a hand gently on my arm and squeezes it. 'It must be terribly daunting for you, having to meet all these strange people.'

'You're not strange,' I say, smiling, and she laughs.

'Come down when you're ready,' she says. 'We'll have tea.' She turns and goes, and Ed comes in and gives me a hug.

'She's lovely,' I say into his shoulder.

'I know,' he says. 'I knew you'd like them.'

And then, naturally, insecurity hits.

'Do you think they liked me?'

'Of course they liked you,' he guffaws. 'How could they not?'

Thankfully he doesn't then expect me to engage in a passionate embrace, he just lets me go and says, 'Shall we go down for tea in fifteen minutes?'

'Sure,' I say, nodding, and Ed leaves the room and closes the door behind him.

I bounce up and down on the bed a few times, because this is what they do in the films when they walk into a fabulously sumptuous bedroom. Then I hang my dress in the wardrobe and touch up my make-up, and shortly after I hear a soft knock on the door, and Ed and I walk down for tea.

I suppose I was half expecting to hate his friends. I guessed they were all much older than me—and, judging by Sarah and Charlie, who must be in their forties, most of them are, but I also thought they'd be those really English county types, who would look down their noses and be incredibly snotty to someone like me, but I was completely wrong.

We walk into the room and I'm dreading it, but as Sarah introduces me as 'Ed's friend', with, incidentally, no special emphasis on the 'friend', everyone is just incredibly friendly, and no one is nearly as smart or as intimidating as I'd feared. In fact, I'd go as far as saying they all seemed very down-to-earth.

I don't want to embarrass myself by scoffing, so I settle into an old sofa and nibble daintily at a cucumber sandwich as Julia (one half of Julia and David) sits next to me and makes small talk.

'It's lovely to see Ed with someone,' she says finally, after we've discussed PR versus being a housewife, which is what she is, we've both agreed that the grass is always greener, how she'd kill for my 'exciting, glamorous' lifestyle, and how I think hers sounds like complete bliss.

'We're so used to Ed turning up on his own to these annual balls, and he's such a good chap, we've always wondered why he's never found himself someone lovely,' she continues. 'But now, it seems, he has.'

I laugh. 'Well, I don't know about that. It's very new. We're really just, umm, friends, right now.'

'But from what I hear Ed's quite serious about you.'

Should she be quite so candid? I mean, she hardly knows me.

I smile again. 'We shall see,' I say mysteriously, because I don't know quite what else to say.

I notice that the men seem to be on one side of the room, presumably discussing business, while the women sit on my side of the room talking about the best places to shop in 'town'. Town being London.

'You're ever so lucky, Libby,' says Sarah, moving to sit closer to me. 'Libby lives in London,' she explains to the rest of the women.

'Where in London do you live?' says a youngish woman who, I think, is called Emily, but I can't quite remember.

'Ladbroke Grove,' I say, wishing I could say Regent's Park, or Knightsbridge, or Chelsea. Among my friends I'm pretty damn proud of living in Ladbroke Grove, because it's trendy, but here, with Ed's friends, I know it's not even nearly good enough.

'How lovely,' says Julia. 'That's bang next door to Notting Hill, isn't it, and there are so many wonderful places in Notting Hill. Tell me, do you go to the Sugar Club?'

'Yes,' I say, my face lighting up because I have actually been there. Once. 'I go there all the time.'

'Lucky you,' they all coo. 'Having all those wonderful places right on your doorstep.'

And then the talk disintegrates into schools that their children go to, so I put down my cup of tea and wander onto the terrace, and sitting on the low brick wall that looks out onto sweeping gardens I wonder what Nick would think if he could see me now.

I turn as a hand rubs my back, and Ed leans down and plants a kiss on my cheek, and what's really sweet about this is that it's in full view of all his friends, and I think about all the men who have warned me about public displays of affection, and I look at Ed and wonder whether, if he was a bastard to me like all the others, I might like him better.

'Do you want to go for a walk?' he says. 'I'll show you the grounds.'

I nod and link my arm through his, and his face lights up at my spontaneous display of tenderness, and he strokes my hand through his elbow. 'I don't want you to get cold,' he says. 'Shall I get your jacket?'

'Don't worry.' I lean up and give him a kiss on the cheek, 'I'll be fine.'

At seven o'clock everyone disappears to their bedrooms to get ready, all having been given strict instructions to be downstairs at eight thirty.

And so much for cold, draughty bedrooms. My room is lovely and warm, and I have an en suite bathroom, which Sarah has filled with delicious smelling bubble baths and soft, thick towels.

I soak for ages, right up until the water is practically cold, then I get out and go into the bedroom to try and reposition the dressing-table mirror to give me enough light to do my make-up perfectly.

And finally, at 8.30pm, there's a knock on my door and Ed's standing there in a dinner jacket.

Neither of us says anything for a while. I'm just so impressed with the difference black tie can make on a man. He looks, well, the word that springs to mind is powerful. He looks like a real man, and that's when I realise that up until now I've only ever been out with boys.

Ed is the first to speak. 'You look beautiful,' he whispers. 'Absolutely beautiful. You'll be the most beautiful woman at the party.'

There. He said it, didn't he? Woman. Not girl.

'You look lovely yourself,' I say, grinning. 'All dark and sexy and mysterious.' I don't mention that the moustache ruins the effect somewhat, because I think I might just about be getting used to it . . . as long as it doesn't get too close to me.

And we walk down the staircase, my hand resting gently on his arm, and maybe I'm imagining it, but I do seem to be wearing the most stunning dress here, and we walk down to meet all those upturned faces, and I do feel, for perhaps the first time in my life, truly, truly, beautiful.

We have an incredible evening. And though the people are slightly older than those I would normally socialise with, they are all so warm and friendly that after a while I start to forget the age difference.

The champagne helps of course.

And God, the champagne. And the food. And the thousands of tiny white fairy lights sprinkled around the trees surrounding the terrace. And the music. And the fact that I am high on the champagne, on the glamour, on the excitement of being at a party that truly looks like something you would see in a Hollywood movie, or perhaps because of the British accents, in a Merchant Ivory film.

It feels like the kind of party that I would only ever go to once in my life, because it is all so magical, and so beautiful, and so special, it could never be re-created. Except, of course, with Ed there would be parties like this all the time.

And the more champagne I drink—which, let me tell you, is a hell of a lot—the more attractive Ed becomes.

And at around one o'clock in the morning I'm thinking, yes. Yes. Tonight's the night. I'm going to do it tonight. And I think that perhaps this whole sex thing has become such an issue because it's been hanging over my head, and that if we got it out of the way it would all be fine, because it's bound to be better than I expect. Isn't it?

Ed's trying to stifle a yawn, and I laugh and kiss him on the forehead, saying, 'It's past your bedtime, isn't it, old man?'

And he snuggles up to me, smiling sleepily. 'I'm not old.'

'OK. Older-than-me-man.'

'That's better. I'm fine. You're not ready for bed. I'm really happy staying up a bit longer. *Ce n'est pas un problème.*'

Oh shut up with the bloody French, Ed. You're about to ruin the moment. But of course I don't say this. I say: 'Come on. You're tired.' I take him by the hand and pull him to his feet. 'I'm putting you to bed.'

Now I know I could have said I'm taking you to bed, but that would have been too obvious, wouldn't it? That would have made him realise tonight is the night, and then we would have both had to walk upstairs knowing that once we made it into the room we were about to, as Jules put it, make lurrrve, and halfway up we probably would have started throwing up with nerves or something.

So we say good night to Sarah and Charlie, and walk upstairs, me leading Ed by the hand. My heart's pounding, I can't believe I'm about to do it, and part of me wants—and God oh God, please don't think I sound like a total prostitute for saying this—part of me wants to give him something, to thank him for all this.

Ed stops outside his bedroom door and puts his arms round me.

'You are the most beautiful woman I've ever seen,' he says, pulling me close. 'What are you doing with me?'

And the way he says it makes my heart open, and I reach up to kiss him on the lips, and when I pull back I smile and say, 'Would you stay with me tonight?' Once the words are out, I suddenly think that Ed might take me for a brazen hussy, and I'd have to say goodbye to my new-found lifestyle.

'Are you sure?' he whispers back. 'I wasn't expecting—'

And I cut him off with a kiss as I open my bedroom door with one hand and pull him gently in with the other.

Sometimes I feel so angry that I think I'm going to scream. It's like a deep well of anger, resentment, fury, whatever, and I have to concentrate incredibly hard, because at any moment it's all going to come flooding out and I'm just going to completely lose control.

This is how I feel this morning. Ed's sitting next to me, we've just driven past Guildford on our way back home, and I want to kill him. He keeps giving me these worried glances, and putting his hand on my leg with a reassuring squeeze, and every time he does it I want to hit him.

And I know I'm behaving like a spoilt brat who hasn't got what she wanted, but the more disgusting I am to him, the more he looks at me with these sad puppy-dog eyes, the worse I become.

So what was his terrible crime?

The sex was crap.

And I'm furious with him for it, which I know is completely unfair, but I can't help it.

So OK, you're probably now dying to hear just how bad it was, so fine, I'll tell you.

I pulled Ed into my room and started kissing him, and the kiss wasn't brilliant, still way too much saliva, so I stopped kissing him on the mouth and started to plant tiny kisses over his cheek and down his neck, which is when I realised what it is about him that turns me off.

It's his smell. Not BO, or anything like that, but just his natural body smell. It seems to be kind of sour, not massively pleasant, so I decided I'd better keep my tongue firmly in my mouth from there on in.

I know, I know. I should have stopped there. I should have realised that sexual chemistry quite obviously hadn't grown, at least not for me, but I kept going, thinking that Julia Roberts admitted in *Pretty Woman* that she never kissed the men she slept with (up until Richard Gere, of course, and who could blame her?), therefore I could have sex with Ed without having to kiss him either.

And because I didn't want to taste his skin, Ed obviously thought that these strange birdlike pecks I was giving him were the way to turn me on, so he started doing the same thing to me, at which point I promptly stopped, because it didn't feel the least bit sensuous, or sexy, or anything other than bloody irritating.

And then he said, 'Do you want to use the bathroom to get undressed?' which was a bit odd, because I thought in the heat of the moment he would just rip my clothes off, but I went into the bathroom anyway with the T-shirt I'd brought to sleep in. When I came out Ed was lying in bed with the duvet tucked up under his chin, and my first instinct was to run far, far away.

But, being the determined woman I am, I squashed that instinct flat, and gingerly climbed into bed beside him. He cuddled up to me and started kissing me again, and I thought, this will be OK, I can do this.

And after a while I moved my hand down and felt the very thing that I had been completely dreading.

Y-fronts.

So I prised them off as gently as I could, given the fact that he had an enormous erection, and Ed started squeezing—actually, perhaps kneading would be a more accurate description—my breasts through my T-shirt, and he did it for so long that I figured I may as well take my T-shirt off myself, which I did, and then he carried on kneading, and I have to say I was about as turned on as a loaf of bread.

And then, before I knew it, Ed was on top of me, and, even though penetration was now the very last thing on my mind, I reached for a condom and put it on for him, because, although he tried, he didn't seem to know what to do with it. Then he was inside me, and there was a look of pure bliss on his face, and he started moving a bit, and then, I kid you not, about six seconds later he groaned very loudly and collapsed on top of me.

And I lay there fuming.

Absolutely fucking fuming.

And while I was staring at the ceiling with his huge weight on top of me and thinking that this, without doubt, was the worst sex I'd ever had, Ed moved his face above mine, grinning like a Cheshire cat, and said, 'That was wonderful, darling.'

And then he must have seen that my face was completely blank, and he kissed me and said, 'Was that OK?'

Well, no, actually, it wasn't bloody OK. It was abysmal, and maybe I should have just nodded, rolled over and gone to sleep, but I couldn't, I was just too damn disappointed and angry.

So that's what I said.

And Ed rolled off me, looking as if he were going to cry, and this in itself made me even more furious, because he's not exactly a child, and how could a man of his age be so completely pathetic in bed?

But he didn't say anything, so I just kept ranting about how sex is a two-way street, and did he really think I would get turned on by ten minutes kneading my breasts, and hadn't he ever heard of the clitoris, and premature ejaculation wasn't exactly enjoyable, especially given that I'd had no foreplay whatsoever, and come to that, did he even know what the word 'foreplay' meant?

And the more I ranted—because by this time I was really getting into it—the more upset he looked. Eventually, when I finished, he tried to put his arms round me and say sorry, but I just stormed off and went into the bathroom.

I sat on the loo seat, wishing I could talk to Jules. After a while I got a bit cold, so I went back into the bedroom, and Ed was sitting on the edge of the bed with his head hung low. He looked up and sighed.

'I really am sorry,' he started. 'I feel awful, it's just that I suppose I'm not terribly experienced, but if you help me I can learn, you can show me what to do. I really do think that we can work this out if we're both willing.'

I harrumphed a bit and said that I didn't want to be his teacher, but then I started to feel I was being nasty, so after a while I said OK, we could work through this, and I got back into bed and allowed Ed to get in and cuddle me, and, I suppose, we both fell asleep.

But the thing is I thought I'd feel better about it this morning, but I don't. I feel worse. Because while I don't believe that sex is the most important thing in a relationship, it has to be, at least, OK. I mean, I know that sex with Nick was completely fantastic, but I also know that it's very rarely like that, and that as long as it's good, you can get by.

And Ed probably is right, I probably could teach him what to do, what I like, but even if, say, technically he learns the right moves, because he's so gauche and awkward it's never going to be sensual and delicious.

And this morning I start thinking about what sex was like with Nick, and the more I think about how good it was, the more I start to resent Ed, and this is why we're driving home in a thick, tense silence.

Not that Sarah and Charlie would have been able to tell. At least, I hope not, because they were so charming and so hospitable. I think, this morning, when we all met up over breakfast, I managed to hide the fact that I'd had the night from hell. When we said goodbye and I thanked them for everything, Sarah gave me a big hug and said we'd have to come down again.

So we hardly say a word on the way back, and when we reach my flat Ed brings my bag inside and says, 'Can I call you later?' and I shrug and say, 'S'pose so,' behaving like a six-year-old, and he just looks incredibly sad and gives me a kiss on the cheek.

And the minute he's gone I pick up the phone and ring, naturally, Jules, ignoring the three messages on my answering machine from my mother begging me to ring her as soon as I get back.

'Uh-oh,' she says, hearing my flat voice. 'Start at the beginning.'

'Just tell me first,' I say. 'Any news from Jamie?'

'Well, yes,' she says slowly. 'He called last night sounding absolutely miserable, so I said he could come over this evening and talk about it.'

'You're kidding!' I gasp. 'Are you going to forgive him?'

'I want to see what he has to say first,' she says, 'because I know that even if I may be able to forgive him, I'll never be able to forget, and I still don't know if I'll ever be able to trust him again, and if you don't have trust, what is there?'

'Love?' I venture softly.

'Yes,' she sighs. 'There is that. Anyway, enough about me. Tell me everything about last night.'

I start at the beginning, describing everything to her, in graphic detail, what the people were like, what they were wearing, the atmosphere, the music, the champagne.

And then I get to the bit about going to bed and I stop.

'Go on,' she prompts. 'You did it, didn't you?'

'In a manner of speaking.'

'Please don't tell me it was awful,' she groans. 'I couldn't cope.'

'It was awful,' I shriek. 'No. I take that back. It was worse than awful. The worst experience of my life.' And I tell her, exactly as I told you, what happened, and when I've finished speaking there's a silence.

'Hello?' I say. 'Are you still there?'

'Hang on. I'm thinking.'

'What are you thinking? Don't say that lust can grow, because I honestly don't think I can go through that again.'

'OK,' Jules sighs. 'I don't think that lust can grow, but I do think that he's obviously inexperienced, and that can be resolved. But,' she adds ominously, 'I also think that you mustn't try to talk yourself round this one. Sometimes I worry that you jump in and do things that you know aren't right, just because you really want them to be right. And I don't mean that this isn't right, I just mean don't try to whitewash over the things that aren't.'

And as she talks I can see my fantastic fantasy life slipping away, and I don't want it to slip away, I want to marry a rich man, someone like Ed, I want to live in a house in Hanover Terrace, but I also see the point that Jules is making. Even if I don't like it much.

'So what should I do now?'

'You don't have to do anything. Just wait and see what happens. You don't have to make a lifelong decision after three weeks, that's all I'm saying. If it doesn't work out, fine. You'll move on.'

And I can see that she's absolutely right, except it's bloody hard to not think about the life you've always wanted when it's right there, at your fingertips. And OK, I have been spending rather a large amount of time recently thinking about how I'd redecorate Hanover Terrace, and maybe it isn't very healthy, but it's a damn sight better than thinking about how to avoid nights down the pub drinking pints with your mates.

'But do you think it is going to work out?'

'God, what do you want me to say, Libby? I've already told you what I think. Look, do you want to come over?'

'Nah. I'm going to stay in and watch the box.' I pause. 'Unless you want me to.'

'No. Don't worry about it. I should get ready for Jamie coming over. Mentally steel myself and all that. But don't worry about Ed, it will all work out.'

'OK, thanks. Isn't that what I'm supposed to be saying to you?'

At five o'clock, just as the movie I've been watching finishes, the phone rings . . . again. And again I don't pick up the phone because it's probably my mother, who hasn't stopped ringing all day, and even though she hasn't left any more messages, every time she puts the phone down I dial 1471 and it's her bloody number.

I just can't face talking to her right now. I wouldn't know what to say, and actually I'm grateful as hell that there's been good TV on all day, because I haven't had to think about Ed, or last night.

But this time it's Ed on the phone, and as I hear his little worried voice I start feeling really bad, so I pick up the phone, and before he has a chance to say anything I apologise.

'I can't believe those things I said to you,' I say, a touch sheepishly. 'I feel like a complete bitch, and especially after you took me to such a wonderful party and you've been so incredibly sweet to me.' I pause for a while. 'I completely understand if you don't want to see me again.'

'Of course I want to see you again!' splutters Ed. 'I was phoning to apologise myself because I know last night was awkward, and I was just phoning to tell you that I'm willing to do anything to make this relationship work. And I know that the physical side is very important to you, and I feel so ashamed that I'm so inexperienced, but I promise you, Libby, I'll learn. I even went out today and bought *The Joy of Sex*. I'm reading it now, and I think I can learn how to, umm, well, satisfy you.'

'Oh, Ed,' I say. 'You do satisfy me, and last night I was just in a really bad mood, and I'm sure we'll be fine.'

'I think so too,' he says, and I can hear the relief in his voice. 'You probably want to be on your own tonight, don't you?'

'Why? What were you thinking?' Umm, hello? Libby? You did want to stay on your own tonight. God, why am I such a complete pushover?

'I just wondered whether you wanted to come over and have supper. It would just be nice to see you and, sort of, make up for last night.'

'OK,' I find myself saying. 'I'll come over at eight, OK?'

'I love you.'

In all my fantasies when the tall, dark, faceless but presumably handsome love of my life tells me he loves me, I melt into his arms, murmuring, 'I love you too.'

But I really don't know what to say.

'I know things haven't been great,' Ed says, holding my hand across the table, 'but I also know that we can work them out, so you might not be able to say that you love me too, which is fine, because I know that you will.'

'I love you too.' What else can I say? And the fact of the matter is, I may not love him, but I love the idea of loving him, and I think, for the moment, that might be enough. And Ed looks so happy I think his smile may well burst off his face.

'I really do love you,' he says again. 'And you make me so happy.'

How can I not spend the night after this?

I walk upstairs, knowing that I have to try everything in my power to make this work. And this time Ed seems to discover that nipples are an erogenous zone. That the clitoris is not just a useless body part. That I quite like soft, sweeping strokes down my stomach.

OK, it's not perfect. He's still slightly clumsy, awkward, and he keeps on saying, 'Is this OK? What about this? Do you like this?' But eventually he slightly seems to get the hang of it.

And well before there is any question of actually having full-blown sex, I find that if I close my eyes and concentrate very hard, it starts to feel nice, and, although I wouldn't normally be so selfish as to just lie there and not do anything while someone is slowly stroking my clitoris and asking if it's OK, I do feel that after last night I deserve at least the chance of an orgasm, and, after what seems like hours, I feel a familiar warmth as the tingling feeling spreads up through my body, and I have an orgasm. I actually have an orgasm.

I open my eyes and smile at Ed, who's looking half pleased with himself and half worried, and he says, 'Did you, umm, well. Was that it . . .?'

And I nod, and he exhales loudly as I laugh, and plant a soft kiss on his lips.

'Thank goodness for that,' he says, and that's when I think that maybe the sex will get better, maybe it won't be so bad, and I pull him on top of me and guide him inside me, and OK, if the truth be known I still can't quite handle kissing him, or licking him, or burying my nose in his neck, but it's a hell of a lot better than last night.

I think we make it to twelve seconds. Not that it matters, because after my orgasm I can quite happily go to sleep, but I want to do this for him, because he is so sweet, because he is trying so hard.

We lie in bed afterwards, talking softly.

And I snuggle into his shoulder, just loving this feeling of being loved. 'How did you learn that all in a day?' I ask eventually.

'I speed-read *The Joy of Sex*,' he chuckles.

'You mean you didn't do any work today?'

'Of course not. This is far more important. You are far more important. Libby?'

'Hmm?' I'm almost asleep.

'I think perhaps it's time I met your parents.'

I'm now wide awake.

'Umm. Why? Don't you think it's a bit soon?'

'Not if we're serious about one another.'

Jesus, the thought of my parents meeting Ed makes me feel sick. My mother would go into Hyacinth Bucket overdrive, and I'd want to die.

'Umm, well, er.' I struggle, unsuccessfully, to think of an excuse.

'Don't you want them to meet me?'

'Of course!' I lie. And it's not them meeting him that's the problem, it's him meeting them. I don't want Ed to see who I really am, who I'm trying so hard to leave behind. 'I just think it's a bit soon, that's all.'

'I think it's a good idea,' he says, with a mysterious smile, and suddenly I think, shit! He's going to ask me to marry him! But it's much too soon for that, and even Ed wouldn't jump in this early on, I mean for God's sake, he hardly knows me.

'OK. We'll sort something out,' I say vaguely, praying he'll forget about it.

'Great,' he says, reaching out for his diary on the bedside table. 'What about Wednesday?'

'I'll have to check with them,' I say, knowing that my parents will definitely be busy on Wednesday, if I have anything to do with it. 'I'll let you know.'

'They could come here for dinner,' he says. 'We could cook.'

'But you can't cook.'

'OK. Well, you can cook and I can help you.'

'OK,' I say. 'Maybe.'

'I love you, Libby Mason,' he says, kissing me before closing his eyes.

'I love you too.'

 # Chapter Twelve

'ARE YOU ENTIRELY SURE you know what you're doing?'

'Not in the slightest,' I groan. 'In fact, I think this may well be a night-mare come true.'

'I'm glad I'm not the only one whose nightmare's coming true,' Jules sighs.

Jamie did go over to see Jules that night. She said she opened the door and her very first feeling was this overwhelming maternal urge, because Jamie looked terrible. 'He'd lost so much weight,' she said. 'He obviously hadn't been eating a thing.'

He'd looked haggard, and miserable, and just completely downtrod-den. Jules invited him in and took him into the kitchen, where she'd spent all day cooking his favourite meal, so the smell of oxtail stew would permeate the air and make him realise just what he had thrown away. Or not. She hadn't, at that point, decided.

Jamie naturally commented on the food, but Jules didn't offer him any. She offered him a cup of tea instead, knowing that he prefers coffee. He said he didn't want anything.

He sat there, on the sofa, with his head in his hands, and when he eventually raised his eyes he looked at her pleadingly and said, 'I miss you so much, Jules. I love you so much. I don't want to be without you.'

And somehow this seemed to empower Jules, who suddenly discov-ered this pool of strength lurking within, and, looking at him, decided that she would make him suffer.

So she told him that he had hurt her beyond measure. That he had broken down every belief she had ever had about marriage. That he had destroyed every dream she had ever had about her future. Their future.

And Jamie apologised, repeatedly, and hung his head in shame.

She said she needed more time, and Jamie nodded and silently left. He turned to kiss her just as he was walking out of the door, and Jules moved her head so he ended up kissing air.

'But Jesus, Libby,' she says, when she has finished telling me this, as we are pushing the trolley round Sainsbury's, me once again having crept out of work slightly earlier than usual, 'it was so hard. So hard.'

She pauses. 'And I've got this bloody work do I've got to go to tonight, which Jamie was supposed to come to, and I'm dreading it.'

'Do you have to go?'

'Unfortunately, yes. Too many good contacts to pass up. Anyway,' she continues, 'tell me again why you decided to go through with this.'

'This' being Ed meeting my parents.

'Because, Jules,' I say in a mock exasperated tone, 'it's going to happen sooner or later, and I may as well get it out of the way now.'

'But it's your parents.' Jules knows my parents. My parents, in fact, love Jules. They think she is the perfect woman, and many's the time my mother has compared me to Jules, with me, naturally, falling short. And Jules likes my parents. I've tried to tell Jules how completely awful my mother is, but she still thinks she's nice, which I suppose I might do as well if she wasn't my mother. Well, maybe not, but I can see that parents always seem a hell of a lot better if they're not yours.

'You don't think Ed's going to take your father for a walk round the garden after dinner and ask for your hand in marriage, do you?' she jokes as I throw a bag of spinach in the trolley.

Actually, that's exactly what I had been thinking, and I can't believe that Jules thought it too. I turn to her in amazement. 'Do you think he might do that? Really?'

She shrugs. 'Maybe. What would you say?'

And suddenly I know exactly what I would say. 'I think I'd say yes.'

She gasps and stops dead in her tracks. 'Yes? Are you serious? The sex is crap, him speaking French irritates you beyond belief, and you think you could spend the rest of your life with this man?'

'Jules!' I admonish firmly. 'The sex isn't crap. OK, it wasn't great the first time, but it's much better now,' and, incidentally, given that I've now stayed at Ed's every night since Sunday, we've had plenty of time to practise, 'and the French annoys me a bit, but not that much, and yes, I can imagine spending the rest of my life with this man.'

Jules shakes her head. 'Listen, Libby, I know things don't appear to have worked out with Jamie, but at least I loved him. I mean I really, really loved him. Are you sure you know what you're doing?'

'Jules, it's highly unlikely that he will propose tonight, and anyway even if we did get engaged we'd definitely have a long engagement.'

'How long? The chicken's down here.' She wheels the trolley down aisle eight.

'A year.'

'Promise?'

'Promise.'

Jules drops me home so I can pick up my recipe books, and I ring Mum just to check she's got the right address. Her voice is all fluttery and excited on the phone.

'Are you sure my green suit will be all right?'

'Mum, it doesn't matter what you wear, we're only staying in.'

'But, darling, I want to make a good impression.'

'Your green suit will be fine.'

'I thought perhaps you might like me to bring some salmon mousse to start with. I made it anyway for us this morning.'

'You think I can't cook, don't you?'

'No, darling. I'm just trying to help.'

'Forget it, Mum. I've got all the food sorted out.'

'Are you sure? It's no trouble—'

'Mum!' Why, oh why, did I ever decide to go ahead with this?

Did I mention that Ed gave me the spare keys yesterday and told me to keep them?

I let myself into his house, lugging the bags of shopping, and go down to the kitchen. There's something very eerie about being in a house this size all by myself, so I turn on the lights and retune his radio to Virgin (it was, unsurprisingly, tuned to Radio 3), and rearrange a few things to make it a bit more cosy.

I must talk to him about getting the sofas re-covered.

I open the recipe books to the pages I've bookmarked and start to read. I went through them last night and picked out a Jules special for the main course, and a Delia special for pudding. I had a bit of a panic about starters, but Jules said I should try bruschetta, so I've got the ciabatta, garlic and tomatoes, and she says all I have to do is toast the bread, rub it with garlic and olive oil, and arrange tomatoes, olives and fresh basil on top, and the bonus is it's completely idiot-proof.

So there I am, seasoning the chicken breasts and boiling the spinach. I'm not entirely sure how to squeeze all the water out of the spinach, plus, what the hell does blanching mean anyway? I boiled it for fifteen minutes, and I stuck it through a colander and put it in a dish with the chicken breasts on top. Jules's recipe says use four large chillies, and I forgot the chillies in Sainsbury's so had to stop at a corner shop and Sod's Law they didn't have any big chillies, only the tiny ones, so I figured four small chillies would equal one big one, so I chop up the chillies and throw them in the sauce.

But a chocolate mousse is easy. I whip the egg whites until my arm is so stiff it's painful, and, although I haven't got a clue what a bain-marie is, I melt the chocolate, butter and sugar in a saucepan, and stir it into the egg whites. (What exactly is folding?)

Jules said make the bruschetta just before they arrive. Ed isn't home yet, and it's a quarter to eight, which means my parents will be here any minute, so I stick the bread under the grill and pile all the used dishes into the sink to wash.

The doorbell goes. I check my watch and it's ten to. Trust my parents to be early. I go to the door and here they are, Mum and Dad, standing on the doorstep. Mum grins expectantly, and Dad looks ever so uncomfortable in a suit and tie.

'Where's Ed?' Mum says in a stage whisper.

'He'll be here any minute. Come in.' I kiss them both on the cheek, and step aside as they walk in, my mother, apparently, struck speechless for the first time in her life by the size of the hallway.

'Do you want the guided tour?' I can't help myself, I want to feel smug for a little while longer. 'Take your coats off and I'll show you round.'

'Do you think we ought?' says my mother. 'Shouldn't we wait until Ed gets home?'

'Don't worry. It's fine,' I say, as I hang the coats in the cloakroom.

And I lead them round the house, while they ooh and aah over the rooms, and even my father admits it's beautiful.

'It's not beautiful,' admonishes my mother. 'It's a palace,' and then she turns to me, and you're not going to believe it but she actually has tears in her eyes. 'Oh, Libby,' she says, clasping her hands together as a tear threatens to trickle down her cheek. 'I'm so happy for you.'

'I'm not married to the guy, Mum,' I say.

'Not yet,' offers my dad, whose grin now matches my mother's.

'You'd better not mess this one up,' says my mum, inspecting Ed's cupboards. 'You'll have me to answer to if you do.'

'Mum, can't you give it a rest just for tonight?'

'Yes, dear,' echoes my father as I look at him in amazement. 'Don't give her a hard time.'

My mother looks at both of us as if she doesn't know what we're talking about, then shakes her head and goes to look at the curtains. 'Fully lined,' she mutters. 'Must have cost a fortune with all these fancy swags.'

'Shall we go downstairs?' The last thing I want is for Ed to catch us snooping round his bedroom, so we troop downstairs and I make them both gin and tonics.

My mum sniffs. 'So what are we having for dinner?'

'Bruschetta followed by, shit! shit! shit! shit!'

I leap up as my mother sniffs again. 'Is that burning I can smell?'

Fuck. Fuck, shit, and fuck again. I open the oven door to reveal eight lumps of charcoal steaming away, and I groan because I know exactly what my mother's going to say. I don't even have to go back into the dining area to hear her say it, because there she is, right behind me.

'I knew I should have brought the salmon mousse,' she says, standing behind me.

And saved by the bell, or key turning in the lock in this case, we all freeze as Ed comes bounding down the stairs calling, 'Helloooo? Hellooo? Anyone home?'

He sniffs as he walks into the kitchen but obviously decides to refrain from commenting, and shakes hands with my mother and father.

'Thank you so much for coming,' he says, his public school accent suddenly sounding ridiculously loud and affected next to my parents' suburban-but-trying-hard-to-escape accents, but he doesn't seem to notice, so I decide not to make an issue out of it.

Besides, I know they drive me up the wall but they are my parents, and I suppose, if I'm pushed, I'd have to admit that I do love them.

'Thank you so much for having us,' says my mother, and I can't say I'm exactly surprised to notice that her accent has also gone up a few notches. Not in my estimation, I have to add.

'No, no, it's nothing. Think nothing of it,' said Ed. 'Did you find the house all right?'

'We didn't have any problems, did we Da—' She stops, having just realised that it's not quite the done thing to refer to Dad as Dad in the company of someone like Ed. 'Alan?'

For a second there I wonder who she's talking about, because I don't think I've ever heard her call my dad anything but Dad.

'No, Jean,' says my dad, putting a tiny emphasis on the word 'Jean', because he seems to think it's as odd as I do. 'No worries.'

My mother gives my father a curt shake of the head, which my father and I understand to mean, don't say phrases like that, but Ed doesn't notice, as he goes over to top up their glasses.

'Da—Alan, don't have another one. You're driving.'

'Oh, what a shame,' says Ed. 'I've got a lovely wine for dinner. I thought, as this was a special occasion, I'd open the Mouton Rothschild. You'll have some, won't you, Mrs Mason?'

'Oh, call me Jean,' my mother giggles. 'Everyone else does.'

'*Mais bien sûr*,' chuckles Ed along with my mother, who seems enormously impressed with these three words of craply accented French.

'Ooh,' she exclaims. 'You speak French?'

'*Juste un peu*,' Ed laughs. '*Et vous?*'

'*Moi?*' My mother thinks this is the funniest thing she's ever said. Christ. Why oh why did I ever agree to this?

'Would you like to sit down at the table?' I say, in my most gracious hostess manner, because I figure the sooner I serve, the sooner we'll be finished, and the sooner they can go.

And obviously the bruschetta is a bit of a non-starter, as it were, so I bring the chicken to the table with rice and vegetables, and Ed goes to bring the wine up from the cellar.

'He's absolutely charming,' whispers my mother the minute he's left the room, still speaking in her 'posh' voice. 'And perfect for you.'

And, despite myself, I breathe a sigh of relief, because finally someone, albeit only my mother, has given me their seal of approval, has told me exactly what I wanted to hear. That Ed is perfect for me.

And Ed comes back, opens the wine, and my mum and dad sit there watching us, waiting for one of us to start before picking up their knife and fork. Eventually I pick up my fork, so my mother picks up hers and takes the first mouthful.

I swear, I've seen cartoons where people go bright red and smoke starts pouring from their ears when they've eaten something hot, but I never thought it actually happened in real life.

Everyone stops, forks halfway to their mouths, and we all just stare at my mother as she sits there gasping, flapping her hands around.

'Here, here,' says my father, holding up the wineglass because that's the only liquid on the table, and my mother gulps the whole thing down in one. 'What's the matter?' says my father.

Now there are tears streaming down my mother's face, and she's trying to speak but can't seem to get the words out, so she points to the food, furiously shaking her head.

'Mrs Mason?' Ed's jumped up and gone over to her, terribly concerned, and I wonder how it is my mother always manages to make herself the centre of attention. 'Is it the food?' he asks.

My mother nods.

'Perhaps I'd better taste it,' says Ed, going back to his plate and gingerly taking a tiny amount on his fork while I feel more and more of a failure. He tastes it, sits for precisely two seconds while it hits his taste buds, then jumps up and runs to the kitchen, and the next thing I hear is the sound of the tap running.

'What is the problem?' I practically shriek, taking a forkful of food. 'My cooking isn't that bad,' and, while my father's still comforting my mother and Ed's still in the kitchen, I take a mouthful.

Aaaaaaaaargh!!!!!!!

I run into the kitchen, shove Ed out of the way and lean under the sink, sticking my entire mouth under the water. It feels like my mouth is about to burn off. I stay there for about three minutes, cooling down.

Eventually, when I'm fairly certain there's no permanent damage and I think I can talk again, I walk back to face the music.

'What did you put in that?' My mother's face is puce.

'Well the recipe said four large chillies, but I couldn't get them so I put sixteen small ones in.'

'Sixteen?' Ed looks at me in horror as my father starts giggling.

'What's the problem? Four small chillies equals one large one.'

My mother's looking at me as if she can't believe I'm her daughter.

'Libby,' she says, after nudging my father, who quickly stops laughing and tries to make his face serious, 'small chillies are four times the strength of large ones.'

'Oh goodness,' says Ed, looking slightly disconcerted. 'I thought you said you could cook?'

'I can cook!' I say. 'But how was I to know that about chillies?'

'I'm sorry, darling,' he says, kissing me on the forehead, which perks my mother up no end. 'I know you can cook. What about pudding?'

I fling my napkin on the table and go to fetch the chocolate mousse, and the minute I open the fridge door I know it's a disaster. It's basically just a big glass bowl of chocolate-coloured slop, and I don't even bother bringing it to the table. I just tip the whole lot into the dustbin.

'Umm,' I say, coming back to the table. 'There's been a bit of a problem with pudding.'

'You know what I really fancy?' says Ed. 'I'd really like a Chinese takeaway,' and my parents both say what a brilliant idea, as I sit there too embarrassed to say anything.

And half an hour later there we sit, my parents in their smartest clothes, at the table that I've beautifully laid with table mats, Irish linen napkins and even flowers in the centre, surrounded by tinfoil tubs of Chinese food, and it really isn't so bad.

Ed seems to keep the evening going by telling my parents all about his investment banking, and my parents look completely riveted, although I'm sitting there half proud of him for making sure there are no uncomfortable silences and half bored to tears.

Finally Ed and I see them to the door, while my mother makes big eyes at me, and I know she's simply dying to get me on the phone to do the post-mortem, and presumably to have a go at me about the chillies, and Ed is as charming as he always is and walks them to their car, and thank God it's over.

When I get into the office there's a message from Jules and a message from my mother. I ring Jules first. 'I'm really not that interested,' Jules says, after she's told me all about her works do last night.

'But, Jules! You said this guy Paul is tall, handsome, sexy and funny. How can you not be interested?'

'Libby, I still love Jamie. I don't know what's going to happen with us, but the one thing I do know is that I don't want anyone to confuse the issue further.'

'But it's only one night, for God's sake.'

She sighs. 'Jesus. You go to a work party expecting to stay for twenty minutes, and some bloody bloke comes along who would have been exactly your type if you weren't married, and . . . I don't know. I'm not interested in going out with him. I just didn't know what else to say.'

'One date isn't going to hurt you. And if you and Jamie don't get back together, at least you'll know there are other men out there.'

'But I'm not sure I want other men. Oh, why did he have to bloody phone,' she moans. 'Why couldn't he have been like all those men you used to meet who'd take your number and never phone?'

'Because he's not a bastard,' I say, smirking. 'And anyway. You never know. You might have a nice time.'

Then I ring Mum. She can hardly contain her excitement, and spends twenty minutes telling me how wonderful Ed is, and how he's the best catch I'll ever have, and how she can see he adores me, and thank God she doesn't mention the cooking.

Just as I'm about to pick up the phone to ring the *Telegraph,* who want to do a feature on Amanda, my phone rings again (trust me, the life of a PR is all about phone calls, personal or otherwise), and it's my father.

'What's wrong, Dad?' My father never, ever calls me. In fact, it took me a while to recognise his voice, so rarely does he actually speak.

'I just thought I'd phone to thank you for last night.'

'Oh! Well, Mum already phoned. Did you enjoy it?'

'Yes. It was very nice. Are you happy with him, Libby?'

What is this? First my father phones me at work, and then he asks me about the state of my relationship. I need to get to the bottom of this.

'Why, Dad?'

'I know that your mother's over the moon because he's wealthy and very keen on you, but I just wondered whether you were serious.'

'You didn't like him, did you, Dad?' My heart sinks.

'Do you want me to be honest?'

'Yes.' No.

'I think he's obviously smitten with you. In material terms he could probably give you everything you needed. But . . .' And he stops.

'Go on, Dad.'

'Well, it's just that I'm not entirely sure he's for you.'

'Why not?'

He sighs. 'Nothing that I can exactly put my finger on, but if you're happy, Libby, then I'm happy.'

'I'm happy, Dad. Honestly.'

'Good. All right, darling, that's all. We'll see you on Sunday?'

'See you then. Bye, Dad.'

'Bye.'

What was all that about? I ring Jules again as I want to know what she thinks of this strange conversation with my dad, plus she'd better have returned Paul's call, so I ring her mobile because I know she's on her way to a client.

'My Dad hates him.'

'You're joking!' she gasps. 'Did he say that?'

'Well, no. But he didn't have to.' And I tell her what he did say.

'Hmm. Could just be parental concern. I mean, Ed is quite a lot older than your other boyfriends, so maybe he's just worried about you.'

'What's Ed being older got to do with anything?'

'OK. Point taken. I'd tell you what I thought of Ed, and you know I'd be entirely honest. In fact, I've just had a brilliant idea. You know that guy Paul? Why don't the four of us go out for dinner? I couldn't face seeing him on my own, it's too like a date, but I could cope if you were there too, and then I could suss out Ed as well.'

'Fantastic!' I say, and it is, even though it will feel completely weird without Jamie, but at least this way Jules will definitely see this guy again. I'm trying to fight Jamie's corner, but I don't think there's any harm in lining up a reserve, just in case. 'When can you make it?'

'Sunday night?'

'Perfect.'

'Libby? Delivery again for you.' It's Jo on the internal phone.

'Don't tell me yet more flowers.'

'Nah. This one's more mysterious. Come and see.'

I go to reception, where there's a large plastic Gucci carrier bag with my name on it, and my heart, I swear, misses a beat.

Jo rubs her hands together squealing, 'Open it, open it,' so I do, but first I pull out the card and read out loud: 'To my darling Libby, for making such an effort last night. I love you. Ed.'

I slowly tear off the tissue paper, and open a drawstring fabric bag with Gucci printed on it, and pull out a chocolate-brown leather Gucci bag. The one with bamboo handles. The one I've always wanted.

'You. Are. So. Fucking. Lucky,' says Jo.

'You've got one of these!' I say, stroking the leather that's as soft as butter.

'Yeah, but I had to pay for it. Three hundred and ten pounds.'

'You're joking!' Now it's my turn to squeal.

Naturally, I have to phone Jules again, and, although she is excited, there's something about her voice, something slightly reserved, that makes me question her until she tells me what she's really thinking.

'I'm worried that it's almost like he's buying you.'

'Don't be ridiculous,' I snort, still stroking my gorgeous new acquisition. 'Three hundred quid for him is like three quid for the rest of us.'

'Still,' she says. 'Lavishing presents on you would make it very difficult for you to leave.'

'But I'm not going to leave,' and for the first time I'm beginning to get slightly pissed off with Jules, which never, ever happens.

'God, I'm sorry,' she says. 'I'm being a complete killjoy. I'm jealous, that's all. And I can't wait to meet him on Sunday.'

'Good. And I can't wait to meet Paul. Oh, and just in case you don't recognise me, I'll be the one with the Gucci bag.'

We get to Sartoria first, having found a parking space almost immediately, which is a bit of a miracle in the West End, and I order a kir, which is what I've taken to ordering these days because it fits my new image as the smart, sophisticated partner of Ed McMahon.

Ed sits next to me and holds my hand under the table, and every few minutes he kisses me on the lips, which, nice as it is to be so adored, is beginning to irritate me ever so slightly. I did try to extract my hand, but then he got that sad puppy-dog look on his face again, so I placed my hand back in his and gave him a reassuring squeeze.

And then Jules and Paul arrive (it sounds so wrong, Jules and Paul), and Ed stands up to shake their hands and say how lovely it is to see Jules again, while Paul stands there waiting to be introduced to me.

Paul seems . . . he seems nice, which I know is pretty nondescript, but, despite being everything that Jules described, he's just not Jamie, and I really don't know whether I could get used to this man.

But Ed is at his most charming, asking lots of questions, not, thank God, telling his bloody investment banking stories, and I'm praying and praying that Jules loves him.

I do get slightly exasperated when most of his hors d'oeuvre ends up on his moustache, but I want Jules to see how close we are, so I pick up my napkin, raise my eyes to the ceiling and wipe the food off, and while Ed looks a bit sheepish, he's also delighted that I'm looking after him.

There is a moment when Jules is talking about someone she works with who's driving her mad by constantly changing her mind, and whom she describes as 'mercurial'.

'Umm, excuse me?' Ed interrupts her.

'Yes?' She stops in mid-flow.

'I don't think "mercurial" is the word you mean.'

Jules stopped dead in her tracks. 'Umm. I think it is,' she says slowly.

'I don't think it is. As far as I'm aware, mercurial means of mercury, i.e. liquid, flowing.'

'I think you'll find it can also mean constantly changing,' she says, and from the tone of her voice I pray that Ed backs down.

'Please don't think me rude, but I think you'll find *The Oxford English Dictionary* defines it as "of or containing mercury",' Ed persists, while I want to die with embarrassment.

'Actually,' says Paul, jumping in to save the day, 'I think you'll find you're both right. As far as I can remember, mercurial means both of or containing mercury, and volatile.'

'And Paul's a surgeon,' I say, trying to break the ice, 'therefore frighteningly clever, so I think we'll all have to agree with him.'

Thank God, it does break the ice somewhat, but from thereon in the atmosphere is slightly less convivial, and every now and then I see Jules shooting Ed daggers when she thinks neither of us is looking.

'Well, I must say,' Ed exclaims as we're about to order coffee, evidently having completely missed the implication of his near argument with Jules. 'It's lovely to meet Libby's closest friend.'

'Thank you,' says Jules. 'And it's lovely to meet you.' This bit was said through gritted teeth. 'Has Libby met your closest friends?'

And that's when I realise that apart from Sarah and Charlie and the people at their party, not only have I not met any of Ed's friends, I haven't even heard about any. Everyone he talks about seems to be a colleague through work, and isn't this a bit strange? I look at Ed to see what he says.

'Ha, ha,' he laughs. Umm, was there a joke? 'I don't really have many friends. To be honest, I'm not a hugely social creature. I'm either in the office or at home.'

'You must be delighted you've met Libby, then,' says Paul, smiling.

'Oh, I am,' he says, beaming at me with relief at being let off the hook.

'I am.' And he leans over and kisses me on the lips.

'I'm just going to the ladies' room. Jules?'

'I'll come,' she says, putting her napkin on the chair as we stand up and walk down to the loo.

'Well? What d'you think?' The words are out of her mouth before the door is even shut.

'He's lovely,' I say. 'A really nice guy.'

'I know,' she sighs, reapplying her lipstick. 'But it's not the same, is it?'

'Well, no. I suppose it's not.'

'Oh Gawd,' she says. 'What am I going to do? I know this sounds weird, but I kind of feel that if I were to be unfaithful as well, then we'd be equal, and then I could forgive Jamie.'

'Are you sure that's what you want to do?'

'No. I don't really want to do it. But I think it's the only way. Anyway, enough about me. Ed obviously adores you.'

'I know that! But what do you think of him?'

'Do you want me to be completely honest?'

Suddenly I'm not so sure, because I know it's not going to be good news, and I don't think I could stand to argue with Jules.

I shrug.

'Look,' she says. 'We haven't exactly got off to a great start, so right at this moment I can't think of many positive things to say, but I can see that he's treating you incredibly well, and for that I'm grateful.'

'You really don't like him?'

'I don't know. I'd need to spend more time with him. But the main thing is that you're happy.'

'You will like him, you know,' I say. 'He's really a sweetheart once you get past all the pompous shit.'

'You mean you can get past the pompous shit?'

'Oh, Jules!' I give her a hug. 'Please be happy for me. He's treating me better than anyone I've ever met.'

'That's what I'm scared of,' she says. 'That you've fallen for the way he's treating you, rather than for the man himself.'

We disengage and I reapply my lipstick. 'I don't think that's the case,' I say, painting on my top lip. 'I really don't.'

'OK,' she says, smiling at me in the mirror. 'If you say so, then I believe you.'

'Did you like them?'

'Yes,' says Ed slowly, on the way back to his place.

'Did you like Jules?'

'She's certainly feisty,' he says.

'You didn't like her, did you?'

'Of course I did,' he says, reaching over to give me a kiss as we stop at a red light. 'She's your best friend, so I have to like her.'

I'm not sure that's entirely what I wanted to hear, plus I don't really believe him, but I'm sure they'll both get over it. Everything will be fine.

We park the car and get out, and just as we're walking to the front door Ed suddenly turns and grabs me, enveloping me in a huge hug.

'I was going to wait,' he says, 'and do this properly. But I think I should probably ask you now. Will you marry me?'

These are the words I've waited my whole life to hear, so why isn't my heart soaring into the night sky? Why am I not dancing up Hanover Terrace with joy? Why do I feel so completely and utterly normal?

'OK,' I say, and Ed's expression turns from worried to rapturous.

'You will?'

'I will.'

'Oh goodness. I think we need to celebrate this with champagne.'

So we go inside and as I sit on the sofa watching Ed open the champagne I wonder why this feels like the biggest anticlimax of my life. And even when he brings me the glass and sits next to me to cuddle me, I still don't feel ecstatically happy, but then maybe no one feels like this? Maybe the whole thing is a bit like a Hollywood film, the passionate love thing, the feeling of ecstasy when you're proposed to? Maybe none of it really exists.

And after we've celebrated for a while I pick up the phone and wake up my parents to tell them the good news.

My mother screams. Literally. Screams.

'She's getting married,' she then shrieks at my father. 'Oh, Libby, I don't know what to say I'm so excited and I can't believe it you're getting married and oh my good Lord I never thought I'd see the day and you're marrying Ed McMahon and he's so eligible and you've got him . . .' I swear I'm not making this up, she doesn't take a breath.

Nor does she add, 'Wait until I tell the neighbours,' but I know that's what she's thinking.

And Dad comes on the phone and just says, 'Congratulations, darling. I'm very happy for you,' and then I pass the phone to Ed and I can hear my mother shrieking delight at Ed, and finally we put the phone down and I think about calling Jules, because, after my parents, she should be the first person in the world to know, but somehow I think I'd rather tell her when I'm on my own, so I leave that call until tomorrow morning and we go to bed.

Chapter Thirteen

'I COULDN'T DO IT!' says Jules, when I ring her the next morning.
'Paul came back here for coffee, and it was awful, Libby. It was
so weird, sitting here knowing that he was going to make a pass, so I kept
getting up for biscuits, and sugar, and things, and it was awful.'

'Well? Did you do it?'

'No!' she practically screams. 'He tried to kiss me and I panicked! I
started blabbing about how I hadn't been separated for very long and I
wasn't sure I was ready to do this. Oh, I feel such a failure.'

'What did he say?'

'He was really sweet, and kissed me on the cheek and said he'd call
me again but he probably won't. What do you think?'

'Of course he will, and by the way I'm getting married.'

'But what should I do when he calls?'

'Jules? Did you hear what I just said? I'm getting married! Ed proposed when we got home last night.'

There's a long silence.

'Jules?'

'Oh my God! Why didn't you call me? You cow!'

'I wanted to tell you when I was alone. So. Aren't you going to congratulate me?'

'I can't believe it,' she says. 'When are you actually going to do it?'

'We never got round to talking about it. But don't worry, I do want to
be engaged for about a year.'

'Promise?'

'Promise. Jules, aren't you happy for me?'

'God, Libby. I'm over the moon. Are you with Ed tonight?'

'Nah. I just want to chill out on my own tonight.'

'You mean I can't tempt you with a Marks and Sparks dinner and a
selection of bridal magazines from which to choose your dress?'

'You've got me,' I say. 'Shall I come straight from work?'

'Yup. I'll get the champagne on ice. Damn. I wish Jamie were here.'

Thank God. That's the first time she's given any indication that she
misses him. 'I know,' I say. 'Me too.'

By lunchtime I think I've told the world, and, though personal calls are normally frowned upon at work (not that you'd know it, the number of times I speak to Jules), Joe said it was fine to make a few this morning, and he sent Jo out to buy champagne so we could have a mini-office celebration. That's what I love about this job: everyone here is so laid-back that they'll jump on any excuse to have a knees-up.

'We'll be doing your PR next,' Joe says, grinning as he pours champagne into my glass. 'Setting up features on the glamorous charity-supporting wife of Ed McMahon.'

I laugh. Although it's not a bad idea. And charity work would be a good thing to do, because other than shop, meet friends for lunch and eventually look after our children, how will I fill my days?

Everyone at work keeps congratulating me, and the champagne's going straight to my head, when Jo—who's been rushing back and forth to pick up the phone in between swigging champagne—shouts, 'Libby, Nick's on the phone. D'you want to call him back?'

'No, I'll take it.' I run to my desk, away from the hubbub, and pick up the phone.

'Hi, Nick!'

'Congratulations. Sal just told me.'

Is it my imagination or does his voice sound just a teensy bit flat? 'Thanks. Can you believe it, me, getting married?' I say.

'Well, not really. It seems like only yesterday that we were going out.'

Oh. I see. Now, all of a sudden, we were 'going out'. Before, we were just sort of seeing one another.

'I'm really happy for you, Libby. I hope he knows how lucky he is.'

'Oh, he does,' I laugh, because it's clear that Nick does have at least some regrets, which is always nice to hear when you were the one that was, to put it unceremoniously, dumped.

'Good. Listen, I can't stay on. I just wanted to say congratulations. I really hope you'll be happy, Libby. You deserve to be.'

'Nick! This isn't like you. What's all this stuff about how lucky Ed is and how I deserve to be happy?' I can't help it. The champagne seems to have loosened my tongue.

Nick laughs. 'I'm sorry. I've been thinking about you recently, and I suppose part of me kind of regrets things not working out. Anyway, I really must go, but we should get together soon. Maybe you and I could celebrate, for old times' sake.'

'As long as you promise not to make a pass.'

'That's going to be a hard one,' he says, and I can hear from his voice that he's smiling. 'But I can promise I won't make more than one.'

'Perfect,' I say. 'One pass will do wonders for the ego,' as indeed will this entire conversation, although I keep that thought to myself.

I put down the phone, thinking it was a shame it didn't work out with Nick. He seemed to fit in so well, so much better than Ed in some ways, and God knows there was certainly passion there. But Nick could never have given me the life I wanted, and anyway it's not whether someone fits in with my friends that matters. It's whether someone fits in with me, and Ed does.

Jules staggers down the stairs under the weight of two cardboard boxes.

'They're in there,' she announces as she drops them on the floor in the kitchen.

We curl up on the sofas to work our way through the magazines.

'You can't have that one,' Jules says in horror, as I show her this fairy-tale meringue dress with layers and layers of stiff tulle shooting out from a tiny boned waist. 'You'll look like a huge cream puff.'

'Oh, thanks a lot. Are you trying to tell me I'm fat?'

'Yeah, really.' She raises her eyes to the ceiling. 'You? Fat? Hardly. I'm just saying that those dresses are really unflattering. I see you in something really elegant and sophisticated. Here. What about something like this?' She slides her magazine over to my lap and points to a stunning ivory sheath.

'Mmm,' I say. 'That is gorgeous.'

'Very sophis,' she says.

'Mmm. But what about bridesmaids?'

'You could do something similar but on a smaller scale. Maybe knee-length or something, in a different colour.'

'Oh God. Colours. What colour?'

Two hours later we're groaning after a major pig-out, and at our feet are piles of pages I've torn out for ideas.

'Listen, what do you think about an engagement party?' I say.

'Hmm. What about an engagement dinner?'

'What, instead of a party?'

'Well, you can always have a party later, but, seeing as Ed doesn't have that many friends, why don't you have a small dinner somewhere and introduce him to everyone?'

'Yeah. Good idea. So have like an introductory dinner, and then have the party?'

'Yup, because it will be a bit weird to have the party when no one's met him. Who will you ask?'

'Sally and Paul. Olly and Carolyn. Who else? Should it be everyone or just the inner circle?'

'Just the inner circle, I think. What about Nick?'

Is that really a good idea? 'Do you think he'll come?'

'Yes. Plus you're always saying you're still friends.'

'But then I need a woman for him. I know! Jo from work! They'd get on.' Actually, I'm not sure that they would, which is why I'll ask her. Jo, like me, would never demean herself by going out with someone with no money whatsoever.

'OK. Then you can ask those friends of Ed,' says Jules. 'What were their names?'

'Charlie and Sarah. Hmm. Don't know. Maybe not. They were really nice but they're quite a bit older. I'm not sure they'd fit in.'

'Fine. Well, have one dinner for your friends and another for Ed's.' And then she stops and sighs. 'You really are going to marry him, aren't you?' she says.

'What? Did you think this was all a joke? Yes, Jules, I really am going to marry him.'

'OK, but let me ask you one question. Are you in love with him?'

I pause. 'Yes. Well. I love him.'

'That's not what I asked,' she says. 'Are you in love with him?'

'Jules,' I say slowly, because I really want her to understand what I'm about to say. 'You were incredibly lucky with Jamie, or at least, we all thought so at the time. You seemed to have found someone who was gorgeous, bright, funny, who adored you, who was your best friend, and whom you completely fancied. But it didn't work out.'

'Thanks,' she says bitterly. 'Rub it in, why don't you.'

'I didn't mean it like that,' I say. 'All I'm trying to say is that you thought you'd found the recipe for a lifetime of happiness, and it still didn't work out. Maybe what I have with Ed would work out. And at least I'm going into this with my eyes open.'

'You mean you're having to compromise.'

'Well, yes, but I think you have to compromise. Not on everything, but I think the most important thing is to look for a good man. A man who will look after you, who will be a good husband, a good father to your children. Someone who can be your best friend, who will see you through the ups and downs.'

'But you have to fancy them.'

'Of course you have to fancy them,' I say. 'But that's not nearly as important as the other things, because the fancying thing, the lust thing, always goes. Friendship is the most important thing.'

'I'm just worried that you might be compromising a little too much, and I could understand it if you were thirty-seven or something, but you're twenty-seven, and it just seems a bit young to be making these sorts of compromises.'

'Jules, I do love Ed, and I know he's very good for me, and it doesn't feel like a compromise to me. He's everything I've ever wanted.'

'In terms of wealth,' she says with a sniff.

'No. Not only that. I can really see us together.'

'I'm sorry, I just don't want to see you making a big mistake. Marriage is such a huge step, you have to be completely sure.'

'I am completely sure. I know that, because being involved with men I'm completely crazy about has only ever made me miserable.'

'You'll never know now, will you?'

'Know what?'

'Whether you'd find someone whom you could fall completely in love with without being miserable; someone who'd feel the same way about you. This is it, Libby. No more adventures. No more getting excited over dates with someone you really like.'

'Yes, and no more tears. No more feeling like a piece of shit when you've been dumped yet again. No more sitting at home crying while you're waiting for the phone to ring. No, I promise you this is right. Ed is exactly what I've always looked for and I know I'll be happy. Let's get back to the engagement dinner. When do you think it should be?'

'What *are* you wearing?' I've just disengaged from one of Ed's smothering hugs, and I look down to see these worn-out, shabby old carpet slippers that are exactly like the ones my grandfather used to wear.

'My slippers,' he says in a bemused tone. 'My favourite slippers.'

'Ed! They're old-man slippers. They're awful!'

Once again he gets that sad puppy-dog expression on his face, and this time it just irritates the fuck out of me. 'Ed, sometimes I think you're a sixty-year-old trapped in a younger man's body.'

'What do you mean?'

'It's only that sometimes you seem so middle-aged.' Shit, I think I've pushed this one a bit too far. 'I'm sorry,' I say, putting my arms round him and kissing him, which, thank God, removes the expression. 'It's just that sometimes you behave a bit like an old fuddy-duddy.'

'I'll throw them away,' he says, kicking off the offending slippers and putting them in the dustbin. 'There! All gone. Happy now?'

'Yes,' I snort, although it's not just about the slippers, and I do worry that Ed lives in another world. That he doesn't really have a clue what's going on, that I really am forcing myself to be compatible with someone who's too damn straight for me.

'Would you listen to me?'

'I'm sorry, darling. I'm in a bit of a bad mood.'

'I don't like Libby when she's grumpy,' he says, sitting next to me on the sofa and pursing his lips for a kiss. I dutifully kiss him and he grins at me. 'I like Libby when she's happy.'

'I'll try to be happy,' I say, and smile.

'That's better,' he says, kissing me again and then kissing my neck and stroking my hair, and I know what this means. Yup. Just like the textbook says. Move number two is hand up to my breast.

'Mmm,' he says into my hair. 'Libby smells sexy.'

And then move number three is hand under the jumper, hand under the bra, bra strap undone (amidst much fumbling, I'll have you know).

'Shall we go to bed?' Ed says as he's pulling off my jumper.

'Why? What's wrong with the sofa?' I say.

'Oh no!' He looks horrified. 'If we're going to play bouncy castles we have to do it in bed.'

'Right. Bouncy castles. In bed. OK.' And I pick up my jumper and walk up the stairs, wondering how I'm supposed to be turned on by the words 'bouncy castles'. Wondering whether sex is ever going to improve with a man who refers to a fuck as 'playing bouncy castles'. Whether 'bouncy castles' is as dirty as it's ever going to get.

And while Ed's pounding away I look at the ceiling and try to picture my wedding dress. And for your information I do have an orgasm, but I suppose if someone, anyone, rubs long enough in the right place it's bound to happen, isn't it?

'That was gorgeous,' he says, when he's finished.

'Mmm? Good,' I murmur, halfway down the aisle once again.

'Libby? Was it, umm, good for you?'

'Yes, Ed. It was lovely,' I lie.

Ed gets up to go to the bathroom, and when he comes back I tell him about the idea for an introductory pre-engagement-party dinner.

'Excellent idea,' he says. 'I'll take everyone out for dinner.'

'Don't be silly,' I say. 'Everyone will pay for themselves.'

He looks at me in horror. 'Libby, you can't invite people out for dinner and then expect them to pay. That's very bad form.'

'Are you sure?'

'I wouldn't have it any other way.'

'OK,' I say, shrugging. 'If you don't mind.' I tell him who I think we should invite and he says fine. And he doesn't even ask who Nick is.

 # Chapter Fourteen

'So COME ON, then, Sis. Tell me all about him.'

'Olly, you're going to be meeting him in about six hours. You'll see for yourself.'

'He's definitely a big hit with Mum, but I'm never sure if that's a good sign or not.'

'Tell me about it. Shit, someone needs me, Olly. Listen, I've gotta go, but you'll be there on time, won't you?'

'Yup. I'll see you then.'

'All right, darling. Bye.' I put the phone down and turn to Jo, who's making worried faces at me. 'What's the matter, Jo?'

'You're going to kill me,' she says. 'I'm really, really sorry.'

'Please don't tell me you can't come,' I say slowly.

'I'm really sorry,' she says, wincing. 'My friend Jill called to check I was coming to her birthday party, and I completely forgot, and she went bananas when I said I couldn't make it, I'm so sorry.'

'Don't worry,' I sigh, completely pissed off but knowing I probably would have done the same thing. It's what single women do. We'll make arrangements, and then if something better comes up, i.e. some event where we're more likely to meet Mr Right, we'll cancel our first arrangements without thinking twice about it.

And I'm not upset, it's just that who the hell will I put with Nick? Thankfully, my phone rings, so Jo takes the opportunity to slink back to reception while I sigh a 'hello' into the receiver.

'Darling! It's me.' 'Me' in this case is Amanda Baker. Since I got her the feature in the *Telegraph* I'm definitely her best friend. Suddenly a light bulb in my head switches on.

'Amanda! I was just this second going to call you! I know this is incredibly short notice, but basically, umm'—time for a little white lie here—'Ed and I decided to have dinner with a few friends this evening and I really want you to come.'

'How lovely!' she exclaims, as I wait with bated breath. 'Actually, I'm not doing anything tonight, and I'd love to come out for dinner with Ed McMahon. And you.'

'Wonderful!' I exclaim, mustering up some enthusiasm from somewhere. 'That's great!'

'Just tell me,' she interrupts, 'is it going to be couple hell?'

I laugh. 'Sort of. But there is a single man there, although I don't think he's your type.'

'That's OK, as long as I'm not the only single person there.'

'Nope. Don't worry,' and, as I tell her where to be and at what time, I breathe a sigh of relief because I'll never have to be ashamed of being single again.

I remember clearly all those times I'd turn down invitations to dinner parties because I'd always be the only person on my own, and those times I'd turn up to find I'd been fixed up with someone awful, and how I vowed I'd never go again until I had a partner.

And now I do, and I never have to ask those questions. I've got a partner. A fiancé. I'm now, officially, a grown-up.

Jules says there are three things that make you a grown-up: radiator cabinets, whisky in the house, and making your bed every morning. But I disagree. I think you're a grown-up when you've got another half. When you don't have to live in fear of other couples. When you don't have to feel you're not good enough.

I make sure that Ed and I are the first to arrive, and we order champagne as we sit down. Ed kisses me and tells me how beautiful I am. Just as the champagne arrives, so does Jules, followed swiftly by Olly and Carolyn.

Ed kisses Jules and shakes hands with the others, telling Olly how delighted he is to meet him, having heard so much about him.

'We're all thrilled Libby's finally settling down,' Olly says, winking at me. 'We're just slightly surprised at how quick it's all been.'

'Ha ha!' laughs Ed. 'I'm surprised myself.'

'So where's Jamie, then?' Olly asks, looking at Jules quizzically. 'Got a big case on again, I suppose?'

Jules manages to pull off a shrug that looks genuine to everyone but me, but then again I'm the only one who knows the truth. 'You know how it is,' she says with a sad smile. 'Bloody barristers.'

'You could have asked him, you know,' I whisper, sidling up to her and pulling her to one side.

'I know,' she says. 'And he phoned today, and I so nearly asked him, but he hasn't suffered enough. Not yet.'

'So what did you say?'

'Well, I told him you were having an engagement do tonight, and I think he thought I was going to invite him, but I changed the subject.'

'How do you feel?'

'Lonely as hell.'

I put my arm round her shoulders and give her a squeeze, and then I hear, 'Libby!' and Sal comes bustling through the restaurant. 'I'm so excited for you!' she says, throwing her arms round me and giving me a huge hug. 'Paul and Nick are parking the car. They'll be here any second.' She looks at the others, who are now standing by the side of the table making small talk, and seems to do a double take when she sees Ed. 'Is that him?' she says finally, sounding surprised.

'Yes. Why? You sound surprised.'

She shakes her head. 'Sorry. God, I'm really sorry, Libby. It's just that, well, I thought you hated moustaches.'

'I do,' I whisper back. 'I'm working on it.'

'You must think I'm really rude. He looks lovely.'

'He is lovely. You'll see.'

'Of course he is!' she says, squeezing my arm. 'He's marrying you, so he has to be!'

'Ed?' I call over to get his attention. 'Come and meet Sal.'

Ed walks over, smiling, and extends a hand, looking a bit taken aback when Sal reaches up and gives him a hug. 'Lovely to meet you,' she says. 'We've heard all about you, but I suppose you're sick of hearing that.'

Ed chuckles. 'Not at all. Not at all. And how do you know Libby?'

As Sal's explaining, I see Paul walk into the restaurant with Nick at his heels, and for a second my heart catches in my throat. He's in his old chinos with his DMs and a scruffy old raincoat, but he looks so familiar, so gorgeous, that for a second I think I'm going to start crying.

'Libby. You look lovely,' he says, giving me a sedate kiss on each cheek. 'Congratulations.'

'I'm so pleased you're here, Nick,' I say, and I am. 'I was a bit worried about, well, you know.'

'Don't be silly. We're friends, aren't we? And I'm dying to know what the infamous Ed's like.' Nick turns and sees Ed talking to Sally.

'That's not him, is it? Please tell me that's not him.'

'Nick! What do you mean? Why not?'

'Libby, he's old enough to be your grandfather.'

'Crap,' I laugh, suddenly remembering Nick's sense of humour. 'He's only ten years older than me. Come and meet him.'

'Umm, is there a reason you've left an empty seat beside me?' Nick leans over the table to me. 'Is my personal hygiene problem that bad?'

I laugh. 'No. Amanda Baker's coming. She's late, she should be here any minute.'

'Amanda Baker?' Nick's eyes widen. 'Sitting next to me? Phwooargh.'

'I might have known you'd know who she is,' I laugh. 'You're the only person I know who watches daytime TV on a regular basis.'

'Speak of the devil,' whispers Nick, as Amanda sashays towards the table, and I suddenly feel slightly nauseous, because what if they do get on? What if Amanda decides Nick's just her type?

'Libby!' she kisses me, then kisses Ed, moving back round the table to sit next to Nick. 'I'm so sorry I'm late,' she says. 'I had to do another bloody interview.' She waits for someone to comment on the fact that she's famous, but no one does, until Nick steps in to fill the void.

'I watch you all the time on TV,' he says. 'I never realised you were a friend of Libby.'

'Yes. Do you like the show?' Her face lights up, happy at being given the opportunity to talk about herself.

Jules rolls her eyes at me as I suppress a giggle, but I watch Amanda very carefully, and, although she's obviously delighted at having found a fan, I can't hear a glimmer of flirtation in her voice. I turn to Ed, who's got his hand on my knee. 'Are you enjoying yourself?' he asks, pursing up for a kiss. I kiss him and nod.

'Are you?'

He smiles. 'Of course,' and looks round the table. 'Who would like some more champagne?'

'Yes, please,' says Sal, proffering her glass.

Ed refills her glass, then says, 'Do you know Amanda?'

'We haven't met,' says Sal, as Amanda looks up at the mention of her name. 'Hello. I'm Sally Cross.'

'How do you do,' says Amanda, a distracted look on her face. 'Sally Cross. That's a familiar name. Have we met before?'

'No, I don't think so,' says Sal.

'What do you do? Are you in TV?'

Sal explains her job, and Amanda's voice immediately warms up. A journalist! Another potential hit to get a feature written about herself! Amanda taps Nick on the shoulder. 'Sorry, but could we swap places for a bit, it's just that it's so rude to talk across you.'

Nick shrugs and stands up, and Amanda pushes past him to sit in his recently vacated seat, as she carries on talking about her career.

'How's the book going?' Olly shouts over to Nick.

Nick taps the side of his nose mysteriously. 'All sorts of things going on, but can't talk about them . . . Yet.'

Olly laughs. 'You mean we're going to be able to read it soon?'

'Time will tell,' says Nick, in his Mystic Meg voice.

'You're an author?' Ed, for the first time this evening, is showing an interest in Nick.

'Aspiring,' Nick says with a smile. 'But things are looking hopeful.'

'What sort of a book have you written?'

'Oh, usual thriller, cloak-and-dagger-type stuff.'

'So if you're not published you must do other work.'

'Nope. The only other work I do is walk to the dole office and back.'

'Oh ha ha! Very funny.' Ed laughs and Nick looks at him peculiarly.

'Yes, well, I'm glad you think it's funny. Unfortunately, it's not a joke.'

'Oh gosh!' Ed colours a deep red. 'I assumed you were joking.'

'I wouldn't joke about a thing like that.'

'I've never met anyone on the dole before,' says Ed, digging himself deeper and deeper.

I decide to step in and help the conversation change course. 'Come on, Nick, tell us what your book's about.'

'You wouldn't be interested,' he says.

'Yes, yes! We would.' Jules joins in with me, and for the next ten minutes Nick holds centre stage as he details the plot for us, while I sit there absolutely staggered, because it is brilliant! Seriously, it is one of the most original ideas I've heard for ages.

'That sounds fantastic!' says Olly, who by now is also listening in. 'You shouldn't have any trouble getting that published.'

'I agree,' says Paul. 'I'd buy it.'

'I hope you will,' laughs Nick, puffing up with pride. 'I expect all of you to contribute to my royalty payments.'

Amanda and Sal have finished their shop talk, and Amanda taps Ed on the shoulder. 'Binky Donnell says hello,' she says, smiling.

'Binky Donnell!' exclaims Ed, his eyes lighting up. 'There's a name I haven't heard in a while. How is the old rascal?'

Nick nudges me and mouths, 'Rascal?' I kick him under the table.

'He's lovely,' she says. 'I had dinner with Binky and Bunny last week.'

Nick nudges me again and this time I can't help it, I start giggling.

'I can't believe you're going to marry someone who has friends called Binky and Bunny,' Nick mutters, when he's finally recovered.

'Oh I see,' I say, 'and Moose is so much better?'

'At least Moose is cool,' Nick says, mock indignantly. 'Binky and Bunny don't exactly have much street cred.'

'How do you know? For all you know Binky drives a vintage Harley, and Bunny's a blonde bombshell rock chick.'

'With long floppy ears?'

'Quite possibly,' I snort, and we both collapse with laughter again, completely unnoticed by Ed and Amanda, who are now shrieking with delight at having so many people in common.

Even Jules shoots me an odd look, and I just shrug, more than happy that Ed's found something in common with at least one of my friends, even if Amanda isn't exactly a friend.

Olly and Carolyn are chatting away to Sal and Paul, and as far as I can tell the evening's a success. OK, so not everyone's really had a chance to talk to Ed, but then that's always the problem with large groups of people at dinner, isn't it?

When the coffee arrives I get up and go to see Olly at the other end of the table. 'Why don't you talk to Ed a bit? Get to know him?'

Olly sighs. 'Libby, I'm not sure what I'd have to say to him.'

'Olly! That's not very nice. This is the man I'm marrying. And how do you know you wouldn't have anything to say to him?'

'OK, you're right. But . . .' he pauses. 'Anyway. He's deep in conversation with your friend Amanda. I don't want to interrupt.'

'OK,' I say warily. 'Maybe you and Carolyn will come over for dinner with us?'

'Maybe,' he says distractedly. 'Let's talk about this tomorrow.'

'God, Oll. Anyone would think you'd taken an instant dislike to him.'

'Libby, we'll talk about it tomorrow.'

'So what did you think?' We're driving back home, and much as I hate to admit it I'm actually far more worried about what my friends thought of Ed, but I won't be able to get the lowdown until tomorrow morning, so in the meantime I want to know if Ed liked them.

'It was a great success.' He smiles indulgently at me.

'No, I meant what did you think of my friends?'

And it suddenly occurs to me that Ed's opinion matters far more than I ever dreamt. And not because I want him to like them, but that whatever he says will be a reflection of who he is, and if he fails to approve, I'm not sure I'll ever be able to see him in the same light again.

'Oh, they were great fun,' he says finally. 'Especially Amanda. I definitely approve of Amanda.'

'It's not about approval, Ed. It's about liking the people whom I love. And Amanda isn't exactly a friend, more of a work colleague, and the only reason you liked her was because you know so many of the same people, probably because Amanda's such a bloody networker.'

'Libby! That's not nice.'

'Sorry,' I mutter. 'But it's true. Anyway, what did you think of Olly?'

'I didn't really talk to him,' Ed says truthfully, 'so we'll have to have him over for dinner, I think. Soon.'

'Yup, OK. But he's nice, isn't he? Is he what you expected?'

'I didn't expect anything, and he seems awfully nice.'

'What about Sal and Paul? Did you like them?'

'Well,' he pauses. 'I'm not sure I'm that happy about you being friends with tabloid journalists.'

'What? Are you serious?' I can feel an argument coming on.

'Darling, I'm not sure I trust them, that's all.'

'But you don't even bloody know them.'

'Don't swear at me, Libby.'

'Sorry. But Sal and Paul are two of the nicest people I know. I can't believe you're judging them by their jobs. And their paper isn't exactly sleazy, plus they don't do news, they write features.'

'Still,' he says, looking quickly at me. 'Oh, maybe you're right. I'm just being a judgmental old fuddy-duddy, but I do have to say I was very surprised that you are friendly with someone like that Nick fellow. He's terribly scruffy. Not the sort of person I'd have thought you'd associate with at all.'

'But you hardly said two words to him.' My voice is becoming more and more strained.

'But, Libby, please. Look at the chap, what does he think he looks like? Those shabby clothes, and as for that business about being on the dole . . . I think it's best if you don't see him again.'

'I can't believe you're saying this. I can't believe you're sitting here'—incidentally, I'm now spluttering with rage—'I can't believe you're trashing my friends. And most of all, I cannot believe how incredibly superficial you're being. You have judged all my friends either by their appearance or by their jobs. Evidently unlike you'—this last bit said through gritted teeth—'I choose my friends because of who they are, and not because of how much money they have.'

I run out of steam then and sit there shaking with anger, and we don't say a word to one another the whole way back.

But as we get out of the car outside Ed's house, I wonder whether I'm being too hard. I don't know whether to compromise on this and try to forget about it and accept that Nick and Sal and Paul are not the sort of people the wife of Ed McMahon should be socialising with. I just don't know what to think any more.

We get undressed in stony silence, and, after I have climbed into bed and turned my back to Ed, he says he's sorry.

I ignore him.

He touches my shoulder and I shrug off his hand, and he says, again, that he's sorry. 'And you're right,' he continues. 'I was wrong. I've been far too judgmental. Libby, my darling, I really am sorry.'

And I turn to him and there are tears in his eyes, and I can see that he is sorry, so when he starts stroking my leg I accept his apology, but I don't feel anything. Completely numb. And when he thinks he's done enough foreplay and is ready to enter me, I still don't feel anything. And then he's inside me, pounding away on top of me, and this time I don't try to picture myself in my wedding dress, walking down the aisle, I just lie there with a strange pain in my chest, and this pain moves higher and higher, and suddenly I'm crying.

Huge, great heaving sobs. And I push Ed off and run into the bathroom, locking the door, and look at myself in the mirror for a long time.

I have never felt so lonely in my life.

Despite myself, as soon as I get to the office the next morning I pick up the phone and ring Sal.

'Well? What did you think?'

'He's lovely!' exclaims Sal, and I start to relax.

'Really? You liked him?'

'He's very charming. Of course. You two look good together.'

'God, Sal. I am so pleased to hear that.'

'Why? Did you think I wouldn't?'

'No.' Yes. 'It's just that it's important to me what my friends think.'

'Did he like us, then?'

'Yes! He thought you were lovely!' And as I say it I recognise the insincerity. My voice has exactly the same inflection as Sally's.

'**I**'m ringing up to thank you for last night.' Why do I suddenly feel that Nick is playing a larger and larger role in my life? I mean, it's over. Finished. I'm getting married to someone else, yet suddenly I seem to be speaking to Nick, or seeing him, far more often than ever before.

'Did you enjoy it?'

'It was lovely to see you,' he says warmly. 'Especially looking so glowing and happy.'

'Am I?' I'm surprised. I never dreamt Ed had that effect on me.

'Very much so,' he laughs. 'You're really going through with this?'

''Course!' I say indignantly. 'I don't go around getting engaged to every man I meet.'

'You're telling me,' he laughs.

I want to ask Nick what he thought of Ed, but I have a horrible feeling that Nick will tell the truth, which is why he hasn't volunteered the information himself, and I don't want to know. As far as I'm concerned my doubts are just pre-wedding nerves.

Jo runs in and tells me Sean Moore's here for the meeting, so I say goodbye to Nick and spend the rest of the morning talking to Sean Moore, his agent and Joe Cooper about his publicity campaign. When we're finished there's a message from Jules.

I don't call her back. Not yet. I go out for lunch with Jo and try to forget about everything, because right at this moment I feel that it's all getting a bit much for me. So we go to the Italian café and order tuna salad on toasted baps, and we sit there and gossip and by the time I step back into the office at half past two I feel human again.

So when Jules calls again midafternoon I'm in a good mood, and I'm totally unprepared for what she's about to say.

'Libby, you might hate me for saying this, but I've just got to.'

'Go on. What is it?'

'Look, I'm only saying this because I love you and I don't want to see you make a mistake.'

'Get to the point, Jules.'

'OK, OK. The thing is, I'm just really concerned that you've been swept up in a whirlwind of excitement, and I'm worried that you haven't actually thought about the reality of it.'

'Jules, you've said all this to me before. I know what I'm doing.'

'OK. But I'm going to say it again, and I really want you to listen to me. Marriage is for life. It's not just about having a spectacular wedding day, it's about spending the rest of your life with that person, for better or worse. What about children? If you have children Ed will want to send them to Eton, and would you really want your children brought up away from you? There are so many other things to consider, and I'm just so frightened that you haven't thought this through.'

I start to feel sick, and immediately jump on the defensive. 'What about you, then? If marriage is for life, how come you keep saying that Jamie has to suffer and you don't know whether you'll take him back? If you really believe what you're saying, then you'll do anything to save your own marriage, and that includes forgiving Jamie.'

There's a long silence, and then I hear a catch in her throat as she says softly, 'I'm trying. And I do believe what I just said, and all I've been thinking about is that I have to find it in my heart to forgive him, because I love him, because he's my husband, and because I don't want to live without him.'

'Thank God,' I practically scream.

'That doesn't mean everything's fine,' she says slowly. 'It's not, and I don't know if it will ever be fine again, but I am going to ask him to come home.'

'Yes!' I punch the air. 'Thank God you've seen sense.'

'Libby,' she says, 'stop changing the subject. You need to know that marriage is not a fairy tale. This has been the most nightmarish fucking thing that's ever happened to me, but I'm willing to work at it.

'Look,' she continues. 'I'm not saying that Ed's not for you. All I'm saying is you need some time out on your own to think about this, to think about spending The. Rest. Of. Your. Life. With. Ed.'

There's a silence while I digest what she's just said, because, even though she's said it before, it never hit home. And now I see that she's right. That this, marriage, means I'll never have another flirtation again. I'll be sleeping with Ed, and only Ed, for the rest of my life. And I remember last night again, and I exhale deeply.

'Libby? Are you still there?'

'Yes.' My voice sounds small. 'I think you're right.'

'I'm not saying this isn't it,' she says, sounding relieved, 'I'm just saying you need to be one hundred per cent sure.'

'I know.' My voice still sounds small. 'So what do I do?'

Jules tells me to tell Ed I've got a pitch coming up, and that everyone will be working late the next few days, and that I'll miss him desperately but I need to prove myself with this one because since I've met Ed I've barely concentrated on work, and if I don't do this, I'll be in big trouble.

And as she says it I know that even though it's going to be difficult to tell him—I can already see his sad puppy-dog expression—it's a credible excuse, and she's right, I need a few days on my own.

'Jules? Thanks. Really.'

'Don't be ridiculous. That's what best friends are for.'

But I still feel nervous as hell as I'm driving over to Ed's that night. I have nothing with me, no change of clothes for tomorrow, and I can see that Ed notices this as soon as he opens the door.

'Darling? Where are your things?'

I can't lie so I say, 'I'm not staying tonight,' and, predictably enough, he looks crestfallen.

'Is something the matter?' I can already see the fear in his eyes, and a wave of sympathy sweeps over me.

'Don't be silly, darling. Nothing's the matter. But I'd love a cup of tea.'

Anything to stall for time.

We go into the kitchen, I tell him we've got a pitch coming up and I'm going to be working really hard the next few days, so I don't think I'll be able to spend much time with him.

Ed is visibly relieved as he puts the tea in front of me. 'Is that all, darling? Don't worry about work. You know I won't want you working once we're married, so why don't you just hand in your notice?'

'I love my job,' I say indignantly, suddenly realising that, at the moment, I do. 'I don't want to give it up quite yet. Although,' I add as an afterthought, 'it's very sweet of you to offer. I feel that I need to prove myself with this. You do understand, don't you?' I sip the tea.

'I suppose so,' he says sadly. 'But I will see you, won't I?'

'God, I hope so,' I lie, reaching up and giving him a kiss. I look at my watch. 'Jesus, I've got to get back. Everyone's working late tonight.'

'You mean you're going back to the office now?'

'I'm so sorry, darling,' I say, grabbing my bag. 'But they'll sack me if I'm not there. You'd better not call because the switchboard will be closed, but if there's anything urgent I'll leave the mobile on. I'll call you tomorrow,' and I give him another peck and run out of the door.

I catch Marks & Sparks just as they're about to close, but the security man is taken in by my pleading looks and he lets me in.

Freedom. I feel free. I can eat whatever I want tonight, and I'm going to be in my flat for the whole night and refuse to answer the phone. I run down the aisles throwing things in a basket. Mini-pitta breads, tara-masalata, hummous, olives. I chuck in a packet of smoked salmon and some chocolate bars. Fuck it. I'm having a blowout.

Then back in the car and on to Ladbroke Grove, but not before stopping at the video store. And while I'm trying to decide between *Sleepless in Seattle* and *Sleepers*, my mobile rings and Ed's number flashes up on the screen. I know it's mean, but I press the busy button on the phone.

I choose *Sleepers*, the last thing I need is to watch a slushy romantic love story where the hero is gorgeous (if you're into Tom Hanks, that is, which I am), and I whiz off home via the off-licence, where I treat myself to a very expensive (that means more than £4.99) bottle of claret.

Home. Wonderful, fantastic home. As I put my meal together, the phone rings, and I hear Ed's voice on my machine.

'Sweetieloviedarling, I tried your mobile but you're not answering. I just wanted to ring and say that I miss you and I love you and I can't wait for us to get married. Don't worry about work, and I'll call you tomorrow. I love you very, very much.'

'Fuck off,' I mutter, as I gather up my food and collapse onto the sofa.

 # Chapter Fifteen

THANK GOD. It's Saturday morning and I've managed to avoid Ed since Thursday night. OK, I know it's only one day, but what's so extraordinary is that I've loved having two nights pottering around at home by myself.

I thought that these 'days off', as Jules put them, would be a time of reflection. I thought I'd be sitting around analysing every aspect of our relationship and trying to work out whether Ed is The One, whether I want to spend the rest of my life with him, but actually I haven't even thought about him. I've been far too busy being happy by myself.

Which I suppose is slightly worrying in itself.

So when the phone rings on Saturday morning, again I leave it because I've assumed it's Ed. It isn't Ed. It's Nick.

I trip over the rug and stub my toe on the coffee table as I'm rushing to the phone to pick it up before Nick rings off, and I pick up the phone shouting, 'Shit!'

'Is that any way to greet your second-favourite man? If I piss you off that much why bother picking up the phone at all?'

'Ouch,' I say, rubbing my toe. 'I just stubbed my toe.'

'Have you looked out of the window?'

'No. Why? Are you sitting on my railings?'

He chuckles. 'Nope. But it's a beautiful day. Far too nice to be staying inside. What are you doing?'

Like I even have to think about it. 'Nothing. Absolutely nothing.'

'Not spending the day with your fiancé, then?'

'Nope. He thinks I'm spending the day in the office.'

'Oops. Do I smell trouble on the West London front?'

'Nah, I just needed a bit of space. Anyway, why are you asking?'

'I thought maybe we could go for a walk on the heath, then maybe have lunch or something.'

'That sounds fantastic!' It does. 'I'd love to.' I would.

'Great! How about I'll meet you outside the cinema on South End Green in an hour.'

'OK. See you then.'

And for the first time in what feels like ages I don't have to worry about what to wear. I sling on my jeans that haven't seen the light of day since I met Ed, pull on some trainers and inch on a tight, white, V-necked T-shirt, and that's it, I'm ready.

And when I reach the cinema at noon, Nick's already there, sitting outside reading the *Guardian*, looking decidedly gorgeous.

'Libby!' He stands up and flings his arms round me, giving me a smacker on the cheek, and as we walk off down the road he keeps an arm casually round my shoulders, and there's nothing sexual, nothing intimate about it, it's just the mark of a good friend, and I laugh as I put my arm round his waist and give him a squeeze.

But then I remember I am the property of another, and I move away from him slightly, just enough for him to remove his arm, and I link arms with him instead, which feels much safer.

'Come on, come on,' he urges, marching next to me. 'If I'd known you were such a snail I wouldn't have asked you to come for a walk.'

'We can't go for a walk yet,' I say in horror. 'It's practically lunchtime and I haven't had any breakfast. I'm starving.'

'OK. Shall we hit the high street?'

'To the high street we shall go,' and giggling together we march up Downshire Hill.

'God, this is beautiful,' I say halfway up the hill, stopping to peer into the windows of a tiny, cottagey whitewashed house.

'Mmm,' agrees Nick. 'This is one of my favourite roads in the whole of London. If I had money I'd definitely buy a house here.'

'Money?' I look at him with horror. 'But, Nick! If I remember correctly, you'd give all your money to the bloody politicians.'

'Ah,' he says, nodding sagely. 'Yes, that is correct. But of course I'd save a few million for myself.'

'You've changed your tune.'

'Yes, well. As you keep saying, I'm really a girl, and isn't it a woman's prerogative to change her mind?'

I laugh and we continue up the hill, idly chatting about this and that, and then I remember how mysterious he was the other night about the book, and what's happening with it, and I ask him again if he'll tell me.

'Can't.' He shakes his head. 'It's a secret.'

'Oh, pleeeeeeeeeeaaaaaaase,' I plead, looking up at him hopefully.

'Nope.'

'What about if we exchange secrets?'

He looks interested. 'You mean you tell me one, then I'll tell you?'

He stops walking and turns to look at me. 'OK. You tell me a secret, and if I think it's good enough I'll tell you. How's that?'

'OK, deal.' And I stand there desperately trying to think of a secret. I could tell him that I cried during sex the other night, but I don't want him to know that, it wouldn't be fair on Ed. Then I think of something. 'I've got one, but you have to promise you'll never tell anyone.'

'I promise.'

'OK. When I'm driving in my car I talk to myself.'

'So? Loads of people talk to themselves.'

'But I do it in an American accent.'

'You're kidding!'

I shake my head.

'Give me an example.'

Reluctantly, it has to be said, I stand in the middle of Hampstead High Street and in a crap American accent I say, 'Did you have a good time tonight? Yeah, it was rilly cool.'

And Nick collapses with laughter.

'I can't believe that,' he splutters, and I start laughing too. 'You are seriously weird.'

And when we recover I say, 'Your turn. Now tell me about the book.'

'No way. Your secret wasn't big enough.'

'You bastard.' I hit him.

'Wanna try again?'

'Nope. You're not getting any more secrets out of me. Now I really am starving, what about here?' We're standing outside a café with tables dotted on the pavement, and I watch a couple leave a tip, then stand up.

'Quick, quick.' Nick grabs me by the hand. 'We must have that table.'

I order a salade niçoise, and Nick has an egg and bacon baguette, but by the end of the meal we're feeding each other our respective meals, making a huge mess, and giggling like children.

And Nick insists on paying, which I feel slightly guilty about, because he really doesn't have much money, but he won't hear of accepting anything from me, and then we leave and walk up to the heath.

And the weather is beautiful. It's a hot, hazy, lazy summer's day, and everyone's smiling, and this is London at its best.

After a while, kicking through the long grass until we're on open spaces, Nick says why don't we sit down and sunbathe for a bit, and I kick off my shoes and fold my arms behind my head, just listening to the birds and watching the trees blow slowly in the soft breeze.

'So,' I say eventually, when we've been lying there for a bit in silence. 'What did you think of Ed?' I don't know why I ask this question, but I suppose I think he'll echo Sal and say he seemed like a nice guy. I'm certainly not expecting what comes next. If I had been, I would never have asked.

'Do you want the truth?' Nick says seriously, and I shrug.

'I think he's awful,' Nick says slowly, while I look at him with a smile because he's obviously joking.

He's not joking.

'I think he is absolutely horrific,' he says, and there isn't even the merest hint of a smile. 'He's pompous, arrogant, and he doesn't fit into any aspect of your life. He treats you like some sort of trophy girlfriend, sorry, fiancée, with patronising comments and pats on the head, and he has completely ignored who you really are because he's just not interested. He probably cannot believe his luck that someone like you would even look at him.

'And to be honest,' he continues, while I sit open-mouthed in shock, 'I can't believe you would even look at him. I think he is quite possibly one of the most awful men I have ever met.'

I'm about to scream at him, to shout 'How dare you,' to splutter with indignation, and fury, and rage, but I don't. Nick just looks at me, waiting for a reaction, and I feel my eyes well up, and suddenly I'm crying. Hiccuping huge sobs, and before I know it Nick has his arms round me, and I'm soaking his shoulder with my tears.

'Sssh, sssh,' he's saying. 'It's OK. It's all going to be OK.' And this makes me cry even more, because I know he's absolutely right.

And eventually I calm down, and pull away and try to smile through my tears, finally absolutely sure that I have to end this with Ed, that I cannot go through with it, and Nick smiles at my wobbly smile, and Christ only knows how this happens, but we're kissing.

His lips are on mine, and they're soft, and warm, and then, before I even register what's happening, my tongue slips into his mouth, and he pushes me back on the grass and a moan escapes me, from somewhere deep down, and I want his kiss to swallow me up.

We can't stop. Neither of us. Not even when a group of teenagers walks past and starts catcalling and shouting things. I am lost in this kiss, in Nick, and I want it to go on for ever.

But we have to stop. Eventually. And as we pull apart and look at one another, my hands fly up to my mouth. 'Oh my God,' I whisper. 'What have I done?'

I didn't expect to be quite so upset, but I cried all night. I cried for the loss of my fantasies, for the loss of my dreams. And I cried at the memory of what it is like to be alone.

Last night, drowning in tears, Nick rang, and this time I didn't pick up the answer phone. He left a sweet message saying that he'd had a lovely time, and that he hoped he hadn't offended me, but if I wanted to call him he would be there.

But I don't want to call him. I don't want to confuse the issue any further, and the only issue that's important right now is Ed.

Ed. I called him. Last night. I managed to calm down enough to pretend there was nothing wrong, although the first thing he asked was whether I had a cold because I sounded sniffly. He told me he loves me very, very much, and he said he'd missed me desperately, and we arranged to meet this evening.

He wants to take me out for dinner, a romantic evening, just the two of us, and I nearly broke down when he said this, because he doesn't have a clue what I'm going to say to him tonight. At the end of the conversation, he said, 'Darling, I think it's time we went shopping for a ring,' and I didn't say anything. I couldn't say anything, and when I said we'd talk about it tonight, he sounded worried.

I feel like I've been drugged. I suppose that crying all night does that to you. You move as if in slow motion, your head too fuzzy to think clearly, and eventually I ring Jules, because I can't do this on my own.

She knows instantly that something's wrong, and orders me over there immediately. They are having lunch with friends, but she sends Jamie off by himself, not, however, before I have a chance to see them together, to see how they are post-trauma. Jamie is being extra affectionate towards her, and, although I can see she is trying to resist, when he puts his arms around her to say goodbye she leans into him and the expression on her face is one of relief.

And when he leaves she sits me down and makes me milky sweet tea without saying anything, just waits for me to start.

Haltingly I start to tell her about Nick, and when I've finished she doesn't say anything for a while, so I start blabbering and everything comes out in a big rush.

'I can't marry Ed,' I say, tears already filling my eyes. 'I can't. He's not what I want, and more importantly I'm not what he wants. Nick's right. I've realised that all this time he's been trying to turn me into the investment banker's wife, and that's not me, it never will be, and I never laugh with Ed, and you were right about everything, about me falling for the fantasy, and the thing is I'm seeing Ed tonight, and he's not a bad person, and I do genuinely think he adores me, and I just don't know what to say to him or how to say it, because however I put it it's going to destroy him.'

'I know it's hard,' Jules says finally. 'But you're doing the right thing. Yes, Ed is a lovely guy, but he's not for you, and thank God you've seen that now rather than a year into the marriage.'

I nod sadly.

'So you're going to tell him tonight?'

'Oh God.' I sink my face into my hands. 'This is going to be the hardest thing I've ever done.'

Jules looks worried. 'But you have to,' she says firmly. 'You have to be very honest and say that you won't make him happy.'

'So I put the blame on myself rather than on him?'

She nods. 'Isn't that what men always do?'

I stay at Jules's all morning, and by lunchtime I'm starting to feel much better. Until, that is, three o'clock approaches and I know that I've got to face my parents for tea.

Jules gives me a hug at the door and wishes me luck, and says I must call her when it's done, and I drive straight to my parents, feeling this cloud of dread hanging over me, wondering how on earth to tell them.

My mother, being the witch that she is, can see something's wrong as soon as I walk in.

'You look like you've been crying,' she says, stepping in for a closer look. 'I hope everything's all right with you and Ed. What's the matter?'

'Nothing,' I mutter, going into the living room and moving aside the newspaper in front of my father's face so I can kiss him hello.

My mother follows me in. 'I know something's wrong, dear,' she says firmly. 'You may as well tell us now, get it out of the way.'

'Uh-oh,' says my father, shuffling his feet into his slippers. 'Girl talk. I'll leave you two alone, shall I? I'll be out in the garden.'

'Come on, then, out with it.'

'Leave me alone, Mum. I don't want to talk about it.'

I sit there with my arms crossed, staring at the mute television picture, with my mother perching on the edge of the armchair.

'I hope it's nothing serious,' she says, and before she has a chance to say anything more I stand up and march outside, saying, 'I'm going to see what Dad's done in the garden.'

My dad's deadheading the roses, and I stand next to him as he hands me the deadheads in silence. My dad and I have never exactly had long conversations, but I know that the only way to do this is to tell him first—yet I don't know which words to use.

'Is it Ed, then?' my dad says slowly, not looking at me, just reaching up to a particularly high branch.

'Yes.'

'Is it over?'

'Yes. Well. Not yet. But it will be tonight.'

My dad just nods and carries on.

'Am I doing the right thing?' I ask.

My dad stops and finally looks at me. 'I couldn't tell you this before. I couldn't even tell your mother, not when she was so excited about having a rich son-in-law, but he wasn't for you, Libby.'

'You didn't like him, did you, Dad?'

'It wasn't that I didn't like him,' my dad says slowly. 'It was just that he lives in a completely different world, and I worried that he didn't really approve of you the way you are, that he was trying to change you into something else.'

God, I never realised my dad was that perceptive.

'And I didn't think you loved him,' he continues, walking over to the bench at the end of the garden and sitting down before I join him.

'You see, the thing is,' he says after we've both sat for a while in the sunshine, 'the thing is that love is really the most important thing. I know it's hard for you to see it now'—he chuckles quietly—'but when I first laid eyes on your mother I thought she was fantastic, and I've never stopped loving her, not for a second. Oh yes, she can be a bit of an old battle-axe at times, but I still love her. That in-love feeling at the beginning settles down into a different sort of love, but it has to be there right from the start, otherwise it just won't work.'

He smiles. 'You didn't love Ed. I could see that.' He sighs, stands up and stretches before saying, 'Do you want me to tell your mother?'

An hour later I'm sitting at the kitchen table watching my mother still wiping the tears from her eyes.

'What am I going to tell everyone?' she sniffles.

I shrug, not bothering to reply.

'You know, Libby, you may not find another man who treats you like Ed treated you,' she says.

'But, Mum,' I sigh, 'I don't love him. I'm never going to love him.'

'And since when was that important? It's far more important to find a good man, and Ed is definitely a good man.'

'But you and Dad were in love when you met.'

'Pfff.' She rolls her eyes. 'That was so long ago I can't remember.'

'Dad told me when he first saw you he thought you were fantastic.'

Her face lights up and she beams as she says, 'Did he? Oh well, I suppose I was a bit of a looker in those days.'

'And he said you were madly in love.' OK, artistic licence here.

My mother practically simpers. 'He was terribly handsome himself, your father. When he was young.'

'You see?' I persist. 'I've never thought Ed is terribly handsome, and I've never felt madly in love with him, but I tried to pretend that that was OK, that I didn't need more, but now I've realised that I do. And I'm really sorry that Ed won't be your son-in-law, but you should want what's best for me, and it isn't him. I'm sorry, but it just isn't.'

My mother opens her mouth as if she's about to say something, but, wonder of wonders, she doesn't seem able to think of anything to say, anything to prove me wrong. For once in my life I think she sees my point, and I think it's rendered her completely speechless.

So finally I head home in preparation for a traumatic evening, and maybe this is slightly sick, but I make far more of an effort tonight. I wear a biscuit-coloured jumper and taupe trousers, and I'm tempted to carry the Gucci bag, but I don't, just in case he asks for it back. I do my make-up very slowly, making sure I look my absolute best, and so when the doorbell goes at seven thirty, I walk towards it feeling strong, feeling calm, in control. As soon as I open the door and see Ed standing on the doorstep, already looking crestfallen, I know that this really is going to be, as I predicted, one of the hardest things I've ever had to do.

But I also know, looking at his face, that I have to do it.

'You look beautiful,' Ed says. 'I've missed you,' and he tries to pull me in for a kiss, but I breeze away to pick up my coat.

'Shall we go?' I say, and I see that he doesn't understand; that he knows he's missing something, only he's not entirely sure what it is.

We walk out to the car in silence, and as we drive Ed keeps shooting me these worried glances.

'Poor Libby,' he says finally, as we pull up to some traffic lights, 'I can see you're exhausted. They've obviously been working you far too hard.'

'I'm fine,' I say. 'Really. There are just some things I need to talk about.'

Ed finally seems to cotton on to the fact that this involves him as well, and for the rest of the journey he doesn't say a word.

We get out of the car and go into the restaurant, and I am constantly aware that Ed is gazing at me with that sad puppy-dog expression. We sit down and Ed looks at me, waiting for me to say the words I now think he knows he's going to hear.

'Ed,' I say softly. 'This isn't working.'

And he looks at me. Silently.

'This. Us. I'm not happy. I don't think I'm what you're looking for.'

And he looks at me. Silently.

Now I expected arguments. I expected Ed to tell me that nothing in life is easy, least of all relationships, and that things need to be worked at, and that he would be willing to do anything to save this relationship.

But I wasn't expecting this. Silence.

'I think you're wonderful,' I say, going to take his hand to reinforce the point, but Ed moves his hand away, which shocks me slightly. I sit back and try again. 'You are loving, giving, you have so many wonderful qualities, but I'm not the right woman for you.

'You will meet someone one day who is perfect for you,' I say earnestly, 'and I wish it were me. I wish I could be the woman you want me to be, but I can't.'

And he looks at me.

And from thereon in it is quite possibly the most awkward, uncomfortable, desperately sad evening I have ever spent. We sit there, Ed and I, in silence, and when the plates are removed and the bill finally comes we stand in silence and walk outside to his car.

And when, finally, we pull up outside my house, I look at him sadly, and twist his key off my keyring. 'You'd better have this back,' I say, and he nods.

'Can I call you?' I say, not because I want to call him, but because I can't just climb out of the car and say goodbye. Ed shrugs, and then, evidently having thought about it, shakes his head, and we sit there for a while, both of us presumably feeling like shit, and then I reach over, kiss him on the cheek, and get out of the car.

He still hasn't uttered a word.

And later that night, while I'm lying in bed crying, because I never realised how much it would hurt to cause that much pain to someone who loves you, it suddenly strikes me that the reason Ed didn't say anything, at all, all evening, was because he was holding back the tears.

 **Chapter Sixteen**

I DON'T BOTHER GETTING UP the next day. I ring the office at half past nine and croakily tell Jo I think I've picked up some kind of bug, and then burrow back under the duvet and sleep for another hour.

At half ten I collapse on the sofa, and watch crap daytime television.

The day passes in a bit of a blur. I try not to think about it too much, because when I do I just feel enormously sad, and when Jo rings from the office and says I've had an urgent message to call Amanda, I think, fuck it, at least it will take my mind off things.

'Amanda? It's Libby.'

'Darling!' she exclaims. 'They told me you were ill and I said it could wait, but your receptionist insisted on disturbing you at home.'

A likely bloody story. Jo would never insist on something like that.

'I'm OK,' I croak. 'Just a bit under the weather.'

'It's just that I had a message from *Cosmo* this morning about wanting to interview me, and I wondered whether you could set it up.'

She rang me at home for that? When she could easily have picked up the phone herself and called. I sigh wearily. 'I'll ring them tomorrow.'

'Great!' she enthuses. 'Oh, and by the way, I had such a lovely time the other night. You're so lucky, getting engaged! To Ed McMahon!'

'Actually,' I groan, knowing that if I don't tell her now she'll be furious when she eventually finds out, 'actually it's all off.'

I think she stops breathing. 'Amanda? Are you still there?'

'Yes. Sorry. It's just that you two seemed so perfect together.'

'Well, we weren't.'

'Oh my God. No wonder you're not at work. Are you OK?'

'I'm fine, and anyway, it wasn't his decision, it was mine.'

'You're kidding?' She's laughing. 'Are you completely mad?'

'Jesus, if you think he's so great, why don't you go out with him?'

There's another silence.

'Sorry,' I mumble. 'I didn't mean to be rude. He's not for me, that's all.'

'Right. Right. I completely understand. Oh well, plenty more fish in the sea,' and a few seconds later she tells me her call waiting's going and she'd better answer it, so we say goodbye.

For a few minutes after I put the phone down I feel pretty damn awful. But then I remember his sad expression, his moustache, his habit of speaking French, and I know that I could never have gone through with it. Not for all the money in the world.

Later that afternoon, when Jules has left the fourth message of the day, I pick up the phone and she says she's coming over to check I'm OK.

'You look terrible,' she says, as I open the door, still in pyjamas. 'You look like you've been crying for weeks.'

'That's how I feel.'

'Come here,' she says, giving me a big hug, and when we pull apart I make some tea, and we sit down as I give her all the details.

'I can understand how hard this is for you, but now you've got to get on with your life.'

'I know,' I sigh. 'It's just that he seemed so hurt, and I don't think I've ever caused anyone that much pain before.'

'You were, as the saying goes, cruel to be kind.'

'Yes. I do know that. Oh God, now I've got to start going to parties again and getting back into that bloody singles scene.'

'It's the best way of getting over someone.'

'But I don't want anyone else. I just want to be alone for a while.'

'What about Nick?'

I shake my head. 'I'm not ready for anything. Although,' and for the first time in what feels like days, a glimmer of a smile crosses my face, 'although it might be worth it again for the sex.'

'Don't you dare get into that whole "just a fling" business again.'

'Jules?' I sink back into the sofa and start giggling. 'You know what? Thank God I'll never have to sleep with Ed again.'

Jules starts to laugh. 'Was it really that bad?'

'No,' I say. 'It was worse.'

Olly phones the next day.

'I heard,' he says. 'Mum called me this morning. Are you OK?'

'I'm fine, Oll,' I say. 'I still feel a bit bruised, but actually I'm starting to feel relief.'

Olly starts laughing. 'I didn't want to say anything at the time but he was awful, you know.'

'What?'

'Oh, come on. I can say it now, but he was a pompous old fart.'

'Oll! Don't be so nasty. He wasn't that bad. Jesus!'

'Libby, I've never said this about any of your boyfriends in the past, but if you'd have married him I think I would have disowned you.'

I'm truly, truly shocked. 'Did you really feel that strongly?'

'Sorry, Libby, but not only was he fuck ugly, he was arrogant too. His only saving grace is his money. Oh, and the fact that he adored you.'

I wince. 'Do you think everyone felt the same way?'

'I wouldn't like to hazard a guess. Look, I'm sorry if you're upset by this, but it's over now, I didn't think you'd mind me being honest.'

'No,' I sigh. 'I don't. Has Mum forgiven me yet?'

'Nah. You know Mum. It'll take her about ten years to stop blaming you for finishing with Ed McMahon. But if it's any consolation, she did say that she understood how you felt.'

'You're kidding!'

'I know. I was as surprised as you. But I think she knows that it wasn't really right. She started banging on about her and Dad, and how in love they were. The woman's finally gone completely round the bend.'

'Oh, Oll,' I laugh. 'You will never know how relieved I am.'

It's been a month, and I really feel fine now. I've rediscovered my career, and no one at work can believe quite how hard I've been working, or quite how much I've achieved, but Jesus, isn't that the best way of getting over being single again?

And OK, so my evenings are slightly harder. Not that I want to be with Ed, it's just that I find myself at a loss for things to do, although my friends have been fantastic, and everyone's been inviting me to everything, and the best thing about going out with my friends again is that I know there's absolutely no possibility of me bumping into Ed. Ever.

Because now I realise that I was living a total fantasy with Ed, generally behaving in a way that absolutely, one hundred per cent, was not me. You see, although I always thought that was the lifestyle I wanted, now that I've had a taste I know that I never again want to pretend to be something I'm not.

Although I'm still slightly thrown when Amanda rings me at work one day and out of the blue asks me if I'd mind if she went out with Ed.

'No, no,' I say, in a falsely enthusiastic voice. 'That's fine.'

'Are you sure you don't mind?' she says, and I know that, even if I did, it wouldn't make a blind bit of difference.

'I'm delighted,' I say, wondering whether they've already gone out, but I don't have to wonder very long, because later that afternoon Jo runs in brandishing the *Daily Express*.

'OK,' she says, perching her long legs on the edge of my desk. 'Take a deep breath. Are you ready?'

I nod, and Jo opens the *Express* and places it on my desk in front of me, and there, in Features, is a piece on London's new It couples. And taking pride of place with a large colour photograph are Amanda Baker and Ed McMahon.

'Jesus,' I gasp. 'That was quick work.'

Jo shrugs. 'Thank God you got out of it when you did. I mean, please. Look at that picture of Ed. Look at that tache. How could you?' And I examine the picture in the newspaper again and start to laugh. 'I know.' I shrug my shoulders. 'What the hell was I thinking?'

Joe Cooper comes out of his office and sees us laughing, and he walks over to see what all the fuss is about.

'Are you OK with this?' he says, looking at me intently. 'If there's any problem I'll put someone else on her account.'

'No,' I laugh. 'I'm fine. I'm just bloody relieved it's not me in there.'

'What are you doing on Saturday night?' Sal sounds excited.

'Noth-ing,' I say slowly, always wary of committing myself before I know what I'm committing myself to. 'Why?'

'Paul and I have decided to have the biggest, loudest, fuck-off party you've ever been to.'

I can already feel my own excitement rising at the prospect of a proper party, something to dress up for, something to look forward to.

'Are you having it in your place?'

'Yup, of course. Paul spent last weekend building a barbecue in the garden, and we're going to have a bar with Sea Breezes and Martinis, and I've got to go out this afternoon and buy a load of fairy lights to string up in the trees.'

I squeal with excitement. 'Who's coming?'

'Everyone!' she shrieks. 'No, but wait. I haven't finished. Paul's got a friend who's a DJ, and he's coming and bringing his record deck thingy to do all the music properly.'

'Excellent. What time will it start?'

'Around eight. And most people probably won't turn up until later, but I definitely want the hard core of close friends there early.'

'How many people?'

'We've got about eighty on the list, but everyone wants to bring friends.'

'Sal, I can't begin to tell you how excited I am.' And it's true. I am.

On Saturday afternoon I do something I haven't done for ages: I start getting ready for the party at three in the afternoon, and, even though it brings back shades of my teenage years, I'm loving every minute of it.

I wash my hair in the shower, then smear a hot wax treatment all over it, cover it in a hot towel and spend the next hour chatting to Jules while it does its stuff.

I use an apricot facial scrub, then three different face packs, all of which I leave on for twenty minutes, and by the time I've finished my face is so tight and shiny you can almost see your reflection in it.

At last, at precisely half past seven, I'm done. I survey myself in the mirror, in my floaty chiffon floor-length dress covered in a dusky flower print, demure until I walk, when the front slit sweeps aside revealing my newly tanned legs (I bought the fake stuff this morning and much to my amazement it left me with smooth brown legs, and no orange stripes). Flat strappy sandals complete the look, and I scoop my hair up into a messy ponytail, figuring I can always loosen it later, should I find someone to loosen it for.

I'm tempted to drive, but I'm planning to really let my hair down this evening (excuse the pun), and call a minicab instead.

There are only a handful of other people there when I arrive, and no one I recognise, but there's a buzz of excitement in the air already, and we all grin at each other and shake hands, chattering about how wonderful the weather is, and what a beautiful evening to have a party.

And the garden looks spectacular. Paul waves to me from behind the barbecue, the coals still jet black, and behind him are makeshift wooden shelves, lined with what I can only assume must be Jello shots.

The trees surrounding the garden are all covered with tiny white fairy lights, but, as Sal says, as she shows me what they've done, we won't get the full effect until later.

'I can't believe what you've done,' I say, after Sal and I have knocked back a delicious lime Jello shot together. 'This is amazing.'

'Do you think everyone will turn up?' She shoots me a worried glance before looking around the garden. 'I mean, hardly anyone's here yet.'

'Don't worry.' I check my watch. 'It's only a quarter to nine. People will start rolling in any minute now.'

And sure enough, as if by magic, people do start arriving, and within an hour the garden is heaving, literally heaving, and the nicest thing about it is that, even though I don't know more than a handful of people, everyone feels like my closest friend, and I'm having a whale of a time dancing with some guy called Dave who isn't really my type but who's a bloody good dancer.

And then Sal switches on the lights, and Paul moves round the garden, lighting the torches that have been strategically placed in the flowerbeds, and the whole night seems to take on a magical quality, and it feels like anything could happen.

Soon there are crowds of people dancing, and although we're outside there's no breeze, and it's so hot I can feel beads of perspiration dotted on my forehead, and eventually I shout to Dave that I'm going to get a drink, and he nods, grins, and turns to dance with the girl behind him.

The only drink to quench my thirst right now is good old tap water, so I push through the partygoers until I'm in Sal's kitchen, and, leaning panting against the sink, I reach for a glass and gulp it down in about two seconds.

'John Travolta has nothing on you.' I jump and with my hand on my heart I turn to see Nick lounging in the doorway, grinning.

'I hope you're not still in insulting mode,' I say suspiciously.

'No!' He looks aghast. 'I was serious. I never realised you were such a good dancer.'

I shrug, secretly flattered. 'How long have you been here?'

'Not long. We got here about fifteen minutes ago. Just in time to see those hips move.'

I laugh self-consciously before asking, 'We?' And then I notice her. Tall, skinny, cropped dark hair in that perfect gamine cut that you can only have when you are tremendously beautiful and live in Notting Hill, and of course she is tremendously beautiful, and I hate her. Instantly.

'Hi,' she smiles, and fuck. Her teeth are perfect. If I didn't know better I'd think she stepped straight out of an American advert for toothpaste. 'I'm Cat.' Great. This gets better. I shake her hand warily, and trying to be polite ask, 'Is that your real name?'

'No.' She shakes her head and laughs. 'My real name's Sophie, but everyone used to tell me I looked like a cat at school and the name stuck.' As I take in her catlike almond-shaped eyes, I note that her voice is immaculately polished, that lazy insouciant tone that immediately marks her out as a member of the upper classes. I wish, instantly, that I had worn something more like her, a plain vest top with baggy combat trousers and trainers.

Nick smiles at me, waiting to see what I'll say next, probably proud as punch that he can show off his new girlfriend and she can be that gorgeous. Well, fuck you, I think, smiling at him graciously as I say, 'I mustn't leave Dave alone for too long,' and with that I sweep past them, ignoring his odd look at me, and go back into the garden.

Dave's still dancing with the other girl, and I tap him on the shoulder and grin at him as he turns, holds my hips, and moves his body perfectly in tune with mine. Over his shoulder I see Nick and Cat walk into the garden, and I throw my head back with laughter to prove I'm having a fantastic time, because Nick's looking at me and quite frankly he can go screw himself. Or Cat. Which he probably will be doing later.

Fuck.

Why does this bother me so much? Why do I care? After all, I really, really don't want a relationship right now, and even if I did the last person I'd be interested in would be Nick. So why can't I take my eyes off the two of them, giggling together in the corner? Why do I feel a stab of jealousy when I remember how he used to do that with me?

I resolve that there's only one solution to this dilemma, and that is to get drunk. Very drunk. I down my next Sea Breeze in one, much to Paul's astonishment, and then start on another one. Much better.

Nick who?

I lose track of time, but soon the world suddenly becomes slightly hazy, and I know that I've probably had enough. More, and I'd run the risk of getting into bed only to have an attack of the deadly bedspins or, worse, throw up at the party. This is just perfect: hazy, friendly, just enough to make me happy. Who cares. I've got no problems other than who to dance with next.

Nick who?

I stagger off to the barbecue, not that I'm hungry, it's just that drinking on an empty stomach is not exactly clever, and I know that if I don't have something to eat, anything, I really won't be very well at all.

I tear at a chicken kebab, not really tasting it, and, as I throw the stick merrily over my shoulder, I see Nick standing by himself on the other side of the garden, and when I catch his eye he starts walking over to me, so I head off in the other direction and make myself very busy flirting with a group of men I've never seen before, who seem more than happy to make me feel welcome.

Ha! That will show him. Nick has skulked off, presumably to find his precious Cat.

The party's in full throttle at two in the morning, despite the neighbours' complaints, but gradually people have started disappearing, and I haven't seen Nick for ages and I'm slightly drunk and very tired and actually I'm now wondering how I'm going to get home.

I go inside, to the living room at the front of the house, which is pitch black and empty, and, bumping into the coffee table en route, I finally make it to the sofa and slump down.

'Fuck!'

'Fuck!' I jump back up to hear rustling, then footsteps, then the light's switched on.

'Libby? What are you doing?'

'What am I doing? What the hell are you doing?' I'm looking at Nick suspiciously as he starts to laugh, and it sobers me up instantly.

'I was just lying down for a bit. In the dark. I know you still have a soft spot for me but did you really have to leap on top of me to prove it?'

'I didn't,' I grumble, sitting down again. 'I didn't know you were there. Anyway. Where's Cat?'

'Gone. She's off to some other party. Her friends are far too Notting Hill for me. I can't stand them.'

I look at him strangely. 'So don't you find it difficult . . . well . . .'

Now it's Nick's turn to look at me strangely. 'What? What are you talking about? Libby, you're pissed.'

'No, no.' I shake my head to clear it. 'I mean, if you don't like her friends, well, it's just that I can't see her getting on with yours, you know, Moose and that lot, and, well . . .' I stumble into silence.

'Libby, what are you on about, all this friends stuff? Cat's always had bloody awful friends.'

I still don't understand, and then it dawns on me. 'Cat's your . . .'

'Sister? Yes. Why? What did you think?' And then he sees exactly what I thought and he roars with laughter. 'God, Libby. You are fantastic. Cat? My girlfriend?' and he snorts with laughter again.

'Well, how was I to know?' I go on the defensive because what else can I do?

'I don't know,' Nick splutters, wiping the tears from his eyes. 'I just, well. Even if she wasn't my sister she wouldn't be my type.'

'No?' I resist the urge to ask him what would be his type.

'No. Look, how are you getting home? You're not driving, are you?'

'No.'

'Thank Christ for that. If you get a cab I'll come with you to check you get home OK, then I'll take it on home.'

'OK.' Actually, I'm not sure that I want him to go back to his home, but maybe I'm just drunk.

Nick calls a cab, and when it arrives we hug Sal and Paul goodbye and stumble into the back seat, and I pretend to look out of the window for a bit, but the only thing I'm concentrating on is keeping my breathing as normal as possible, because the fact that it's so dark in here, so quiet, and that there is a gorgeous, sexy man sitting inches away from me, is making it very, very difficult to pretend that the only thing on my mind right now is friendship.

And then we're outside my house, and we just sit and look at one another as the cab driver taps his fingers impatiently on the wheel.

'Shit,' Nick says suddenly, slapping his palm on his forehead. 'I knew there was something I forgot to tell you.'

'What?'

'It's a long story.'

The cab driver, who's listening, sighs, and I say, 'Do you want to come in? You can always call another cab.'

'Great!' he says, reaching into his pocket and pulling some money out. 'I'll get this,' and he follows me inside the door.

Nick closes the front door behind me, and stands in front of the light switch, so as I fumble to turn on the lights I don't feel anything. Except

340

Nick's hand. He grabs my wrist and places my hand on his cheek, and I can't help myself, I start stroking his cheek, and then I'm tracing his lips, unable to see anything, but knowing his face so well from memory, and then his lips are open and he's gently sucking my finger into his mouth.

I gasp, and Nick pulls me very gently towards him, and our mouths find one another's in the darkness and Nick leans back against the wall, holding me tightly, kissing me slowly, sensually, until I think my legs are going to give way.

And then very gently he moves round and, holding one arm out to guide him, falls slowly onto the sofa, pulling me with him, and within seconds my dress is round my waist, and I am moaning softly as he gently teases me with his tongue.

And the only thing that's going through my mind is how did I do without this for so long, how could I have ever settled for anything less?

Nick's hand moves up my thigh, stroking, gliding, as I groan into his neck and softly bite the skin there, and I reach down for his belt buckle and listen as his belt clicks undone, and I unzip the zipper of his trousers and stroke the length of his hard-on, and he inhales sharply before kissing me again.

We move to the bedroom, and we make slow, languorous, passionate love, and after we have made love, after we have murmured to each other and are lying in bed, side by side, with Nick's arm round my shoulders, gently stroking my hair, I remember he had said he had something to tell me.

I lean over and kiss him gently on the nose. 'So what was it you had to tell me, then?' I whisper.

Nick opens his eyes. 'Actually, there are two things.' He pulls his arm out from under me and sits up in bed, taking my hand. 'Libby,' he says seriously, while I start to get worried. 'I know you're probably not ready to hear this, but the thing is, well . . .' He stops.

'Yes?' I prompt, not having a clue what he is going to say.

'Well, the thing is that I think I might be in love with you . . .' My mouth falls open, and he gulps before continuing. 'I'm not entirely sure because it's a bit of a new feeling for me, but it's just that I haven't been able to stop thinking about you, and I don't know whether it was just the timing last time, that I wasn't ready, but now I think I am, and you may not even want me, but I just had to say something, because every morning when I wake up you're the first thing on my mind, and every night before I go to sleep you're the last person I think of, and I have no idea what you are going to say but I wanted you to know.'

And I sit there, my heart racing at hearing these words, at hearing them from Nick, at seeing the expression in his eyes which are glistening with emotion, and I know he means it. I know that he is in love with me, and not the way that Ed loved me, not because I would make a good wife, or for any of those other superficial reasons, but for me. He loves me for who I am.

And suddenly I realise that although I've never thought about being in love with Nick before, all the right ingredients are there. I fancy him. I like him. He makes me laugh. I love being with him. And I start to feel all sort of warm and glowy, and screw the other stuff. Screw the stuff about him having no money, and living in a bedsit, and not being what I thought I wanted. I'm just going to go with this and see where it ends up.

'Nick,' I say, leaning down to kiss him. 'If I'm being really honest, I don't know how I feel about you yet, I think it's still a little early for me to talk about love, but I know that I do love being with you, and I'd like to give it a shot. Just being together, I mean, and seeing where it goes.'

Relief spreads over his face.

'So,' I say curiously, after we've snuggled up and kissed for a few minutes. 'What was the other thing? You said you had two things to tell me.'

'Oh yes. That. It's nothing major. I've got a publishing deal!'

JANE GREEN

For the past ten years Jane Green has made a career out of being professionally single, and her books, *Straight Talking*, *Jemima J* and *Mr Maybe,* have all reflected what it is to be young, female and single in the Nineties. But in January 1999, just as she had completed *Mr Maybe*, Jane Green left behind 'singledom' when she said 'I do' to David Burke, an American investment banker. She had met David on a blind date organised by a friend and quickly realised that she had at last found the man for her. 'From the moment I met David it all just felt so right. I trusted him and he became my best friend in a very short space of time. We just got on amazingly well.'

In her single days, Jane had a similar lifestyle to that of her heroine, Libby Mason, working in the media and living alone in north London. Like Libby, Jane tended to fall for the wrong men and was once tempted to settle for a rich man she didn't love. 'I went out with an incredibly wealthy man who lavished presents on me and whisked me off to exotic locations at a moment's notice,' she recalls. 'I am ashamed to admit that

it was very seductive, like stepping into the film *Pretty Woman*. But all he wanted was a trophy wife and that was certainly not my scene,' she says with a laugh. So did she base Libby Mason on herself? 'Oh my God, no. You don't think that, do you? My readers won't think that, will they? She is the least likable character I have ever created—materialistic and shallow. But I have worked in PR and the men she encounters are similar to the types of relationships I have had.'

Her own happy ending to the single phase of her life has coincided with what Jane considers to be the beginning of the end for 'singledom' type novels. 'It all began with *Bridget Jones*, and now the sequel has just been published I think the genre is almost exhausted. I sat down to write another, but I thought, I can't do this any more, I've moved on from this. So my next book is very different and about a group of university graduates who meet up ten years after a big falling-out and it's called *Bookends*.'

Jane and David are now eagerly awaiting the birth of their first baby and Jane can't wait to be a mother. 'I have been fighting the maternal instinct ever since the age of four and believe motherhood is my true destiny,' she says. And then, once again, she asks me worriedly, 'My readers won't really think I'm like Libby, will they?'

Jane Eastgate

VALERIE BLUMENTHAL

Saturday's Child

After a desperately unhappy childhood, during which Isabella was sent from one foster home to another, she now feels content with the way she has shaped her adult life. Then, one Saturday morning, a small child flashes a sunlit smile at her. On a wild, uncharacteristic impulse, Isabella abducts the child and flees from her carefully crafted life. The path ahead is full of dilemmas, heartache, even danger, but also with something that has always eluded Isabella—genuine love.

LIES. FLIES. BREEDING LIKE.

'So why did you do it?' he asks her.

'I did it because . . . Do you know the French word *éclat*?'

'I'm not sure. I'm not much of a linguist.'

'*Éclat de: éclat de soleil.* A burst of sun. That's what her face did. And inside me I . . . it singed me. I can't explain it. It wasn't something I can just explain.'

'But it was out of character.'

'I suppose so. Until then I'd never done anything out of the norm. My life was very structured.'

But leading up to it were pointers, had she chosen to tweeze them from her subconscious and examine them. A random collection of influencing factors, accumulated over the years, which a psychologist would have latched on to with a satisfied snap of the fingers.

'And you regret it.' Spoken with the rhetoric of assurance.

She wraps her arms round herself. Looks tiredly up at him. At her peeling nails. At the window with no view and her silver reflection in it.

'Isabella? Surely—'

She turns back to him, and he is struck anew by how her face can switch from plain to beautiful with a flicker of expression in her eyes; she shakes her head as she thrusts out her palm in a typically eloquent gesture: 'What can I say? How can I possibly regret it?'

The night before she did it. And there she is, in her flat, on her bed with its antique silk Chinese cover, having frenetic sex with her lover of one and a half years. Peter, soon to be twenty-seven, is thirteen years younger than her. Since she has known him he has become more assertive. Perhaps she has contributed to his confidence; and now, having assisted him in worldly ways, he can fend for himself. He is an actor. When she first met him he was hopeful and shy. He used to be needy of her common sense, her attention. But nowadays his own attention span has a low threshold. So—this is not love. It never is, and she does not expect it. And whatever this is and was, is about to have run its course. Which, as an intelligent woman, Isabella knows is to be anticipated.

'See you when I get back from Nottingham.' And when is that? He hasn't said. And an affectionate slap on her backside at six o'clock in the morning as he departs.

She rolls over and lies on her tummy amidst the devastation of the bed. Diffused greyish light sieved through the muslin curtains. Her limbs are heavy and aching. Emptiness washes over her. Of late this sensation—hard to pinpoint—is something she has been experiencing more and more, and it is disturbing for a woman who believes herself to be so purposeful, levelheaded and certain of what she does and does not want.

It is Saturday, and it unfolds. Saturday, August 31. Isabella will have reason to remember the date. She goes about her usual routine: puts the kettle on, grinds coffee beans, opens the curtains to bright sun and the geraniums in their terracotta pots outside on the patio shedding night's moisture. Herself dry-mouthed, early-morning-dry-skinned. Invasive middle age drying her out. Not everywhere yet, thank God. Picks up Garibaldi and fusses him.

'Yes, you're getting middle-aged spread too.' She can feel his purrs reverberating against her throat. Talking to the cat, to herself, to her car, to her furniture, which she is forever moving around. An old maid. That is how people will one day look at her. Maybe they do now. In fact she was married once: a youthful attempt to put wronged childhood behind her with this most grown-up of declarations: I do.

She has her coffee, and an orange because it is slimming—it acts as a diuretic—while listening to *Today* on Radio 4 and simultaneously read-ing a manufacturer's promotional report on its latest HGV, which she has to translate into both Italian and French. Washes up, baths, gets dressed, waters the plants, packs a few things into an overnight bag, puts enough food and milk into Garibaldi's bowls for twenty-four hours, and leaves her flat. Isabella is a woman like thousands of others as she locks the door behind her and walks towards her car: she has several close friends, is independent, attractive, successful, social, vivacious, childless by choice. There is nothing irrational or obsessive about her.

But this morning she is rather tired, a little deflated. She does not analyse these feelings as she climbs into her seventeen-year-old MGB GT; is more concerned with getting the thing to start. 'Come on. I'll sell you if you're not careful.' When, after several turns of the engine, it does, she is jaunty with relief. 'A new battery for you,' she says, pushing in a tape. Her car is her single eccentricity; it has an insouciant style, she says when people tell her she should change it for something more reliable. And Isabella has great style.

Off she heads, up Hampstead High Street—coming to life at ten o'clock—towards the North Circular. The sun's brightness piercing the windscreen and her eyes; and she reaches for her sunglasses by the gear-lever. Domingo as Pagliaccio singing of his anguish. And how much shelf life does her relationship have left? They could stagger on for a couple of months, but it would be better to slide out now.

Dissatisfaction swilling about in her. And she does not care to examine this. Isabella has evolved into the woman she is without self-questioning; past, present or future.

The traffic is light. Halfway down the North Circular she realises she has not bought her friend anything, and when she comes to a shopping parade she pulls in there and parks. Wanders past various shops: a greengrocer's, launderette, chemist's, newsagent's, Indian restaurant, off-licence, twenty-four-hour Spar, butcher's, hairdresser's. Outside the newsagent's is a child strapped into a buggy. She decides to buy a bottle of something and perhaps a box of chocolates as well. Goes into the wine shop, where she declines the offer of help from the young male assistant, preferring to browse on her own. She has plenty of time. She does not have to be in the Cotswolds for a couple of hours. There are no other customers in the shop. In fact the precinct is a fairly dead sort of place altogether. A pass-through zone without soul.

She takes her time and settles on a Chilean Chardonnay.

'Do you sell chocolates—you know, praline types?' she asks the assistant as he rolls the bottle in green tissue and tapes the ends.

'No. The newsagent's or Spar might.'

She thanks him, leaves the shop and makes for the newsagent's a couple of doors away. The child in the buggy is still there.

'Hello,' Isabella says to her as she pushes open the door.

The toddler gazes back. She has grave, shadowed eyes, a frail pixie face. It strikes Isabella that the child has been left alone for a long time:

she was at least ten minutes in the off-licence, and who knows how long it was there before that? She is a further ten minutes in the newsagent's by the time she has bought a box of chocolates, *Vogue* for herself, and filled in a lottery card on an impulse. And when she comes out, there is the child, silent in her buggy, playing with a knitted toy of some sort.

This can't be right—to leave it so long by itself. There is no sign of the mother among the disinterested passers-by. She hovers uncertainly, thinking that perhaps she should enquire in one of the shops. The mother might be in the hairdresser's, it occurs to her. And in she goes—hit by the drone of hair dryers and cheerful female voices.

'Is anyone the mother of a little girl outside the newsagent's?' she asks a stylist in the middle of winding hair round tiny perming rollers.

'No, love. They're all grandmas in here.'

The other possibility is the launderette. Music blasting within. The thudding, whirring and spinning of machines. Sitting around are three men, a teenage girl, a weary-looking faded blonde.

'Excuse me,' Isabella shouts above the hubbub, 'has anyone left a little girl outside the newsagent's?'

Blank eyes stare at her. One of the men leers. 'No, but I'll take you home, darlin'.'

She makes a quick exit and returns to the child, crouches beside her. 'Where's your mummy, then, eh?'

At that moment the girl drops her toy. Isabella picks it up and gives it back to her. 'Here's your rabbit.'

It happens then. The *éclat*. The child's smile is like a brilliant flash. It illuminates her face in a burst of light as she curls her fingers round the knitted toy, and Isabella is rooted to the spot, seared by an extraordinary rush of emotion. Slowly she straightens up and rests her elbow lightly on the buggy's handle. Within those few seconds the transition has taken place. Isabella has gone from being one woman to being another. And inside her is this incomprehensible yearning that is almost painful in its intensity.

She waits another couple of minutes. The child is silent, solemn, clutching her rabbit. Several people go by, then comes a lull. Isabella is conscious of the acceleration of her heart, and at one point she realises she has been holding her breath. Another couple of minutes elapse as she prevaricates and does battle with the overwhelming urge that has seized her. And then the child drops the toy again; deliberately, it seems. Again, Isabella retrieves it. 'Poor rabbit.'

She strokes the child's hand. Its dimpled smallness, its softness, make her throat snag. The child doesn't smile this time. She stares at Isabella with an unfathomable expression. And suddenly it is as if someone is galvanising Isabella forward, and she is walking briskly away, pushing the child in the buggy in the direction of her car, expecting at any moment to feel a tap on her shoulder: *Excuse me, madam, what do you think you're . . . She's got my child. She's stolen my little girl.*

This isn't me. I'm not doing this. She increases her pace.

She arrives at her car and unlocks it. Her fingers are trembling to such an extent that twice she misaligns the key with the lock. She realises that she no longer has the bottle of wine, or the chocolates and the *Vogue*, that in her urgency she has mislaid them. There is no question of going back. She unstraps the infant and is about to lift her inside when it dawns on her there is no special seat. The next immediate problem is that try as she might she cannot make the buggy collapse.

'Are you having a problem?' a voice behind her says, making her leap. And she wheels round.

'Sorry, I didn't mean to startle you. I just wondered if you wanted any help.' A young man is grinning at her.

'It seems to be jammed.' Shaking her hair forward; hiding her face.

'You've obviously not mastered it yet. We've got one of these. They're very nifty when you get used to them. May I?'

She nods, watching intently as he raises the buggy's lower bar with his toe, presses down on the handles, and lifts the safety lock behind the seat. The buggy collapses, folding up like an umbrella.

'*Madre*,' Isabella says. 'That's brilliant.' Corrects herself quickly. 'I mean you are. I just couldn't get it to work.'

'No problem.'

'Well, thanks anyway.'

The man is still grinning at her, just standing there. What's he hanging around for? She is worried he will notice there is no child seat in the car.

'Love the old MG. It's a Jubilee edition, isn't it? Want to sell it?'

'No, no. Thanks so much. You've been awfully kind.'

She watches him disappear into the Spar and lifts the child into the car. In the back, on top of her luggage, is her cardigan-jacket and she rolls this up and pads the girl with it; then she fastens the seat belt snugly round her. Shuts the door and double-checks it.

'That'll do. That'll have to do. Oh, *madre*.'

Her armpits are sticky with perspiration. She reeks with it. Pungent, unfeminine. She can smell herself. And the day is stifling.

She climbs in her side—the MG starts first time—and drives off, back towards Hampstead. Imagines blue lights in her mirror, baying sirens closing in on her. Every traffic light, every holdup, tests her nerves.

She had long red hair and was wearing a white dress—Isabella can hear the young man describing her at this very minute—*racing green, Jubilee-edition MG. She seemed tense.*

At regular intervals Isabella takes her eyes off the road to glance at her small passenger—so strangely quiet, gazing about her, the knitted rabbit on her lap. 'Almost home,' she says, and stretches out to touch the froth of light hair. 'Don't you talk? How old are you? Two? Three?'

She parks a few yards away from the red-brick Victorian building where she has her garden flat, and sits on for a moment slumped over the steering wheel, her forehead pressed against it. Here, in the leafy familiarity of her surroundings, rationality claims her once more and she knows that she must take the child to the police. She feels a sense of loss as though she has just miscarried.

'We'll go indoors for a bit. I need to unwind first.'

The child seems to like her chattering. A spark of curiosity comes into her languid eyes. There is a square Elastoplast on her forehead which Isabella only notices now that her fringe has been blown back.

Oh, *madre*, and she must phone and cancel Sally. She cannot possibly drive there now. She lifts the child from the car, leaving the buggy inside it, and, holding her by the hand—what a strange and enchanting sensation it gives her: like a small bun in hers—walks the short distance to her gate.

Four steps lead from it down to her front door. And suddenly the girl becomes rigid and starts screaming.

'What is it? Hey—shush—what is it?'

Isabella doesn't know what to do. She is afraid the neighbours will hear . . . *My sister's little girl* . . . The words are already on her lips.

The child is beside herself, her face red and contorted. Isabella scoops her up. 'Hey—*cara*—what is it? Nothing's going to hurt you.' She has a soft voice. It draws people to her, her low soft voice, as much as her red hair and Latin dark eyes. The mixed dominant genes of her Scottish mother and Italian father.

The sobbing subsides. The child's body relaxes against her, after its initial resistance. But she has weed. Her jeans are drenched.

'You see, you're all right now, aren't you? Look, we'll carry you down, and then you'll be fine. Did the steps frighten you? Look—one, two, three, four—here we are. Safe and sound. This is my home.' Isabella sets her down carefully and unlocks the door.

Garibaldi greets them, tail upright, its white tip quivering.

'Ca',' the child cries out, pointing. 'Ca'.'

'You can talk!' Isabella bends to hug her, laughing. 'Yes, he's a cat. His name's Garibaldi.' She strokes the cat, who rubs himself against them both and winds his tail round the child's legs.

The child giggling with pleasure, repeating, 'Ca', ca'.'

Isabella leaves her there in the sitting room to make her phone call from the kitchen. Her friend answers after interminable ringing.

'Sally, it's Isabella.'

'Oh, hi. I was in the garden picking tomatoes to shove in the salad.'

'*Cara*, I can't come.'

'You're kidding. Why?'

'I—' Sally is her oldest friend. They were at Bristol together. They founded an all-female rock band. Isabella had been going to tell her the truth as it now is; she has picked up an apparently abandoned child and is about to take it to the police.

'I think I've got flu,' she, who never lies, says instead.

'Oh, no. I'm really sorry. I was really looking forward to seeing you. We all were. It's been ages. Oh, shut up, Geoff—' Her husband. 'He's yelling something. Hang on. What? Oh, he says he was going to slaughter you at ping pong . . . What? Oh, and he says to give you a love bite on your delicious bum.'

'Tell him don't be too sure to the first; and that I value our deep friendship too much for the second. I'm sorry to let you down.'

'It can't be helped. Get better soon. Dose yourself up.'

'Shall do.'

She rings off. Her first lie.

In the sitting room the child is on all fours by the armchair, behind which Garibaldi has taken refuge.

'So what are we going to do with you, then, eh?' Isabella says from the doorway. At the sound of her voice the child looks up. 'Ca',' she states.

'Can you say anything else? Would you like a drink?' Isabella does not use a 'baby' tone; would feel foolish doing so. She speaks gently, but as she would to an adult. She holds out an arm. The child looks at her blankly. Isabella goes towards her and picks her up. Feels her flinch.

How strange: Isabella knows not the first thing about children; has always been outspoken about not wanting them, about how they upset the order, the balance of one's life, are demanding, self-centred. Yet this seems completely natural. Instinctively she knows what to do. And Isabella, who has attained the age of nearly forty and has never held anyone special nor been held dear in return, finds that she now craves both. She is captivated by this small, mysterious person. A warmth of pleasure is seeping into her, filling some hitherto unrealised vacancy within her.

In the kitchen she gives the child some utensils to play with while she pours orange juice into a mug. The child sits on the floor, without attempting to play. Isabella is conscious of her eyes on her.

'Don't you want to play, then? Here's your drink, anyway.' She joins the child on the floor. 'I'll help you, shall I?' Holds the mug while the child sips—frowning up at her slightly, her fingers curled on top of Isabella's. And Isabella, who scarcely ever cries, who cannot remember the last time she cried—not when her mother died, and never since—finds her vision blurring.

Halfway through drinking, the child loses interest and pushes the mug away. The orange juice spills down her clothes and on the tiled floor. She stares at the pool as though in terror, then her features crumple and darken, and the hysterical screaming starts again.

Isabella immediately enfolds her in her arms.

'Hey, what is it? *Cara*—what's the matter? It's only a bit of spilt juice. Shush, there. It's OK. *Cara*, it's OK.'

Hot cheeks against her own. Small juddering chest against her breasts. The sweet scent of her hair. And once more the child is soothed and the sobbing dies away. But she has weed again. Even her shoes are wet. Isabella decides to wash her clothes and stick them in the tumble dryer before going to the police station.

'Let's get you cleaned up a bit, shall we?'

She has never undressed a child. Has a sudden recollection of herself alone, playing with a doll in the flat above the restaurant. Her parents hollering at each other from the kitchen below. 'Be quiet,' she shrieked through the floorboards, stamping her foot. 'Be quiet, be quiet, be quiet.' Nobody heard her, and systematically Isabella pulled the doll apart, limb by limb, before wrenching out the hair. She must have been about seven.

The child stands up obligingly. She is tiny, skinny, like a little worm. Isabella tackles the jeans first. They slide easily over her hips, falling about her ankles.

Isabella, kneeling, stares, appalled. Her legs are smothered in bruises.

'*Madre mia. Madre mia,*' she repeats against her hand clapped to her mouth. She feels quite, quite sickened. She draws the child to her—compliant now—and rocks her against herself without saying anything further. Then she resumes undressing her, bracing herself. She peels down the saturated knickers with great care—there are more bruises to her cup-sized buttocks—next takes off the wet shoes and socks. She is so fragile, her legs whisker-thin; and she is so quiet, steadily regarding Isabella, with that expression which Isabella now recognises as wariness. It is shattering to see it in so young a child's eyes. Gently she unbuttons the cardigan. Her upper arms are in the same state as her legs and buttocks.

'Poor *cara*. Poor, poor little *carina*.'

And Isabella cannot help herself. With one arm encircled round the child, she brings the other across her own face to shield it, and she starts to cry. Except for a slight sound that escapes her throat, the crying is contained within her.

She takes control of herself once more.

'Well, this won't do, will it,' she says to the child.

It is then that she sees the note attached by a safety pin to her T-shirt. She unfastens it. The message, written in blunt pencil in an ill-formed hand, says, 'I cudn help misel. im skert wot il do. her nem is hana. don luk fo me.'

This time, when she comes to the decision to keep the child, it is not with the unreasoned rashness of earlier, but with a sober sense of inevitability. Even as she makes it she is afraid. Isabella is perfectly sane. She knows that what she is contemplating is legally wrong; that it defies logical explanation. That by her actions her life is about to be disrupted. That from now on she will be living a lie. How strange, it strikes her, that the words *rash* and *rational* should sound so similar and have almost the opposite meanings.

And she is rational, a few minutes later, as she snaps away with the Polaroid camera, capturing on film the child's naked body, closing in on the bruises; weeping within herself, raging within herself: How could anyone? How could *anyone* . . .?

That evening, when the child is asleep in the double bed, which the night before had been a sexual trampoline, Isabella sits at her desk in the neutrality of her living room. Garibaldi a sleek whorl on her lap. In a hardback notebook she writes: *Today something extraordinary happened. I am going to keep a record of events, both for my own purposes and for possible future evidence.*

At approximately ten o'clock this morning, Saturday, August 31, I stopped to do some shopping in a parade off the North Circular Road. Outside a newsagent's . . .

She is truthful about her initial impulse; the child's sunburst smile, her own atypical covetous yearning. It is important to mention this first instinct in order to show her subsequent change of mind and intention of going to the police.

I have reached my decision to keep the child for a number of reasons . . .

And what are they? The shock of seeing the pathetic body? The fact the police might think she herself has inflicted the injuries? The powerfully protective emotion the child has evoked in her? An inexplicable rapport? A sense of fate? Most of all, fear for the child: that at best she will be put into care, shunted from foster home to foster home, at worst returned to an abusive parent, another casualty of red tape.

And the child has a name now. Hana. Hannah.

Do not look for me, the mother requested.

Isabella, whom fate conspired to have stop at a shopping parade that particular morning, has been granted the mother's permission.

'ISABELLA, *CARA* ISABELLA,' her father murmured through the shadows in a dove-throaty voice, when she was nearly thirteen.

'*Che cosa fa*, Papa? What are you *doing*. Don't do that.'

'*Scusi. Mi scusi* . . .' stumbling back away from her with a half sob. '*Facevo niente*.' I wasn't doing anything.

She was saved from facing him the following morning. He was gone.

Her mother, her sharp-tempered, sharp-featured mother, was left to run the restaurant. Her mother, with her excoriating Scottish tongue, who drove herself and her daughter to the brink, pushed and pushed. *Show me what you did at school . . . No, I said you can't go out . . .* The lights of Sutton in a string piercing the unlined curtains of the flat while she did her homework. Her mother's sewing machine on the same table; and the globe on its stand. Hated. Enforced geography. Her mother would test her, covering place names with the end of a pencil.

'Do you want to end up with the same life as me?' she said, when Isabella protested. 'Don't think I haven't seen it: generation after generation of repetition.'

From the restaurant below old Neapolitan melodies drifted upwards selling impossible dreams. For the next year, evenings after homework, weekends, holidays would find Isabella in the tiled and stainless-steel kitchen, peeling onions and potatoes, slicing courgettes into matchsticks, filling aubergine shells with stuffing, opening giant cans of plum tomatoes. She could hear the diners' laughter and the indistinct hum of conversation through the glass in the upper part of the dividing door.

Who was this woman who was her mother? Why had she borne Isabella, when plainly motherhood was another encumbrance? Why had she married Isabella's father? Or he her? Presbyterianism at odds with Catholicism. And did her father huddle in the confessional box and admit to that night's aberration?

'The sod,' her mother said the morning he went. 'Well, don't think we can't do without him.' And as if to prove it she was wearing lipstick for the first time in years.

There is no indication the child misses her mother. Isabella tries to visualise her. A stereotype composite is all she can muster to her imagination: a young—maybe under twenty—weary woman whose man has done a runner; no money; a damp room in one of those godforsaken streets off the North Circular, in a building where half the windows are boarded up. Not a bad girl, judging from the note—there was love apparent in it—just desperate. That anyone can batter such a tiny creature, whether the victim be human or animal, is beyond Isabella's comprehension; yet she feels sympathy for this woman. Perhaps she is suffering from depression. Perhaps she has an ungovernable temper that takes hold of her. Perhaps she is of below-average intelligence. Certainly she is ill educated. There is no doubt she needs help.

The child has turquoise eyes in certain lights, grey in others. Troubled eyes. With the wisdom of hindsight, does the mother regret abandoning her daughter? There must be some ambivalence. Such an act could not be undertaken without a measure of grief.

And if the mother is aware of the outrageousness of what she has done, then, equally, so is Isabella of what she has done. For both, the deed is irrevocable.

There has been nothing on the news, to which Isabella has listened every hour on the hour for the last day and a half. No anguished, pleading, repentant mother (and what would Isabella do if there were?). No police message. No 'missing child' report in the papers.

Monday. And the scales this morning revealed she has lost just over three pounds. Anxiety has always suited her body.

They have spent the weekend getting to know one another. Everything, but everything, is new to Isabella, yet she has slipped naturally into this alien role: feeding the child, dressing her, holding her on the toilet, wiping her little bottom, massaging arnica cream into her bruises, which are changing colour, becoming a dull cadmium and merging into each other. She talks to her constantly. All Hannah can say is 'Ca'', when she catches sight of Garibaldi. She responds to Isabella with a tilt of the head, a light in the eye, or wary mistrust. Twice Isabella has elicited from her that brilliant burst of a smile which drew them together in the first instance. The peculiar empathy she feels towards the child makes her sensitive to her needs, moods and terrors. Isabella is instinctive in her handling of situations and in her reactions. She is fairly phlegmatic by nature—quick to become irritated, slow to anger. She has a wry humour, sees humour where others might not. Some people find her too self-contained, dauntingly independent; but she exudes down-to-earth calm, and this seems to be communicated to the child, who no longer flinches at Isabella's touch.

But at nights she whimpers, and sometimes wakes, sobbing. And bathing her poses a problem. Hannah cowered when Isabella led her into the bathroom and ran the water. The frightful wailing started up and she shot naked into the hallway.

And yes, Isabella has received a visit from a concerned neighbour. 'I'm looking after my sister's little girl,' she explained. 'She's homesick.'

The child screams when she wets herself. She screams when she drops or spills anything. And Isabella realises that these were crimes that resulted in punitive treatment. From her horror of the outside steps Isabella can guess at the form one punishment took. There are other things that trigger hysteria: the hair dryer, any sudden loud noise, a raised voice on the television or radio, the dark, cigarettes—until now Isabella smoked moderately, between five and ten a day; no longer. All these are clues that enable her to build a picture, and which she assiduously records in her report.

All I have done, she wrote last night, in conclusion of yesterday's events, *is circumvent bureaucracy*.

This woman had no conscience, sneered the bewigged, robed figure pointing an indicting finger, in Isabella's sleep. Or was it sleep? *No sense of right or wrong. There were no mitigating circumstances. She twisted the situation to her advantage, to satisfy a whim, because—to coin an expression—her biological clock was running down.*

Isabella sitting up in bed, hugging herself, arms in an X round her chest and shoulders, deliberately slowing her breathing. Beside her, the child's regular, deep breathing; honey-smelling moth-wing exhalations from her slightly parted mouth. The hall lamp was on and the door ajar, and the bedroom was partially illuminated by a prism of light. It allowed Isabella to decipher the outline of Hannah's face on the other pillow, the fluffy hair, and her hand curled and lost in it. So sweet. So sweet. And Isabella was like the she-wolf in the *Jungle Books*, filled with protective tenderness—and that had been the name of her rock band at university: the She-Wolves; Isabella had been lead guitarist—and she lay back again, positioning her own body in a sickle shape round the child, not quite touching; inhaling her skin.

And now the sun glints through the kitchen window onto the wheaten head of the child and the copper hair of Isabella, on whose lap Hannah sits, being spoonfed muesli with warm milk and brown sugar.

The telephone has rung several times during the course of the last couple of days and she has not taken any of the calls. Has stood by the answering machine, pen poised to write down the messages: a couple of friends—one of them Sally, enquiring if she is better; a man she has met a couple of times out hacking on Hampstead Heath. He is a banker or something. Last time she told him her phone number. Useful to have him in reserve, although he is rather British and pink-looking. The mother of the boy to whom she gives private French coaching to say he has got chickenpox, which suits Isabella fine. The final call was her agent, just a few minutes ago, reading out a fax he will be sending to a firm of French publishers with whom he is trying to negotiate a deal. If it comes off she will be a few thousand pounds better off and will be kept occupied for several months. The book concerned is a 600-page tome on the influence and development of rural France through the ages.

The trouble with Isabella's work is that it can be lonely, isolated, and at times boring. But sometimes there are challenges, sometimes the material itself is interesting. There is always plenty of work to be had and it can be fitted into her own hours; if she is busy during the day, she can work through the night. Then there are the business, political or press conferences—perhaps half a dozen a year—where she will accompany a personage and be on hand at all times, ready to interpret speeches, questions and responses. These can be fun, and are well paid. And you never know who you might meet. Over the years she has had quite a few dates this way.

On the mantelpiece above the fireplace, the testimony of her independent and busy life is displayed: invitations to parties, book launches, a first night, private views, previews, an embassy dinner. Isabella is the provider for her own social life, her career, her well-being. A strong woman. A survivor by necessity. In her wardrobe hang several designer-label outfits. In her wallet are advance tickets for the theatre and the opera—the Coliseum. And she is about to turn her back on it all. She has no plans, no formulated thoughts other than she must get away.

There are things to do first.

It is a ten-minute walk to the motor accessory shop in Haverstock Hill, and on the way there they meet a woman with a labrador on a lead.

'God,' the child says from the buggy, stretching out her arm to it, and Isabella bends to hug her. Then realises she knows the woman. She goes to the same Latin American dancing class on a Monday evening.

'Hello. I didn't recognise you out of context for a minute.' She tries not to sound as flustered as she feels.

'Well, you're recognisable anywhere. That hair,' the woman responds.

The words play in her head for a few seconds: recognise her anywhere. Instantly recognisable.

'I didn't know you had a child.' The woman smiles at Hannah, who is leaning sideways across the buggy, fingers outstretched towards the labrador's nose.

'She's my goddaughter.' It comes to Isabella easily, so easily. And now, with the adrenalin of confidence, she is inclined to embellish. 'I've got her staying with me for a bit. So I shan't be coming to class tonight.' Has only just remembered it is tonight. The days have lost their sense.

'That's a shame. Well, have fun with your goddaughter. See you soon.'

And they part. No problems there. No difficult questions or protracted small talk. Her goddaughter. And in a way is she not? Her magic little gift from God. Except Isabella does not believe in God.

Dave, in the motor accessory shop, knows her well. She is always popping in for things.

'Wish I was that car, the way you cosset it,' he said to her once.

Isabella is not a woman to take umbrage at a bit of innocent leching. She herself enjoys flirting. Far from finding it demeaning, she sees it as empowering. And men like Dave have always existed, will always exist, will never change, and cannot fairly be expected to change. She cannot see where the harm is; it is all meant in a light-hearted way. She has had arguments with other women over this. There are always heated quarrels in the Women of the World Awareness group to which she belongs. It amuses her how the evening always degenerates. Last time someone attacked her for pandering to the male ego.

'Why don't you reserve your venom for important things?' she said, exasperated. 'Real exploitation, discrimination, harassment, subjugation, abuse, physical mutilation in Third World countries. These are what women's rights are about in the nineties, the issues to be tackled. Whether or not some of us flap our eyelashes at men rates zero on the Richter scale of importance.'

Remembers being coquettish to her father to get what she wanted. Never imagining.

'Mornin', all.' Dave grinning his broken-toothed grin at her as she enters, struggling with the door and the buggy.

'Blimey, that was quick.' Gestures to Hannah. 'Didn't know they came out so big nowadays.'

Hannah stares at him impassively.

'She's my goddaughter,' says Isabella. 'Dave, I need a child seat for the car. Oh, and a new battery.' As she spots one on the shelf.

'Your MG got seat belts that cross diagonally and over the lap, or just the lap?'

'The diagonal-and-lap one.'

'That's fine, then. You could have one of them Euroseats. They fit on anything. Basically, they sit on your car seat, front or back—front in your case—and you just shove the car seat belt round it.'

'You don't have one now?'

'Cor, you don't expect much, do you? My son will be coming in a bit later. I dare say I might just be able to get hold of one and nip up lunchtime, say. Install it for you. Fit the new battery for you too. If you're nice to me.' A suggestive wiggle of the eyebrows.

'You're brilliant.'

'Yeah. And look where it gets me.' Gives an exaggerated grimace.

Isabella wandering up and down the colourful aisles of Mothercare, pushing the trolley with Hannah tucked inside, legs threaded through. And no one so much as glancing at them. Well, who would have guessed she would ever find herself doing this? Into the trolley goes a fold-up toddler chair and a potty seat, a collapsable bed-rail, boxed sets of plates and mugs. She is carried away by the novelty of it; transfers Hannah to another trolley and fills this one with clothes, books and toys. She cannot recollect the last time she had such fun.

'You've had a spree, haven't you?' comments the woman on the till.

'She's from Bosnia. I've just adopted her,' Isabella says without a second's hesitation. 'We're starting from scratch.'

Her own ability to lie astounds her.

In the chemist's a few doors along she enlists the saleswoman's help in choosing a hair colorant.

'And I'd have sworn you was a natural redhead,' the woman remarks.

'Just to cover the grey, you know.' Isabella waves her hand ruefully around her hairline.

'Happens to the best of us, luv,' says the woman, patting her platinum fringe and sighing.

'Shall we go north or shall we go south?' she says to the child—rocking on the corduroy horse and cooing to herself, something Isabella has not

VALERIE BLUMENTHAL

heard her do before. A contented, heart-warming sound. At first she had
not seemed to know what to do with the toys and had sat, surrounded
by plastic animals and people with their own playhouse, showing only a
mild curiosity. With Isabella's encouragement she had begun to pick up
the little figures and place them in an order. But it was the unveiling of
the horse that did it, that drew from her a spontaneous cry of delight
followed by real laughter.

'A job in Italy's cropped up. I'll be gone at least a month,' she tells
several friends on the phone.

'Drop me a line,' says the banker, who turns out to be a lawyer.

'Cornwall,' she says to her agent. And gives him her mobile number.

'It looks hopeful,' he says, and reads her the fax he has received from
the French publishers.

Southwest.

'"I want to go south, where there is no autumn, where the cold doesn't
crouch over one like a snow-leopard waiting to pounce . . ."' Tom had
read to her from the collected letters of D. H. Lawrence in his drawn-out
upper-class accent which, when she'd first met him, she thought he was
putting on as an affectation. Later she learned that his parents were in
fact upper-class liberal intellectuals. His father was an Oxford don; his
mother a Jewess distantly related to the Rothschilds, a writer and
researcher on Russian history.

She remembers a week in Cornwall—their honeymoon, actually—in
a tiny fishing village on the Roseland peninsula. Tom taking endless
photos in the rain. What was its name? She could find it on the map.
Also remembers a half-term spent in Falmouth with her mother. Has
more memories of Scotland. Is her Scottish grandmother still alive? If
she is, then no doubt she is still vituperative, exercising the eroding
power of her vocal cords on the other inmates of the old people's home
where she ekes out her days. Or perhaps she has been silenced by
senility. Isabella wastes no pity on her. She owes her nothing. Her
grandmother made her own choice, when she marked the card of her
granddaughter's fate.

Isabella coaxing Hannah into the bath. She herself lying in there surrounded by bobbing toys, clapping her hands enthusiastically.

'It's fun. You're really missing out, you know, Hannah,' Isabella says to
her. Lies back with an 'A-a-h'.

The child jumping up and down excitedly. It obviously strikes her as
very funny to see Isabella in the water. In one hand is a Gromit wash-
mitten . . . And now the child is stretching out her arms to be lifted

inside the bath. Isabella has won. It has taken nearly an hour. Later it will all be faithfully recounted in her report. But meanwhile she opens the bottle that is on the side and lathers the contents over Hannah's head, making a turnip of her fine hair. Thirty minutes later it is the same mid-auburn as Isabella's.

A while later, when the child is asleep, she begins preparing for the morning: puts clothes and toys directly into a couple of newly purchased holdalls—pores over the road atlas to plan her route, does an hour or so's work, a company profile from Italian into English. Then, finally worn out, she pours herself a glass of red wine and switches on the television. She is too tired to eat. Has she taken on too much. How will she fit in her work? The child is a full-time job.

So many emotions and thoughts sparring in her head. It will take a while to adjust from one life to another; from having no responsibilities to being weighed down with them—she who had deliberately cultivated a trouble-free existence. At times she has the sense she has strolled into a play in which she sees herself in the third person. At others she is wrenched into awareness of the outlandishness of what she has done.

She watches the news again. And following this, on Channel 4, a gentle documentary about the close bond between a cerebral palsy victim and his carer. The film so moves her that instead of turning off the television she waits for the credits.

It was written, produced and directed by Tom.

It takes her almost an hour to load up the MG, squeezing things into every possible niche. And then she realises she has forgotten to make a space for Garibaldi and his basket. A further twenty minutes is spent rejuggling. The child watching with apparent interest from the buggy.

One of her neighbours—a prissy, shabby, beige man who makes her flesh creep—is coming towards her.

'Hello there. Are you going away?' Eyeing the child.

'To my sister's. This is her daughter. Hannah, say hello.'

Hannah says nothing.

She is thankful it isn't the same neighbour who investigated them a couple of days back when the child's hair was its natural blonde. Had forgotten about that. Slams the door, says a hurried goodbye to the man and whisks the child indoors just as she starts screaming at the shock of the loud bang.

Isabella is a private sort of person; likes to remain anonymous except with people of her choice, and although she has lived at the same address for many years she still barely knows her neighbours. Wishes now that she did, so that she could entrust someone with a key, to keep vigil and forward her mail. As it is, she will have to return on a fortnightly basis.

Just as she is about to lift Garibaldi into his basket, he pins back his ears, leaps out of her arms, shoots through the cat flap from the kitchen onto the patio, and streaks up the fence. Where he sits glaring and swishing his tail. She unbolts the door and approaches him gingerly. He contemplates her slyly until her fingers are within reach of him, then down the fence he springs, into the next garden.

'Grabla, Grabla,' states the child, pointing to where the cat had been.

'You clever girl! Yes, *carina*. Grabla. Ga-ri-bal-di. And he's a bad cat as he's run away.'

The child frowns, as though trying to comprehend.

For the next couple of hours her inane cries of 'Dinnies' do not entice him, since he has already eaten his fill. And next door's bird table provides limitless entertainment. In the end it is the neighbour's terrier which drives him back onto his own patch. This time he zooms through the flap from the other direction, straight past Isabella and into her room, where he entrenches himself under her bed. Eventually she manages to disengage his claws from the carpet and pluck him out.

'Horrible creature,' says Isabella as she fastens the straps of the basket.

Almost lunchtime when they set off, taking the North Circular, passing the very precinct. She grips the steering wheel. *A young man running along the pavement: That's her. I recognise her. That red hair. And the car* . . . And in a room somewhere, does a mother mourn? Only when they hit the M4 does she begin to relax. Distancing herself from the scene of her crime. She is a criminal. She, Isabella, is a criminal in the eyes of the law. Switches on Domingo and sings along with him, drowning out Garibaldi's plaintive mewing from the back. Beside her, the child giggling.

A couple of hours later they stop just before Exeter at a Granada service station off the M5.

The noise of machines blasts at them as they enter the building: gunfire, zinging, rattling, sirens howling. Groups of youths and girls gathered round, cheering each other on. She can feel the child's whole body tensing, shrinking against her.

'It's OK. Hannah, *carina*, nothing's going to hurt you, I promise. Shall I carry you?'

The child's legs wrap themselves round her waist. Her hair is silky beneath Isabella's chin. Her glance darts about, as they head first for the Ladies' then the restaurant. So many new experiences within a few days. What must she be thinking? What must she be feeling? Does she wonder where she is? Where her mother is?

'You can make something of yourself. Not like me,' Isabella's mother said, not long before she died. 'Don't chuck it over some man.'

And later, when she was in hospital, anger in her eyes because there had been only hard work and disappointments. She went out with another kind of light in her eyes, whispering from St Luke.

It was winter, and there was a lovely cool silence in the room. And what would happen to her? she wondered, standing composed over the deathbed which held no shocks. A tall fourteen-year-old with her red hair pulled back in a ponytail; dark eyes like lacquered stones.

What must it be like, Isabella often thinks, to have such implicit faith? Not a flicker of doubt. One is going to a better life, and that is that. Her mother: dutiful, if not loving. And perhaps she loved in her own way. How old, when she died of lung cancer? No more than forty.

'Don't come to me. I can't have her,' said her grandmother.

They have entered the county of Cornwall, land of lore and legends and soft burred voices. Bodmin Moor spreads bleakly either side of the road, the skeletons of disused mines adding to the sense of isolation. The countryside becomes more undulating and her spirits lift. The sun lowering and evening setting in. The child asleep, head lolling onto her chest. Garibaldi has long given up meowing, is apparently reconciled to being in a basket for ever. Isabella turns off towards St Mawes.

It is growing dark. On her right is a lane, narrow like an artery, and she takes this turning. The lane descends steeply in a series of wishbone bends. High banks either side of her obscure the countryside. Overhead the trees arch to form dense-leaved tunnels. The banks become hedges, and through gaps she catches glimpses of dusk-gentle pastureland and grazing animals. Suddenly her headlights pick out a fox, and she stops, thrilled. It turns its head leisurely, to stare for a few seconds directly into the beam, blinking, the richness of its coat gleaming in the light, then it saunters in front of her car across the lane.

A mile or so on, she passes an illuminated mill selling antiques, and shortly after it comes to the village of Zerion. On the corner of a small junction of lanes is an inn: the Fox's Retreat. And now tiredness consumes her. It is virtually dark, and she doesn't feel like driving any further.

The place is fairly busy, and the low hum of voices, the laughter, are curtailed as everyone turns to look at her standing there half in the shadows of the doorway.

'I've left my little girl asleep in the car,' she calls across to the man behind the bar. 'I can't really come in. Could we have a room for a few nights?'

'Sure. Hang on a tick.' Smiles at her, finishes pulling a pint, hands it to his customer, wipes his palms on the sides of his thighs, and comes across the room to her. Accompanies her to the car.

'Nice old motor . . . You've a fair bit of stuff,' he adds mildly, when he sees everything.

'Oh, it's not all for now. We'll only need a few things.'

'I wouldn't leave anything valuable overnight. Your guitar. You should bring that in. And is that a laptop computer?'

'Yes.'

'I'd bring that in.' He has a warm, glutinous Cornish accent.

'A cat,' she says, unstrapping the child, and gesturing with her chin to the basket at the back. 'I forgot to tell you I've got a cat.'

And he has two Dobermans, at whom Garibaldi vents all the day's frustrations through the mesh of his basket as Isabella carries it inside.

The landlord banishes the dogs into a lobby and shuts the door.

'Gods,' says the child sleepily, hanging on to Isabella's other hand.

'Gods?' The publican looks askance.

'Dogs,' Isabella says in a mother's proud tone.

The staircase is steep and uncarpeted. She can see the child's face puckering in readiness; sets down the cat basket and whisks up Hannah. 'My daughter's afraid of stairs,' she says.

'I'll take the cat,' he offers.

They follow him upstairs to a broad landing.

He unlocks a door and goes inside. He puts the cat basket on the floor and parts his arms in an expansive gesture. 'Here you go, then. Not grand, but plenty of room for the three of you for as long as you want.'

'This is perfect.' She flops down onto one of the twin beds with its flowered nylon cover.

He leaves her, and returns twice more with her other items.

'You might need this'—holding up the bag of cat litter. 'And I also brought you up an old newspaper to put under the tray.'

'Thanks. You're very kind.' She pours litter into the tray and releases Garibaldi from the basket.

'Grabla,' cries the child, running towards him.

The cat glares at her and dashes under the bed.

'He's been cooped up for hours,' Isabella says.

'Poor thing. Well, I'd best be getting on downstairs. The name's Dick, by the way.'

'I'm Isabella. This is Hannah.'

'Hello, Hannah. How old are you, then?' He crouches down to the child's level. She stares blankly back at him.

'She's very shy, I'm afraid.'

He straightens up—she hears his knees cracking. 'No problem. So, what about food? Do you want to eat something?'

'Well, I am a bit peckish, and all Hannah's had since lunch is some chocolates.'

'Hows about I bring it up to you on a tray?'

'I feel so guilty. Your waiting on us like this.' Turns the force of her eyes upon him.

'Rubbish . . .' Locks into them for a couple of seconds. 'It's no trouble.'

They eat in front of the television. The child sits on her potty, tugging at a toasted sandwich with her fingers and teeth and cramming pieces into her mouth.

'Hannah wee-wee,' she announces, tottering up from the potty.

'Clever girl.' Isabella hugs her. The child is progressing daily, hourly; witnessing it fills her with pleasure.

She washes her then tucks her in bed. It is their first night in separate beds. She reads to her and shows her the pictures. Kisses her. Turns off the main light, leaving only the lamp. The child follows her every move.

Barely nine o'clock, and she herself is ready for bed, exhausted. She cleans her teeth, washes, tiptoes to the loo next door and returns to the room. The child is still half awake, eyes in watchful slits, but does not seem perturbed by Isabella's short absence. There have been other examples that would indicate she is used to being left on her own.

There is so much I will never know, she writes in her report, in bed.

From downstairs, now the television is switched off in the room, she can clearly hear the conversation from the bar directly below. Some people are discussing her.

'I reckon she's a businesswoman. She had a mobile phone with her. And a computer. Did you see? One of them yuppies from the city.'

'Not with a kid that age.'

'Well, I reckon she's an actress. I'm sure I recognise her.'

This is nothing new. She is always being told she looks like someone. Susan Sarandon or Sigourney Weaver; some actress from *EastEnders*.

'Good-looking woman and all,' says another man's voice downstairs.

'Oh, I don't think so.' A woman's sharp tones.

Isabella smiles. Such a predictable response. She finds it sad that some women can't acknowledge others' attractiveness without bitching.

And then comes another man's voice. 'Well, if you ask me, she's running from something. You don't drive all that way with a kid and a cat and all that luggage on spec.'

Feels a chill run through her.

ISABELLA SEEMS SO SELF-ASSURED and poised. There is no bitterness apparent in her features. Her eyes are mink-soft. There is determination in the set of her jaw but not aggression. She is a woman of inherent good taste and style, yet she had no yardstick. What happened to the child who stamped her foot unheard, and dismembered her doll as her parents hollered out their mutual frustrations at each other?

Perhaps that act of destruction was partly responsible: she had lost her most treasured possession and thus only punished herself. Tantrums were replaced by sulks. But sulking was only of use when there was someone at whom to aim it.

When her mother died, different rules applied. She had to endear herself. Isabella the chameleon. And yet the guise she assumed was never conscious. She was never deliberately one person or another. She watched and learned, picking up a bit here, a bit there; and each place she went brought out another aspect of her character and she became the woman she is today. Whoever that is.

The screeching of an owl from the churchyard opposite pierces her sleep and wakens her. For a moment she cannot think where she is, and then, in the aureole of the night lamp on the table beside the child's bed, the pink room comes into focus and she remembers.

She had a pink bedroom once. And she went into it after school one day to discover a dress—a skimpy thing she had seen and hankered after and bought with money earned at the hairdresser's on Saturdays—cut into pieces. She said nothing. Determined to be no trouble. And when she tried to work in the small pink bedroom—it was perhaps eight foot by six foot, and she hung her clothes on hangers on the door—on would go the pop music in the room next to hers. Louder and louder it became, drowning inspiration.

'Everything all right?' The woman, kind, hearty-bright-voiced, would come in with bulging string shopping bags and dump them with a 'phew' and puffing out of cheeks.

'Any volunteers to unload?'

And Isabella would oblige.

The woman's troubled glance shifted towards the other girl, her daughter, the same age as Isabella, who would slam upstairs to her younger brother's room. Giggling from within.

A year, Isabella lasted there. Making her fifteen.

Zerion sprawls, with its anachronistic amalgam of architectural styles, in a brook-bound cobweb of lanes within the bowl of three hills. There is that end-of-season feel about it this Wednesday morning, like an empty bag of sweets in which one rummages among the sugary deposits for a piece worth eating. The weather has broken.

It gives the locals something to talk about, the change in the weather. And in the newsagent's-cum-post-office-stores in the lane that runs along the base of the neatly mown triangular green, the proprietor is telling another woman that she welcomes the breeze and the cooler temperature, that her legs have been playing up in the heat. When Isabella enters with the child, she breaks off. Both women swivel and assess her openly. News of the visitor has already reached their ears via one of the men from the pub last night, who has just been in for his *Mirror*. And Isabella, who is used to London, where one can go anywhere without attracting attention, knows that in a small parochial community like this she is likely to find herself the butt of gossip. And so she injects a friendly liveliness into her tone when she wishes the two women good morning and comments on the weather, before asking for the local paper.

'It'll be the *West Briton* you want. There's a Truro edition for round here. It comes out tomorrow, Thursday.'

The proprietor, a mealy-faced woman, takes off her bottle-glass spectacles and rubs them on her lilac crochet pullover, considers Isabella through watery eyes for a couple of seconds and resites the glasses.

'I've got one from last week at the back of the shop'—she has obviously decided in Isabella's favour—'I could let you have it if you like.'

'Oh, but I'll pay for it.'

'That's not necessary. I was only going to chuck it. It's out again tomorrow.' Disappears through a doorway behind the counter to fetch it.

She is left alone with the other woman, whose right arm is in a sling. A good conversation-opener.

'What have you done to your arm?'

'I fell down the stairs,' the woman says, staring at the floor. Isabella immediately regrets the question; knows that her husband is violent. She pretends to sift through the postcards. Is relieved when the other woman returns.

369

'I'm hoping to rent a cottage in the area,' Isabella says. 'That's why I wanted the paper.'

'Are you now?' The proprietor regards Isabella keenly. 'For a holiday, you mean?'

'No. Longer than that. Maybe a few months.'

'Ah.'

The women nod wisely at each other, then at her. And she can see them thinking: It's true, then. She's run off. Sympathy clear in their faces. She gives the tiniest of nods herself, as acknowledgment.

The woman with the sling says, 'There's nothing in Zerion that I know of.'

'Actually, I really wanted to be in Pengarris Cove.'

The child butting her face against Isabella's legs, tugging at her pullover for attention. She hoists her into her arms.

'Pengarris Cove's just a couple of miles from here,' the post office woman says. 'There're only holiday places to rent there.'

The other woman swirls her lips round contemplatively. 'What about old Timothy Abell's place? That's been standing empty.'

'Oh, that'd never suit the likes of her.' The post office woman shakes her head slowly at Isabella. 'That's not for you. For a start it's only got an outside toilet.'

'Who's Timothy Abell?'

'Was. He died a month back. And Lord knows what state the place must be in. He was more'n ninety when he died. And looked after himself till the day he went. Bad-tempered old goat he was. Hadn't spoken to his daughter since she got pregnant by that . . . what was his name?'

'Collett. Will Collett, you mean, from Penzance way,' the other woman obliges.

'Yes, that was him. A married man. But for goodness' sake, a woman has to take what she can get sometimes. And she gave all her best years to her father. Any rate, he kicked her out. And Will Collett wouldn't have nothing to do with her. She lives in Truro with the kid. He's funny in the head. Backward, I mean.'

'How do I find out about the cottage?' she asks.

'Babs Carrick at Pengarris post office is bound to know. It's down the hill on the right, next to the Sun Inn.'

Isabella thanks her and leaves. Guesses she has given them plenty to talk about. As she steps out of the shop, her hair blows across her face and she pulls it back and tucks it into the neck of her pullover. Does up the top button of the child's collar. 'You mustn't catch cold.' Pulls forward the buggy's transparent hood. Next to the post office is a garage which, according to the metal sign swinging and creaking musically from the corrugated roof, does servicing, repairs and MOTs. She rummages in her bag for a pen and paper to jot down the phone number.

In the yard a young man is tinkering with a battered white van. He is staring at her, and she has the impression he has been doing so for some while. She is both self-conscious and disquieted.

'Creepy guy, creepy guy,' she says to the child.

She follows the left diagonal of the green, past the terrace of thatched cottages whose front doors are approached via miniature bridges traversing the brook; the butcher's, with its cheerful cardboard pig alongside a suspended carcass (this always strikes her as rather sick); the art gallery in a converted chapel.

'Blustery day,' one or two people remark to her.

And an elderly woman on a cylindrical cob plods by, waving to everyone in general.

They arrive at the duck pond, to the side of the church, whose tower can just be glimpsed through the lich gate. And somewhere among the pines and the yew in the little graveyard is the screech owl that woke her in the night.

'Some folks round here are superstitious of it,' Dick, the publican, told her at breakfast this morning. 'They're supposed to be a death portent. Full of old wives' tales this place is.'

And here she is, back at the pub, and her car, parked outside.

She unlocks it and lifts the child inside, fastens the seat straps round her and passes her the knitted rabbit and her new bear, whose ear Hannah has taken to sucking. Folds up the buggy with the expertise of an old hand and puts it in the back. The garage mechanic's glowering eyes remain with her and disturb her.

The lane to Pengarris Cove is winding and narrow, and several times she has to pull in for an oncoming vehicle. Then, ahead, she has her first glimpse of the sea, turbulent and mossy green. She has a passion for the sea, is always thrilled by that first sighting of it.

The descent into the village becomes steeper, and as her foot grips the brake the MG clunks metallically. Either side, pastel cottages cling to the lane. Subtropical plants blaze out from gardens. Flower baskets hanging from lime-washed walls swing in the wind. She slows when she comes to the Sun, and notices the post office immediately after it. But there is nowhere to park, and presently the lane splits into two, one fork veering sharply to the left and climbing, the other carrying on for a few yards before shelving in a cobbled slipway onto the cove. At the apex of the lanes, the Ship Inn leans forward from its Tudor gables.

Outside, a group of people are sitting in the courtyard.

She deliberates about taking the left fork; the incline seems almost perpendicular. Resolutely, she puts her foot down on the accelerator, and the MG crawls upwards. She grits her teeth all the while during its painful progress. Laughs with relief when they reach the top.

As she stands outside the car, the wind lashes at her hair and cheeks. Seagulls squeal and careen overhead.

'Buds,' the child says from the buggy, pointing upwards.

The rocky western headland rises in gorse- and bracken-clad cliffs and sweeps out to sea. There it divides, one prong jutting out in a long tusk, the other embracing the cove like a protective lover. She can see a row of cottages and behind them a bleak-looking chapel. Perched on the end of the 'tusk' is a lighthouse. The opposite promontory is softer, cultivated on the upper slopes.

Up here, along this stretch of road, the houses are hidden from view at the end of long driveways, their names attached to gates or discreetly placed among rhododendron hedges. She instantly latches on to the name 'Rhododendron Drive'. Here there is a sense of prosperity. The lawns are emerald from sprinklers.

For a few minutes the wind dies down, and in the brief lull she catches the sound of a lawn mower; then of something much closer. It is coming from the scrubby bank somewhere near her feet: crickets. How rarely she has heard crickets in England. Their tintinnabular whirring fires her senses and triggers a keening in her towards something indefinable yet somehow important.

Slowly, she walks down the hill with the child in the buggy. Old buildings cascade on top of each other, their rooftops forming staggered layers. Alleys splay from the lane and terminate in courtyards or in steps leading through shadowy arches onto the cove.

At the Ship Inn she unstraps the child, who automatically reaches for her hand. The spontaneous gesture of trust plucks at her emotions. The child is so diminutive—she barely comes up to thigh level—and Isabella is filled with a fierce protectiveness; wonders again how anyone could inflict harm on so small a being.

The entrance to the harbour is marked by the small weatherboarded coastguard's office and the old granite boathouse with a ramshackle hut tacked on to it. Fishing boats are hauled up on a concrete hardstanding, and beside one, on a square of canvas sheeting, a tangle of cuttlefish writhe balletically. The child stares with huge, transfixed eyes. A couple of other fishing vessels rest on the shingle, and a man repainting the registration number on the hull of his touches his denim cap in greeting.

They pick their way between heavy chains and mooring blocks, lobster pots, nets and seaweed towards the sea.

The tide is out, leaving a glistening tongue; and they stop just short of where the lip of wet sand begins. The child frowns, as though puzzling at the expanse of water before her; turns to Isabella as if for explanation.

'It's called the sea,' she says, gesticulating with her arm. Repeats the word several times.

'Sea.'

'That's it! Yes, that's it, *carina!*' Whirls her round in a circle. Their laughter. The child's laughter. High peals. Such a beautiful sound. For Isabella it validates everything she has done over the last few days.

One or two people are watching them, smiling. Fleetingly she sees themselves as others might: a mother and daughter playing together. Alike with their red hair.

She puts her lips to the child's ear and points to herself.

'Mummy.'

The child does not react. Engrossed by the serrated rim of the sea rolling in and out.

The village's main street has few shops: a chandler's, a barber's, a tea-room, a chemist's that also sells knitwear, and the post-office stores, wedged between a pair of disused lime kilns and the Sun. She remembers from years ago that it was less spoilt than other villages—too small, maybe, or too remote. And there is no bathing beach.

Displayed outside the post office is a basket of sea urchins on an elm stool. Round like ogen melons, purple, and speckled with raised white freckles, they look as if they have been crafted from porcelain. HELP YOURSELF. £1.50 EACH. PUT IN BOX, is written trustingly on the card threaded onto a long stick like a flag in their midst.

Babs Carrick is in her late forties or early fifties. She is well groomed and has an American accent.

'Canadian actually,' she says, when Isabella comments on it. 'And I thought I sounded thoroughly Cornish.'

She has an easy smile; striking, Nordic features.

Isabella explains she is looking for a cottage to rent. 'Somebody mentioned Timothy Abell's cottage,' she says.

'You kidding? That place is a dump.'

'Well, is there anywhere else you know of in Pengarris?'

'Wee-wee,' says the child.

Isabella is caught by astonishment. Tries not to let it show in her expression.

'I'm so sorry. Do you have a loo she could use?'

'Of course . . . And that's another thing,' Babs Carrick says, leading the way. 'Timothy Abell's cottage only has an outside one.'

But there is nothing else in the village, and she digs out the estranged daughter's number for Isabella. Writes down her own also.

'You can always come and have a civilised bath in my place,' she says. Adds, 'I do hope you rent somewhere near here. It would be nice to have someone to . . . well, you know what I mean.'

Instinctively knows she has a friend.

The cottage is a five-minute walk from the centre of the village and is one of the row she noticed earlier on the western headland; the last of a whitewashed terrace of four.

Standing in the shelter of the porch, out of the buffeting wind, and with her arm about the child, Isabella can hear the sea slapping against the rocks; can look out onto the entire harbour. Behind the terrace the hill forms a steep escarpment with clumps of purple heather between yellow gorse and bracken.

The cottage's windows are sixties replacements carved into walls that must be at least two foot six thick. Through the filthy glass she can just make out a small square room with khaki walls and an armchair on rockers. She wanders round with the child, squinting through other foggy windows. Discovers the outside toilet. It is a stinking cubbyhole of leaves, mud, cobwebs and old urine. But it could be cleaned up, and it is only a stone's throw from what appears to be the kitchen. She tries to imagine them living here; visualises white paint over the anaglypta, rugs, plants, a few pieces of decent, inexpensive furniture.

That evening she rings Timothy Abell's daughter. Her voice is curiously monotone. A meeting is set up for the following morning. Afterwards, she accesses her answering machine.

'Hi, it's me,' says Peter. He sounds like the hesitant boy she first met. 'Where are you? I've tried you twice. I need to speak to you. Could you ring me?' Articulates the number clearly.

She does not write it down. There is no need to phone back. It is only to tell her he wants to break it off. And what does she feel? Nothing.

Her agent: 'I'm sorry, I lost your mobile number. Let's hope you access this. We've got the deal. Phone me ASAP.'

She does so. He sounds ebullient. He is young, enthusiastic, only recently set up on his own.

'Well, congratulations,' he says when he hears her voice. Tells her a contract is being drawn up. 'Five thousand. Split the usual way: signature, delivery, publication. Six months to do it. I thought that fair.'

She works it out: ten pages a day, six hundred pages in sixty days—

leaving her time for other work. But there is the child to look after, and the cottage to make habitable. Calculates: at least ten days before they sign. She can organise the cottage in that time. Another week settling in. And then she can get down to work.

'OK.'

'You don't seem very excited.' He sounds nettled.

'No, no, it's great, really.'

She gives him her mobile number again, and tells him she'll let him know her address for the contract.

She eats downstairs by herself. The child took longer than usual to go to sleep—overexcited. Every ten minutes Isabella slips upstairs to check on her. Only one other table is occupied, by an elderly couple who do not speak to each other except for the briefest of exchanges.

She used to see this with her own parents. There was either silence or yelling; rarely anything in between. But her father looked at her, Isabella, with love. Was her mother jealous of their closeness? And with that one fleeting error he demolished it.

She finishes her own meal—chicken in a mustard sauce—and goes over to the bar to get a second glass of red wine. Several men are drinking there. Dick is chatting to an immense, bearded man wearing jeans tucked into hiking boots. Lizzie, Dick's wife, appears, pink-faced from the heat of the kitchen, bearing a plate in either hand.

'Chicken all right?' she throws over her shoulder to Isabella.

'Delicious.'

'That'll please her.' Dick breaks off from his conversation with the tall man. 'It's the first time she's made it. She was fretting.' He refills her glass.

'So you've got the MG,' the man with the beard says.

'Yes.' She can't believe his height. He must be six foot six or seven.

'I used to have one. An earlier model, though. Chrome bumper.'

He is as softly spoken as he is immense. A rolling accent like treacle falling off a spoon. Open, honest features.

'Go on, Aidan.' Dick leans over and stabs his shoulder with a finger. 'Tell her what you've got now.'

'No, it's not impor—'

'He's got an old Aston, and an XK150.'

'Leave off, Dick . . . I'm doing up the old Jag,' he says to Isabella; looks apologetic and embarrassed, as though afraid he might appear to be showing off. And she warms to him.

'Aidan owns the garage on the corner of the green,' Dick informs her.

'Oh, how funny. I made a note of the phone number from your board outside, as my car's always going wrong.' As she says it she can clearly see the mechanic on the forecourt, his gaze lancing her. Banishes the image. 'In fact I think the suspension's collapsed.'

'More'n like. Car's so low on the ground. And these lanes won't help.'

'I'm beginning to realise that.'

'There's a concealed dip in the road between here and Pengarris that'll do the trick, if nothing else does.'

'I found it. Twice.' There and back. He laughs when she recounts it. His laugh is a deep rumble like a mild earth tremor.

She has her red wine, buys one for Dick, and another for herself. Offers to buy one for Aidan.

He declines. 'I'm old-fashioned like that,' he says. 'It feels wrong having a woman pay. I'll do the next round.' Assertively.

It transpires he has a blues group, and plays at local gigs or pubs.

'I used to have a group at university. The She-Wolves, we called it. I was lead guitarist.'

'You never!'

They smile at one another. She is aware of feeling slightly tipsy: relaxed, warm, vivacious. And of fancying Aidan.

'If ever you need a female guitarist,' she says.

'Well, I might just take you up on that.'

'You two should do a deal,' says another man next to him, rather drunk and slurring.

'What's that, then?' Aidan asks. His black moustache and luxuriant beard are speckled with foam from his beer; he surely cannot feel it, but must know that there is a tendency for this to happen, as he wipes it away with the side of his hand.

'She plays in your group and you fix her suspension.' The man cackles raucously. Pulls his features into an insinuating leer.

'That's enough, Ed.' The humour gone from Aidan's voice.

'I have some work to do,' Isabella says abruptly.

And she does. Although this is not the reason for her sudden urgent need to leave. Nor is it the drunk man's remarks, which don't bother her. Framed in the doorway is the intense-eyed figure of the mechanic, just staring at her. How long has he been standing there, unnoticed?

And in echo of her thoughts, Aidan calls out, 'How long have you been standing there, Luke? Come and join us.'

The young man sidles over. He has a curious, silent, crablike gait. His head is shaven to a stubble.

'This is Isa . . . Mrs . . . What's your surname?' Aidan asks her.

'Mercogliano.' She can barely force her own name from her lips.

'Mrs Mercogliano's got an MG. Suspension needs seeing to.'

On the bar stool beside him, Ed guffaws. The newcomer mumbles something unintelligible and will not now meet her eyes.

'Is that an Italian name, then?' Aidan asks.

'Yes. Excuse me. I really—' Flings her hand out apologetically and hurries upstairs without finishing her drink. She feels quite unreasonably unnerved.

The child is whimpering in her sleep. Stops when Isabella strokes her forehead and hair.

She switches on the lamp by her own bed and sits down at her laptop computer on the extra table Dick has put in the room.

Wednesday evening, September 4. What is she doing here? And on the mantelpiece of her kitchen in Hampstead is an embossed invitation for tonight for the opening of a new play at the Royal Court. Another world. And later there will be a party: a lot of air-kissing and performance postmortems, and canapés and champagne.

She finishes the company profile. Writes up her report on the child. Gets ready for bed. The long-delayed rain rapping against the window.

She lies beneath the duvet, corpse-stiff, remembering: the second place she was sent. The boy, the son, had the same look in his eyes as the mechanic. The same obsessive, almost deranged look that drew and mesmerised and repelled. She had blocked it, along with other things.

Dreams. In them a man's arm encircles her tenderly and protectively. She doesn't know his name or who he is, but this is not as important as the feeling of safety and the sense of secure love transmitted to her soul. A very great contentment spreads through her from the arches of her feet. She knows she wants to stay with him for ever.

THE WIDE-PANNING countryside, the fecund hills, remind her. She was about four, and it is her earliest recollection of an outing to the countryside. To Box Hill.

Her father took her. She went alone with him. He drove them in his newly acquired, secondhand, red Singer Gazelle. From time to time he pressed her hand as he drove. Innocent contact. She remembers him saying, 'Isn't it nice to be just the two of us, eh?' He always spoke in his native tongue to her. His English never seemed to progress much. Her mother had had to learn Italian. She remembers him singing on the journey (which seemed so long, endless). He had a fine singing voice. Her love of opera stems from him. '*La donna è mobile*,' his baritone would let rip. And he would swing his head in time from side to side and glance at her for her reaction, grinning.

He was stout and on the tall side of average, with a large head crowned with wavy metallic hair of which he was overtly vain—she would often catch him combing it. He could be morose one moment, jovial the next, with a boisterous humour and a delight in pranks. That same boisterous streak could quickly escalate into rage or tumble into sorrow. She saw similar traits years later in Tom.

That day at Box Hill they had cool drinks and lunch at a table outside a hotel; it was summer and she can even remember her dress, pale blue with smocking and puffed sleeves. Children dressed up in their best for outings in those days, she muses.

Remembers something else, an incident that nearly put a blight on the magical day, but not entirely. There was a tennis court a few yards from their table and she was watching a couple playing when, before her eyes, a bird flew into the wire netting that fenced off the area. It seemed to fling itself straight at it. For a minute it struggled and fluttered, its head caught in the mesh, one wing at an unnatural angle, then the beads of its eyes closed and its small body dangled. She began screaming, standing there at the net, and her father and several other people came chasing over. What's wrong? What's happened? And all she could do was scream and sob and point. And into her father's loving, protective arms she was hoisted up and cuddled and crooned over. Nothing untoward. Nothing except paternal concern and devotion.

Does not wish to think of him.

They come to Aidan's garage. He is alone outside, changing the wheel of a car. On his head is a baseball cap pulled down against the drizzle. His overalls are stained. She toots and slows down, and he comes towards her smiling, wiping his hands on his thighs. He approaches the driver's side of the MG and bends to window level, almost filling it with his face and beard. She unwinds the window. Unreasonably glad to see him. Has the urge to wipe the rain from his beard.

'I was thinking of you earlier,' he says with complete naturalness. 'So how's you both, then?'

'Fine. We're on our way to Timothy Abell's cottage. I'm hoping to rent it.'

'It could be made nice,' he says thoughtfully, nodding his head; the first person not to be negative.

She is heartened. There is a dependable quality about him. If he states something then one knows it is so.

'That's what I think. Look, I'm sorry if I seemed abrupt last night. I realise I dashed off rather quickly.'

'Well, you did a bit,' he agrees. 'I don't blame you, though. It was getting a bit . . . how'll I put it? Heavy?'

For a second she is tempted to tell him the truth: it wasn't that, it was . . . but the mechanic is his employee. 'Well, I'd better—'

'I was thinking,' he interrupts. 'I mean, it's probably a bit presumptuous'—rubbing his beard then his thick eyebrows—'but I was wondering if you'd like to come to one of our gigs some time.'

'That would be nice. Oh, *madre*—' Remembers the child suddenly. 'I can't. There's Hannah.' Who, at the mention of her name, looks up sharply from playing with her bear.

So, she *does* know her name.

'I dare say Lizzie could keep an eye on her, though she might be a bit busy. Otherwise there's Sophia. You remember Luke, the chap who works for me? You met him last night. Sophia's his wife. She does child-minding and cleaning. She's Italian too, or half, or something.'

'Oh, I'm not sure.' She wants nothing to do with the mechanic.

'You've nothing to worry about. She's ever such a nice girl. I know Luke can be a bit . . . well, between you and me, he's a bit of an oddball, but he's great with engines. She's not like him. I don't know what she sees in him. She loves kids. I could arrange for her to come to the inn.'

'I'd love to, then. Thank you.'

'Saturday? How would Saturday be?'

'Fine. Yes, fine.'

How extraordinary: she is shy. Isabella, with all her worldliness, is struck with shyness.

'Seven fifteen? I'll tell Sophia to be with you a bit before that. You'll want her to get to know your daughter.'

'That's a good idea.' Unused to a man who takes charge, or to one who is considerate. Unaccustomed to not being at the helm.

He straightens up slowly. 'See you, then.' Taps the window edge.

'Remember the dip in the road,' he calls out as she drives off.

A tea-coloured sky. The twin headlands enshrouded in mist. The village huddled beneath a cloak of fine rain. A sludge-grey sea.

Janet Abell is waiting at the cottage. She is probably about fifty, although it is hard to tell. She has a rosebud mouth which reminds

Isabella of a knot in a balloon, and lachrymose blue eyes. Her voice is the same as it was on the phone, like a well-rehearsed automaton, as though she has only learned with effort what to say in what context. Her conversation itself is normal enough, but the flat monotones convey no emotion. Her mannerisms are gauche and ill-coordinated.

Her son is with her, an overweight Down's syndrome boy of about eight or nine who stands like a heavy, truncated tree in the entrance, his hand slack in his mother's, thick pink tongue lolling like a salmon steak out of his gaping, drooling mouth. Hannah does not take her eyes off him. Isabella senses her tensing and picks her up.

'You'll be—wanting—to look—around,' Janet Abell says in her robot tone. 'I'm—afraid it's—a—mess. I haven't set—foot—in here for—years.'

The whole place is shambolic, but from the glimpse she had yesterday she had not expected otherwise. The sitting room has obviously not been touched since Timothy Abell's death. The carpet is like a dog with mange. The ceiling is tobacco-stained. In the grate the charred remains of logs poke out from a bed of ash. The low plastic-topped table still has bottles, mugs and glasses upon it, and an ashtray heaped with cigarette butts. She can smell the staleness, the dank, the tobacco; the old man's breath and irritability and loneliness. But there is a phone, she notes.

The kitchen is poky and greasy, separated from the scullery—where the sink is—by a door; she would remove it to create a sense of space. Off there is a bathroom of sorts. It has a half-bath with a ledge to sit on. Upstairs. The bed in the larger bedroom is unmade. Imprinted with the old man's hollow. Did he die in it? The wooden floor is swayed like an old horse, and his clothes are strewn about: underpants, grey trousers, a beige cardigan-jacket. The odours of age and sweat and cigarette smoke. She finds this evidence of his personal life terribly poignant.

'I'd clean—it—up for you—first—of course,' Janet says, after Isabella tells her she would want to paint the inside. 'It's—disgusting,' she adds. And for the first time there is the faintest inflection in her voice.

When Isabella asks about the furniture, a note of vehemence creeps into her tone: 'I'll get the—lot—burned. I'll be—glad to—burn it. His—clothes—too. He were—cruel, he were. This—weekend. I'll—do it—all—this weekend. You can—have it from—Monday.'

'How will you shift the furniture?'

'I know—someone.'

The 'someone' hangs mysteriously in the air. They discuss a fair rental.

'Oh no—that's—too much,' Janet protests when Isabella suggests £400 a month for a period of six months. 'Specially as—you'll be—prettying it up like.'

She has a point. They settle on £200 for the first couple of months and £400 thereafter. In the kitchen Isabella writes a cheque out in advance, for the first instalment.

'Oh no, that's—not—necessary.'

'Please, take it.' Thrusts it towards her across the Formica worktop upon which is a plate with the congealed remains of a meal. Timothy Abell's last supper. She is suddenly filled with pity for him, cantankerous though he obviously was. Sorrier, by far, for this woman with her hard life and its lack of chances; her lost love, her strange, gauche mannerisms, and her son.

'You're very—kind.' Janet folds the cheque carefully and puts it in her purse. Fastens the press-stud slowly and firmly.

'No, I'm not. You've done me a great favour.'

And does Isabella truly believe she will be here six months hence? Who is to say what will have happened by then? She can only be thankful when another uneventful day has passed.

'Fears for the safety of a two-and-a-half-year-old girl, missing since the weekend, are growing,' says the solemn-voiced newsreader.

Isabella, at her computer, sits upright. She is rigid with shock. Her heart seems to stop beating completely.

'The mother, Mrs Winnie Edwards, today made an impassioned plea for the return of her child.'

And there she is, the mother: 'If anyone has got my little daughter . . .' Too overcome to talk, tears pouring down her cheeks.

And tears down Isabella's. Swallowing down hysterical laughter. Sagging into her chair.

The woman is black. Afro-black. The child is called Louise.

But how is it that until now she has heard nothing, read nothing, about this missing girl? Could Hannah's absence, too, have been reported without her being aware? The mother's anguish haunts her.

She was one of the youngest in her year at university: a month away from her eighteenth birthday. Teamed up with Sally straight away: a winsome fair-haired girl with lashings of black mascara, and a humour at odds with her convent school background. In their second term they formed the She-Wolves. In the third she met Tom. Married him in the summer vacation after a night of incredible sex. He was seven years older than her, and was a reporter for the *Western Daily Press* when she met him; but he had higher ambitions. He was restless, passionate, fearsomely knowledgeable on numerous topics, self-centred; spoke—in his upper-class accent—at the rate of a runaway hare, or when bored would sit in hooded-eyed, excluding silence. He was pro-devolution, anti-monarchy, anti-Establishment and a Doppelgänger for Steve McQueen. Like her he loved both opera and rock music. After their wedding they headed southwest on his Harley Davidson. She recalls roaring away on the bike after saying, 'I do'. The only other time she has ever done anything impulsive.

Tom drained her emotionally at times and buoyed her at others. Everything about him was so extreme: his obsessions, his generosity, his opinions, his impetuousness—so opposite to her steadiness.

'I'm going freelance,' he announced one day in March 1977, when they had been married a year and a half.

'I'm going to Vietnam,' he said a week later, after three days of barely speaking. 'They need reporters out there.'

And returned more than a year later when she had graduated and taken a job. She read his articles meanwhile, heard him over the airwaves, saw him with a microphone in hand, vocalising in his crisp, incisive tones about the problems of the new republic. So strange seeing him, the stranger she'd married, on television, in his khaki shorts, with his tousled bleached hair and charming smile.

After the initial flurry of letters and a couple of hopeless attempts on the telephone, the correspondence dwindled. There were perhaps two or three perfunctory letters over nine months, written by someone who could have been anyone, to someone who could have been anyone. She was married, but not. She longed to be angry with him. He returned an alcoholic and a womaniser, unable to settle to anything.

'This country stinks. People are so petty. Petty, prurient, pusillanimous.'

'So why did you come back?'

'Sometimes I wonder.' Looking through her with loveless, lonely, icy eyes which made her shrivel.

It struck her he would never be satisfied for more than a few months at a time.

'You're drinking too much.'

'Don't nag.'

'*Madre*, this is hopeless.'

'Yes, it is.'

Divorced before she was twenty-five.

It takes ages to drive the few miles to King Harry Passage, as she has to keep pulling over to make way for cars coming in the opposite direction. Once she is forced to reverse about 100 yards along the lane. Gives a V sign to the tractor who just keeps coming at her.

They park in a line of other cars and wait for the ferry to clunk across the Fal from the opposite side. Stands outside the car, her arms tight round the child. The air bracing. The seagulls and kittiwakes screeching and circling and diving.

She counts the cars as they are driven off, enunciating clearly for the benefit of the child.

'Twenty-three,' she says as the last vehicle disembarks.

Then it is their turn. They are guided onto the boat by a brown-faced young ferryman.

From the belly of the boat there comes a metallic grating, as gradually the ferry slides forward, then gathers pace, and they are conveyed across.

The child gazes, bird-curious, all about her, her face undergoing a rapid sequence of expressions. She seems to hesitate, then her features concertina and her skin darkens. Isabella hauls her onto her lap just as she begins to bellow.

'*Carina*, everything's fine. We're on a boat. Look, we're crossing the water to the other side.'

She quietens. Nowadays it does not take a lot to calm her. She trusts Isabella. One day maybe she will not be scared of the unknown. Isabella hopes upon hope that she will be there for that day.

They are fourth in line to disembark. She feels light-headed, as though she has stepped off a fairground ride.

Beside her, Hannah sleeps. It occurs to her, as she drives, that so long as she has the child she will never again be alone. And her obsessive dread of her own death, which sometimes has kept her awake at night, has for the moment been quiesced. Is this one reason, she wonders, why people want children? To enable them to confront their own mortality?

In Truro she parks in Lemon Quay, beside the Pannier Market. The cathedral's spires loom over the city. A Zeppelin balloon floats overhead.

The child stirs. Eyes opening—befuddled, then clearing. Her dazzling smile. 'Mummy.'

Joy lancing through her. It floods her head. She can barely contain it.

It seems that each minute brings a new surprise; and each to her is a reward that she wishes could be stored so that it could be recaptured at will, as one can look upon a photograph. In the past she has seldom bothered to take them. Now she has a reason: And this was my daughter when she was two and three-quarters . . .

Who is she fooling?

But already she cannot conceive of life without Hannah. In a short space of time her own happiness has become inextricably linked to this small person's.

They turn into Lower Lemon Street, a cobbled lane lined with shops. Midday, and the city is bustling. Isabella weaves the buggy between the legs of shoppers.

A commemorative statue in Boscawen Street draws her attention, and she stops to read the plaque on the plinth. It is dedicated to a soldier killed in the Falklands in 1982. *Madre*, how long ago that seems. And yet not. She can remember all the controversy at the time. And the shock of seeing Tom on television—referring to an idiotic war perpetrated by a batty English female führer for her personal vanity. For a couple of minutes he raged uninterrupted, watched by millions of astonished viewers, herself included, until a hand yanked the microphone from him, severing his invective midstream. The papers were full of it the next day: he was being sent home in disgrace. Unrepentant. And until a few nights ago she saw or heard nothing more about him. So now he is making documentary films.

Through the web of streets she and the child wander. In Smith's she buys a book on child psychology. Browses in Monsoon. Shares chicken nuggets and chips out of a paper bag with Hannah. Through the open door of a fish restaurant with Mediterranean-style awnings waft the tobacco odours of char-grilling. I might eat here some time, she thinks. Take Aidan? Knows he would never permit that. *Her* taking him. And what of romance, with him or anyone? Now there is the child, what time, what chance for romance, or lust?

A policeman directs her to a furniture store. She finds it behind wrought-iron gates: three floors of rattan, pine, rugs and terracotta in a Victorian warehouse. She can order everything she needs from this one shop. Tells the salesman she wants it delivered in a week's time.

They head for the cathedral; and even as they stand by one of the great arched doorways she can feel desolation pressing down on her, that familiar darkness taking hold.

'Ny agas Dyn Ergh', a notice says; and underneath, the Celtic is translated: 'Welcome to Truro Cathedral'.

Just inside the entrance she falters. Yet it is her very reluctance which impels her to go in. Face her phobia.

It is always the same: the apocryphal, sinister atmosphere wrapping round her like a carapace. It is as though her own death is rearing before her, mocking at her atheism and the residue of guilt, the sense of blasphemy she still feels and which occasionally induces her to pray; in case. Her mother so peaceful as she died.

'Hannah go. Hannah go.' The child beginning to sob loudly, raising her arms to be picked up. The sobs becoming wails that rebound off the stone and are hurled from wall to wall, ricocheting in piercing shock waves across the vaulted ceiling.

Fumbles for two pound coins in her wallet as a donation. Grabs Hannah, grabs the buggy.

The glorious fresh air. Fresh drizzle on their faces, and the moist leaves of the trees in the square.

The child is tranquil again.

'Poor Hannah. Poor little *cara*. Were you scared?'

And one day will it befall Isabella to tell her about God? . . . Well, this being may or may not exist. Some people believe . . .

When she was a girl religion was a fact, as much a part of her life as the restaurant and the rows. The computer age, but a decade away, was a mere hint, like the wash on watercolour paper before the tint is applied. PC meant police constable, and he usually rode about on a bike. Women did not sue for sexual harassment. *Madre*, what does she know about bringing up a child in today's world? Where are the guidelines for her?

I'll be honest with her. The main thing is to be honest.

Honest? How can she be honest when she has acquired the child by deception in the first place?

*B*ruises *almost gone,* she writes in her report that evening. *Hannah has strung words together for the first time, and has expressed her needs. Her progress is staggering. Doesn't this prove that what I did was correct, if unorthodox? She called me 'Mummy'.*

Up springs the prosecutor in her head. *This woman does not know the meaning of honesty. She has been living a lie through the child, even going so far as to encourage the little girl to call her 'Mummy'. Ladies and gentlemen of the jury . . .*

Isabella extinguishes the prosecutor's malevolent flame; she plans the evening's work. And has a sudden image of Aidan, his big, bearded face grinning at her from beneath the baseball cap.

She is absurdly excited about seeing him tomorrow. In London it would not occur to her to go out with someone like him. Like him? She cannot know what he is *like*. But the owner of a tinpot garage in the middle of nowhere? Then she immediately chides herself for being superficial, too image-conscious, and for intellectual snobbery—all of which have no place in her life now. She wonders how old he is. Probably at least her age. And that will make a change. And now she worries that he might not be attracted to her at all, that he only asked her out of kindness, because she mentioned about the She-Wolves.

Isabella is like a teenager about to embark on a first date; tingling at the prospect of seeing Aidan. Tomorrow will be the eighth day, exactly a week since she abducted—I did not abduct her, she was sent to me—the child.

REMEMBERS: THE THIRD PLACE. They were both teachers; serious-minded, decent people with their own three children: one daughter at university, a shy, studious son a couple of years younger than herself and another, much younger daughter. They were a pleasant family, not affectionate or demonstrative—she cannot recall any of them kissing or hugging—but encouraging, open-minded and respectful of other opinions.

She was closest to the young daughter. Read to her. Played the guitar to her, which she had recently taken up. Plaited her long, mousy hair. I like you, the girl said, looking straight ahead of her. And Isabella can remember the glow within her that this gave her.

It was a contented six months. But the area was rough, and the father was beaten up one evening when he tried to prevent some youths from stealing his car. He died in hospital a week later.

This time they advertised her. She saw it in the local paper. Like she was a dog or cat: 'Isabella is an intelligent, attractive, well-adjusted girl of nearly sixteen . . .' Shopping for a family. She felt so humiliated seeing that advertisement. Perhaps more than anything it brought home to her her true situation. Impermanence. She was important to no one.

I matter. She covered a page of her Latin exercise book with it. And in French, another page: *Je suis importante*. And Italian: *Sono importante*.

Sophia is a small shrew of a girl with sleek olive skin. A ring through her left nostril emphasises her long razor nose, and is incongruous with her otherwise conventional dress. She has silky brown hair cut in a slanting bob. Isabella has never seen such silky hair, gleaming like glass.

It transpires that both her parents are Italian and that they have a restaurant in Fowey. Isabella extracts this information from her after several false starts.

'How funny. My parents had a restaurant too.'

The girl's eyes stray towards the television: a game show. Raucous laughter. 'Theirs is a fish-and-chip place,' she says.

'So do you speak Italian?' Isabella asks her, trying to draw her into further conversation.

'No. I was born here. The odd word, that's all.'

She tucks her hair behind one ear, and briefly meets Isabella's enquiring gaze with shy eyes that are like raisins.

But she is good with the child. With the child her shyness disappears and her expression becomes animated, her voice takes on a warmth. Hannah seems contented enough. Isabella hovers in the doorway.

'I'm not sure when I'll be back. It might be quite late.'

'It doesn't matter. We'll be fine, won't we, Hannah?' Sophia says, touching the top of the child's head.

Sharp-toothed jealousy nipping at Isabella. She wills Hannah to resist Sophia, to run towards her and cling, shrieking, to her legs.

She glances at her watch. Seven seventeen. She is two minutes late.

'I'd better be going.'

'Bye, then.'

'Yes, bye. Bye, *cara*.' Raising her voice to the child. Blowing a kiss and waving.

'By-ee' comes back to her, as the child glances up. The By-ee, the sweet little wave, buoy her. Smiling all the way along the corridor and downstairs to the crowded bar; and at Aidan, who is looking at her as she makes her way towards him. He dwarfs everyone else around him. She feels a fanning of pleasure within her.

'Hello,' he says.

'I'm sorry. Have you been waiting long?'

'Only a couple of minutes. But I think we should make a move.'

He is wearing a black suit and a white shirt whose top two buttons are undone. Dark hair springs up from his chest. She finds it hard not to keep looking at him; is unsure where to rest her eyes. For a woman whose calm confidence in all situations has often been commented upon, this is extraordinary, this sense of gaucheness with Aidan. She cannot remember ever having been so physically affected by any man. Perhaps Tom. But she had been an impressionable girl then.

He opens the car door for her with old-fashioned gallantry.

'It's beautiful,' she says, tucking her knees into the Aston.

'She was a wreck when I got her.' Easing his bulk in beside her.

He drives off slowly. Silence is a mist between them. Her need to speak pinches her throat. She is still not sure whether or not this is a 'date', and therefore how to act accordingly. Feels disadvantaged. Perhaps he is a man who doesn't like to talk when he drives.

'You look pretty.' Aidan turning briefly to her—his teeth white in the darkness of his beard.

'Thanks.'

Nobody has ever told her that before; only her father, when she was a child. But not as a woman. Attractive, yes. Striking. Unusual. Even handsome. Occasionally, beautiful. But pretty, never.

'I wasn't sure what to wear,' she confesses. And now it occurs to her that the black trouser-suit she settled on matches what he is wearing.

'So, how did you get on with Sophia, then?'

'She seems nice. Very quiet, like you said. She obviously loves kids.'

'She does. To tell the truth that's why she married Luke in the first place. It was no secret. She was pregnant.'

'So she's got a child?'

'It died. Cot death, it was.'

'*Madre*, how awful. Poor girl.'

'Yeah. And now she's stuck with Luke.'

'Perhaps she loves him.'

The mechanic manifests himself: crablike, sinister.

'Who knows? Anyway, what about the cottage, then? You taking it?'

'Yes. From Monday.'

This topic keeps them going for about five minutes.

'You'll need some help doing it. I could help you if you like.'

Which means he intends to see her again. She sits back.

'Where are we going?'

'Falmouth. A wine bar. We're booked at ten for an hour. I'm taking you for a meal first.'

'Oh. That's nice.' A surprise, for sure.

'I wasn't sure what kind of food you'd like.' Takes his eyes off the road for a second to look at her. 'You being so, well, smart.'

'I'm not. Really I'm not.'

They park on the Moor, in the centre. A few people stop to watch as Aidan manoeuvres the old car into a space. He attaches the security device over the steering wheel and they get out.

He guides her by the elbow across the street; the few seconds' contact ricochets through her. Cool night settling. Illuminated shops, pubs.

He has a long stride. Walks slightly apart from her now; a head-up-eyes-forward walk. She is starting to be more comfortable with him, with the way he takes charge. A man with entrenched values, she guesses, who could be stubborn. But fair.

They go down some steps. Between a sail-maker's and an antiquarian bookshop is tucked a restaurant guarded by a huge old ship's figure-head. Fishers, says the name painted on the white wall of the building.

'You looked as though you might like fish,' he says, pushing open the door.

'I do. I love it. I hardly eat any meat.'

The inside is decorated with marine artefacts, ship's instruments and shells; nets are slung across the ceiling.

'I really wasn't sure where to bring you.'

The thought he has put into the evening touches her.

A girl comes over and shows them to their table. Most of the others are already occupied. Theirs looks onto the harbour. The water blinking in black and silver crescents. Boat masts nudging each other. Momentarily she feels a surge of intense, pure happiness.

He is observing her. 'You have a very expressive face.'

'Do I?' She is taken aback. Can feel the heat rising in her neck. Bends her head to study the menu. She chooses charcoaled brill with a lemon sauce. Melon as a starter.

'I'm not very good on wines,' he says. 'I haven't a clue really. Do you want anything in particular?'

'House wine's fine.'

With Peter she would have wrested the wine list from his hands and taken charge.

'White, then? I know that much. White with fish.'

'That's fine.'

Though in fact she tends to have red with everything, even with fish.

'So, is it true, what folks are saying,' he asks her, when the waitress has taken their order and returned with a bottle of Sauvignon blanc, 'that you've run off?'

His eyes are so kind. They spill honesty.

'In a way.'

'Was he bad to you, then, your husband?'

'Aidan, I don't want to talk about it.' Which of course makes it sound like an affirmation.

'OK, then.'

'I didn't mean to be rude.'

'You weren't. And I wasn't meaning to be nosy. It's only I don't take out married women as a rule.'

And she has the same code. Does not go out with married men.

So now he will not want to see her again.

'But you're separated, so that's all right.'

They both take a few sips from their glasses.

'What about you?' she says.

'Divorced. I've got two lads, aged fifteen and twelve. We rub along fine now, the ex and myself. She's living with someone else. The lads seem to like him.'

The waitress appears, bearing Isabella's melon and his giant prawns. Vivaldi's *Four Seasons* playing softly in the background.

'You aren't jealous?' she asks, when they're alone once more. 'I mean, about the boys having another man about the house.'

'No, why should I be?' He sounds genuinely puzzled. 'Jealousy's so negative, isn't it? I'm still their dad. It's up to me to show them. Be there for them.' He snaps the leg of a prawn decisively.

So—that is the preliminaries dealt with.

He is so reasonable; speaks with reassuring common sense in his accent that makes her think of rich soil and fertile plains. Possibly he is rather too serious, too literal; she cannot imagine him cracking jokes or having the quick repartee of the men she has known. Tom, for instance.

'How did you start, with cars?'

'As a young lad motors fascinated me. I was forever tinkering when I should've been working. I did a couple of years at university, then I dropped out.'

'Where? What were you studying?' She can't help being glad at this piece of information.

'Exeter. Zoology. I've always liked animals and nature. I seriously thought about training as a vet. I wish I had, now. My father was head gamekeeper and forester on a big estate Bodmin way, so I grew up with wildlife all around me. Well, his boss collected classic and vintage cars, and I suppose you could say I became obsessed. So the die was cast, so to speak. Anyhow, when I was at Exeter I got hold of this old Austin Seven for next to nothing, then a Morris, and sold them both for a fat profit after I'd done them up. Somebody asked me to restore a 1940 Alfa Romeo—and that was it. I told the old man I was leaving university. He went ape.' Laughs at the recollection. His laugh is a slow, low grumble.

'So, anyway, now I've got the garage. It does OK. It's steady. It doesn't thrill me, but I'm my own boss. It pays the bills. And I've got time for other things.'

What other things? she wonders.

They have scarcely touched their food. The waitress peers over towards their table, at their plates, and flits past. She has a provocative walk, a microskirt, big, china-blue eyes, but his gaze does not stray.

'I'm sorry, I've been talking too much,' he says, cracking open prawn shells in quick succession and munching. 'These are ever so good. Almost sweet. Want to try one?'

She nods and he feeds her one with his fingers, smiling at her as she takes it between her lips. A desirous warmth rippling slowly up her inner thighs. And what is he feeling?

'Tell me about yourself. I've been banging on.'

'No you haven't.'

The next course arrives and they wait awkwardly while the girl sets their plates before them and lays fresh cutlery.

'Well?' he says.

His expression is interested, patient. He is not handsome—his face is too broad, his upper lip too thin, his grey eyes rather small and nondescript; but their directness is compelling. It is a good face, a face to trust. It occurs to her that she hasn't been in this situation for years. Her boyfriends have invariably been much younger and she has played a role: sometimes the femme fatale, sometimes the mother. Always in control. And in between the longer relationships have been the shorter flings. Since Tom there has been nobody with whom she has come close to falling in love. Never has she known what it is like to lean on a man or depend on him in any way, or reveal any vulnerability.

She prods at her food with her fork.

'My job, you mean?' she says.

'Well, it's a start.'

'I'm a translator and interpreter.' She takes a bite out of the fish. The brill is succulent, tangy-fresh.

'That's interesting. Now that's *really* interesting.' He leans forward across the table towards her, elbows resting either side of his plate. When he smiles she notices he has a dimple in his left cheek, just above the beginning of his beard. 'I knew you'd do something a bit different.'

'How? How did you know?' Tilting her chin; flirtatious for a moment.

'Everything. The way you dress. Your manner. It's just a way with you. So what do you have to do, in your work?'

She explains it to him, tells him about the book contract; the journals, the brochures and company reports, magazine features.

'It fits in well with your daughter, then, your job.'

'Yes.'

'What's her name? I'm sorry, I've forgotten her name.'

'Hannah.'

And for the last hour or so she has not thought of her once.

Reproaches herself. Would a real mother have done the same?

'Aidan, maybe I should check she's all right.'

'You do that, then, if you're worried.'

She makes the call on her mobile from the Ladies' in between the main course and the dessert.

Aidan's eyes are pinned on her as she makes her way back to the table, past other diners, several of whom glance up at her. She feels self-conscious under Aidan's gaze.

She takes her seat again, pushes her chair in, then back slightly. Their desserts are on the table: sorbet for her, toffee pudding for him.

'She's fine, apparently.'

He senses her despondency. 'Then that's all due credit to you.'

'What do you mean?'

'That she's fine. She obviously feels secure. You've made her feel secure. You should be glad.'

She had not thought of it like that. Eight days. And a half. And she has made the child feel secure. Isn't that an achievement?

'Thank you for saying that.'

'It's only the truth. So, what did you do today, you and Hannah?'

'We walked. It was wonderful. We found this beach about a mile away—'

'Tregurran beach?'

'Yes, that was it. It was empty. It was wonderful. We ran . . .'

He watches her intently as she speaks: her every facial expression, how she uses her hands.

He asks for the bill. He will not hear of her contributing.

'Not now or ever,' he says firmly.

He clearly regards a woman paying for a man as demeaning. Yet she does not have the impression he is chauvinistic. He seems to like and respect women. On balance she decides she doesn't mind.

The wine bar—Matisse, it is called—is in Church Street, in a basement beneath a tailor's. The place is decorated with Fauvist prints. It is seething, much the same as anywhere in London. She asks if he gets nervous performing.

'I will be in front of you.'

'Of me?'

'Yeah. It's far worse performing in front of someone you know. And worse still when you fancy them rotten and want to impress them.'

The remark coincides with the appearance of the other two members of the group, a bass guitarist and a drummer, both younger than himself.

He finds a stool for her in a shadowy corner near the front. She feels conspicuous. The group leader's woman. That's how it must appear. How funny. Herself *here*. And what was originally in her diary for this evening? Was tonight the opera? She doubts he has ever been to the opera. Does he ever got to art galleries? Does he ever read the arts pages of the Sunday papers? Does he *read* the Sunday papers? *Madre*, do these things matter?

He handles the guitar competently, even sensitively; his voice is lyrical and easy to listen to. She relaxes, relieved. And she sits up proudly, wanting to be noticed. Aidan's woman.

At half time he comes over to her with a glass of beer in one hand and in the other a glass of red wine for her. Crouches by her stool.

'Thank you.' She takes the glass from him. 'You were all very good. I really enjoyed it. You've got a lovely voice.'

'That's the seal of approval, then.'

He brushes the flat of his hand across his glistening forehead.

Does his beard make him hot? What would he look like without it? She would like to comb her fingers through its denseness.

The last song of the evening is Clapton's 'Wonderful Tonight'. It is a slow number, and most of those who were not already dancing now get up. Soldered together, they sway and grind. She feels like a voyeur.

'"It's late in the evening, she's wondering what to wear",' sings Aidan. '"She puts on her make-up and brushes her long red hair".'

And he catches her eye. Did anyone notice he had exchanged 'blonde hair' for 'red'?

They finish at just gone eleven. Pack up. They say their goodbyes. Friendly but detached.

In the car he explains to her, 'We've got nothing in common, apart from the band. It's a business deal, that's all.'

Her right hand rests on the edge of the seat, near the handbrake, his on the bulb of the gearlever. A couple of inches from each other. She is acutely conscious of his.

'Well, this has been a bit different from your usual nights out, I expect.'

'What do you mean?'

'Don't you usually go to fancy sorts of places?'

'Sometimes. More often not. I go to all kinds of places.'

'But London,' he persists. 'If you're from London . . .' Shrugs and leaves the sentence trailing.

'Why are people who don't know it so afraid of London? You only take in bits at a time.'

'So will you miss it? London?'

She thinks of all the things she used to do. Sometimes every night of the week was accounted for.

'It's rather soon to tell. But I don't think so. We go through phases, don't we? That phase is past now.'

'I seem to have been doing the same things for years,' he says. 'I'm probably a bit of a stick-in-the-mud.'

'What do you like to do?'

'Well, there's the band, of course. And my lads. And walking. I love going for long walks, spotting wildlife. Then there's the cars. And reading. I do like to read. And music. All kinds of music. I like—you know—quiet things. My house took nearly three years to do up. It's still got no curtains and bits and pieces. I'm not very good with that sort of stuff. Women are better at that. Would you like to see it?'

Come and see my etchings.

'I'd love to. But Sophia will be waiting.'

'Five minutes. It'll only take five minutes.'

He turns down an unmarked lane about a mile from Zerion. She worries that his home will be in atrocious taste and she will be put off him. Does not like this trait in herself.

It is a converted stable block, fenced off in its own garden from the main house to which it once belonged.

Inside the timbers and rafters have been sandblasted and left exposed. The floor downstairs is flagstoned throughout. The kitchen and living room are open-plan.

'It's wonderful.' Ignoring the maroon sofa and armchair, which is on teak rockers.

He looks like a pleased boy.

'You did everything yourself?'

'I enjoyed it. And it took my mind off things. You know. The divorce.'

'Yes. It must've been a difficult time.'

There is a slightly protracted pause. She wonders why he got divorced. Wishes Sophia weren't back at the inn, waiting.

'So, now you've seen this place, do you trust me to help you with the cottage?'

'It doesn't seem fair.'

'I'd like to. I'd enjoy it.'

'Done, then.'

'Well, I suppose the five minutes is up, Cinderella.' Regret in his tone.

'I suppose it is.' And in hers.

'I don't want to push myself at you,' he blurts out. 'I mean, maybe you don't want my help with the cottage. It was rather presumptuous.'

She smiles. 'You said that before. About being presumptuous.'

'Did I?' He takes a small step closer to her. 'When?'

'When you asked me out. Well, not out. When you asked me—you remember—on Thursday, to hear you play.'

'Yes, out. I was asking you out. And it did seem presumptuous, with a sophisticated woman like yourself.'

'I'm not sophisticated.'

'Come on, of course you are.'

'Not deep down.'

He seems about to take another step towards her, then to decide not to. The air crackles between them.

'I really like you,' he says with quiet intensity. 'But I don't want to do anything out of place, that's all. You've obviously been through a lot.'

'Please don't worry.'

'If ever you need anyone to talk to, I'm a good listener.'

And now he does move towards her, enfolding her very gently in his arms; just holds her there—she feels small and protected—before his face bears down on hers. He lays his lips almost chastely against hers, then he presses and parts them, again with that same gentleness, and his tongue seeks hers. His beard is soft against her nose and cheeks, not coarse as she'd imagined. He clasps her chin in one hand and with the other lightly traces round her eyelids. She closes her eyes with pleasure.

'Such beautiful hair.' He caresses the crown of her head. 'The colour of a red squirrel.'

He pulls away from her. 'I must take you back.'

'All right.'

But it is not. Her body is desperate for him. Every nerve ending alight.

Outside the door of the inn he says, 'I hope—before—that you didn't think I was being—'

'Presumptuous?' she finishes for him.

His teeth flashing under the streetlamp.

'Well, you might've thought I was rather . . . fast.'

Fast. How that takes her back. She hasn't heard the word in that context since she was a girl. Fast? How little he knows about her. *How* little. Oh, *madre*, she can never get involved. Not with him or anyone else. That is her penance.

'You look sad.'

'I'm not. I'm fine. It was a wonderful evening. Thank you.'

'It was for me too. So, see you Monday, at the cottage. I can easily put in a couple of hours after I've finished at the garage.'

'That's terrific.'

He kisses her good night. She hears the throb of the car's engine after it is out of sight.

Sophia is asleep on her bed. The child asleep in hers, sucking her thumb, the knitted rabbit and new bear lodged under her chin. The nightlight lends a soothing glow to the room. Garibaldi runs towards her with one of his little chirrups, and she picks him up. She touches Sophia's shoulder, and the girl wakes instantly.

'Oh, hello . . . I hope you didn't mind.' Sitting up.

'I'm sorry if I'm late.' Speaking softly so as not to waken Hannah.

'No, it doesn't matter,' Sophia says on a yawn, getting up. 'She was so good. No trouble at all.'

'That's great. How would you feel about coming again?'

'I'd like to.'

'I'm moving to Pengarris. Would you be able to help me there also?'

'Yes.'

'What about transport?'

'I've got a Mini.' Pride in her tone.

Isabella pays her. Takes her phone number.

'*Ciao*, then, Sophia.'

'Oh, I know *that* word.'

For a moment her pinched little face is almost attractive.

'*Ciao*, then,' she says back. Looks quite perky as she leaves the room. Bonded by a casual word in Italian.

Isabella does not wash or clean her teeth. She smells and tastes Aidan. Lies between the nylon sheets and relives the evening.

Madre, what now? Where do we go from now, Isabella, cara?

MONDAY. THE TENTH DAY. And her London answering machine bears down on her with her other life. Her French language student is past the infectious stage and is ready to recommence his coaching. *Why haven't you got back to me?* demand several acquaintances and also her accountant. *I'm afraid we shall have to charge you for your missed appointment,* says the dentist's receptionist. A stream of calls needing a response; there is satisfaction in ignoring them. But the mail: she can visualise it, like a slag heap by the front door; pamphlets sticking through the letterbox, alerting the world to her absence. She will have to go to London soon. Dreads it. At least she has an address now to where the mail can be redirected: 4, The Rise.

And on this tenth day summer is back: a brilliant yellow, insect-strumming day. The sand glints where the tide is out. The light dazzles their eyes and heat seeps into their pores. The sea inhales in hisses then exhales in sighs, drawing back then building up into a ledge that curls slowly forwards before breaking.

'This is unbelievable,' Babs Carrick says, lying back. 'Who'd have thought?' Squeezing her eyes against the brightness.

They are picnicking on the lower slope of the eastern headland. The child pulls up daisies and places them singly into her plastic bucket. Humming. This is the latest development, the humming.

'He was a sculptor and potter,' Babs says of her husband to Isabella beside her. 'We met when we were both in Ontario. I was staying in a friend's log cabin for the summer vacation. He was camping. He was fifteen years older than me. I quit university and returned to London with him. It was that simple. Thirteen years ago he wanted to come back to Cornwall, where he grew up, and we bought the shop. He fell ill four years after we'd moved.'

A sculptor and potter with multiple sclerosis. She did not try to prevent him. They discussed it together: the best method, the implications, her life afterwards, without him.

'I'd have helped him, if he'd wanted it.'

Isabella ponders such heartfelt and selfless love. She cannot conceive what it must be like—to possess it, then to lose it.

'And you? All this gossip about running away from a violent husband.'

She takes an apple from the plastic box and crunches into it. Its juice runs down her chin.

'It's not quite like that.'

'Will you go back to him?'

'There's nobody to go back *to*, Babs.'

Which could mean anything; could be taken literally, or not.

'I didn't mean to press you,' the other woman says. 'Look, if you ever *do* need anyone—'

'I know. Thank you.'

Aidan had said virtually the same.

'Do you know Aidan—?' Breaks off, realising she doesn't know his surname. 'He's got the garage in Zerion.'

'Aidan Argall. Sure. Everyone knows him. He's a nice guy.'

'He's going to help me with the cottage.'

Babs sits up and narrows her eyes shrewdly. 'Good. You can trust him. He's his own man. I wouldn't think he shocks too easy.'

She feels a glow at Babs's words, this endorsement of his character. And in just a few hours' time she will be seeing him.

Babs points out the fishing boats beyond the narrows. 'One of them will be old Charlie. He's your next-door neighbour. You can always tell Charlie from the other men as they pass on their way down the lane to the cove at six in the morning. You can hear him dragging his gammy leg. His twin died at sea five years ago.'

'How dreadful.'

'Charlie married his sister-in-law, Joyce, a couple of years later. That set the old tongues wagging, I can tell you. They're like young newly-weds. It's real funny. Did you know a television documentary's being made here soon?'

'No.'

How long is it since her attention has strayed from the child? Seconds? Minutes? But suddenly where Hannah was there is only the toy bucket on its side.

'Hannah—she's gone.'

Panic sweeping through her. For a few seconds she is rendered utterly useless; can only stare at where the child was a moment ago.

'She can't have gone far,' Babs says. 'We'll look in different directions.'

Her calm penetrates Isabella's immobility. She calls the child's name. Clambers up the headland, round a bend, calling, frantically calling. Another bend. She hears the humming first.

The child, on her hands and knees. Her angel's smile.

'Rabbit,' she exclaims, pointing.

'Oh, *madre.*' Relief flooding her. '*Carina* . . .'

She falls to her knees beside the child, and clasps her to her. Then she holds her away at arm's length. 'You mustn't run off. It's naughty. You understand, Hannah?'

It could be the reproval in her voice, or it could be that a key phrase has triggered some memory, but the child becomes corpse-stiff. Her face becomes red and she struggles to free herself. She lashes out, bellowing, raining blows against Isabella with her fists. Isabella is shocked. Has never seen her like this.

'Rabbit. *Rabbit* . . . Hannah *go.*'

The shrieking magnifies, ripping across the headland, so that the entire village must hear.

Isabella is bone-pale. 'Please, *carina*, please.'

She is too drained to deal with this attack. She clings on to the child as she beats Isabella's shins with her sandalled feet. Finally the hysteria wears itself out. The child burrows her drenched face in the crook of Isabella's arm.

'Mummy. Mummy,' she whimpers.

Isabella is too enervated to move. Hangs on to her for all she is worth. Afraid that the growing bond between them has been damaged.

'Isabella, you mustn't feel bad,' says Babs as they walk back to the shop. In her buggy the child gives small judders as she sleeps.

'I took my eyes off her. Anything could have happened.'

'But it didn't. It wouldn't have in those few seconds. God, my kids were always in scrapes. It's a miracle they survived. Sometimes I completely forgot about them. Why don't you put Hannah into playgroup?' Babs says. 'It might be good for her. There's one near Zerion. I'll dig out the number.'

They part outside the shop. Isabella thanks her.

She pushes the child in the buggy slowly up the hill, past secret windows and sleeping cats. Failure straddles her. She stops outside Timothy Abell's front door.

'WELCOME,' Janet Abell has written on a sheet of paper which she has anchored under the door knocker.

The note jolts everything into perspective and causes an instantaneous reversal of mood. What is there, after all, to be dejected about? The child is safe, and that is what matters.

'There's this legend,' Aidan says, rollering white over the anaglypta in the sitting room, 'claims a giant used to inhabit these parts. If he didn't eat a child a day he would become ill. Then one day he got ill anyway, and one of the little girls he'd kidnapped to eat tended him until he recovered. But he'd grown to love this little girl and knew he could never eat a child again. So he went off to die. He dived from this headland into the stormy sea and was changed into a rock. The boulder on its own a little way out—that's supposed to be him.'

'I've never known a place with so many legends.' Isabella, painting the door. Beside her, the child daubing with her own brush.

'But he was rather noble, I reckon, don't you?'

He lays down the roller carefully in the foil tray, comes over to her and kisses her with the child between them.

'Mummy and man,' Hannah says.

'If you knew how I've been thinking about you,' he says against her

399

lips. 'I've been—' Shakes his head and releases her slowly. 'It's not right in front of your daughter.'

'You didn't seem particularly glad to see me.' Teasing him. In fact she had anticipated how he would be and was unsurprised when he greeted her as he might a casual acquaintance.

She sits down on the dusty floor and he joins her.

'I felt awkward. I didn't know what you might be feeling. For all I knew you could've regretted . . . everything. And then I thought, why should a stylish woman like her . . . I mean, I'm out of your league.'

'I wish you'd stop thinking that.'

'I will, then.' Slapping his own cheek lightly; grinning at her.

'Something awful happened this morning.'

She relates the incident. He listens attentively.

'She's just strong-willed like her mum.'

She stares at him. He takes her hand and massages the knuckles.

'I like your hands.'

'They're ugly—big and square.'

'Rubbish. They look capable. Practical.'

He becomes serious again. 'Look, it's hard being alone with your child,' he says, reverting to their earlier conversation. 'Worrying all by yourself. I understand that. I'll mend the fence for you. Make it safe for her. That'll be one less worry.'

He is so kind. She has never met anyone like him.

'I've never met anyone like you,' he says.

She smiles.

'What are you smiling about?'

'No, nothing . . . Just, thank you so much for everything.'

'Don't be daft.'

'I'm not . . . Aidan—'

'Yeah?'

'Listen—there are things . . . I don't want you to think I've misled you.'

'Look, I've told you, I'm not about to drag confidences from you that you're not ready for. Maybe one day, when we know each other better, you'll feel you can tell me.'

She loves the soft modulations of his voice; the round, sleepy vowels. And now he is looking at her with his steady, unmasked gaze. Her body is going mad with its need for him.

'I haven't stopped thinking about you,' she says.

'I could come and help you Wednesday evening, if you like. You could come back to me after. Both of you. I could fix a meal.' He raises his eyebrows quizzically. 'I'm busy tomorrow night,' he adds.

So will Wednesday be The Night? And what is he doing tomorrow?

He furnishes her with the information. 'I'm going to Bath to look at an MGA. I'll be back late.'

He is without guile or games. He offers up his no-secrets life on an unadorned platter. One day he will be so disappointed in her.

'To work,' he says, hauling her up from the floor.

And for the next hour, as they transform the room, they scarcely exchange a word. But there is companionship in their silence and in their working together. And every so often the glance of one will meet the other's and become a protracted communion. While beyond the open window, against a red, dipping sun, the gulls return at leisure to their outposts. And indoors, the child chants in her funny, tuneless voice: 'Mummy-man, Mummy-man, Mumm-ee.'

Please let it continue.

Tuesday, September 10. And who could have imagined, a fortnight ago, that this particular morning would find her delivering a child to a play-group in Polhearn Community Centre, in Cornwall? 'Bring her tomorrow,' Margaret the playgroup leader had said on the phone.

'Well, good morning, Hannah,' she welcomes both of them as they enter hesitantly, and stoops to grin into the child's face like an ugly gargoyle. Hannah stares warily back at her. Her hand tightens in Isabella's.

'Hannah go. I go.'

'It's all right, *cara* . . . She's shy, I'm afraid.'

'They all are in the beginning. Now just look at them.' Margaret gesticulates towards the children filling the room, at small girls and boys forming into groups or running to the two helpers.

'You're welcome to stay here until she settles.'

They stand pressed close together, outsiders; both observing: the one the children, the other the mothers. And from the surreptitious glances in her direction, Isabella guesses she is known to several of them. What rumours have been circulating? Adheres a smile to her lips. And meanwhile the child's expression is one of puzzlement.

'Come on, everyone,' calls Margaret, clapping her hands. 'Get ready for our singsong.'

She organises everyone into a wide circle.

On Hannah's other side is a small girl who announces herself as Becky. She takes Hannah's hand firmly and swings it up and down a few times. She is as talkative as Hannah is taciturn.

'A-one, a-two, a-three,' cries Margaret. 'Ring a ring of roses . . .' They all join in.

Afterwards the children are paired. Becky has commandeered Hannah. It is extraordinary for Isabella to witness her opening out, copying the other child, becoming bolder by the second.

'No, not in there,' Becky is saying adamantly as Hannah places a plastic farm horse in a pigsty. She points to the stable. 'Horses go in stables.'

'In there?' asks Hannah, moving the horse.

When she leaves on her own she feels oddly redundant. Oddly sad. No longer needed. She drives off in the direction of Pengarris. Suddenly she can clearly remember her own nursery school: the piano by the window, with curly candlesticks attached to brackets. The teachers seemed inaccessibly old. They were all nuns. One of them, with the pink-rimmed eyes of an albino rabbit, had an amputated finger. She played the piano in prayers. Isabella remembers the crunching discords as they sang 'All Things Bright And Beautiful'. Afterwards they painted, wearing blue overalls, and made potato men, and learned the alphabet. Twenty assorted kids kept in strict disciplinary order.

And then it is several schools later. Isabella is in her teens, and loutish boys with cracking yodellers' voices take bets as to the size of her breasts and who will be the first to touch them. Jealous girls. Always alone. Always observing. Thinking, thinking.

I matter.

Half a mile or so from Zerion there comes a grinding-metal sound as she applies her brakes down the hill. Determinedly she carries on through the village and towards Pengarris.

The sun is a glaring spotlight through the archways of branches. And the grating noise becomes constant. When she goes to apply the brakes on a descent her foot seems to be pumping nothing.

Her hands are clammy on the steering wheel. She changes into first gear—there is a protesting whine from the engine—and applies the handbrake, and in this lip-biting way makes it to the bottom of the hill. There she pulls over, half on the verge, half in the lane. She ponders what to do: she could call the AA on her mobile, walk either to Pengarris or back to Zerion for help, or risk driving to Aidan's garage. She settles on this course and turns the car round. Prays there won't be any oncoming vehicles where she will have to stop on an incline. Slowly, the MG clunks its way along the lanes. She draws up outside the forecourt and climbs out.

From behind the half-pulled doors she can hear revving, and peers inside. A figure with a torch is bending over the open bonnet of a Ford Escort. She knows it is Luke, and she experiences that same unaccountable apprehension again. She approaches him purposefully.

'Hello,' she shouts over the bent back in the navy overalls.

He straightens slowly and turns round. He says nothing. His eyes are pale in the grime of his face.

'My car brakes have packed up.' Keeps her voice brisk. 'I think it's the discs.'

He rubs his hands down the flanks of his overalls—his arms are extraordinarily long and simian—and still with no word, walks over to her car, with his curious gait.

'Key,' he states, when he sees it is not in the ignition. His teeth are like a rabbit's the way they protrude over his lower lip. She gives him the key and stands aside; and he brushes past her—apparently deliberately—climbs into her car and starts it up. He depresses the brake pedal a few times before driving into the garage and onto a ramp.

She has followed him inside, and now suppresses mingled anger and nervousness, watching as he unscrews and removes the front wheels. His ears are very small, she notices, pinned to the bullet of his close-cropped head. She can sense a latent violence in the set of his neck.

'I'm sorry Sophia was so late the other evening,' she says, in an attempt to break the tension.

He grunts and goes into the office where she can see him making a phone call. Can hear the mumble of his voice but not what he is saying. Fury brews within her. She is angry for allowing herself to be intimidated by him.

He reappears.

'Do you always dump your customers to make a phone call?'

'I've just phoned for the parts.'

'Oh.' And now she feels stupid. 'So when—?'

'This afternoon.'

And he turns his back on her. Starts working on the Escort again.

Her contract for the book has arrived, and back in her room she starts to read through it.

Lizzie from the pub gives her a lift to the playgroup to fetch the child.

'So, what's this I hear about you going out with Aidan?'

'I—' She is stunned by the forthrightness of the question. Lizzie goes out of her way to be friendly to her but is, she knows, suspicious of her: this London woman come to ensnare the local men.

She resists a sharp retort. 'He's helping me with the cottage, that's all.'

Hannah and her new friend are waiting, dangling soggy paintings.

'She was good as gold,' Margaret says.

'Diff'n' car,' the child observes when Isabella lifts her into the back of the Volvo.

'By the way,' says Lizzie, as she drives, 'you had a letter. Did you see it? I put it in your room. Something formal and brown. It looked like it might be a legal document.'

'Yes. It was a book contract from my agent. Thank you.'

'Oh.'

From that 'oh' it is obvious to Isabella she had assumed it to be connected with her 'divorce', and had been anticipating a meaty discussion which she could relay.

At the garage that afternoon, she writes out a cheque. Can feel the mechanic's breath on her neck.

She stands up and edges towards the glass door of the office.

'The suspension's next,' she says, still trying.

He ignores her as though she has not spoken.

She assists the child into the car. Is strapping her in when the mechanic mutters something that stops her in her tracks. She is mistaken; surely she is mistaken. Her face is burning as she climbs into the driver's seat. She is conscious of his eyes following her every move.

She had thought he said, I want to fuck you.

MY *INTERESTS/HOBBIES*: wrote Isabella when she was sixteen and a half and living with a childless couple in their early sixties, a retired physicist and his botanist wife. *Animals, all types of music, dancing, the guitar and singing with it, cinema, current affairs, swimming, going to exhibitions, reading, fashion.* She wore skimpy tops and tiny skirts. Bum-grazers they were known as at school.

My favourite book ever: Le Petit Prince.

Worst book: Jane Eyre.

Best person: She wavered here, trying to think of a single person who really meant something to her. Anyone. Left a blank.

Worst person: Now she had no hesitation. Wrote down the name of the sighing social worker who made her feel like a no-hoper.

Likes: Her likes were what nourished her. They prickled her flesh, sweetened the air for her, imbued her with hope. *I like the sun on my neck—it makes me warm yet shivery. Eating sandwiches on park benches. The noise of pouring tea and its orange trickle from the spout. Hills. Red-brown newly turned soil. Pavement art. Sand. Platform-heeled shoes. Street markets. Richard Burton's voice, Steve McQueen's entirety! Being barefoot. My newly pierced ears . . .*

Her list of 'likes' covers a whole page and could go on further. It surprises her. She had not thought there were so many things.

Dislikes: Getting up in the morning. Grey sky. School. Foster homes. Narrow-mindedness. Meanness. Snobbery. Prejudice. Crocodiles. Cruelty. Purple and maroon—they make me think of dying.

My appearance—best points: For this she had to inspect herself in the mirror screwed to the door of her room. It elongated her slightly, she knew that, as she always looked fatter in shops. She had asked the woman for the mirror—hesitant to make this request.

'I can't see how things look on me,' she explained.

'But of course, my dear, you have to tell us what you need.'

Both she and her husband were completely out of touch with young people and with today's world, with anything that was light-hearted or scandalous. But they tried so hard. The botanist would make clumsy attempts at affection; but these self-conscious demonstrations from an elderly woman with dingy skin, a centre parting and short socks and brogues filled her with repugnance. Nevertheless she was grateful for their efforts and for the two years of stability provided by this, her last port of call. And there were things she learned from them. Knowledge was everything; and hers was continually expanding.

I like my hair, she wrote. *My eyes. Eyebrows—they're dark, whereas you'd expect them to be the same as my hair. My skin's OK. It's rather fair and goes red easily, but I've not got freckles. I like my breasts and shoulders and being tall.*

Worst points: I don't like my nose—it's sort of craggy. And my chin's too big. My face is too large—a bit blobby. My bottom and thighs and hips are too big.

My aims/ambitions: To go to university. Travel. I never want children. I like animals better. I'll have a cat. And I'll live in my own flat or house with lots of plants and beautiful things. People won't laugh at me or leave me out. I'll wear lovely clothes and have a sports car. I won't ever rely on anyone else. I'll make it all happen.

There is an air of tension this evening between Isabella and Aidan, but it is of a very different kind from two days ago. This evening it is the almost unbearable tension of expectation.

'I got the car,' he says in the kitchen—he seems to occupy the entire area, even on bent knees as he fixes the cat flap.

'Is for Grabla,' says the watching child, whose speech in the last couple of days has put on a spurt that astounds and excites Isabella.

'She's really not in bad nick,' Aidan says. 'She'll be lovely done up. She's that traditional cherry red. And the leather upholstery's very fair. I could sell her on easily.'

She smiles at his enthusiasm. 'It,' she corrects him, stopping in her painting of the kitchen shelves to inspect them. 'A car should be "it".'

'Well, that's as maybe. But I think originally the usage would have come about because of ships. Seamen cherished their ships like a woman.'

'More, probably,' she says cynically.

He pauses then, in his fitting of the plastic flap into its frame. 'I cherished my wife,' he says reflectively. 'I've always thought it important a man does things like that. She didn't want it.'

She turns to look at him—he is stretching one leg from its cramped position and jigging it about; their eyes meet and hold.

'Sometimes you get this expression,' he says. 'It completely belies how you come across. It's so vulnerable, so soft and dark and warm and sad, it'd melt an iron foundry. I had this fox cub when I was a lad. Ever such a spiky little creature it was, but it loved its tummy being rubbed and it'd get an expression in its eyes just like yours.'

'For the record, I love having my tummy rubbed.'

'For the record, I love doing it. All over, in fact.'

He stands up—his head almost brushes the ceiling—and she goes over to him and kisses him. He parts her lips and for a second his tongue coils round hers; he touches her breasts through her T-shirt—then stands back. 'This won't do. We're supposed to be working. And your daughter—I'm funny like that.'

'You're funny about lots of things . . . I haven't told you about my car,' she says, when he is about to cut in. She recounts yesterday's incident.

'I'll get it completely overhauled for you. It'll take a couple of days, but we'll do everything. The suspension. The lot.'

'That sounds expensive.'

'No. I'll only charge you for parts at cost. No labour charges. I hate to think of your driving something unroadworthy.'

Emotion swells within her. She rubs at a white paint stain on the inside of her wrist.

'You're so kind to me.' She finds his kindness one of the most seductive things about him. She has the sense of taking refuge.

'Maybe I've a vested interest,' he says.

But she is afraid of Luke doing the work on her car. Imagines him tampering with the engine.

'Would you be doing it, or would Luke?'

'I don't know.'

When she makes no comment he raises his eyebrows enquiringly.

'Is there a problem?'

'Not really. I just . . . He gives me the creeps. The way he just stares and says nothing. It's . . . unnerving.'

'You don't have to have anything to do with him.'

'I know, but I want to use Sophia sometimes. And I'll need to phone her to arrange it.'

'Look, he's harmless, I'm sure. It's just his way. He's shy, more'n like. You probably terrify the wits out of him.'

'All right.'

'I mean, someone like you, well . . . Listen, put him out of your mind. As for your car, I'll see to it myself.'

'*Madre*—Hannah, no!'

The child has the paint tin poised at her lips, about to drink from it. Her face crumples in readiness as Isabella rushes over.

She plucks Hannah up and cuddles her before she has the chance to start screaming.

'The paint will give you a pain in your tummy, *carina*.'

'Hannah bad?'

The small face scrutinising her own; tears standing out in her eyes.

'No, *cara*. You're very good. But the paint will hurt your tummy.'

The child's features settling once more.

'Paint hurts tummy,' Hannah states, nodding wisely; and slithers down, patting her little belly protruding in dungarees.

'She's bright,' Aidan remarks.

She is inwardly jubilant: *that* is how to tackle the problem of reprimanding her. Now that she knows the child has a reasonable level of comprehension, she only has to explain to her.

'You're good with her. Patient . . . I want to make love to you,' he says softly.

She goes up to him and rubs her face against his arm. The child runs over also; and here they are in Timothy Abell's kitchen, which smells of paint, the three of them, enfolded together. The moment is so utterly beautiful in its sweetness that she can hardly breathe.

Beyond the window the tide is high. A few boats are still out. She recognises the red hull of Charlie's, the furthest away. She met him and his wife for the first time yesterday evening. They were blatantly besotted with one another—this sprightly woman with her silver perm, and the grizzle-haired, lame man with his salt-worn skin and dreamer's blue eyes. He explained about the tides to her, in his verbose way, how they were related to the gravitational pull of the moon. Joyce poured out elderflower wine into the best glasses.

'He knows so many things, Charlie does,' she said, passing cheese-flavoured biscuits on a green plate patterned with pink roses.

Seeing them together, Isabella wondered if they had always been in love; if Charlie had been jealous of his brother beforehand and Joyce had felt she had married the wrong brother.

Aidan can cook. Really cook. He eschews a garlic crusher for a sharp knife and proceeds expertly to chop then crush the clove together with salt with the flat of the blade. Brushes the chicken quarters with virgin olive oil before rubbing in the garlic mixture and then squeezing fresh lemon on top. He is efficient, graceful as he works. *The Archers* is playing on the radio, and so they don't talk.

It is a scene of such total and unusual domesticity that she cannot keep the smile from flickering on her lips.

He puts the chicken under the grill. *The Archers* comes to an end, and the familiar signature tune is severed as he switches off the radio.

'Sorry about that. I'm addicted.'

'You and several million others,' she says.

He is a good animal artist. Coyly he shows her ink drawings and pastels of dogs and horses he has done, and of a badger from a photograph he took at night by flashlight.

'You're so lucky. I wish I could paint. Landscapes. The sky.'

'Have you tried drawing or painting?'

'Not since school. Anyway, I was hopeless.'

However, she would like to write. But whenever she writes more than a few hundred words it seems that she is delving too far into her own psyche.

He catches the pursued look in her eyes. 'Isabella? What's wrong?'

The past is what is wrong. In leaving London and the accoutrements of her self-styled success, she has left behind the identity she created for herself. She is having to confront herself anew.

'I'm going to check Hannah,' she says, dodging his arm, his concerned, honest eyes.

The door to the spare room is ajar to allow the landing light to filter through. The child is asleep in a sausage-hump beneath the duvet.

He appears in the doorway, blocking out the light.

'Is she OK?'

'Fine.'

'And you? I thought . . . I thought you might have gone off me.'

He holds out one arm towards her then, motioning to her. She gets up and goes to him, into the enclave he has made for her.

'I've turned off the grill,' he whispers.

'Oh? And why would that be?'

'I don't want to do . . . to be—'

'Presumptuous?'

She feels his arms relax, the gentle laughter vibrating through his body. 'I'd rather like you to be. If *you* would.'

He gazes at her thoughtfully for a few seconds then leads her across the short gallery of the landing to a closed door. Opens it. His expression is faintly self-conscious as he closes it once more behind them. The room is fairly large; white-walled and with a brown, worn carpet. Brown and blue open-weave curtains droop from the window, and the only furniture, apart from the bed, is an ugly oak wardrobe and a modern pine chest of drawers. The bed has a garish purple and yellow duvet cover over it and matching pillowcases.

'I'm not much of a one for interior design,' he says, apparently seeing the room for the first time, as though through her eyes.

'Not many men are,' she consoles him. 'It's perfectly all right.'

'It's not. It's all wrong. But I can't quite say why. I mean, before I had no reason to be fussed. The women I know—have known—well . . .' He leaves the sentence trailing.

She knows his nervousness is not only about the room.

'You're so stylish. Even in jeans and trainers you somehow manage to look it. And your accent. Well, the Queen's English and all that. I feel a right bumpkin.' He sounds quite anguished.

'Shush.' Slaps his thigh. He captures her hand. 'As for my accent—my mother was Scottish and my father was Italian.'

Was Italian? He is probably still alive. Maybe remarried.

'I cultivated my accent,' she says. Her eyes alight on the simple wooden cross above the bed. 'Are you religious?'

'I'm a committed Christian. Does that bother you?' His defensive tone. His hand slipping away from hers.

'No.' But, curiously, it does disturb her. She is so anti-religion herself.

'I'm not heavy with it. I just believe in trying to be a decent human being. Fair. I like to examine things from different perspectives.'

So here they are in his room, discussing style, accents and religion, and the scent is rapidly growing cold. They seem to be becoming snarled in knots, whereas a few minutes ago there was only a single thought in their minds. It is as though they cannot clamber back through the haze of misunderstanding to that point.

'Kiss me?' she says, tilting up her face.

'Oh God, Isabella.'

He stumbles towards her, and steadies her as she almost loses her balance, holding her upright again, his mouth fierce on hers. They don't speak. His large fingers manage to untuck her tight black T-shirt and hitch it over her head. He hesitates then, gazing at her in her black lacy bra and, impatient, she undoes it herself and lets it slip to the ground. She stands before him: broad-shouldered and slender-waisted. Her breasts are heavy but firm, quite widely spaced; the coral tinged nipples protrude from their pale aureolae like tiny stalks.

He bends his head and submerges his face between her breasts, then cups each one in turn, sucking at them, tugging gently with his teeth so that a succession of ripples shoots up between her legs. The sensation of his beard on her flesh further increases her pleasure. She bends her head backwards, arching her throat with a sudden spasm, then she pushes him away from her and they undress themselves hurriedly, almost tripping in their urgency.

He has a fine body, carrying more weight than she expected round the waist and stomach, but not flabby. The hair is thick on his chest, tapering to a badger-stripe over his belly. She runs her fingers over his body.

'No.' He sinks slowly to his knees, stroking and caressing her all the way down. He kisses her navel, lets his tongue travel over the sweep of her tummy, and stops just above her line of hair.

Her whole body is electric and keening.

She finds herself lifted up, and he lowers her slowly onto the bed. He massages her for some minutes, then enters her with a sudden lunge so that she cries out with surprise and pleasure. He is so deep, so swollen. She doesn't think she has ever known anything like this.

They lie curled towards each other, limbs round limbs. The aftermath of lovemaking. The hot, silent, nothing-moving room.

'It was amazing,' she says into his beard.

He tells her, 'I've never experienced anything like it.'

She nestles into him, catlike, and he traces her form with his fingertips—his hands are rough-textured, but coupled with his sensitive touch, the effect is sensuous.

The sweet sheen of contentment within her. And just at this moment something very akin to love.

She thinks of the child. 'I hope Hannah didn't hear anything.'

'The door's really thick,' he says. 'But go and check her if you like.'

She gets up slowly, reluctant to leave him. She can sense him watching her as she pads over to the door.

The child is fast asleep on her tummy, her face half turned. When Isabella touches the back of her head lightly she does not stir. Her breathing is the heavy, rhythmical breathing of tiredness and of satisfaction. This morning she went again to the playgroup. Becky hugged her hello. How important, friendship, Isabella muses. The wonderful thing about making love with Aidan was that it was making love with a friend. It occurs to her that, with the possible exception of Tom, she has usually been the dominant one in bed. With Aidan she wanted only to revel and bask in all the different sensations he aroused in her, and in the awareness of an intimacy and closeness that went beyond these.

She returns to him. He is getting dressed.

'I thought we should eat,' he says, coming up to her to kiss her.

It is night now. She goes over to the window, naked. There is a figure by the trees, lit by the moon. She ducks.

'Aidan, there's someone outside, by the trees.'

He comes over immediately and looks out.

'There's no one as I can see,' he says, after several seconds. 'I'll go down and check with the torch.'

He leaves her. Suddenly her sense of being safely cocooned is ruptured.

She pulls on her jeans and top—she doesn't bother with shoes—and goes downstairs. He is bent over the cooker, and she puts her arms round him. The smell of the chicken grilling, the sound of vegetables boiling, and Domingo—she is certain it is him—singing from *Tosca*.

'You like opera?'

'My mum was an opera fanatic. She was a music teacher. Yes, I like it.'

'Oh.' This makes her almost unreasonably happy.

'By the way, there was no sign of anyone. Maybe it was someone looking for the main house, came here by mistake.'

He dishes out the food. Huge portions on their plates. She lights a candle in an old beer bottle. They sit down opposite each other and raise their glasses in a toast.

And how will it change things, their having made love? Aidan is not a frivolous sort of man whose emotions can be toyed with. He has no veneer. Eventually he will expect her to offer some explanation for why she is here.

He says, 'I want you to know I'm not like some men who . . . well, let's face it, a lot of men will do it just for the sake of it. Look, I don't just go with any woman. It has to mean something. Tonight—it was over a year since I last went to bed with a woman.'

'You're kidding.' Herself barely a fortnight. She felt ashamed.

'I suppose I'm a romantic. An idealist.'

And she is afraid she will be the saboteur of this idealism.

It feels so right sitting across the table from him, in his lovely house with its appalling taste.

'Won't you tell me about your childhood? I know next to nothing,' he says. 'I want to know what's made you you.'

He instantly notices the panic, followed by the guarded clouding over, in her eyes, and seeks to reassure her.

'I'm not trying to drag things out of you. Just something. Your parents, for instance.'

She cuts up a piece of chicken, eats it, and lays down her knife and fork on the plate. Takes a long sip of red wine.

'My childhood,' she says, as though reciting the title of a book. And proceeds to tell him what she has told no man—not Tom, who said only the present mattered; no other lover, because every one of them was inconsequential. She misses out nothing . . . Her father has just entered her bedroom and she is woken by his hands; now he has gone for ever; her mother has died. And there she is: young girl free to good home . . .

Aidan's eyes spilling compassion. The total silence around them. The flickering candle.

She talks for two hours. He grips her left hand across the table, and sometimes his grip tightens at a particular revelation.

She stops speaking when she has reached the age of eighteen and is about to meet Tom.

'HOUSE,' SAYS THE CHILD.

They have settled into Timothy Abell's cottage, along with dozens of rodents that Garibaldi has, in the last fortnight, been rapidly decimating. They are everywhere: running down the tea towel, appearing from behind curtains, tucked in her Wellington—as she discovered when she slid her bare foot inside.

Every day she goes for a walk. On one walk she saw a red squirrel. Aidan had told her they were virtually extinct everywhere in Britain except Scotland. She stopped still, astonished and entranced. Aidan said it must have escaped from somewhere. In bed he calls her 'My squirrel'.

He has taught her to distinguish between the various gulls and she is learning to recognise them for herself. She still confuses the common gull and the kittiwake, but she can tell the difference between the others. She will sit high up at a particular vantage point near the lighthouse where every inlet, projection, every crevice in the rock face of the other promontory, can be clearly identified through Aidan's binoculars—a spare pair he had that he has lent her.

Over the last few days the wind has been strong, shrilling around the headlands, and the rain heavy on occasions, but she never fails to go for her walk, sometimes with the child, sometimes alone when she is at playgroup. Being fair-skinned she has never been partial to extreme heat, and the weather suits her complexion. The bracing air has coloured her cheeks. The salt and the wind have lightened her hair a shade and caused it to curl slightly. She has given up wearing any make-up; feels fitter, is leaner than she has been for years and has more energy. She is cautiously happy.

On a shorter walk they came across a hollow oak in a spinney. There was just sufficient room for the child to climb inside. Hannah's Tree, they have named it.

She marvels at the child's progress in just over a month. She is hardly recognisable. As for Isabella herself, she has entirely adjusted to her life here. Looks upon her previous incarnation, as she calls it, quite disparagingly. It was an existence she had pursued because it had been the one lodged in her mind since the age of sixteen. Here, with Aidan, with the child, it is as though all her senses have been awakened. It is perhaps the nearest she has come to being her real self; and she has yet to become acquainted with this woman.

Aidan has remarked on the change in her. He knows more about her than any man. He knows about her views and her values. Knows her sexually in the minutest detail. He knows her every gesture and expression. He also knows her not at all:

She loves the changes in the weather as autumn sets in. She loves the longer evenings and the wind's eerie whistling through the gaps round the windows. Loves the view at night of the staggered lights glittering from the village like a lit birthday cake (and in a few weeks she will be forty. *Forty*.).

And she has become used to watching the lighthouse's rhythmical signals—two long, three short—winking on-off, on-off, like irregular heartbeats through the bedroom window; used to the smell of a fresh catch on the beach; to hearing the front door of Charlie's cottage shut behind him as he limps off at ten to six in the morning, and his whistling dies away; to the cockerel's rousing proclamations. And later in the morning, Joyce will be pegging out her husband's dungarees on the washing line where they will flap in the breeze.

Everybody in the village knows or recognises her by sight, and generally their curiosity has abated. There have been offers of help, words of advice. She has been touched by people's kindness.

Charlie presented her with a squid and Joyce gave her a bouquet of dried heather for luck the day she moved in. They came for supper that evening; Aidan cooked the squid as she couldn't bear to touch it. Over dinner, as the evening wore on and one wine bottle was replaced by another, Charlie became more and more loquacious and began to ventilate his outrage about the commercial fishing industry, about European rights and about the government.

'I'll be telling all this to them television people,' he said. 'We don't want no politics brought into our livelihood.'

And under the table Aidan's foot sought hers, and his eyes shone secret smiles; and the child slept sprawled across her lap.

When she was walking on Tregurran beach with Hannah a few days ago a spaniel came bounding across to them and leapt up at the child, bowling her over so that she toppled backwards onto the sand.

A woman came running over. 'I'm so sorry, I'm most awfully sorry.' Yanking the spaniel off. 'He's just young.' She was attractive, in a manicured way, middle-aged; a surgeon's wife, she told Isabella.

'We're having a drinks do on Sunday morning,' she said. 'Do come.'

She has accepted, but she is wary. Recognises a type. Who does voluntary work and wears gold jewellery to walk the dog, has drinks do's. And lives in 'Rhododendron Drive'.

Also on Tregurran beach she met the woman on the cob. They were splashing about in the sea, the water up to the horse's hocks. She noticed Isabella and rode over. She was ruddy-faced; a tough complexion and gunmetal eyes; gunmetal hair in a long plait hanging beneath a headscarf. She introduced herself as Mary Anne Evans.

'As in George Eliot,' Isabella commented.

'Precisely.' The woman looked at her keenly. She was also a writer, she said. Of pornography.

'*Madre!*' Gives a burst of laughter. 'What fun. I suppose you must be used to people's reactions.'

'I am. Mostly the blustering kind.'

'Well, you did rather throw it into the conversation in a kind of "I bake cakes" voice.'

'Talking of which, please come round one afternoon for tea. I think I like you, which is rare.'

Then there is Aidan whom she has seen most days since she has been here. Last night they played the guitar and sang together. She sat curled at his feet, while the child lay on the rug, reaching up to twang at the strings and chuckling at the discords, joining in their singing in her odd, flat tone.

'I feel so comfortable with you,' he told her in bed, rippling his finger down the cleft of her rib cage. 'Does that sound boring?'

'No. I take it as a compliment.'

'I feel very strongly for you. You know that, don't you?'

'Yes.'

'Is that—?'

'Presumptuous?'

She could feel him grinning in the dark.

'No. For once, no. I was going to say, premature.'

Oh, *madre*. She so longed to reciprocate, to say the same back.

'It's not that it's premature. Not that. It's that there are . . . complications in my life. Real complications that can't be brushed aside.'

But he was not deterred. 'I don't care what it is,' he said, taking her face between his great hands, loving her with his entire body. 'Not when there's this. Whatever it is, it doesn't matter.'

And now, at 7.45 on this rainy morning, Wednesday, October 2, she is about to set off for London. Watches from the child's bedroom window for Sophia to arrive. A van pulls up instead of the expected Mini. She recognises it. Two people get out. Luke is with her and they are both coming to the door. She doesn't want him in her house, experiences that tightening sensation in her chest which she has whenever she sees him or even hears mention of him.

Sophia looks embarrassed. Blurts out, without saying hello: 'My car's clutch has gone so Luke's brought me. He's thirsty. Could he have a glass of water?'

Can't he ask for himself?

But: 'Hi. Yes. Come in,' she says with her usual air of calm, motioning them both indoors.

In the scullery she pours him a glass of water, and he takes it from her without a word. She fiddles around at the sink to pretend to be busy herself, but inadvertently catches his eyes over the rim of his glass. They are reptilian. She stares back at him. His eyes narrow and an evil expression that chills her comes into them. She tries not to flinch, held in this eye-lock, and it is he who drops his gaze first; yet she senses she has antagonised him.

When he finally leaves and the van rattles off, it is as though a spring has been released in Sophia. Her relief is palpable; she becomes quite garrulous.

'You've done more to the cottage since I last came. New shelves. Plants. The futon. Everything looks really nice.'

'You really don't mind staying overnight? Sleeping on the futon?'

'No. Luke only ever watches videos. You know, horror videos and such. He loves those . . . I could clean for you as well, if you wanted.'

Isabella pictures the mechanic in front of the television, engrossed in a violent scene.

'It's just the other evening you said you've got masses of work and you didn't know how you'd do it.'

Isabella focuses on her. And although a moment ago she had been thinking she would not use Sophia again because of her husband, she now hears herself saying that she will need her twice a week and they must discuss a suitable wage.

The girl's face sparkles. 'I've brought Hannah some jelly babies. I hope she likes them. There you are, darlin'.'

Hannah thanks her, as Isabella has taught her. She says 'fank' instead of 'thank'.

'Dear little thing—how she's come on, hasn't she?'

Sophia bends to kiss her. Jealousy nudges at Isabella.

'I've been really looking forward to this. You know—staying the night.' She says it shyly, confidingly, her eyelashes sweeping downwards over her thin cheeks.

'You will remember to keep the gate shut *all* the time.'

'You can trust me. Really. I'll be really careful.'

And what of the baby that died of cot death? *Was* it cot death? How long ago did it happen?

She finds it so hard to leave. Picks up Hannah—who wraps her legs round her—and kisses her several times.

Hampstead High Street is bustling in the rain. Irritable faces beneath a ceiling of umbrellas. Dodging feet. Music spilling out from shops whose lights reflect into the day's greyness. The dark outlines of people browsing in Waterstone's. Crowded cafés. So familiar. All so familiar. And once the very encapsulation of everything she had fought to achieve. Cosmopolitan, arty Hampstead with its affluent left-wing, liberal-thinking clientele, its intelligentsia, its cliques. And now she wants to be able to view it with disdain so that she can whole-heartedly turn her back on it a second time.

And here she is, pulling up in the nearest vacant spot to her flat . . . and getting out of the car, walking towards the building, past the dripping maples, treading polished leaves. And manic fingers hammer the keyboard of her chest as she descends the steps to her own front door.

Gloom and unloved darkness greet her. As she expected, the mat is heaped with mail and there is more stuffed through the mouth of the letterbox, but there is nothing out of the ordinary. Isabella tiptoeing about with a burglar's stealth. Her flat reproaches her. There is a curious deadness about it, removed of all personality. The place is untidy with evidence of her hasty departure: clothes on the back of a chair, the child's toys that could not be squeezed into the car.

In the kitchen she makes a black coffee—the water erupts from the tap. While the kettle is boiling she switches on the radio in an attempt to impart a sense of normality to the atmosphere. Coffee in hand, she plays the messages on her answering machine—writes down new ones. Wipes clean the tape. Starts to go through all the correspondence, getting rid of the junk mail first. One particular item catches her attention. It is a photograph, sent by an animal welfare charity, of a Chinese black bear in a capsule no bigger than itself. There it will remain imprisoned until the end of its days. The picture horrifies her and she immediately writes out a cheque for twenty-five pounds. Nevertheless she cannot banish the picture from her mind: the bear's muzzle jammed against the end of the cage, the despair in its eyes.

She has the need to free herself of the image—gets up from the kitchen table and systematically sets about cleaning the house. An hour later it looks as it always has done. But—she feels only an affectionate detachment towards it. Rather like returning to a lover only to tell him she is leaving him for good.

In her room she sorts out more things to take back with her. Most of her clothes fill her with distaste. Chic dresses; power suits. Others—impulse buys—she has hardly worn and is unlikely to do so; and she has the idea of giving them to Sophia.

Towards four thirty she is suddenly hungry and realises she has not eaten. Decides to go to Café Rouge for one of their delicious *croques au saumon fumé* with fries. Locks up the flat and walks to the High Street—losing herself in the anonymity of rush hour. Frayed-tempered drivers.

Queues at the bus stops. The tube vibrating beneath her legs. And into the newsagent's.

'We haven't seen you for ages,' the little man beneath the huge turban says. His cheeks are like Italian grapes, and he has the most beautiful white teeth, the most perfect lips she has ever seen.

'I've been away.' And then a thought occurs to her. 'Mr Shastri, your wife, she wouldn't . . .'

His wife comes downstairs from the flat above the shop, a wiry woman in an emerald sari, and it is arranged that she will come in once a week to dust over Isabella's apartment and generally keep an eye on it. Isabella pays her in advance and gives her her phone number and address. Arranges to return in the morning with the spare key.

At the post office she fills in forms to have her post redirected. 'With immediate effect' she writes.

Café Rouge is full. She has to wait. The gay waiter, with whom she used to discuss Peter Greenaway films, chats to her meanwhile. Finally she sits at her usual table by the window, with her *croque* and fries and a cappuccino, reading her magazine and watching the Hampstead types scurrying by.

Later she calls Sophia. The phone rings about fifteen times before it is picked up. Her armpits become damp with anxiety.

'I was bathing her,' the girl says. 'I couldn't get to the phone.'

'It doesn't matter.' Relief flowing through her. 'How are you both?'

'Great. We had a lovely day.' She sounds animated as she relates it to Isabella, who lies on her cool silk bedspread, lazily tripping her fingers up and down her body.

'I can't wait to get back,' she says.

She piles up the car and sets off early the following morning. When she comes to Bodmin Moor she calls Aidan on his mobile phone from hers. He answers, and she feels an almost dizzying rush of pleasure when she hears his voice.

'So how's you? How did you get on?'

'Fine. I got everything done that I needed to.' Hesitates. 'I missed you.'

'I did too. I couldn't put you in any kind of place. You were just kind of floating.'

'I pictured you in your bed. Do you want to come over later?'

'I could be persuaded.'

She can tell that he is smiling also. *Madre*, I love him.

Halfway down the main street of Pengarris something is going on. A Toyota Land Cruiser is parked, and alongside it, blocking her passage, is a red Alfa Romeo with its hazard lights blinking. She realises it must be the television team. Quite a gathering of locals are also hanging around, gawping. Babs is among them and waves to her; then the man who is double-parked darts into the road to move his car. Gestures apologetically towards her. She only catches a glimpse of him, but she recognises him instantly. Twenty years later. Grey-haired now, but unmistakable as he scrambles into the driving seat and revs up the Alfa.

Tom.

Back at the cottage the child runs up to her and flings her arms round her. It is her most effusive action to date. Sophia looks relaxed. There is a smell of tomato soup and toast from the kitchen.

Sophia helps her unload the car.

'My rocking horse,' the child exclaims when Isabella carries it indoors, and immediately clambers onto it.

'I love you, *carina*.' Isabella puts her lips to Hannah's.

Hannah reaches up and touches her eyelids. 'I love Mummy.'

Isabella is astounded. She cannot believe what she has heard. Hugs the child tightly.

'I've got some things for you,' she says to Sophia. 'I don't know if they'll be any good.'

She lifts out the top layer of clothes from the case. Sophia holds her hands to her face in disbelief, half weeping; exclaiming over each item as she picks it up.

'Most of them will need altering. You're much smaller than me.'

'I'm good with a needle and thread.' Her face is flushed. It is obvious that few favours have ever come her way. More than anyone, Isabella understands what this means.

'It's not charity. I don't want you to think that. I don't want to seem patronising.'

The girl doesn't reply. Shaking her head as she holds a red satin skirt against her, and laughing.

'I'll take you back now, if you like,' she says softly.

The Land Cruiser and Alfa have gone. The narrow street is quiet again. She wonders whether she can avoid meeting him.

Seeing Tom has completely unsettled her.

Aidan has bought her flowers. He kisses her passionately then grabs the child and swings her into the air.

'Who's as high as a mountain, then? Who's as high as a mountain?'

'Me. Me. Me.'

It has become a ritualistic game. And she loves to watch the two of them, the giant of a man and the tiny child. His presence has become so dear to her. And he talks of the future: 'We'll celebrate your birthday in style. I want to take you out properly.' Or: 'I'll make sure your roof's properly insulated for winter.' Or: 'We must remember to put antifreeze in your car.' He assumes that nothing will change, except for the good. And his bits and pieces are all round the cottage: a comb, his tooth-brush, a motoring magazine, his drill . . .

And she had not thought it possible, but sex with him improves and improves. And this night, as he moves his pelvis against hers so that her body arcs with longing for him, he tells her that she must have gathered by now that he is in love with her. That he could never make love like this otherwise.

All under threat.

'Are you crying? Oh, my sweetheart, don't fret,' he says in his tender, rolling voice that has come to mean the landscape itself to her. 'We'll sort things out, whatever they are.'

'. . . So, *CARA*,' Isabella writes to Sally in the first of her explanatory letters, 'I suppose we all get to a stage where we question ourselves—our needs, our directions; apparently it was my turn to reach that stage.' So far, so true. 'And now for the big shock. I have adopted a child. She is from Bosnia . . .' She wishes she had thought to tell everyone this in the first place.

It is easy to lie on paper. The recipient is distant, both literally and emotionally. It is as though everybody she knew before Hannah has ceased to exist. Is she callous? Is there something lacking in her? She does not *feel* a bad person, yet she has concocted an elaborate lie to her oldest friend.

She is disappointed in herself, as she signs off her first letter.

The surgeon's wife glides around with a plate of tiny whirligig sand-wiches. Her daughter is fulfilling her duty with a large dish of cheese croquettes spiked with cocktail sticks.

'Absolutely marvellous food, Deirdre,' someone yells across the room.

'. . . so I told him he could expect his knees to outlive him by ten years,' the host, an orthopaedic surgeon, is saying in a voice intended to be overheard, glancing in her direction for verification. He has already admired her leather skirt, and 'the wondrous colour of her hair'. A man who has affairs, and his poor wife probably knows it. Isabella is surprised the woman took the risk of inviting her.

Everything about the party, about the house, about the guests, is as she predicted. Rhododendron Drive.

'So you've just moved here, have you?' the man with whom she has been talking for the last few minutes asks.

'Yes. About a month ago. Well, a couple of weeks in Pengarris itself.'

She is planning her escape from this man; has to her relief seen Mary Anne arriving, draped dramatically in a dark green cape.

'Rather odd your picking somewhere like this to live, isn't it?' Eyeing her out-of-place skirt and tight top.

'It's a good place to bring up a child,' she says in response to his comment. Excuses herself then, as he is about to question her further—and catches his disapproving frown when she waves to Mary Anne before making her way across the room to her.

'Thank God, a human face,' she says.

'Dear girl, how delightful. What a splendid outfit.'

Mary Anne kisses her and immediately regales her with biographical details of everybody in the room: 'The man you were talking to—dreadful, parsimonious type. A widower. I'm sure he drove her to her death. She became an alcoholic. He's a magistrate. He'd have us all behind bars if he could . . . Now she's nice,' Mary Anne says. 'A psychotherapist, or whatever they call them . . . And that rather beautiful woman in a tragic kind of way, the one by the door, is lesbian and has just nicked the Amazon with her from *her* husband with whom she was originally having an affair . . . My dear, our host thrives on the local scandals. He laps them up. Makes him feel modern. His wife has to go along with it. But look at that rictus of a smile. That is not a happy woman.'

'*Madre*, Mary Anne, you take my breath away. So have you shoved them all in a book?'

'Singly, dear girl. Not *en masse.*'

'I shouldn't think anyone feels safe with you.'

A couple of hours later, and she is about to leave. The surgeon corners her in the front porch. Leans his arm over her, resting his hand against the Fibreglass pillar so that she is blocked.

'So nice to have such a delightful newcomer to these parts. Do give us a shout if we can do anything. That's what neighbours are for. I sometimes go jogging your way. I might drop by.' A meaningful look in his eyes which she wouldn't trust peering at her femur, and he draws back his arm. The arrogance, the . . . presumptuousness (a fleeting smile, as she thinks of Aidan). The sheer male conceit. She makes her getaway, and steps out into the misty cold.

She can hear laughter and chatter through the open window of Charlie and Joyce's cottage, who are looking after Hannah. The melting odours of roast beef drift outside. One of Joyce's records is playing.

There is no bell, and when nobody hears her knock she lets herself into the lobby. Charlie's Wellingtons are propped against the wall, a pair of heavy woollen grey socks draped over them. Through the glazed door she can see Hannah sprawled on the living-room floor playing with some cookery utensils. Charlie, Joyce, and a man whose face is averted are sitting close together, poring over what looks like a photo album. But she knows who it is; and her heart is thwacking against her sternum as she turns the door handle.

They all glance up as she enters.

'Hello, dear, did you have a good time?' Joyce.

'Well, I bet you knocked them for six in that get-up.' Charlie.

'Mummy!' Hannah bounding up.

'G-o-o-d G-o-d,' Tom iterates slowly.

'We were friends at Bristol, when I was at university,' she says. Shoots him a warning look. She can see he is enjoying the situation. His eyes, navy and thick-lashed and slightly compressed between loose skin now—which doesn't detract from his attractiveness—glint with relish. And even after all these years that well-remembered expression has the same effect on her, irritating her on the one hand so that she wants to wipe it from his face, and on the other drawing her, so that she finds herself wanting to appeal to him.

She is shocked that all this time later and despite Aidan he still has that power over her. His greying hair is cut in the same style as it was then. It grows forward and he wears it very short. His face is fleshier but his jaw is still firm with the defined cleft that he used to say was the mark of a good lover. And yes, he was good. But silent. She never knew what he was thinking, and sometimes he made her feel as though he were a voyeur on the act, spying on her pleasure, and she became inhibited under his tireless, detached gaze.

He is wearing a safari jacket over an Aran pullover. Jeans. Heavy lace-up shoes. He looks what he is—somebody connected with the media. So bizarre and disconcerting, sitting a few feet from him. After that initial incredulous exclamation he has shown no sign of anything except amusement. And what is his impression of her? Does he see a middle-aged woman? *Such* kids they were. Extraordinary to think they were married. He is drinking water, she notices. Earlier he refused Charlie's offer of whisky.

Charlie is beaming with the repleteness of Sunday bonhomie.

'He's OK, this friend of yours,' he tells Isabella. 'Agrees with me about things, y'know.'

'*Most* things, Charlie.' Tom leans forward to rest his elbows on the low table in front of him. Smoking. 'Isabella will tell you I'm always objective.' Wrinkles his forehead quizzically at her.

His voice is still the same. Still exaggeratedly refined.

'I wouldn't agree you were always objective.' Thinking of his irrational behaviour when he returned from Vietnam.

He turns to Charlie. 'You see, Charlie? Never appeal to a woman's better nature. They don't have one.'

Joyce observes them shrewdly, her eyes going from one to the other.

Tom glances across at Isabella. She knows he is angling to be alone with her, and when she stands up to leave he does also. Annoyance pricks her: that he automatically assumes he can come back with her. And later Aidan is coming. She wonders what Joyce is making of it all.

She unlocks the door to the cottage and he follows her inside. He has a jaunty, rather swaggering way of walking, hands in pockets, so that the jacket is pulled tight over his bottom. And now for the first time he seems unsure of himself; ill at ease as he pads about jerkily, making small noises in his throat that she takes for approval. He throws himself onto the futon-sofa then immediately springs up and goes and sits in the cane armchair, where he leans back and makes fists in the air. She had forgotten what an unrelaxing man he was.

'I'd love a coffee,' he says meekly when it is clear she isn't going to help him out with conversation. 'This is quite a surprise, Bella.'

'Would you rather have something else? Wine?'

It only takes a little humility on his part to soften her.

'I don't drink any more. I've been dry for nine years.'

'Oh.' Resists a biting comment. 'Good for you.'

'It's all right. I haven't become boring.'

'Isn't that for others to judge?' Hears the primness in her own tone, and quickly addresses the child before he can retort.

'Do you want to come and help me make coffee?'

The child accompanies her into the kitchen. Tom has lit a cigarette and is scouring about for an ashtray. 'There aren't any ashtrays in this place.'

'That's because nobody here smokes,' she says, skirting round him to get milk from the fridge. 'Hannah hates it.'

'So you make the rules here, do you?' he says to Hannah. Who takes no notice of him. Occupied with arranging shortbread on a plate.

'You look in bloody good nick for your age, I must say,' Tom tells Isabella. 'Dammit, for any age, I mean.'

'Thanks.' Her back is turned. He cannot see her blushing. His comment has confused her. He is making her confused, anyway.

'You're married, then?'

'That would be telling.'

She carries the tray into the sitting room. He does not offer to carry it for her. As Aidan would.

After trying out various chairs again he finally selects the sofa, perhaps in the hope she will sit beside him. She takes the cane armchair he was in earlier. Hannah empties a box of fuzzy felts onto the floor. Isabella watches with a wry smile as one by one Tom eats all the biscuits.

In between mouthfuls he talks about the film.

'It'll take two or three weeks, depending on the weather. It could take up to four.'

He explains that besides filming the men fishing, he wants to show their daily lives. 'You know, getting up in the mornings, putting on their gear, mealtimes. That kind of thing. I want anecdotes. Recollections. Drinking in the pub . . . All the background. I want it to be a complete portrayal of a fishing community.'

'It sounds wonderful. How many of you are there?'

'Three of us. Myself, my cameraman, and an assistant. We've worked together for years.'

'I saw something you did a month or so back—about a guy who had cerebral palsy. It was very moving. Uplifting, even.'

'So you liked it. Good.' His eyes shine. He seems genuinely pleased at her approval. That he takes his work very seriously is evident. 'It was all credit to the young man. He was an inspiration to everyone.'

Are his eyes becoming suspiciously pink? Surely not.

But: 'God, I get emotional nowadays,' he says.

She is astonished. This is a new side to him, and she can feel herself warming to him. So very strange, this turn of events.

'How long are you renting this place for?'

'A few months.'

He considers her for several seconds, obviously wondering what she is doing here. But doesn't ask.

'Well, well. I expect it brings back the odd memory or two.'

She is reluctant to share reminiscences with him. Alternates between wanting to be friendly and shying away warily.

'Shit, we burnt up a few lanes on the bike, didn't we,' he says.

'Too many.'

'You were terrified.'

'Well, you were *mad*,' she accuses him.

'Yes, I was, rather. Anyway, I've changed.'

'Is that a fact?'

'I believe so. When you give up booze you go through a fair bit of crap. You have to undergo therapy. And I attend AA meetings once a week still. Yes, sure it changes you.'

'So, what made you switch from reporting?'

'I . . . how best to put it? I was booted from the Beeb. I rather disgraced myself on a particular job. Then my drinking got slightly out of hand and my career took a nose dive. Then a chum asked me to do the script for a documentary, and I thought, I like this. It was a great feeling, actually: recognising you've found your vocation. Quite simply, it's the most important thing in my life. The people I meet, the places I get to, the experiences I've had . . . I've seen such heartening courage, such unexpected kindness in the most unlikely places.'

She is struck by his fervency as he talks. But then he always had that passionate intensity which could change into obsession and destructiveness. Has therapy evened out his extremes of mood? Battened down the dark side of his character?

Stroking Garibaldi, who has just sprung onto his lap. 'Could I have a drink of water? I'd fetch it myself, only I can't move.'

'I'll get you one.' Smiling at the sight of him with the cat—now rotating on his chest so that Tom is presented with its backside and quivering tail. She can feel laughter bubbling up inside her. All so strange, all so strange, she thinks again. Longs for a glass of wine.

'Do you mind if I drink wine in front of you? I won't if it's a problem.'

'No, go ahead. I'm fine about it. There's always booze at my place for guests.' The way he says *my* suggests to her that he is single.

There is no doubt he has been through a lot during the last few years. There is no doubt he is a clever man, a creative man, a fascinating man, a difficult and mercurial man, an attractive man. There is no doubt he is a man to whom it is almost impossible not to be drawn.

She pours some Rioja into a glass and quaffs it.

'What are you making?' she hears him asking Hannah in the sitting room.

'I make cat like Grabla.'

There is a long pause. 'Do you like cats?' Tom says.

He sounds so unnatural; it is obvious he has no children. This time Hannah does not bother to reply.

A scattering of flashbacks come to her. She giggles as she finishes off her glass of wine.

'What were you laughing at?' he asks when she rejoins him.

She hands him the water; puts her own refilled glass on the table.

'I was thinking of a game of Scrabble we had—'

'Which I, of course, won.'

It was true, he nearly always won, and was petulant when he didn't.

'That wasn't the point.' And she reminds him of the time.

He laughs also. Between them is a semblance of ease. Tied youth. An entire chapter of their life. He lives in Ealing, he tells her, but is thinking of going to Chile for a year. Restless as ever, she teases. Not restless, he says. He just has a questing nature. That's surely not a bad thing? For a moment his eyes hold hers.

His eyes linger on her for a few seconds, then he gives one of his abrupt movements and motions towards her guitar. 'Play something.'

'Oh, no. Not now. Really, I'm not in the mood.'

'Don't be so bloody coy. Isabella. Bella. P-l-e-a-s-e.'

'Mummy play g'tar.' Hannah jumps up and down.

She feigns an exasperated sigh and holds up her hands in defeat. Fetches the guitar.

She strums a chord and begins:

'"Have you seen the old man in the closed-down market, kicking at the papers with his worn-out shoes? . . ."'

The first song that came into her mind. And too late she remembers she used to sing it when they were going out. He lies back on the sofa, eyes shut, head going from side to side in time to the song. Garibaldi purring on his thighs. Hannah on her tummy on the rug, humming.

And into this small, intimate scene enters Aidan, bearing the last rose from his garden and a soil-encrusted marrow.

She sets down the guitar immediately. She can feel the colour rushing into her cheeks. And she goes over to him, framed in the doorway, looking hurt and startled. Covers her awkwardness with a flurry of words.

'You're half an hour early—this is Tom—we met when I was at university—and now he's making the documentary here—isn't it odd?'

Babbles on that the pair of them would have so much to talk about—knowing they would have absolutely nothing in common; conscious of Tom homing in on the marrow and grinning incredulously. She dislikes him just then; is so sorry for Aidan. Wishes she could embrace him there, proudly, passionately, in front of Tom. But she can't. The truth is she is torn between them. And annoyed at Aidan for turning up early, and for embarrassing her; for wearing his purple track suit and for just standing in the doorway like a yokel, so dumbstruck, with the rose in one hand and the blessed marrow in the other.

AFTER TOM LEFT they sat apart either in strained silence or struggling with a stilted conversation that was an endurance for both and saddened her. She longed to be able to talk to him as a friend, but his expression—simultaneously wounded and aloof—deterred her.

After scarcely an hour he got up to leave.

'Aren't you going to stay and have a meal? I bought some salmon steaks.'

'Thanks. But no. I think you've got a bit of sorting out to do.' Dignified. He was so dignified. And his jaw came forward obstinately. She knew that proud look. She wanted to tell him she loved him; but the word was not one to utter lightly so far as he was concerned. Love and reliability were linked.

'No, I don't have. He's someone from my past that's all.' She reached out for his hand. It lay in hers like a frozen fish, and she released it.

'He's your type,' Aidan said flatly. 'Clever, witty. Good-looking. I can see that. You've known each other for years. I'm just an ordinary bloke. I do up cars. I don't make films. I don't want to get in the way. I've more pride than that.'

'You're not in the way.'

'Even so.'

And he left. And now it is exactly a week since she has seen or spoken to him; yet she realises it would be wrong for a multitude of reasons to contact him. Tom's re-entry into her life has introduced one complication too many. He won't leave her alone. Phones her between takes from his mobile, takes her out to dinner, calls round uninvited with champagne for her while he drinks apple juice. Discusses topical affairs and opera and issues where she is obliged to think quickly—and can admit to herself that, yes, their conversations are stimulating. She reviews her relationship with Aidan soberly and tells herself that it would not have stood a chance anyway.

'I'm phoning from Charlie's boat,' Tom yelled over the crackling line one afternoon. 'Can you hear me? I just called because I'm happy.' And rang off.

He has tried to get her into bed, but on the whole has been respectful when she has refused. If Isabella were to analyse her feelings towards him she would say that now that she is used to him again, they are more sisterly than anything.

Hannah does not like him. She stares at him with mutinous eyes. Tom stares back, pulling idiotic faces, wiggling his fingers, growling in his throat, in a vain attempt to draw a smile from her.

'Your daughter doesn't like me,' he says this evening.

'She's very particular about whom she likes,' Isabella says.

He knows no more about her than he did a week ago, and seems unbothered. Likewise, she has asked him nothing. He has not mentioned Aidan to her, and it is obvious he assumes she can no longer be seeing him, since he has visited her every day or asked her to meet him at the Ship Inn, where he is staying. She adds arrogance to his list of failings.

Oddly, about his work he is not in the least conceited. He is modest, loves approval, and takes a boyish delight in what he is doing that she finds rather sweet.

He has filmed Charlie bringing Joyce tea in bed at five in the morning; Charlie pouring himself cornflakes in the kitchen, Charlie shaving and simultaneously cracking jokes; putting on his thick socks by the front door. A camera close-up of his withered leg . . . Follows him down the lane where he meets up with another fisherman, Rickie, and his son. And at this hour in the morning the light is grey on the greyness of their faces as they prepare the boats on the hardstanding.

'Nick's a great cameraman,' Tom said, as the video showed Charlie leading the line out from the pulley attached to the davit. Later the lens focused on struggling mackerel as they were hauled aboard. And now here was the lighthouse, and the waves were lashing the rocks; the rain began to drive down, and the rivulets streaked down the creases of Charlie's cheeks as he steered the boat . . .

'We had to stop filming then, and pack up the equipment to stop it getting wet,' Tom told her.

Sometimes she is almost on the brink of allowing herself to feel something deeper for him—and then with a gesture or word or action the moment will be severed.

She keeps hoping Aidan will ring. Or is he waiting for her to do so? She can't. There is too much to explain. Imagines what he must be thinking of her. Bitter, no doubt. And that grieves her.

But this evening Tom is with her. They are having supper on trays in front of the television, watching a documentary made by someone Tom knows.

'Thousands of children and young people go missing every year,' his acquaintance says. 'What happens to them? Where do they go? How is it possible for them to apparently disappear into thin air?'

'Split infinitive,' mutters Tom, gnawing on a chicken drumstick. 'Hey, Bella, don't get up. I want you to see this.'

'It's late. I've got work to do.' Avoiding his outstretched hand.

Goes over to her computer and opens *Rural France through the Ages* at page ninety-three. Tries to block out the tormented voice of a mother:

'She were just three year old. One minute she were with her friends in the park. Next she were gone. You'd think the police would've found some clue, wouldn't you . . .'

Against her will Isabella watches the woman blowing her nose into a handkerchief she pulls from her cardigan sleeve, and her own eyes start to water.

'. . . The English influence in the fourteenth century is much in evidence in the bastide towns of Aquitaine,' Isabella keys onto the screen.

'Bella,' Tom calls across. 'Do you remember that night in the B & B when we were here together and we were bonking away in our room and you were making a hell of a racket, and the landlady . . .'

'I thought you were watching the programme.'

'I am. That doesn't prevent the train of thought.'

She could hardly forget. Does not wish to think about sex with Tom. 'I don't want to discuss it.'

'Dear oh dear. Has the lovely Isabella become a prude in the autumn of her years? Or perhaps it is a case of: And so she pined, and so she died forlorn, imploring for her pot of yokel clotted cream to the last . . .'

Isabella striding furiously over to the television. Switching it off and yanking out the plug.

'Out,' she articulates with quiet precision.

He looks amazed, then pretends to shrink back in fear, throwing his hands up. When she doesn't smile, he says, 'Christ, Bella, don't take things so seriously.'

And that is his trouble. Except for his work, he takes nothing seriously.

Her shoulders drop. She makes a tutting sound, and returns to her computer. And a minute or so later the television comes on again, and a father metaphorically beats his chest over his ten-year-old son's disappearance after a family quarrel.

For half an hour, until the programme finishes, they don't speak. Then from his reclined position on the sofa, Tom says: 'Contrary to what you might believe, I have been doing a fair bit of thinking. And yes, I did behave pretty badly towards you. But meeting you again like this . . . I don't know what your situation is now, or even what you're doing here, but you know I'm not the conventional sort who's going to start sermonising about—'

She gets up then and goes over to him. Gives him a quick hug across the sofa. He gets up also and tries to pull her into his arms.

She resists. 'Go now,' she says gently. He taps her chin and nose with his forefinger and he is gone.

She clears up the sitting room and turns off the lights, and is poised on the stairs when what sounds like the creaking of the outside gate stops her in her tracks. She runs up the remaining stairs to her room and presses her face up to the window, squinting to see. But it is too dark. It is Tom. It is bound to be him, chancing his luck a second time. Smiling at the cheek of it, she opens the window and calls his name. There is no response, and she shuts the window once more. Uneasy.

She is persuading herself that she was mistaken about the gate when there comes another noise. A dull crash this time, which she recognises as one of the flowerpots falling over; they regularly topple onto their sides in the wind. But there is no wind tonight. Therefore somebody must have collided with it. She is suddenly afraid. And now another sound, thin and metallic, comes from downstairs: the letterbox flap opening and closing. Fear crawls up her arms like scarabs. She unplugs the bedside lamp and armed with this creeps downstairs. She can hear the unmistakable creak of the gate again, and the whine of a car starting and driving off down the lane. She switches on the light and immediately sees the envelope poking through the letterbox. Written on it with a black marker pen is a single word: SLUT. She stares, horrified—then realises it is bulging with something inside. Very slowly, dreading what she will find, she opens it. A used condom falls out, oozing milky semen. For a couple of minutes she remains nauseous with repulsion; too shaken to think what to do.

Her first instinct is to dial 999, and she goes over to the telephone. Is poised to dial, when through her abstractedness it occurs to her that this could be unwise. Trembling, she dials Tom on his mobile instead.

'It has not been possible to connect your call. Please try again later,' recites the computerised voice.

Aidan, Aidan. Lifts the receiver again and transfers it from hand to hand. I'm frightened. I need you. I'm sorry. And then a terrible thought causes her to replace it. Suppose it was him? Suppose this was his revenge? Not Aidan. Oh, *madre*, no. She inspects the single word again. The writing slopes backwards while his slopes forwards. There again, he would have disguised it.

I *know* him.

She prevaricates about whether to phone Babs. But she is reluctant to involve her. Isabella is not used to running to anyone with her problems. At this moment, though, she feels utterly alone. Resolutely, she takes the envelope and goes outside to flush it down the loo. The other cottages are in darkness. The light streaming from hers shines on the shrubs, and on the pot lying broken on its side.

In the cottage the phone is ringing and she dashes inside, then stops as she reaches it; her heart commences its thudding march again. The answering machine cuts in with her recorded message followed by the hum. There is a pause of a few seconds, then:

'Slut,' whispers a voice. And the person hangs up.

She dials 1471 and is informed: 'You were called today at twenty-three-oh-seven hours. We do not have the caller's number.'

The taste of threat lacquers her tongue.

In her small room with its sloping ceiling Hannah sleeps with one arm flung outside the duvet, her rabbit and bear pushed against her turned cheek. The glow from the nightlight delineates her small humped form. Isabella touches one of her springy curls and lays her cheek against the child's.

Is filled with a lonely sense of desolation and impermanence.

On the way back from the playgroup in the morning she slows when she comes to Aidan's garage. The mechanic is just visible in the shadows of the open doors. She drives past a few yards, changes her mind, reverses and parks. She will not, she resolves, getting out of the car and walking towards the workshop, be intimidated.

At the sound of her footsteps he turns, and briefly an expression of surprise flits across his face. His rabbit teeth form an irregular fringe over his lower lip. And now he angles his head back and slants his eyes in a leer at her.

She faces him squarely, says with a cold clarity she does not feel: 'I'd like to speak to Aidan, please.'

He seems to be deciding whether or not to respond. Then he crouches down so the curve of his back is presented to her, and busies

431

himself sanding the filler above the wheel arches of a Land Rover.

She tries to muster authority into her tone. 'I just asked you something.'

'He's not here,' he says at last. 'He's in Bristol.'

His grating voice seems to be emitted through the padded rings of flesh at the back of his neck.

'The car's suspension needs doing. I want to book it in.'

He stands up reluctantly, disappears into the office and reappears with the diary. 'Thursday of this week.' He goes back to work on the Land Rover.

She lingers, torn, trying to decide whether or not to leave a note for Aidan. The need to see him right now is almost overwhelming.

'Do you have an envelope?'

'In the office.'

She goes in there. On the desk is a framed photograph of Aidan's two sons leaning against one another, laughing. She tears a sheet from a notepad and scrawls on it: 'I miss you.' Hesitates, and adds: 'I love you.' Stares at what she has written—those three small words of such magnitude; finds an envelope in the drawer and puts the note inside. She marks it for his attention and puts it by the photo.

Sophia is at the cottage, having let herself in with her own key. Isabella does not mention having just seen her husband.

'Hi. Coffee?' she asks, without looking up.

'Love one.'

Sophia goes into the kitchen, and Isabella sifts through the post on the table in the sitting room. Recognises Sally's handwriting on one of the letters and reserves it to read with her coffee.

Sophia brings it to her, with a couple of biscuits on a plate. She is particularly quiet. Lately she has lost her shyness and usually chatters away freely. Isabella glances at her. The girl's eyes are puffed and red.

'Hey, what's up?'

'You're so good to me,' the girl blurts out. 'I love coming here. I don't know what I'd do if I didn't have this job. I really like you. I love Hannah.'

'Well, I'm not about to give you the push, I can assure you. You're a godsend as far as I'm concerned. So what's the real problem?'

'Oh, I don't know . . . Look, I shouldn't say anything . . .' She sighs several times and presses her wrists against her bent head. 'It's Luke,' she says. 'He's so strange sometimes, that's all. And after Grace died—'

'Your baby?'

'Yes. After she died . . . well, you know, I . . . well, you know, didn't feel like . . . well, in bed. Doing it, like.'

'Of course. I can understand that.'

'And he's always angry with me. And he goes out at night sometimes, and I don't know where he's off to. He wasn't always as bad as this. He's got worse . . . Sometimes I think he's crazy . . .'

Her skinny body is hunched taut with the effort of not crying. And all Isabella can do is murmur banalities.

But she knows the identity of last night's visitor.

And now she recollects the mechanic's surprised expression when she strolled into the garage. Had he assumed, therefore, that she would guess it was him, that she would not dare come near him?

'Perhaps he just drives around,' she says to Sophia. 'Clearing his head.'

'Maybe.' She sounds unconvinced.

'Did you have a good relationship before?'

Sophia puckers her lips contemplatively. 'Fair. I mean, he was always very silent. But courteous. I like that. And when he said anything nice, you thought, well, he must mean it as he never spoke much. I didn't think I'd ever meet anybody. So . . . And then I got pregnant. And we married.'

'You don't have to stay with your husband if he makes you unhappy.'

Sophia looks shocked. 'Oh, but I'm Catholic,' she states in a tone that staunches all further comment.

When Isabella is alone she reads Sally's letter:

Darling Issi,

This is the first second I've had to put pen to paper since I received your bombshell of a letter. Why the hell didn't you put your address or phone number on it? Anyway, I'll just have to assume this will be forwarded to you. You're amazing! What a truly wonderful thing to go and do. I don't know how you kept it so quiet. I'm longing to see you and to meet Hannah. Although I don't know when. I have to tell you things are pretty atrocious here. Geoff was getting frightful headaches and has been diagnosed with a brain tumour. He is going into hospital tomorrow to be operated on, and frankly I'm bloody terrified. We're both clinging on to each other with that awful fear that there's no time left. If it's malignant the chances aren't good, because not only is the tumour large, but the cancer could spread further as a result of disturbance from the op. The worst of it is trying to appear positive with the kids, and having to go about doing things as normal, when in you is this awful ache that feels like a tumour itself.

For God's sake, phone. Actually I'm rather hurt you haven't, but no doubt you've got your reasons and all will be revealed.

Much love to you, Issi, and to your Hannah. Pray for Geoff, even though I know you don't believe in anything. Cross your fingers too.

Sally XX

Isabella lays the letter down on the table. She has been unforgivably selfish. Reproaches herself for thrusting aside Sally of all people. And the letter was written four days ago. By now Geoff will have had the operation.

As she dials the familiar number she is apprehensive. Childishly, her fingers *are* crossed. And when Sally finally does answer, she knows from her quavering voice that it is bad news.

'*Cara*, it's me.'

'Oh God, Issi.'

She listens helplessly to the storm of sobbing at the other end, saying nothing, filled with bleakness; waits for the sobbing to abate.

'Geoff died. He had a massive brain haemorrhage under surgery.'

Shocked tears streaming down Isabella's face. Geoff? It is not possible. Gentle, overweight, balding, amiable Geoff. And weren't he and Sally a brilliant couple together? Her oldest, most loved friends.

'*Cara*, I'm so desperately, desperately sorry.' She can scarcely speak, unable to hide the fact that she is crying also. 'Is your mother with you?'

'Yes. She's been staying since . . . oh goodness, I've lost all sense of time.'

'When's the funeral?'

'I'm not sure. Friday maybe. I'll phone you. I don't have your number even. And I haven't asked anything about you. I'm so—'

'Don't be stupid. Don't worry about me. I'm fine.'

But she is not. She wants to rush upstairs and howl. She gives Sally her telephone number, makes her repeat it, and says goodbye. And sits on, slumped by the phone.

Tregurran beach is deserted. She takes her shoes off and carries them. The tide is out, and beneath her bare feet the sand, swept into peaks and scoops by the wind, is cool. The sea is rough: moss swathes rolling over each other, crashing on the shore and sluicing over rocks. And she stands at the edge, the current tugging her feet, sucking the sand from beneath them so they are implanted in shifting troughs that massage the balls of her heels. The roar of the sea is a colossal sound that fills her head. She walks about aimlessly; comes upon a stick lying where the sand is more compact, and with it draws the outline of a woman. Hopeless. She is hopeless at drawing. And she is reminded of the conversation she'd had that evening with Aidan, the first time they made love, when he showed her his paintings. Pain wrapping round her.

She sits with her knees huddled to her chin, staring out to sea.

Some way out are a couple of fishing craft, rising and disappearing with the swell of the waves. Tom and his colleagues were going out today to get some shots of Charlie in his boat from a distance. It is definitely them, as when she lifts her binoculars she can see that one of the vessels is larger than the other, and can make out Charlie's red hull.

Aidan's binoculars. She still has his binoculars. They will provide an excuse to see him. How will he react to her note?

She lies back, covering herself with her waterproof jacket. Tom, Aidan. Aidan, Tom. Hannah, Hannah. She half dozes; motes floating in the air are distorted through the cracks of her eyes and become images that merge in a contrapuntal stream: her father stroking the blade of his nose as he worked on the restaurant's accounts; her mother's old-fashioned underwear drying on the kitchen radiator; Geoff's teasing grin as he served the ping-pong ball; Aidan's steady grey gaze scorching her . . .

She is on the point of sleep when the air is split by what sounds like an explosion. She sits up with a jolt of fright. Peering out to sea, she can just decipher what seems to be a spiral of smoke. She looks through the binoculars. And now, clearly, she can see a thick plume sweeping into the clouds, and flames beneath it engulfing the smaller of the two boats as it lifts on the waves. Knows with certainty that she has just witnessed a terrible disaster.

MONDAY, OCTOBER 14.

Everything is chance, Isabella writes in her report book, which has become more of a diary. *I am beginning to realise that virtually everything is circumstantial; a sequence of cause and effect. What choice did Hannah have when her mother left her or when I took her? What choice did I have when my father came to me that night and left the next morning; when my mother died; when I was sent from place to place? Therefore, do we have no responsibility? Does our responsibility begin and end with behaving honourably towards one another? Do we have a choice in loving?*

A moment of lapsed concentration killed Charlie.

Tom is devastated.

'We couldn't see what was happening from our position,' he tells her that evening, drinking coffee after coffee and smoking cigarette after cigarette in her sitting room. 'It was very rough and the boat was pitching about. I was just thinking, There'll be some great shots . . . Nick was closing in on him with the zoom. And then I heard him say, "Christ, Charlie's engine's on fire." We yelled out to him, but he couldn't hear a thing over the wind and the sea. Rickie was driving our boat, and he turned at right angles to cut across Charlie. But before we could make it there was this massive explosion as the fuel tank caught.'

Tom pauses, looking anguished as he relives the incident.

'We couldn't get close,' he continues. 'You felt so powerless, just watching the flames engulfing Charlie and the boat . . .'

Doesn't finish the sentence. His mouth twisted, cheek muscles drawn in. She cradles his head against her and strokes his hair as she would Hannah's. She feels no need to comment. Her own emotion is, at this point, almost overwhelming.

'Joyce is remarkable. It's like she was expecting it. Apparently he used to keep an old oil rag in the boat. She reckons that caused the fire. She said he'd become forgetful recently. She took it so calmly when we told her, but you could see what she was really feeling.'

'She's been through it before.'

'You think that helps?' he says sharply, edging away from her.

'I didn't say that. Only I imagine it might make you more on your guard. You realise nobody's inviolable.'

'I marvel at you, I really do. Sometimes I don't think you've got any feelings. Nothing ruffles you, does it?'

What does he know? Something snaps in her.

'When did you ever trouble to find out what my feelings are? You're completely selfish,' she shouts, gripping his arm and shaking it in fury. 'You crawl back out of the woodwork, thinking you can take up where you left off, thinking you're this wonderful, reformed, irresistible man and nobody else thinks as profoundly as you . . . I could, I could—'

Piercing shrieks come from Hannah's room. Isabella's tirade is cut off, and she releases her hold on Tom, who is looking astounded, and dashes upstairs. Hannah is jumping up and down on the bed, tugging at her hair, her mouth a giant 'O' as she lets rip scream after scream. It is terrible to hear them, to see her like this. What half-buried experiences have just been resurrected? *Madre*, how this takes her back to her own childhood.

'Oh, *carina*, I'm sorry. Sweet Hannah, shush, it's all right.'

She hoists the child into her arms and gathers her close. She is filled with self-reproach.

'Mummy cross,' sobs Hannah, wrapping her legs round Isabella's waist like a frog; and her body gives tiny involuntary convulsions.

'Yes. But not with you, *carina*. I wasn't cross with Hannah. And I'm better now. I promise I won't be cross like that ever again.'

Tucks her back into bed, reads to her, sings to her. The child's features become peaceful once more. Her elfin face peeps sleepily over the Dalmatian-patterned duvet. And Isabella goes downstairs—avoids looking at Tom—and into the kitchen.

What does he know? What does he know?

Pours herself a glass of wine, which she gulps down, and refills it twice more. Its oaky warmth caresses the sorrow in her throat. Too much has happened. Everything seems to be collapsing.

'You think that'll help?' Tom regarding her from the doorway. 'You're punishing yourself. Nobody else. Not me.'

Coming towards her and trying to prise the bottle from her. She resists him and it crashes to the ground, where it splinters into fragments and the remainder of the wine snakes along the floor.

They both stare at it. Abruptly, the light of her rage shrivels. In deference to Charlie, in deference to Geoff, in deference to a small child upstairs who has undergone her own traumas, they must not quarrel.

This time when Tom requests to stay the night, with a simple 'I need you, Bella', she does not reject him. She is slightly drunk, but not enough to prevent her from being aware of what she is doing.

First, she goes about the evening's routine in the usual way. She uses the loo outside, washes and cleans her teeth, switches off the lights, locks the front door, checks Hannah, and finally goes into her bedroom. Tom is almost undressed. His body is good for a man of his age; though she likes chest hair and he has virtually none, and he is rather on the thin side.

Used to Aidan's body. She gets undressed; he makes no move to help her and she feels, as she used to with him, self-conscious. A sense of detachment comes over her, so that even as she stands there naked, even as he stoops to fondle her breasts, with a murmured 'How could I have forgotten these?', and puts his mouth to her nipple; even as she looks down at his bent head and can feel her nipple hardening as a natural response despite her not being aroused, it is as though this were happening to someone else. She wants to get it over with.

She is compliant, but that is all. She feels like a prostitute, going through the motions.

'It was nothing like that twenty years ago, was it?' Tom says, lying on his back, his arm loosely round her neck. So: he enjoyed it. And was it good for you, dear? Slightly hysterical giggling repressed in her head. Over in six minutes.

'I don't remember,' she says.

She wonders when she can decently get up.

Silence between them.

'You remember my best friend Sally?' And she tells him about Geoff.

'That's awful. Why didn't you mention it earlier?'

'I only heard this morning. And Charlie rather eclipsed everything.'

The day seems to have gone on for ever.

'Charlie,' Tom says heavily. 'I have to admit I'm in a bit of a quandary. I mean, I shouldn't really be thinking about it now—it seems disrespectful—but I don't know what to do about filming. I'll have to come to a decision pretty soon. The awful thing is it would give a whole different dimension to the film. It could be amazing. Really poignant. But that sounds as though I'm exploiting his death, which is the last thing I'd want to do. Maybe I shouldn't go on with it.'

'Ask Joyce.'

'Yes, of course. That's what I must do. I'll ask her first thing tomorrow.'

His voice is muzzy, and she slips out of bed, puts on her dressing gown and goes downstairs to do some work. Wide awake now, her mind leaping about with thoughts, whereas a short while ago she had longed for sleep and to put the day behind her. First, she needs to pee. All the wine has gone straight to her bladder.

She unlocks the door and steps outside, straight into a prism of light. Briefly she is dazzled by the torch flashing up in her eyes, then it drops away and there is a scurrying of feet from behind the bushes, down the cutting and towards the lane.

He has been skulking about again. Oddly, now she knows who it is, she is less afraid.

The next morning. And Tom, a skimpy towel fastened round his waist, is in the bathroom, shaving. The buzzing of his electric razor is like a bumblebee trapped in a glass. Aidan used to shave round the neat outline of his beard with a hand razor. It was a feat of geometry.

She is glad when Tom has gone. He exhausts her. It was probably a mistake to have sex with him; on the other hand it hasn't really changed anything. It is as if it didn't happen. She feels neither closer to him nor more distant.

Upstairs, when she is kneeling to dress Hannah, doing up the belt round her pale little middle with its protruding bellybutton, Hannah traces an outline with her finger round Isabella's lips.

'Mummy smile,' she says.

Isabella clasps her tightly. 'Oh, *madre*, you're special. Have I ever told you you're the most special little girl in the world?' She draws back slightly from her. 'Do you want to make me smile, then?'

Hannah nods solemnly, her malachite eyes burrowing into Isabella's.

'OK, then. Look, I'm going to smile. You can help me.' And taking Hannah's fingers of both hands in her own, she raises them to the corners of her mouth and smiles hugely.

But there is little to smile about. The whole village is in mourning. And when Isabella goes to see Joyce later that day, Joyce is wearing brown.

'I don't have anything black,' she explains. 'I wore this for Phil's funeral too. I don't suppose Charlie would mind.' Gives a small half-laugh which ends up as an extended sigh. 'I told Tom he should do the film. "Make it," I said to him, when he came to see me this morning. Charlie was so proud of being in it. Well, it'd be like a tribute to him in a way, wouldn't it?' Stoic, this second time. But her eyes are bemused, and she is stooped-shouldered. 'You tell your friend Tom to make that film the best thing he's ever done.'

When Tom phones she gives him Joyce's message.

And: 'I want to be on my own tonight,' she says.

'That's good. So do I,' he replies tersely.

And she remembers how childish he can be when he is peeved; how everything has to be on his terms or not at all. So at the moment he is newly infatuated, but Tom's enthusiasms are in the place where he happens to be; and then he moves on.

Missing Aidan is like an ulcer that keeps flaring up.

There is a small incident that afternoon. The cottage is cold and she lights a fire, before remembering she needs to go to Babs's shop for one or two things. She lets the fire die down first, then puts the guard in front of it. She walks to the village with Hannah, buys the things she needs and chats to Babs for ten minutes. When she returns, the fire-guard is pushed to one side. She is mystified. Her first thought is that someone has been here. But the cottage was locked and the windows shut, and there is no sign of forced entry.

Thursday morning. To her surprise, Aidan is at the garage alone. When she sees him she feels almost weak. They say hello awkwardly. Politely he asks how she is. She lies that she is fine, as he holds himself so aloof and untouchable, haughty, in his oil-streaked overalls.

'I saw your car was booked in. I told you I'd do it myself.'

'There was no need. I couldn't have expected—'

439

'I keep my word,' he says. Implying? She feels as though she is being strangled, all her emotion stifled within her.

'Could I have it back this evening? I have to leave for Gloucestershire early in the morning.'

He lifts his eyebrows slightly, and she blunders on, wanting his sympathy: 'My best friend—the one I had the rock group with—her husband's just died. The funeral's tomorrow afternoon.'

'I'm sorry.' A gentler note creeping into his voice.

'It's awful.' She is close to tears.

He looks down at her, and a gamut of expressions flits across his face as he clearly does battle with himself.

'Come into the office for a bit,' he says, after deliberation. 'Do you want a coffee?'

'If you've time.'

She sits on one of the leatherette chairs and watches him spooning instant coffee into stained mugs and adding the water.

'So there's Charlie's funeral too, next week. Monday, I gather.'

Tells him how she heard and saw the explosion from the beach.

'I realised who it was. They were filming.'

Wishes she had not raised that particular subject. The air is taut with significance. She stares round the office. The photograph on the desk reminds her that he has not mentioned her note.

At the risk of being humiliated, she asks, 'You got my note?'

'What note?'

'I left you a note when I came here on Monday morning. By the photo of your sons.'

He frowns. 'I didn't know you came here. I thought you rang and booked in. I didn't get a note.'

So Luke took it. Did he read it? Should she tell Aidan about him?

He is busily searching for it, first behind the photograph, then beneath the desk. 'I just don't know what could have happened to it.' The puzzle over its fate absolves him from having to ask about its contents.

She finds it almost impossible to drink her coffee. Cannot swallow.

'Aidan, I'm very sorry about what's happened.'

Her hand is close to his on the desk.

'Forget it. You never made any promises.' Moves his hand. 'You were fair all along. It's my fault for getting involved.'

'But it wasn't like that. I felt the same.'

As he glances at her sharply, Sophia's voice calls out, 'Anyone around?' And his features cloud over once more.

'I'll drop your car off later. Luke will follow me and bring me back to the garage.'

A surge of determination seizes her suddenly.

'No, I *won't* let it go just like that.'

Stands up abruptly and, taking his face between her hands, kisses him with great tenderness. She moves away as he begins to respond.

'I meant what I said. I still do. If you'd read my note you'd have realised. You're too bloody proud, that's your trouble.'

She leaves the little office. Doesn't need to turn round to know that he is standing there, with his shoulders forward, flummoxed, rubbing his beard. And she still has his binoculars.

She is one of the first to arrive at the Cotswold church, and waits outside. When she sees her, Sally breaks down.

People arriving, hanging around outside in the drizzle. Subdued. Funeral etiquette. Faces she hasn't seen for years, others encountered more recently. One or two people come up to her and enquire about the Bosnian orphan they have heard she has adopted. And then she spots someone she recognises slightly and tries to place. He comes over to her.

'Hello. I didn't know you knew Geoff.'

The pinky-fresh complexion and large ears; kindly, downward eyes.

'You don't remember, do you? Out riding. We met riding. I rang you.'

'Of course, I'm sorry.' The banker. No, solicitor. Neil something.

'I've phoned a couple of times, but I got your machine and didn't bother to leave a message.'

'I'm staying in Cornwall for a while.'

She is actually quite pleased to see him. Remembers from riding that he was self-effacing with a good sense of humour.

'London's loss,' he says.

He tells her Geoff was a client of his, but they had become friends, he explains. And as he says it his droopy dark eyes become moist, as do hers. He touches her upper arm in a way that has no hidden motive.

'So how long is the "while" for in Cornwall?' he asks.

'A few months.' Waving her hand vaguely.

'I don't suppose you'd want a boring old solicitor turning up one day, would you? I could stay in a bed and breakfast, or whatever.'

She hesitates. She does not want to mislead him. 'I *am* involved with someone,' she says. Even if this is no longer the case.

'I wouldn't have expected otherwise. And if you weren't, I'm not the sort to impose myself. I'd be glad to see you as a friend. My wife died sixteen and a half months ago of breast cancer. I happen to be that rare man who *likes* women.'

The 'sixteen and a half months' touches her. He counts every day.

She writes down her number for him. 'I've got an answering machine there also. Leave a message this time.'

He gives a jocular military salute. A widowed man of about her age, unwillingly flung into the den of divorced lechers and confirmed bachelors. Perhaps in time he and Sally . . .

Right now Sally is wending her way with her daughters into the church, to the ghostly traces of the organ. Her fair hair is lank and flat. The two girls are like wilted tulips. They form a single clinging, weeping nucleus, surrounded by close family: Sally's mother and sister, Geoff's parents, his brother. The rest of the congregation packs in around them.

I hate churches. I hate death.

The image springs up before her, realistic and horrific, of her own decaying skeleton.

Neil is sitting beside her, and she reaches for his arm instinctively.

'It's the first funeral I've been to since my wife. I hate churches,' he whispers.

And they hold hands to comfort one another.

She had thought she would stay at Sally's, but realises there is no room. She kisses her friend goodbye, promises to visit soon, with Hannah.

It is 6.30pm, and she heads back to Cornwall, anxious to see Hannah. The owl from the churchyard skims low in front of her headlights through an arch of trees as she drives through sleeping Zerion.

And in his converted stable, is he asleep? I love you, Aidan.

One funeral down, one to go.

Past midnight. Weary from driving. Glad to be back. But Sophia is not on the futon in the sitting room. Isabella frowns, disturbed. Can hear sounds from overhead in her own room, and listens for a minute. Then, with foreboding, she tiptoes upstairs.

They are having sex on her bed. Sophia and Luke. He has her pinioned beneath him. Sophia notices her and lets out a shrill cry.

'Get off me,' the girl begs, struggling, as Isabella just stands there, dizzy and speechless.

Luke doesn't budge, leering across at Isabella, his slight, muscular body poised over his wife's, his hands tight over her wrists. Then, still with his eyes fixed on Isabella, he gives a final thrust, and throws his head back silently. And rolls away from the girl.

Sophia, weeping, rushes up from the bed and grabs her clothes.

'He insisted—it was his idea—he made me—I didn't want to.'

Isabella trembling to such an extent her teeth are chattering.

'Get out of my home.'

It is all she says. She can only wait for them to leave—Sophia, hysterical, dishevelled, is already downstairs. Luke deliberately takes his time.

'See you,' he says softly, as he sidles out of the cottage.

She goes into Hannah's room. The nightlight glow of innocence. The fluff of hair. The rabbit and bear on the pillow.

Isabella lies down carefully beside her. She stirs.

Murmurs, 'Mummy back.'

'Yes, *carina*. Mummy's back.'

Dear Isabella,

I'm so sorry about what happened. Luke came round in the evening and refused to leave and said he would do all kinds of things if I didn't do what he wanted. I've taken your advice and this morning I've left him for good. I'll really miss working for you. I feel terribly upset about everything and I'm really depressed, to tell you the truth. I don't know what I'm going to do and I'll miss Hannah awfully as I really love her. She became like a daughter to me.

Lots of love,

Sophia

The letter, in neat, rounded writing on lined airmail paper, is hand-delivered two days later while she is out. Sophia has enclosed the key, and some jelly babies for Hannah. There is no contact number for Isabella to reply to.

She is preoccupied and constantly anxious; finds it hard to sleep, hard to concentrate on her work, and drags herself about lethargically, plagued with uncertainties and fears. Perhaps she should return to London now that her friends know of Hannah's existence and sufficient time has elapsed for her to be confident there is no police search. What reason is there to remain here? There are several for not doing so: a warped stalker, a shattered love affair and constant reminders all around, the invidious gossip, and a spirit of gloom that has settled over the village since Charlie's death. Yet this village, the whole area, has won her over: she has grown to love the landscape, the pace of life, the harshness and the gentleness, and to feel that this is where she belongs. Also, having only recently begun to discover aspects of her character long suppressed, she is unwilling to revert to her old lifestyle and the other Isabella.

Hannah is happy here. But she has fallen out with her friend. Becky spent an afternoon with them and Isabella took them for a walk to Hannah's Tree. Two of them could not squeeze into its hollow and the other child monopolised it. Tears were the outcome, and the adult-devised treaty between the two is frail. At playgroup the pair studiously avoid one another.

Hannah's love affair, it seems, like her own, is over.

Sometimes, lying in bed, reflecting on everything, she contemplates emigrating to Italy. She has retained her dual nationality. But the problem of a passport for Hannah seems insoluble. She goes over and over this in her mind; worrying about the future, the prospect of having to show a birth certificate or adoption papers—depending on whether she claimed Hannah to be her own natural daughter or not. Her thoughts hop from one thing to another at night. Her own mortality obsesses her. The ghoulish image of her disintegrating corpse keeps recurring. And there is plenty of time to brood, lying by herself in bed; dispirited that Aidan has not contacted her after their meeting; listening to autumn rattling the windows; falling asleep, apprehensive. Fuck me, her father says in the mechanic's voice, pulling the sheet back from her adolescent body in its flannel nightdress.

Early this Monday morning she walks with Hannah to the cove where, from the boathouse, they watch three young men unchaining the boats from the mooring blocks and pushing them down the ramp. Inside are strings of lobster pots tied together. 'Joyce', as Charlie had painted on his boat's hull above the registration number, is conspicuous by its absence. It used to be in the cradle on the concrete apron.

'Be back in good time, lads,' she hears someone call.

For later today it will be these three young men who will bear Charlie's coffin.

'That must be Joyce's daughter next to her,' she whispers to Babs, who is sitting beside her in Zerion church, and indicates a fair-haired, square-jawed woman with a bulldog stance. 'She looks very formidable. I wouldn't want to cross her.'

'I think you could hold your own,' Babs whispers back.

Isabella swivels her head; spots Janet Abell a couple of rows behind them, and mouths hello. Janet's bland face appears to respond. The whole of Pengarris and half of Zerion crowding into the Methodist church, come to pay their respects. Tom arriving with Nick and, simultaneously, Aidan. The two men end up sitting beside one another in the corresponding pew to Isabella, on the other side of the aisle. Tom winks at her. Aidan opens the prayer book in front of him, inclines his head forward, and closes his eyes.

The vicar begins his address, his voice resonating off the whitewashed stone walls. He is elderly, with a face that has receded like a turkey's. 'Who, here, did not love Charlie Minear—? Who, here, was not enriched in some way by him? I know I was . . .'

Hannah's hand biting into Isabella's. She can feel the child's body tensing against hers.

'Do you want to sit on my lap, *carina*?'

'I 'fraid. I 'fraid.' Her voice piping out. Reproving heads turning.

'I know. Here, come onto my lap and you'll be fine.' Lifting her over.

A few seconds later: 'Man's cross,' Hannah says loudly.

More heads swivelling. Finally, after several more interruptions, when she senses Hannah is about to start bawling, they leave. Make their way down the aisle, with everyone's eyes on them. And tomorrow they will all be discussing her, the disruption of Charlie's funeral service, how the vicar had to halt his address. She will apologise to Joyce. But she, more than anyone, will understand.

She sits on the bench outside, Hannah half lying across her. Can hear them singing 'For those in peril on the sea'. The leaves all round are dropping, with the barest popping sound.

'I don' like church,' says Hannah. She pronounces it 'jush'.

Isabella soothes her forehead.

'I don't either.'

She waits for everyone to come out. Tom comes over to them.

'Well, you provided a bit of light relief.'

'It was rather embarrassing.'

'Oh well, I shouldn't worry. Give everyone something to talk about when they've got the weather out of the way. Actually, it was a very moving service . . . You've been avoiding me.'

'It was getting out of hand,' she says.

'I don't agree that it was. Can I come over later?'

'You don't give up.'

'I'm going back to London tomorrow anyway. We've finished the job.'

She receives this news with a mix of emotion: a sense of loss, of an ally departing, and relief, like an amphibian coming up for air.

'Bella, contrary to what you may think, I do care about you. I'd like to stay in touch.'

'I would too.'

'The only thing is, I live with someone. So be careful about phoning. She gets a bit narky.'

Thank God she didn't get involved with him.

The rain pelting down as Isabella drives back from taking Hannah to playgroup, the trees leaning in the wind, leaves cascading; and ahead she sees the Aston nosing slowly out of the lane where he lives. Accelerates to catch him up. Hoots. Flashes. Is he deliberately not slowing? Finally he brakes and stops. She gets out and runs up to the car, head bent against the rain. Jazz blaring out. At least he would genuinely not have heard her hooting. He switches it off. He is wearing his suit, she notices when he opens the door, the same one, but with a bright tie and a carnation in the lapel.

'I was following for ages,' she says. 'You look smart.'

'I'm going to my cousin's wedding in Exeter.' His gaze meets hers briefly then is averted to the dashboard.

'I need to talk to you.' Looks at him despairingly.

'There's nothing to say.' Turning off the engine, nonetheless.

'Yes, there is. I've got your binoculars, for a start.'

'You can keep them.'

'Please, Aidan.' Her hair plastered to her head, to her face; the rain penetrating her pullover and trickling down the polo neck.

'Let's just leave it, eh? I'm not just going to come running now your friend's gone. That's not me.' Turns on the ignition, revs the engine.

She cannot bear to watch him drive off. Lays a preventive hand on the steering wheel, and says quietly: 'He's not a "friend", he's my ex-husband.'

His jaw is slack with astonishment. He turns off the ignition once more. 'Jee-ee-ze.' He makes his clicking-of-tongue noises and rubs his beard. All the familiar reactions. Which makes her smile.

'He wants you to go back to him, I suppose.'

'No. We divorced years ago.'

'But I thought—'

'Please come round this evening? After the wedding?'

'Yeah. Yeah, I'll do that.' His features relax. Perplexity in his eyes, but warmth too. 'I'll be late, mind. Ten, maybe eleven.'

'It doesn't matter.'

Ludicrously happy suddenly. Outlandishly, wildly happy.

'God, you're beautiful,' he says.

He climbs out of the car and embraces her. His huge hands form a 'Y' round her chin, and he kisses her.

'Your poor suit,' she observes, when they move apart.

'It'll dry.' He glances unconcernedly down at himself. He grins his open grin that she remembers.

He gets back in the car and holds her hand through the open window. 'I don't want to leave you. But I'll see you later.'

'Drive carefully. The conditions are awful.'

Madre, if anything were to happen to him now. Comforts herself that at least the car is solid enough to see him out of most kinds of trouble.

It is a few minutes after nine thirty. Schumann's Piano Concerto is softly playing. The fire is smouldering. The champagne is in the fridge.

'After the annual harvesting the fields would, for a limited time, become common property . . .' Isabella types on her computer.

She can't work any more. Grasshopper-on-edge as she waits for Aidan. She gets up and goes for a walk around outside. The night is damp, slightly foggy. She uses the lavatory, then returns indoors.

Her computer has stopped working. She presses the relevant keys, but to no avail. And then she realises: the CD has also stopped playing. She bends down to check the plug and sees that it has been pulled out.

And the fireguard has been removed from in front of the fire.

She straightens up slowly. Her body is rigid.

The mechanic is here.

She makes for the door—just a couple of strides—but he is there first, appearing from the kitchen. He captures her hand with his. In the other is a flick knife, blade open.

She opens her mouth to cry out, but he presses against her, his jaw thrust up to hers. She can feel the knife blade against her throat, and he lightly plies it back and forth there, sadistically teasing.

'Don't yell. You might wake the child,' he says.

He stinks. Onions. Beer. Lust.

'What do you want?' She can hardly form the words between her clenched teeth. She feels almost paralysed with her fear.

'Now that's a daft question.'

She leans against the door for support. He studies her assessingly. And now he is trailing the knife towards her stomach and with its tip is lifting the fabric of her jumper.

'Kneel,' he orders, in his hoarse rasp.

She slides down onto her knees.

'Now crawl round the room. Go on, *move*.'

She scrubs round the room like an amputee, and he follows, prodding her with his foot, kicking her back. She makes no attempt to disobey or argue or plead; knows that the first two would incite and the last excite. She would not, anyway, be able to speak coherently. Round and round the room she grovels.

This isn't happening, this isn't happening, this . . .

He hauls her to her feet. 'Get undressed.'

She has on a black silk-knit tunic over her leather skirt, and lifts it slowly over her head, sobbing dryly. Her hair crackles with electricity. She caves her shoulders forward, trying to shield her breasts, acutely conscious of her womanliness, of her body being private to her, and of the black half-cup bra she'd put on for Aidan.

He is riveted to her breasts. Spittle forms in one corner of his lips. He jiggles the knife about, taunting her. She can scarcely breathe.

She puts her hands up to herself protectively.

'Aidan will be here soon.'

'Liar! Whole village knows it's finished. You've been whoring around.'

His face looms over hers; the flashing row of his teeth. The flashing line of his knife. And she shrieks out as a scorching sensation zips down her right arm to the elbow.

'I'm not playing games.' Unbuckling his belt with one hand and gripping her wrist with the other. 'Now get your bra off.'

Her arm is dripping. It is too sore to raise to unfasten the hooks at the back. She struggles with her left hand but is trembling so much she can't locate them. And all the while, through her pain, through her fear that he is going to rape her, mutilate her, while he abuses and debases her, is the deeper terror that he will actually kill her.

He undoes his jeans and drags them off, over his trainers. He is not wearing pants. His erection is like a glistening pole, purple and veined.

'Get down on your knees.'

Weeping, she crouches and he forces back her head and pushes his penis into her mouth. She gags as he jerks it down her throat.

Suddenly he pulls out of her mouth, and she immediately retches. Vomits there, in front of him. He stares in disgust.

'Clean it up. I can't have that near me.'

Propels her into the scullery, knife to the small of her back. From under the sink she takes a wad of paper roll, a cloth, and a bottle of disinfectant. She scarcely knows what she is doing.

In the sitting room he watches as she cleans the carpet. Relishing her degradation, as she scrubs on all fours, in her leather skirt and laddered black stockings. His erection has died and he is angered because of it.

She does not screw the disinfectant lid back on. A vague idea forming in her mind.

'Get the rest of your clothes off,' he orders, when she has finished.

She undresses under his gaze. Steps out of the skirt, peels down her hold-up stockings, and finally her G-string briefs. Shivering and ashamed and defenceless.

He lifts the knife to her pubic hair. Sweat pours from her armpits down her sides. For a second they are face to face, and she knows her opportunity is now or not at all. With a burst of resolve she reaches out for the bottle of disinfectant and flings the contents in his eyes.

He lets out a bellow and presses his knuckles to his face, rocking in agony. He has dropped the knife and she snatches it up and stabs him hard in the shoulder with it, barely aware of what she is doing.

Screaming insanely, regardless of Hannah upstairs. Savage in her released rage and retaliation. Kicking out and clawing at him as, half blinded and bleeding heavily, he tries to lock her in a hold and they grapple towards the table. On it she catches sight of Aidan's binoculars, and she grabs them just as his hands encircle her throat. Brings them down, with every fragment of her strength, on his head.

He falls back, partially across her.

'*Mummy, Mumm-ee!*' Hannah shrieks upstairs.

Isabella, collapsed on the floor by the sofa, just a couple of yards from Luke, whom she may or may not have killed.

And Aidan opens the front door and steps inside.

AIDAN CALLS HER MY DARLING, my little love, my squirrel . . . He nurses and cossets her, cooks for her, lies beside her in bed, caresses her without having sex, wakes her when she is writhing about in the midst of a nightmare. For a week he scarcely lets her out of his sight; has organised a friend to take charge of the garage. He shops for her, helps with the housework, shepherds Hannah to and from playgroup.

Her arm is stiff but healing. The mental wounds are slower to heal.

At Truro hospital, where he drove her that night, they told the weary-eyed registrar she had stumbled over a ceramic plant-pot in the dark, gashing her arm on a broken piece as she fell on the concrete.

'Nasty,' he commented, having worked a sixteen-hour shift. Looked sceptical. Had heard it all before.

They have told people in the village the same. She is touched and surprised by their concern.

She has no energy, cannot concentrate for any length of time, frets about falling behind with her work, can't be bothered even to read the papers.

He reads extracts to her, picks out amusing stories in an attempt to elicit a smile from her: how two keen 'twitchers' in a leafy suburb had been hooting to each other from their gardens for the past year, each believing the other was an owl responding.

And she might begin to laugh, but then her laughter alters and the tears are trickling down her cheeks. Often she does not realise she is weeping. She will be sitting at her computer or in front of the television, staring ahead and crying silently. It is impossible to exorcise the ordeal from her mind. The images are replayed constantly.

But Luke has removed himself temporarily from the village.

'She won't dare do nothing,' he jeered weakly, when Aidan threatened him with the police and elbowed him, bleeding and half undressed, out into the night. Left his trail all the way to the van in the lane.

He is right. She does not dare.

The horror of reliving every detail in the witness box.

Ms Mercogliano, I understand that since you have been living in this area you have acquired something of a reputation where men are concerned.

And, says the smirking barrister, *there are other factors which have come to light, that His Lordship might be interested to learn.*

Nevertheless, she is afraid that by not taking action she is leaving the door open for the mechanic; that when he returns to the village he will seek her out. Unfinished business.

Aidan tries to reassure her this is unlikely. She remains unconvinced.

'His resentment will have built up in him,' she says. 'Eating into him. He'll want revenge. He's not balanced. Not normal.'

'Then report him. For your sake. For other women's sake.'

'I can't. Stop making me feel guilty.' She is not in the mood for objectivity and becomes angry with him, accusing him of being insensitive.

Fear, specific and unspecific, is with her the whole time. She whips round at every unexpected noise. Normal things that once went unremarked now give rise to panic in her. And she is concerned that Luke has a copy of her key, recollecting the afternoon she returned from Babs's shop to find the fireguard in a different position.

Aidan changes the lock and fixes a safety chain; attaches locks to the windows also. He blames himself for what happened.

'You told me you mistrusted him. And I was dismissive.'

He reproaches her, too, for not confiding in him.

'But it came to a head when we'd had our . . . rift,' she says.

He castigates himself over this also, for not trusting her.

'Although, if you'd been more open in the first place, there'd have been no need for any jealousy. I'm a man as likes to know where he stands. That's all I ask.'

They have still not discussed Tom, although she senses he is longing to. She does not have the energy to deal with the inevitable questions that would arise. Her body is repellent to her. It feels desecrated, as though it will never be clean again.

She has told Hannah she is not well.

'Mummy not well,' Hannah says sorrowfully. 'I make better.' Puts her arms round Isabella and kisses her.

And will Aidan grow impatient with her? She is not used to being feeble or to being pampered. Has always been so self-sufficient.

'I'm angry with myself,' she tells him today, on their first walk since it happened. 'I didn't react the way I'd always imagined I would in a situation like that. Everything just went from me. I disintegrated.'

'But your life was at stake, for goodness' sake. He had a knife jammed to you. You're brave, little love. You're brave.' Enfolding her in his arms as she breaks down.

Hannah rushing over to them from the spot where she was filling her pail with sand; clasping their legs, demanding, 'I want hug. I want hug.'

Laughing through tears. Aidan stooping to hoist Hannah onto his shoulders for a piggyback.

The fishermen go about their day as usual. No Charlie whistling, dragging his foot and outpacing them. The village without him is gradually slipping back to normal. The Sun Inn resounds once more to darts matches and beer-drinking competitions and karaoke nights.

A fox is on the prowl, having dispatched Joyce's bantams and a couple of other people's chickens, besides the surgeon's wife's pet ducks.

For Joyce it has been one thing too much. This catastrophe, so minor compared to the other she has just been through, has defeated her.

'I don't know as I'll bother replacing them,' she tells Isabella. 'All that work for nothing. And without Charlie I don't need all those eggs. I can get them from Babs.'

Days passing. Storms lashing the headlands. The sea mountainous; and the men go out regardless, in challenging spirit, in their yellow oil-skins. She falls asleep with the blinking of the lighthouse and wakes to the lament of the foghorn. Tregurran beach is brown with tossed wet sand, dead bracken blown from the cliffs, and banks of seaweed.

Mary Anne is in bed with flu. Telephones Isabella: 'Would you like to ride Nabokov? You'll have to tack him up yourself. I can't move.'

She leaves Hannah with Joyce. It is the first time it hasn't rained for four or five days. The lanes are slippery. Branches and leaves are strewn about. Nabokov picks his way with a cautious rhythmical clop. It is the slowest two miles she has ever accomplished. When they come to Tregurran beach he puts on a spurt, and with a swish of the tail and the tiniest of bucks he canters towards the ragged hem of the sea. He slows a little and she slackens the reins and lets him trot of his own accord into the waves. Needles of salt scour her cheeks. The wind tears at her hair. She laughs in pure exhilaration; pure, obliterating, transient happiness.

In the evening Aidan drives her to Falmouth to see a production of *Lady Windermere's Fan*. They leave during the first act—driven away by an old man on Isabella's other side who takes up half her seat besides his own with the spread of his belly and thighs, his walking stick, and a stinking bag of fish that becomes more overpowering by the second.

'Poor old guy,' Aidan reflects. 'There's something very pathetic and lonely about it, if you think, isn't there? A man of seventy or eighty at the theatre alone. Bad chest, bad hip more'n like, and a bag of fish he'll cook for himself.'

They walk to a nearby Italian restaurant, converted wine vaults reached via steeply angled steps. They cause her to remember when she took Hannah back to her flat.

Today something extraordinary happened . . . At approximately ten o'clock this morning, Saturday, August 31 . . .

Is that all it is—only just over two months ago? It seems incredible.

The restaurant is fairly busy this Friday night. She recognises a couple from the surgeon's wife's party. They recognise her also, smile hello. The woman gives Aidan a friendly little wave.

'I do her car,' he says, as the waiter shows them to a table in a secluded corner.

During the meal she becomes aware that his fingers are drumming on the table, then wandering up to his beard, then his hair. Grabs his hand as it moves towards the candle, about to tackle the dripped wax.

'So, what's up?'

He tilts his head from side to side and studies her contemplatively. 'All right,' he says finally. 'The other evening, well, *that* evening, you were going to tell me about Tom . . . I haven't mentioned it as I didn't want to upset you. But it's bothering me. I need to know, Isabella.'

Aidan's right hand is tanned, with pale threads of ancient scars traversing it. What were the incidents that caused them?

'We were married when I was at university. He was a journalist then. Anyway, after about a year he went out to Vietnam as a reporter. By the time he returned I'd graduated. He was impossible to live with. He hated being married. So we divorced. That's all there is to it. When he turned up here it was the first time I'd seen him since we split up.'

He nods slowly, plainly not satisfied. 'But you said you'd run away from your husband.'

'No, I didn't. Others said it. *I* didn't. They just surmised.'

'You're not married, then?'

'No.'

'Then Hannah's father—?'

She doesn't answer.

'Why won't you tell me? I'm an open book. You know everything about me. You're not being fair.' He raises his voice in frustration, and she leans forward and lays her finger against his lip.

'I adopted her.' It isn't entirely a lie. 'I can't tell you any more.'

His voice is flat with hurt. 'You're so secretive. It's insulting, you know that? I thought we trusted each other.'

She feels a quickening of panic. She is so afraid of driving him away a second time. She cannot conceive of their not being together. Has come to value him more than anyone she has ever known.

'Please, *caro*, don't be hurt.'

Her eyes are black with tenderness, and he gazes into them.

'I love it when you call me that.' Sighing.

Neither of them speaks for a moment. He swirls his sautéed potatoes round in the tomato sauce. Pushes the plate away from him.

'You'll tell me one day, when you're ready?'

'Yes.'

God knows how. The postponement of playing her own executioner.

'I suppose that'll have to do, then. Just a couple of things. Are the police involved?'

She doesn't answer.

'Isabella?' he presses her.

'No. But they might be one day.'

And now he really will tell her he's had enough, that under those circumstances he must finish with her. Who could blame him?

She feels him touch her face, his hand gently lifting her chin so that she is forced to look at him.

'You haven't hurt anyone, I mean physically? It's a terrible thing to ask, but—'

'No. Never in my life.'

'And you haven't taken any money, nothing like that?'

'*Madre*, no.'

A child. But no money.

'I trust you.'

And in two days' time it will be her birthday. Her fortieth. And Hannah's third. She has decided they shall share a birthday. Has bought her a swing that Aidan will put up in the garden, on the patch where Timothy Abell used to dig his potatoes. And what if it were her birthday? Would her mother be remembering when she gave birth?

'Do you want me to tell you the best birthday present of your life?' Aidan says on the phone, from the garage.

'Keep it as a surprise.'

'Are you sure? Are you sure you don't want me to tell you that new people have moved into Luke's place? That he's left the area for good?'

For a few seconds she experiences a sense of relief. But it is quickly replaced by an odd deadness. In her head he has not gone for good. His quiet, brutal voice is in her ears. His face leers over hers. She is consumed by images.

Among her birthday cards is a letter from Neil:

Dear Isabella,

It was splendid to see you a couple of weeks ago, albeit at such a tragic occasion, and I just wanted to scrawl an impulsive note.

Long day, today. Had to represent a client in court. A bit of a yawn case, but I mustn't complain. It pays the bills. Well, some. If ever you need a good lawyer . . . Joke. You seem like a woman whose life is thoroughly in order.

As I mentioned to you, I have no wish to impose on you, and should hate you to feel obliged in any way, but it would be lovely to escape from London for a few days and have the bonus of seeing you again, as a no-strings 'chum'. I wonder if I could trouble you to give me the name of somewhere local to stay for two or three nights. Ideally the

middle or end of this month would suit me, as December tends to get silly
with work. But you must tell me when it would be convenient for you.
    That's it for now. My youngest is yelling for her fish fingers.
    All best wishes,
    Neil

She is glad to hear from him, and writes back immediately with some provisional dates and the telephone number of the Ship Inn.

Aidan has bought her a gold-link bracelet for her birthday.

Tears in her eyes. He fastens it round her wrist, and she stares down at it, settled neatly there; rubs her thumb round it.

'It's beautiful. I shan't ever take it off.'

'You might need to sometimes.' He grins down at her.

'And for Hannah . . . For Hannah,' he teases gently, holding the untidily wrapped parcel aloft before giving it to her.

'P'esn't for me, p'esn't for me,' she squeals, dancing around with Becky, who is reinstated as her best friend.

It is a cloth doll with yellow tresses and ribbons. 'My name is Hannah,' it says on the pink box. They are at his house. Balloons hang in the hallway. HAPPY BIRTHDAYS, he has painted on them. The paint has dripped.

In the garden, in the deepening dusk, the girls run about, in and out of the cypresses.

They wait for Becky's mother to come; Aidan shields them from the cold, one either side of him, within the cave of his jacket. They are tiny beside his hugeness, snuggling against him.

She settles Hannah in the spare room for the night. Goes downstairs into the open-plan kitchen, where he is preparing dinner for the two of them.

I don't deserve him.

The ticking of the kitchen clock. Classic FM on quietly. He is grating nutmeg into fettucini, then blending in an egg yolk. And she creeps up on him and covers his eyes with her hands.

'Guess who loves you.'

He prises her hands from his eyes and grips them; turns round to her, his expression serious. 'No. I want to hear you say it.'

His gaze flows into hers. She is drowning.

'I love you.'

'And I love you.'

It solves nothing. Probably complicates it. But, *madre*, the relief, the joy, of saying it. The relief, the joy, of hearing it.

And after dinner, after the champagne, the cake, the single red rose, the Cointreau, she goes to bed with him and lets their love wash her body clean.

SHE HAS TWO WEEKS. Perhaps one day she will review them as the happiest she knew. Two weeks. Thirteen days to be precise. Remarkable for being unremarkable, for the fact little happens.

She will look back and remember Guy Fawkes Night, and the village gathered round the leaping bonfire on the eastern headland. Hannah's anxious little hand slotted into hers. Aidan's arm round her neck. The air alive with the zinging and crackling of fireworks.

Will look back on the dinner party she gave, when Babs flirted with the vicar, who entertained them with card tricks, and Mary Anne and Joyce discussed sex in old age.

Will recall the glow of pleasure she felt when she was asked to give a talk about her work at a WI meeting. And on winning the karaoke competition at the Sun—the teasing, and laughter around her, and buying everyone a round of drinks; and when they toasted her she knew she was finally welcomed into the community.

Will remember the comparative serenity, the peace of mind she felt during that period. Time on 'hold'.

Loving Aidan. Loving Hannah.

Will remember reading to Hannah in bed from *The Wind in the Willows* and her rapt expression. The rabbit and bear either side of her.

And then it is Saturday. Thirteen days since her birthday. Eleven weeks since that other Saturday. And like that other one it unfolds. Saturday, November 16. Isabella will have reason to remember the date. She goes about her usual routine; puts the kettle on, grinds the coffee beans, opens the curtains to bright sun . . . and silver grass. Fusses over Garibaldi. Feeds him. Gets herself ready. Wakes up Hannah. Dresses her—she has learned to fasten the buckles of her own shoes. Makes them both breakfast. Ten o'clock; and they go outside. She pushes Hannah on the swing.

'Higher.'

The phone is ringing. She lifts Hannah down from the swing and runs indoors to answer it.

It is Neil, finalising arrangements for his visit. They chat for a bit.

She has been five minutes at most. Returns outside.

Hannah is not about. Where is she?

The gate is open, and Isabella feels a twinge of alarm. But she suppresses it; reminds herself of that other occasion on their picnic, her needless panic.

'Hannah,' she calls from the garden. '*Cara.*'

No response comes, and now Isabella's fear is clutching at her, and she runs to the gate and peers left along the cutting towards the lighthouse and right towards the lane. There is no sign of the child.

'*Hannah!*'

Her panic taking hold of her. And she runs down the cutting towards the lane. From here there is an unhampered view to the village, and she can see that, apart from an elderly couple hanging on to each other and pushing a shopping basket on wheels, the little street is deserted.

Up the hill she runs, her breathing catching in her chest, her arms waving about in an uncoordinated way; past the car park, past the surgeon's house, in the direction of Tregurran beach.

'Have you seen my little girl?' she shouts to a gardener hoeing the edge of the driveway. No, he is afraid he hasn't.

Of course, she would not have ventured this far. She turns and tears back in the direction from which she has just come.

'*Hannah! Hannah!*'

Back down the cutting, making for the steps that lead to the cove. Gruesome images of the child's body on the rocks below filling her head.

It is high tide; only the two uppermost steps are exposed. Dear God. *Madre.* Dear God, dear God . . . Isabella muttering to a deity she has never believed in.

'Isabella, what's happened?' Joyce's rollered grey head out of her open window.

Doesn't hear her. Running about distractedly. Stumbling up the embankment that leads to the chapel, pushing the door, then tugging it, in case the child has gone in there; but it is locked fast. It always is.

For another half-hour she searches. By now it is approaching eleven. There are people about. They see her running directionlessly, crazed and dishevelled. Someone takes her elbow as she sobs that she has lost Hannah, that Hannah has gone, Hannah has gone . . . And whoever it is leads her back to the cottage. She dashes upstairs into the child's room.

She lies on the child's bed, smells her vanilla skin and sweet hair on the pillow and duvet. Resigned. Knows she will never again see the child.

Aidan drives her to Truro police station. Two of them interview her. One is a woman. They are sensitive in their questioning, soft-voiced. A cup of tea arrives, and they encourage her to drink. Are patient when she can hardly whisper. Aidan's concerned eyes next to her, his hand almost crushing hers.

Her face is haggard. She huddles doubled up in the chair in the clinical white room, nursing her stomach, while they quiz her, taking her painfully step by step through the morning, which has already assumed a distant, unreal quality.

'Try not to worry,' the woman officer says.

'Five minutes,' Isabella says. 'I wasn't even five minutes.'

'You mustn't blame yourself.' Glancing at her male colleague.

'Is there anyone she knows that she might've gone to?' he asks.

She shakes her head.

'You look after her yourself?'

And through her anguish she realises that, however subtly masked the question might be, he is trying to ascertain whether she herself might have harmed the child.

'Yes. I had someone for a few weeks who helped out. But she left.'

'Why?'

'She moved from the area.'

'Do you have a contact number?' the woman asks her.

Again she shakes her head.

They address Aidan. She doesn't hear what they ask him, or his replies. Fixated by a fly traversing the ceiling. She knows the child is dead. One day a fisherman will find her. And did her real mother feel like Isabella, as she gave up her child? The drip-drip of haemorrhaging longing?

Isabella has failed the test of motherhood. She could not guard the child from harm. And maybe, after all, God exists, and this is his punishment; he has meted out his own brand of irony.

'We'll keep you closely informed,' the WPC assures her.

'I want to die,' she says, as Aidan helps her up from the chair. Isabella, who is petrified of death.

News of this kind circulates fast. Over the next few days she is besieged by visitors. Everyone rallying round, trying to keep her mind occupied, attempting to console her.

She wants to be left alone.

And all around are reminders of the child. But there is no sign of the knitted rabbit. Gone with her.

The days drag and pass.

DISTRAUGHT MOTHER FEARS WORST, runs the headline in the *West Briton*. Four lines in the *Independent*, and maybe other papers, for all she knows. How does the national press hear about these things?

'It's their job,' Aidan tells her.

'I hate them,' she says.

He tries to persuade her to eat: 'You can't just give up. Please, squirrel.' Holding his own fork to her.

'I can't. I'll be sick.' Pushing it away.

'We're not giving up,' the police say.

From the shore she watches a boat set off with police and rubber-clad divers. Overhead a helicopter lumbers in slow, monotonous circles between the headlands and hovers round the narrows, sending the gulls squealing.

She lies awake night after night, with Aidan's back curved against her, plagued with ghastly, vivid imagery. Found on a Saturday. Gone on a Saturday. Saturday's child. Nowhere child. On loan for eleven weeks. She herself was born on a Saturday.

And now it is Friday; the afternoon. She sits on the swing in the drizzle, absently levering herself back and forth. Hears a car turning into the cutting from the lane and watches with bleak presentiment as it draws up outside the cottage.

They get out of the car: the woman sergeant accompanied by a man she has not seen before. He is not in uniform. The twin thuds of the car doors shutting. Of her heart. She does not stand up as they approach via the open gate—no need to bother about it now—and come towards her, grim-faced.

'We've found her, Isabella. She's fine,' the WPC says.

She stops swinging. Stares at them both with disbelief; a smile spreading across her face, becoming laughter. Laughing and crying.

In her emotion she does not register their sombre expressions.

'Your childminder took her, Sophia Gundry.'

'Sophia? *Sophia* took her? Not Sophia, surely.'

'Yes, that's correct.' The man speaks for the first time.

The woman officer looks from him to Isabella. Compassion puckering her forehead. There is something wrong. They are too serious. And why haven't they brought the child with them?

'Where's Hannah? What's happened? Why isn't she with you?' Her voiced raised and high-pitched with her sudden anxiety.

The man steps forward. He introduces himself as Detective Sergeant . . . She doesn't catch the name.

'I'm afraid Mrs Gundry has made some serious allegations against you,' he says.

The blood pumping back and forth in her ears, like the sea.

'What kind of allegations?' Hears her voice from over the horizon.

'That in fact you are not the child's mother. Apparently she read some diary you'd been keeping. Miss Mercogliano'—he sneers over her name—'I have to inform you I am arresting you on suspicion of abduction.'

'Ms,' she says faintly. 'Not Miss. Ms.'

So. It is over.

THE WPC LEADS HER DOWN a linoleum-floored corridor—it reminds her of the hospital where her mother died—to the charge area, in Custody. It is a large room with a computer on the table. The young woman motions for Isabella to sit down. She seems uncomfortable, having switched from her role of consoler to that of arresting officer.

The detective sergeant enters with a short, rotund man. He is introduced to her as the custody sergeant, and he positions himself in front of the computer, gives a small nod to his colleague, who begins speaking in a monotone:

'This person has been arrested at sixteen fifty-seven hours this day, Friday, November the 22nd.'

Was arrested, she notes. He doesn't know his tenses.

'To summarise: for the past three months she was caring for a young child on the pretext of being its mother, when this child subsequently went missing. The child was duly found at eleven oh-seven today, having been abducted by a Mrs Sophia Gundry, who for a short while was employed as a childminder and cleaner by Miss Mercogliano.'

'Ms,' she murmurs, polishing the Formica of the table with her fingers.

'For God's sake.' The detective sergeant rolls his eyes heavenwards. 'I was saying—Mrs Gundry was taken in for questioning during which it emerged that *Miss* Mercogliano is not the mother, she herself abducted the child. Mrs Gundry claimed to have seen a diary that Miss Mercogliano kept.

'After hearing Mrs Gundry's statement I drove with WPC Harries to Miss Mercogliano's rented home at Pengarris Cove and arrested Miss Mercogliano for the abduction of a child against its volition.'

The custody sergeant stops typing and turns to Isabella. 'Ms Mercogliano,' he says, acknowledging her preferred prefix, 'you have just heard the arresting officer's account. Do you wish to add anything?'

'No—yes, I do. I did it for the child's good. I did not take her against her own volition. She had been abandoned.'

And where is she now? She despairs at the thought.

The custody officer forms his lips into a moue and scrutinises her.

'Ms Mercogliano, the allegation against you is extremely serious. I am authorising your detention here for twelve hours, pending enquiries. Because of the weekend interlude, you will not be heard in the magistrate's court until Monday.'

He exchanges a few words with his colleagues, nods curtly to her and leaves the room.

She immediately turns to the other two: 'Hannah—who's looking after her? Where is she?'

They are not at liberty to say, the detective sergeant tells her.

'Please. I have to know.'

The child she was nurturing so carefully, so instinctively. The child screaming, confused, wetting herself, calling for Mumm-ee.

The WPC takes pity on her. Tells her that a local social worker, a conscientious family woman, has taken her into her own home until suitable alternative arrangements can be made.

'Look, you must remember she's alive. She's safe, at least,' she says. 'Yesterday you thought—'

The detective sergeant glowers. 'I think you've covered the matter now, Constable.' He presses his hands together, making a steeple with his fingertips pointed. 'Miss Mercogliano, I am informing you of your rights. They are as follows. You are entitled to consult the Code of Rights book if you wish. You may also make two telephone calls . . .'

And she suddenly remembers—it had completely slipped her mind—Neil is arriving this very evening. Perhaps he is already here. She starts to laugh, then cannot stop. Tears flowing from her eyes. Gasping. She cannot get her breath.

The WPC makes her put her head between her knees. Isabella is dimly aware of her voice, of her asking the detective sergeant to fetch a glass of water, of the blood pumping through her ears and behind her temples.

Gradually her breathing pattern is regulated. She drinks the tumbler of water that the WPC is holding out for her.

She sits back, recovering for a few moments, ignoring the detective sergeant, who is shifting about impatiently in the chair opposite her.

'I just need to make one call,' she says, when she is composed.

He pushes the phone across the table towards her.

She dials Aidan's number. He answers. His ripe bass; tender with gladness at hearing from her:

'Where *are* you? I've been trying to ring you. I drove to the cottage. I was worried.'

Matter-of-factly she explains what has happened and the reason for her arrest. Self-conscious with the other two present. A withering inside her as she listens to the change in his tone—flabbergasted shock, then an edge of strain. Already distancing himself.

'I'll drive there now.'

'No,' she says forcefully. And asks him to contact Neil on her behalf at the Ship Inn.

She replaces the receiver with a sense of painful inevitability, clamping her teeth together to prevent herself from betraying her emotion in front of the detective sergeant.

Out of the corner of her eye she sees him getting up, going to the door. He tells her the WPC will search her; appraises her with contempt when she looks horrified, before making his exit.

'It's standard procedure. I'm sorry, Isabella,' the WPC says. And her expression is genuinely so.

Afterwards she is led up a flight of stairs and along a corridor, then halfway down another. Her cell is about nine foot by twelve, the walls adorned with graffiti, and with a wooden bench which she is told also serves as a bed. Behind a brick partition is an aluminium toilet; whose wooden seat has been stuck down. The reek of shame.

'I'm afraid I have to take your belt and bag.'

The door clunks behind her. Alone with her sense of unreality. Unbelievable that she should find herself in here. A few months ago, as she went about her normal, chic, ordered existence, who could have imagined this?

The WPC appears with a paper cup of tea and *Woman and Home* and *Good Housekeeping*. An hour or so passes. She reads how to make bramble jelly, and how to disguise a pear-shaped body. In her opinion the woman in the photograph looks better before her makeover. Muted voices outside the door. The sound of a key in the lock.

'Well, I always fancied being locked in with a beautiful woman,' jokes Neil, coming up to her and kissing her on both cheeks.

'So why did you do it?' he asks her.

'I did it because . . . Do you know the French word *éclat*?'

'I'm not sure. I'm not much of a linguist.'

'*Éclat de: éclat de soleil*. A burst of sun. That's what her face did. And inside me I . . . it singed me. I can't explain it. It wasn't something I can just explain.'

'But it was out of character.'

'I suppose so. Until then I'd never done anything out of the norm. My life was very structured.'

But leading up to it were pointers, had she chosen to tweeze them from her subconscious and examine them. A random collection of influencing factors, accumulated over the years, which a psychologist would have latched on to with a satisfied snap of the fingers.

'And you regret it.' Spoken with the rhetoric of assurance.

She wraps her arms round herself. Looks tiredly up at him. At her peeling nails. At the window with no view and her silver reflection in it.

'Isabella? Surely—'

She turns back to him, and he is struck anew by how her face can switch from plain to beautiful with a flicker of expression in her eyes; she shakes her head as she thrusts out her palm in a typically eloquent gesture: 'What can I say? How can I possibly regret it?'

'It's ridiculous you're being held over like this,' he says when she has recounted the circumstances to him. 'I'm going to kick up a fuss. After you've given your statement we'll try and get you out of here.'

'It's such a relief to see you. I'm sorry—I forgot everything. It was supposed to be a break for you. Will you represent me? As my lawyer, I mean.'

'Of course, if you want me to.'

'I'm so sorry,' she says again, close to tears.

The interview room is on the ground floor. It is the same room where six days ago she was questioned gently and comforted, and Aidan sat beside her gripping her hand all the while.

'You do not have to say anything. But it may harm your defence if you do not mention, when questioned, something you later rely on in court . . .' the detective sergeant cautions her.

She recalls as faithfully as she can the sequence of events of that Saturday morning three months ago. He refuses to believe she had intended to hand the child over.

'You should have taken her directly to the police, without going home.'

'Don't say anything,' Neil advises her. 'My client has no further comment to make,' he says.

He does not succeed in having her released from custody.

'The thing is,' he says, 'they *know* you're not a threat. They realise you're not likely to go around grabbing other children. They probably even believe your story. But the problem is it doesn't fit in anywhere, doesn't relate to a case history they can look up. Abduction against volition—and on paper, that's what it is—is deemed to be an SAO and as far as the police are concerned, that's all that's relevant.'

'What does SAO mean?'

'Serious arrestable offence.'

'*Madre*, the things I'm learning.'

'Isabella, this will be a Crown Court job. And you must be prepared for a lot of publicity. It's an unusual case, to say the least: an abandoned, abused child abducted, and then abducted again.'

His eyes stray round the room then rest on her. 'I hate the thought of you stuck in this dump . . . Listen, as soon as I leave here I'm going to get on the phone. Find out who the best local barrister is.'

'It's all going to cost a fortune.'

'Not for my part, it won't. But a good barrister doesn't come cheap.'

'Oh, *madre*.' She slumps back on the bench.

'You mustn't brood and despair. I know it's easy for me to say that. But . . . I'll come and see you tomorrow. On Monday we'll go for bail. Two days. That's all. Be strong. You *are* strong.'

She used to think she was. Now she is just so weary.

'I landed myself in this. I can't be self-pitying.'

'Tell me, did you really think you'd get away with it? How could you have kept up the deception?'

'I don't know. I don't know what I thought,' she answers truthfully. 'I only knew that I wanted Hannah's welfare.'

He takes her hand. He still wears his wedding ring, she notices for the first time; finds that very poignant.

'You're so kind. Thank you for everything.'

'We're chums, aren't we?' he says, getting up.

At the prospect of his leaving she is suddenly afraid.

'Joyce, my next-door neighbour, has a spare key to the cottage. My report's on the bookshelf between Delia Smith and Webster's dictionary. The photos and the mother's letter are inside.'

'It'll be my bedtime reading tonight. I'll go directly to the cottage now. What do you want me to tell Joyce?'

'The truth. She'll hear soon enough anyway. Everybody will. And could you ask her to feed Garibaldi, my cat? Poor little Garibaldi. Poor Hannah. Oh, *madre,* Neil, I'm so *scared.*'

A policeman enters bearing supper on a tray: a bowl of tomato soup, three triangles of white bread, sparsely buttered, jelly, and a plastic cup of water. He sets it down on the bench and goes out. A moment later the key jangles in the lock again. This time it is the WPC.

'I've got hold of some toothpaste and soap for you. And here's a letter. It's a copy. The original had to be kept as possible evidence . . .'

Night has fallen. She reads the letter while having her soup (she is surprisingly hungry):

Dear Isabella, Sophia begins.

> *You have no idea how sorry I am about everything—taking Hannah and then telling on you but everything got out of hand and after that awful night when you found me and Luke I was really miserable. I stayed with my parents for a bit but we weren't getting on so I left there and my dad paid for me to rent a flat except that it was just a room really. Every day I used to drive from St Austell back to Pengarris trying to get the nerve to speak to you. I hid near the chapel and watched you and Hannah together playing. I longed to talk to you but didn't dare. I knew she wasn't your real daughter because the time before the last that I worked for you I found your report as it fell out when I went to get the Delia Smith. First of all I was really shocked that you'd nicked her and then when I saw the photos of darling little Hannah all bruised I knew you'd rescued her really and it was a good thing to do so I never said anything when I next saw you and you were always so kind and gener-ous to me. Well last Saturday I hid in my usual place and I hadn't any thoughts in my head about taking her or anything but suddenly you went into the house and there was Hannah all alone and I went over to speak to her and she was so pleased to see me it just happened.*

> *I want you to know she missed you. I looked after her really well but she kept asking for Mummy and Grabla—*

'Oh no.' The words escape her in a small moan.

> *I was going to give her back I promise. I was planning how I'd just drop her off when you were inside the cottage. But it turned out that*

Janet Abell lives near me and saw me with Hannah and phoned the police and so they came and found me. I have to go to court about taking Hannah but they are not keeping me here. I was here for nearly eight hours and now I'm waiting for my dad to get me. He's going to be livid. The nice policewoman says she'll give you this letter. I feel really awful about getting you into trouble. I hope they let you go too.
　　Love,
　　Sophia

She takes off her shoes, but other than that she does not undress for the night. She cannot think she will sleep, on this plank of a bed, with the pungent smell from the toilet permeating the cell, with her mind churning and every thought and uncertainty leading to an entire new set. Loose threads flying. Yet she is mentally and physically exhausted. She rolls over onto her tummy. A finger of light penetrates through the eyelet in the door. In this most unlikely of bedchambers she sleeps properly for the first time in a week.

She wakes at just gone seven, almost drugged; fuzzy-mouthed, having slept for nine hours. Washes herself in the tiny basin. Breakfast is brought in by a policeman who has obviously been on night shift. He is pallid, except for the fierce acne on one cheek.

'Ah, breakfast in bed,' she quips as he puts the tray on the bench.

She lives for the rattling of keys. And what must it be like day after day, year in, year out? She might yet discover for herself.

And now it is later on in the morning and this particular rattling of keys heralds Aidan. She springs up as he comes in. He kisses her awkwardly, briefly, his lips landing on the corner of her mouth.

'I recognise that wrestling-with-yourself look.' She attempts to be light-hearted. But it falls flat. She wishes he had not come.

He denies it. He says he is sorry to see her in here, that's all. He tells her he met Neil the previous evening, after he had visited her.

'So you got the full story.'

Pause. Waiting for him to comment. 'So?' she pushes him.

'Well, it's just I believe there's a proper way of going about things.' Avoids looking at her as he says it.

'I'm not expecting you to stick by me.'

When he makes no reply to this she feels suddenly cold.

Belatedly he says, 'Of course I will. I mean, when you took her you were probably mixed up.'

'When I took her initially, maybe. But when I decided to keep her, I was utterly clear about what I was doing.'

She knows it is not what he wishes to hear.

466

'Look, I can't make the truth palatable for you,' she says to his back. 'I've got my own worrying to do. Frankly, all I care about is what is going to happen to Hannah.'

But this isn't so. She cares desperately about him also. At this moment all she craves is for him to hold her. It is too much to expect. She is more trouble than it is worth to him. In the comparatively short time she has known him she has been nothing but trouble.

'Is someone feeding Garibaldi?' he asks suddenly, turning round. His face is ravaged.

'I told Neil to ask Joyce to.'

'I could—'

'You don't need to concern yourself.' Which comes out far more harshly than she intends, so that she immediately apologises.

They are diagonally opposite each other, just a couple of strides away, facing one another like soldiers come face to face across a trench.

'What are you doing this weekend?' she asks, trying to make normal conversation.

'There's a gig I'm playing at tonight.'

'Oh yes, of course. I forgot.' A gig. Ordinary life. His reality.

'And my lads are coming tomorrow. They'll spend the night. But I can get away to see you, if you're still here.'

'There's not much point. Is there?' A dry thickness in her throat like a bone trapped horizontally. She gives a small cough.

'Yes. I want to see you,' he says, his voice cracking.

'It'll be all round the village soon. After the hearing on Monday.'

He pulls a grimace. He has evidently thought of that. It disturbs him, as an intensely private and, above all, honest man. Sucked into the vortex of her scandal. Judged because of her. And he has two school-aged sons: *Your dad's girlfriend's a child-snatcher.*

Understands his predicament.

He kisses her goodbye. For a few beautiful seconds his kiss holds her. His grey eyes, slightly bloodshot this morning, search hers unhappily. He tuts. He sighs. He shakes his head. He stumbles out. A man whose conscience will not be able to provide easy answers.

Neil visits in the afternoon.

'You look surprisingly rested,' he remarks, kissing her on both cheeks. She notices a food stain down his Aran jumper.

'I've had a lot of time to do just that,' she answers wryly. 'Resting and thinking.'

'Well, I've also been doing some thinking.' Sitting down next to her on the bench. 'I tell you, your report was an eye-opener. I've taken charge of it, along with the photos and the mother's letter, for safe-keeping. My God, those photos . . . There's good news and bad news,' he goes on. 'They've successfully applied for an extension to the twelve hours. You're being detained until the hearing on Monday morning. The police are trying to trace the mother.'

He notices her crestfallen expression and touches her arm.

'Now look, the good news is what we have to focus on.' He claps his hands with deliberate heartiness. 'I did quite a lot of ringing around various contacts yesterday evening and I got the name of an excellent-sounding barrister with a formidable reputation.'

'Does he charge formidable rates?'

'She. Well, as I mentioned yesterday, good barristers don't come cheap, but she charges less than her equivalent in London. Anyhow, I took the liberty of phoning her at her home last night and summarised the case. She was fascinated by it and is keen to take it on. She agrees with me that as an indictable offence the matter will be beyond the jurisdiction of the magistrate's court, therefore you won't be putting forward a plea. The thing to focus on is getting you bail. I'll be talking to prosecution before the case is heard, so he knows the full circumstances. Now, you mustn't worry.'

'Could you bring me a change of clothes? I need a change of clothes.' Flicking her hand disgustedly over her leggings and long, shapeless jumper.

'With pleasure. I'll have to check it's permitted, though.'

The key in the door. Four o'clock, and a woman officer she hasn't seen before brings her a cup of tea and a couple of digestive biscuits.

'Could my . . . lawyer have some tea also?'

'I think we might manage it.' The woman goes out and returns a few minutes later. She is big, unfeminine, with a heavy black fringe.

'I warn you, it bears no resemblance to the real thing,' Isabella tells him.

'It's hot, anyhow,' Neil says.

For a short while they don't speak. She takes a biscuit and blows on the steam rising from her cup.

'You wrote something in your letter a few weeks ago,' she remembers. 'It was quite ironic.'

'What was that?'

'You wrote that I seemed like a woman whose life was thoroughly in order.'

'Well, you did. That's how you came across.'

'I once believed it myself. And when I got your letter I was just recovering from a trauma. You must've read about it in my report.'

'I didn't know whether to raise that subject or not. Since you have . . . You should have reported him, Isabella.'

'I couldn't, for the reasons I wrote.'

'Maybe you'll decide to when all this is over.'

Another, longer silence.

'You know I met Aidan last night?' Neil says. 'He came to the Ship.'

'Yes. He visited this morning. He told me you gave him the full story. Did you show him the photos?'

'That's right. I thought it might help, when he realised . . . Anyway, so how's he taking everything?'

'Badly. No, not badly. He's confused.'

The bone of pain is in her throat again.

'I love him, but he can't deal with what I've done. Do you know, Neil, before this I can't remember ever having told a lie. Oh, maybe a fib to save someone's feelings, but never a proper lie. And I tell you something. I'm glad that part is over. The lying.'

'Will you do me a favour? Will you tell Aidan not to come tomorrow? I can't face seeing him in here again.'

TEN O'CLOCK THIS MONDAY, November 25. Hers is the first case to be heard in courtroom number one.

'The whole thing will be over within ten minutes,' Neil says, observing her frozen expression. He gives her elbow an encouraging squeeze as she is about to walk in.

She feels everybody's eyes on her. Cannot, for several seconds, bring herself to do anything but stare at the ground. Dimly aware of movement and muted voices. Hesitantly she raises her eyes to look around.

Her impression is of a large, modern room, about thirty feet in length. From the main doors there are three rows of tip-up chairs where a few members of the public—there for free theatre, she presumes—are already seated. Along the opposite wall are another couple of rows of seats with tables for the journalists. There are four of them this morning, scribbling away, in between looking across at her. She feels a wave of pre-emptive antagonism towards them. Now her glance wanders to the Clerk of the Court at his raised desk, in front of the lawyers, and finally towards the Bench, on a dais a few feet across from her. One woman and two men. In the middle, on a larger chair than the other two, presides the chairman. He is balding, and sits pole-upright. Lances her with glacial eyes. She feels a jolt in her ribs—has recognised him instantly. The man from the surgeon's wife's party.

Mary Anne's gleeful remark comes back to her: *He'd have us all behind bars if he could.*

'Next case is the Crown versus Miss Isabella Mercogliano, Your Worship.'

The prosecutor stands: small, with receding hair and a non-existent mouth.

'This is a matter which can only be heard by the Crown Court,' he says, 'hence no plea is being offered.' He proceeds to outline the case.

The journalists' hands flying across their notepads.

'Abandoned child . . . Drove home with . . . Abused . . .'

She is conscious of the chairman peering at her over his bifocals which he has just put on.

I am not ashamed. I am not ashamed. Repeating it over and over; as, when she was a young girl, she had covered pages with the words: *I matter*—in three languages.

'I invite you to commit the defendant to the Crown Court without hearing any of the evidence,' the prosecutor concludes.

The Clerk turns to Neil. 'Do you agree there is a prima-facie case?' he asks.

Neil stands up. 'Yes, I agree.' And sits down again immediately.

The chairman looks across at Isabella. 'We commit you to Crown Court to stand trial.' He says this in a slow, ringing tone, as though condemning her to be executed.

Neil gets to his feet again and addresses him: 'Your Worship, I would ask you to grant bail for my client. I've discussed this with my friend'—turns briefly to the other lawyer—'who is in agreement.'

He sits down once more and the other man stands. 'Your Worship, I'm instructed that the prosecution will agree to bail on the accused's own recognisances.'

'Very well,' says the chairman. 'We grant the accused conditional bail.' He looks at her severely. 'You will be heard at the Crown Court, on Tuesday, the 7th of January. Your passport must be lodged with this court by two o'clock this afternoon. You must present yourself to the same police station of your choice each Monday, and under no circumstances are you to have contact with the child. If you do not comply with these conditions you could be liable to arrest.'

But—for the moment she is *free*.

She goes with Neil to the WRVS-run canteen. And there, at a table with an older man she presumes to be the father, is Sophia.

She feels no animosity. Sophia has been caught up in her own web of circumstances. She goes up to the table.

'Hello, Sophia.'

The girl seems to shrivel into the chair. She can't meet Isabella's eyes.

'Isabella, I'm . . .' It is obvious she does not know what to do or say.

Isabella touches the girl's cheek—thin, drained of colour. 'It's all right. There's no need to say anything.'

Tears come into Sophia's eyes.

'Bye,' murmurs Isabella. 'Good luck.'

They have their coffee by the window.

'So now we get moving,' Neil says. 'I'm taking Eileen—the barrister—your report, et cetera, this afternoon, and the copy of Sophia's letter. And she's been kind enough to squeeze us in for an appointment tomorrow afternoon, before I go home.'

'*Madre*, you're going back tomorrow? Some holiday this has been. Can't you take an extra day?'

'I'm afraid not. And there are the girls.'

'Yes, of course. Neil—I couldn't have managed without you. Your wife must've loved you very much,' she says softly. Takes his hand as he sucks in his lips and momentarily his features buckle.

Outside the building photographers are waiting with their cameras. Neil grasps her elbow and hustles her down the street.

And now it is sodden evening and Timothy Abell's cottage is his, not hers. The cold outside needles through the gaps round the windows and door, while inside the night storage heaters do little to relieve the draught. She lights a fire, opens a bottle of wine, then picks up Garibaldi and cuddles him. After his initial enthusiastic greeting, then his subsequent sulk period, he is back to his normal self. The computer has a film of dust on the screen. And tomorrow she must recommence work. And there is a pile of letters to wade through. Messages on her answering machine. She is listless. Does not know what to tackle. And wherever she turns there is the child.

Waiting tensely for Aidan to arrive. A knock at the door—and here he is, in his purple track suit. The barest glimmer of a smile, followed by the lightest brush of his lips against hers. He takes the glass of wine she gives him and only comes to sit beside her when she pats the cushion.

Neither knows what to talk to the other about. Every subject seems barbed. She curls up against him, lonelier than when she is without him. She *is* without him.

Yes, the gig went well, he tells her. Yes, the boys are fine. But eventually he can no longer avoid the topic.

'So, when's the Crown Court hearing?'

'The 7th of January. I was surprised they actually gave a date, but apparently that's how the system here operates.'

Silence. She, squeezing her eyes shut, her face hidden by her hair.

'How . . . I mean, how do you feel about it?'

'Fatalistic. I've just got to try and get on with things.'

The problem with them, she realises, is that they are both naturally poor communicators, reticent about their true feelings.

'Let me explain just one thing to you, without trying to justify myself,' she says. 'I didn't want her to go through what I went through.'

'Well, now she is anyway.'

The implicit disapproval in his remark makes her defensive.

'You're a little intransigent, don't you think?'

'That's as maybe.'

She longs to hear warmth in his tone. Tries to keep her voice even: 'Do you still love me?'

He turns to her. His expression is tormented.

'That's the problem. I do.'

'And you regard loving me as a problem.'

'I didn't say that. I—I don't *know* you.'

'No,' she agrees. 'But nobody ever can know anyone completely. You know various aspects of me, better than anyone else has ever done. They haven't changed. And I never lied to you.'

'No.' On a sigh. 'To be fair, you didn't. You warned me. I shouldn't have—'

'What? Got involved? Of course not. Neither of us should.'

'Oh, I don't know, I don't know . . . I want you so bad still. I want everything back the way it was.'

'So do I. But it was spurious.'

He relaxes a little. Their talking seems to have helped. He lies back, the upper half of his body reclined on the sofa-futon.

'I hated seeing you in that place. It was terrible.'

'I've committed a crime.'

Feels his body stiffen when she says that.

He stays the night. They make love. But it resolves nothing. And afterwards each of them lies awake for much of the night.

They get up early the following morning. She piles on clothes to keep warm. He does not have breakfast with her.

'I need to get my head round this. I'm not saying this is it. I just . . . I can only give you my support if I work things out in my own time.'

'Well, that makes sense.' Tries to smile. Her mouth doesn't comply.

They kiss goodbye. Lovingly. She knows it is over.

And now to face the world.

Babs says calmly, 'Seems you're a page-three girl.'

She has made page three of the *Daily Telegraph* and the *Daily Mail*. TODDLER IN ABDUCTION DRAMA, ABANDONED CHILD ABDUCTED NOT ONCE, BUT TWICE.

'Oh, *madre*.'

'I know you better than to make snap judgments,' Babs says. 'There's more to this.'

They chat until a customer comes in. She ignores Isabella. And it is to be a foretaste, she realises as the day progresses.

But Joyce tells her: 'Your solicitor showed me the photos of the little mite. Seeing those, who could blame you? Maybe in the eyes of the law it *was* wrong. But I saw how you were with her. You made that little girl happy.'

The people who matter, she thinks. But not Aidan.

Eileen, the barrister, is in her fifties, with a brisk manner and a high, domed forehead like Elizabeth I. Her desk is a mass of papers. Among them Isabella notices her report and the photographs. After a few polite preliminaries she comes directly to the point.

'Having read your statement and report and seen the evidence I think it likely that if the case proceeds you may well be found guilty of the charges,' she says, drawing deeply on a small cigar. She holds up a preventive finger as Isabella is about to interrupt. 'However, it seems to me that there are very strong mitigating circumstances in your favour, and I would hope that I could persuade the prosecution to do a deal with us. If you plead guilty they will take this into consideration and also you won't have to give evidence or be cross-examined. Of course, it is not for me to tell you what to decide.'

'Is it likely I'd go to prison?' Isabella asks.

'I would say the most probable outcome would be a non-custodial sentence.'

'What does that mean?'

'A suspended sentence. Possibly eighteen months.'

The meeting is over within twenty minutes.

'What was your opinion of her?' Neil asks, outside chambers.

'Daunting. Efficient.'

'That's exactly what we want.'

'What do you think we should do?'

'Follow her suggestion. You?'

'Yes. I suppose so.' She huddles into her coat. Drizzle. Winter. She longs for summer. Italy. When this is over . . .

'Not sure?'

Shop windows gaudy with Christmas decorations. Another year about to expire. Why is she so afraid of death? What is so great about life?

'No, it's all right. I *am* sure. But—I'll have a criminal record, won't I?'

'The risks attached to pleading not guilty are very high,' he says gently.

'It's all right,' she says again. 'I've made up my mind.'

They walk back to their cars. He is driving directly back to London. Over the last few days they have become close. She knows she will miss him. They come to his Rover first.

'It's so strange here now,' she says, as he beeps open the car door. 'There's nothing. Without Hannah . . . And Aidan . . .'

'I'm on the other end of the phone. I'll be thinking of you.'

He hugs her. An enveloping bear hug.

Her agent rings. She manages, finally, to calm him. Sally phones. 'It's my turn to listen,' she says. But, generally, she does not bother to take calls. Stands by the answering machine. In case. Never Aidan.

The locals react in various ways. Some cut her dead; others are ill at ease and behave unnaturally. She has her small team of backers: Babs, Joyce, Mary Anne, Janet Abell and, curiously, Deirdre, the surgeon's wife. When she ventures into the Sun on her own one evening everybody stops speaking. It is excruciating. Then conversation starts up again, artificially loudly, and she departs without saying a word.

LONDON DIVORCEE AND LOCAL GIRL IN CHILD KIDNAPPING SCANDAL, shrieks the *West Briton* on Thursday.

And she knows she cannot remain here. She applies for a court hearing so that she can return to London.

The first week of December. Her last walk on Tregurran beach. A cement-toned sky in which the sea's horizon dissolves. She wishes the day were fine, that she could have her final, proper glimpse of the sea.

Later on the fog will lift, but she will be gone. *Madre*, how sad she is, but has no right to be, since there is nothing she has not instigated.

The car is packed up. As many of the child's toys as will fit are squeezed into corners. Everything that she bought for the cottage, including all the furniture, she leaves. 'Keep it for yourself or sell it,' she wrote to Janet Abell, enclosing the key in the envelope. 'Thank you for your kindness.'

She posts her note to Aidan: '*Caro*, the Isabella you knew, and the one you didn't, loves you. Remember that.'

Off she drives, away from what she had come to regard as her sanctuary, through the village, past neat gardens with gnomes and Christmas wreaths, cottages with cobalt-blue shutters; and Babs's post office; and clucking chickens. Not a single goodbye. She has gone, they will realise later—left without a word. And Aidan's garage—quickly past there, with her hankering heart. Out of Zerion, no child in the seat beside her. What has happened to the knitted rabbit? Does she still have it? Has she become watchful and withdrawn again? Have the fits of hysteria recommenced? Where is she? Tears blurring her vision so that she has to swerve to avoid an oncoming livestock carrier. It hoots long and loud as it judders by with its bleating contents. The snow drives down.

Mrs Shastri gives her back the key.

'So you won't be needing me to come in any more,' she says, without a trace of condemnation in her lilting voice. Yet every newspaper on her shelves carries a story about Isabella.

She unpacks. Reacquaints herself with her flat. Mrs Shastri has kept the place in immaculate order. And now her computer is in its old position, the guitar is in the corner where it always stood. There are new invitations to prop on the mantelpiece: exhibitions, fashion shows, openings, conferences. There is only herself and Garibaldi. It is as though nothing has happened.

Christmas approaches. She sends no cards. Stacks the ones she has received in a pile on a table, then, in a mood of defiance, strings them up round the fireplace and under the windowsill. No card from *him*. She spends the days working, catching up on the book; goes for walks on the heath; riding with Neil. Whatever she does, wherever she goes, a sense of pointlessness accompanies her.

Neil telephones.

'They've found her.'

'Who? What are you talking about?'

'The mother. She's a druggie, apparently, with a five-year-old son in care, and has a past conviction for child abuse.' He sounds jubilant.

'How did they find her?'

'Social workers were worried as it seems they'd been keeping an eye on her for some time, and suddenly the child was gone. They became suspicious. The *other* bit of excellent news is I've just heard from Eileen. The prosecution have agreed to the lesser charges in return for the guilty plea. The judge is sure to accept his recommendation. It's almost certain to be a non-custodial sentence . . .'

As she replaces the receiver she tries to register some feeling. She feels nothing.

It is on the nine o'clock news: 'The mother of a young girl recently at the centre of a most unusual and complex case has finally been traced. The twenty-two-year-old woman, who is not yet being named, already has a son in care and has past convictions for child abuse and possession of drugs. The plight of three-year-old Hannah, abandoned nearly four months ago outside a newsagent's in North London, has touched the hearts of the nation. Meanwhile, Ms Isabella Mercogliano, who found the child in an abused state and is accused of abducting her, before, in a bizarre twist, the child was abducted from *her*, is regarded by many as being something of an avenging angel . . .'

She lies in her bed with its silk cover—where sex was always on her terms, where love never happened, and which no mad mechanic ever sullied. She knows she cannot revert to the person she was, but nor does she need to dismiss her entirely. She realises her total rejection of her old life was extreme. Equally, her infatuation with Cornwall was extreme. How much of it was to do with the child and with Aidan? She cannot separate the place and the personae. Perhaps now she can become more objective. She does not have to eschew one lifestyle for the other. Does not have to scorn one place in order to appreciate the other. One day she will go back there.

She thinks of the mother. Twenty-*two*, *madre*. The no-hoper girl who is destined to sink ever deeper, she thinks. Of her own mother and her implacable determination that the wheel of repetition be broken. Of her father and how he has influenced her life and her attitude to men.

'All sorts of people can become foster carers and adopters,' she reads the following morning in the *Ham and High*. 'Children in this area need local people to offer them a home. We can help you explore whether fostering or adoption is right for you. We will provide training, individual support, finance. To request an information pack telephone . . .'

It commences as a tiny dot within her, then it grows, fans out, infusing her with heat.

All sorts of people? Even someone with a criminal record? Surely she is advantaged because of her unique relationship with the child?

All at once she is invigorated with purpose. If it takes every penny she has, if it means harassing every authority, if it entails going through all the courts, she will not give up until she has explored every avenue to achieve her aim. She will grasp this hope.

That is the first thing that happens, this Saturday, December 21.

The second thing occurs later in the day. It is the afternoon, and she is working at her computer; Garibaldi on her lap; Roberto Alagna singing Puccini. And she gets up to answer a single, short ring of the doorbell. A young woman stands there.

'I'm sorry to trouble you. You don't know me—but was your father's name Filipo?' she asks.

Dark. Thick, coarse hair. Raptor nose. The eyes. There is no mistaking the eyes. Her own.

They stare at one another.

'Come in.'

Isabella shows her inside. Makes tea.

'What a lovely flat,' the visitor says, sitting on the cream sofa, stroking Garibaldi, looking round her and lingering over the framed, enlarged photo on the glass table of the child on Tregurran beach. And beside that, Aidan, resembling a South American explorer.

She found Isabella through all the publicity, she says. It took her a while to pluck up courage. She is a secretary, she answers, in response to Isabella's question. Nothing high-powered. Staring at Isabella with open curiosity. Isabella continues to question her politely. Within herself she is trembling. All sense of time has become distorted. The cubbyhole of her childhood is exposed.

'He was a wonderful father,' the young woman says of the man they both knew differently.

So he is dead.

'He loved opera,' she reflects, as Alagna sings of his love for Tosca. 'We always made him turn it down. He played it so loudly.'

'Did he ever . . . touch you—molest you? Sexually, I mean.'

'Mol*est* me? Papa mol*est* me? What are you saying? How dare you? You're mad. I should've realised, with what you did.' Putting down her cup and saucer and standing up. A stocky figure in a too-tight miniskirt.

They part stiffly. Will not see each other again. Their own truths exchanged to gnaw at them. Why me, not her? *Did* he with me? Did I imagine it? *Did* he with her and she has forgotten? Or maybe she was lying to herself. Why was she so quick to tell me he was a wonderful, father?

He is dead. Let them each cling to what she wants to believe. To what Isabella needs to believe in order not to have wasted twenty-seven years.

The third thing.

She puts on her coat and opens the front door to go for a walk. As she does she sees someone getting out of a car a few yards up the road.

He sees her simultaneously. Is walking towards her slowly, in his purple track-suit top, with his long, swinging stride. His shining eyes flowing into hers as he approaches; while she remains where she is, disbelieving, incapable of moving a limb. Trying to smile. Not to break down.

It is the uncertainties which enable one to continue hoping.

VALERIE BLUMENTHAL

Sitting at a scrubbed pine table in a cosy Oxfordshire cottage kitchen filled with the aroma of freshly brewed coffee, Valerie Blumenthal talked to me about her life and writing career. Visible along a narrow passageway leading to her front door, a huge German shepherd dog sat keeping a watchful eye on us. This, she told me, is Schubert. He looks terrifying, but turns out to be a gentle giant, and the same is probably true of Henry, her recently acquired shire horse, kept in an adjacent stable. For a woman on her own, these big, strong animals must provide welcome companionship and a certain feeling of security.

Valerie Blumenthal was born in Hampstead and spent much of her childhood and youth in London. One event that seems, to a large extent, to have set her course in life was the birth of her only daughter, Ingrid. She was just twenty-one at the time and recently married, but the relationship didn't last and she found herself raising Ingrid alone. Having to cope with single motherhood left her stronger and more self-reliant, and she is now a woman determined to make the most of her time and her many talents. As she puts it, 'I didn't go to college, but I went to the university of life.'

She not only writes, but also paints and sings. At eighteen her one ambition was to go to the Royal College of Music but, because her piano

playing did not match the high standard of her singing, she narrowly failed to get in. Instead, she did some modelling and then worked for eight years in her father's London-based wine company, during which time she also started to write. Now, besides being a fully-fledged novelist and freelance journalist, Valerie Blumenthal also holds creative writing classes and runs a one-day-a-week therapeutic writing workshop at a local prison. This last experience has, she says, been immensely fulfilling. 'I do think that if you find yourself on your own for any reason, it's a good time for self-development. It's important to use the time to understand oneself better and, hopefully, other people.'

Already Valerie Blumenthal is at work on her ninth book, which will be set in a young offenders' institution and will gradually reveal, through flashbacks, why a young man has been put there. 'Like all my novels, it will be about the psychology of a particular human drama,' she explains.

Throughout my visit, Valerie Blumenthal talked with ease about herself and her life. However, she never lost an opportunity to turn the conversation back to me. As I departed, I was left with the impression that she is deeply and genuinely interested in people and what motivates them, and this is, without doubt, what makes her so perceptive and successful as a writer.

Sue Poulsen

Originations by Rodney Howe Ltd
Printed and bound by Maury Imprimeur SA, Malesherbes, France

601-005-1